CONFLICT OF INTEREST

"Wonderful reading—full of nitty-gritty details . . . thoroughly engaging characters!"

—*Washington Post Book World*

"Mr. Whitten reveals enough of his trade to stock several journals in school seminars. [He] tells a good, informative story."

—*New York Times*

"Whitten . . . is at his best. . . . The writing is smooth and well-paced. The characterizations . . . are excellent!"

—*Los Angeles Times*

THE ALCHEMIST

"A highly volatile blend of national politics and the essence of evil . . . Mr. Whitten is an elegant sylist with a flair for both language and action and will hold you spellbound!"

—*New York Times*

"A shrewd and entertaining writer. . . . Kinky . . . a brisk, semi-tough study of power and love, the intoxication of public life and non-negotiable private satisfactions."

—*Times* Magazine

MOON OF THE WOLF

"A superb and exciting style, a gift for atmosphere grounded in thorough research."

—*Washington Star*

"You are swept along at a very rapid pace from the first page! I found this a tingler and very good reading!"

—*Columbus Enquirer*

PROGENY OF THE ADDER

"Mr. Whitten has a enviably professional skill in developing . . . his tale!"

—*New York Times*

LESLIE H. WHITTEN, Jr.

THE LOST DISCIPLE

THE BOOK OF DEMAS

LEISURE BOOKS   NEW YORK CITY

For Phyllis

A LEISURE BOOK®

November 1990

This edition is reprinted by arrangement with Atheneum Publishers, an imprint of Macmillan Publishing Company.

Published by

Dorchester Publishing Co., Inc.
276 Fifth Avenue
New York, NY 10001

For further information, contact: Atheneum Publishers, an imprint of Macmillan Publishing Company, 866 Third Avenue, New York N.Y. 10022.

The name "Leisure Books" and the stylized "L" with design are trademarks of Dorchester Publishing Co., Inc.

Printed in the United States of America.

Acknowledgments

I am grateful to the following people for their help, without implying that they approve the use I made of it: the Reverend Ron Albaugh, Patrick Anderson, Richard Bast, Martie Chidsey, Charles Colson, André Condon, Joan Czarnecki, Perry Knowlton, Lucette Lagnado, Rod MacLeish, Judith Martin, William B. Moore, Jr., Edward Motsinger, Jr., Evan Oppenheimer, Berry Richards, Phyllis Richman, Susan Richman, Carol Eisen Rinzler, Jane and Paul Stam, Tom Stewart, Margaret Talcott, the Reverend Dr. Patricia Thomas, Mrs. Leslie H. Whitten, Sr., Phyllis and Andrew Whitten. These libraries were especially helpful: the Montgomery County Library, Four Corners branch; the Library of Congress; the Libraries of Lehigh University. I drew heavily on these books for historical reference, preeminently *Daily Life in the Time of Jesus*, by Henri Daniel-Rops, Servant Books, Ann Arbor, Michigan; but also *Paul of Tarsus*, by the Right Reverend Joseph Holzner (although our views of Paul are often at odds), B. Herder Book Company, St Louis; *The Westminster Historical Atlas to the Bible*, the Westminster Press, Philadelphia; *The Jewish War*, by Josephus, translated by G. A. Williamson, Penguin Books, Baltimore, Maryland; *The Search for the Twelve Apostles*, William Steuart McBirnie, Tyndale House Publishers, Wheaton, Illinois; and these versions, *inter alia*, of the Bible: Revised Standard Version, Thomas Nelson, New York; King James Version, John C. Winston Company, Philadelphia; *The Book*, Tyndale House Publishers, Wheaton, Illinois; *The New Testament in Modern English*, translated by J. B. Phillips, The Macmillan Company, New York. To cite the some two hundred other works drawn upon during the nine years since I conceived this book would require a bibliography beyond the concept of this novel.

The Thessalonian Apograph, as a specific document, does not exist, although many of its characters, events, and quotations are historical. Demas lived, but all that is truly known of him is in the three cited passages of the New Testament. The persons, institutions, and events involved in the discovery of the Apograph are fictional, as is the Tiflis Microapostolic Fragment and all its words.

From the Epistles of Paul

Colossians 4.14: "Luke, the beloved physician and Demas greet you. . . ."

Philemon 23–24: "Epaphras, my fellow prisoner in Christ Jesus sends greetings to you, and so do Mark, Aristarchus, Demas, and Luke, my fellow workers. . . ."

2 Timothy 4.9–10: "Do your best to come to me soon. For Demas, in love with this present world, has forsaken me and gone to Thessalonica. . . ."

THE BOOK
OF DEMAS

Foreword

By VIRGINIA P. JONES-HAARWIJK, *Collmann Professor Emeritus, School of Middle Eastern Theologies, Brampton University, Brampton, New Hampshire*

A manuscript, popularly known as the Book of Demas, but more properly identified as the Thessalonian Apograph, written in aqueous-based lampblack on papyrus scrolls circa A.D. 450, was discovered by me and a graduate assistant, Berenice Galipulluci (M.A., University of Turin), on August 14, 1986. We were working under a grant from the Reges-Macedonia Foundation, studying records found in the so-called "third crypt" of the Church of Saints Paul and Secundus in Thessalonike, which had been excavated January–June, 1982.

The Apograph, a type of transcript, was amid packets of land records dating from the early fifteenth century. How the work made its way there, we were unable to determine. With the gratifying help of the Department of Classics, Brampton University, and of other graduate students under my supervision, we translated the document. Written in grammatical Greek, the work, we suspected, was originally composed circa A.D. 64. From internal evidence, including anomalous and colloquial spellings and mistranscribings, however, we deduced that the scrolls we found were a copy of a version dating back at least to A.D. 300.

The Apograph claims to be an autobiographical work of one Demas Faevolian of Borhaurus, once a town in Judaea. It covers the period from his birth to his thirty-sixth year. I say "claims," for I have come to the reluctant opinion that the manuscript *may* be spurious.

Admittedly, there is a distinguished minority among the few who have examined the Apograph—e.g., Professors Ray L. Armstrong, Lehigh University, and Rolf R. Mohn, University of Durham (England)—who have made cogent arguments for the authenticity of the supposed Demas's work.

My doubts are based on the unlikelihood that a manuscript of this importance could have existed from A.D. 64 until A.D. 450 without having been cited in any hitherto discovered ecclesiastical or other historical document. These doubts put me in an awkward position—that of a mother who has lovingly raised a child only to begin to fear when the child is in his or her teens that the offspring was never hers.

To carry the analogy one step further, the mother, nevertheless, has a duty to give the child every possible access to a worthwhile life. It is for this reason that I am publishing *The Lost Disciple*. For even if the Apograph does not predate A.D. 450, it deals at a far closer distance than the present with the life of Jesus and the apostles and comments explicitly on the Gospels, the Acts, and the letters of Paul. It tells in detail of a time that is largely lost.

Its author, whoever he may be, and for all his literary failings and excesses, had a vivid, if crude, imagination, a basic understanding of the interrelation of the sensual and the devout, a bold sense of adventure, and certain analytical skills. Demas, or the False Demas, if that is the case, obviously had a classical education, was curious, and had read widely.

On the other hand, he admits to a spiritual "shallowness," which, in the context of his supposed mentor St. Paul, seems to be his own "thorn in the flesh."* This honesty about a pervasive yet seldom self-recognized human failing (if the candor is ingenuous, rather than guileful) may give internal weight to those who argue for the manuscript's authenticity.

Demas states his purpose in writing the manuscript was to reveal with naked truthfulness his life, with its vices in stark view, so that his followers could better assess the worth of certain epistles and a life of Jesus Christ he planned to write later. While no such further writings have ever been discovered, no one disputes the existence of a historical Demas, as evidenced by the aforementioned biblical citations. Indeed, if the material is what it purports to be, it would solve many important enigmas and contradictions in the New Testament that have puzzled us for almost two thousand years.

Vide Colossians 4.14; Philemon 23–24; 2 Timothy 4.9–10, *Holy Bible* (New York: Thomas Nelson & Sons, 1952).

I early perceived that to put our rough translation into proper English, and to subject it to the necessary peer reviews so that it might be published as a work of scholarship, would take several years. While I was making the funding and time arrangements for this Minervan task, I learned that a copy of my rough translation had found its way into the hands of a New York publisher.

He intends to reduce it to modern English as rapidly as possbile and to publish it as an *authentic* work of the first century A.D. with a foreword so certifying from two unaffiliated professors, one, *mirabile dictu*, a sociologist. Brampton University, the Reges-Macedonia Foundation, and I have sued to block this publication. Meanwhile, to forestall any similar effort and to protect ourselves against the possibility that we should lose our suit, we decided to preempt the field with our own "popular" edition of the Apograph.

The publishers of the edition in your hands had my rough translation rendered into idiomatic English in fifty-one days, with substantial accuracy. I heartily endorse this work in the interest of competition, but urge scholars to withhold final critical judgments pending my academic edition. Meanwhile I offer certain explications:

1. The writer has inserted quotation marks around exegetic and other material. I am told this makes the book more "accessible" to modern readers. For historicity, however, he has generally used ancient measures for distance, weights, etc.

2. He has used a number of anachronisms, e.g., "book" occasionally for "codex" or "scroll," and such words as "mesmerized" instead of "hypnotized," as in my translation, the original Greek being *hypnotikos*. ("Mesmerized" is an artificial word derived from one Franz Mesmer [1734–1815], who practiced hypnotism in Vienna during his latter years. *Ab uno disce omnes . . .*)

3. Ideally, the length of sentences and the lack of paragraphing and chapterization should have been left as in the original. In addition, there are inconsistencies in use of modern and ancient place nouns—e.g., "Massilia" for "Marseilles" and "Joppa" for "Tel Aviv," but not "Roma" for "Rome," or "Tyrus" for "Tyre." "Palestine" is also used in a modern context.

These considerations aside, the extravagant activity of the Apograph's "Demas" from his birth to the end of the manuscript remains intact, this popular version thus capturing the spirit of a time that in so many ways was like our own.

THE BOOK
OF DEMAS

I

My first encounter with Paul of Tarsus was on a day when the air was parched, the hot dust thick in the streets of Scythopolis. It was fall, I was seventeen and had been sent off to school a few months earlier by my father for good and sufficient cause. The justice of my banishment did not make it any less difficult to bear. The other youths at the academy were here by desire, or at worst by default. I alone was here solely as punishment. I had disgraced our family, hardening even my gentle mother against me, and so in addition to the isolation and emptiness in this distant place, I felt the void that comes from the withdrawal of love. I filled it as best I could by studying.

On the day Paul came to Scythopolis I was in my room reading Athenodorus. I remember it because I was struck by coincidence. Athenodorus, friend of Cicero and Strabo and the teacher of Augustus before he became emperor, was from the unlikely city of Tarsus, and the voice from outside, didactic, high-pitched, challenging, was also from there, or so it stated in accented Greek: "I am Paul of Tarsus in Cilicia. . . ."

The man's words carried over the jeers of my schoolmates. I slipped a stylus into the scroll to mark my place, and went into the academy yard to see what was going on. Twenty students, along with a dozen townspeople, children, a donkey, and two mongrels, were before the speaker. He was short, with a body like that of a wrestler, and wore a coarsely woven *chalouk* and weathered hobnailed sandals. His face was badly pitted. I judged him to be in his early forties.

". . . Young men," he was saying, "you have followed me the

breadth of Scythopolis like runners in a long race after the pacesetter. But, as you know, in athletic contests only one receives the prize, a perishable wreath. Why not compete in a race where all can win imperishable laurels? For the race that I run and invite you into is toward the kingdom of heaven. And our pacesetter is Christ Jesus whose message I bring and who rejoices with all of us when we win. . . ."

Christos meant "the Lord's anointed" in Greek, which was *mashiah* in Hebrew, a language I knew slightly from my Sadducee mother's side of the family. The Messiah was the prophesied king who was going to deliver the Jews from us—the Romans. My father was a Roman tribune, and it was as a Roman that I regarded myself. Be that as it may, claims that this person or that was the "Messiah" or "savior" or "King of the Jews" were pepper in the eyes of both Sadducees and Pharisees.

". . . A runner," the Cilician was saying, "does not run aimlessly any more than a boxer beats at the air. Yet that is what you do in your lustfulness and your pride, destroying both the contest and your athletic bodies, which are the temples of God. Do you not know that he who destroys God's temple will himself be destroyed, for the wages of sin are death eternal?"

His voice rose at moments almost to a war cry, then fell so low we had to bend toward him to hear, its tone never deferential like the peripatetic Stoics, Epicureans, and Cynics, who harangued us from time to time. Nor was he deranged like the hirsute flagellants, the scabrous neo-Dionysians, and the beggars who passed through the city assuring us they would soon be back reincarnated as the Great Living Ram of Gold.

"The message of Christ Jesus," he said, "is fulfilled in a single sentence: 'You shall love your God first, and secondly you shall love your neighbors as yourself.' For even if I speak to you in the tongues of angels and have not love, I am a noisy gong or a clanging cymbal. And if I have prophetic powers, and understand all mysteries, and all knowledge, and if I have all faith, so as to remove mountains, but have not love, I am nothing. If I give away all I have, everything, even delivering my body to be burned, but have not love, I gain nothing. . . ."

I listened, enthralled by the poetry pouring from this unlikely vessel: "Love is patient and kind; it is not jealous or boastful; it is not arrogant or rude. Love does not insist on its own way; it is not irritable or resentful; it does not rejoice at wrong, but in right. Love bears all things, believes all things, hopes all things, endures all things. Prophe-

4

cies will pass away; tongues will cease; knowledge will fade. Love never ends. When perfect love comes, all that is imperfect will disappear forever. . . . Through love, we shall understand fully, even as we become fully understood. Faith, hope, and love abide, these three. But the greatest of these is love."

In my loneliness, I had seldom been more susceptible to these words, could hardly have been more ready for them. Paul had churned the vapors of my heart into living blood. Yet even as I began to commit the words into my mind, I felt the return of my dry melancholy. I knew that this stranger, for all his eloquence, did not in himself have the means to make me whole.

Around me, students shuffled their feet in the dust. There were a few "Well done"s, a few nods of approval, but mostly "Bah"s and catcalls. Paul, after all, had chided us for lustful excesses and for arrogant atheism, the last kind of accusations that sixteen- to twenty-year-old sons of rich men wanted to hear. And they had not been touched by the other things he had said.

Paul searched eagerly among us as if looking for one or two who might dissent from the rest. His eyes lit on mine for an instant and I shuddered within, but gave him no sign that his words had reached me. He turned toward the arch of our yard. The road outside led to Jerusalem. From the shadows by our wall, two men, dusty as Paul, both taller and one younger, moved up beside him. The younger handed him a creased leather pack and the three struck off through the arch.

Still bewildered, I approached Tullo, an acquaintance, to ask him about the speaker. Before he could reply, there was a hubbub outside the wall. We heard angry shouts in Aramaic, the resounding thumps of sticks striking flesh, cries of pain. As one, we crowded through the arch, and in the dirt of the street saw a tangle of bodies: the three visitors and two burly townsmen. Circling the struggling heap like wild dogs around a fallen goat were three more local men with broken staves, swinging at Paul and his two disciples whenever they found an opening.

Although the majority of my schoolmates urged on the bullies, two of the older boys shouted for the attackers to forbear. That failing, they ran at one of the circling men. I rushed at a second. I was tall and sturdy, and when I struck the man at the waist with my shoulder, I knocked him over.

But a dozen schoolmates rose up, pulled us away and cursed us. In minutes, the three strangers had been bloodied and brought to their feet, their arms gripped behind them. They stood straight, faces composed, before their five foes. The leader of the ruffians approached Paul, panting, and said in Aramaic, "You have spoken against the Law of Moses. We will teach you a law of our own."

Paul looked up at his bearded attacker and said in perfect Aramaic, "I am a Jew and I preach not only to Gentiles but to Jews like yourselves, and according to the Law of Moses."

The leader hesitated, inarticulate before a man of words, then noisily hawked and spat at Paul's mouth. Paul flinched and the sputum struck him on the cheek. Passively, he accepted the insult. The chieftain nodded at one of his band, who, quick as a ferret, lashed his stick against the side of Paul's head. The Cilician dropped to the ground, eyes rolling.

Next the man with the stick drew back to strike the younger of Paul's disciples. But this disciple, unlike Paul, wrenched free, brought his fist around as smoothly as if it were a leather sling, and tumbled the townsman backward. The rabble chief, his own stick cocked, moved irresolutely toward the young disciple, who grabbed him by the beard, jerked his head down and brought up his knee to meet the man's face. Screaming, covering his bloody face with his fingers, the injured man reeled away.

Those who a moment ago were so eager to beat the three itinerants had less stomach for blood now that they saw it flowing so copiously from their comrades. The two disciples helped Paul, who was still dazed, to his feet. From the street, the pair gathered up the rough garments, bits of cheese and bread and other belongings that had been tossed from their shoulder sacks during the fight. The young man, glaring defiantly, and the older assistant, with downcast eyes, took Paul's arms gently. Without a word, but also without interference, they walked toward the Jerusalem gate.

That evening, I spoke with Tullo. His father was a centurion in Jerusalem and Tullo kept himself informed about what was going on in all the provinces. "Did you ever hear of this man Paul?" I asked. He had not. "And this Jesus he talks about?"

"I think so—a man the Jews prevailed on us to let them crucify fifteen or so years ago. I was too young to remember, of course, and anyway no one can keep account of things like that."

"And this one, Paul, what did you think?"

"Fair Greek, good Aramaic," said Tullo, who fancied himself a judge of elocution, "analogies badly mixed. Typical Jewish sophistry . . ." He blanched with embarrassment. He, like many of my classmates, tended to forget that I was half-Jewish. "I am sorry, Demas—" he began.

6

"It is no matter," I interrupted him untruthfully.

Back in my room, I picked up Athenodorus. Before I had extinguished my lamp, I had come to these stern words: "Live with your fellowmen as if the gods watch you. . . ." Had I behaved during the fight as if the gods were watching? Probably the answer was yes, if the watching gods were the pagan gods to whom my father and we other Romans paid lip service; or my godlike Stoic father himself, who had tried to teach me there were no gods; or my mother's father's God, the God of the Jews.

But how would this Paul's God of love have regarded my violent intervention? "Love endures all things," Paul had said. He had followed that precept, accepting the phlegm in his face. Yet his young disciple had fought back. With a sharp calamus, I jotted down on a scrap of papyrus what I could remember of the Tarsan's words.

II

♦•♦

Borhaurus, where I was born and grew up, was a busy town of ten thousand on the highroad from the port of Joppa to Jerusalem. In its early days, Borhaurus had been fortified by the Jewish king Solomon, and it was near here that Jewish warriors had slaughtered their most dangerous enemies, the Amorites. Called "Bor-haruz" by the Jews, it was still three-fifths Jewish. But because of its position on the great trade route from the sea to the east, and from the gradual migration of nearby rural pagans, it was now two-fifths polyglot. These "strangers among us," as the Jews called them, were originally Samaritans, Phoenicians, Idumaeans, Peraeans, Syrians, Egyptians, and Greeks.

The architecture of the city was as mixed as its peoples. To the Jewish town's jumble of cube-shaped wattle-and-daub houses and its angular alleys and lanes, the Greeks and, more recently, the Romans had brought order. They had torn down ancient neighborhoods and built them anew. Borhaurus now had two wide, straight streets, each punctuated by squares in which fountains flowed at hours regulated by the water warden.

In the new section, a forum had been cleared, and here, on market days, the merchants set up stalls for copper goods, jewelry, ironmongering of every imaginable kind, yard goods from Ionia and beyond, embroidery from Persia, purple dye from Tyre, cosmetics and scents, balsam from Jericho, cedar and cypress furniture, wines from Galilee, Cyprus, and even Campania.

From the bronze caster I bought grooming combs for my pony, bronze nails for my rabbit hutch. I sponged up the market's smells, sounds, and sights. Mutton dripped on cook shop braziers; pistachios popped open in hot pans; rosemary, cumin, mint, garlic, and cinnamon from the far east scented the air; sweating men hand-milled baskets of locusts into bitter powder to be mixed with honey and baked into cakes. The Babylonian silk dealer in pantaloons with a gold ring in his nose hawked his fabrics in demotic Aramaic. The Phoenician tattooist decorated the hands and foreheads of wincing devotees of Sandan and Baal with grotesque faces and pictographs.

Most of the houses in Borhaurus were lime-washed, one-room dwellings. Some families shared their single door, tiny window, and tamped dirt floor with a goat and sheep or two. They pitched tents of woven goat hair on the roof to house guests or as sleeping space for adolescent children.

There were also two- and even three-story clay brick houses in Borhaurus. Their loggias surrounded courtyards. On warm afternoons, one could hear the idle laughter of gossiping women from the awninged balconies.

Our own house was made of limestone. Its two stories were shaped like a wicket, with the fourth side an eight-foot-high wall topped with shards of glass. The floors were of cypress. Our water was piped to the kitchen and the toilet closet and thence into the town's cloaca. The homes of my wealthy Sadducee relatives were similar, except for mezuzahs on the doorposts, and the absence in accordance with the Torah of any humans or gods in their carved or painted decorations.

When I returned from visits to Grandfather or my Jewish cousins, I passed lesser dwellings, those of the poor, and heard the sharp voices of women in the open or beneath lean-tos, preparing meals redolent of goat and lentils simmering in olive oil, rancid and sweet. At dusk, their houses were dimly lit by the flicker of a single lamp.

On Friday evenings, between the first and the third star, as the chill set in with the death of the sun, the Jewish communities waited the bleat of the *hazzan*'s Sabbath horn from the highest tower in Borhaurus. He blew two mournful yet demanding notes three times, the first time to summon the last of the workers from the fields, the second to tell devout Jews to close their shops, the third to advise Jews to light their oil lamps. At that instant, all over Borhaurus there was a glow in the windows of our Jewish neighbors.

The extremes of Borhaurus were less pronounced than in cities like Jerusalem or Scythopolis, but no child was unaware of them. A few blocks from our house were alleys caked with drying and rotting garbage scavenged by dogs and buzzing loudly with flies. One day, a playmate and I came upon a half-dozen people mesmerized before a gasping woman. Her skirts were above her hips and her life's blood was still flowing from her womb. Also bloody, but like a long, stringy sausage, was a tube connected to a wrinkled pale thing that I saw was a dead baby.

She was a beggar, a young leper, an outcast even from the poor. The flies were everywhere on her and her gory infant. It did not occur to me or my friends that we could or should do anything. We stood like the rest, fascinated, appalled. At home, I told father about it. Not unkindly, he said, "They are nothing to us. If we were to care about them, it would take all our time. There are too many of them for us to bother."

We Romans were the newcomers, and as conquerors we had imposed on Borhaurus many of the trappings of Rome. While the Jewish majority had its complicated religious-civil system of courts and police, Father, as tribune, could overrule them whenever he felt obliged to do so. Only he, for example, could order executions. If the offender was a Jew and the offense a capital one under Mosaic Law, however, Father turned him over to the Jewish council for stoning. Father's Roman auxiliaries—we called them legionnaires, although they were mainly Samaritans and Syrians, for Jews were exempt from conscription—were the enforcing arm of his absolute but generally benign power.

The majority of the Jews, who had their own large quarter, were Pharisees and their adherents. They believed in every jot and tittle of the Jewish Law's oral and written interpretations since Moses. Besides the Torah, they accepted as Law the prophetic, psalmic and other books, the canonical legal code with all its tractates, the commentaries on this code and the Midrash. They were the Jews of intellect and scholarship from whom came most of the scribes, the scholars of these diverse writings.

They disdained all who were not Jews, and thus they were fervent in their opposition to pagan Rome. Yet, it was the Pharisees who made up the majority of the Jewish Council, which, under Father's suzerainty, did the day-to-day governing of Borhaurus except as regarded Roman citizens.

The Sadducees, from whom my mother's family and thus I sprang, had largely accommodated themselves to the Romans. Indeed, Grandfather and many other well-to-do Sadducees (and some Pharisees) had bought Roman citizenship for themselves and their progeny. The Sadducees presided in the Temple in Jerusalem and in four of the five synagogues in Borhaurus, living well, even luxuriously, on fees from sacrificial animals and grains.

To both Pharisees and Sadducees, my mother was a renegade, for there was little intermarriage between Jews and Gentiles. Indeed, some Jews said her two miscarriages after I was born were God's punishment on her for marrying a Gentile. Contrarily, it was a matter of comfort to them that a Jew was the wife of the Roman tribune, who, it was therefore assumed, would be sympathetic to the needs and demands of the Jews.

Before he gave the hand of his daughter to a pagan, my grandfather, perhaps the richest man in Borhaurus, had exacted a curious concession from my father, then a Roman captain obviously selected by Rome for higher position. Once a week, Grandfather was to be allowed to take the first-born son, and, as it proved, the only child, to the synagogue.

Since Father's ambitions were for advancement in Judaea, he recognized the wisdom of this further tie between ruler and ruled. He was confident that his own rational skepticism would overcome any tendency in a son of his toward faith in the God of Abraham, even though he understood that Grandfather, because the Jews trace lineage through the mother, regarded me as a Jew, if an uncircumcised one. Yet, to give Father his due, he respected the courage and wisdom of Judaism and the frequent beauty of its writings.

Grandfather, beginning when I was four, took me to the main synagogue, although not often on the Sabbath. It was a sturdy rectangular stone building with a red tile roof and with columns inside dividing it into three aisles, and a gallery for women. Grandfather was a crafty old proselyter: we made side trips after our observances to a sweet shop, and I swiftly came to identify the synagogue with freshly made honeyed candy. But my visits had more than just this contrived appeal. The elders treated me with respect even when I was a child. I was awed by the male rhythms of their chants, the assertive prayers, their melodious singing of the psalms.

The synagogue was filled with mysterious things, some of them behind a heavy curtain, which, despite their sanctity, I was allowed to explore: the brass-adorned chest; the leather scroll cases, but not the scrolls themselves; the horns and trumpets, some of metal, some of horn, all studded with rare stones that glowed dimly in the light from the high slotted window; the misshapen, faded palms and flowers and six-pointed stars painted high up on the stucco walls, the dark gallery.

The smells in the curtains of dried mint, of cedarwood in the ark, of rich, oiled leather, of nard and balsam that the men rubbed in their armpits to mask their sweat: these odors combined in my soul with the sense of a vague, powerful God, a God who was present for every Jew each moment of the day, advising, praising, criticizing. Gradually, I

11

came to be sure that, while I did not understand God, he was never *not* there, both as a presence in me and outside me. My father's dry Roman unbelief was no match for all this magic.

❀

One night, the two mastiffs who were freed at night to prowl our courtyard as warders growled longer than usual. I was used to their voices. Whenever an animal or person passed outside our walls within their sniffing or hearing powers, they responded. I assumed that night it was to some tavern straggler urinating in the street. I fell securely back to sleep. It seemed only moments later that hands stuffed cloth into my mouth while other hands snatched me from bed. Terrified, I struggled against the three men who had grabbed me up. With complete stealth, they carried me onto the gallery. Using a ladder, they lifted me to the roof, then crept across the roof tiles, lowered the ladder, and passed me down to the street.

In the moonless night, I saw a fourth man waiting for them as lookout. They shoved me into an alley, where I was sure they would kill me. I tried to tear the cloth from my mouth, but the man who held it there cuffed the back of my head with his left hand. "Roman mongrel!" he hissed. "Any more and your throat is cut, ard your whore mother's, too!" They dragged and pushed me toward the town wall through an alley I knew well by the stink of garbage. At the wall, they handed me up the ladder, then down the other side.

The darkness made the fields outside Borhaurus with their stubble of flax and wheat treacherous. The men cursed in low voices. To make walking easier, my guard unhanded me, with a threat to stab me if I tried to run. To reinforce his words, he pricked my neck with his short dagger before he put its point at my back. I touched my neck and felt the wet blood, and cried silently. A short dagger—*sica*, in Latin—meant to me as it did to all boys in Palestine, *sicarii*. They were the fanatical and murderous wing of the Zealots, Pharisaic extremists. The *sicarii* were determined not just to drive the Romans from Palestine, but also to kill all Jews who cooperated with them. They had murdered the nephew of Herod the Great because, though Jewish, Herod had let a Roman eagle be placed above the main gate of the Temple.

There had been no *sicarii* in Borhaurus, but the short dagger and their insult to Mother, their calling me a "mongrel," made me shake with the fear that I was in the hands of a band of them from elsewhere.

Still, near as I was to panic, I had some hope they meant to hold me for ransom. Otherwise, why had they not slain me already?

We reached the highroad to Lydda. They rushed me along for a half hour before stopping at an overgrown lane. I gathered that they had gotten directions, but were not sure this was their turning. Decided at last, they marched me through waist-high thistle and brush. The smell of scrub turpentine trees pierced the heavy night air. The lane ended at a broken shed on a deserted cattle graze. The men searched around until one of them grunted. The others, with me in tow, joined him by a well. One dropped in a stone and they waited for its splash far below. I screamed involuntarily. These men were going to throw me in. My captor, their leader, slapped me into silence.

"Stab him first," said one. The two underlings who had not spoken gave affirmative growls. My abductor squatted to look into my face. In the dim starlight, I could see little but a man with a full beard and Levitical sidelock curls.

"Little man," he said fiercely, "I want you to listen carefully. If you say the words I order you to, I will do as my comrades suggest against my own better judgment. I prefer to let you drown slowly so that when your body is found with lungs full of water, your swine-eating parents will know you suffered and reflect on it all the days of their lives—may they be short."

He paused to let me fully understand. He had obviously not had much experience with children. Frightened as I was, it was unthinkable that I would make what might be the intelligent choice of an easy, quick death—since the alternative gave me hope for a few more minutes of life.

"Say, 'My mother is a harlot, worse than Jezebel, a whore traitor to all Jews.' Say you abominate her with the curses of Ebal." I remained silent, from paralyzing fear, not from stubbornness, for I would have said anything to preserve my life. Indeed, if he had reversed the options, I would have called her worse. He slapped me. "Say she spawns Roman mongrels; say she is a hole for the deposit of Roman shit." He had begun to make a litany of it, seeming to care less now about whether I answered than about relieving his hatreds. "Say she welcomes the filthy discharges of pagans through all her orifices."

I thought of my gentle mother and of what he might mean: acts I had heard described by the children of our servants, things I was unsure of but knew had to do with urine and babies. Even in my fear I angered. "You welcome filthy discharges, else you would not say and do these things."

The man who suggested I be stabbed interrupted. "We are wasting time. Do what you will and let us be gone."

The squatting man paused, then said rapidly, "Say your father is an idolater, a murderer of Jewish babies, a drinker of our blood, a defiler of the Lord's Temple. Say you curse him. . . ."

His words tumbled out with a spray of spittle, for he had a slight lisp. It was his saliva in my face as much as his words, although his words had also enraged me, that made me slap his hairy cheek with all my might.

With an oath, he grabbed me up and did not so much drop me as hurl me down the well. I shrieked. My foot struck a rock jutting from the well's side, sending a slash of agony up my leg. My head hit the clay wall, but by luck only glancingly. My face scraped dry dirt, my teeth raking earth into my mouth. I flailed my arms and legs, instinctively forestalling a fatal collision with the well wall.

I hit the water feet first and felt them jam into muddy bottom. The water was only shoulder high. My mind worked frantically. If the men above thought I might not drown, they would find some way to kill me even if it meant coming down by rope to do so. I spat dirt and began to beat at the water. "Help me!" I screamed. "I can't swim!" Then I realized I was shouting in Greek, our family tongue, and switched to Aramaic. "Oh, help!" As I splashed, I mixed my cries with gurgles.

For ten, fifteen minutes, I churned and screamed, from time to time ducking my head into the water, which tasted of rotten moss, then spitting and making choking sounds. I made my splashing and cries grow weaker, my gagging more frequent. At last, I uttered a hopeless cry and submerged, blowing up bubbles before surfacing quietly beside the wall. I listened, hearing nothing but the faint moan of the sluggish night air blowing across the mouth of the well. Then I heard one of the men say, his voice made sepulchral by the well, "Done."

For hours, I did not make a sound. Pain set in from my neck, my mouth, my face, and most of all from my left foot. I was sure some of my toes were broken. It was cold in the well, and I gritted my teeth together lest they chatter. From time to time, I dared to look up at the round mouth of the well. The sky was brighter than the dark water only by a few stars.

I thought of working my way up by scraping footholds with my fingers. But the clay was dry and the well too wide for me to brace myself across it as I climbed. I thought of tearing my nightshirt into strips, tying them together and attaching an end to a rock, which I would throw from the well. But it would never reach that far, even if I could find a rock. Hours passed.

My great fear had drained me of energy. I fought to remain conscious. But the drifting images that precede sleep wafted through my mind. I smelled the garlic and pickle odor of the terrible man's breath as he besmirched Mother and Father. His dark head changed to a housetop, then a dark jumble of dog shapes, a ropy ladder, a great flapping cloth and I was swept into sleep.

I woke coughing and spluttering, for my head had slipped into the stagnant water. My first thought was that my abductors would hear me thrashing and choking. But I realized they were gone. I fought further sleep and began to construct fantasies. I imagined a tree fell and a branch dropped down for me to climb; a wild dog sniffed me and yowled and a hunter came and discovered me. As I built these pipe dreams, I slipped again into sleep and again water filled my mouth and nostrils and awakened me.

The dreams came again, ever more fanciful. I heard the welcome thuds as a tunnel was dug directly to where I stood and I crawled out; Father was lowered with a rope around his ankles and lifted me up; I urinated until the well was full enough for me to swim out. I awoke, in fact urinating.

Finally, it was dawn. The sky was a round window of soft, untouchable blue. I waited silently, huddling at the well's side, fearful still that the men might return and throw in a torch to see whether I was dead or alive. But when the edge of the sun showed above me, I began to call, again and again, each time listening for a response. My voice grew hoarse and I spaced my shouts.

During the day, I heard the caws of crows, and once a dove sat on the side of the well and purred to a mate before taking wing. They were free. I imagined myself a crow, a dove. I considered what other animals I would want to be if I had to give up being a boy in order to escape. Perhaps the wise ibis, or, with the world so dangerous, a lion, or a wild boar too ferocious even for lions or hunters to meddle with.

I was hungry. I thought of the dove falling in, of my plucking it, eating its tender flesh raw, drinking its warm, clean blood. A fly did drop to the water and spun until I squeezed out its life. I dug a tiny ledge in the clay wall and put the fly there. Mosquitoes moved on the black water, and when one lit on my face, I killed it and added it and several others to the trove. I could look on them as provisions. It gave me a game to play, whether I decided to eat them or not.

The day began to darken, at first so slowly that I could hardly discern it. It was with the coming of night that I began to fear I would never get out, that no one would think of this deserted cattle graze. I began to cry. The well was like Sheol, a gray, drizzly place, the afterworld of the synagogue. Hitherto, I had not given a thought to the synagogue or its God. When I had imagined being saved, it had been by the father I worshipped, not Grandfather or his God. I recalled now the warmth of the synagogue, the feeling of security that had come with the smell of the incense and ancient cedar, the patient droning prayers of the tall, sure men in their shawls.

It was dark. I must eat. I must sleep. I sipped a little more of the water. I did not dare gulp it or I would vomit. I thought of my little store of bugs. No, I would not eat them. I recalled a chant from the synagogue: "Thy words were found, oh Lord, and I ate them." I thought of God's words falling from his mouth and tasting like pomegranates. Oh, how I longed for a pomegranate or some other soft, juicy fruit. The chant begged God to deliver the Jews from the hands of the wicked. If only he would deliver me from the well. He had the power to. Why was he unwilling? Because I was not a Jew, but a Roman? Because he was the God of the men who had thrown me in the well? But, no, he could not be. From my five years in the synagogue, I knew enough to be sure that while God might be unpredictable, he was not wantonly cruel.

Then had I done something to deserve this? No, nothing evil enough for this. Perhaps God did not know all that was going on in the world. That would explain why he left me in this well. And why the baby of the leper beggar perished before it even had life. And why Mother lost two babies.

I must attract God's attention. In a loud voice I said phrases from the synagogue: "Oh, Lord, my refuge in time of trouble. . . . Deliver me from the evildoers. . . . Be not a terror to me, although men have dug a well for my life." No, that was not it.

The mud on my injured foot was making it itch. But it was not mud: something was fixed to it! I grabbed in the water, screamed at the pain when I touched my toes and brushed a slimy, wriggling leech. I snatched it up and pinched off its head, then, breathing hard from my exertions, put it on my shelf.

I remembered Daniel being saved, and I thought of God coming down and fetching me from the well as he had come into the lions' den and shut the lions' mouths. But I could remember nothing of what God or Daniel had said at the time.

As the night went on, I slipped in and out of consciousness again, my dreams now muddled with courtyards and squares and excavations. Each time I dozed, I awoke with a mouth full of the nauseating water, the price I paid for a minute or two of half sleep.

Again, I tried to focus on the synagogue, and then I remembered another chant: "On the third day he will raise us up." "Lord," I said in the darkness, "on the third day, raise me up." If I could just get through this one night, it would be the third day. I saw the phrase written in big Greek letters. I said it aloud in Greek, and then Aramaic, and then I said it over and over in the Hebrew of the synagogue. I promised I would keep God in my heart, if only he would raise me up.

My stomach began to ache and I voided my bowels, unable to stop myself. I began to cry. By dawn, I was so weak from the wasting of my body that I could hardly keep from slipping beneath the fouled water. I thought of what a relief it would be to let my legs turn to dough and to go under and breathe in the dirty water for a few moments and be done. But, no, that was to die.

I was dizzy and knew it was the result of not eating. I looked at the dark niche where the leech, the fly, and the mosquitoes lay, but I could not eat them. It was the third day now, but I no longer gazed at the blue sky with hope.

A beetle fell, and almost without thinking, I pinched off its head and ate its body, a mere bit of crackling crust. I thought that the beetle must have done me some good since I did not vomit it, so I ate the fly and the mosquitoes, not even minding their slight bitterness. Then I ate the leech. I vomited, or rather gagged, for there was nothing substantial in me but bile.

I had long since stopped listening to sounds from above me. My eyes were closed, and phantasms, broken bits of memory and of unknowns, whirled in my aching head. I was losing awareness of myself, of time passing, of everything. I faded in and out of delirium. To retain some center, I prayed over and over in a rasping voice I hardly recognized as my own: "Lord, raise me up on the third day."

At times, I did not know whether I was awake or asleep. But I screamed with the horror of being in a nightmare when I heard a voice shouting "Halloo!" I was certain it was the men returning who had put me in the well. Yet, I heard apprehension in the voice, and a peasant twang. I looked up and saw a bulge, a head outlined at the well's mouth against the afternoon sky. "Help me! Help me!" I called.

"I heard you praying," said a man in crude Aramaic. "I hasten to get rope." I did not want the voice to go, but, yet, I knew I was saved. And because the man had called down to me as I prayed for help, I knew my savior was the God of the synagogue. Whether I thought at that time that he had saved me for some special purpose, I cannot remember. I can only recall sobbing, "Thank you, God, thank you . . ." over and over.

The man must have taken an hour to return. He let down a rope and instructed me how to tie it around my body and hold my arms tightly against my sides while he slowly hoisted me up. When he grabbed me at the top and eased me to the ground, I saw with a momentary panic that he, like the man who had thrown me in the well, had the curled side hair of the devout Jew.

The man carried me on his back. My left foot was in too much pain and my right leg was too weak for me to walk. At his crude hut, he put me on his pallet. I told him I was the son of the tribune, who would reward him. He looked at me first with disbelief, then wonder, and went, as I directed him, to Father.

Father, a centurion, and a captain, all armed, came out on horseback. Father ran to me and held me in his arms, sobbing, the first time I had ever heard him do so. Before we left, he put a purse containing gold in the hand of the herdsman—he was a land poacher with a few head of cattle in the underbrush. The man held it for a while and then uneasily gave it back. "Great sir, I cannot take this gold," he said. "Our father Moses himself has given us God's order that we shall love our neighbor as ourself, and to take gold for doing the work of God would be worse luck than losing a wolf tooth."

Father and the two officers stood amazed. But Father was never at a loss for words. "Then," he said, "will you let me rent you this land so that you need no longer fear that your poaching will bring on you the wrath of Rome, its owner?"

The herdsman looked even more distressed. "Great sir, my cattle will not be fat enough to sell until fall, so I cannot afford to rent. I must needs just go if you order it. . . ."

The man's worn goatskin purse was on the woven thistle table. Father took from it a quadrans, scarcely enough to pay for a piece of bread. "For this, it is yours to graze as long as you live," said Father. "Let me have your hand on it, kind herdsman. Tomorrow I will deliver to you a paper of rental and I will be in your debt forever."

Father ordered the man to say nothing of his discovery of me. At home, he gave our servants commands, on pain of torture and death, not to say I had been found. Mother brought me broth, and as I ate, Father had me go over every moment that I had spent with my abductors. He nodded approval when I said I had struck the man, and took note of his short dagger and the nature of his curses. It was not until the third recounting that I recalled the lisp. Father looked at me aggravatedly. "Demas, that is the most important thing you have remembered."

Father had me remain within our gates and when we had guests, in my room. Each night for a week I lay in my bed in fear until, unable

18

to bear it any longer, I went to my parents and begged them to let me crawl in with them as I had sometimes done when I was three or four. But Father, who had no doubt about the depths of my terror, sent me back to my room with a kind admonition. My door to the gallery, however, was locked.

Only Nathan ben Zev, the most talented physician in our region, was admitted to see me, and he under the most awful oath of silence. Despite his ministrations, the last joints on my left foot's two smallest toes were permanently stiffened. They remained deformed and nailless. Ever after, I had a slightly peculiar walk, more like a sailor's roll than a real limp.

Three weeks after my abduction, Father held obsequies on the basis that I would never be found. Another two weeks, and a letter was delivered to our door by a sailor. He had been given five drachmas and the guarantee of more from us by a man in Joppa who had kept his *couffieth* pulled over his lower face. The message contained directions to the well and a legend in Hebrew: "You will find him poisoning the well there as Roman and Jewish traitors have poisoned Judaea."

Five days later, three Zealots who had fled Borhaurus two years before were arrested by the Romans in Jerusalem, returned to Borhaurus, and subjected to "the wheel," a chariot wheel and axle to whose hub the victim's foot was lashed. The wheel was slowly turned while men held the suspect's shoulders, wrenching foot at ankle, calf at knee, and thigh at hip. By that time, guilt or innocence was generally established. The third Zealot screamingly remembered as his knee popped that he had told one Gaddiel, a *sicarius* with a lisp, of the location of the well. The two innocent Zealots were given small gold stipends as recompense for their crippling.

Two months after that, Gaddiel was found by the Romans in Alexandria, questioned, and returned to Borhaurus. He was already mad from his interrogation, part of which had been to pull an inside-out hedgehog's skin over his face, blinding him, a favorite torture of Herod the Great. He had confessed, but would not name his coconspirators. Father had him and the local man crucified at the place of execution, an abandoned quarry outside the walls. The Borhaurusian was put to death that evening with a spear thrust, a charity that Father, unlike most Roman officials, extended to those he sent to the cross. But he made an exception for Gaddiel. It was three days before he died.

Father took me there on the second day in hopes the man would hear him when he told him I was there to witness his dying. But I do not think the *sicarius* understood. His purple tongue half choking off

19

his words, he paused only a moment before hoarsely resuming prayers, some of them the same as I had uttered from the bottom of the well, along with curses similar to those he had mouthed that night against my mother and father.

◈

Father's power and Mother's wealth gave my early life the illusion of tranquillity and order. But even without the lasting terror of the well, I would have had no doubt that it *was* illusion. Rome had subdued Greater Palestine sixty-four years before I was born. Under the emperor Augustus, two of its regions, Idumaea and Samaria had cooperated with the Roman authorities to further Augustus's dream of a new Rome between the Jordan and the sea. Galilee and Judaea, lands of the Jews, were recalcitrant. One still heard how they sided with the Parthians and tried to sabotage the reign of Herod the Great, even though he rebuilt the Temple and Jerusalem more grandly than ever.

Caligula, Augustus's great-grandson, was emperor during my early adolescence. Beneath the regular march of the hours, the rich, plentiful meals, the servants and slaves, the seemly clothes for every pursuit, Roman officials were a threatened and frightened people. Fear of Caligula's homicidal folly penetrated the calm of our lives, and evil came to the land like hungry lions emerging from the scrubby brush of the Peraean mountains, vicious and unpredictable. On any day, a colleague of Father's, a neighboring tribune or even a procurator, might be summoned to Rome for execution, or exiled to some bare island. Or he might be found poisoned by his own or an unknown hand, and a sycophant of Caligula's would expeditiously arrive to take his place.

Caligula's insanity led Father and other administrators all over Palestine to yearn for his death. When these Romans visited our house, their whispers abated if I came into the room, but not before I heard snatches of incendiary talk: ". . . madman . . . incestuous serpent . . ." and once from Father himself: ". . . this lethal clown."

When I was fifteen, Caligula was assassinated, not by a man incensed by his excesses, but by one he had slanderously called a homosexual. *Sic semper tyrannis. Semper*, but through fortuities. By comparison, the reign of Caligula's successor, Claudius, was benign.

By then, to most appearances, I was a model Roman youth, the son of Junius Faevolian. I preferred a simple Roman tunic to the silk robes trimmed with fur, the golden chains, the white turbans and the shoes

20

of embroidered jackal skin that my grandfather, my uncles, and even my cousins wore.

I emulated Father's talk, his taste in foods, his brash riding style. He had been educated in Rome; his late father had been a minor member of the Senate; his grandfather, Drutus Faevolian, had been censor. I trained in swordplay and with other weapons both on foot and on horseback. Before I was eleven, I had wrestled, boxed, thrown javelins and discuses. I had also run and jumped, though less well than my fellows because of my toes.

My academic tutor was a sad, fleshy Greek named Aesubius, made a eunuch in Iconium forty years before by barbaric Moesian allies of Rome. He was a simple man, more learned than wise, his pleasures food, literature, and wine, in that order. I was more taken with the chatty Herodotus than Thucydides, with Sappho and Anacreon over Pindar. Aesubius also schooled me in the Romans on orders from my father. There, I much preferred Ovid with his lewd humor and Catullus with his eroticism to Vergil.

"*Ab Vergilio ad vinum ad venus*"—from Vergil to the vine to venery—Father once described my education to a friend at table, to my mother's embarrassment and my amusement. Father was premature: I had just begun sampling the second and had only speculated on the third of these curricula.

In my mid-teens, I accompanied Father into the field with the Borhaurus garrison for their two weeks of exercises. I was already tall, broad of chest, a bit thick at waist. I had his gray eyes and his Roman nose—a patrician face except for the wide mouth and dimpled chin inherited from my mother. In the field, we lived in tents, made forced marches with full packs, and kindled fires of wet, smoky wood with flints and tinder. I even learned to cook an edible stew.

I never lost contact with my Sadducee cousins, particularly Ezra, who was my age, but even taller, and thin as a sword. He and other aristocratic Sadducee youths outraged strict Pharisees, who looked on all Roman sports as sinful, by working out at the Xystus, a colonnaded square named after the great paved agora and sports area built by Herod in Jerusalem.

The Sadducees excelled at close-in dagger fighting. Secretly, some of them admired the *sicarii*. In our games, we used knife-sized dried carob pods tipped with pitch. We fought ferociously with and without small shields; the loser was he who was most smeared with pitch. We contested in view of the roof of a two-story house belonging to pious Jews. From this overlook, leading Pharisee citizens and even rabbis often cheered on the young Sadducees in their "knife" battles with us Roman youths.

While Pharisees and to a lesser extent Sadducees followed strict rules about sex, Romans regarded with easy tolerance everything but infidelity by their own wives. As a child, I saw sexual symbols above the doors of the town's two brothels and the prostitutes and catamites lazing in their doorways. And when I was twelve, two slaves, in exchange for four quadrantes from me and a friend, made love with acrobatic variation.

Yet, an abnormal timidity, perhaps related to my foot's deformity or the aftereffects of the synagogue's stern tractates against fornication, or both, made me fear physical love. My friends, steaming in the baths, told of conquests too explicit for me to doubt. I burned with jealousy, yet said—and did—nothing.

In the spring of my seventeenth year, the emperor Claudius's legate for Palestine, Barga Persullus, made his annual visit to the provinces. He was an amiable man, understanding of small bribes and other minor peccancies, merciful when he discovered large ones. His wife, Visilia, traveled with him. She was a straight, flat woman of forty with bark-brown hair beneath an embossed, but unjeweled, silver diadem. Her toga was always newly pressed, its folds as regular as the severe lines of her matriarch face.

On the second night of their visit, they sat in our box at the theater. As Barga, beaming from Father's best Falernian, lurched up convivially to acknowledge the audience's applause of his presence, he turned his ankle and pitched forward. His wife adroitly grasped the back of his toga, but lost her own balance, and tumbled after him with an indecorous display of white thigh. Barga was screaming in agony, the blood already running from where his shinbone had broken through his hairy skin.

Nathan ben Zev and his son came quickly to our home, to which Barga had been taken, and set and splinted the leg. Next day, the physician examined the leg and urged Barga not to move from his bed for at least four weeks. We made the second floor of our guest wing an infirmary. I was designated page to run messages, fetch medicines, and otherwise tend the patient's and his wife's needs.

While Barga did his best to read dispatches and dictate replies, he spent many hours drugged with poppy tea, an infusion called "lion fat," which upset his stomach less than myrrh. Our servants carefully lifted him to the toilet closet, but his wife, with my help in turning and lowering him, gave him his daily bath. I discreetly left the room when she washed his generative parts.

One day, I brought his letters to him and found the door slightly ajar. Through the crack, I saw Visilia Persullus on all fours atop him, her head enveloping his member, his face buried in her loins. Her white toga was bunched around her middle as she rocked back and forth faster and faster like a praying mantis until they both uttered low cries.

When later I came up to deliver the dispatch, Barga was asleep. His wife scrutinized me with her amaranthine eyes. I blushed so deeply that I was sure she suspected I had seen them, and I felt without knowing quite why that she might purposely have left the door ajar. In any case, the scene of domestic prurience simmered in me next day like a greasy lamb stew. When her back was turned, I imagined her naked white buttocks through the matronly toga.

After supper, she sent me to the apothecary for a special oil scented with storax to rub on her husband's bedsores. My heart beat faster; my palms sweated. I knew, and I knew she knew, that she had half a *choinix* of the oil remaining from her last purchase. I nervously climbed the stairs with the oil. Visilia Persullus was outside her door. I could hear the legate snoring in the adjoining room. With only an affixing look, she guided me through her doorway. I began to tremble, not from eagerness, but from the most abject apprehensions.

"Stop shaking," she whispered peremptorily from the darkness. She took the container of oil from my hand, put it down and folded her arms around me with extraordinary gentleness. I calmed slightly. She led me to her bed, and without letting go my hand, eased us both down. She took off her toga, and helped me from my garments. I tried to recall the lust that I had felt for her all day. But gentle as her kisses were, their insistence defeated my imagination, and it was only by a reperformance of her part in what I had seen through the crack of the door that Visilia Persullus was able to make even half a man of me. Ashamed, and yet relieved, I left in confusion.

I delayed going to the guest wing next day until just before supper. Not only did I feel guilty about seeing Visilia, but I worried that my looks might betray us to her husband. When, at last, I went, I was too agitated to enter the room until I saw that Barga had regressed. His wife had just taken the cup of cloudy poppy extract from his lips.

"Demas," he groaned, "you have been loyal as Ganymede. If you ever need a position, ever anything within my powers, it is yours." He held out his hand in pledge, and I, wiping my moist palm on my tunic, took it. As I left, his wife nodded, perceptible only to me. I hesitated. She nodded again; this time the invitation was unmistakable.

That night in her arms again, although fear seized me lest I be precipitant, she slid me between her wet nether lips as my climax

23

began and thrust up snugly and enclosingly so that I was deep inside. When I was done, I pressed my face between her breasts. She held my head to her warm skin, making no effort this time to find her own pleasure. I was a whole man.

Almost every night thereafter, I went to her. In the darkness, her clean, agile flesh made real all my dreams of a Cytherean Aphrodite. One night, coitus freshly completed, she took her lamp from the cabinet where it burned and studied me before her full-length mirror, watching herself as she touched me. "Ah, Demas," she said, "you are beautiful." I thought less of love than of hiding my mutilated toes. But those, also, she knelt and touched. Her words and the caress of my toes were, to me, gifts of worth beyond calculation.

Perhaps it was inevitable that one night her husband, now in a lighter splint and able to stump around the room with a cane, should break off his snores without our noticing. The door between the two rooms opened and I saw his jowly face made demonic by the small lamp he held in his hand.

"I will come to you in a moment," Visilia said firmly, as if she were ordering him to lift his chin so she could shave his neck. I lay cold as a corpse with fear. Barga hesitated for a second and then exploded.

"Whore! Whore!" he shouted, "filthy whore!"

She jumped naked from the bed and ran to him, propelling him into his own bedroom even as he screamed. I could hear her voice desperately and uselessly trying to calm him. But the alarums had already sounded. Clothes in my arms, I rushed past two of our servants—suddenly dumbstruck—as they climbed the stairs two at a time to aid Barga.

❁

Barga and Visilia left the next day. Father, Mother, the highest local officials, a representative of the Jewish Council, turned out to bid them good-bye. I watched from my room, to which I had been banished, worrying serially about whether I had hurt Father with Rome, Visilia with her husband, and myself with my family. When they were gone, and Father came in, I was prepared for exile, disinheritance, or worse.

"I assume that what I believe is true, that it was she not you who initiated this?" he said, sorely galled. It gave me an easy way out, but not one I could take.

"I was as eager as she," I said. "I loved her."

"Love?" he snorted.

I looked at the floor, not answering, waiting for his anger to diminish, aware that, as he did with every problem, he would soon analyze the options in terms of what was least likely to damage him, the family, and Rome, in that order.

"I must make some gesture," he said at last. "The man was our guest, and disabled as well. The servants will talk. The whole town, all Palestine, will know that you put horns on the legate of the emperor." He grew angry again. "My god, Demas, you are a fool. Surely you had brains enough for some discretion. If your inamorata"—he pronounced the word derisively—"were a Jew, she could be strangled or stoned to death, and you, perhaps, along with her."

He talked about detailing me to the legions in Syria, and even about sending me to one of the harsh Hebrew schools in Jerusalem. In the end, he settled on the academy at Scythopolis, one of the ten "Greek towns" in Palestine called the Decapolis. It was far enough away to be perceived as punishment, but not true exile.

III

As a going-away gift, Father gave me with characteristic irony the love poems of Catullus. My Roman friends gave me a javelin, a bearskin for my bed, a gladiator's helm. Ezra gave me an ornate Judaean dirk. It was keen as a razor, with a jeweled grip and a horsehide scabbard. With it, he enclosed a carob pod broken in half. My mother, her brown eyes even larger than usual with suffering, gave me a silver comb. In all of this, she had not asked me a single question.

At Scythopolis, we studied literature, history, ethics, philosophy, aesthetics, drama, poetry, music, and rhetoric, in all of which my good Aesubius had taught me well, and military strategy, medicine, the engineering of aqueducts and roads, in which he had not. The instruction was more Grecian than Roman, although Thermopylae was not taught as history or ethics, but as a failure of Sparta's military intelligence. We also worked at athletics, not just the pursuits of Borhaurus, but chariot racing and mock gladiatorial contests with net and trident.

In my second year, a combination of social pressures, lust, and curiosity led me to the city's upper-class brothel in a former temple to Artemis. On my first visit, the cheeks of the girl I picked were so rouged with *sikra*, her eyes so darkened with antimony, that it was only when she spoke that I realized she was no more than fifteen. Her palms were dyed orange with privet powder and she smelled of lily, but there was also a suggestion of rotting fish emanating from her private parts. For all her diligence, she might as well have been a marble maenad and I a granite Silenus.

26

Walking home from that unclean temple, I passed the place where Paul had been beaten. Our bodies are the temples of God, he had said, and if we defile them, we are doomed to death eternal. Harsh words, much like those of the elders arguing the tractates. Nevertheless, some months later, I went back to the brothel and chose a woman well into her thirties. She was an ignorant Greek from Pergomum, but kind. In her limestone chamber, its walls draped with threadbare rugs against the dampness, I was reassured of my manhood.

But that was no longer enough. Visilia Persullus, though I now realized she had been predatory, perhaps even with other youths before me, had been a person of intelligence, of quality. That lacking in physical love, the rest, it seemed to me, was only thrown seed. This time as I passed where Paul was pummeled, I thought of his words about love. They had been poetry, anything but harsh. Yet I wondered whether he had meant to apply them to physical love, even between married people.

When, at twenty, I left the academy and returned home, I had a reputation as a forceful debater, a passable writer, an aggressive wrestler, boxer, and swordsman, a good horseman and fair gladiator, a person who was neither pagan nor atheist nor agnostic, one who would argue philosophy but kept his thoughts on religion hidden. I left with high academic honors, but I think my teachers wondered, as I did myself, just what was synthesizing in my head, my heart, and my soul.

In Borhaurus, I was startled at how much older Father looked. Mother did not—until I regarded her more closely and saw that the cosmetics she had so carefully applied for my homecoming hid new lines. My short letters home and Father's and Mother's to me had fixed the terms of my return. For one thing, I would not follow Father into the legions. That left medicine, literature and the other arts, and engineering, all of which had interested me, but not sufficiently, and politics, administration, and pedagogy, which had not interested me at all. More or less by default, I agreed to Father's recommendation of the law.

I read Roman and Greek law, along with a good deal of Jewish law, since the Mosaic Law, with all the Talmudic variations, was the legal code of Borhaurus's majority. After a few months, Father found me a clerkship with an elderly lawyer. He handled land disputes, inheritance matters, rights-of-way, debts, torts, but not complaints by or

27

against the military, or other problems that touched directly on the order of the city and thus would come before Father.

Law came to fascinate me. Perhaps it was the visible impact of its applications, or, however fitfully, its respect for fairness. Or perhaps it was that I had always been a secret busybody and being in a law office made me privy to everything in the city's mind, heart, and intestinal tract.

I learned about the ownership of forest lands near Gideon by our neighbor's cook, recently manumitted, which made him richer than our neighbor. I found that the chief priest of the temple of Jupiter held a lien on a Pharisaic synagogue. I discovered the lengthy criminal record of an aged oxen that had trampled townsmen's gardens four times yet avoided the butcher's knife because its owner was a third cousin to the water minister of the late King Herod Antipas.

One evening, I passed through the small square on which stood the mud brick jail, the constabulary, and a few mean shops. At the window of the jail, I saw two hands on the bars and a tramp's weathered face leaning between them as he spoke hoarsely to a half-dozen listeners.

With a few minutes to idle away, I began to move closer. I heard voices behind me, turned and saw two husky men, one of them a leather craftsman named Ahiam. They were carrying an adolescent boy toward the jail. The youth's head lolled back and forth, and his eyes were abstracted with the mental pain of the badly disturbed. His body was properly proportioned, but abnormally loose, like meat in a sack. The bearers, both Jews, looked nervously at my Roman clothes. Then Ahiam recognized me and nodded. Taking a good purchase, they raised the lad to where the vagrant could put both hands in his hair and steady his head. The crowd around the window increased.

The jailed man's skin was dirty, his hair uncombed; two of his front teeth missing. His pale brown eyes withdrew to some far land as he began to pray in Aramaic, but with the cabbagy flavor of Galilee. "Lord Jesus Christ, son of the true God, beloved leader, hear your old comrade Andrew. . . ."

His words surprised me. Jesus was the "Messiah" that Paul had preached about on that parched day four years ago. But Paul had been an intelligent rhetorician. Had the ministers of his dead leader fallen away to this tatterdemalion?

". . . Master," the prisoner was going on, "this child has been brought to me by two unbelievers who are nevertheless good Jews like us. If it is your will to help him, please, please, give some of your steadiness to his head and your light to his eyes, and your strength to his poor body. It will also probably convert these two worthy men to our path. Master, believe me, we need all the followers we can bring over in this town."

Although this Andrew saw that his prayer for the youth was having no effect, he continued to pray, in much the same fashion, and ever more earnestly. The two men began to shift under the weight. At last, after almost a half hour, the vagrant preacher took his sweaty hands from the boy's hair. His face reflected his dismay so excruciatingly that I averted my eyes.

"I am sorry," he said to the two men. "I must not have believed I could do it strongly enough. Our Savior just was not with us. I could die right here over raising your hopes and then letting you down."

They lowered the youth, his head still swaying. Ahiam, who evidently was the boy's father, reached through the bars and awkwardly squeezed Andrew's wrist. "You tried hard, brother," he said. "Yes, you did," agreed a woman, the owner of a rag shop across from the jail. The audience dispersed. The magic show was over. It had disappointed. I was moved by the old supplicant's failure, the desolation in his eyes. He was no charlatan. He had sought nothing for himself, only for the boy. I came to the window. The prisoner held his head in his hands, from remorse or fatigue or both.

"You," I addressed him. "Have your prayers ever worked?"

He looked up. The trappings of the orator, sorry as they were, were gone.

"Sometimes. Rarely."

"Then why try? It makes a fool of you."

"Why not try? Jesus told us to preach his word, forgive sins and do miracles, and the others do them fairly often." He brooded on it a moment, then went on, his tone more acerbic. "And what if I am a fool? Who cares? The sands of my time on earth are running."

"Why? What are you charged with?" I asked.

"Incitement to riot. But I am innocent."

I smiled. *Everyone* in jail claimed he was innocent. But incitement to riot was a serious charge. Why had I not heard of the case? I wondered. "Incitement to riot?"

"So they say. I was trying to tell a few people about Jesus, our Savior and Messiah, and here I am."

I smelled a dead jerboa in the bed straw. "Tried *where*?"

"On the synagogue steps."

For him to call *anyone* a Messiah on the synagogue steps was a sacrilege. "You're lucky you were not beaten into gruel."

I thought of Paul all but challenging the rabble to assault him. "You

29

people are lunatics. Does your Jesus ask you to get yourselves killed? Do you know a man named Paul?"

"Paul, a Tarsan?" said the unkempt man. "All of us know him—" he paused an instant before adding—"and admire him."

"Some more than others?"

The prisoner smiled, bad teeth on either side of the gap. "Thou hast said it, not I."

That pricked my curiosity. The Cilician's memory had fretted me like a small stone in a sandal. "I saw him beaten once." I started to say I had tried to help him, but why explain myself to this beggar? "Has this happened to you before?"

"Unhappily. And when the Jews see old scars on my back, they'll know I was whipped before and declare me incorrigible. This time, they'll cut out my tongue. Or stone me."

I studied the man's face. There was a kind of gallantry in him. I had not been able to help his coreligionist. Why not accord him a fragment of help? What would it cost me? A talk with Father, a visit to Grandfather?

"My grandfather is on the Jewish Council . . . if you will stop this stupid preaching, not rile things any further, I will go see him." I started to tell him my father was tribune, but held back.

He groaned. "Good young man, I cannot."

"Cannot shut your mouth to save your tongue? Or your life?" I was both surprised and angered. Why try to save a fool like this? But I imagined the pincers pulling the tongue, the quick dumbing slash of the knife. "Listen, madman, would you at least leave town?"

"I would do that," he said. "Our master told us if people won't listen to shake the dust off our feet and move on."

That night, I spoke with Father. He had heard of Andrew's case at the daily meeting of Roman functionaries. I made my arguments with what I hoped was judicial aplomb. "Except on his 'Messiah,' he is not deranged. He is stubborn, yes, but well meaning. He does not deserve death or maiming." I hoped my last word would make Father think of my foot.

Father shifted in his chair. "Demas, his braying on the synagogue steps about some beggar being the coming King of the Jews . . . Why, he might as well have dropped his *saq* and unloaded his bowels."

"But a poor vagrant . . ." I said. "Can we just stand back and let them cut his tongue out? Or stone him to death?"

"Well, it's Oriental, yes, but it's also a Jewish, not a Roman, matter. The man, under their Law, is a blasphemer. And in this case, most of the Sadducees agree with the Pharisees."

I recalled Father had once said to Mother, "Your father and the rest of the Sadducees dread the arrival of a Messiah because he would overturn the system. The Pharisees dread his arrival because he would not."

Mother had smiled. "And you Romans?"

"We dread him," Father had answered, "because we would have to kill him, and by so doing would unite the Pharisees and the Sadducees."

Thinking of these delicate relations between Rome and the Jews, I said, "You could let it be known that Caesarea"—where the procurator, Rome's supreme voice in Palestine, kept office—"was looking for precedents from the Jews themselves to use in punishing obstreperous Jews. You could suggest that a flogging would go unnoticed in Caesarea, but that a public linguaectomy or a ritual stoning could not be kept quiet. And the next ones, God forbid, might be performed by Romans on Zealots, or perhaps the precedent might be used by Rome to remove other parts of any *sicarius* who got caught."

Jewish Law discriminated against men with deformed or mutilated genitals. They were not allowed to serve as priests or even enter religious assemblies. Raising the possibility of Roman castration of Jews would divide the council's fearful Sadducees from the vengeful and obdurate Pharisees.

"Spoken like a true lawyer," Father responded with mild disdain, then with unkind bite, "or like one of your old synagogue prefects arguing about whether you must fish a fly out of your soup with one or two fingers on the Sabbath. No," Father said, "I will not lie that way." But he gave me a tight smile, signaling a major concession. "I might let them know it is *conceivable* Caesarea would use this case as a precedent for sentences of mutilation against Jews. That much is true."

The next day, I went to Grandfather's, one of the few houses in Borhaurus with a garden: a fragrant corner in the court with imported roses and native jasmine. His cedar floors were covered with rugs from Persia, his walls with tapestries from Greece. He financed caravans to the one, ships to the other, and used the money from trade to make high-interest loans (but through a pagan factotum, for he would not dream of personally violating the adjurations of the Mosaic Law against usury).

"Demas, Demetrius." He made a mild jest at my name, a derivative from that of several Macedonian kings and a Greek sculptor. "You are so stern of countenance that I can only postulate you are seriously in debt or seriously in love."

Immaculately and richly robed in a long-sleeved lounging chethomene, Grandfather hugged me, kissed me on each cheek, and waved me to a hassock beside the low couch on which he reclined. A black slave, a rare Ethiop, appeared at the doorway and Grandfather nodded. Soon the best fig and nut cakes and date juice in Borhaurus appeared.

I told Grandfather my purposes, explaining that to cut out the tongue of this miscreant or to kill him would encourage other members of his cult to come to Borhaurus, either to seek followers or to give their lives up to martyrdom.

He shook his head. "This is much ado over the tongue of a disgusting renegade who would save a great deal of wasted breath if he lost it. If I help, it is not for him, but for you, and to prevent my Pharisee brethren from behaving like Scythians, and thus shaming all Jews."

"Then you will make common cause with Father?" I knew from experience it was best to tie Grandfather down precisely. He was subtle enough for a seeming yes to prove to be a no.

"Make common cause? Certainly not as such. It would only stimulate my colleagues' choler. But I will *independently* recommend we confine ourselves to a scourging."

I greedily put four cakes on the tiny gold plate given me. Grandfather rolled his eyes in mock astonishment. I knew he loved me, perhaps second among his grandchildren only to Ezra.

"What do you know of the Jesus this man is preaching?" I asked, munching.

"That the Pharisees had him crucified in Jerusalem, that he supposedly worked miracles, sometimes on the Sabbath, that he appealed to the rabble. His is a cult of the *am-ha-arez*"—circumcised, but illiterate, despised Palestinians who had abandoned Mosaic Law.

I told him about Paul, saying he seemed anything but *am-ha-arez*, at least as far as his intelligence was concerned. Grandfather took a fastidious taste of fig cake. "Demas, in every group of the dispossessed there are able opportunists who ride it for power or money and eventually rise above it. If this social law were not true then how— those five hundred years ago in Rome—would such plebeians as the Faevolians have ever advanced to patricians." Grandfather had pronounced his bon mot for the day. We could now catch up on family and town gossip.

IV

The Jewish Council made a pageant of punishing Andrew. It took place in the afternoon before the main synagogue. Grandfather wore a turban of white silk. His linen robe, dyed deep blue, was trimmed at collar, cuffs, and hem with ermine as gleaming as his beard. On his hands, he wore four rings, and around his neck a gold chain with a jeweled Star of David pendant. The other four Sadducee council members and the dozen Sadducee community leaders were only slightly less ornate.

In contrast, the Pharisees wore no jewelry. Their robes of tightly woven wool were gray, black, or dark blue and, save for blue tassels laced with gold threads, were without trim. They wore black-and-white silk prayer shawls, embroidered with grapes and pomegranates, over their heads and chests, and large phylacteries tied on their foreheads and hands.

The chairman of the council carried a Torah, signifying the religious nature of the punishment. The vice chairman held a scroll of laws and interpretations. Many of these same men had been familiars of the synagogue when I had been a child. I resented their part in this present rigmarole in much the same way that I had resented Father's oblique insult to them.

Even so, I understood the pomp. Since the last of the Jewish Hasmonean kings had been crushed a hundred years ago, the Jews had desperately clutched what power remained to them. Their ceremonies were the strongest evidence that even under Rome, they continued as a nation. The ritual flogging of a blasphemous mendicant became a

33

restatement of their judicial independence. Throughout the empire, Rome wisely permitted such steam vents in the boiling caldrons of its subject peoples.

Three thousand men, women, and children had turned out for the chastisement. They filled the square, some standing on boxes and carts. Every rooftop was crowded. The voices were like the humming of countless bees. By dint of Father's office, I stood among the soldiers atop a rampart overlooking the square. They were distant enough not to offend the Jews, but near enough to act in the unlikely event of disorder.

Andrew, naked except for a loincloth, was led by a rope around his neck from the side of the synagogue and all noise ceased. A wiry drover in his fifties, the *hazzan*, or combined beadle-clerk-scourger, stepped up with his two grown sons. They tied Andrew's arms to the lintel of a doorframe anchored with building stones. His stretched body faced the synagogue.

Better the double-strip lash of the drover, I thought, than the whips knotted with lead or the knuckle bones of sheep that the Roman legions used to punish troopers. And better a whipping than a Jewish ceremonial burning. In these, the condemned man was shoved into a pit of manure up to his waist and covered with flax fibers that were ignited with a stick, and the stick was thrust burning into his mouth.

Andrew slumped miserably, a far remove from the proud bearing of Paul and his two disciples before the ruffians in Scythopolis. The chairman of the council walked officiously down the steps and stood before the bound man. I could not hear what he said, but knew it was an anathema. The procedure had been delineated a thousand years ago. Andrew nodded his head and made a response. The chairman went back to his place. The vice chairman raised his arms toward two heralds bearing rams' horns who blew the eerie bleats one hears during the high holidays.

The *hazzan* whipped the lash through the air twice, then brought it down on Andrew's shoulder with a crack that we could hear even on the ramparts. Andrew's body jerked forward against the bonds so hard that his feet left the ground. Again, the drover flogged. I watched, sickened. Halfway through, the scourger moved from Andrew's back to his front. A few more lashes and Andrew sagged in a faint. One of the whipper's sons threw a bucket of cold water on him. When that did not revive him, the drover put a flacon of salts under his nose.

In all, he was hit forty times minus one. The blood ran down his torso and streaked his legs. If he had been a sexual offender, he would have gotten a third of the lashes on his genitals. Andrew was fortunate: his crime was of the heart.

When it was over, I made my way to the jailhouse, where ordinarily a flogged man was allowed to recover, but Andrew had already been expelled from Borhaurus. At the Joppa gate, the blind beggar, a fixture, told me that an hour ago he had heard the soldiers releasing a prisoner there. Thinking the freed man might have a quadrans or two left, the beggar had solicited him.

The blind man grinned at me toothlessly: "This prisoner said, 'All I have is thirty-nine stripes and I would not give them to my worst enemy.' Then, Sir Demas, he was on his way, to Modi'im, he said." I gave the beggar a half-dozen quadrantes.

Modi'im was a long walk. If robbers saw Andrew, they would kill him for his rags. Aware I was inviting Father's anger, I harnessed my stallion and a mule. I told Mother what I was doing, to her displeasure. I softened it by adding that I needed to go to Lydda anyway to get some polished cypress for shelving. I assured her I would stop in the inn at Jalon, a town along the way, before nightfall.

I stocked the mule's saddlebag with Samnium wine, bread, ewe cheese, ripe olives, pickled fish, pomegranates, and medicinal oil. I had been on the road for an hour when I saw Andrew limping along. He heard the animals' hooves and turned, smoothing his tattered robe in hopes he could beg passage on the riderless mule. When he recognized me, he shuffled toward me, and as I drew up, took the bridle of the big black horse.

"You ran away without paying my legal fee," I joshed him gently. He looked sly. "Well, I will give you the robe off my back, but I would rather give you the back in my robe."

I dismounted and told him I had business in Lydda, but that we could treat his back and eat. Then I would take him to the Modi'im turnoff, where he could keep the mule blanket and sleep away from the road safe from robbers. Andrew's stomach was unready for food. When he eased himself out of the top of his robe, I saw the scars from old floggings and the wide, gooey welts of the new. I was amazed he had been able to walk as far as he had. He rubbed the oil on his shoulders and more gingerly on his chest. I salved the wounds on his back.

"Bad, but not the worst," he commented. "Some Romans up in Tiberias, vicious sons of dogs—pardon me for saying it to a Roman— laid them on four years ago with leaded whips."

"Why? Why would Roman soldiers beat you?"

"Sport, just sport," Andrew said, not without bitterness. "A follower of Jesus Christ is fair game for everybody. We have no power on this earth. Those soldiers had me dancing with one hand over my eyes and the other over my parts. The Jews show a little respect for a man's organs of generation. Unless you have raped your mother-in-law or some such, of course."

It was dark by the time we reached the Modi'im turnoff. I would not make it to Jalon tonight and would, like him, have to sleep out. We walked the mounts well off the road to a copse of oaks too scrawny even for timber cutters. While I got out the food, Andrew gave the animals feed from the mule's side bags. I soon had a small fire going. Though it was winter, the midday heat had been sweltering, but tonight it might chill below freezing. I dug the wax seal from the amphora with the dagger Ezra had given me and passed the wine to Andrew. He drank deeply, eyes closed. "I could cry, it's so good," he said with a broad smile.

I had never seen anyone with so little malice. Was it really not there, or did he learn to tolerate torment and accept the tormentor the way street fire-eaters learn to live with heat and smoke in their throats?

"I wonder at you," I said. "You have been whipped from Baalbek to Beersheba; your teeth are falling out and the gods alone know what else; you cannot work a miracle; you cannot turn anyone to your God. But here you are, cheerful. You do not even hate the people who beat you. . . ."

He saw my curiosity was not merely rhetorical. "If you believe in Jesus, Sir Demas, it is all quite simple." He tried to tell me about turning the other cheek, and loving those who hate you, but it all sounded like a poor student reciting imperfectly learned lessons. He sensed he was failing to reply in a way that would mean anything to me and looked unhappy.

"Could I just tell you how I came to know Jesus?" he asked. "That might be the best way to answer you."

"Will it explain why you are like you are?"

"If it doesn't, then I don't know how to . . ."

We had a whole night ahead. "Tell it, then," I said.

He looked for a while at the fire, recollecting, then commenced: "It all began twenty years ago, when we were fishermen in Galilee, my brother Peter and I. Late one afternoon, we were casting our nets from shore because a squall was spitting and hissing, and along came this man, younger than us, in his late twenties. When we had drawn in the nets, he told us he was Jesus, son of Joseph, the carpenter of Nazareth. We thought at first he might be selling oars or bait traps. But, no, he said he was a preacher and that he felt what he had to say

36

would change things. He needed people to help him. We started to move away, saying we were fishers, but he nodded at the nets and said, 'If you follow me, I will make you fishers of men.' "

I put sticks on the fire, and Andrew thought I was getting impatient. But in fact the wine had made me feel content, unhurried. The stars were huge and lustrous and their and the moon's cold silver made the woods look like one of Ovid's magic forests, all sheen and filigree.

". . . That night he ate with our family, and two of our partners, James and John, and their father, Zebedee, came by. Jesus talked about how God had inspired him and how he regarded God, in a way different from how he felt about Joseph, as his father. We knew he was not, in one sense, anything more than the son of a carpenter. Yet he knew our law, the prophetic works, the histories, like a rabbi. But he didn't *talk* like a rabbi. He said that all the rules and regulations, all the 'if this, then that' of all the scrolls of the Law and all the rabbis' wisdom of the centuries, could be summed up with one simple Law: Love God first, and love our neighbors like ourselves. . . .

"Peter is younger than me, and smarter, and he said, 'Everybody already knows about loving God and man. *That's* in the Torah.' And Jesus said, 'Yes, but *I* am saying that even if you forget everything else in the Torah, *everything*, and practice that one rule, you will find life everlasting.' 'You say *everything*,' Peter said, 'the Sabbath observances, the rules for food, the Ten Commandments . . . ?'

" 'I am saying *everything*,' Jesus said.

"For hours we talked, and every time we raised a situation where his rule would not be enough, he explained why it was. John said, 'Well, that is something so simple even I could preach it.' And Peter and James nodded, and even I thought that it was easy to remember: Love God; love man. Deep in the night, he said, 'So who among you will be first to come with me?' And he looked at me. I wasn't married, and I had never heard anyone like this before. Just imagine, Sir Demas, that you were standing by a lodestone as big as a mountain but did not know it, and you had an iron kettle in your hand. The kettle would draw you right to the mountain. You would think it was enchantment. That was the way he drew me, and so I said yes. And Peter said, 'Well, somebody has to go along and take care of Andrew,' and they all laughed, Jesus, too. Peter was not getting along with his wife, anyway, but truly that was not the main thing. And John said, 'We may never get a chance to do anything like this again.' And his brother James said something like 'If we don't like it, we can always come back.' "

"So you followed him as he asked? Just like that?"

"Yes, and even then we knew we were doing the right thing. It was as clear as when lightning hits near the boat on a dark night and you can see every piece of rope, every nail, every splinter, even. That clear."

In the firelight, Andrew's face seemed a bearded mask, something ancient, mythic, absorbing, so deep was he in his thoughts.

"Now, remember, I am a Jew, so I never knew what it was *not* to have a God. But my mind was cluttered about what that God was. Jesus showed us he was simple to understand: powerful, but a God of love, not rules and punishments and more rules. When I understood that, I knew no man could ever hurt me again. I knew I was happy and always would be in the work of following Jesus, doing what I could."

Andrew had a bardic sense of people and distances. He talked awhile of the long marches, the songs along the way, the laughter and foolishness and comradeship. "Ah, it was good times at the end of the day when we were all together on the road. I tell you, even a young unbeliever like you would have seen how grand it was. Jesus called me 'Old Protokletos'—it meant 'first-called.' The others picked it up, and it became a joke. Sometimes, the master would question us on what we thought about something and he would go down the list—Peter, John, Thomas, and so on—and at the end, he and the rest of them would shout, 'And what about Old Protokletos?' I knew they were having a little raillery, and I liked it."

When Andrew talked of Jesus, it was with the admiration of a loyal career corporal for a brilliant lieutenant destined to become a general. After a while, I turned him toward the death of Jesus, and he gave me a quick look and then said Jesus had come back to them from the dead, and I interrupted.

"Did you see him?"

"No, but the others did," he replied vehemently.

"Your brother?"

"Well, he was not as sure as some were."

Such things just do not happen, I argued.

"Sir Demas," he replied, "we believe or we don't. You asked me why I was cheerful. I have told you. I was happy in the three years I was with the master and I have been happy ever since, and I hope he will let me join him again when I die."

I found it as natural to talk about myself with this stranger as he had found it natural to talk with me. I told him about my family and my youth, including why I was banished to Scythopolis. I spoke of my conviction that there was a God, one perhaps different from the God of the synagogue, yet a presence that was everywhere, a force that had saved me from the horror of the well for some special reason. Andrew nodded in agreement.

I came back to Paul, and how he had seemed two people, one a scolding runt and one the bearer of words about love that I had thought so important I had written them down. Andrew smiled knowingly, just as he had at the jail.

"You are not fond of him. That much is clear," I said.

"Well, Paul is sincere," he responded. "When he talks, you know Jesus is in him. And he gets things going. He has brought dozens, hundreds, to us in Antioch, Cyprus, Pamphylia. He's in Jerusalem now, reporting about it. He has all the accomplishments I lack. I admit that. Paul is the sun of our earthly sky, and while our sky may be a millet seed to you and Rome, it is everything to us. But Paul is preaching things I never thought the master was saying."

"When he talks about love, it sounds to me that is *exactly* what your Jesus was saying."

He took up the amphora—I was glad I had brought a large one—drank and belched defiantly. The drink was bringing out a streak of belligerence in him I had not seen before.

"Oh, yes, on that, yes. But consider this: Paul talks like a Roman hangman, pardon the expression, about fornication and gluttony and drunkenness and so on. Now, Jesus did not say fleshly lapses are not wrong. Some are disgusting. But it did not seem to *me* that Jesus felt they were in a class with hatred, and rage and greed and cruelty, things like that. If parts of Paul's preaching catch on, then I think we will sound like a herd of fanatics, mean as pigs and just as unforgiving."

"But surely *someone* remembers what *Jesus* said about these things. You were all with him."

"We *all* remember," said Andrew with a sigh. "That's our trouble. We remember the way we want to. Nobody wrote down at the time exactly what he did say."

"So Paul's version—"

"He got most of it from talking with Peter and the rest of us, and adding a little here and there out of his own head. Paul never even saw Jesus except, he says, in a flash of light that blinded him for a while."

That surprised me. I had thought from Paul's tone that he had been a companion of the dead man. I considered this new God Andrew preached: a self-taught eccentric whose obstinacy led him to a cross, an orator whose words were already beginning to be lost in controversy. But I was getting drowsy. The fire had burned down. The night had gotten cold. The wine was gone. "It's time to bank the coals," I said.

Andrew, however, had stubbornly made up his mind to go on to Modi'im. He feared the head of his coreligionists there, a fuller, would hear news of his beating and think he was dead. Andrew wanted to arrive first to assure him he was alive. I argued, but it was useless.

"The Furies damn you, then," I cursed, giving in. "Get on the mule. I will take you on to Modi'im." Now he argued, saying he would be safe alone, but I had also made up my mind.

V

❖❖❖

We were an hour down the road at a small stream in bright moonlight when I heard scrambling on stones. I saw one man come out of the creek bed, a second from the other side of the road where he had lain, two others close behind him, all armed with pikes. Brigands! I felt a stab of panic.

My horse whinnied and shied as the first of them clutched my reins. Behind me, I heard the voice of the second and third robbers and Andrew's shouts. Negligent from the wine, I had left my scabbard secured to my saddle instead of belting it at my waist. The first brigand saw me frantically grabbing at the scabbard and tried to wrest it from my hand. In effect, he held it for me. I snatched out the short broadsword, my instincts mitigating my fear, and with one stroke hacked into his neck where it joined the shoulder.

He screamed and fell, the reins still in his hand. The stallion reared, tumbling me to the ground. Seeing me helpless, the fourth brigand wheeled toward me. His leather cuirass gleamed like copper in the moonlight. He lunged with his pike and I parried with my sword, but the impact knocked the weapon from my hand. His pike head plowed into the soil, and I grasped it desperately with both hands. The robber dragged me toward him as if I were an impaled hare on a stringed arrow. He called out to one of his comrades to dispatch me while I was helpless.

I released the haft, throwing him off balance, came to one knee and clawed at my waist for Ezra's dagger. The pike man lunged again. I dodged and sprang up, catching him around the waist. He saw the

41

dagger, dropped his spear, and feverishly gouged with one hand at my eyes while he fumbled for my wrist with the other. With all my might, I drove the razor-sharp dirk into the cuirass. So stiffened was the leather that only the point stung him, enough for him to howl. I jerked up the back of his cuirass at its cross-laced closure. In this murderous simulacrum of love, I stabbed again, this time into the soft flesh above his pelvis.

Struck to the death, he vomited food and blood. My knife was fixed in his vitals. I could not get it out. One of the two remaining robbers left Andrew and lurched muddily from the creek where he had been holding the mule. I grabbed up the dropped pike with my aching right hand. Andrew was manfully wrestling the other cutthroat in the bushes, from the sound of their thrashing. But the bandit thrust the old man aside like a bushel of wheat husks and he, too, scrambled toward me. The pike I held was far heavier than a throwing javelin. Nevertheless, I cocked my body like a bow and hurled it as best I could at my closest adversary. The conical iron point whizzed past him, but buried itself in the second man's gut. He fell, body thrashing.

I rushed toward my sword. Then, the unimaginable happened. The man I had speared, in his rolling dance of death, spasmed so violently that the shaft of the planted pike whipped around and hit me in the temple. Dazed, I tried to raise my sword, but could not. The final robber drew back his pike, targeting my unprotected torso. I had a weird presentiment of the deadly iron entering my chest.

In that eye's blink, Andrew threw himself between me and the pike head. I felt the spear jar, not into me, but into Andrew. His breath rushed out as we fell. I squirmed from under him, the sword still in my right hand. The brigand freed the iron head from Andrew's lower side. I crawled backward like a scorpion, my eye on the pike head, blooded with my deliverer. The man jabbed, but the spear slipped between my arm and my chest. I jumped to my feet and the man stalked me. But I had a new ally: a scalding rush of anger. This man had struck, perhaps killed, a hero, my friend and savior. I was armed. I was a Roman.

When the pike man thrust, I savagely chopped. When he swung, I parried, some of my skills from our gladiator contests in Scythopolis coming back to me. As his weariness brought down the pike head, I slashed the pike to the ground and stamped on it, dashing it from his hand. He turned and fled and I ran after him, knowing I dared not help Andrew while this man lurked in the woods or summoned other highwaymen. Though large, the man was not agile. He crashed through the underbrush.

As I drew up on him, he tripped and quickly curled into the ball of an unborn child, crying hoarsely. His hands cradled his head. I chopped. The blade severed his wrist and he flopped over. His face, dappled by the shadows was like that of a fetus, the eyes bulging but closed. With disgust for him and for myself, I shut my own eyes and hacked again. When I looked, I saw I had all but beheaded him. The blood had jumped up my arm like a fountain.

In the gorse, the mule and horse grazed together, men's lives and deaths all alike to them. Andrew lay beside the road, groaning. His robe was bloody, but the blood was dark. The bright red blood that carried life was still in him. I pulled up his robe. The wound was deep and wide, and beneath the ooze was a gory mess of punctured entrails.

I cut a strip from my tunic, made a compress and held it helplessly on the wound. Andrew's eyes were full of pain, but he mustered a smile, blood on his lips from the ruptured vessels inside him. I lifted him slightly to slip my belt under him and bind on the compress. Even that small movement increased the flow of blood. If I tried to put him across the mule, he would bleed to death. I wet another swatch of my tunic from the water bag and wiped the dirt from his face and from around the wound, trying desperately to think what to do.

"Not much left, hunh?" He read my thoughts. He closed his eyes. "Dear Jesus, what a day."

"As soon as the blood has congealed a little," I improvised, "I am going to get you on the mule. Modi'im is not an hour away."

"Two, three hours," he corrected me. He raised his hand feebly just above the ground. The fingers trembled like willow leaves in a breeze. "Come now, Demas"—he had finally dropped the "Sir"—"don't lie to Old Protokletos."

"How could I lie? You saved my life. I can . . ."

Andrew snorted a little laugh, then grunted in anguish from it. "You can what? You can certainly stick a pig. But you can't get me off the ground. No, my boy, I want to say something while I still have my wits. It's going to distress you, but I want to say it. Just let me catch my breath for a second."

I had thriftily thrown the wine amphora into my saddle bag. I gave Andrew the last few drops. He commenced in a low voice, conserving both words and volume. "Now listen. I have left only the plainest words." He took a breath, and coughed blood. I wiped it from his lips. "At this moment, I could ask you to give me, to give Jesus, your life in return for mine and you would do it. I know how you Romans are. And for you, maybe it would not be such a jump, because of your grandfather and the synagogue and whatever God you already have in you. . . ."

43

"I would, Andrew," I said. "I would." And it was true. I was in debt to him for my life. Whatever terms for repayment he asked, I would meet them. He understood.

"I could ask you to take up what I am putting down, to go from one cold, uncaring town to the next, preaching to ears that do not want to hear."

"I would do it."

The dying Galilean grimaced. "I know, I know, but I am not asking you to climb into these old sandals. What I do is not conscript work. You would come to hate it and Jesus, too, and then what kind of stupid bargain would I have struck?"

I was silent. I was the more deeply sorry because he was saying, and truly, that I could not honestly worship his God, and that to say I could would be to pay Andrew for my life in bad coin, coin unsuited for my great debt.

"You would be so good at it," Andrew said, beginning to drift. "I was clumsy. A fellow like you, with a fast tongue and good Greek and Latin. Why you could bring over as many in one day as I could in a half year. Another Paul . . ." He was listening only to his own thoughts. "I suppose I ought to ask you to take me to the creek so I could baptize you. That's how we mark you as belonging to Jesus. It would be such a triumph after all these dry years, a Roman tribune's son, grandson of a rich Sadducee. Even Peter would click his teeth over that."

Suddenly, my tears began to drop. Was that all he wanted, the poor old trooper? A little honor on earth and in heaven? I took his hand. "Andrew, I do not have to believe the same way you do. You saved me. You are the finest man I ever knew. Andrew, my old friend, baptize me!"

His words and his death that I could do nothing about were clawing under my skin, grabbing at my heart. I began to sob, the tears running through the dirt on my face and into my mouth. "Andrew, I could *try* to worship your Jesus. I love you so I must love the God that I can see is in you."

"Oh, Jesus," he said, his voice suddenly loud, "it is such a temptation." He opened his eyes and saw my face. It must have looked like mud flats. He smiled. "No, I know what is right. I am too close to seeing the master again, and I won't take the chance." He breathed deeply and gave a little cry from the effort. "Here, we are wasting time. What I want you to do is this and when it is done, no more talk of debt, all right?

"That little oil flask will do. Take it to the creek and fill it with

44

water. I am going to bless it. The oil will keep it from getting stagnant. Seal it up. Think over what we have talked about. When you have a day or two, go to Jerusalem and find my brother at what we call the Apostolic Council, on Celicus Street. Tell him what happened to me. If he is on the road, tell James; he's the brother of Jesus and the head of the council." He paused, then recommenced in great pain. "If by then you think you want to be baptized, I mean for yourself, not for me, then maybe you would want this water used in the ceremony. I would be very proud. . . ."

He gasped and I started to go for the flask and to the creek, but he held me with his trembling hand. He was trying to find the strength to say something else. When he did, his voice was so low it was hard to hear. "It would be like having a son of my own. I never did, not as far as I know"—and he was too weak to smile at his small bad joke—"and the way my poor old loins got whipped and caned over the years, and not even for sexual offenses, I probably wouldn't have been able to anyway." He stopped, and in spite of his beard and the streaked face I could see the flush of death was on his skin. He was in agony. I moistened another piece of my shredded tunic and put it to his lips, but all he did now was mouth "Go."

So I rushed to the pack for the half-empty flask, then to the stream. When I got back, he was barely alive. He blessed the flask in a whisper and kissed it. ". . . If you have absolutely made up your mind you do not want to be one of us, then give the flask to Peter or James so they can use it to baptize somebody else. But if you still have not made up your mind, then save it until you are ready . . . because I think you will be, Demas, you will . . ." He shut his eyes. "Christ Jesus, take me up," he said aloud and died.

I covered my face with my tunic and wept. At last, when I could, I put the mule's saddle blanket over Andrew and tied up the animals. I did not think I would be able to sleep, but I wrapped my cloak around me and lay on the stallion's blanket. My body was at the end of things. I went to sleep beside the road with the five dead men around me.

Just after dawn, I awoke. I washed my sword, my dagger, my face and arms and Andrew's face. I wrapped his body in the blanket, and tied him on the mule. I took the road toward Modi'im. That was where he had been going and that was where I was going to see he went.

In Modi'im, I asked the first townsman I saw if he knew a fuller who "talks of a minor prophet, one Jesus, a dead Galilean." The man looked at my bloody, torn clothes and at the body strung across the mule. However, he heard my Roman accent and so did not question me, but directed me to the shop of one Rechab. The fuller was built like the barrels in which he kept his moist yeasty-smelling earth. There were stacks of clothes, two wide cleaning tubs, a press with two thick screws for squeezing clothes, and strutted half globes and tripods for drying and bleaching them.

I told him briefly what had happened since Andrew came to Borhaurus. He kept interrupting me with groans, as if he had lost a son or wife or a business he had spent a lifetime building. I could understand how for the people who belonged to the little cult, the loss of one of the few who had actually walked with their God Jesus would be a tragedy. We carried Andrew's body through the front room, which was without windows to keep the fuller's clay from drying out. In a second room, his living room and kitchen, we put the body, its makeshift cerements now stiff with blood, on his table.

Rechab's wife, a quiet, worn woman, came in and he quickly summarized my report then told her to get the "church" together. I was eager now to be on my way, and asked him whether I could buy a fresh tunic from him. He found one of exquisite byssus linen. Clearly, the creditor it had belonged to was a fashionable one. He vigorously shook his head when I tried to pay. I started to bid him farewell, but he said, "I had hoped, sir, that you could tell our congregation of our great brother's last days. It would mean something to us all our lives."

I did not want to be part of his ceremonies. I wanted to leave this unfamiliar world where my instinct to help Andrew had thrust me. But the events since the robbers attacked us were like a rain-swollen stream overflowing its banks and I was caught in the currents. I had to ride them out.

In a few minutes, the fuller's two adolescent sons came in. Then men and women began crowding into the room, all Jews, common people save for a shopkeeper or two and one young woman. She was taller than most of the men, a finger or two shorter than I, and with a strong, womanly figure. Her Jewish robe was as simple as the other's, but of costly woven bleached wool. Her belt was embroidered with saffron crocuses. She was, I judged, eighteen, her chestnut hair combed back as a woman's, not a girl's. Her eyes were dark sea blue, a rarity in Palestine, and her face had the leanness of northerners, perhaps from some Greek ancestor, or far-ranging Scythian or Circassian or Gaul.

The older women, with careful, worn fingers, loosened the belt I had tied around Andrew. They worked in silence on the battered corpse, touching the wounds with alum to close them, rubbing the scars with unguents, scenting him with nard, myrrh, and aloewood. The young woman—one of the others had called her Deborah—

cleaned Andrew's face with a perfumed cloth. I was sure he had never smelled so good or been so tenderly handled in life. When they were done, his skin looked younger. His hair and beard were clean and combed, the hair banded with a piece of gold-trimmed linen. His mantle was embroidered at the hem with rams' horns.

We men stood by awkwardly, I regarded by the others deferentially despite my age, and thus made more awkward yet. My mind worked busily on the words I would say to help Andrew, as Grandfather might say, go with dignity to the gates of Sheol. Is it shameful that I also hoped my talk would lodge me in the thoughts of the young woman called Deborah? Is it ludicrous that I was embarrassed lest she see the slight roll in my walk and posit that I had deformed toes?

In the Jewish manner, the women wrapped Andrew in a shroud, veiled his face with a *soudarion* and ritually tied his legs together with linen strips. The women went first in the little procession through the flax field to a cave a hundred yards behind Rechab's house. There Andrew was to lie with several other believers who had died in recent years. Last came a boy with a flute, playing mournfully, but not well.

I was weary but nervous, my thoughts and emotions agitated. One minute, tears came to my eyes as I thought of Andrew throwing himself in front of the spear. The next, I watched with covert fascination the swing of the young woman's body as she stepped past the flax stalks. The fuller and three other men carried the poles of the funeral litter. They put it down by the thick, flat stone that blocked the door of the cave. Rechab placed a key, the Jewish burial emblem for a bachelor, on Andrew's chest.

That done, the fuller turned to us and spoke with humble assurance to his God. It was a departure from the portentous way that Greeks and Romans address Zeus or the formal way Jews call on Yahweh. Rechab asked God and Jesus in simple words to witness our sadness over Andrew's death and our gladness that Andrew was now with them. As if he were talking to an old and reliable customer, he asked Andrew to intervene with God and Jesus to help this band of worshippers in Modi'im. Then he turned to me: "We thank you, Master Jesus, for sending us this young man who so selflessly helped your servant Andrew. We beg you to keep him forever in your sight until that day when he comes to you as freely as he has come to us."

I felt a flash of resentment over his assuming, as Andrew had done, that I would one day become part of his sect. But his look and his words of loving gratitude disconcerted me far more than his simple presumption. I wrestled to control myself. The fuller waited considerately, then asked me to tell them of Andrew's final days. I obliged succinctly and far less ably than I had hoped I would.

They sang a psalm in Hebrew, one I knew well from my childhood days in the synagogue. Its theme was that even a sparrow finds a home, a swallow a nest, and those who find a home in God are blessed. I might have joined in, but did not.

As they sang, I heard the clear voice of the girl, lower than those of the other women. I dared to look at her, for she, like the others, was gazing at Andrew. The winter sun beat down. In my nostrils was a mix of odors: the aromatics on Andrew that rose exotically because of the sun's heat, the rural smell of cattle and dried plants, my own sweat.

The voices were continuous, the melody not rising and falling by great leaps, but repeating at different levels. The young woman's face was beautiful. She seemed to burn with life, and I, recently so near dead, burned as well.

The song ended, bringing my thoughts of Deborah up short. Two of the men pushed back the stone. I helped ease Andrew's body into the cave. The ceremony was over. I looked for the young woman so I could introduce myself, but I felt a touch at my sleeve. It was the oldest of the women. She took my hand and kissed it, and a second older woman did the same. I thought, well, these are emotional people or they would not be in this emotional cult. Still, it made me uncomfortable. Another of the women lifted my hand to her lips. Behind her was the young woman. My heart banged in my chest. She looked as embarrassed by the hand-kissing as I was.

"Please," I said to her in Greek. "Please do not do what they did."

"I was not going to," she answered in Greek, more academic than colloquial. "I was merely going to thank you." Then, recognizing, as I now did, the snobbishness in our using the lingua franca of the middle and upper classes, she changed to Aramaic. "You are Roman?"

"Yes, half. My mother is a Sadducee." The proprieties, even, or perhaps especially, in these odd circumstances did not give me much time. In as low a voice as I decently could, I said, "Your name, I heard them say, is Deborah."

"Yes, Deborah, daughter of Sirach ben Isaac."

"Deborah bas Sirach, if I come here again, where may I find you?" She faltered. "I do not know."

"Then I will . . ." I started, trying to find some means of opening a way to see her again. But Rechab's wife and some of the others had gathered around. My time with her had run out.

"It would be complicated . . ." she began. Rechab's wife had taken my hand in both of hers. Deborah stood in the group briefly, then with a guarded look left with two of the women who had already turned toward the house.

I walked back with the fuller and several other men and they helped me feed and water the stallion and the mule. Except for Rechab's wife, the women had gone. The fuller held my bridle as I mounted. He was not quite ready to let me go, wanting to say something that would bind me to them. But the words that might bring me back to Modi'im were not his to say.

VI

✦✧

I went on to Lydda and bought the shelving, but did not linger. On the road back to Borhaurus, I felt elated. My excitement, I knew, was partly Deborah bas Sirach and the fact that I was alive. Yet, the fact that a brave man had died for me was, perversely, integral to my elation. Andrew had lived a life in which he loved God and then his neighbor. He had died in the absolute belief that he would walk forever with Jesus, who had taught him that simple way of doing things. When I thought of that, feeling as I did enormous gratitude and love from my incandescent time with him, I could not be sad, only joyful.

That night, I told Father what I had done, omitting my encounter with Deborah bas Sirach and my peculiar uplift on the road back to Borhaurus. He tried to be vexed over my helping Andrew, for it would hurt him with the local Jews if they learned of it. However, he was so proud of my prowess against the brigands that he found it impossible to scold me.

"But, Demas," he said. "One word of warning: these Nazarenes, as they are called, are becoming a problem in Palestine. We are fortunate that none are in Borhaurus. My fear is that they will try to exploit the fact that a Roman tribune's son helped one of their leaders, attended his burial."

"They only know me as Demas of Borhaurus. . . ."

"One inquiry of anyone in Borhaurus is all it would require for them to identify you. Go to Jerusalem, get your business done, come home. And then put them out of your mind."

The sight of Jerusalem from the heights above the Gennath gate always filled me with a mix of wonder and uneasiness, and not just because I was the provincial come to the city. Jerusalem was the tug in my Roman body of my mother's blood, my knowledge of how long Jerusalem had been the city and the symbol of all Jews' Jewishness. I rode past the crumbling limestone tomb of the traitor King Absalom, at which devout Jews still threw stones as they passed. Inside the walls, the cobbled street soon became so narrow I had to dismount. My stallion bumped the panniers of donkey and camel drivers, who muttered angrily.

In this quarter, shops were hollowed shallowly from the bases of two-story buildings that hung over the street like massive women in close converse. Under colored sackcloth awnings, merchants raucously hawked vegetables, bread, clothing, jewelry, charcoal, oil, cosmetics, metalware. The air smelled of garlic, cooking lamb, and people living too close together. Here strode, shoved, and shuffled Jews in all the raiment of Judaea: brown-, blue-, and gray-striped robes, shepherd's coats of woven camel and goat hair, fancy shirts embroidered with silver threads and worn over tunics, women's shawls decorated with ribbons of silk.

Suddenly, at the end of a moldering street, I seemed to see a giant white volcano erupting gold. It was the Temple, its gilded roof giving back the sun's brightness undiminished from above massive walls that towered sixty cubits. As if drawn by the lodestone mountain Andrew had imagined, I walked down the vile street, through a cavernous door in the wall and entered the Temple's vast outer court. Columns tall as six men, marble balustrades, wide flights of stairs glistened as if in some architectured dream. Platform rose on platform: how well mad Herod had realized his vision of majesty! He had rebuilt the Temple, more magnificently by far, all agreed, than it had ever been in Solomon's day.

The din was inescapable: the contentious debate in Grandfather's synagogue was multiplied a hundredfold by the voices of priests, doctors of the Law, the cries of money changers, all augmented by the cooing of pigeons, and baaing of sacrificial goats, the chatter of veiled women, the clink of coins. I breathed in the faint scent of cedar and incense, then smelled abruptly on a wisp of breeze the reek of burning meat as the entrails of a sacrificed animal in the inner court were thrown on a fire. Here, truly, in all its complexity was Israel, the ancient land of my mother, alive and powerful.

Celicus Street was in the lower city. When I rapped, the door opened a crack. A youngish voice asked me what I wanted. His eye took in the stallion and my Roman clothes. I told him I had a message for Peter or for James, but he waited for more.

"One of your people, Andrew, was killed by brigands. I was there and promised to bring word of it." The man gasped and opened the door. He was in his early forties, with a handsome, weak face turned ashen by the news.

"You are sure? Dead?" He grunted three times as if from jolting chest pains. Hardly seeming to know where he was going, he led me into the well-furnished house across mosaic floors. In a spacious, low-ceilinged room, a half-dozen men looked up at us.

"Andrew is dead!" the doorman blurted out.

Every face in the room looked as if it had been lashed with a whip. The oldest of the men, in his late fifties, with the sere look of one of Borhaurus's efficient and humorless senior civil servants, stared at me, the messenger. "Dead," he said, rather than asked.

"I am to speak with Peter, his brother," I said.

"He is not here." He nodded at the man who had let me in, and the man left. "Thomas will get him. He is near."

"Is there a James?"

"I am he," the civil servant said. "And you are . . . ?"

"It does not matter. I promised only that I would tell Andrew's story."

James seemed to accept discretion as both need and right. That notwithstanding, he introduced the others, perhaps as a proffer of trust in me that I could reciprocate or not. Their names were vaguely familiar from Andrew's tales by the firelight: Matthew, Bartholomew, Philip, John.

"We are grateful to you for coming," James said courteously but without the warmth that the words implied. "We had heard only that he was in Borhaurus."

We waited nervously for the arrival of Peter. The anguish in the room was almost palpable. The man named Philip, white-haired and a little hesitant, looked particularly ill at ease as if something were on his mind that he did not want to broach with a stranger there. But his anxiety was too much for him. "Paul?" he asked James.

"I do not think so."

"I was sorry. After so many years of thinking about Paul's words and my talk about him with Andrew, I would have liked to see him. Philip's question and James's answer made them all shift uncomfortably. The one named John began to recover from his shock and seemed about to dispute James on the issue of Paul. But at that moment, there were voices at the street door and Peter appeared with Thomas behind him. He was a bluff man, bigger than his brother Andrew, with the same peasant look. Without any move to take my hand, he embraced me impulsively.

"You came to tell us," he said, distraught but wanting to show his thanks. "You are certain?"

"I was with him when he died," I said. My stomach was tightening.

Peter put his hands to his face and groaned while we all waited unhappily. At last he calmed and dropped his hands. His face was streaked with tears as he signaled us to sit. But seated, he gave another great moan as if an unseen hand had struck him in the pit of his stomach. Thomas rose quickly, put his hands on Peter's shoulders from behind and kneaded them. At last, Peter looked up at me with red eyes.

"Begin," he said. "Please. I do not know your name."

"I am a Roman who was just passing that way with an empty mule. Let me leave it at that." I made my story concise, as much like a lawyer's presentation as I could, trying to suppress emotion even when I told of Andrew interposing himself between me and the spear thrust. When I was done, they asked me some few questions. How many followers of Jesus were present at the fuller's? Had Andrew been badly disabled by the lashing?

"Sir Roman, you were decent beyond all need to let him ride your mule," said John, who was slight and balding, his hair wisping in a corona. "It was like him not to wait until morning to go to Modi'im," added Bartholomew, a stocky man with a hedgehog beard. "Andrew had more courage than any of us," said Peter effusively, trying hard not to break down again, "more than me, more than any except Jesus himself. God made a great hero when he made Andrew."

The others looked embarrassed. They loved Andrew, I could see, but as someone who never quite succeeded, never quite measured up. Andrew had said as much himself. Well, in my view he had been the best of them. He and the fuller, Rechab, had given me a taste of something more, well, godly than these others among whom I sensed such discord. Here, only Peter seemed cut from heroic cloth. I took out the flask of oily water.

"I am giving it to you as he asked," I said to Peter.

"It will be an important relic for us," said James officiously. "We

53

will seal it forever in remembrance of Andrew, the first-chosen of our Lord."

I recoiled. "He wanted it used for baptisms." On that he had been definite.

"He was in the midst of agony. It would be better to keep it sacrosanct. We have preserved some of the stones used to kill another of our brothers, Stephen. And drops of the holy blood from our brother James who was beheaded—"

Well, I thought impulsively, you are not preserving this. "I have changed my mind. I am keeping it," I said. If any of them had a claim to it, it was Peter who was not making any.

James was taken aback. His administrator's mind was trying to understand my action, something I was not sure I could do myself. "Then you are thinking of baptism for yourself?"

"No," I said. "I am not certain why, but this flask means something to me." I looked at Peter.

He fixed me with his brown eyes, less pale than Andrew's, but more thoughtful. "Keep the flask. I am honored that it is in your care, young Roman-just-passing-that-way."

They saw me to the courtyard, where my horse was tied. All shook my hand warmly, even James. Peter embraced me again. "Thank you for seeing Old Protokletos to his grave," he said. My throat began to constrict with the beginning of a sob. I took the horse's bridle. Thomas accompanied me to the street to point out the best way to the Gennath gate.

"Shall I walk with you a bit?" he said.

I had hoped he would. I felt shaken, in need of talking to someone about that meeting. Because he was younger than the others, I felt more comfortable with him. I noticed the weave and tailoring of his tunic, fine cloth cut more Roman than Palestinian. Although a Galilean, he spoke good Greek.

Down a cobbled street I could see the "Mariamne," part of Herod's marbled palace and named by him for his wife, the last of the Hasmoneans, whom he had murdered in a moment of insanity. To the right was a fortress of gigantic limestone blocks manned by legionnaires and named by Herod the "Antonia," after his friend Mark Antony. We found a bench in its shadow.

"Your council reminded me of a gathering of disputatious Roman administrators," I said. "It was a surprise to me after Andrew and his stories of your days and nights on the road."

"Movements are not built on the nostalgia of pure, humble old men, however wonderful they are," Thomas said.

I knew institutions had to be well organized to survive. Rome, without its administration, laws, army, roads, aqueducts, taxation, the whole system meticulously structured, would not be able to hold Gaul, Illyricum, Egypt, much less Thrace and Palestine and the upper Rhine, for a day.

"A religion ought to have more idealism than an imperial government," I said. The Apostolic Council did not even practice Jesus' rule among themselves. Paul had been in Jerusalem. And when one of them had suggested they invite him to hear my story, James had meanly barred him. What kind of charitableness was that? I chided Thomas with the contradiction, mentioning I had heard Paul years ago while I was in Scythopolis.

He sighed and said that I had come at a particularly contentious time. He explained that Jesus and the original disciples had worked almost entirely with Jews. While Jesus had sometimes eaten with the uncircumcised, which horrified devout Sadducees and Pharisees, he had not gone out of his way to enlist them. Quite the contrary. He generally avoided them. Neither Jesus nor the disciples had really *understood* Gentiles or their pagan religions, Thomas went on. They had been simple Galileans, taught that Gentiles were unclean enemies.

Then Paul had arrived on the scene—a Pharisee, yes, but extremely well educated and raised in cosmopolitan Tarsus, a city with every kind of race. He had begun his ministry in Damascus and Antioch of Syria, both also polyglot. So it had been natural for him to convert Greeks, Syrians of all kinds, Arabs, Parthians, Elamites, Romans when he could, any Jews who wanted to join, even the occasional Libyan or Egyptian.

"He thinks that distinguishing between Jewish and non-Jewish followers builds a civil war into the movement," said Thomas. "But we, well, they"—the Apostolic Council—"do not even *want* Gentiles unless they are first circumcised and agree to follow the Mosaic Law."

The council was trying to work things out with Paul now, perhaps with Peter officially being called Apostle to the Jews and Paul Apostle to the Gentiles, although everyone knew Paul would convert Jews if they came his way. In Antioch, the headquarters of Paul, Jewish and non-Jewish followers alike were simply called "Christians."

"They are giving Paul what he wants," Thomas said. "He would take it anyway. Paul is fishing in the great pool. We are fishing in little Palestine, which we have already fished out."

"Why not go everyplace in the empire where Jews have settled? Alexandria, Ephesus, Rome . . ."

Thomas looked defeated. "We should, we should. But Paul is so good at it. We have never figured out how to do it."

I glanced at the sun. There was time to see Paul. He was obviously the most interesting person in this movement. I had the best of reasons: to tell him about Andrew. Besides, it would satisfy my curiosity over whether Paul's brilliant sermon about love was merely one rare diamond in a quarry of gravel, or evidence of a mine of such gems.

Thomas correctly assessed the course of my thoughts and preempted them. "How would you like to visit Paul for a few minutes before you go? He gets under your skin, doesn't he?"

Paul's quarters were several shabby streets away, against the wall of the Water gate. "Paul likes to live where he can make a rapid exit," said Thomas. "Do you like ironies? Six hundred years ago, King Zedekiah escaped from the window of a building on this same spot while Nebuchadnezzar was besieging the city." We climbed a narrow staircase to the second floor. Thomas knocked and at the same time said quietly, "It's Thomas." I heard two bolts thrown. The small alcoved door opened.

"Welcome, welcome," said Paul with forced heartiness.

"Andrew is dead," said Thomas gently, "killed by brigands."

We were still at the threshold. I could not see Paul's face. For a moment, there was silence. Then he uttered an agonized "Oh." A minute passed before he recovered enough to say sorrowfully, "If ever there was God's own, it was Andrew."

"I have with me the young Roman who brought us the news," Thomas said. Paul stepped back so we could enter. The room was minuscule, its table by a tiny window neatly stacked with papyrus and wax tablets except for a small writing space. Beside it was a raffia basket of scrolls.

Paul was even less prepossessing than I remembered. His face was pitted, his wrestler's build small, his legs bandied. He looked at me intently, his eyes among the most unusual I had ever seen, jet black, like peas made of polished ebony squinting from half-open pods.

"I thank you for coming, young man, and you for bringing him, Thomas." The words were cordial, the tone awkward. I thought: Here is a man who fares far better with audiences than with individuals. "Do the rest know?" It was barely a question. Thomas nodded. The brief interchange had told Paul everything he needed to comprehend the affront to him by the council.

"I heard you years ago in Scythopolis," I said, looking for a way to overcome my own discomfort. "You and two of your assistants were beaten outside our academy gates." I started to tell him I had tried to help him, but I did not.

Paul considered a moment, then recollected. "Barnabas. And young Tractus."

"The young one knocked down a man who spat on you."

"Tractus. He loved me well, but perhaps the Lord not well enough. He was impulsive."

I was startled. Did he really believe people should take that kind of injury and insult? Andrew, whom he had just praised, had fought the highwaymen like an old tiger. "You mean you are sorry this Tractus hit him?" He nodded without comment and turned to other matters, leaving my curiosity unsatisfied.

"You came to tell me of Andrew," he said. "I loved him."

He spoke now so simply, so sincerely, that he seemed a different man from the dogmatist of a few seconds ago. I told him everything I had told the others. When I was done, he fixed me with those penetrating eyes.

"You are fortunate, young man. A man filled as few are with the goodness of God gave up his life for you. I would I were a tenth the man Andrew was."

Surely, I thought, Paul knew that Andrew saw him as a dangerous distorter of their dead leader's message. Yet the love he expressed for Andrew sounded genuine. I felt intimidated by him as I had not been by any of the others. "He did not have so high an opinion of himself," I said.

"Yes, but now he is where he will be honored for what he was on earth. He had no hubris. Nor was there any meanness in him." He smiled, showing small, even teeth. "Andrew did not have to pray for goodness as the rest of us do. He never had an idea of what it was to be without it."

We talked a little more of Andrew, and Paul said he assumed I did not plan to use the flask of water for my own baptism. No, I said, I did not.

"You are not ready," he told rather than asked me. "If I thought you were, I would not let you go so easily. However, you have one foot in the water." His tone was chaffing. "May I pray you will decide to step in the whole way?"

"There is certainly not enough water in that flask to immerse me," I bantered back.

"Nonsense," Paul said, "there is enough in there to drown you."

❀

The day after I returned from Jerusalem, I visited Grandfather. On the lower floor, where the offices were, Ezra was working. Already, it was assumed he would be Grandfather's successor, for he was a genius with figures, had much of Grandfather's charm, and not a little of his subtlety and his knack for conspiracy. Through the grapevine of masters and servants, he had heard of my fight with the robbers.

"Your dirk saved me," I told him, patting it. Yet, even as I said it, I felt uneasy, thinking of the last robber curled in a ball while I slashed my sword into his defenseless flesh.

Upstairs in Grandfather's sitting room, I recounted what had happened since Andrew's scourging, including my trip to Jerusalem. Grandfather questioned me, then grinned. "But that is not really why you are here. Were it only that, Demas, Demetrius, it would have been another week before you came my way."

I protested, but he rolled his eyes comically, and I confessed to my meeting Deborah bas Sirach and my curiosity about her. He took bites from three cakes before settling on a small date pastry. Then he began:

"Her father is a Pharisee member of the council in Modi'im. I encounter him from time to time. He is a founder of brass and sits in the front row of the synagogue"—a place of honor accorded theoretically to devout elders, but more often in practice to those who contributed most.

"Two of his sons are rabbis in Jerusalem, graduates of the school of the great Shammai." He said it with sarcasm. The late Rabbi Shammai had prescribed the strictest possible interpretations of the tractates, positions that Grandfather ignored. "The third and youngest son, Bediah, will take over his business. The daughter is famous for her blue eyes—" my face must have given me away—"as it is obvious you already know. The father of her father was the son of a rich marble cutter in Amphipolis, all supposedly Jews, although I suspect a touch of northern Gentile blood there. The mother is impeccable. One of the brothers of Judas Maccabaeus is back there someplace. . . ."

This genealogy was his way of approaching what I really wanted to know. It also occurred to me that Grandfather might have a second motive. Although he had helped arrange—for practical political reasons—

his daughter's marriage, and liked and respected Father, he neverthe-less resented her being married to a non-Jew, an occupier of his homeland. What better—is "justice" or "revenge" the fairer word? —than for the Roman's son to marry a member of a distinguished Jewish family?

"The girl is fractious. But if she wanted to rebel against her father, for which I cannot totally blame her—in truth he is a most authoritarian person—there were tolerable paths she could have followed. For exam-ple, there is a woman dealer in flax in Gibeon and even a female ships' chandler in Joppa." Grandfather smiled widely, showing stained teeth failing from too much soft, honeyed food.

"These occupations are shameful for a woman, yes. But impossible, no. However," and he was serious again, "instead, a year ago she joined the cult of this fuller. She meets with them in the man's grubby shop, she the daughter of a Pharisee council member and descendant of a Maccabean. She makes her father's position on the council and in the synagogue difficult. In sum, she is an extraordinarily strange young woman in whom only a most strange young man would be interested."

I ignored the insult and begged Grandfather to learn what else he could and to keep my confidence. It was not an unusual request. Grandfather made a point of knowing everything about everything. I was sure he had paid informers in Father's administration, as well as in his rivals' businesses.

"Let us return to other things," he said. "Four murderers, hunh? With these strong arms? I have always heard that we have blood lines to Joshua."

He rose a bit feebly from his couch and beckoned me to follow him into his dressing room. Hanging on an armorer's tree was the most beautiful coat of mail I had ever seen. It was of bronze, each leaf crafted individually so it overlapped only as much as necessary to protect the wearer.

"From Ecbatana, I am told," said Grandfather. "It will dent under terrible blows, but no ordinary blade will cut through it. And not much more than half the weight of iron."

"Beautiful, beautiful," I said, touching it, feeling the cold perfection of its leaves, the sturdiness of its buckles and cured and recured leather straps. I waited for him to tell me to try it on. He called in his slave, and in a moment I was clad, from neck to greaves.

"Media has always made better armor than men," said Grandfather, "with the possible exception of Cyaxares. I shall have a Roman helm made for you," he said, "unless you would prefer a Judaean model."

59

"I love it. I love you," I said, knowing I did not have to answer his not-so-sly barb.

He walked me into his bedroom, a large room with a coffered ceiling, where I could see myself in the mirror. Grandmother was long dead and Grandfather had not remarried: he sometimes summoned in the cook, a sturdy woman in her forties, or so Ezra had told me. "You look like a warrior king . . ." he said with unaffected pride.

". . . Come to put the Hasmoneans back on the throne," I finished for him, knowing how that jest would please him.

For four days, I worked arduously to catch up with my law studies so I would feel no dereliction in going to Modi'im. I could see no honest way of hiding my intentions from my father. Even so, I told him only that I had met a young Jewish woman of good family among the Nazarenes and wanted to see her again. He pressed his lips together, angry that his advice to avoid members of the cult would not be heeded.

The fuller greeted me warmly but lapsed into nervousness, too polite to question me about why I had returned. There was nothing to do but ask him bluntly, "Where can I find Deborah bas Sirach?" He looked at me with astonishment, and then stammered that she was no longer in Modi'im. Her father had been furious when she joined Rechab's group, but thought it was merely a childish phase. She had spoken seriously to her father after the burial of Andrew about leaving home to live with a Nazarene woman and he had sent her away, to Greece, Rechab had heard.

For days, I had thought about talking with her, discovering what she was like. I had even imagined, with flicks of guilt, how it would be to make love to her. I was not prepared for the collapse I felt. I could hardly believe she had been removed, perhaps forever, from contact with me.

"Where in Greece?" I asked the fuller.

"I do not know, Sir Demas, she was not allowed to bid us good-bye." He was taken aback by my consternation, and felt he should add something, if only something benevolent. "Wherever she is, she will do the work of the Lord," he said.

I groaned. What concern was that to me? Doing her Lord's work, it was true, had brought her to me. But doing it had also taken her away from me.

On the way home, I thought romantically of going to Greece to seek her out in such towns as Thessalonica and Corinth, which had large Jewish populations. More realistically, I went again to Grandfather. A week later, he sent word for me to visit him. "Deborah bas Sirach is somewhere in Asia Minor," he said. "I do not know where. If I did, I would tell you."

I grunted unhappily. Asia Minor could mean anywhere from Ephesus to Armenia, from the Black Sea to Pamphylia, hundreds of towns, thousands of miles. Even if I were so foolhardy as to search, it would be like seeking a single tiny chip of stone in a mosaic the size of Borhaurus. "I thought Greece . . . ?" I said miserably.

"A story Sirach ben Isaac has put out. He sent her to relatives. With two servants, virtually under arrest."

Thereafter, when I saw Grandfather, I always carried with me that unspoken question. His unspoken response was always "Nothing." In fall, on the way to Lydda, I turned off to visit the fuller. But there was no word from or about Deborah.

Early in the next year, Grandfather told me that Sirach ben Isaac had been crippled by an apoplectic stroke. A few months later, he died. His third son, Bediah, seven years older than Deborah, moved with their mother to Ni'im, closer to the highroad, the better to conduct trade with Joppa and Lydda. Perhaps now Deborah could come home. But she did not.

I found ways of passing the time pleasantly. I courted one young woman after another. I thought sometimes of Andrew, of my journey to Jerusalem and of the magnetism of the missionary Paul. From time to time, I drank and gamed with old friends. I went infrequently to Lydda's law library, occasionally combining it with a visit to its brothel when my bias against mere "thrown seed" proved inadequate to quell my lust.

Many afternoons, I exercised at the Xystus, although now Ezra and my Jewish cousins came less often. The distance between Jews and Romans in Borhaurus, and everywhere, was growing, and it was changing the structure of Judaean society. Younger brothers of Jews I had grown up with imitated Romans at our worst, our arrogance and our dissoluteness, wearing their hair long and sprinkling it with gold dust to make it glitter in the sun. Yet, contradictorily, they pretended to an idealistic devotion to the *sicarii*.

Only a few could throw a discus. Many were no better than street rowdies. Their fathers no longer tried to control them, yet indulged them with money, paid off victims of their shoplifting, vandalism, and assaults, and hoped age would tame them.

Two years after the death of Andrew, when I was twenty-two, I became a lawyer and established a practice of my own. I handled land disputes, merchants' suits, estate law, again nothing that would touch on Father's immediate jurisdiction. On occasion, I made trips to Jerusalem for clients. Although I was tempted to visit Thomas, I did not. Like Deborah bas Sirach, the Apostolic Council had been a barren sowing.

VII

One steaming day during my first summer of practice, I returned from Caesarea, where I had presented a *jus gentium* appeal. Drowsy from the trip and from too much lunch, lulled by familiar far-off sounds—the low bray of a donkey, children's pipy voices—I put down my head and dozed. Two sharp knocks on my doorjamb awakened me. I was unsure for a moment where I was, yet, at the same time I was anxious to appear the alert lawyer in case it was a client. It was Deborah bas Sirach.

"Demas Faevolian?" she asked, in obvious distress.

I gave my head a shake, astonished, thrilled, foolish, all at once. It had been three years since I had seen her. And here she stood, beautiful even with her face tightened in worry. I looked for a way to defend my drowsing. "Yes, he. Why of all days am I . . . ? How did you find me? Where have you been?" She was still standing at my sill. "Come in, come in, the sun will burn you up out there." I seated her in my one expensive chair.

"I have something important—"

"Did the fuller tell you I came looking for you? I heard you were in Greece, then Asia Minor. I had no idea what town."

"Kybistra, it was a depressing place." But she hurried on urgently. "Something has happened, something terrible . . ."

Truly alert now, feeling even more foolish for my personal remarks, I nodded for her to go on, and found a wax tablet on which I began taking notes.

"We, Rechab and I, came to Borhaurus yesterday, and are staying with Dathan, who is one of us." Dathan was a master worker in terra-cotta tiles and other kilned wares, but I had not known he, or anyone, in Borhaurus was a member of their sect. ". . . Late in the day, Rechab went to the well and talked about Jesus to a few women drawing water there, telling the story of how a woman at Shechem offered Jesus water, and he gave her the living water of salvation.

"While he was preaching, two Sadducees, about eighteen or nineteen years old, came up. When they heard Rechab speak of Jesus Christ, they cursed him and one drew a curved dirk and said any more of that and his head would go into the well. That frightened the women away, except for one, and Rechab asked the young men to pray with him and the woman for friendship. That infuriated them, and they said there were no false prophets in Borhaurus and that there had best not be any by sundown.

"That night, after we were asleep, there was pounding at the door. We made no answer, trying to think what to do, but they beat harder. We were sure they would break it down, so Rechab unlocked it to go out as a hostage for our safety. They snatched him away into the night."

She clutched and unclutched the bottom of the chair. My sympathy for her and my outrage at the young hoodlums increased simultaneously.

"Dathan's wife stayed with the children and Dathan and I ran to the barracks. It took a while for the soldier on duty to wake up a corporal, who finally called the captain. We begged him to help us, pointing out that Rechab had been talking by the well on Roman ground, not on religious land. The captain knew Dathan and, I think"—she said it with unhappy embarrassment—"liked me."

In spite of the story, I smiled. That would be Thaddeus Bariponte, a renowned rake, but a responsible officer. He had taken me riding when I was a boy and was the captain who had come out with Father the day I was raised from the well.

"He took a half-dozen men with him and began a search. We looked everywhere for Rechab, but could not find him, or the people who took him, either. This morning at first light Dathan and I began again, and outside the gates, two hundred paces off the Lydda road, we heard groans. In the underbrush, we found Rechab, half conscious." She shut her eyes and swayed back in her seat, getting herself under control. When she opened her eyes, in their blue depths I saw hatred, raw and undiluted.

"They had burned out his eyes with brands, telling him they wanted to be sure he was not distracted from seeing the heavenly land he preached about. And they had crushed his foot with a great stone so he could not run for help."

"Oh, the Dark Gods," I groaned, thinking of that honest, inarticulate man who had presided with such dignity over his little flock when we buried Andrew.

She fixed me unwaveringly with her gaze. "We have come to you because we want to preach Jesus Christ in Borhaurus. And we want justice against the men who blinded Rechab."

There it was, stark as a sentence of death without appeal. If I took this case, I would alienate Father, for as tribune he would be the person who tried it with me as prosecuting lawyer, putting him in an impossible position. Besides, the maimers, although wastrels, were certain to be sons of wealthy Borhaurusians. Father could not sanction his son tearing the town apart on behalf of an interloper, a fanatic member of an outlandish and despised cult. For the same reason, it would sunder me from my friends, from the town where I had grown up.

Yet to refuse would be to forfeit the very self-respect that Father himself had so often encouraged in me. Besides, as indistinct as my God was, I was sure he did not like cowards. If I turned away, I would also forfeit Deborah, about whom I had dreamed so much and now might come to know well.

But how dared she plunge me into this boiling fat? She was not a simpleton. "You know this case will destroy me," I said angrily.

She looked intimidated, but undeterred. "Yes, we thought of that, and we are sorry because you have already helped us, but Dathan said no other lawyer would take it." She paused. "And we prayed and are sure Jesus means for us to come to you."

"Oh, *Jesus* wants it? Well, Furies take Jesus!" I barked.

But I went with her to Dathan's, where Rechab was on his back in the bedroom. His eyelids were blistered and sunken where the jelly had been stabbed from the sockets with the burning sticks. He could only hold my hands in his horny, powerful fingers, mumble words of thanks and try to cry from eyes too ruined for tears. My anger against Deborah and these Nazarenes with their foolish, dangerous God was as nothing to the hatred that engulfed me against Rechab's attackers.

That evening, when I told Father I had taken the case, he looked at me as if a maniac was before him. I felt woebegone, my righteous anger dissolved in the enormity of what I was doing to Father, to our family. "I am trapped, Father," I said.

"Do not tell me you are trapped, idiot!" He lost his temper, as he rarely did. "There are sound arguments you can make to yourself that will let you refuse with honor. You owe nothing to these people. An old dead man, not they, saved your life. Four of the five who beat this

Rechab—oh, we had no trouble finding them; they *bragged* about it—are Roman citizens through their fathers. Besides, the man brought this on himself."

"He was blinded, Father. His foot was crushed. He is crippled for life."

He flinched. His fury began to subside. "I do not accept you as his lawyer, only as his carrier of messages." I did not argue the point; it could wait. "Let us suppose," he went on, "something could be worked out whereby the families made a substantial payment to the fuller—just how much could be negotiated. The young men would be informally banished for a time. The fuller and his—your—friend would leave town. Dathan would be compensated for the trespass upon his house."

I waited for him to say more, but that was it. "And the case itself?"

"Well, all the principals would be gone, so there would be nothing before me. It is a workable proposal."

I was numbed. Was this the father I had revered? Presenting me with this shoddy bargain? Certainly, since my return from Scythopolis I had seen him make compromises. But an intervener for torturers? "The fuller will not agree," I said desperately. "He wants to preach here."

Father burst out at me again. "Preach here? Then he is a lunatic. And I, it seems, have *raised* a lunatic."

"Idiot" *and* "lunatic" were too much. "A lunatic speaking legally by a public well," I said, my own voice rising, "and another lunatic bound by his oaths to defend him."

"Well, 'legally' may be an issue. . . ."

He was calming again, regretting what he had called me. But even as I tried to quell my own ire, I was determined to have my say. "He was speaking legally, taken from a house where he was legally resident, dragged out in violation of every Roman law since Romulus and Remus. Feloniously blinded and crippled!"

"Demas, we are trying the case before an empty hearth." He shut his eyes and waited until we were both breathing more slowly. "Will you talk to him, try to get him to be reasonable?"

I was aware I was trembling. "I will present what you propose to him."

"Without prejudice?"

I resented the question. "Father, do not provoke me. I will present it to him as his lawyer, not as a message carrier." This time, he was wise enough not to challenge me.

That night, unable to sleep, I recalled those austere men in light armor who long ago had come to our house and talked with Father of the death of the tyrant Caligula. The remembrance made me forlorn and left me isolated in my own home.

In the morning, when I went to Dathan's, Deborah came to the door. Her face was flushed, but this time from the heat in the cottage. Three young children were at the table where she was feeding them porridge and goat's milk. "The others are in the bedroom asleep," she said. "Talk softly."

"I had not imagined you were so domestic," I said, making uneasy small talk. I could not forget she had brought Father's wrath on me, had precipitated my disappointment in him.

"I am not very domestic," she said curtly. "I have generally tried to avoid such things. For the time being anyway, I have other things I must do."

From the bedroom, I heard Rechab moan and speak and then other voices. I went in and found the fuller still in great pain, but the clean bandages around his head made him look a little less like Oedipus. I put Father's proposal before him. His lips moved in silent prayer before he spoke.

"Will your father reconsider? He is just. Dathan told me. If I do return swiftly to Modi'im, would they give us this payment and let Dathan use it to build a simple meeting place and carry on a ministry here without persecuting him?"

"I think it must be yes or no, Rechab," I said. "They will not tolerate any kind of ministry." I hesitated, not wanting to impugn my own conscience. "You realize that a yes would be easier for everyone, including your lawyer."

Rechab ignored my suggestion. "Can you tell them of my hope for this compromise that I propose, Sir Demas?"

I sighed. "If you can forgo the 'sir.' " I smiled. His own cracked lips also parted, but more in a grimace.

Father, of course, refused Rechab's plea, and with the breakdown in our negotiations, a caldron began to bubble in Borhaurus. To stoke the flame, first a few twigs—a handful of cult followers—then a forest of Nazarenes came to town, some from as far as Hebron and Gaza. They pitched their tents of goat hair or sheepskin or ragged cloth outside the walls. More campfires glimmered with each passing evening. Soon a hundred had come, then two hundred.

The blinding of the fuller, a hardworking tradesman and the offspring of common folk, stirred sympathy in many Borhaurus households. They saw Rechab not as a member of a fanatic sect, but as a poor Jew maimed by profligate sons of rich men for bravely defying the social order. By extension, they viewed him as a victim of Roman rule, of the high priest in Jerusalem, of all the nameless powerful "theys" who ran their lives from above. What Jew did not know that at Sepphoris forty years ago, Rome and their Judaean puppets had crucified two thousand Galileans seeking freedom? Indeed, Israel's history was full of rebels seeking to throw off insufferable yokes.

Rechab's religion, too, had this heady revolutionary air about it. The Nazarenes preached that the downtrodden were the salt of the earth to whom the world belonged by right. Its dogma was simple enough for anyone to understand. It had no complicated rules governing every action in life, no endless and costly sacrifices of animals, of remembering this holy day, this ritual act, this line of the Torah. It demanded only love of God and love of one's neighbor. Judaism, with its centuries of layered complications, and paganism, with its ambiguities and contradictions, were senescent, ripe for replacement.

The threat and appeal of the new creed did not come only from its earthly message, but from its view of the afterlife. Pagans, save for the most benighted, no longer believed in the gods and their Hades. The afterlife espoused by the Pharisees and Sadducees was not unlike Hades, a lifeless Sheol. Jesus' vision of life after death, by contrast, was one of sweetness and dignity. In exchange for present misery, it offered, however meretriciously, an eternity of joy free from arbitrary rulers.

This promised paradise for the miserable held great dangers for all government authority, it seemed to me. For if a man had nothing to lose and a heaven to gain by his death, how willingly he would die! And desperate men who were eager to die for causes were lethal to law and order. Rechab's faith, for all these reasons, made inroads among Borhaurusians, and the court case, no matter what its outcome, would only bring more of the alienated to the Nazarene fold.

Once it became certain the trial would proceed, Father was obliged by law to give us the names of the defendants. Their leader had been Menah ben Tahath, son of a rich Sadducee, the other four, two of them Pharisees, were also from wealthy families. Deborah helped me prepare Rechab to testify. We coached him on how to describe the faces of his assailants, how to listen hard to their voices, since he could not see them and point to them. We rehearsed him on the precise sequence of events. Deborah was as quick as I, or quicker.

With our mutual respect, soon came trust. It was not long before we discovered we liked to talk with each other about ourselves, and sought occasions to do so. However, in spite of Grandfather's warning about Deborah's "strangeness," I found her ideas about what a woman was supposed to be so astounding that sometimes I had a hard time believing she was not playing some elaborate joke on me.

"Before I joined Rechab," she once said, drawing her thickish brows together, "I was beginning to hate my father and my two oldest brothers just because they behaved like men. They sat in the front of the synagogue talking about God's love and justice and then came home and screamed at Mother and me to find softer shucks for the privy. To them, we were female goats, useful, even necessary, but animals, objects. Half the human race! And not important enough for men to consider what we might be doing, when they wanted their bottoms wiped. Father Abraham! Do they think men told Judith and Jael to fetch shucks and empty their morning slops?"

"Maybe Judith did empty slops," I said.

"Well, we will never know, will we? Men wrote the holy books. Women washed the styluses."

Nevertheless, she was grateful her father had required her to know the Torah. She had loved reading not just those five scrolls, but the other Jewish writings, and anything else she could find as well. Her youngest brother, Bediah, the one who had *not* become a rabbi, had used her to practice his Greek, an obligatory tongue for anyone going into commerce. She and he had read Homer aloud, then the histories and tragedies.

As we talked, I imagined Deborah with her hair coiffured, in a handsome stola with a fibula of delicately crafted gold at the neck, a personage I could transpose easily into my own world. One day, I found her behind the house, helping with the wash, dressed even more like a crone than on my first visit.

"Are you determined to look like a peasant for the rest of your life?" I asked, meaning it to sound like banter.

"I will let you know when you can start dictating my style of dress, Sir Demas," she answered flippantly.

Another time, I told her of my visits to the synagogue. I tried to explain how I felt about the indefinable God I had found there who had heard me when I called from the well.

"God in the Torah *is* indefinable," she said. "He says love your neighbors as yourselves, just as *Jesus* tells us. But he also tells Moses to make certain the Israelites totally destroy the tribes fighting them, men, women, and children. He says to stone a man to death for

69

incest. Yet Lot, the only man God found holy in Sodom, fathered children on *both* his daughters, and he was not punished. The simplicity of Jesus makes it no longer necessary to debate these contradictions."

When I asked her one day about how she had become a Nazarene, she responded eagerly. It had begun, she said, when she was fifteen and heard people singing in the fuller's house. She had listened at the window, and when the familiar hymn ended, the fuller had reminded them that Jesus had said the only important things were to love God, and their neighbors as themselves.

At home, her father and two oldest brothers had been finding her defiant, ill tempered, anything but a good daughter and sister. In subtle ways, she had let them know she thought them hypocrites for treating her and her mother like slaves, and her father had forced her mother to beat her. The next day, she had returned to Rechab's on the pretense of needing a robe cleaned and had told him that she had eavesdropped on one of their meetings and if their God was as Rechab described him, she wanted to join them. Rechab had recognized her as the daughter of a Jewish Council member and was fearful. But he had prayed for guidance and finally he had said, yes, he would talk with her about Jesus. She had gone back four times before he invited her to a meeting. There, the other members had agreed with Rechab that they would take her in.

"They treated me like an adult, and they treated me like they would want to be treated themselves. And after a few awkward moments, I felt I had found a new kind of home."

Rechab had asked her to tell her father that she had become a Nazarene. She had told him, and, he had slapped her for the first time in her life, and forbade her to go to any more meetings. When she had gone anyway, he had locked her in and she had refused to eat. After two days, Bediah had heatedly told their father that the shame of her starving to death would be much greater than the shame of her belonging to a sect that did, at least, keep the Sabbath with other Jews even if on the next day, Sunday, they met as Nazarenes.

The father had freed her, but after the burial of Andrew, when she had wanted to move out, her father, as Grandfather had told me, had sent her away. Then, well after Sirach ben Isaac was dead, Bediah and her mother had finally worn down the two older brothers and they had let her come home.

We argued about everything, and I once told her she was well named, for Deborah means "bee" in Hebrew. And, indeed, she had stung me: I was falling in love with her. I dared not tell her lest it force on her decisions that would complicate our friendship. And so we sparred, a means perhaps of my keeping a safe distance from her. For example, she scorned my admiration for Herodotus on grounds that he had repeated as fact stories about animals with two heads, and other absurdities.

"No more ridiculous," I said peevishly, "than stories about a carpenter who becomes a beggar, then God, then invites his crucifixion on purpose so he can come back to life."

"*Jesus* is no goat with heads on both ends of his body," she retorted. "People *saw* him alive after he was dead on the cross, just as we see the sun or the moon. If you were blind from birth and someone described the sun, you would find that unbelievable, and in the same way you find Jesus unbelievable."

"You are saying I am blind?"

"On this subject, yes, I am saying you are blind."

"And I am saying you are pathetically deluded."

VIII

✦✧

When I was a child and worshipped Father, I had wondered why he was not emperor. Now, in spite of our estrangement, as I watched him function so proficiently under the unprecedented strain on his town, I thought how fortunate Rome would be if he were. For instance, a handful of Nazarenes, angered that some of their coreligionists had been beaten after straggling into a lower-class Jewish quarter, went in themselves as a provocation, and were also assaulted. At about the same time, Jewish adolescents ran through the Nazarene encampment with clubs, knocking over tents.

Greater violence appeared imminent. But Father, with the approval of the Jewish Council, restricted speakers of *all* persuasions to neutral squares unless expressly invited by residents. When a few Nazarenes defied the edict, they were jailed, and when several town youths again ventured into the camp, Father's soldiers arrested them and returned them to their parents with a warning that they would be jailed next time.

Meanwhile, Father sent a sanitation officer to lay out with the Nazarenes the placement of their privies. He assigned hours when they could use the town wells so as to avoid clashes. He ordered a physician to hold a clinic in the tent town each morning. The conservative members of the Jewish Council grumbled that Father was too lenient on the strangers. But most of the citizenry were relieved that Borhaurus was tranquil.

Early on the day of the trial, the Nazarenes—among them thirty Borhaurusians already recruited to the new God—began to move through town to the court square. Arcades made up three of its sides; the Palace of Justice with its limestone Corinthian columns was the fourth. Armed Roman soldiers stood in the arcades. By the time of the trial, four hundred Nazarenes and two thousand townspeople had clogged the square.

I had bought the fuller a handsome brown tunic to wear. Dathan's wife had combed and banded his hair, and Dathan had trimmed his beard. I wanted Rechab's tidy appearance to contrast sharply with the scabbed cavities where his eyes had been. This bit of theater would not affect Father's judgment, but would make it easier for him, if he chose, to rule for Rechab. The town would understand that an attack had been made on a man of substance, and that therefore the sentence was just.

The Nazarenes stood out in the crowd, for many carried palm fronds, a symbol of the last and fatal visit of their Messiah to Jerusalem. Others, more audacious, carried thistles or twigs from thorn trees bound on staves. These suggested the crown of thorns pressed on the head of Jesus by the Romans in mockery of his followers' claim that he was king of the Jews. The inference as to Rechab was obvious.

When we arrived, the Nazarenes waved their peculiar standards and pressed toward Rechab. Lictors with their short batons cleared a path. The Nazarenes reached past them to touch Rechab, some seeking his blessing, some with encouraging words. Deborah, dressed in a white robe, guided him, her hand on his arm. Dathan, whose complaint of trespass was being tried by Father at the same time, followed. Then I came in my Roman best, but wearing the Sadducee dagger that Ezra had given me outside my tunic as a quietly defiant emblem of my half-Jewishness.

Inside, the audience was standing, for by custom there were no benches. They had been admitted by tokens, half given to leading Borhaurusians, the rest first come, first served. The five defendants were dressed simply, looking as unthreatening as rabbinical students. They sat in the dock behind their hoary lawyer, the most distinguished of Borhaurus's Pharisee advocates, as schooled in Roman law as in Judaic.

A herald announced the opening of the session and Father came in, straight as the fasces of the lictor who preceded him. His scepter of office was carried by a page behind him. He nodded first to the defense lawyer, then to me, his stern features showing no partiality. He pointed to our side, signaling us, the accusers, to put on our case first.

Deborah guided the fuller to a small bench below Father's dais and he commenced in a firm voice: "I and Deborah bas Sirach were called

73

by the God we believe in"—I had implored him to keep God and Jesus out of it as much as possible—"to come to Borhaurus to spread his word and help our brother Dathan, the tilemaker, set up a ministry."

His heavy mouth and gruesome eye sockets had been facing Father as he spoke, but he turned his head as if seeking out Dathan, and there was a gasp of shock in the audience at the unexpected sight of his maimed face.

The fuller testified with neither rancor nor fear, but simply, as if he were telling a customer about different types of cleaning. He described the incident at the well, saying one of the youths had threatened to cut his head off and throw it into the well.

I interrupted: "Can you tell us which of the two at the well said this?"

"Sir, I wish the Lord would give me back the power to point them out to you, but I can only describe them in words. This one was tall, the oldest, with a face like that of a fox, but without the whiskers, and large, long hands."

Menah ben Tahath puckered his lips unhappily at the description while two of his codefendants grinned, then quickly put on serious expressions.

The fuller told of the evening at the house of the terra-cotta worker, making a point, as I had advised him to do, of their having drunk nothing. He said he had not fought when the five men called him out lest they harm Dathan's family and because "my God believes we should turn our other cheek."

The defense lawyer picked it up. "And yet you do not now turn the other cheek in seeking revenge on these young men."

I objected, and Father overruled me, but it gave Rechab time to phrase an answer he had been mulling over. "I believe in turning the other cheek at such times of physical conflict, but I am also a good Jew, and I believe in the Law of my fathers . . ."

He told how the five took him through alleys, and "knowing now that I would not resist, they began kicking and beating me until I fell to the ground. For one of the kicks . . ."

"Go on," I prompted.

". . . was to my parts of generation . . ."

"And when they saw where they had injured you?"

"One of them said that would make sure that I did not sire any little Nazarene bastards in Borhaurus and they laughed. Then their leader said, 'Let's make doubly sure,' and since I saw they wore those little daggers, I was afraid they would do to me the worst thing that can be done to a man. . . ."

There was murmuring in the courtroom. Just as Jews do not allow sexually mutilated men in the priesthood, so sexual mutilation under Jewish Law is a barbarism; Jews do not even make eunuchs of their enemies.

"In pain as I was, I got up and ran. But they ran faster and tripped me. I saw a passerby but did not shout, fearing the young men might do me even greater ill. . . . They dragged and half walked me to your Joppa gate. There, a town constable questioned them. Their leader, the tall one, said I was a drunkard who had vomited on his father's door. I tried to speak up, but in truth I must have sounded and looked drunk and the young men hooted me down. Outside the gates, a blind beggar lay before his fire and asked for money, and one of the youths threw him a coin, and grabbed up a brand from the fire. . . .

"They kicked and punched and pulled me five, six hundred paces, abusing me and my religion. And now I was frightened, terribly frightened, for there was only the noises of night birds and the empty road and the brand. Its flame had gone out, but it still glowed like the eye of a demon."

Father interrupted. "Counselor, move this along a bit."

"Yes, sir," I said.

"They threw me down and three held me while the others put the brand into tinder and built a fire. I prayed under my breath, for each time I prayed aloud, they stuffed dirt into my mouth." His voice fell. "I prayed for death so I should not have to suffer while they cut or burned my parts."

A low groan came from several men in the audience. Father nodded at the herald, who called, "Silence, else all will be evicted!" The fuller turned and I told him to continue.

"That was what they were arguing among themselves over doing. The leader said, 'Crush his foot.' I was sure my time was near because they would not do that except to keep me from breaking away and running. Being in such terror, I kicked, but four held me tightly while the other, not the leader but the fat, short one with the beginnings of a beard"—everyone's eyes found him in the dock—"struck my foot with a great stone.

"I screamed and the fat one stuffed dirt in my mouth and I bit. He and another one beat my foot with rocks. I never before suffered such pain, and I knew my foot was being smashed beyond repair, as has proved to be—"

"Fuller, stop a moment," I said.

I undid the bandage on his foot. Rechab winced. The foot was swollen, with lines and blotches of purple, puffy as a rotted chicken

75

and almost the same shape. The front rows of the audience twisted their heads to see. There were grunts of compassion and anger. I bandaged the foot. In Father's eye, I thought I saw a steely suggestion of humor at my showmanship.

"Go on," I said. "Please be more concise."

"More . . . ?" asked Rechab.

"Shorter."

"The tall one pulled up my robe. I feared now they would cut me, so I thrashed, almost throwing them, but three held me while he took his knife out. 'So who will do it?' he asked. One said, 'You,' and another said, 'It's too much. I won't stay.' The tall one said, 'The eyes, then,' and he picked up a brand from the fire. I tried to struggle but they held me fast. . . .''

Rechab swallowed. He stopped talking and his shoulders began to tremble. It was ghastly. He was making the noises of weeping but there were no ducts for his tears.

"Go on, Fuller," I said.

"I felt pain such as I cannot describe when they put the brand to my left eye. When they drove it in, I screamed and I remember no more, for when I came to this time the pain was equal in both eyes." He stopped but did not again lose control. Quietly, he said, "And I knew, sirs, that I was blinded."

There was a great exhalation of breath in the courtroom because at the end, they, as I, had been listening without breathing. I glanced at the maimers. Their faces were pale but without expression.

The old lawyer asked Rechab again about the few injuries he had inflicted on the youths with his kicks and bites, then turned to the talk at the well. In more detail than I would have liked, he had the fuller repeat what he had said about Jesus being the Messiah and son of God, and about Jesus' alleged return from the dead, all mortal blasphemies to traditional Jews.

After Deborah had led the fuller back to our table, I called the woman who had lingered by the well. She described the threats as Rechab had and, again, my white-bearded opponent forced her to dwell on what he called, over my objections, the "blasphemies" and "sacrileges" spoken by Rechab.

The town constable reluctantly testified to the identities of the "young gentlemen" who had passed his way, saying that the stranger they were assisting had seemed drunk to him. I had thought of summoning the beggar, for after I gave him two drachmas, he remembered the incident. But we both knew if he testified against the youths, he invited a silent knife thrust or club blow some night while he slept by his fire.

Deborah, Dathan and his wife, all corroborated what they had witnessed of Rechab's story. The youths' lawyer drew from all three the fact that the fuller had not called for help as he was led away. The old owl was not leaving any cracks undaubed.

He put on his own case with the thoroughness that had brought him his reputation and his mansion on Merchants' Row. Each of the youths swore to their dedication to the Torah and to Jewish ritual. Small wonder, the lawyer suggested, that public mouthings about a crucified felon being the Messiah and coming back from the dead might distress these devout young men.

I looked at the front row and saw the fathers and other male family of these hyenas: powerful, cunning men, here to remind Father of their prestige, their influence in Borhaurus. Through the self-enforced impassivity of their well-fed faces, there broke occasionally, like glitterings of fires in deep woods, hatred, anger, resentment, and shame.

The five defendants had been well coached. All told the same story: no one had drawn a knife or threatened to behead the fuller, and they had only meant to lead him out of town. But on the way he had uttered revolting blasphemies. They had thought he must be drunk. When finally they ushered him outside the gates, he had assaulted two of them. They had sent him fleeing and built themselves a fire, but he had thrown rocks at them. They rushed him and he all but bit the finger off one. In an understandable response, they had thrown a stone, which must have struck his foot. When the madman still came at them, they had jabbed at him with the brands.

The fuller, hearing such lies, cried out to Father, "Not true, Sir Tribune, as Christ Jesus is my judge."

"Enough, Fuller!" Father quieted him.

I whispered urgently to Rechab that outbursts like that could lose us the case by default. I suddenly hated the old lawyer for letting his clients bear false witness, in violation of his own Law as well as Rome's. Still, I could not shatter their stories. Each backed up the lies of the others.

For rebuttal, I called Rechab's doctor, a Parthian surgeon in Borhaurus who ministered mainly to the poor, but did not dare to get in bad grace with the Pharisees and Sadducees.

"Could the blow of one stone have so damaged a foot?" I asked him. He looked uncomfortable.

"It would be hard to say."

"But you told the fuller that bones were broken from heel to toe," I rebuked him. He looked even more ill at ease but said nothing. It was only after I got Father to order him to testify or go to jail that he admitted the truth about his diagnosis.

By now the sweat was running down inside my toga. I could think of nothing I had not done. I looked back at Deborah, who was signaling me with a rapid pinching of her lips. "Sir," I said to Father, "may I consult my client for a moment?" I went back to Rechab and asked him in a whisper whether I had forgotten anything. At the same time, I glanced at Deborah's wax tablet.

"When last at synagogue?" she had written. Rechab, meanwhile, was telling me what liars the youths were, as if I did not know. It took a moment for me to fathom Deborah's message. When I did, I went to the dock and firmly reminded the youths that they had sworn that their devoutness brought on their anger against my client. I addressed Menah ben Tahath: "When, young man, were you last in your synagogue . . . ?"

The skinny hoodlum looked to his lawyer for guidance. This had not been part of the preparation. The lawyer smelled the vulture on the roof and objected, but it was he who had opened the synagogue door and it could not be closed.

"I could call your rabbi to assist your memory," I reminded Menah. Father ordered him to answer.

"I cannot remember."

"Was it a week before this incident?"

"I cannot remember."

"But the incident was only ten days ago. Surely your memory is not so faulty. Some things you remember in excruciating detail. Was it two weeks before? Three? Four?"

Again, he could not remember

"Menah ben Tahath," I demanded, "can you remember going a single time to synagogue this year? Answer, or I call your rabbi! *He* will not lie."

"Answer!" ordered Father, exasperated with the evasion.

"Perhaps once," Menah said falteringly.

"Perhaps once? Yet your piousness, your devoutness, was so great that it led you to blind and cripple my client?"

My opponent objected properly and successfully, but my point had been made. One by one, I questioned the others. Only one went regularly to synagogue and he solely under parental duress. Done, I risked a look of gratitude at Deborah.

It was the custom in our courts for the tribune and his two legal advisers to retire for no more than an hour and then to bring in their decision. The theory was that a case was best ruled on when the evidence was fresh in the judge's mind.

Father was back in a half hour. The audience immediately became still, tense. I was sure I had won. When I saw the grayness and strain on his face, I thought it was because he knew his ruling would anger powerful elements of the town and cause him trouble in Caesarea. He did not look at me, or anyone, but after the prescribed invocation of the names of the emperor, Minerva, and the Roman Senate began reading from his notes:

"I, Junius Faevolian, make the following findings: that Menah ben Tahath, of Borhaurus, and"—he read the names of the other four—"are guilty of a felony of the fourth category under the statutes of the eighth year of the reign of the Divinity and Emperor Augustus . . ."

Deborah, Dathan and his wife, looked enraptured and even Rechab smiled. A cry of "Justice!" went from the Nazarenes in the court, along with a groan from the town fathers and their allies. The youths looked as if they had just suffered what they had originally planned for the fuller.

But the face of the Pharisee counsel was alight with devilish joy. For he knew, and I suddenly remembered, that a fourth-degree felony included trespass, but did not include injury of a person. The finding meant that Father was going to find Rechab had been done no *criminal* injury—that the five animals had acted justifiably. I put my head in my hands.

The herald shouted for order, and when it was restored, Father read on as steadily as if he had not, for me, become as corrupted as an Asian satrap bought with gold and child harlots.

". . . in that they took by illegal trespass from the home of Dathan, a tilemaker of Borhaurus, one Rechab, a fuller of Modi'im, and that the defendants"—he said those vile and now victorious names again—"did in fact injure the foot of and blind the said Rechab. But I find that, while these acts were, *lato sensu*, legally reprehensible, *stricto sensu*, the defendants are not guilty because of the extreme provocation both by word and deed given them by the said Rechab."

This time, if there was any outcry by the Nazarenes, it was drowned out by the cheers of the Pharisees and Sadducees. Even as the herald threatened to clear the room, a mingled cry of dismay and triumph sounded from outside, where someone had taken the news. When all was quiet in the courtroom, Father continued. I looked at him, perceived his pain, but felt only the hatred of the betrayed.

Father read the penalties. They were severe, but meaningless: three hundred drachmas to be paid to Dathan by the defendants for trespass, with Menah ben Tahath, as the ringleader, to pay an additional fifty. Father rose and his entourage convoyed him from the room. There was a burst of happy chatter among the freed criminals and their allies. The five hugged each other and then their parents. The Pharisee lawyer glanced at me. All in a day's work, his look seemed to say.

The audience, except for the few Nazarenes, shoved toward the door. The fuller, Deborah, Dathan and his wife, stood as if they had been stunned with cattle clubs but had not yet fallen. In the nearly empty room, the fuller cleared his throat and said without confidence, "The will of God is done."

IX

❖❖❖

Outside in the sunlight, the four hundred Nazarenes waited silently. The townspeople had dispersed except for a few of the curious on the edges of the square. The fuller, helped by Dathan and Deborah, reached the steps. He squared his thick shoulders and, freeing his arm, raised a crutch to the crowd as a greeting. For a long minute, they waited for him to speak. But he could not summon up his words.

In the awkward vacuum, a voice near the front sang out boldly. "Oh Lord of hosts, even the sparrow finds a home. . . ." It was the hymn that Rechab's people had sung as we buried Andrew. A few around the singer picked it up and soon all four hundred Nazarenes were singing. ". . . And the swallow a nest for herself where she may lay her young . . . Blessed are those who dwell in thy house. . . ."

When the song ended, Rechab found his voice. He held up his crutch again, this time for attention. "Brothers and sisters in Christ," he said, his words carrying into the square. "What can I say to thank you? Only this: that in travail for Christ there is joy. When I heard the judgment, my heart fell into despair. But even as I walked out to you, it seemed a voice spoke, saying that though blind, I would see the light of Jesus more strongly than when I had eyes, that though lame, I would walk in his ways with stronger steps. . . .

"No, do not be tempted to think that Jesus fell away from me today, for he was with me a thousand times more than if we had prevailed. Think: what are two eyes and one foot to the sixty eyes and sixty feet which are ready to be baptized into us? Is that not a fair bargain: to buy with these three pieces of flesh eternal joy in heaven for thirty souls?

81

What if Borhaurus has taken my sight? In exchange, I have bestowed on Borhaurus a new kind of sight, the sight of the kingdom of heaven!"

I was dumbstruck by the transformation of this humble man, untrained in elocution. His words had soared. My admiration expanded to the disinheriteds in the square, far away from their homes, but, unlike me, not solitary, not defeated. I shook my head to bring my loyalty back to where it belonged, to myself.

". . . And thirty will not be all," Rechab was saying. "There are among us today other stray sheep seeking a new flock, a new shepherd. Bring them in, brethren, for before we are done, my poor eyes and foot will be redeemed not just thirty or fifty but a hundredfold." Rechab was panting. It was his first full day out of bed, he still had a fever, and he had been in court for four hours. He was getting hoarse.

"Before you go back to your homes, I ask you to pray for me, for those who have helped me, not just followers of our Lord Jesus, but for this brave young Roman who took my case, yes, even though his father was my judge—" Rechab turned, seeking me in the wrong direction—"and pray for those who injured me, that they may find their way to repentance and salvation, and for the tribune, that from this trial which must have caused him pain, he will find wisdom and courage."

❁

That evening, I ate lentils and lamb shanks at Dathan's, where we gloomily discussed the trial. Even Deborah was polite enough not to say what was on all their minds: that my father had given in to cowardice. Rechab, for all the inspiration within him during his talk, had lapsed back into pain and feverishness.

Later, when I went home, it was to Mother's room, where, as usual, she was embroidering. I told her I was moving out in the morning. She reached for my hands and I took hers, so soft, so indulgently tended. Father would have told her what had happened. Tears ran down her plump cheeks, streaking the still-unremoved powder. At the sight of her wordless weeping, tears came to my eyes, too.

"It was time, anyway," I said.

She shook her head, holding my hands until her tears stopped and she could talk. "Go talk with him," she insisted. "Do not abandon him, not this way."

I could not answer. The accumulation of anguish had finally breached what self-control I had left. I kissed her and went to my room and began to pack the tunics and sandals that I had paid for, along with Grandfather's armor, Ezra's dirk, my javelin, and other things not bought with Father's money. I knew that leaving behind my stallion, my broadsword, an ornamental shield that Father had given me, would hurt him. I wanted it to.

When he came to my room, I ignored him. "Do you mind if I sit?" he asked. I went on with my packing. He sat on a brass chest, another gift from him that I would not take. "Can you stop packing and talk?" he asked. "I have shown you more courtesy, Demas, when you have come to me with your problems."

"I am removing a problem from you tomorrow," I said.

"I came to talk with you, not to hear edicts." He waited for me to answer, and when I did not, he went on. "This thing was turning Borhaurus into a shambles."

"You did what you knew was wrong. You knew the fuller deserved justice."

"There are compromises I have to make. You have always known that."

"Compromises up to a point, Father. This went past the point. I know it; you know it; the whole town knows it, even those who are most pleased by what you did know it."

His gray eyes narrowed in anger, then he closed them and put his thumb and forefinger to them. "How easy for you to be the household judge," he said.

I could not spare him. "You could have found them guilty on every charge, fined and banished them, then, for balance, deported the fuller and"—I could not bring myself to say Deborah's name to him—"his deputy."

"No, I could not," he said wearily.

All along, at some level beneath awareness, I had feared it: Caesarea. He went on. "Caesarea did not even want me to find them guilty of trespass. I had to wring that out of Cumanus. He was adamant, adamant. . . ."

He shook his head, knowing I would assume the rest: Cumanus, the procurator, that is Rome, had felt a Nazarene must not prevail lest it stir an already restive population into even more sedition. The more so in this case where the leading Pharisees and Sadducees were in agreement.

Even so, a man of honor would let himself be pushed only a certain distance. It was as if I had seen cowardice through his skin, malignant and spreading. He had done what he did to preserve the status quo: his position, the family's, our wealth. He had done it at the expense of his integrity, the thing I had valued most in him.

When he spoke again, his voice was dry, without force. "If I had defied them, Cumanus made me understand I would be recalled. There is a point beyond which I could not be driven, but I was nowhere near it. I was not prepared to lose everything for the sake of a fuller."

"Not just for a fuller," I said, suddenly understanding how he was manipulating me, trying to make me more sympathetic to him than he deserved. "You knew you would lose me, too."

He looked at me, no authority in his face, merely fatigue and age. I had not been able to see the oldness until now, when he had become a stranger. "I thought I might," he acknowledged. "I hoped I would not. But even if I had been sure, I would have . . ." He looked for a kinder word to describe what he had done, then gave up ". . . capitulated. There were too many others, too much else at stake."

Again, I felt as if I would weep. There was the formula: justice for the fuller equaled giving up the status quo. Serving injustice equaled giving up me. Ergo, the status quo equaled more than me. It was precise, intellectual, functional.

"Does it matter to you, Father, that you taught me principles and they became a system I lived by, and that what you did in that courtroom left me with worse than nothing—a garbage heap, a cloaca? Does it matter to you"—my voice rose as I began to feel wrath beneath my despair—"that you who taught me to revere honor were, in fact, *dishonorable?*"

He jerked from his chair as if to strike me. His face writhed. I had said words I was sure would create a breach between us forever. Abruptly, his hand gripping his wrist, he reined his anger. His breath still coming fast, he said coldly, self-protectively, "It mattered a great deal to me, Demas, but as you have observed, it did not matter sufficiently."

I had put by enough money to buy a gelding, and had enough left for a month's advance on two small rooms. They had their own entrance on a court common to seven other tenants. The last occupants had removed themselves but not their rubbish. Deborah, upset over her responsibility for my break with my father, volunteered to help me make the place habitable. We heated water, scrubbed floors, white-washed walls and ceilings, arranged my belongings.

My brown bearskin made my narrow bed a cozy couch. In one

corner, I kept my armor on its "tree." In another, on a polished stand of oak, I put the bust of Socrates I had won as a debating prize at Scythopolis. By late afternoon of the second day, the rooms looked like a home. Deborah and I were sweaty and speckled with whitewash, hungry and thirsty.

"Do they expect you back?" I asked.

"Not for a while," she said. "Is there more to do?"

"Just if you want," I said, heart suddenly speeding up. "I have a fiasco of Falernian. Could we buy some lamb and bread? The first meal in the new house?"

"I am the worst kind of cook."

I was afraid she was saying no. "We can spit the lamb and salt it and hope for the best," I said. "You go buy, I will have the coals ready." I forced money for the food on her. As she went out, I felt the sudden silence. For two days, there had been our serious talk about Rechab's case, about our families, and our chatter, our cleaning and decorating, the ordinaries of moving in. If I felt loss over her leaving for a few minutes, how would it be when she went back to Modi'im? I grouped the coals on one side of the hearth and thought if she could not learn to cook, I would. I opened the wine, the remainder of a dozen fiascoes paid me as a fee by a wine merchant.

Deborah came back with the lamb, bread, and two pomegranates and knelt to unwrap the scrap papyrus from the lamb. Outside our door, the day was fading. The firelight silhouetted her, not in prayer, but simply kneeling, this tall, beautiful woman at a timeless task. I went to her with a cup of wine and held it to her lips so she need not wipe the grease from her hands to take a sip.

"Deborah," I said, "I love you. I loved you in Modi'im and I love you now and I might always love you. I love you so much that when you go the best part of me will die. . . ." I stopped, afraid it would all flood out of my eyes and drown whatever chance I had of her ever loving me in return. She sipped the wine as I held it there, safe from having to reply so long as it was at her mouth. At last, she looked at me, the wine moistening her parted lips.

"I know that, Demas, but I do not know what to do. Some of the time I feel so natural with you. And sometimes I feel I want to close you out of my life—" she took the cup, greasy hands or no and had another sip—"because feeling that way protects me. I *care* what you have done for me"—she slipped and quickly corrected herself—". . . us. But . . ."

I thought I knew what she was going to say. I could not bear to be told by her she did not love me so soon after Father had as much as said the same thing. It was throwing me down the well all over again. It was less painful for me to say it myself. ". . . But you do not love me. Or if you do, it is only in the way you Nazarenes love. You are all so busy loving Jesus and each other and even your enemies in *that* way that you never love in the way I love you."

"No," she said sharply, "you are wrong. I was not going to say I do not love you. I was going to say that when I feel as I did at the trial, proud of you, admiring your bravery and sacrifice, then I am confused, uncertain. So it becomes less complicated—less frightening—for me to close you out."

"But why do that? Why not just—"

"Oh, Demas." She stopped me. "Do you think I have not been working all this out in my mind? For weeks. And I had it all in such order. And now, curse you, my logic seems so silly compared with . . . Demas, we have problems," she finished lamely.

She looked so serious, her observation such a monumental understatement, that I laughed. She began to laugh, too, but uneasily, then cut it short and looked at me. I leaned toward her, not wanting to steal anything she might not want me to have. I kissed her lightly, briefly. When she did not draw away, I kissed her that way again. I looked into her sea-dark eyes and saw no resistance, none at all.

When I kissed her the third time, my lips lingered, and after a few seconds, hers moved gently as if they were made of tiny fingers and she, blind as the fuller, must explore my lips to learn what they looked like, what they were made of. Suddenly, she pressed harder. I took her in my arms, her hand still holding the wine cup. I felt the good flesh at her waist, and I was so aroused, I was dizzy. The breath rushed from her nostrils onto my face.

At last, she broke, but held her cheek on mine. "So," she said with warmth that bordered on happiness but also held in it a great resistance, "so that is what it's all about." She took a deep breath, then shook her head to escape from what she must have seen as some sort of thralldom. "I do not even know whether you like your lamb well cooked or not," she said, fumbling with the salt, pepper, and rosemary, part of the kitchen larder Mother had packed, "and I have never cooked at an open hearth."

"Then maybe we should kiss instead of cooking."

She shook her head. "You have just taught me about kissing, and it almost burned me alive. Now I am going to learn about shish kebabs. On my own."

When, with a few false starts, she had cooked the lamb, we sat before the fire cross-legged like children. The skin was crackly and the meat inside was pink and succulent. We wiped the grease from our hands on the fresh bread, and ate the bread. We washed the food down with wine. For dessert, we ate the pomegranates, spitting the seeds in the fire, where they popped.

The wine emboldened me. I pushed a wisp of hair behind her ear, too intent to smile. I spoke of how companionable we were, of how we had seen each other under trying conditions and not found each other wanting, of how we were the right ages.

"Just suppose, Deborah, *suppose* we were to marry. Even in your religion, young people do. They eat by the fire and perhaps they make love by it. They raise their children into good people, one parent yielding to the other on all sorts of things. We could live anywhere you wanted: here, Modi'im, outside Palestine. I could practice law wherever Rome is, which is everywhere, and you could have your ministry. I could buy you Roman citizenship and our children could be Romans. You could raise them as Nazarenes. I would be happy with that."

For a time, she said nothing, her eyes a little unfocused. Then she wiped her hands on her old skirt and took my face in them—how hot they were—and studied my eyes. As if to remind herself of what had happened, she kissed me again and then a second time. Then she shook her head again.

"Demas," she said, "do not 'just *suppose*' that way with me. I could not be your wife and be what I want to be to Jesus. That is what I have been practicing to say all these weeks." Suddenly, she began to weep. I tried to kiss her, to defeat this ultimatum with another embrace, but she put her cheek again to mine. She held me that way, both of us kneeling on the worn wooden floor. I felt my heart slow its millrace.

"I have seen what happens to women when they marry," she said. "I have seen my mother, my brothers' wives, even Bediah's. Your mother is the same. The men and then the children absorb them. . . ."

"Deborah, I am not your father, your brothers, my father. I am not like them. I swear I would never be."

"No, not today. Not tomorrow. But, Demas, where has anyone seen it any differently? Not even Jael, or Esther. Or Andromache, or the goddesses. If by a miracle you did not become like men everywhere, how do I know I would not force you to—"

"That's ridiculous. I would not let you change."

"But, Demas, I would, I would. Out of love for you, out of love for our children. Surely you see that with men it is not the same. Moses, no doubt, was the partner of Zipporah at home, but it was not she who led the Chosen People out of Egypt. We women keep the family afloat, our husbands feeling brave and worthy. We stuff our children's dolls with husks, are your . . ." She was warming to the subject, but amended what she had been about to say, which I suspected was "goats." ". . . handmaidens. No, you would not be like my father, but you could not help being a man.

"And even if all this could be worked out, there is the problem we started with. If I were your wife, I would devour you and my love for you would devour me. There would be nothing left for Jesus, nothing for all this that I believe, nothing, not a thread, not a speck of dust. I would be only love."

She capped her hand over mine. Her voice, though, came from the head: "There is a story about Jesus that the fuller tells, that Satan took him up on a mountain. He said if Jesus would give up his father, God, then Satan would make him king over the whole world. Jesus said no without a second's consideration."

I thought that was the end of the story and started to argue the analogy, but she shook her head to silence me.

"The point is that Satan promised Jesus the wrong thing. He should have promised him a fire and a strong friend and children and good food and wine and laughter. He should have promised him love. That would have made the choice so difficult that I wonder if even Jesus could have said no."

"If Satan had been able to promise love," I said, "he would not have been Satan. It is the sense of God in me that lets me promise you love, Deborah."

She threw some pomegranate seeds on the coals, not bothering to eat the sweetness from around them, and said with sudden emotion, "I cannot accept that love, Demas. In Kybistra, during those long years, I said I would do certain things, with Jesus' help, if I got back to Modi'im. I am going to do those things. I made promises to the fuller. He chose me as his assistant on the basis of them. But, most of all, I made promises to myself and to Jesus. So you see, in a way I am already married. I feel him so much in you. But I belong to him."

I must have looked as downcast as I felt. Everything I had to offer was not enough. And the competition was not even corporeal. There was no way to compete.

"I am not saying that this need in me to be Jesus' will not be fulfilled as time passes, that someday I may not want—very much—to marry you. But please, please, Demas, do not tug at me now. It hurts too much."

Perhaps because I looked so forlorn, she gave me a peck on the lips, friendly and nonprovocative as a sister's or aunt's. Then, slightly stimulated from the touch, she looked wistful herself. I put another piece of wood on the fire. It steamed for a short while before flames sprang from it. My words had been weightless, powerless. I lighted a lamp. The room was small, warm, ours. The armor glinted dully. The homely face of the philosopher in the corner on his stand looked like a friendly daemon's. The bed with its thick, soft covering was a wish, a temptation without hope. We cleaned up, more distant, but with our conflict resolved—unhappily for me—for the time being.

We walked through the dark streets to Dathan's. When we reached his garden, we could see the glow behind his shutters. I stopped, but she took a pace toward the house.

"Not yet," I said.

In the starlight, she turned as naturally into my arms as if we had been lovers all our lives. There was no caution, no reservation, because the warm room, the bed with its bearskin, were far behind us. Again, I did not press hard on her lips, but let her press mine. She held the kiss, exploring my lips in that measured way as leisurely as if she had already forgotten what they were like and wanted to take her time remembering. Her hands were behind my head, my arms around her waist. She let her body sway into mine for an instant, breasts, belly, thighs. And then withdrew and ran silently to the house without looking back.

Rechab had been overly optimistic about the trial bringing in a hundred followers. Still, the original thirty had grown to sixty and Rechab had formally named Dathan the minister of the new church. Before the trial of Rechab, he had seemed only an able terra-cotta maker, just another tradesman. He had made tiles and pottery wares; the town had paid him for them.

Now he seemed taller, broader. He had become a leader, and not just of poor workers and the dispossessed. He had named a young mason as his assistant, and among the members were a disillusioned scribe; a hardworking leadsmith; a bent gray man I sometimes used for clerking. Peter and Dathan were not unlike Vercingetorix and Arminius and King David, simple men, untrained in any civil or military skills, who rose from the masses and became leaders at the precise moment when they were most needed. The same, I thought reluctantly, might be said of Jesus.

X

Rechab's eye sockets were healing, but his foot was worse. The Parthian doctor wanted to cut it off rather than risk spread of the infection. The fuller prayed and said God wanted him to go home. I would have accompanied him as escort even if Deborah were not with us. I had become more bound up with him than any lawyer ever should with a client. Before we departed, Rechab's admirers loaded his and Deborah's mules and my gelding's side bags with gifts for Rechab and the Modi'im church. Then they gathered around us and sang. "There is a river whose streams make glad the city of God. . . ." Their religion, I knew they meant, was the river. And the Nazarenes were its streams.

We had padded the fuller's foot, but still he gasped involuntarily when the mule shifted gait to avoid rocks in the road. Yet, for the first two hours he was caught up in the excitement of the trip, of going home to his shop and his church work. Rechab's wife, who was doing what she could with both the business and the church, had sent word they had ten prospective Nazarenes as a result of the events in Borhaurus.

Deborah and the fuller discussed the ten's coming baptism, a site for their larger congregation, changes in their observances. She was resourceful, eager to help him with duties requiring sight. Their social differences evaporated in their common fervor. She, now living with an old woman in Modi'im, was learning to weave, generally a man's trade. Like dedicated rabbis, the ministers of the Nazarenes were all self-sufficient.

As we plodded along, I thought about Rechab, blinded and in

danger of losing his foot, who nevertheless was optimistically talking of the future, cheerful as Andrew. Such men could live bravely and uncomplicatedly on earth because they were already half in heaven. How easy it was to conjure up a picture of Rechab limping down a lane on his crutches in the afterlife, Andrew beside him telling stories of the days with Jesus, the two of them comparing a fuller's life with a fisherman's.

We passed groves of lemon, citron, and oranges. One worker, seeing Deborah, brought us three oranges. The orchards gave way to stands of laurel and wild pomegranate, then snarls of cactus and tall prickly pears. Despite clouds, the day grew warmer. The fuller complained that his foot hurt more, but he did not want to stop. After a while, in spite of, or perhaps because of, the pain, he slumped in the saddle and drowsed.

Late in the afternoon, the clouds grew dark and fat drops of rain began to fall. Off the road ahead there was a grove of olives. I led my horse and Rechab's mule toward it. The fuller's foot was hurting so badly that he gritted his teeth. By the time we were in the shelter of the trees, the rain was hard and steady. We put the fuller's goat-hair cloak on the ground and helped him onto it. He was in such agony he could hardly talk. We undid the bandages. His toes were like great purple sausages, and from his equally discolored ankle, rootlike veins, filled with angry dark blood, had begun to reach upward toward his knee.

We had to get him to a surgeon. But when we tried to move him, he shouted hoarsely in pain. More traveling might send the poisons higher, infect his whole system and kill him. Deborah and I decided I should gallop to Modi'im, now closer than Borhaurus, find a physician and bring him to Rechab. I tightened my saddle, cinched my new broadsword to it so I could reach it easily, then knelt beside the moaning fuller. He pulled me down to kiss my cheek.

"If I am not here when you come back, Demas, I will be in heaven with my master praying for you," he said. I gripped his hand and swallowed hard, suddenly again reminded of Andrew.

The rain became a drizzle halfway to Modi'im. I clattered up at the fuller's house two hours after sunset. His wife and I could not get the surgeon to go with us, only an animal healer who quickly packed a small brazier and an ominous-looking leather sack in which tools rattled. A church member went, too, the three of them on borrowed donkeys. It was well past midnight when we got to the fuller. The rain had dripped through the olive leaves and Deborah had propped her cloak over the fuller like a tent. She was bedraggled and worn, but

91

smiled with relief as we stumbled up. Rechab woke from his fever dream and greeted us wanly.

"Get a torch lit," said the animal man. "Put the brazier over here." He was a small, officious man with a self-confident air. I hoped it was warranted. We soon had the brazier and two torches burning. The animal doctor poked gently at Rechab's bloated foot, then squeezed his calf, then the knee, then the calf again. He squatted by the fuller's head. "Rechab, I can do no more than I can do," he said.

"I know," Rechab said. "God be with me."

My stomach felt twisted from the riding and the lack of food. The sight of his monstrous foot made my guts churn. The healer ordered us to carry Rechab a short distance away so he could void. Afterward, we brought him back by the fire, where his wife cradled his head and gave him wine. We stuck the torches in the wet ground just beyond where Rechab might kick them.

The animal doctor heated a poker in the brazier's coals. Beside Rechab's leg, he placed a long knife and a small saw. He put on a leather apron, strapped a belt around the fuller's upper leg, slipped a smooth stone under it to press the artery in the thigh and tightened the belt. He bound a second belt around the calf, just above where he planned to cut. Rechab began to sob. The healer gave the fuller's wife a piece of folded goatskin.

"Rechab," he said. "I want you to bite the skin. Do not open your mouth. Not even to pray." The animal healer signaled me, Deborah, and the Nazarene to kneel and hold down the fuller. Rechab, the skin in his mouth, clutched Deborah's arms. Her lips moved but I felt no tremor in her body. The oil on the healer's saw flickered liquidly in the yellow torchlight. For an instant, he rested the saw blade on the leg. Then, with one deft stroke, he cut through the meat and to the bone. The fuller screamed, the sound made nasal by the compress in his mouth.

The blood spurted onto the ground, but quickly subsided to a dribble as the animal man sawed at the two calf bones. The fuller bucked and Deborah and I wrestled his good leg to the ground. But the Nazarene was unable to hold the pitching right leg, whose foot and ankle were held on now only by a flap of skin.

The healer cursed as the lower leg flailed around like a throwing stick. The Nazarene jumped astride the thigh and pinned it to the wet ground. One more long stroke and the surgery was done. The animal man flung the foot and ankle into the brush. He scrambled to his feet and got the hot iron. My stomach finally rebelled. I turned my head and vomited. Into the oozing stump, the healer pressed the poker, here, there. I smelled the scorched flesh and retched again.

The fuller had fainted, but his body jerked with muscular spasms. I was humiliated at my weakness. When the poker was hot again, the healer thoroughly singed the wound. He loosened the top belt slightly, let the stump redden with the fresh blood, then retightened the belt. Deborah went to where Rechab's wife knelt by his head as if paralyzed. She took the older woman in her arms. The fuller moaned.

"He's alive," said the animal man self-congratulatorily. He wiped his bloody hands on the leather apron, and carefully bound the fuller's stump with a clean rag dipped in unguents. Then he looked for the wineskin and everyone but Rechab and I took long draughts.

A dreary, misty dawn had grayed the skies by the time Rechab became conscious. Groggy and suffering as he was, we put him side saddle on the most tractable donkey and rode slowly into Modi'im. After we had installed him in his own bed, I stole a few moments alone with Deborah outside the house.

"When can I see you?" I asked.

"In a week? Make sure you convince Rechab you've come to see him." She smiled wearily. "But then you lawyers are good at doing things like that."

❈

The time I had expended on Rechab's case had reduced my finances. But I soon found that I had a new kind of client. My willingness to challenge the Pharisee and Sadducee elders brought me small merchants—both Jews and pagans—who had suffered injustices from the rich but had not found a lawyer who would take their cases for anything less than half the settlement.

Grandfather's ornate litter couch arrived before my office one day, carried by two dark-skinned Cyrene slaves, the Ethiop walking beside it. Heads peered from doors all around the arcades to see what dignitary had come to see me. The Ethiop parted the curtains and the old man, resplendent in silk and gold, glorying in the impact he had made, stepped out and raised an arm cuffed in ermine toward where I stood in my doorway.

"I have a case of Roman constitutional law I would like to pursue with you, Counselor," he said when we were inside. "It is against the Divinity and Emperor Claudius." I blinked with surprise. "Because I have heard you are so courageous, I want you to file suit against him for reinstatement of our Hasmonean dynasty with eighty-nine years' back payment of wages."

We both laughed. "If I proved successful," I said, "the Hasmonean kings would confiscate all your property because you are Borhaurus's most dedicated collaborator with Rome, a Roman citizen, and . . . the grandfather of a lawyer for blasphemers."

He laughed again, but when his face lost its merriment, I saw how he was aging. I could more easily bear to see age in Father. Unlike him, Grandfather had never played loosely with what I needed: his love and fidelity.

I excused myself, went three doors down to an office of hired clerks, and dispatched one for citron juice and honey cakes. When I came back, Grandfather and I made small talk about clients and my new abode until he was ready to tell me why he had come to see me. He made a question of it.

"How fares the daughter of my late friend in Modi'im?"

I swore him to discretion and told him I was serious about wanting to marry her. "But her religion stands in the way. I have not given up persuading her otherwise."

He nodded. "Her religion is absurd. I cannot tell you how to overcome her objections. But I can tell you that her and this Rechab's faction are by no means the worst of the Nazarenes. They maintain their ties with the synagogue, I am advised. Indeed, the fuller survives in Modi'im *because* he has not totally deserted the synagogue and the Law. *He* was enlisted by this sect's leaders in Jerusalem, who, though disgusting, remain in contact with the Temple.

"There are others who want to throw the Law out into the gutter as if it were swills and who thereby bring down the wrath of every Jew in Judaea on their heads. Dathan"—and now I saw the true purpose of Grandfather's visit—"is of this latter group, I am sorry to say. His terra-cotta work took him to Antioch, and it was there that he was sworn into their wing of this sect."

Grandfather was never wrong about such things. Though surprised, I tried to minimize what he had told me. "I know there are doctrinal differences," I said.

"*Unhealthy* doctrinal differences, Demas," he corrected me as the clerk brought in a copper tray. When the man had gone, Grandfather went on, "If you should ever be so love-giddy as to ally yourself with this cult, Demas, make sure it is with the Modi'im, that is the Jerusalem branch."

I was silent, thinking through what Grandfather was saying. Did he sense the appeal—even aside from Deborah—that this sect sometimes had for me? I was not ready to talk with him about that. "I gather you are telling me that Dathan's branch is in danger? He will listen to me. His was the only part of the case I won."

"Clients *never* listen to their lawyers outside court," observed Grandfather. He tasted a cake and delicately put it back on the tray. "There is also the matter of your poor family. Do you think if I arranged a little family supper . . . ?"

"Not yet, Grandfather."

"Well," he said, "as a general principle I would say it is wiser for fathers and sons to be speaking to each other than not, even if it is across wide chasms."

That afternoon, I went to see Dathan. He and two other men were planing a ridgepole. It was for an open-sided structure they were building to the right of the shed where Dathan stored his tiles, bowls, jugs, and other products. He broke off his work and wiped the sweat from his bald pate.

"Our meeting place," said Dathan, "the fruits of your labor. From the money you got us." His jauntiness belied his expression, and when I told him my news, his face clouded further.

"My grandfather is trying to warn you to be more circumspect, Dathan. This construction will just make the Jews angrier. Let me at least attempt to sound someone out about it before you go any further."

"Borhaurus has already let me know how it feels, Sir Demas," he said. He walked me toward a clump of weeds at the end of a row of chopped corn. We were out of sight of his comrades. From the weeds, he pulled a cross of fruitwood. The upright was a little over a half cubit in length. On it, tied with a leather thong, was a long shard of terra-cotta tile. "My wife found it outside the front door yesterday morning," he said.

I turned the thing over in my hands. It said plainly that the maker of tiles was going to be tied to a cross if he kept stirring things up. Caesarea and Father should have foreseen the message their cravenness would give those in Borhaurus who hated the Nazarenes. Or had they foreseen, and did not care? Unable to do anything about Father or the haters, I spilled my bile out on Dathan.

"So you blithely build your meeting place, whistling while cripplers and gougers of eyes warn you that if you do not stop, they are going to spread you on a tree."

"There is more yet to come, Sir Demas," he said, churlish, but at the same time amused at my misplaced pique. "We have taken in a young Pharisee, and Cyrus the weaver." Cyrus was a Gentile, and a stream of Gentile Nazarenes would further break Borhaurus into hostile camps.

"You could accommodate yourselves to Borhaurus the way the fuller does with Modi'im," I said, "but you refuse. A meeting house, Pharisees, Gentiles, next it will be Romans."

I felt him stiffen, resenting my intrusion. "I love Rechab," Dathan said. "All followers of Christ love each other. But I was baptized in the Antioch church and we take in whoever comes to us in good faith."

I was still fuming, but saw it was useless to argue further with him. Dathan waited for me to calm, then touched my arm and said with a placating smile, "How can I give my friend a gift I have made him when he remains angry with me?"

I started to upbraid him again, but he took my arm and led me toward his storage shed. There, he lifted from a shelf three small pitchers, each shaped differently.

"This is a Jewish pitcher. It holds a *log*," he said, handing me a squat, sturdy pitcher. "This"—and he gave me one with a long, graceful handle—"is Roman. It holds a sextarius. And this one"—it had an embossed flower and a fluted lip—"is my own design. We will use ones like this for the wine in our Communion. All hold the same amount. All are made of the same clay. All sit peacefully on the same shelf. I wanted you to take payment from the money you obtained for me. But since you would not, these pitchers are your fee."

After I had them all settled in my hands, he gave me a quick embrace. The gift and his hug had turned away my wrath. As I walked toward the courthouse square, I thought, It is bad enough that they are threatening a good, if pigheaded, human being. They are also threatening an artist and poet.

When I returned to Modi'im, I went first to see the fuller, telling him I was on the way to Lydda and had come to see how he was. He was submerged in his own misery. "This is a great deal to bear, Demas. It is easier to tell you that than the rest of them. You are not a follower of Christ. I can feel woeful around you all I want."

I laughed and put my hand over his big paw where it lay on the bed and gave it a shake. "You are a tough old rooster, Fuller. A little bit and you will be turning the multitudes toward your Jesus with the best of them. Better. People can see what you gave up for your Christ. You are a living legend. I only wish I had represented you more ably in court."

"No, no, nobody could have," he said.

I could see him brightening. I hated to cloud him over by telling him about the threat to Dathan, but Rechab had tied his life too closely to Borhaurus for me to spare him. When I finished, he looked somber, but not daunted.

"Borhaurus sowed the wind when it found those boys innocent," he said, "and it will reap a whirlwind. Will your father give Dathan and his people any protection?"

"Possibly. Just to keep the peace. He may have a soldier go by Dathan's at night now and then. I am sure he will put down any real riots." I told Rechab of Dathan's meeting house, and of his new Pharisee and Gentile members.

Rechab pondered the situation. "I fear for Dathan. He will no more compromise than our beloved Stephen, who was stoned because he would not bend, not even by the hair of a flea. Dathan should take his family and go to Antioch while he can. He has terra-cotta thighs"— tilemakers form tiles by shaping them on their thighs—"he can make money anywhere. Borhaurus will fall on him and his church like rats on a poor man's baby and kill them in a night of bites."

"That is true, Fuller," I said, "but is it not a little odd for you to be counseling flight?"

Rechab smiled. "Jesus did not go to the cross on the second day he preached, Demas. He had work to do first. Dathan should use his gift before he risks his life." Rechab turned toward me with those dreadful sockets. "You see, I knew when Jesus sent me to Borhaurus that something might happen. It did. I was made . . . like this. And the church of God has grown there."

Deborah was alone and weaving at her landlady's. She sprang up when she saw me. All week, I had imagined her falling into my arms, but instead she merely squeezed my two hands in hers. She put aside her work and took some bread and cheese and olives from the larder to go with the wine I had brought. As we walked out of the town, I told her of the threat to Dathan and the other happenings.

From the hill where we spread our lunch, though hidden from the road by pines and firs and clumps of broomcorn, we could see the sun on the Mediterranean more than twenty miles away. But Deborah seemed anxious, beyond the natural anxiety from her new duties in the church. "I am having a difficult time, Demas," she began cautiously. "I have prayed about what we said and did with each other and I do not get a simple answer. It seems,"—she smiled sadly—"that Jesus wants me to make up my own mind about this. I am torn between a love that brings, brought, will bring me again, peace and joy, and your love, which brings me excitement and turmoil—" her voice dropped— "and need."

"And warmth and laughter."

"Yes, that too. But for me to love you now the way you want is for me to lose the person I have become. All the things I said about women and families and men, all the things I said about Jesus, seem even truer today than when I said them." She looked miserable and took my hands for support, not affection.

"Deborah," I said. "Don't make up your mind to anything yet. We have time to let things happen the way they will. What we have, believe me, is rare."

"But rareness is the problem. Can't you see? You *are* rare: brave, and good, and humorous, and loyal. But if I let myself cling to you, where is my love for Jesus? Where am *I*?"

"You say Jesus makes you happy, Deborah, then why are we so unhappy now?"

"I was joyous until you came along," she said, near to tears, "then you bumped into my life like an ox in a narrow street, sticking your horns into everything that was in the way."

"*I* bumped into *your* life? Did I bump into *your* law office . . . ?"

"No, no, I am wrong about that. I apologize. But not about the rest. Demas, you made love to me with your talk, you know you did, then we kissed . . . oh, I let you. But you courted me, Demas, not I you. Even on that day in Modi'im when we buried Andrew, you did . . . and ever since we saw each other again." With effort, she curbed her tears. "What did I know about love? What did anything I read about Medea or Jason, or Helen or Paris, or David or Bathsheba, tell me about *my* lips, *my* body, *my* heart?"

"You love me," I said. "And I cannot stop loving you. Perhaps I could learn not to if I thought you could cut me out of your heart and put me on the ground like a fish to die. Perhaps to save myself I could stop. But you *cannot* cut me out. You think you are married to Jesus. But in terms of how we live, he is only an *idea*, a magnificent idea, but he cannot touch your lips. Singing hymns is not going to get you kissed. Jesus is not going to get you pregnant with some wonderful little baby."

I took her in my arms and she did not draw back. She breathed hard with her agitation, her breasts heaving against me. At last she calmed. In that embrace, I knew I was losing her. When we broke, she saw the tears welling in my eyes and blotted them with her fingers. "I cannot stand it, Demas, I cannot. Please, please, you must let me be alone for a while."

I waved a final plea like the tattered banner of a defeated army. "Let me come back in a week, and in the meantime . . ." Surely, she would have me as a patient suitor, waiting on the periphery of her love.

"No," she said. "Please. No more. I have a fragile-enough hold on things, on what I know I must do. If you come back before I am ready, I will have to brace myself all over again." She begin to cry anew. Demas, let me have some time."

"But if you change, if you . . . ?"

"If I find a way," she said, relieved that at last I was sparing her, "if I can think of some way to bring things together, I will come to you, or get word to you."

XI

✷✣✷✣✷✣✷✣✷✣✷✣✷✣✷✣✷✣✷✣✷✣✷✣✷✣✷✣✷✣✷✣✷✣✷✣✷✣✷

I waited, hoping every day to hear from her. A week passed and there was nothing. I knew it was futile to go to her. Like a plumb lead in the wind, my bitterness swung between her and her religion. Even if I could overcome her fears that I would absorb her, her Jesus would remain as an adversary I did not know how to fight. Sometimes I thought of the Nazarenes as a legion of lunatics getting themselves blinded, crucified, scourged, stoned, and otherwise mutilated *in order* to deny themselves normal lives. Two, then three, weeks went by.

I concentrated on my work and began to make money. I put in Campanian and Cyprian wines, fine oils, I bought new clothes and furniture. I visited home when Father was away on his duties. I saw Grandfather, Ezra, and those friends who had ignored or forgiven my affront to Borhaurus.

Dathan and his Jewish followers no longer even came to the synagogue. From his meeting place, the voices, stronger every Sunday, sang out lustily the psalms of David. Prominent Jews said to each other, "Even our music has been stolen."

It was not long before the most extreme of the Pharisees began talking about how God had told his Chosen People to eradicate the worshippers of Baal in their midst, to make their altars as dust. Were these blasphemers any less pernicious?

But Borhaurus was not a town whose decades of orderliness could be destabilized in a few days. The blinding of the fuller, although symptomatic, was still an aberration. Indeed, the meeting place, despite the threat, went unharmed. Yet, gradually, Nazarenes found old Jewish friends no longer had much to say to them. Nazarenes who kept the dietary laws were told by kosher butchers they had patronized for years that the cuts of meat they sought were sold out. Those seeking loans to carry them until payday, or until the next harvest or the next order for brasses or rags or charcoal, were now told no money was available.

The first outbreak of violence was among the children. Nine- and ten-year-old sons of Pharisees waylaid two Nazarene boys on the way home from school. Then a Nazarene orchard worker coming back late to the town was set upon by four young assaulters. They had tied cloth over their faces so he could not identify them. I was sure Menah ben Tahath was becoming active again. Dathan came to me seeking justice for the orchard worker. I went to one of Father's legal advisers. I had known him for fifteen years, had contested with his younger brothers at the Xystus. "Are you going to do anything?" I asked.

He looked unhappy. "Every case will be dealt with. On an *ad hoc* basis."

"*Ad hoc* is not the way the law is written." Every criminal case was supposed to be prosecuted under specific statutes, no matter who committed crimes against whom.

The legal adviser lowered his voice. "Well, *ad hoc* is how all these cases are going to be handled from now on."

"*All*? Father?"

He shook his head negatively. That meant Caesarea.

Some of Dathan's members wanted to take revenge. Their target was Menah ben Tahath. But Dathan dissuaded them, saying the tenets of Christ were under test. The beatings continued until few Nazarenes ventured out after sundown. As if Dathan's continued seeking of followers among the sons of wealthy Jews and among Gentiles was not enough, he invited the fuller to preside over a mass baptism.

Rechab visited me on the way to Dathan's. He wore an embroidered and cowled robe tied at his waist with a white silk rope. I liked his prosperous and ceremonial look. While he had reservations about baptizing Gentiles, he was determined to let the people who had taken his eyes and half a leg know that far from diminishing his spirit, they had elevated it. Deborah and three other Modi'imians were with him. There was no occasion for me to draw her aside, not that she seemed eager for me to try.

Rechab invited me to the baptism and I went. It was held at a pool called Gadessera, where I had swum as a boy. The pool was surrounded by date palms, myrtles, and rushes, a cool place where caravans sometimes watered. The approaches were trampled smooth and hard by hundreds of years of hooves. Deborah, as Rechab's deputy, and bald Dathan waded into the pool followed by the new members. About two dozen troublemakers shouted oaths and imprecations while the new members were immersed. Rechab blessed each new member. As Deborah walked from the pool, I saw with agonized eyes how the wet cloth clung to her thighs.

Back at Dathan's, the Nazarenes held what they called a love feast. It was a little awkward, since the fuller's Jewish followers, lest they commit an act proscribed by Mosaic Law, did not want to eat at the same table or under the same roof with Dathan's Gentiles. They solved it Talmudically, or at least sophistically, by all eating outside on benches, not tables.

I approached Deborah shortly before the Modi'im group left. "How are you?" she asked, her voice tense and defensive.

"Busy," I said. "Worried." Then lest she think I meant worried about her, us, I added, "About Dathan, the town . . ."

"You have not gone back with your family?" There was curiosity in her voice, but also a desire to keep things safe.

"I see my mother when Father is not there." In the past, we would have explored it. Now she merely nodded. The seconds were running. "If I came there . . . ?" I asked. "I have stayed away on purpose, thinking if I gave you time . . ."

"No," she said. "Please."

"You got me out of your mind with great ease, Deborah."

"No," she said. "Do not do that either, because it is not true."

"Then why . . . ?" My mouth tasted like potash.

"Demas," she said tightly, "I have built up this pathetic little wall. I want to be happy in the garden behind it. But the wall is not very strong right now. So just let me be."

One night, the sturdy mason roused me. Men had come into Dathan's shed and smashed his wares. Awakened, Dathan had ordered his wife to lock the door behind him and had run out in his nightshirt. He had been knocked down, and when he staggered up, had been hit again, this time with a club. When all was silent, Dathan's wife had come out to drag him in and had seen that the night raiders had set the meeting place afire.

As soon as the mason and I were out of the center of town, we saw the glow. When we arrived, the planking beneath the tile roof was still afire. Several benches inside for the crippled had been pulled out by the arsonists and were burning. Roman soldiers, I noted with outrage, had cordoned off the fire so the Nazarenes who had hurried to the scene could not put it out. I found Dathan in bed, his scalp split, the fringes of hair bloody, but his skull unbroken. He could identify no one. There had been only enough light for him to see masks. I was sure that Menah ben Tahath was responsible. "Next time, it will not be just your wares and your pate," I said.

"Demas," he said, "please do not carp. I hurt too much. If they come, the will of God be done." He closed his eyes as if to dismiss me. But I was not disposed to be that charitable.

"The will of God, my Roman arse," I persisted angrily. "It is the will of these night jackals that is going to be done."

Once so steady, his hands began to pick nervously at their calluses as if his fingers had lives of their own. I waited. At last, he opened his eyes and fixed them on me.

"Tell me what you would have me do, Demas?"

"Go someplace else. I will hire you a wagon. These people will burn down the house next time with all of you in it. They do not even think of you as humans. Go, please, Dathan."

"Then, that is what you would do?" he persisted.

No, I thought, of course not. But I never would have tumbled into this poisonous broth. "That is entirely irrelevant," I said. "What are *you* going to do?"

"First," he said, his trace of smile almost lost in the pain and fatigue, "we are going to rebuild the meeting house."

"No," I urged him, "no. This has got to have a stop. Murder is waiting for you every night of your stupid life." He studied me, all his irony gone, nothing between us.

"Demas, it is you who are stupid. If they kill me, they will have left behind someone who will do far more for God than I in my ignorance and stubbornness could ever have done."

I would like to have thought he was making a speech about the mason. But it was me he was talking about. I returned home, Dathan's words adhering to me like a curse. The night's infernal events had left my nerves pitted and untrustworthy, my emotions no longer safely contained in their housings. I hated the town, hated Father for standing by while this happened to Dathan, hated venomous Caesarea and distant, unwise Rome.

Dathan had not heeded my warnings, but as I calmed, I asked myself why he should have. Whom did his message harm? No one. Was it an evil message? To the contrary, it was a message of love and bravery, as Dathan was loving and brave. Like all men of good will, he preached that one should treat one's fellow decently. And unlike the gods of Jews and pagans, Dathan's God was not one of punishment, but of self-sacrifice and unfailing benevolence. Yes, but why, if Dathan's God had any power at all, had he let these things happen to his followers? "Why?" I asked in the night. "Why?" That was the question.

I went back to bed, but could not sleep. I got up, knelt, and began to pray, not to Dathan's God, for I did not know him, but to mine, powerful and good, but fickle and not always there to hear me. "Please God," I said aloud to the God of the synagogue, who, after all, had saved me from the well, "let Dathan live and continue his work. And if he dies, let him be wrong about what he said to me. Do not lay his toil at my feet."

The destruction of the warehouse and meeting house only increased the zeal of the Nazarenes. I had always underestimated eastern fanaticism. I went to see Dathan to plead again with him. He heard me out, then told me he had not lost a single member. In fact, as a result of the night attack, he had been approached by several more young Jews and Gentiles from good families.

Two weeks later, halfway through the night, Dathan's wife beat on my door. Her eyes were crazed, the children cowering around her skirt. The night raiders had set fire to their house. Dathan had rushed them, giving her and the children enough time to escape.

I grabbed my sword, ordered her to wait with the door locked, and ran to their house. Ahead, the flames again flared on the night sky. When I got there, citizens and soldiers were milling around. The exterior of the house was of clay bricks and terra-cotta, but its wooden door, stoop, steps, roof supports, and interior were all afire. Sword drawn but forgotten in my hand, I pushed though the crowd.

Even in my worst forebodings, I had never imagined what I saw. The night attackers had stripped and crucified Dathan, using the new ridgepole as the upright and a plank as crosspiece. They had lashed the cross to one of the scorched brick corners of the burned meeting house. Great spikes in Dathan's feet, hands, and shoulders held him to the cross. His throat was cut, and from a great slash in his belly his intestines looped out.

The mason, who lived down the road, sleeping fitfully since the last raid, no doubt, must have heard the shouts. He had snatched up the hatchet he used to break bricks and had run up the hill to Dathan's home. A few other men had arrived at the same time but had not dared to hinder the work of the dozen masked men. The mason, unable to bear the screams of pain from his dying leader, had broken through the murderers. He had first tried to pull Dathan free of the spikes. But that had not been possible. His wrenching only made the tilemaker's dying a greater agony.

Seeing Dathan could not be saved, the mason had clambered up the cross and with a single merciful blow had cut Dathan's throat, almost beheading him. Covered with blood, the mason had dropped to the ground, sprung to his feet, and chopped madly at the killers. They had slain him at the foot of the cross. The Roman soldiers arrived after a cruel delay.

One of them saw me with my drawn sword and because I was in a common tunic, started to arrest me. It was the captain, Bariponte. I was shivering as if with an ague. "Get a hold on yourself," he said recognizing me. "Sheathe that thing."

I obeyed, too shocked to talk. When I found my voice, I was close to hysteria. "Thaddeus! What is this? The whole world has gone insane. . . ." I could feel myself slipping. Bariponte took my biceps in his hammy fist and gave me a shake that would have pushed me to the ground if he had let go. I looked again at the man on the cross. With his head flopped grotesquely on his chest, Dathan was like a dead bird on a thorn. He was a strange red-brown color from his own blood and from the guttering light of his burning house. Some Roman soldier, out of charity, had thrown his cloak over the body of the mason.

Bariponte released me. "Demas, this is dungeater's work," he said with bitter disgust. "And it is not over yet."

My mind snapped. "Not over?" I raved. "Not over?"

"*Not over!*" he roared into my face, so close I could smell a hurricane of garlic and strong wine. It brought me around. He left me there, I, like those near me, staring up at the dead man. I felt faint, as I had imagined epileptics must feel before a seizure. Something seemed to wash out of me, and then a different something washed in.

"It is over for me," I said aloud but to myself.

I went home, and as understatedly as I could told Dathan's wife what had happened. In the morning, I bought three sturdy donkeys and a pack mule and sent her and the children out with several other Nazarenes fleeing to Antioch. As it turned out, she would have had to go anyway. At noon, Father put the town under martial law and ordered every Nazarene man, woman, and child who would not recant his or her faith to be gone by nightfall.

Dathan on the cross had swept away every barrier between me and the Nazarenes. If they must go, then I must go, for I had become one of them. Only my theology remained to be sorted out. I bid good-bye to Mother, Grandfather, Ezra, my closest cousins, and my few Roman friends, but made a point not to see Father. I packed, not forgetting Dathan's three pitchers and the flask of water Andrew had blessed—it seemed a century and a world ago. Before I left, I helped five fellow Nazarenes to secretly bury Dathan and the mason near Gadessera.

XII

╍╍╍╍╍╍╍╍╍╍╍╍╍╍╍╍╍╍╍╍╍╍╍╍╍╍╍╍╍╍╍╍╍╍╍

I was the first to bring the news to Modi'im. The fuller began lamenting like the most devout Jew, rocking back and forth on his chair, groaning, praying aloud for any number of people: Dathan, the mason, the dispossessed, even the Romans and the murderers. Summoned by the fuller's wife, the congregation gathered in their new meeting place, the large second-story room of a weaving shop with its own outside staircase.

Deborah arrived, and as I staggered up from a bench, half dead from exhaustion, she took my hands briefly but without reserve. Wearily, I told the forty people everything I knew. Many of Dathan's followers would be coming to Modi'im, some in transit, some to stay. The fuller's flock began talking about how they could welcome them, not omitting how they would prepare the synagogue leaders and the civil authorities for the influx.

The meeting recessed with a prayer, and I silently knelt with them. As we rose, Deborah gave me a look of surprise, but Rechab was already asking her to organize a group to meet the refugees on the highroad with food. I volunteered, and sat in a corner to wait. When I wakened, they were gone and Rechab was offering me a bed in his house. I chose the comparative quiet of an inn, but guided him home first. He walked without crutches: a carpenter had constructed for him a wooden calf with a shoe and with rods for strapping to his knee and thigh.

At his home, he asked me to take a moment to see the improvements the church had made on the tomb of Andrew. Outside the cave was a cross carved from a single piece of hardwood and anchored into a gray marble cube. Around it were roses and a circle of marigolds. I breathed in the autumn smells, the dry marigolds, the perfumed roses, and the faint scent of mint and hyssop and looked at the cross.

"Rechab," I asked, "will you baptize me, with all my confusions on me?" My fatigue and sorrow mounted from the pit of my stomach into my voice. "I am unsure of so many things," I said, "but I know I have no life if I am not one of you."

His arms came up, his fingers trembling to find my hands, and when I put them in his, he clutched them fiercely. "How I have prayed for this!" he said. Then, suddenly joyous in the midst of horror, he hugged me so hard I stumbled.

I slept all that afternoon and on until just after dawn. As I lay on my straw mattress, the vision of Dathan on the cross assaulted me, making me dizzy with hatred. I tried to fix on Rechab's words about Borhaurus taking his eyes and his giving the town a sight of a new world. But I focused instead on going back and inflicting Jesus on the town as punishment for its viciousness and for Father's betrayal. I knew that being a Nazarene meant forgiveness, but the idea of pardon stuck in my gorge.

It was not until evening, when Deborah was ready to walk home from their upper room, that I had any time alone with her. Rechab had told her of my request to be baptized.

"This is not just a reaction to Dathan?" she asked, not so much expressing doubt as looking for assurance. "Should it be so soon? You do not really *believe* in Jesus as God."

"Deborah"—I smiled—"more slowly. In the first place, you are wrong. I do believe. I believe a God is inside me—"

"But you already believed in your vague way about that God, ever since your grandfather's synagogue, or anyway since you were in the well. When you were ten."

"Nine, but the well is as good a place as any to start, because last night I was raised from the well for the second time. I had not wanted to come out even though the stagnant water was up to my shoulders again and Paul and Andrew and Rechab and you were all telling me how to get out. But it was Dathan who tied a rope around me and jerked me up. Two weeks before, he said if they killed him, I would take up his cause. I swear it. I was not ready to hear those words, Deborah. I fought them, prayed against them. But Dathan knew it was time to say them. He fixed them on me as surely as Medea put the wedding dress on Creon's daughter that burned off her flesh.

"When I saw Dathan dead, the only calm voice in me said,

'Demas, you belong with people like that poor brave, foolish man up there. *He* is the kind of man you want to be. You do not want to be a spiritual desert like your father or merely wise and benevolent like your grandfather or contented like Ezra.' I even thought that if being like Dathan meant dying like him, then that would be what I would have to do and God grant me a friend like the mason to make it be quick. At that moment, Jesus entered me and stood by the God of the synagogue who had been there all along. Beneath Dathan's cross, I felt my old empty life was over, and a new life was taking its place."

"Demas," said Deborah, moved, but determined, "I am not disputing you. . . ." But then, of course, she did, reminding me of my arguments in the past months against the divinity of Jesus, the holy ghost, the resurrection.

For all her seriousness, I laughed. How exciting it was simply to be talking this way with her again. "Deborah," I said, "I do believe Jesus is the son of God, as we all are, but he more than us. I admit I am vague about the holy ghost. But so are you. I believe Jesus is resurrected in the courage and goodness of Dathan, of the fuller, of you. I believe your faith in Jesus helped make you that way. Andrew, Rechab, Dathan . . . They were nothing until they found Jesus. Look at Rechab now. What is my father, what was your father, by comparison? Nothing! But worse, because they began with so much."

The fuller, with Deborah as my sponsor, baptized me in a stream that ran through a Nazarene farmer's land. Rechab's forty faithful and the Borhaurus refugees bore witness, although there was some feeling I should have been circumcised first. The fuller, an able politician when he strove to be, pointed out that I was a Jew through my mother under Mosaic Law. Besides, I was the grandson of a Sadducee council member and, he extemporized, I was praying over the matter of circumcision. It sufficed.

The fuller waded into the stream, his wife on one side, Deborah on the other, to make sure the fast-moving water did not topple him. I came out to them with Andrew's flask in my hand, and gave it to Rechab. He asked whether I believed Jesus was the son of God and had been resurrected, whether I felt the holy spirit was within me, and whether I was contrite for my sins against God and man. I answered "Yea." I felt some stiffness in Deborah over my replies, but she and Rechab immersed me and then the fuller poured some of the water from the flask on my head. It ran down into my face and I could still smell its faint perfume.

With Deborah gripping my arm, Rechab said, "In the name of the Father, the Son, and the Holy Ghost . . ." Then we stumbled out of

109

the stream and all those present gave me a hug. When I took Deborah in my arms, our bodies in that loving, familiar posture, she seemed about to kiss me on the lips. We could not do it, not possibly, but there would have been a rightness to it all the same. Exalted is not too strong a word for how I felt.

❁

The refugees from Borhaurus, uprooted from where their families had lived for generations, found the new town as foreign as if it had been Cathay. We procured supplies for those going on to Antioch or other places, and dwellings for those who were staying. I gave them legal advice on what could be done to sell homes and goods in Borhaurus *in absentia*, and wrote letters for the illiterates. I began a small practice, taking only the poorest clients unwanted by the town's two lawyers.

As I watched the Modi'im Nazarenes getting along with the town, and vice versa, I saw how few compromises Dathan would have had to have made to have functioned in Borhaurus. I began to speculate on what would be needed to get Father to lift or modify his edict so that the Nazarenes could try there again. The more I thought of it, the more it intrigued me, and the more I seemed the person who best could implement it.

❁

I could not pursue my courtship of Deborah without some encouragement, and she gave me none. She never came to the clay-brick cube I had rented, and I felt constrained not to visit her. We spoke often while we were working with the refugees and during other church tasks, but seldom intimately or alone. Yet, I still believed that love lurked in her like a leopard in the underbrush, and that one day it would spring out and ambush her.

I sent notes by travelers to Mother, Grandfather, and Ezra, assuring them all was well. They wrote back gossipy letters, sometimes, but not often dealing with controversy. Each communication, whether carrying good or ill news, made me mull over how I could find a way home. How much of this desire was based on homesickness, on disappointed and vengeful feelings toward Father, on genuine zeal to bring Jesus, and peace, to my hometown, I would have been hard put to tabulate.

110

More news on Borhaurus came from an unforeseen quarter. The leather craftsman, Ahiam, in Modi'im to buy cured jackal skins, a local specialty, saw me in the street, and I stopped him. I recalled it was he who had futilely brought his son to the window of Andrew's cell. When I asked him about Borhaurus, he told me hesitantly that another killing had occurred.

A fanatic follower of Dathan had sneaked back into town and preached provocatively from the synagogue steps in emulation of Andrew. He had been confined in the synagogue cellar until nightfall, but instead of a lashing, he had been released to an angry mob of young Jews who had stoned him to death. Father had issued an edict, making such summary punishment a capital crime, but had done nothing to apprehend the malefactors.

Before we parted, Ahiam nervously but determinedly said, "I confess to you, Sir Demas, I had once thought of joining with Dathan. It is good I did not, but I feel . . ."

He wanted to say he felt ashamed but could not bring himself to. "You were wise," I said, wanting to soften his discomfort. But he would not be palliated.

"No, it was a lack of courage—and of gratefulness."

"Gratefulness?"

Ahiam looked even more uncomfortable. "I saw you at the window of the jail three years ago, Sir Demas. With the follower of Jesus, Andrew. Since that day, the mental affliction has slowly been leaving my son. He"—and tears came to the leather craftsman's eyes—"can say simple words to us, can walk, if poorly, and even help me with certain tasks."

I embraced him impulsively, astonishing him. "I will pray that he will continue to improve," I said.

The death described by Ahiam was not the last. Two more men, Ezra wrote, both Antiochians, chained themselves to a column in the synagogue, where they preached that Jesus was the Messiah and that Mosaic Law was dead. The elders were horrified, but did not dare defy Father's new edict. They went swiftly to the barracks to summon our legionnaires. But masked men entered the synagogue and cut the preachers' chains. Father's soldiers found their two bodies in the synagogue square, their ripped tongues still gripped in hot pincers. Yet Father still did nothing to enforce his new ukase. Ezra said it was rumored that Menah ben Tahath and his gang were responsible. I cursed vengefully. Menah had become in my mind an apostle of Satan.

Hate had bred the *sicarii* and bands like Menah's. Now, the letters told me, it gave birth to their demonic complements: young pagans and Jews as well, who, claiming to be followers of Dathan, dishonored him with retaliatory violence. A Pharisee on the council was assassinated outside the door of his mistress. A second council member was assaulted and identified his assailants as two Sadducee sons of merchants of prestige and wealth. The youths claimed they were carrying out the will of the Jesus of Dathan, and to my amazement, "Paul of Tarsus." They were exiled.

By spring, Father's soldiers were patrolling the streets at night, a measure never before necessary in Borhaurus, even when Jews rioted in nearby towns during the procuratorship of Pontius Pilate twenty years before. My thoughts about returning to Borhaurus began to obsess me. In my anger and hate after the death of Dathan, I had vindictively thought of going back so I could force Jesus on the town as a punishment. Now I knew that Jesus could save it.

I worked at plans for a return, listing officials and members of the Jewish Council who might abide us, drafting manifestos and arguments I could present to Father on how the Nazarenes might further peace by filling the dangerous spaces now occupied by fanatic perverters of our faith.

When the next report of violence reached us from Ezra, I went to Deborah's lodgings and asked her to come outside with me. "I am going to find a way back to Borhaurus," I said.

"No," she answered, shocked. "They will kill you. Why?"

"Because Jesus has called me to," I said, half jesting, for it was the kind of remark she made when she did not fully want to explain things.

After she stopped protesting, I told her why I thought I could succeed, explaining in detail the strategies I had conceived during the past months. By the moonlight, I saw all color drain from her face, leaving it a pale oval before me. Borhaurus remained for her a place of blood and fire.

Next morning, she came to my house, where I was belatedly laying flagstones across my muddy front yard.

"I am going with you," she said.

Her blue eyes were lightened and speckled by the early sunshine. Simultaneously, we reached out our arms and caught each other, spattered with mud as I was. Straight, womanly, brave, and, beneath that plain robe, infused with all the world's voluptuousness, at that pledging moment she seemed as lovable as life and the joyous day, as noble as dead Andrew and Dathan, as the fuller, as the energetic, brilliant, and wise man we called our God.

The idea of Deborah's going did not please the fuller. She, as his deputy, would be leader of such a venture, and although he had accepted her in Modi'im, he was of the Jerusalem faction, who would consider it unsuitable, even sacrilegious for a young woman to head an entire church. From what I had learned from Dathan and knew of Paul's views, her role would not have been any more welcome to the Antiochians. They also held a traditional Jewish, that is Oriental, view of women.

But it was pointless for Rechab to argue. He knew her inflexibilities as well as I did. She told him she had prayed all night and—as I inwardly smiled—that she had heard the commands of Jesus. Neither of us asked what rationale underlay the "commands." Whatever they were, when we ended our talk with the fuller, I was even more certain than I had been that he was not blind enough not to see we were drawn to each other.

I would have preferred to take up where Dathan left off: accepting all who came in good faith, building a new meeting place. But to avoid immediate arrest or martyrdom, we needed to give Father and the Jewish Council guarantees that we would soothe and not exacerbate the festerings. I wrote a letter to Grandfather outlining our ideas and asking for an early answer.

While we waited, Deborah and I planned, generally in the evening, sitting on a stone wall outside her lodgings. We talked of our mission, philosophy, religion, everything except how we felt about each other. We decided that while she would be *de facto* leader—I was, after all, an aristocrat, uncircumcised and only half-Jewish, besides being junior to her as a Nazarene—we must develop a permanent minister from inside Borhaurus. Several Borhaurus refugees in Modi'im suggested Ahiam, the leather craftsman. Through a refugee's brother still in Borhaurus, we got word to him of our intent and he agreed to talk with us but only if we obtained permission from my father and the Jewish Council to come back to the town.

Grandfather, true to his sense of drama, arrived one day at the building housing our upper room. He was in his four-wheeled chariot, as luxurious as a small room. Deborah, her elderly landlady, Rivka, and I were cleaning the flue. We looked like the lowest servants of the lowest *am-ha-arez* peasant. Nothing disconcerted Grandfather. His Ethiop helped him down, and with a blink of elderly lechery at

Deborah despite her sootiness, he held his turban and bowed deeply from the waist.

"I have not seen you since you were a little girl," he said beguilingly. "I profoundly regret the death of my friend Sirach ben Isaac. But I am delighted to see that he left behind such a beautiful and talented daughter." Unaccustomedly embarrassed, Deborah wiped her sleeve across her face, streaking her cheeks even more. He looked at my own dirty face. "Demas, if I may say so, you might consider changing the immersion rites of your sect to daily rather than once in a lifetime."

He held my arm tightly for support as I helped him up the stairs. We seated him while Rivka hurried out for wine and cakes. He recounted the routine family news quickly: everyone in good health save for Aesubius, who was gouty but had volunteered (and been gently rejected) as bodyguard for Grandfather on his trip to Modi'im. I smiled—yet was touched—at the thought of this fat and enfeebled would-be Achates.

After more amenities, Grandfather spoke of the unrest in Borhaurus, citing new bloodshed, and then referred to my letter: "It has brought me here in a role more official than is my wont. Rome, in the person of your father, Demas, and the council of which I am a member, have made me their ambassador extraordinary and plenipotentiary to your leader, Sir Rechab. Should we not await his arrival?"

I looked at Deborah. Rechab had gone to Lydda to speak with their minister about a joint baptism. Deborah explained that she was the leader of our church in Rechab's absence, and Grandfather tranquilly turned his attention to her.

He cleared his throat. "Let me begin with a little *ad hominem* family anecdote. One of my great-grandnephews, Samuel"—a youth I knew slightly—"has earned himself a fine and a caning for chiseling 'God is love' on a minor synagogue. He is a member of a virulent faction of your cult, Antiochian in origin. This boy is not the only one smitten with this fever. . . . On the other hand, your sect here, once this business of a crucified criminal being the Messiah and dead people coming back to life is accepted as sham fit only for a bazaar, seems less poisonous."

Although Deborah's face, like mine, had reddened at Grandfather's insults, she kept her voice controlled: "Dr. Asa ben Hadek"—I sometimes forgot he had half earned, half bought a doctorate in Judaic Law—"here in Modi'im, as you must know, my church works within the general synagogue. On the Sabbath, most of us worship with our fellow Jews. Are you suggesting that the council

114

in Borhaurus might accept us if we established a church there on a similar basis?"

"Well, Deborah bas Sirach, we *do* extrapolate from the message my grandson sent me that any new branch of your sect would be less incitive than that of your unfortunate, and I mean that sincerely, coreligionist, the tilemaker. The council is aware of the appeal of any new movement in these terrible times. We have seen the attraction among young Jews to the Zealots, the *sicarii*, the Essenes, and to these unspeakable night raiders. The majority of us know that extremism will eventually bring down on us the mailed gauntlet of Rome. . . ."

He was getting exercised, remembering, as he often did, the Roman slaughter of Jews at Sepphoris and, in lesser numbers, at Jerusalem and elsewhere, bestialities that gouged beneath his urbanities to profound and bloody old hates.

To give him time to recover his composure, I said, "No one wants that, not even Rome."

"Just so, Demas," he said, still hot, "but to banish our own children—whether they harbor the views of Menah or of these Antioch hyenas—is figuratively to devour our own."

"So the council proposes . . . ?" Deborah inquired.

"Please, do not rush me." He smiled. Rivka came in with unmatched wineglasses, and right behind her came the Ethiop with Grandfather's usual rich assortment of date, fruit, and nut cakes. The slave first started toward me, but hearing Grandfather pointedly hum, veered to Deborah. She daintily plucked a small date cookie from the tray and Grandfather said, "Take, take, my dear, and you, too, dear sister." He nodded to the old woman. "Take four, five." Both took.

Grandfather recommenced: "The tribune, who between us . . ." He looked at Rivka and the Ethiop and slipped into Greek. ". . . never really liked the idea of banishing everyone," and then he was back in Aramaic, ". . . is in a position now to be cooperative."

"Caesarea . . . ?" I asked.

"Cumanus has his hands full. One day, he executes a Roman soldier for tearing and burning a book of the Law, the next he slaughters a dozen Jewish revolutionaries. And tomorrow"— Grandfather shrugged—"he may be recalled to Rome and punished. He wants calm; he must have it."

In my excitement, I broke in again: "Then are you saying the banishment can end? The council, Father, and Caesarea . . ."

"Demas, please, more control. Those *already* banished, Dathan's people, have been properly punished and may *not* return. However,

115

those who now *become* Nazarenes and are willing to abide by the laws of the community would be allowed to reside."

It was a serious concession.

"You are saying if we do not affront Rome and the synagogue, we will not be persecuted?" asked Deborah.

"Your bluntness does not become such a lady," he chided. "I might add the word 'officially' to your characterization."

Ah, there was the rub. "*Officially* persecuted," I said. "In other words, we would still be renegades who might need a lesson taught us now and then? In which case, the town would stand by and let the murderers molest us or worse, and their crimes would not be prosecuted?"

"*Please*, Demas, for a lawyer . . ." he said.

Deborah tried to return to the issues, lest our bickering tear apart the beginnings of our accord: "There will be Gentiles who will want to join us. What is your view on that?" But I had barked Grandfather's old shins. "Demas, you are behaving like a nasty little street merchant. Can you not see what they are giving you? Even the Gentiles, so long as they linger on the fringes, could be, um, associated with you."

"You are right," Deborah said tactfully, "these are major changes. But Rechab will ask us why we failed to inquire about this point which I agree Demas raised in a most ungracious fashion." She did it so well that both Grandfather and I smiled.

"Indeed," he said, "I was about to assure you that the tribune has promised that so long as your sect is reasonable, the laws of Rome will be enforced with equal severity against malefactors of every faith, including those who harass you."

That tied the knot. I could hardly believe we had won. But Deborah ventured one more solicitation: "It is important for us to know the city's view on our building a new meeting place."

"I would not advise it," Grandfather said. "It would remind people of the last unhappiness. I would wait until the Pharisees, scribes, and other punctilious guardians of our ways get accustomed to you, staying in contact with them so everyone knows where everyone else stands and there are no surprises. Another point: your sect in Jerusalem attends various synagogues among the four hundred or so there—one for every trade and every flea-infested tribe of Asians professing Judaism. I suggest you attach yourselves to a synagogue in Borhaurus that will accept your money, let you attend on the Sabbath, and otherwise ignore you."

Deborah, without even trying to conceal her excitement, told Grandfather that we must talk first with Rechab, who might feel it was necessary to consult with the Apostolic Council. But she assured him it was safe to advise Borhaurus that in principle its terms were satisfactory. He rose, kissed her hands, and I helped him down the stairs. In the sunlight, I saw how tightly the skin stretched across his skull, and my heart yearned over him. The Ethiop unloaded the wagon's larder of costly wines, smoked meats, rare nuts, cakes of all kinds. It would make a feast for our next baptism. When Grandfather was seated in his chariot, I took his hands in mine and kissed one and then the other. He pulled me to him, torn tunic, reek and all.

"Demas, I am proud of you even when we disagree." To Deborah he said, "You are a worthy daughter of David, and as obdurate as your father. But prettier." Then, all guile and affectation gone, he said, "You are also brave young people. You know, of course, that they—" his voice broke—"those terrible ones among us, could kill you if you come back no matter what we try to do."

The three of us were silent, his warning taking all the softness from the spring day, all the fragrance from the breeze. Grandfather recovered first. "But that is highly unlikely with such diplomats as you will prove yourselves." And with a wave, he was off toward Borhaurus.

Now that Rechab was reconciled to our going back, he was enthusiastic over Borhaurus's proposal. And why not? It was patterned on Modi'im's arrangement, which he had worked out on his own. Besides, he had hoped his bloody visit to Borhaurus would lead to something like what we were about to achieve. As for asking permission of Jerusalem, he was adamantly against it.

"They are as bureaucratic as Caesarea. I will *tell* them next time I am there that we are in Borhaurus and that they must warn Antioch to stay out. If I *ask* them for a decision, they will begin by debating how hot the fire was in the Burning Bush. They are masters of the useless, the unrelated."

The Sunday before we left, the church in Modi'im held a celebration for us with a baptism of new members, love feast (with Grandfather's delicacies), and a Communion. On the actual eve of our departure, Deborah and I ate at Rivka's. She cooked a stew of two rabbits taken from her garden snares, lentils, beans, barley, onions, coriander, and the last of the black pepper Mother had given me when I left home.

The smell of the stew filled the house. After we had eaten, the three of us sat in front of the fire, drinking more wine, shelling and eating

117

pistachios, walnuts, and almonds. The fire's wavering flame cast the shadow of the loom on the rear wall as if it were some huge jerky war machine. Rivka began to nod, secure in her old woman's world: a mélange of Christ, warm coals, vinous calm. Deborah and I spoke in Aramaic so as not to be rude, but when Rivka had drowsed off, we slipped into Greek.

We were going to bring Jesus back into Borhaurus on a permanent basis. We talked of our plans, our families, Modi'im and the people here, more comfortable than we had been since that night we had cooked lamb on my hearth. Rivka half awoke, mumbled a good-night and shuffled off to bed. Deborah and I fed the animals and packed light meals for our trip.

In passing me or getting me out of the way so she could retrieve a dish or container, she found ways to take my arm, touch my back, even once lean against me. At one point, tense with hope, I took her two hands and waited for some sign that I could kiss her, but she slowly withdrew her fingers, and gave me no more of the touches of a few minutes before.

I knew, however, that in this unusual, even sensuous way, she had told me that she wanted me. Left now with a heart that was beating faster, with quickening desire, but with no further overtures by her, I became the pursuer. I touched her shoulder, her cheek, as we cleaned up. She did not avoid me, seeming to welcome my hands—passively, for I could feel her thinking that to be otherwise would ignite us. I was heavy with want. And I knew from the way she evaded my eyes that beneath her seeming lethargy she was stirring in spite of herself.

When we finished our chores, she hastened to get me to the door, then, indecisive as she seldom was, she walked me as far as the well. The night was chilly, moonless, the stars in their millions cold in the black sky.

"I wish you were in my arms," I murmured.

"I wish I were, too," she replied. "It seems perverse for us to talk as we did tonight, with no walls between us, and then not be able to hold each other with that same kind of . . . honesty."

"So why should we not?" I whispered. "Because it seems perverse to me, too."

Then I sighed unhappily, afflicted by the thought that there might be a rightness in *not* making love just before we begin. Rechab, the church, too, perhaps, must suspect us. Yielding to desire would certainly complicate our mission, and in ways we could not even conjecture.

Unaware of my reservations, she put her hand on my shoulder, her mouth close to mine. I realized the wine had reached her. "Demas," she said, "I am not going to begin in Borhaurus, take these chances, without kissing you." She pulled my head to her. When she broke, she kept her body lightly against mine.

She had been raised a Pharisee and, for all her revolt against her father, believed, I was sure, that she must be a virgin when she married. I sensed this wrenching fission in her between flesh and upbringing. But my poor body had grown up under a lenient code. My rational inhibitions flown, I ran my hand down the valley of her spine, caressing the ridges on either side until I reached her waist. Gently, gently, I eased my fingers to her buttocks.

Almost in spasm, she thrust her body to me, and I pulled her into me. She gasped and I kissed her without restraint as she ground against me until I could scarcely control myself. But, suddenly, she pulled her lips away, and with an outrush of breath, separated our bodies.

"No, Demas," she said. "No, please!"

I groaned, and she, breathing if anything harder than I, took my face in her hands. She stared in the darkness at eyes whose tormented expression she could not see.

"I love you," I said. "And this is killing me."

She held my face a moment more, and started to say something, but then, after a brief, hard embrace, she released me and said she must go in, leaving me confused and frustrated.

Outside my house, I poured gourds of cold water on me from my cistern and scrubbed with natron. It tasted bitter and salty as it ran past my mouth, but the ordeal took part of my mind off Deborah and her melon-sweet flesh.

XIII

Borhaurus lay between two low hills. It was blessed with more rain than most of Judaea, and from the road, one could see lush early summer foliage and patches of flowers in its parks and small gardens. In late afternoon, as I rode toward the Joppa gate alone (Deborah would come after I had prepared the way), I thought theatrically of Julius Caesar looking across the Rubicon and of Joshua assessing the land of Canaan.

I had grown a light beard, knowing it would make me appear both older and more Jewish. With it and my simple tunic, I went unrecognized. For an hour or two, I walked aimlessly in the town, avoiding places where I was well known. For this short time, I wanted simply to feel Borhaurus again. How intense were the old memories: here I had seen a steer break through a fence, here I had bought a hoop and stick, here I had cut my hand jumping on a cart, through this window I had seen a fat woman strike a thin, sick man and knock him down. At sunset, with both regret and anticipation, I went home.

When our porter saw my garments, he set his face as he would for any other commoner knocking toward dusk. Then he saw who it was and his eyes widened. "Master Demas!" He scuttled across the court to our living quarters. I waited. It was home but no longer my house to enter at will. I heard a small scream from Mother, then Father's strong tones. He loped toward me, looked at me for an instant, perhaps wondering as much what my mind held as I did his. Then stiffly but vigorously, he embraced me, and arm around my waist guided me toward the court. "You are back: I am glad," he said. Mother had restrained herself to let Father greet me alone, but now she rushed toward me, hugged me and wept, saying my name. Aesubius, my old tutor, limped across the court, arms outstretched.

A servant quickly laid my place at table. I had forgotten the luxury of tender veal, soft-boiled eggs, snails fattened in milk and fried in garlic, lettuce, everything served on thin plates with silver utensils. Aesubius, who ate with us, alternately beamed at my gluttony and looked deprived as he ate the steamed salsify and boiled tunny that gout had made his menu. While we ate, we skirted any talk that might create discord. After the meal, Father led me to the living room, and Aesubius followed us in. Father noted my surprise. "Aesubius has become my Nestor," he explained. "Would that Rome had such a one." The meeting was mild beyond my expectations. Father confirmed his agreement with the conditions and rights that Grandfather had delivered to us. Only a point or two required exploration.

He said firmly, "Asa told you that the Gentiles could be enlisted so long as it is done discreetly. But I do not want you to seek out Romans, and by that I also mean the auxiliaries."

"We can agree not to solicit them," I replied, "but if they come, Father, we cannot say no."

He put his hand to his brow. How much older he seemed, even in these three months, how much less decisive. "They will not be disposed to join you anyway, or so I hope. . . ."

We talked until midnight, and at the end Father asked whether I wanted to stay in the house until I was settled. He was courtly, but my sleeping there for more than the night was something neither of us really wanted.

Next day, I found rooms much like the two I had before, and, through Ezra, got recommendations for several lodgings for Deborah, all with enough space for her loom. She came to town two days later.

It did not astonish me that even as we reassembled her loom, she set our personal rules of behavior. "I cannot let myself want you," she said. "To smell the berry again might be to eat the bushel. I cannot think about turning people toward God and myself toward you at the same time."

"We could be careful," I argued. "Why would you feel guilty about something so beautiful?"

"I do not feel guilty," she said defensively. "I admit that it made me feel, well, whole to hug you that way."

I gave her a morose leer.

"Oh, in the name of Abraham, Demas, *almost* whole. Why force me to feel combative? Surely you understand. Even if we could put aside the morals of it, which I cannot, the risk would be too great. If we were caught, it would destroy us, all our work, everything."

Next day, we went to Ahiam's shop. His son's head still spindled, but with labored movements the youth was putting a wet reeking muleskin on a stretcher. Andrew would have beamed over the "miracle." Ahiam, once he was reassured he would not be officially harassed, agreed to be baptized and to help us. It was not our most enthusiastic conversion, but it was the one we most badly needed for our beginnings.

We visited Grandfather, who treated Deborah, dressed severely but elegantly in a dark gray shift with a narrow silver-laced girdle, like the aristocrat that she was. He arranged a meeting for her with several temperate Jewish Council members, to be held without my half-Gentile presence. I spoke with the husbands of my two Sadducee aunts and several Jewish family friends to assure them I had not grown horns, and to ask them to pass on that conclusion to their acquaintances. Deborah made similar calls on several Pharisees who had been friends of her father.

These sallies were useful, but our real strength, as expected, proved to be among the poorest Jews who had turned their backs on Judaism; and the despised *am-ha-arez*. With these groups, Ahiam was particularly effective. Like the fuller, he was evidence that in this life, too, there was hope, if not for the most deprived, then for their sons, and thus that ours was truly a religion of change.

At one extreme among our converts was a man who collected dog feces, used in tanning, the only Jew I had ever known whose wife had been allowed to divorce him—because she was allergic to his stock in trade. At the other was the son of a wealthy Pharisee merchant. Their questions were much the same regardless of their class. Would it be weeks or months before Jesus and God the Father came to judge the wicked? (We told them we did not know.) Would there be signs such as earthquakes, great storms, waves upon the land, to announce the Day of Wrath? (We doubted it. If it came—Deborah said *when* it came—it would arrive like any other day.)

Did Jesus shuttle between heaven and earth? Or did he and God govern only from heaven? (We thought we could feel them in our hearts always, but particularly when we were living by their simple maxim of love.) Would the good who died before the Day of Judgment go to heaven? (Jesus would not discriminate.) And the most dangerous: to achieve heaven must one not also be faithful to the Law of Moses? (Jesus, we always replied carefully, thought that all rules that helped men to be better human beings were good.)

My distant cousin Samuel, the youth who had defaced the synagogue, was the inquirer who subjected us to the most severe questioning. He had been a scholar of the Torah, had changed paths to study the Hellene classics and was now reading Roman and Judaic law. Deborah and I, by turns arguing and bullying, first had to sway him from the thought that the Antiochians or any followers of Jesus advocated violence even against our enemies.

"But how is Jesus Christ different from Socrates and Cicero, who preached the same basic message and also died for doing so?" he asked us one night.

"Neither Cicero nor Socrates was the son of God," said Deborah. "Neither established a religion to change the world."

"So you believe God impregnated the mother?"

"I do not know," said Deborah. "I believe God was so much in him that he can be called the son of God. I am disposed to believe she was a virgin." I wanted a say on that one: "I believe Jesus was the corporeal son of his earthly father."

"And you both think he came back to life?" he said.

"I do, and most literally," said Deborah, then she and Samuel looked at me for my dissent.

"It is less easy for me," I said. "I saw Dathan upon the cross. I know he died in pain, but also, I believe, in a kind of exaltation. Once I accepted the possibility that I—that any of us—might die the same way, my fear became assessable. I feel a peace, a usefulness that is always present even when I am not joyous or even happy, and I attribute that feeling to my becoming a Nazarene. In that sense, Dathan and others are resurrected in me, as Jesus returned to life in them, and so to life in me, as, if you see him in me, he will be in you."

"It is clear that followers of Jesus do not *have* to agree with each other in everything," he said, actually relieved.

A week later, he decided to join us. "Kinsman," I said with a smile, "I am pleased to find that you are more Platonic than Mishnaic, but more Nazarene than either."

It sometimes irritated me that Deborah had so few questions about the resurrection, the miracles, the holy spirit. But she was, after all, a child of the Pentateuch, with its magical burning bushes, parting seas, God-inflicted plagues, pastries from the sky. Without a qualm, she could preach to a group of new converts that "such miracles are attested to by our forefathers in the days of Moses, and so are the miracles of Jesus, our Messiah, by the Apostles who were with him day after day almost into our own times."

Soon, we had twenty Borhaurusians ready for baptism, ten upon the brink, and dozens of others interested. We had overestimated the numbers who would be deterred by the murders and other violence. It was a tribute to the stature Deborah had earned (and an anomaly in that few Jewish men, much less council leaders, allowed women to speak with them as equals) that it was she who successfully argued the case that we should be allowed to conduct a baptism. None of us liked begging for the council's forbearance—the less so since they placed on the baptism mean-spirited restrictions—but, as Deborah said, "We knew it would either be this, or coming to Borhaurus with crosses over our shoulders for our own crucifixions."

So we agreed to do without a lengthy love feast, and to hold only a short Communion beside Gadessera. We were determined, however, to make up for these curtailments by inviting one of Jesus' original disciples to baptize our new members. We wrote the Apostolic Council in Jerusalem asking Peter to preside, and if he could not, then another of the apostles.

Peter was on the road, but the council sent us word that James or Matthew, sons of Alphaeus, would come, and on the morning of our baptism, James arrived. He and his brother had reputations as the most narrow-minded of the original Apostles. Prior to the baptism, James, who was small and wiry, with a pinched ferret face, met with us in Deborah's sun-filled room. He spoke mainly to Ahiam, looking uncomfortably at Deborah even when she brought in date cakes, wine, and berry juice.

"James"—Jesus' brother—"asked me to congratulate the three of you. It is the talk of the council." He paid us more compliments. "But we have some concern about whether your"—he fixed on Ahiam—"two main assistants should be . . ." He looked for suitable words. ". . . foreigners and female."

"Foreigners?" I broke in, "Deborah bas Sirach's father was on the Jewish Council in Modi'im, and I, though I am half-Gentile, come from here. And as to—"

But Deborah needed no defense from me. Evenly, but from a cistern of anger I knew well, she said, "We feel that *all* of us, men and women alike, know the master. He belongs to us, just as he belongs to you who walked with him."

Now Ahiam, not natively eloquent, but becoming more so, spoke up. "If Demas and Gentiles like him are not welcome in our church, sir, then Jews like me are not either. And Deborah bas Sirach, although not from here and a woman, has risked her life for Christ Jesus. They and Christ Jesus chose me and I choose them. I am the minister, but they are my eyes and ears and mouth, and although I know it embarrasses them for me to say it, my brain."

"You are carrying Nazarene humility too cursed far, Ahiam," I said.

I turned on James. "The Apostolic Council conceded to Paul that Gentiles can come into the church as full members. We have chosen to come under Jerusalem, not Antioch, for a number of reasons. We plan to contribute to your needs as the other subordinate churches do. But I tell you—" I looked at the others, wishing one of them were saying it, not I—"that if you attempt to run our affairs, you will lose us."

James sipped rapidly at his wine. He was a simple man, intimidated by Deborah's and my education, by the fact that I was a Roman. He was at ease only with Ahiam, who was staunchly allied with us. He took what refuge he could in his rank.

"You could not operate without our blessing," he said snappishly. "Paul is in Greece or someplace. Moreover, he did not even know the master—"

Deborah cut him off. "To satisfy Jerusalem and this city, our Gentile brothers and sisters, while complete in our own hearts, have been on the fringes in public. To keep peace, we are not immediately building a meeting place. Our hopes for a festive ceremony tomorrow have been turned into austerity. We can bow no lower than that to the passivity of Jerusalem."

James did not like being put in his place by a woman, but Deborah when in a dudgeon was commanding in voice and look. Out of charity, she continued in a more kindly tone. "We are honored that one who knew Jesus, who shared in his days and in his victories and sufferings, should be here for our first baptism. But the streets of Borhaurus are stained with the blood of our friends, our brothers in Christ. You in Jerusalem must let us redeem their agony in our own way, and with the assistance of the Messiah we all pray to."

Ahiam and I nodded in solidarity. James still looked as if he had bitten a worm in his date cake. He said, more surly than defiant, "I will take back your message to the council and we will pray for your success."

At Gadessera, beneath the acacia and jujube trees, Deborah, in an embroidered chethomene from Modi'im that made her look like the goddess Diana, gave the introductory talk. The stream that fed the pool accompanied her voice like music. The shadows of the trees softened her face. I was breathless with love for her, ensorcelled.

The presence of James did give it a specialness. But in contrast to Andrew's loving, humble, and balanced words about Jesus, James preached a Jesus of hard rules. He spoke as Paul might, but without Paul's message of love or his fiery juices. We all parted with Christly embraces, but I felt little of Christ when I hugged his small, bony disciple.

Later in the week, there came a more godly Nazarene: Dathan's widow. Word of the relaxation in Borhaurus had reached her and she had wanted to come home. She had never been as inflexible as Dathan. If anyone made an issue about her, I would argue that she had voluntarily departed several hours before Father's decree, so did not legally come under the ban against returning exiles.

She had news in abundance about the Borhaurus pilgrims and Antioch. Two of the twenty-seven had died en route and two others had collapsed and abandoned the journey in Damascus. The rest had been welcomed in Antioch as near martyrs. At the church there, she said, Jews and Gentiles mingled; there was hardly even lip service paid by Christians, for that is what we were called there, to Mosaic Law. The Sabbath, Saturday, was ignored by the Christians, whose meetings, baptisms, and love feasts were held on the Lord's Day, Sunday, all without harassment.

Paul, the leader of the Antiochians, was on a mission through Asia Minor—far places like Lystra, Kolyaeum, and Troas. He had also established churches of importance in Thessalonica, Corinth, although not Athens, and many other large cities. In so doing, he had been jailed, been beaten, been dangerously sick, and crossed snowy mountains, seas in winter, ravines, deserts.

I thought of the little apostle with his ropy muscles trudging through snow, burning his tired feet on hot roads, his apple face wrinkling under foreign suns. As Dathan's wife spoke, I thought of our grueling tasks of organization, our ambiguous, depressing dealings with the Jewish Council and the Romans, of our future allied to Jerusalem as represented by men like James, son of Alphaeus, of the sore fissures within my family, of the grubby law cases I was taking to help with our finances.

What a joy it would be to kick my heels together, shake off from me the dust of Borhaurus, leave the church to Ahiam, and set off with Deborah over the slopes of Taurus to proselytize in Greece, Dalmatia, Italy, and beyond. Then I sighed. Even if there were not all the work still to be done here, Deborah would not marry me.

The wife of Dathan and her children settled quietly in Borhaurus. Some of our extreme members sought to enlist her as a rallying point to confront the Jewish Council and to rebuild the meeting house without the council's acquiescence. But she rejected the offer. She had seen enough of the violence that comes with Jesus. Now she wanted his peace.

XIV

One of our prospective followers, a cosmetics grinder, had come without a sponsor. He was more often out of a job than in one and was frequently drunk. I suspected he was a spy for the Romans or the Jewish Council. Deborah and Ahiam also felt uneasy. We questioned him closely, then asked him to go home and pray for further guidance. He did not come back. To keep other moles out of our garden, we inquired about them of the refugees in Modi'im and with others we were certain were solidly with us.

We kept no lists of potential members. In Rome, Claudius was ailing, gossip had him being slowly poisoned, and the rumors of change blew from a different quadrant every month. We did not want names around for Father's and the council's spies—or for other unknown and perhaps violent enemies—to seize.

It was inevitable as we baptized ever more people that we would encounter trouble from within. Those pushing us to challenge the council more aggressively were mostly young, often well educated, and some, I felt, were motivated as much by hostility against Pharisaic fathers as they were by zeal for Christ. They began to agitate for a new meeting place to replace our upper room, which was overcrowded with a hundred and fifty members. Their demands were reasonable, for we had been peaceable and abided by our concord, and we deserved more concessions. If we could not build inside the city walls, then why could we not build outside?

We leaders were also eager to build, but not if it meant bloodshed. Deborah and Ahiam went time and time again to the council members who had been willing to hear us out, seeking acquiescence, but they were upset already about the numbers of their sons who were coming to us. I spoke with Grandfather and Father. Both discouraged a new building. We were doing so well, they argued, and there had been no attacks on us. Why create tensions? When the time was right, they would give us a signal.

"*I* am getting a signal from God that we ought to go ahead," I said petulantly to Deborah.

"You are mixing up God and your impulsions, as usual," she said.

"Perhaps. What is he telling you?"

"To wait."

"You are mixing him up with your timorousness."

"Perhaps." She smiled.

So we waited.

One evening, Ezra came by. "Demas," he said, "this talk about a meeting place is stirring trouble again. People are throwing dust in the air"—a timeless Jewish way of expressing outrage. I poured us wine and took a solid swig. "The Romans have put pressures on the worst of those seeking to harm you," he said, "and two, three of them have moved to Lydda, still . . ."

"Menah ben Tahath?"

"He is one." His father, Ezra said, had finally disowned him. He was in Lydda anyway half the time, gambling and whoring. "They have a little group there, talking about themselves as *sicarii*, as Zealots. Anything that will bond together those who hate your . . . sect."

I felt death's chill in the room. These were men who would throw people into wells or crucify them. It was one thing to confront them face to face. It was another to walk at night not knowing when I might get knifed in the back. I could not hope Ezra was mistaken. He would have learned it from Grandfather, whose spies were paid enough never to make mistakes.

"How much support do they have in town?"

"Enough. A dozen perhaps that they can rely on for . . . the worst. They are getting money from some of the Pharisees who hate you for all the right reasons—because you follow your Jesus *and* are the son of the tribune."

"Would Father prosecute them if they attack us?" Ezra would be more likely to give me the truth of this than Father.

"I think so, if you do not stir up things with your building. But we are not dealing with Decapolis logicians, you know. What Grandfather and I are saying is that you should wear a sword and move someone in at night who knows how to handle arms." His skinny features broke into a smile. "I do not mean Deborah."

I pulled a long face and he chaffed me. "Ah, you are saying she is too pure for that sort of thing."

"As well proposition a stone."

"I do not believe you," he said.

But he should have. She had kept us to the dicta she had laid down on her first day in Borhaurus. I had not touched her.

In spite of the town's advice, the pressure continued from within our group to build. Those in favor cited the analogues with the rebuilding of the Temple in Jerusalem, the symbol that Judaism existed as a religion. A meeting house, they argued, would symbolize our existence as a faith. It would also exemplify what Jesus did time and time again: defying the Pharisees. Apprehensive, we leaders again visited those on the Jewish Council who would see us. I spoke with Father. Again, they warned us. But now most of our congregation wanted to build. We three yielded, and bought a plot a half mile outside the walls. With no ceremony except a blessing by Deborah as the most senior minister, we dug holes and set the brick corner posts.

I knew Borhaurus: we would not escape with both our defiance and our skins. I thought again of Ezra's advice to wear a sword and call in a bodyguard. But I chose not to heed it, lest by making a show of warding off injury, I invite it. I found what consolation I could in the shrugging words of Rechab—and Dathan—when they were overtaken by events they could not or would not act upon: God's will be done.

I was therefore unprepared when, the night after we set the corner posts, four masked men broke through my door just after midnight. I struggled, but they held me down, stuffed cloth in my mouth so I could not shout, and beat me while one of them with repeated blows efficiently smashed my nose.

The Parthian who had tended Rechab examined the swollen, pulpy, discolored flesh and shook his head. I would look gladiatorial for the rest of my life. The symbolism did not escape me: my nose had been the most Roman feature on my face.

My initial reaction, like that of Rechab when he was blinded, was to

130

hate. But I did try to imagine how Jesus would have reacted. Philosophically, the hurdle of forgiveness did not seem high. In practice, it seemed unleapable. I now felt like badly damaged goods, mutilated at both head and foot. My middle face was swathed in bandages, my rib cage broken, my eyes black, and I felt twice my age.

Angry visitors soon crowded my room. Mother wept and Father, seeing the ruin of his nasal legacy, cursed through his teeth. I hoped it would translate into action against those who had maimed me. Deborah was correct toward him but by no means deferential. She had more than a few debits on her ledger against him. Grandfather fumed and Ezra was so full of fury that he could hardly talk. It was as if the shed blood had been his own, which of course it was.

No one was sure who the four assailants were, but our first problem was not them but our own members. We had among us enraged men who were willing to guess and in whom—though who was I to censure them—Jesus' message of forgiveness and meekness had not taken full root. We calmed them with difficulty.

Mother asked me to come home for a while. Gently, I told her no. A ferocious Gaul who had retired from the Roman legions after being partially lamed came to stay with me at night. He had married a woman from Borhaurus and both were in our church. Still powerful at fifty-five, he slept on a mat before the door, sword by his side, a spear in the corner.

Some church members felt we should still try to finish the meeting place, but the potential killers were doubtlessly also arsonists. Why rebuild, particularly outside town, when they were sure to put our labors to the torch? At the opposite extreme, there were some who took the "other cheek" doctrine so literally that they regretted that I had tried to fend off my assaulters.

Ezra visited me one evening. The Gaul had sensed in my cousin the same raging hatred he had for my attackers. Ezra's commercial aptitudes had given him a smattering of every language in the eastern Mediterranean, and he exchanged a few words in Gallic with my bodyguard, to the man's pleased nods and smiles.

Ezra told me quietly in Greek that Father's informers had identified the one local man who had beaten me. He had been questioned by "special interrogators," that is two torturers. They had extracted the names of my other assailants along with four of his fingernails. Then he had been released and expelled from Borhaurus to join his comrades in Lydda if he dared.

"Menah ben Tahath?" I demanded.

"Yes, he wore a mailed glove just in case your nose was as hard as your head."

"Will Father do anything?"

"Well," Ezra answered indirectly, "your father has many pressures on him."

The Gaul went with Ezra to the door where Ezra bid him goodnight and spoke a few parting words in Gallic.

Next noon, I went by the house and asked Mother if I might come to supper. My swollen nose, my eyes ringed now with the light orange and purple of recovery, drew an agonized look from her. That night, when Father saw me, his face flushed with anger. I asked him whether he planned to act.

"No more show trials, Demas," he said resignedly.

"You have been told to do nothing?"

"That is more or less correct," he said.

"How long are you going to bear this?" I was ready to cry. But he was not going to fall into the trap his feelings had set for him.

"That is my problem," he said, "not yours. I am immeasurably pained over what they did to you, but you and I are beyond your having the right to question me about my conduct."

The Gaul came by to escort me home. He read in my eyes the refusal of Father to act, and limped beside me, muttering curses. Next evening, he asked me if he could be spared for two nights. His wife was complaining about his absence, he said. He had asked another Nazarene, a smith bigger than he, if less proficient in arms, to take his place.

On the third night, he returned and ate cheerfully of the honey and cinnamon cakes Deborah had made for us. A day later, Ahiam came by just before sundown. A friend from Lydda had brought news that Menah ben Tahath and a second exile from Borhaurus had been found dead four miles from Lydda in an area frequented by bandits. The victims had last been seen at a tavern in Lydda, and none of those with whom they ate and drank remembered them saying they planned to do anything so foolish as journeying outside the walls that night.

Even their heads had been hacked into small pieces. They were identified only by their bloody garments and their purses, from which all the money was gone. There was hardly enough flesh left for the obsequies, for wild animals had run off with much of their remains, the most ghastly fate imaginable for Jews. In ancient times, the enemies of Judaea had left fallen Jewish warriors for the dogs as an insult, and the dread of such a fate had come down undiluted to this day.

"Even devils like these do not deserve it!" Ahiam said. "No Jew could do this to another Jew."

No, Ahiam, I thought, you are mistaken. When the Gaul came that evening to take up his vigil, I pulled the curtains shut, picked up his sword from where he had put it on the floor and held it under the oil lamp. I saw no blood on it. It gleamed from a recent pumicing. I regarded him closely, trying to draw an answer from his pale foreign eyes. But he only looked back at me, unblinking. I would get no more than that from Ezra.

I wondered where the money of the victims would turn up? As an anonymous contribution toward rebuilding the meeting place? Deborah had heard of the murders from Ahiam by the time I saw her next day. "Who did it? Do you know?" she asked.

"No, I do not."

"Is that the truth? You suspect something. Where was the Gaul? I heard they were cut as if by some superhuman power, skulls and all. In fact, where was Ezra?"

"Do not even think thoughts like that."

She looked unhappy. "What are we as Nazarenes supposed to feel when such things happen? Do you think there will be retribution taken against us?"

Perhaps not right away, I said. Reduction of the two men to shashlik would dissuade our enemies for a time. "The God of the synagogue says it is a good thing for men to avenge wrongs," I said. "Search your heart. How do you really feel about it?"

She looked at my nose as she pondered, even reaching out to touch it gently. It gave me a feeling I was not entirely ugly, was still attractive to her. "I think," she said, "of Peter cutting off the high priest's servant's ear the night they arrested Jesus. Jesus became angry and told him to put up the sword. I wish I felt that way, but I do not."

"I would like to ask Peter what Jesus really told him that night," I said. "Perhaps he said, 'Why stop at one ear?' "

XV

❖❖❖

Our church would never be safe while the surviving attackers and their coconspirators in Borhaurus were at large. Nor could we three pretend to be true leaders, particularly to our more bumptious followers, if we did nothing to eliminate their threat. So our posture was as Rechab's had been: we would forgive the sins of the men who had maimed me, but not their crimes. In other words, we would pray for their salvation, and, meanwhile, demand that Rome locate and prosecute them.

So, when Father did nothing, we told him and the Jewish Council rather than conferring with them about it that as a Roman citizen I had appealed for prosecution to Felix, the new procurator.

Two weeks later, we got action in an unexpected way. Aesubius burst into my office at midday, jowls trembling. "Demas, they are making your father go back to Rome! You must withdraw your appeal!" I was open-mouthed. Borhaurus without Father? It was unimaginable. He had spent his adult life here. Even in our estrangement, perhaps especially in it, he *was* Borhaurus. I loped out the door with Aesubius breathlessly following.

Father and Mother were in the living room. His weary face tightened when I came in. "They have had enough," he said bitterly. "Your appeal was the final straw." Felix, he said, did not want to set a precedent by refusing to try a case brought by a Roman citizen. Yet for him to try it would make it seem Rome doubted Father's fairness. And if he required Father to try it, there would be the undignified spectacle of a father hearing a case in which his son was not merely lawyer but chief accuser. Finally, there was the disruption of this second trial pitting Jews, even renegade Jews, against Nazarenes.

"Aesubius said if I withdrew my appeal . . ."

Aesubius had just puffed in, and Father glanced at him, irked by his naïveté. "It is too late for that to matter," Father said and went on. "Besides, this is an opportunity for Felix to give his brother-in-law a job. He will be the new tribune of Borhaurus. I suspect anyway that Felix felt I was tainted by Cumanus and Cuspius Fadus"—Cumanus's predecessor.

Aesubius interrupted loyally. "You are free of all taint, Sir Junius, as free as you humanly could be."

Father gave him a wry look, then turned to me. "Demas, what is done is done. The brother-in-law of Felix is a decent-enough man. He will work out some compromise that will not disrupt the accords we have made, what is left of them." He was calm now. "You do realize that you are going to be in jeopardy as long as you are here." I was moved by his concern in the midst of this disaster that I had brought on him.

He went on. "Is there any point in my urging you to come with us? You could go on with your belief"—he could not keep the sour taste of the word out of his voice—"so long as you kept it to yourself. I will not be going back in any disgrace, Felix has assured me of that. There will be a new position, one of some stature. I could find something for you in Rome, or you could practice law there or somewhere else outside Judaea."

"No, Father," I said. "Thank you."

But he was not looking for thanks, even genuine thanks. He had sought to save me from myself and I had rebuffed him. "I taught you to be principled," he said angrily. "And you became too principled by half. Your principles have made you a prig, Demas, a prig intent on being a martyr."

He had lashed out at me when I, too, was trying to make peace. "Perhaps," I retorted, "instead of calling me names, you ought to cast a stoic look at your own principles. Maybe instead of thinking about what Christ has done to you, you ought to think about what he could do for you."

It was just the kind of remark that would bite him because it had elements of truth in it. Aesubius started to intervene, but Father cast a curdling glance at him. "Bloodshed, disorder, hatred! That is what he has done for us."

I had spilled some of my bile and felt relieved. But I did not want us to part this way. "No, Father," I said, "not those things. Love. Do you think hatred led me to this? Who better than you knows I never had time for hatred?"

At that, he looked torn. "Demas, I know you mean me well, and are trying to make things up with me. But to me this creed of yours is swampy, structureless." He paused. "I swear I am not trying to provoke you. You are my only child, my son. I have never understood what appeal this Jesus has for you. At first, I thought you turned to it out of revenge, and frankly that was convenient for me to believe. But in my heart I see I was wrong, or largely wrong. Then why? You see it has wrecked our family, changed everything. Was it the synagogue? I know now I was a fool to let Asa . . ."

It was, in a different form, the same question I had asked Andrew. For a long minute, I said nothing, then I tried.

"Father, by the time Dathan was killed, I was coming to feel I had to be either with them or with everyone else and when I saw him dead, there was no longer any choice. These are brave people, full of joy, and they are also simple people, either like Rechab, born that way, or they became simple, like Deborah. They . . . we . . . believe that Jesus told us to love God first, and, secondly, to treat our neighbors as we want to be treated ourselves." I stopped, feeling inadequate.

"A weak bowl of porridge for anybody to get crucified over," Father observed. I felt in him the same frustration with my words that I felt.

"It is a porridge that nourishes me," I said. "Before I ate it, I was empty. Now I am full. I was incomplete and I am whole. I take the Communion, just bread and wine that has been blessed, commemorating the last supper of Jesus with his disciples, and I feel full of holy joy, as silly as that may sound to you. I have a focus for my life, a cause I can fight and work for." I stopped, then said, "And if necessary die for."

"You are arguing that the tilemaker was right, not a fool to throw his life away?" he asked incredulously.

"Yes," I said, "not a fool! Right to take the risk! Because . . ." And I realized that in justifying my faith to Father, I was peeling away my own incomprehensions about Jesus as if he were a miraculous fruit with many skins. "Dathan on the cross was the embodiment of Jesus on *his* cross, just as I would be if I were crucified for my belief. . . ." In my excitement, I came to my feet. "As all men who die for him are that embodiment, and will be down through all the ages that men live. And that for all the agony a person would be suffering, he would be in joy or even at peace, because he had done right." I was astonished at my own vehemence.

It had also jarred Father, for he looked defenseless for a moment. But only a moment. When he spoke, distance was back in his voice. "Demas, your Jesus is like the maps we had in Germany, *Terra*

136

Incognita written all over them. And, like bad maps, the result for anyone who follows him is death, which is what you are saying—death for Dathan, your old Andrew . . . brave deaths, yes, but death nevertheless. And, of course, he himself was, when all is said and done, a suicide."

"Yes," I said, "a suicide. That is the enormousness of it. Maybe he was misguided, maybe even insane, talking about being the son of God. But he did believe that he was, and he did *know* he was dying for mankind."

I had said what I wanted, and Father had heard me out. I knew that at last he understood. But that was all. I thought of trying again. But what was there left to try? We no longer existed as a family. Nothing remained but the final good-byes.

Yet, an instant later, I was proved wrong, as I so often was when I thought I was most percipient. In the silence, Mother spoke—my soft, passive mother. "You are not ready for Jesus, Junius, but I am." She began to cry.

I had never seen her cross Father before, and I was both astounded and stirred. This comfortable, kind woman whom I loved so much and so simply had somehow during these months, without any but her knowing it, found her way to the foot of the cross.

Father respected her tears. He said nothing until she stopped. "You cannot be serious about this?" he asked her quietly. She nodded yes, still too distraught to speak. He glanced at me, a cold glimmer in his eyes, the look of a man who never entirely loses sight of the ironies.

Before they left for Rome, my hands shaking, I baptized her, using more of Andrew's holy water, wondering if her husband, my father, would ever by some miracle join us in her new faith.

❁

As Father had predicted, his successor was a decent man. Felix would not order the criminals tried in Roman court. But he and his brother-in-law worked out a compromise. The Jewish Council was provided with the names of the two remaining perpetrators and six coconspirators in Borhaurus. The council dispatched one of their members to Lydda, who pointed out to the survivors that so long as they went without punishment, they risked the fate of Menah ben Tahath and his friend. The council also held over them the possibility that Rome would try them, with the punishment likely to be death, or at best mutilation.

All eight men agreed to submit themselves to synagogic justice. They were thoroughly whipped in the basement of the synagogue. A Nazarene passerby saw them limping and being carried from its rear door on the way to their enforced exile. For our part, we agreed not to construct a meeting place unless the new tribune and the Jewish Council changed their minds. It was a bowl of thistles for us to swallow, and our dissenters talked of breaking with us. But finally even the majority of them, constantly reminded by the wreck of my nose, eschewed actions that would bring on us all more bloodshed.

In good weather, we held services by the corner posts on our land. We also honored Dathan and the mason with a cross of marble blocks sunk in the earth over their grave; we had reasonable hopes it would not be vandalized. I no longer needed my Gallic bodyguard. He returned to domesticity. But I had a door of double thickness with heavy hinges and locks installed, and I slept with my sword and dirk beside my pallet.

The more benign disposition of the town set the stage for Deborah's return to Modi'im. The council had come to feel that Ahiam would deal honorably with them, and he had become a leader not just in name but in fact. And I had shown myself trustworthy even if I was still widely regarded as a traitor to both my Roman and Jewish birthrights. So it was possible for the church to survive without her. Whether I could was another matter. I sensed in myself and in her, too, a kind of desperation.

We had seen each other daily, and even without the entwining of sex, we had become loving friends, tried both by crisis and workaday tedium and found worthy. Her departure would mean we would see each other only rarely. The powerful, if impalpable, intimacy between us would be at best suspended. I felt her drawing toward me physically as she had that night before I left for Borhaurus. And I found ways to touch or even take her arm, as if to make some point in a conversation. She did not flinch. Once, just as in Rivka's kitchen, as we both looked at a message, she leaned against me. Just being near her sometimes made me feel giddy.

One night, snug under my bearskin, I had dozed off when I half heard a soft knock. My arm thrashed for the sword, even as I heard, "Demas," and recognized Deborah's whisper.

I had bathed before I went to bed, and wrapping around me the sackcloth I had used to dry, I opened the door. I could see her only in silhouette. As she slipped in, I smelled her breath, sweetly anised, but also scented with wine—to bolster her will? I knew she, too, had bathed, for she smelled of wild rosemary, which she rubbed on herself after washing. We stood shivering on the rough board floor.

"Say something," she said.

"What are you doing here?" was the best I could manage.

"I am standing here and I am cold."

"Well, the only warm place here is the bed. . . ." I was too nervous to finish, my mouth suddenly dry, my heart banging my ribs like a small newly caged animal. I could feel her nervousness, too. I inanely recalled an obscure Pharisee sect that believed the Mishnah taught that engaged couples could go to bed together, even kiss there, so long as they kept on their clothes. It was a means of making sure that the marriage would be a passionate one. Should I propose that?

"Demas," she said practically, "drop that wet thing on the floor. What is it?"

"My towel. I have nothing else on."

"I can feel that," she said, putting her cold hands on my back and drawing me to her.

Despite her Pharisaic upbringing, fidelity to Jesus and other misgivings, she had decided that it was time. And even though in a removed compartment of my mind, I was enumerating all the reasons that we should forbear, I took her in my arms.

She stiffened. I felt sick, fearing her resolve had faded and reason had prevailed. I bent to kiss her. She raised her hand and covered my mouth. "Wait, Demas," she said determinedly, "I must say something, before you and before God. I must say why I am here. It was only by whim that Menah ben Tahath did not kill you. He could as easily have done so. There are other Menahs waiting for us in the lives we have chosen. They could kill you. Or me. Only a fool would think otherwise. And if that happened, we would never have held each other the way we want to. Never, never at all. I cannot take that chance, Demas. God does not want me to take it strongly enough for me to stay away, now that we are parting, perhaps never again to be as close as we are now. That is what I wanted to say."

She stopped and smiled. "Every minute since the Gaul left I have been imagining how it would feel to kiss your nose." She did, light as a mayfly skimming a pool, then pushed back my hair and sighed and I kissed her.

I helped her undo her toga and pull her shift over her head. She stood before me, letting me look at her by the single small oil lamp. I stared at the dark nipples I had never seen, the small emphatic hole of her navel, the bush of dark hair within which I knew lay the treasures of my dreams.

She looked at me silently. At last, she reached out, touched my nipples lightly, feeling their miniature hardness. She ran her hand down my body and I thought I would have to back against the wall to

139

keep from falling. We eased down onto the pallet, abandoned ourselves to the touches of our skins, our mouths, chests, pelvises, thighs, even rubbing our feet together, my deformed toes notwithstanding and, at last, irrelevant.

We made love for an hour, two, I pausing when I was on the verge of spending. Once I dropped my face to her mount, something I had never done with anyone. Indeed, I knew from my Jewish cousins it was forbidden by the Mishnah. I savored the clean hay smell of her, ignoring the discomfort to my nose, her hands gently holding my head to her. It occurred to me that she had imagined these touches, these acts as graphically as I had. When, at last, I entered her, ever so slowly, she caught her breath in pain, but forced me to go on. Once there, whatever her body's needs, I could not wait. She held me in to her, and when at last my body relaxed, she kissed me gently time and time again. "Oh, Demas," she sniffled. "Oh, Demas." We clung together, the bearskin fallen to the floor. My hand was in her sweated hair, and hers was in mine.

We were wordlessly happy, knowing there was no use in saying anything, not because there was nothing to say but because there were no words we knew to say it. All that night, we talked and made love and slept and made love. We rose well after dawn and ate breakfast, but she not leave until noon.

When she did not return the next night, I took her arm while we talked in the morning and whispered, "Come to me. Tonight. I die if you do not." She gave me a desperate glance. That night again we made love. The touch of our naked skins was like the instant flames of torches in dry cornhusks.

❀

"It has gone beyond all control," she said one morning, the perspiration beaded on her upper lip, her face wanton in surfeit. "We are lost and do not even want to find our way back." She looked solemnly at my naked body. "Better that we were ministers in a cult of Priapus," she said.

We should have been seeking candidates for her myriad jobs, assigning her contacts to me and Ahiam, reorganizing schedules and committees. We did not. I gave up any pretense of devoting myself to my law office as she did to her loom. Caught up in our voluptuary indulgence, our lives selfishly began to become only each other.

"Marriage would actually cool us," I once said. "It would permit us to turn outward again."

140

"I cannot, Demas. Nothing has changed except that you have become my drug. Even if we were married, I cannot imagine enough of this. When I give you up, I only pray Jesus will take me back." I kissed her on each lid, but she pushed me away. "Tomorrow, Demas, I must think of something besides you. I must make plans to go." But tomorrows after tomorrows came and went as we made up excuses to postpone her return to Modi'im.

In our fools' paradise, we thought our meetings would go unnoticed, our looks unread, that we were so attuned to the town that we would pick up the first hint of suspicion. I should have known differently. One afternoon, during a coupling so shattering that both of us had cried out, there came a knock on the door. We looked at each other in alarm.

"Who is it?" I said, expecting the voice of a neighbor.

"Rechab," was the answer.

I knew in that single word that Deborah and Borhaurus had ended for me. I did not even look at her. She, with the egoism of all illicit lovers, would also be thinking only of how much of her own life had been destroyed.

"Can you come back?" I said to the closed door.

"Demas," he said, his voice low, "I know. I am sorry."

"Let him in, then," said Deborah. "Rechab, just wait until—"

"It does not matter, Deborah bas Sirach," he said miserably, "I can see nothing. And the porter's boy who led me here has gone."

I opened the door and reached out to lead him in. He recoiled from my touch. It was then that I felt the full guilt of what we had done. We had preached virtue and had been hypocrites whose hypocrisy, if discovered, could have been used by our enemies to destroy all our work. We had endangered those who had placed their faith in us. We had recklessly put at risk their livelihoods, their homes and possessions, even their survival. We had thoroughly betrayed them.

I settled Rechab in the single chair, intolerably aware that the room smelled of sex. Deborah and I stood beside the disorderly pallet, both of us looking at the torment on that blasted face. How awful for him, I thought, to unmask friends such as we. He began to rock back and forth in anguish.

"What am I to do?" he said at last.

I, and surely Deborah, too, could feel him thinking of all we three had been through together, the ordeals in which we had tested each other: she and he in Modi'im, the three of us in Borhaurus, where I gave up my old life to be his lawyer, our tending him when he was blinded, and when his leg was amputated, his baptism of us both, binding us all together in Jesus.

"We do not know, Rechab," Deborah answered for us both.

"How widely known is it?" I asked.

Stumblingly, he said, "I heard it from the sister in Modi'im of a woman here who saw you late at night embracing in a side street. You," he said, speaking to Deborah, "had baptized the woman and found her work in a weaving shop when her husband was sick. She will tell no one." Good deeds coming home to roost, I thought, but small comfort. Rechab had prayed for guidance. Then, using a pretext, he had asked an elder to bring him to Borhaurus, hoping to discover he was wrong.

"Then two people besides us three know," I said.

"It no longer matters," Deborah said. "Rechab has forced us to decide what we lacked the courage to decide for ourselves." I read her thoughts. The humiliation of being discovered had made it impossible for her to see herself as she had: a virtuous woman successfully carrying out the work of Jesus to the exclusion of all else. That illusion was now demolished.

"She will not marry," I appealed to Rechab. "That would solve everything."

"It would solve nothing," she said.

I could feel the space widening between Deborah and me. I wanted to reach across and touch her, to chain up the breach before it grew greater. "We love each other, Rechab," I said.

Deborah spoke again, but to my earlier words. "I cannot marry, Rechab. If I do, I give up Christ, assuming he still wants me. I cannot be halfway about him. . . ." She nodded at me, then realizing Rechab could not see, said, "I mean about Demas. Nor Christ, either. Least of all now. I am making a choice."

I felt my stomach fall like a hut into an earthquake chasm. I was losing her! What good was any more talk? I was losing this transcendent part of my life. Jesus might be all things to her; he was not to me. I had put him aside for her. "I do not know if I can bear for you to go," I said humbly.

She sat, her shift now draped around her, her shoulders slumped, her face still flushed with the heat of our love, also thinking, I knew, of what we meant to each other. At last, she sighed and said, "Demas, there is nothing for me to do but go." She put her head in her hands, then lifted it. "Rechab, if I come back to Modi'im, what can I do?"

The fuller smiled and directed his scarred sockets toward where she sat, just as if he could see her in all her sorrowing beauty. "Why you would be just what you were before," he said. "If Jesus did not condemn the Magdalena, how can I condemn you?" Simple decency. I looked up at Deborah and smiled and she smiled back, both of us with tears Rechab could not see. He had sought a parable and found one about a whore.

Four days later, Deborah left with warm dignity as if nothing had happened. And nothing had in terms of the people she had worked with. They loved her and with such good reason. When she, Rechab, and the elder were on their mules—I had tried to give her my gelding—I stood by her for a moment. The two men started off and I held her bridle a moment. When she had broken with me before, I had only dreamed of what I was losing. Now, truly, I knew. I was coming to understand hell.

"I am not giving you up," I said.

"Demas, we forfeited our chances." I could see her mind was hardened. But she had relented before.

"No, we forfeited nothing." I was frantic. "We did not leave our work and run away. We harmed no one. We did not even marry. We set such terrible, terrible limits." Surely that counted for something.

"We found ways to stay within some limits," she said, "and ways to circumvent others."

The dark and hopeless well I had fallen into as she rode away grew only more agonizing. I was tortured by the absence of her voice, her skin and touch, the look of her as she worked, relaxed, made love, and by the unhealing wounds of my guilt. I fasted and prayed, not to Jesus, for I had taken his bride and I was sure he would not spare me, but to the God of the synagogue. I did not pray for direction or forgiveness, but only for God to take away the aching depression and guilt that made me, at times, contemplate the releasing nihil of death.

"Raise me up," I begged God, "raise me into the light."

After three days, I ate a little bread, but vowed not to return to life until I knew what I would do. My self-denial was childish compared to the ragged mystics I had seen holding forth in Scythopolis, ribs all but poking through their skin, preaching abstinence even from nourishment. But I understood now how abasement could help mollify the devils within. I thought of going to see Deborah, if only to have someone with whom to explore my grief. But I could not do that to Rechab, to her, or to myself. For I was sure she would reject me.

Ahiam came to me. I saw that he thought I was behaving oddly in withdrawing just when Deborah's departure made me most needed. I told him I was praying for guidance in a new direction. He accepted it, although not without doubt.

Ezra also came. "She has gone and it is killing you," he said.

"Yes, gone, and yes, it is killing me." He waited for me to go on. "It never happened to you?" I asked.

"No," he said, "it never did. I never let myself fall in love with anyone."

"But you love."

He nodded yes.

"What should I do?" I asked.

"You are certain she will not marry?"

"No. She feels in a sense she is already married."

"Yes, well, we and the Romans put thorns and a cross on him. That is bad enough. But you and she have put a cuckold's horns on him. It cannot be comfortable for you, or for her."

XVI

❖❖❖❖❖❖ ❖❖

If Borhaurus had been in crisis, I would have stayed. But Ahiam and the elders were a varied yet homogeneous group. I worked hard for a few weeks to arrange matters so I could efficiently pass to them what power I had. I had thought of becoming a lonely mendicant for God, casting off all complication. But that was ridiculous. I had something to offer, my organizational skills. And Jerusalem could use them.

Before I left, a letter came from Mother. Father, who enclosed no greetings, had been asked to draw up a plan to reform the empire's tribunal system. I went by to see Grandfather. He knew nothing of my carnal love with Deborah, but the other upheavals of the last few months had sapped him. He was sick in bed, yet gowned in a glistening silk gown with an ermine collar, his turban dwarfing his head. I knew he missed my parents, and I was sorry to tell him I, too, was going. He put the best face on it he could: it was Jerusalem, the lesser of the sect's two evils. I bid good-bye to Ezra, leaving in his keeping, along with other possessions, a box in which I had carefully packed Dathan's three pitchers.

Just outside the Jerusalem gate, I said good-bye to Ahiam and our flock. Come to see me off were hard men like the smith and my erstwhile Gallic protector, young Sadducee women with the brisk smell of cassia, the old rag lady who so long ago had spoken sympathetically of Andrew; Samuel, Dathan's widow, the collector of dog feces. There were children newly baptized and toothless crones with whiskery kisses and sepulchral breaths. I hugged them all, tears in my eyes, feeling proud and blessed in spite of the absence of Deborah.

145

On the trip to Jerusalem, I wore my armor for protection and because I felt a rightness to it. At times, charmed by unfamiliar hills and patches of woodland, by purplish ploughland and rustling corn, my spirits rose. But when Deborah nagged my heart, I felt as arid as the red ravines I passed where only thistles grew. I could have reached the city in a single day, but I did not push myself or the gelding. I stopped for the night in Gibeah, the capital of King Saul, another and greater leader whose passions had brought him low.

Early next day, I began the climb into the highlands that led to a ridge where I could see Mount Scopus to my left and the city itself in a bowl before me. In the burning sunlight, it had never seemed so august, its marbled towers, its arcades by public pools, its palaces glistening in gardens browned by summer.

Beehive metropolis! "If I forget you, oh Jerusalem," the men of the synagogue had chanted, "let my right hand wither, my tongue cleave to the roof of my mouth. . . ." As always happened when I saw the city, I felt the eastern beat of my mother's blood. Men of all lands had conquered Jerusalem, traded in her, mated with her daughters. She was a city awash with martyred blood, conspiracy, corrupt luxuries. But she survived, a great city when Rome was a field for wolves!

✦

A porter answered my knock at Celicus Street and looked at my armor with suspicion. I gave him my name and position and he bolted the door before going to inquire. In a moment, Thomas came, also took a look at the armor—and my nose—and embraced me. I explained the nose—he had heard of the incident—and he led me into the empty conference room.

"Now, about the armor?" he asked. "I thought Nazarenes were wearing sackcloth and ashes this year. We have heard wonderful things about you," he went on, and hearing no sarcasm in this somewhat sarcastic man, I assumed the reason for my departure from Borhaurus remained a secret.

I told Thomas I had done what I could in Borhaurus and said I hoped I could find something to do for the Apostolic Council. I talked about my legal career and tried modestly to put before him my administrative abilities.

"They would never accept you for work with them unless you were circumcised. This place is not Borhaurus. They would make you swear to the whole *aleph-beth*"—the alphabet. "We are still doing things as if we were a country synagogue in Galilee."

"My mother is a Jew . . ." I began. But why should I plead race. If I had wanted to become a Jew, I would have done so before I went back to Borhaurus. I could scarcely believe that after all I had done and suffered for the church the Apostolic Council would discriminate against me. Yet, when eight years ago Paul had tried to wring from them approval for his conversion of Gentiles, they had, in effect, delayed it for five years. And to this day, the council—petty, parochial, jealous of its small position and its dogma—was still undercutting him.

Thomas raised his arms and let them fall and slap his thighs. "None of it is fair, but that is the way things are. Perhaps one of them would take you on the road even with your"— he smiled—"genital disability."

"Would you take me?"

Thomas was flattered. "Probably, and thank you for the compliment. But I was never that good at it. I am a dog more at home in the stable than the fields. Whatever good I can do is here."

"Then who?"

"John, perhaps. Philip, though he is getting on. Peter . . ." He looked at me shrewdly. "Paul is in town." He had come straight to Jerusalem from his long journey without even a stop in Antioch. "He is making his report to the Apostolic Council. Come if you want. Other visiting ministers will be there."

About forty men—all but myself dressed in Jewish clothes—crowded the conference room, the same one where I had given the report of Andrew's death three years before. Peter came to me and gave me a hug and the others who had been there greeted me. Paul was animatedly talking to a group of youngish men. He was tanner, perhaps grayer, but otherwise no different from when I had seen him in his garret. He saw the activity around me, squinted nearsightedly, and sent the older of his companions, a man of some forty, to Thomas to—I was certain—inquire my name, which Paul must have forgotten. The man went back, whispered to Paul, and Paul came to join the group.

"Demas, Demas," he said expansively, "so you decided to step into the water with us after all?" He might have forgotten my name but he remembered our conversation.

James, the brother of Jesus, presided over the meeting. But Paul dominated it, his impelling voice detailing the churches he had set up, Derbe, Thyatira, Assos, exotic towns I had seen only on maps. He speckled his Aramaic with precise Greek words like jewels thrown on a coarse blanket. But his allusions, skillfully used to buttress his opinions, were invariably from the Torah and the other Jewish books, not the Greek classics.

When he had concluded his report on his travels, he said that two thousand drachmas were needed for a seminary to train missionaries in Damascus and a seafaring mission in Corinth that would send sailorministers all the way to Spain. He reminded the council that when Jerusalem's Nazarenes were starving eight years before, it was he who had brought to them a gift of gold from the Christians of Antioch. There were nods around the table, but only Peter stood up.

"I say give him two thousand, no, twenty-five hundred. We can use it, but he can use it more. Paul is doing what we should be doing." Peter's presence, like Paul's, was compelling, but from something physical, emotional, rather than intellectual.

James pulled nervously at his white beard, which he wore so long, some said, because of his adherence to a Mosaic tractate that recommended beards never be cut lest some holiness be in the discarded hair. He looked around the table at the other disciples. John nodded firmly in assent to Peter's proposal. The rest glanced uneasily at each other. Peter glared at them.

"I *want* that money for Paul," he said threateningly, although what lay behind the threat I had no way of knowing. "Philip? Thomas?" Unenthusiastically, both nodded assent.

Bartholomew, Matthew, James, son of Alphaeus, and James, chairman, were not willing to make it a majority. Peter fumed.

"Fifteen hundred, then. Sheol take us, what is fifteen hundred? Four laborers' yearly pay. The man has won thousands of followers, been jailed, hided. It's a miracle he is here."

"Five hundred," said James, the chairman.

"Five hundred?" shouted Peter. "Are we going to sit here bartering like mongers of slop pots? A thousand, James, in the name of Jesus. Why must I do this?"

I could see why James, a creature of consensus, stayed in power. And why Peter never got any. James polled the council quickly with his eyes, sighed and said, "Eight hundred."

"Our brethren in Damascus and Corinth thank you," Paul said, making no effort whatsoever to hide his scorn.

Peter looked at Paul, who, it was well known, had once been his antagonist, then turned on the council: "Whether you give him two thousand or five hundred or one, Paul is the future. We are drying up here. When we die"—he meant the disciples and James—"this council will blow away like dead leaves." His voice rose to a shout. "A church *in foreign lands, with foreign people* will survive, and ours will not!"

"No! That is untrue!" Matthew cried. He had been a tax collector and was the only one doughty enough and loud enough to try to shout down Peter. "We have our successes: in Hebron, Gaza, Jericho, all churches as healthy as any of Paul's."

I felt hurt. What about Borhaurus? Modi'im?

"Borhaurus," interjected Thomas.

"Jericho and Hebron?" asked Philip. The names seemed to bring him back like an elixir of life. "They are not *our* successes. They are *Peter's.* Hebron—"

"Enough!" roared Peter. He calmed. "Enough. Why, every time, must it come to this?" There was a sudden silence, the sadness and embarrassment so thick it could almost be touched.

"We fail him," said John quietly, "and we who knew him best fail him most."

When it broke up, I went to Peter and asked him whether I could visit him in the morning. He was still shaken, unable to extract himself from the emotional tangle. "You heard Philip," he said to me, but only because I happened to be at hand, "he's right. We flourish in Hebron and Jericho but only because I water them with my blood." He looked at me, came back to my question. "Come early," he said glumly.

Paul and his disciples, neither of them the men I had seen in Scythopolis, stood talking with John, Thomas, and two visiting ministers. The younger follower of Paul, about four years my senior, wore a collar embroidered with rams beneath his light cloak. He was sleek as a seal. The other man was burlier, with wide-apart eyes and a frizzly beard.

With hardly a break in his talk, Paul sent the younger man to me. He introduced himself as Timothy, eyed me curiously, and asked me whether I could visit Paul on the morrow. Yes, I said, in the afternoon. I tingled at the prospect.

Next morning, at Peter's comfortable quarters in the lower town, he was packing his mule's saddle bags for a trip to Hebron. The two-day journey on indifferent roads, I thought, would not be easy for a man sixty or so.

"I get sick, sick, sick of it," he said, picking up from the night before. "Everything has gone wrong."

"I thought I wanted to work with them," I said.

"Doing what? Translating the Roman Rules of Legislative Behavior?" His remark pleased him, lifting his mood a little.

"No," I said seriously, "you mentioned organization last night, or rather the lack of it. I thought there might be a place for me in helping to do that sort of thing."

"Demas, my boy," he said with gruff familiarity, "the council is unorganizable. And you are a *shaygets*—a young Gentile—"in the bargain. So, forget about it."

"I thought they had finally agreed that Gentiles—"

"The council agrees to things and does nothing. I am supposed to be the apostle to the Jews, not just here, but all over the world, and here I am riding off to do handholding work that a twenty-year-old could do. A baptism here, a funeral there, that's all any of the rest of them do anymore."

"John? Philip?"

"More than the others. But poor old Philip . . . And nobody can understand John except for another mystic. Besides, John couldn't organize a one-bed whorehouse in Gomorrah."

My choices were diminishing. "But you keep at it."

"As you see. As Andrew did."

For all my experience at Borhaurus, for all the things that had happened to me, coarse and ill educated as Peter was, he awed me, and not just because he was the primary person picked by Jesus to carry on his ministry. He stared at me, waiting.

"Could I go on the road with you?" I blurted out.

He stared at me, reading me as best he could for a full two minutes, then said, "Why not? Old Protokletos would want it."

My heart leaped. My words came out in a jumble. "There is this thing of circumcision. I do not care about the operation. But taking on belief in the Mosaic Law, becoming a Jew, something I am not, to achieve an end . . ."

"Well, it would be more like *saying* you were a Jew. Circumcision does not mean that much to me personally. But even Paul forced Timothy to be circumcised so as not to rile some Jews they were working with. Of course, when *we* wanted Paul to get a Phrygian, Titus, circumcised, Paul refused—even though if Paul had told him to let us cut stones and all, Titus would have said, 'Chop!' Paul cuts foreskins to suit his time and mood.

"He can afford to. He never operates in a Jewish town. Think about them: Antioch, Tarsus, Thessalonica. . . . What he does is go *first* to the Jews in a town. They are a minority, pleased to have a scholar

150

speak in the synagogue, one who has traveled. Paul ingratiates himself. He avoids saying who in his party is circumcised and who is not. He does not *oppose* the Law, he *seduces* people away from it.

"By the time the synagogue is aware that he is overturning what they believe as sure as Jesus overturned the moneylenders' tables, Paul is baptizing Jews *and* Gentiles. The synagogue leaders start tearing up their clothes and grinding their teeth and Paul runs out of town one step ahead of a burning in the manure pile."

"But did Jesus not do the same thing?"

Peter glanced at the sun, and began to look impatient. "Jesus, Jesus, Jesus. Well, on Gentiles, he did and he did not. The few times we did take them in, Jesus found obscure things in the Law to permit it, that is, he used the Law against itself. He abided by what he believed of it, and on the rest kept his tongue in his teeth enough to stay out of trouble." His face clouded. ". . . Until he decided trouble was what he had to have."

"And was crucified."

"Yes." Peter was somber. "It sounds as if I am being critical. But you do not follow him twenty-two years, not me or the others, either, unless you know there never was anybody like him and never will be." How much like Andrew he sounded. Was a quarter of an inch of foreskin all that important to me?

"If I could do it, when could I start?"

"The day after, if your stave's not too sore." He thought a minute. "I noticed you talking with Paul's man. You are thinking of him, too?"

"He asked me to come see him this afternoon," I hedged.

"Well, you have seen how I stand up for Paul at the meetings, but on some things Paul is preaching gull droppings."

His vehemence surprised me. And, yet, Andrew had said much the same thing. "What do you mean? Just in a nutshell."

"You *cannot* put it in a nutshell. That's the problem. But as one example: Paul thinks that looking at a woman with lust in your eye is just as sinful as cutting out a man's heart, robbing his shop, raping his wife and daughter on the way out, and stomping his dog to death when it barks at you. Of course, I am exaggerating, but—"

"But what did Jesus say?"

"Well, he never said *that*."

I could see he wanted to be off. "Demas," he said cinching the saddle, "if you have a choice, there is something else you ought to know. I am not going to be here forever."

I thought he was telling me he had some kind of slow and incurable disease, or that he was philosophizing about dying, but that was not

151

what he meant at all. He saw my confusion and went on: "You probably realize I am stuffed up to my gills with Jerusalem. The council knows what I am thinking of, but I do not want it to be known yet to the churches. I am leaving in a year or two. Maybe Rome."

Leaving the council? Jerusalem? Christ's *Petros*? I was too surprised to answer. And Rome: with Father there, could I go? But perhaps until Peter left . . . ? It was another confusing fact to weigh. Peter checked the bags a last time. I held the bridle while he mounted. I thought of my discussion with Deborah at the time Menah ben Tahath was cut in pieces. "I have one last question, and perhaps I should not ask, but did you cut off someone's ear when they arrested Jesus?"

He was amused. "I certainly did: the high priest's slave's." I walked beside his donkey as we left the stable yard. "A great pig of a man," he said, "heavier than I am, tall. Jesus, you know, was not all that big and this fellow grabbed him. Jesus did not particularly like to be touched. Not many people understand that. He preferred to be the toucher. Well, I got his head in the crook of my elbow and took off his ear."

"And Jesus said . . . ?"

" 'Put up the sword.' He had decided he was going to be crucified and was burdened enough. He did not want any sideshows to worry about. He said something like, 'The cup is poured and I am going to drink it and therefore do not interfere.' John would remember the words better."

"But what did Jesus *feel* about your doing it?"

He looked up as if to summon back from all those years ago a clear picture. "I know you are thinking about the business of turning the other cheek," Peter said. "But to answer you as honestly as I can: Jesus sort of expected that kind of behavior from me. And, remember, he was upset, too, freshly betrayed, even though he thought he would be, by Judas, one of us. So maybe, just as a lesson in justice, he might not have minded me taking off the other ear as well. But it was not something he would have done himself or told me to do."

We were passing the pool of Siloam, where Jesus, as Rechab had heard it, gave sight to a blind man. Miracles were something I wanted to ask Peter about, too, and there was no time now, and there might not be unless I took up his offer. He would be back in a week. I bid him good-bye at the gate and watched him plod steadily down the long road toward Hebron.

When I arrived at Paul's garret near the Dung gate, similar to his former pinched quarters, he greeted me warmly, then went back to a small table by the window. He made a few more hurried scratchings on a wax tablet already almost full of his tiny, neat handwriting.

"Notes for letters," he said. "By evening, I must have them dictated to Silas"—the older man, I assumed—"or Timothy." This was an example, then, of his famous efficiency. In spite of his meetings with the council, he had not curtailed his correspondence with Antioch and its allied churches.

He motioned me to the chair at the table, the only one in the room, and stood by the wall, making me feel like a prisoner being questioned by the prosecutor. "You stay busy," I said.

"You, too, from what I hear," he replied. "How many turned to Christ Jesus in Borhaurus? Three hundred?"

"Two hundred actually baptized. Probably another hundred very sympathetic to us, on the way." Why did Paul make me feel that I was talking about the Borhaurus Nazarenes, brave people, good friends, *brothers and sisters*, as if they were sheep to be counted at day's end?

"A remarkable accomplishment," he said. His tone changed. "If I may be impertinent, and if what I hear is true, I would have wished you had compromised a little less."

That raised my neck hairs. How could any stranger really know what we had been through? "We did what we had to do," I said. "Antioch is a long way from Borhaurus. So is Jerusalem."

He laughed, that fine laugh I had seen and heard before and sensed even then was rare, a laugh that had in it as much humor over his own foolishness as the world's.

"You have been here three minutes and I have already put myself on your list of people you are asking God to help you to forgive. Let us begin again. What brings you here?"

In answer, I told him briefly of my childhood, my trips to the synagogue, my experience in the well, my life up to the death of Dathan, and, in more detail, my decision to become a Nazarene and my work in Modi'im and Borhaurus. I did not mention Visilia Persullus or speak much of Deborah lest his sharp mind slice into the facts. I told him I had only felt fulfilled since becoming a Nazarene and, believing my work in Borhaurus was done, I had come to Jerusalem "But they do not want me unless I am circumcised. I am undecided about that. I have thought of preaching and organizing on my own or with someone else."

"Well," Paul said, "I am glad to hear 'organizing.' There are many unaffiliated saints on the road. But what do they accomplish? These good people come to a town, talk about Jesus without knowing what they are saying, get everyone agitated, and then move on, without putting down any roots for our master. The next week someone else comes claiming to be the Great Goatgod and they all forget Jesus and start making a religion of courting their neighbor's wife or their neighbor's . . . goat."

"In Borhaurus, our intent was to put down seeds that would take root. Organization was extremely important to us."

"Yes, of course it was. You are a Roman," he remarked.

I could not help smiling. He had said it with a touch of scorn. Yet it was common knowledge that he or his father or grandfather had bought Roman citizenship for him.

"And you are not?"

He looked nettled, then smiled. "Well deserved," he answered. "Yes, my father paid five hundred drachmas three months before I was born for the prerogatives of Rome. But to return to where we were. You were saying you were also thinking of a mission with 'someone else.'" He was still smiling. "Perhaps the dangerous, frightening, heretical Antiochians?"

"Yes, definitely. I had also thought of Thomas, John, Peter . . ."

"Thomas is not on the road and John, well, he is too often with the angels to get much done. Count on it, only Cephas—Peter—or I would do, if you are serious."

"I would not have become a Nazarene if I were not serious. I did not have an unpleasant life, you know. I may be a bit shallow, but I have never taken vows lightly."

"Yes, that *is* a very interesting point. Being shallow and being serious are *not* mutually exclusive. It remains to be seen, however whether you *are* shallow. You talked with Cephas?"

"And Thomas. As you said, he does not want to go. It was Pete who said that I would have to be circumcised."

"Such a forbidding consideration for the Jews. A pity."

"But you did it yourself with—"

"With Timothy. I should not have. He was raised a pagan. Though his mother is Jewish, his father, dead now, was a Roman aqueduc engineer in Lystra. But at the time it was expedient. I have done wors than that." He looked reflective, sighed, and came back to me. "So with Cephas, you left it at . . . ?"

"That I would think about it."

"Arrogant, arrogant. Our savior's *Petros* invites a Christian *infant*— only a year, is it not?—and you *think* about it. Most young Christian would have legated themselves to death by stoning for such a chance.

"Peter did not make me feel that way."

"But I do?"

The talk had become intense. "Yes. You seem to be putting me on trial. Peter did not."

"You think not, unh?"

"I am a lawyer. I did not come here to play games. I know you are much older. I know you are a hero, even a hero of mine. But this inquisition is not necessary."

"Ah, Demas, it is. I do not buy donkeys in the dark."

Peter had taken only two minutes to invite me. I thought of breaking off the interview with Paul at this point and leaving. He was boring irritatingly beneath my skin. But if I turned down Peter, then there *was* only Paul.

"Well," I said, more than a little nervous, "ask, then."

He rose and went to the corner by the door and brought back a round of barley bread, two cucumbers, a knife, and a large cruet of water. We ate, and between bites, he said, "I am satisfied that you have given me the best answers you could about why you came to Christianity. They seem honorable. But your account raised other questions. I am curious as to how you feel about your father, for example?"

It seemed an odd place to recommence. But Paul must have known that younger men cast him, perhaps unkindly, in the role of a second father, so therefore his question was not odd at all. "I understood his need to compromise," I answered. "I felt he went beyond what he had to. Ultimately, he should have taken a stand even if it cost him recall."

"Or his life?"

"I do not think it would have come to that."

"But if it had?"

"Then probably he should have risked it."

"And the lives of his family as well?"

"I would not have asked that of him."

"You have not yet told me how you *feel* about him."

"At first, I was angry, lost. This monument of behavior, his example, had turned out to be made of sand. I remain resentful, and yet I also feel his absence. But I cannot let myself be burdened with what Father and I did to each other."

"How does he feel about you?"

"He loves me," I said, feeling freed of something in saying it. "He wishes, as I do, that things had been different. But it appears he cannot even write and tell me this."

"And your colleague, Deborah bas Sirach? You spoke little of her, but I am told she was the leader in Borhaurus. Most unusual, a woman, and therefore a most unusual woman."

What did he know? "You mean how do I *feel* about her?"

"Yes."

"I love her and I respect her."

"And she you?"

"The same, I am sure." The currents were becoming treacherous. I must swim well or I would, as far as Paul was concerned, drown. "What you are looking for is a delicate way to ask me what there was between us." I felt him tensing. "We were involved in this cause, dedicated to rebuilding a church in a town where the last minister was martyred. It was hardly the place for a dalliance."

"Yet, under other circumstances . . . ?"

I resented his probing, and repaid him by dissembling. "As I said, we had a cause and she felt, in a sense, married to Jesus Christ. Besides, she was raised as a Pharisee. Her attitude on chastity would have been that even if I had sought . . . favors, she would have said no."

"There was no talk of marriage? I ask now because . . ."

"Because you do not want to be left in the cart tracks by a bridegroom deserting you for a bride? I do not think we could marry. There was something in her"—and my heart curled at this great falsehood—"that was not going to be acceptable for me in terms of wife, motherhood, homemaking. . . ."

"That is an involved answer."

"Yours was an involved question."

"There were other women?"

My lying done, I felt I could face anything, even telling the truth. "I did what others did. I am a normal man." He waited. "I had my share of flirtations. And when I was at school there was a prostitute or two. I was not an angel, but perhaps less lustful than most."

"You say 'a normal man' as if lust were intrinsic to normality. Do you think it dwells in us all?"

Long ago in Scythopolis, he had said our bodies were the temples of Jesus and were demeaned by lust. I had the feeling sexuality was something that both fascinated and repelled him. Tread cautiously, I thought. "I think it exists in most people to some extent," I said. "But one can more or less push it out of his mind. How have you handled it?"

I had ambushed him. He was patently nervous. "It has not been a problem for me as it apparently has been for you and, as you say, most

156

people. I am blessed on that score. However, I do believe it is better to marry than to burn with—and because of—lust. Let us move on. I know about your fight with robbers at the time of Andrew's death. You killed all three?"

"Four."

"Four. To protect your life . . ."

"And Andrew's . . ."

He nodded. "Yes, Andrew's, too. I am frankly at a loss as to how Jesus would have responded. Certainly, if it had happened in the first week of his ministry and he had turned the other cheek, he would have been killed and there would be no Christianity. So let us say you were right to fight them off. Did you have to kill them all?"

"Three, yes. The fourth I could have spared."

"Then why . . . ?"

"He had tried to kill me. He had mortally wounded Andrew. Even so, I had a thought of letting him go. But he would have been in the woods while I was tending Andrew's wounds. I could not risk it. I might if it happened now."

He questioned me about my Jewish relatives in Judaea, about which Roman officials I knew, about my finances and my health. We discussed my law skills and how they might be useful to him as well as a means of making money for me on the road. He asked me, pointedly now, whether I could take orders.

"You may recall," he said, "that on our last visit you reminded me that I took a beating in Scythopolis. I told you I disapproved of Tractus fighting back." Once again, I marveled at his memory. "Do you think you could take such a beating if it were in the interests of our work?"

"Well, to what end?"

"If I asked you to do it, I do not think I would want to be questioned. The point is, it could have a desirable effect on students, or townspeople."

I felt my nose, remembered my anger.

"It would be difficult, very difficult," I said. "I understand the benefits, and yet . . . well, I would try."

We had finished eating. He had said he wanted to dictate his notes by evening. Perhaps to Paul that meant midnight. He was tired, too, for he leaned against the wall as he questioned me. He asked me what I thought about drunkenness, sloth, gluttony, cruelty, envy, and so on. I answered as I had preached in Borhaurus: that I was against them all but made distinctions in how intensely I felt about each one. It appeared he was going to argue the point, but he moved on.

He asked me about whether I believed in Jesus as the son of God, his miracles, his dying for the sins of mankind, his resurrection and the certainty of a Day of Judgment. I made myself something more of a believer than I had preached, while admitting to some doubts. Again, he only nodded, as if he were aware of my watery views but wanted to hear them from me.

"I suppose you are interested in what I believe," he said, and I knew the interview was coming to an end.

"I have the feel of it from your questions, and from what people say about you," I said.

"And that is?"

I said I believed that he loved Jesus and God, and believed that Jesus was the redeemer of mankind, that he saw them as son and father. His words on love of God and man in Scythopolis, I said, had affected me so much that I had written them down and, as a minister, had used them in my conversations and sermons. I said I was sure he also believed in sharing the wealth, in hard work, in organizing as the secret to strong churches, in poverty for Christ's ministers, in courage, in truthfulness, in loyalty.

"Not at all off the mark," he said, "but something wants to be added in fairness to you. I suffer from a touch of scorn, which is the first cousin to hubris. Jesus so far has not seen fit to grant my prayers and relieve me of it."

He talked of Jesus differently from the disciples. They talked of Jesus as if they sensed God in a man. Paul seemed only theoretically to sense man in a God. But then, of course, he had not been with Jesus, seen as the others had that Jesus, like all of us, dropped his *saq*—loin cloth—to defecate.

Shadows dimmed the room. The sun had left the single window. "You have been impressive," he said. "You have lived up to my reports." There was no manipulation now, just a statement of his feelings.

At that moment, I liked this small, brilliant man; no matter what his decision on me was going to be. I had been slippery about a good deal of the theology, and I had been dishonest about Deborah. Still, I was willing to be judged on what I had said and not said. "What do you really think of me?" I asked him. "Nobody has ever put me through anything like this before."

"Well," he said, "you are skeptical, undisciplined, rebellious, recalcitrant, probably reckless, and your idea of Christianity is different from mine, perhaps more different than I know." I must have looked unveiled. He smiled, not the dazzling one, but one of fatigue and satisfaction. "And if I invited you on my next mission . . . ?"

I gasped. "To where?"

"First to winter in Antioch. Then, I think in spring along the coast to Ephesus and on to Philippi, Thessalonica, Corinth, it is by no means fixed. And it is by no means certain that after Antioch you would still want to come—or that I would still want to have you. But *if* I asked you . . . ?"

"Well, *if* you did, I would surely pray over it."

And so I did, mulling the pros and contras of Peter and Paul. But try as I might to review only the issues, my thoughts of Deborah interposed themselves between me and my decision. I would be closer to her if I went with Peter, at least until he left Judaea. Yet, if I were in Antioch, might that not tempt her to leave behind her old life entirely and join me? I willed my mind back to the merits. With which disciple could I better serve God? That was the true criterion. It was dawn before I decided: Paul, if he would have me.

Timothy came to my inn at ten and found me sleepless and logy. I knew from his suppressed excitement that Paul was going to ask me to join them. At his room, the apostle beamed. No words from me were needed. On my face he saw that I would go. I embraced him, Silas, and Timothy. There was a sense of purpose in them that made me want to cry out in joy. But their characters were of a less bumptious nature, so I satisfied myself with smiles.

When Peter came back, I told him of my decision.

"I knew you would not be circumcised," he said, not angry at me, but angry. "So we lose you to Paul. And the church of Jesus in the bargain if we keep making imbeciles of ourselves."

XVII

⭒⭒

Despite the dissensions within the council, the disciples all turned out to bid us Godspeed. Only the years separated them from similar mornings when they had taken the road with the master. I was infused with love for this dwindling band who had never given up, never, for all their human failings, ever forgotten the central message of their leader.

Also seeing us off were veiled women and women who had found in Jesus the freedom to put aside their veils, children, farmers in town for the day, men of every craft, a few civil servants, even four Roman auxiliaries in cuirasses who had joined the church. The soldiers had brought two fox tails and some red rags, pagan good luck talismans that the apostles good-naturedly helped tie to the heads of our donkeys.

Peter and John were going with us to Antioch as peace ambassadors. They had talked Bartholomew into changing his vote and Paul would now get his two thousand drachmas. Although I had sold my gelding so I could ride a donkey like the others, I wore my armor. Peter, Timothy, and I carried broadswords, for the sixteen pounds of silver drachmas would be tempting booty. The whole church in Jerusalem knew of it and a few foolish words could apprise the city's fraternity of thieves and thence their brigand brotherhood in the hills.

James, his sparkling beard streaming down his chest like a waterfall, wore a robe with bright blue tassels and a deep blue-and-gold embroidered shawl that could have adorned a high priest. He had brought an earthenware jug for the Communion that was said to have been used at the Last Supper.

In his homily after the Communion, James said, "We hear many versions of Jesus' words. Sometimes even we who knew him best sound like magpies in a field of grain. That is because some of us remember one thing, some another. But we are all still guided by the greatest of the commandments, to love God and man. And so I urge you to live by that golden rule. Preach it to your neighbors. Forgive sins in the name of Jesus Christ."

I was exuberant. For the moment, Deborah was out of my mind. Like these aging men had once done, I was going on the road for Jesus, offering, encouraging, a faith that would make the lives of those who heeded me immeasurably fuller, as it had made mine. Kissing cheeks, we said loving farewells. As we left, members gave us letters for friends and relatives in Tyre, Sidon, Antioch.

We passed the marble colonnades around the spring of Gihon, where Solomon had been crowned, and the pool of Bethesda, where Jesus supposedly had healed cripples. From the pools ran walls of long, thick stones, each drilled, then grouted with lead to carry water all through Jerusalem. Single file we passed the massive Temple. I wondered whether Paul, who looked briefly distracted, was thinking of Stephen, who was martyred there. Or was he merely brooding over mundane organizational problems in Antioch?

We crossed the jammed bazaars, traversed the shadowy street where Jesus had carried the cross, and at the Damascus gate, we waited while a sheep herder drove through his noisy, smelly flock.

Once out of the city, riding past acres of grain in the hot sun, fantasies of Deborah flitted in my brain. Certain configurations of fields, I knew, would always remind me of places we had walked, old walls of places where we had sat. I would find her in roses or the sweetness of hyssop, and summon her up when I saw wine and laughter together on a girl's lips, or a face in the shadow of a loom's upright, or white linen drawn against the thigh of a tall woman as she walked. Then Peter or John would see a familiar landmark and tell us a story of the days with Jesus—and Deborah's enthrallment of me would abate.

On the second day, near Shechem in Samaria, we stopped for lunch by a well. "Oh, Father Abraham," said John—it was a quiet exhalation rather than an invocation—"how many years ago, Peter? Right here, the same well, the same broken wall."

"Twenty-three, twenty-four?"

"The windlass was just worn wood then, not iron like now, thanks to you Romans, Demas"—with John one could believe such remarks were guileless—"and the day was like today. Jesus was sitting on the wall, oh, about where you are now, Silas, tired as a mule at harvesttime, and I was, too, so we two waited for the others to go to town and bring back food."

A woman, John said, had come to the well and Jesus had asked for a drink. She had been snippy because generally Jews shunned Samaritans. Jesus had bantered with her and said, "Everyone who drinks from this well eventually gets thirsty again. But whoever drinks the water I give him will never thirst." Still cheeky, she had asked for some of that water, and he said both she and her husband would get some.

"And she said, 'Sir, I am unwed,' " John recounted, "and Jesus fixed on her as if he were looking inside her head, and said, 'So you are, and you are not yet thirty-five and have had five husbands and the man you live with is not one of them.'

"Well, her eyes almost sprung from her head. 'You are a prophet, straight down from Mount Gerizim,' she said, and Jesus told her, 'Woman, believe me, neither on Gerizim nor in Jerusalem do they worship the true God. For the true God promises our salvation and I am his son and Messiah.' He said it with such authority it frightened her and she ran toward town.

"About that time, Peter and the rest of them came back. Jesus was shaken by what he had said and they asked him what was the matter. 'Why, I just told that woman I was the Messiah, the son of God,' he said. It was the first time he had ever said it so openly. . . ." John chuckled. "Andrew had gotten some special ewe cheese for Jesus and said, 'Well, thanks be to God it's nothing serious. I was afraid you had lost your appetite.' " Even Paul smiled.

"We went in to Shechem and brought over dozens," Peter picked up the story, "but we left no one behind to tend the crop. And today there is no church at all there, just weeds."

We passed Mount Gerizim and headed toward Mount Ebal, the animals straining upward. From our high point, we could see towns and villages, Thebez, Tirzah, Dothan, Samaria itself, the country of the old Jewish judges. As we descended to the ruined towers of Thebez, Paul told of Gideon, who had worshipped a golden idol. Years later, a woman had pushed a millstone from one of those towers on the head of his son by a concubine, Abimelech. Pedantically, Paul drew the moral lesson: the lust and idolatry of Gideon had been punished even unto the second generation. Peter laughed. "Paul, Paul, spare us the sermon. You tell these marvelous stories that we have all forgotten. Let them stand by themselves. You are preaching to believers."

While Peter was our leader and John his deputy, Paul had a special place. Over the years, his face and back had been scarred, just as theirs had been. He had been imprisoned in the same kinds of cells and had been hit by equally hard stones.

I wondered if the sweet poignancy for all three of them on this trip did not have to do with their being alive when so many who had been on the road with them were dead. At times, they must have been sure that they, too, were going to be killed, only to escape. Despite the sometimes appeal of martyrdom, each day must seem to them as, when I thought of the well, it did to me, a gift that might well never have been bestowed.

My armor was dusty and had rubbed blisters. I padded the bronze with rags, but did not take it off. Only recently, the Romans had crucified twenty minor brigands and sent a robber chieftain, Eleazer, who had plagued this region for twenty years, to Rome in chains. But they were still plentiful.

Outside Ptolemais, the Mediterranean breezes dried the perspiration within my armor, cooling and refreshing me. It had been years since I was last by the sea, when Father had taken us to the beaches of Joppa. From the bluffs, I looked at the royal blue carpet stretching to Greece, to Rome, and beyond. I heard the growl of surf, the yawk of birds, and smelled the salt. Soon we saw the port with its sails. Its mariners' calls drifted faintly to us on the wind.

In the days since I had left Borhaurus, my yearning had metamorphosed Deborah into a beautiful phantasm, not always benign, often a temptress, a tormentor. Intellectually, I knew that was unfair, but my pain had been in my soul and in my body, not my mind. But here by the sea I felt promises of far places, a life of undomesticated adventure. The vision of this freer life unshackled me, at least for a time, from Deborah's ghost.

In the town plaza in Ptolemais, a small crowd was gathered around a skinny man naked except for a loincloth. We reined in and listened as his bright mad eyes assessed us.

"Brothers," he adjured us, "I preach the God Yes! He tells us to say yes to everything: yes, I believe in the Olympian gods, yes, in Yahweh of the Jews, yes, in Astarte, yes, in Iris and Nut of the Egyptians, yes, in the Dead God Jesus, and in the gods of the people beyond mountain after mountain to the east, in Krishna and the elephant god Ganesha, in Ghendak and in Chen-su, and in Akatar. Yes!" he shouted. "In love, hate, caresses, rape, disease, health, death, everlasting life." His voice rose hysterically. "Yes! Yes! Yes! In the eternal Yes of God!"

I happened to be beside Paul. "He preaches the divinity as sponge," Paul said. I smiled, but kept my own counsel.

We took the coast road north, staying nights at the homes of Nazarenes. Peter and John, Galilee fishers, were smitten with the seafishing towns, Achzib, Iskandaruna, Tyre. These were in Jerusalem's territory, for the churches had been established by members of the Apostolic Council.

But, in Sidon, it was as if we passed into another country, the land of an ally, but foreign. For here began that vast territory where followers of Jesus were Paulists who called themselves Christians. It was a name I already preferred to Nazarenes. In these domains, as in those we had passed, we did no proselytizing, thus reducing the possibility of discord.

We detoured by way of Damascus. It had been Paul's first stopping place twenty years ago after he was blinded by what he said was the lightning of God. From Damascus, he had gone to Arabia for three years to draw together his thoughts about the new religion of Jesus Christ. Then he had met Peter in Jerusalem and spent two weeks absorbing his stories of Jesus. But disillusioned with the stagnation there, he had returned to Tarsus to work as a tentmaker in his father's large shop and to brood for five years. It was there that the legate of the church in Jerusalem to Antioch, the same Barnabas I had seen at Scythopolis, had found Paul and called him to Antioch.

Now, after all these years, Paul returned to Damascus as a hero bearing the thousand drachmas to set up a seminary. The Damascenes feasted us for two days. We left full of food, wine, and happiness, but as we approached the coast again, drizzles began to dog us. Silas had a cold and our spirits slumped.

We were five miles out of Tripolis when dimly ahead we saw a horseman with a half-dozen or so men behind him, some mounted. The leader posted on his horse like a military man. Three of his men were on donkeys, three straggled behind on foot. As they approached, I saw the horseman's cuirass was Roman. He wore no other armor. He was a Goliath, with arms thick as deer haunches.

Peter cried out in Aramaic with just the right mix of cordiality, vigor, and authority, "Where are you from, friends?"

"From Palmyra," said the horseman in Greek. "I am a soldier of Rome." His great stallion was badly in need of grooming. *Ex*-soldier, I was certain, a deserter, from the looks of his unshaven face, one of those powerful hulks who could neither give nor take orders and were useful in battle only when they were angered at the enemy. He turned cruel and stupid eyes on me. "Who goes with you in such strange armor?"

"We six are brothers in Christ," said Peter.

"My men and I will need your asses," said the horseman. His heavy tones bulged with threat. He looked back to see if there were any other travelers behind him. His pike-bearing footmen and the raggle-taggle donkey riders, armed with swords, spread across the muddy road, blocking it.

"They are not for sale," said Peter, "but we would buy safe passage from you with the gold of heaven. Will you accept Christ Jesus as your master and pray with us?"

It was an odd proposition. The Roman twisted his face. "No man is my master," he said.

"Then Caesar and Rome are not your masters either," said Peter. "Let us pass, brother, and we will pray you will find your way to kneel before Christ Jesus during your journey."

The deserter had made up his mind. "It is a long journey and they," he nodded his head at the three mountless men, "do not plan to go it on foot." His minions cackled and he guffawed at his own wit. At the same time, I saw him feeling the pommel of his long broadsword in its badly worn leather scabbard.

Peter pulled his sword from the sheath and put it across his blanket saddle. Timothy and I also drew. Paul had an oak staff lashed to the side of his donkey and he untied it. Silas fished in his pack for a food knife. I quickly passed Ezra's dirk to him. He was clumsy, but it would serve him better than an onion chopper.

Only John, agitated but resolute, made no move to find a weapon, but he bumped his donkey up toward the front so his life would be equally at hazard if anything happened. It was not as if anyone would question his bravery: only he among the disciples had the courage to wait with the mother of Christ and the former courtesan, Mary Magdalene, at the foot of the cross as Christ died above them. I wished now, however, he were more warlike.

Because I was in armor, I felt I should take the brunt of any attack. I edged my donkey a step forward, letting it seem the animal was shying.

"I would take my hand off that sword if I were you, legionnaire," I said, "and tell your men to let us pass."

"The young man speaks for us all," said Paul. "Let us pass." This was a different Paul from the one who had taken his beating in Scythopolis. Perhaps with these rodents he felt there was no religious or political point to be made by passivity.

The deserter's horse took a side step as its rider tightened the reins.

"Seize their donkeys!" he ordered his crew in broken Aramaic. The footmen pointed their pikes at us. The mounted men raised their swords. In spite of the chill drizzle, I felt my hand sweating on my hilt. I was watching the Roman. I had forgotten how a war-horse towers over a donkey. The rider's muscles swelled as his hand tightened on his sword grip. Suddenly, he wheeled the horse and pulled the enormous blade from its scabbard, intending to crash it down on Paul. But he never even got it raised enough to swing.

My broadsword was sharp as a razor, for I kept it in Roman order, and with a single motion I whirled it back and around. With this momentum and all my strength behind it, I hacked into the giant's unprotected thigh. The man bellowed as his horse reared, flinging him backward but not throwing him. His far foot had caught in the stirrup. Blood spurted from the leg.

I scrambled off the donkey as a pikeman ran at me. He struck my armor at the shoulder. The spear slid and he slammed into me, costing him his balance. I staggered, but he fell. As he put a hand down to raise himself, I slashed. The bloody sword cut through his elbow as if it were a skinned rabbit. He looked at the cleaved forearm, his widened eyes unbelieving. His mouth formed a voiceless "O" as he gripped the gushing stump. The two other spearmen had rushed to help him but saw the fountain of blood and stopped, transfixed. It was then I saw their faces. They were mere dirty boys, not yet turned eighteen.

"Back," I howled, feinting at the spearmen's heads. Their paralysis broke and they jerked rearward, one stumbling and falling on his back. I rushed up as if to impale him and he screamed, "No, no, no!" I stamped his arm, and he released the lance, which I kicked off into the mud.

The shrieks of their leader were hideous. His gigantic horse reared in panic, whipping its rider this way and that as his leg rained blood. To my right, Peter grappled with a mounted man, both roaring as each tried to topple the other. The remaining brigands on donkeys, like drunken Dionysian dancers, twirled and flopped, too occupied with controlling their steeds to fight. Timothy had dismounted and, sword drawn, faced the last armed pikeman, trying to reason with him.

We were dealing with rural pagan cowards, newly recruited by this oaf, who had probably deserted when he was demoted into some unit of Palmyra auxiliaries. He had promised them spoils, no doubt, and they had taken three donkeys in their initial foray, perhaps without a fight. There was not a warrior among them. The spectacle of their chief, his half-severed leg slapping the horse, his life's blood spurting;

of the one-handed pikeman spinning voicelessly on the ground; and of Peter, now slamming his adversary's head into the mud, demoralized the rest.

The man in front of Timothy listlessly dropped his pike and Timothy stuck it neatly in the ground. I hurried to Peter, squatted, and knocked his opponent in the side of the head with the pommel of my sword, feeling very Christian about not taking the surer course and putting my sword in his guts. The final four wallowed through the mud into a field where they waited, far enough away to escape if we pursued them.

Timothy caught the bridle of the frantic horse. The wreck of the Roman lay on the ground, his good leg, still in the stirrup, pointed heavenward. I went cautiously around the animal and cut the strap. The sight of the fallen horseman's gory leg reminded me of Rechab and I began to get sick. Paul hurried up, dropped his staff and put his worn leather belt around the man's upper thigh as a tourniquet much as the animal man had on Rechab. Paul's face was oddly reposed, as was the unconscious Roman's, unlikely twins. I put my sword down by Paul.

"Here, take the rest off," I said, then turned to avoid retching. Timothy and John were putting a tourniquet on the severed arm of the pikeman. I realized I had committed all the carnage, even the bashing of the man who lay in the mud holding his aching pate. But my colleagues were repairing it.

The uninjured brigands all stood in the field now, wondering what we planned to do with their wounded comrades. They had managed to calm their three donkeys. Paul shouted over at them that we would help them rig a litter with cloaks so they could carry the Roman and the one-handed man, too, if he could not be helped on foot. The bandit I had hit in the head began slithering toward the other four. When the robbers saw we did not hinder them, two cautiously came and dragged back the man with one hand.

"Cephas," said Paul, "we must take the Roman to Tripolis. The others would leave him for the animals. He is not of them."

Peter looked at John, who agreed with Paul. "The Romans will take him off our hands and put him on a cross," said Peter.

"We must try," said John.

My feeling was that we had shown more forbearance than they deserved already. I would have put the Roman out of his misery. He was not a brave adversary, just a murderous brute. But John was morally right. Yes, his head would end on the walls of Tripolis, but we would have done the godly thing.

We put the Roman across his horse, but three miles down the muddy road his tongue lolled out and his eyes rolled up. We buried him in a shallow ditch. I would have liked to have kept the stallion to curry it into military condition. But I saw the wisdom of turning in such an obviously Roman beast to the garrison in Tripolis.

The Romans let us camp in their courtyard. By the fire, Peter, Silas, and I drank more wine with less water than usual. We talked of the fight with the robbers, and what it meant to turn the other cheek and to love one's neighbor next only to God.

"The question for Demas just before he swung his sword," Peter said, "was whether he should love and be a good neighbor to Paul or to the deserter. He chose Paul, thanks be to God."

"How do we draw lines?" asked Silas, "Suppose they had been seven poor, crippled brothers on the way to Tripolis to visit their dying mother. Should we have given up our drachmas and our asses and walked?"

"The asses, yes; the money, no," said Peter, "and picked up the asses when we got to Tripolis if they had not stolen them."

"Here is a more complicated dilemma," said Paul, "suppose we were all ridden with fever and crossing a mountain pass in winter and found Silas's same seven brothers shivering for lack of cloaks. Should we give them our cloaks, even if by doing so we risk death which would prevent us from ministering the bread and wine of life to thousands on the other side of the mountain?"

Peter grabbed Paul's cloak at the shoulder and gave it a rough but friendly shake. "The missioners are you, Paul, and I know what you did because Barnabas told me. You gave up the cloak and cursed near died of your chills." The rest of us joined in Peter's laughter and Paul, delighted to be discovered, blushed, his face happy as a homely child's who has, to his surprise, pleased his playmates.

"But bring it back to today . . ." Peter said, when the raillery had died down.

"Ideally," said Paul, "John's actions were the answer."

"I'm glad you said ideally," said Peter. "You were whacking around with that stave. . . ."

"True," said Paul, "I look at some things Jesus said as general principles to which I aspire, and others as explicit directions, which I must heed."

"Well, *that*," said Peter, "was the way Jesus looked at it. He would say one thing and do another. He said don't preach to Samaritans, then did. He said 'Blessed are the meek,' but was like Gog and Magog when he was kicking pigeon cages and whipping sheep and heifers out of the Temple. And John, remember he said never call anyone a fool or we would wind up in hellfire, then lo and behold I was at dinner once with him and some Pharisees, and he called them fools to their faces. I can't even remember why."

"Then should we be preaching him as perfect?" I asked, emboldened by the wine.

"I cannot say that I do," said Peter. "I preach him as a brother, a human who was here and told us the ways of God and then became one. It seems to work." But did it? Or did Peter hold together his churches by the strength of his personality, his own great decency and energy and humanity? Was he not less a revealer of Jesus' and God's words than a demigod himself, sometimes more Olympian than Christian? When he left for Rome, might his churches not shrivel up and disappear like leaf mold?

Paul, if he was thinking as I was, and I suspected he was, did not do the uncivil thing and say it. Instead, he temporized: "Speaking only for myself, I do not preach an incomplete and faulted God. There may have been contradictions in the master, but to preach a halfway god, in my view, is to invite defeat. I preach a God without faults. We—and Timothy and Silas can bear me out on this—urge our followers to emulate the perfection of Christ Jesus in order to achieve their own perfectibility. We offer them God's salvation in a life beyond this one if they exert themselves in trying to be good."

"It brings more over," Peter said a little harshly, the wine beginning to talk. He threw a log on the fire. "God knows it brings more over, but it's hypocritical."

Paul's wrinkled face pursed, but he did not lash back. Instead, in the grip of his iron will, he inflicted on himself his iron honesty. "I accept that, Cephas. I accept the sin of hypocrisy. I bear that cross. I do not like to carry it. But I bear it for the sake of the many." Unlike most evenings, we broke up uncomfortably, even John looking solemn.

Yet, in the morning, the sky cloudless, the sea breeze landward, the red tile rooftops of Laodicea ahead, we again rode on as boon companions. To the north around the most distant cape was Antioch, third city of the empire after Rome and Alexandria.

Paul had been away on this second of his missionary trips for three years. He had first come to Antioch as a follower of Christ ten years before. Now he was the heart and soul of its church. Because of his trips, the church did not have to put up with his authoritarianism day in, day out. It could honor him for his great strengths, knowing he would soon be on his way again.

As we approached Antioch, faster-moving travelers saw Paul and

excitedly greeted him, taking into the city news of our arrival. A crow
poured out to meet us. They churned around us; children pointe
dogs barked. Motley, joyful, formless, we marched toward Antioch. A
the gates, a contingent of Roman soldiers, the sun bright on their ches
armor, blocked us. But their captain recognized Paul, perceived th
peaceful nature of our progress, and shouted an order. The soldiers fel
in at our sides, confining our parade, yet also licensing it.

Singing the thanksgiving hymns of David, we tramped across th
Corso's enormous paving stones, pristine marble columns on eithe
side. I craned my neck, aware but not caring that I was the quintessen
tial country lawyer come to the megalopolis. Looking down the Cors
to the mountain beyond, I saw at its foot a gleaming golden statue c
Jupiter, eyes seemingly fixed on us.

Such richness I had never even dreamed! Fountains, public baths
canals, five-storied palaces, some Grecian, some Roman, some wit'
squat Oriental balconies on every floor. Then, suddenly, we turne
from the Corso, passing drab factories for cloth and metal goods
stonecutting shops and the huddled houses of workers. Our song
soared skyward, amplified by the buildings on either side that cuppe
them like a pair of giant hands.

In the midst of this happy turbulence, I felt for the first time not ju:
the joy of Christianity, but its might. From a few families in th
quarter of Epiphania, the church had grown into a powerful an
many-hued mixture of Greeks, Romans, Jews, Cyrenes, Phoenician
Syrians of a half-dozen minor races, Nigers, even Scythians and F₂
Asians.

To the Roman authorities, most of them at heart agnostics, th
Christians with their busy meeting place on Sidon Street were just on
more exotic sect. In Antioch, the Romans tolerated them all. Amon
its half-million people were worshippers of the Olympians, of Astarte
Attis, Isis and Osiris, Sabacia, Sandan. There were even a few ne
Molochians who carried out clandestine human sacrifices from time ▪
time.

The rich Jewish community had built a majestic synagogue th
displayed the massive silver lamps and burnished copper pots stole
from Jerusalem by Antiochus IV. It accepted not just pagans wh
embraced Judaism, but the "proselytes of the gate" who attende
services even though they generally ignored Mosaic Law.

Our marchers stopped. In front of our church building, five elde
in pristine linen robes held out their hands to us. Paul dismounted an
kissed the stone steps at the feet of the chief elder. Then, happy as
freshly coronated king, he gave the old man a great hug, and intr

duced Peter, John, and the rest of us, who also embraced the elder. The crowd loved it, standing on their toes to see. Timothy—but none of the rest of us—also kissed the steps. The gesture offended the Aesubius in me.

That evening, bathed and in a clean Jewish-cut robe loaned me by the couple giving me and Silas room and board, I went to the love feast, held on tamped ground behind the church. If ever Paul, Peter, and John needed to see the reflection of their greatness, the celebration provided it. One after another, Christians came up to them to touch them, pat them, shake their hands, embrace them.

Paul looked bibulous with happiness. But that would be all he would be drunken from. He waved off all offers from people wanting to pour him more wine. Peter let the wine flow into his cup. Gray-haired and handsome in his brawny, florid way, he was surrounded by men and comely matrons. The women had that air of self-possession one sees in those who have gotten what they want in life but would not mind getting more. Peter looked like he wished he dared oblige.

Church men turned a goat, a sheep, and an ox's haunch on spits, and dispensed wine from engorged skins hung by the legs from cross-beams. At long tables, women served vegetables of every kind from shallow baskets, and bread ranging from heavy wheat rounds to tiny honey cakes. When we had all made a good start on the food, the feast was adjourned—to be picked up after the Communion. A whole second day was planned. But the Antiochians had wisely divided the feast into two parts this evening lest the Communion be beyond the powers or even the inclinations of the celebrants.

The church was crowded, and there were worshippers outside the front and rear doors. Peter preached. His booming Greek, fogged with the accents of Galilee, made him sound as if he came from some distant, primitive time. He spoke of the night before the crucifixion, how Jesus had told him and John to find an upper room and how they had arranged for a meal of goat stew, vegetables, bread and wine. Judas had gone with them.

"We had to let him, he carried the purse," Peter explained, to laughter. They had just begun eating the good food, Peter continued, when Jesus, calm as a man saying he had just bought a new tunic, told them he would not be with them for such suppers again because his next meal would be in heaven. They had questioned him, and he had said he was going to be betrayed but would be preparing a place for them with God.

They had pressed him about the betrayer, but he had shaken his head and they had gone on with the feast. Peter said that when they were about half finished, Jesus, who had just broken his bread into pieces and was about to dip one in goat gravy, stopped as if something amazing had just occurred to him. "He hit his bowl with his spoon to quiet us," Peter recounted, "and asked us all to take a piece of the bread he had broken. 'Whenever you are together eat a piece of bread and consider it my body,' he said. And he poured a cup of wine, and passed it around and said, 'And when you share a cup as we are doing, think of it as my blood, the blood of the *new* covenant.'

"He was like that, wanting to leave us with something important, but easy to remember. A couple of us began to cry," Peter said, "especially this one," he put his arm around the slight frame of John. "And ever afterward, when we are sharing a meal, we call it a love feast, and then we share the pieces of bread and the wine and call it the Communion. I can tell you, my brother and sisters, if he were here tonight in body as he is in spirit, he would be wonderfully happy.

"Like John and me and most of the rest, he was a simple man from Galilee, except for his great brain and spirit. Like us, his Greek was bad. Like us, he hardly even knew how to talk to Gentiles, much less get along with them. But also like us, he would have learned on the instant here in Antioch from the love you have shown us, and he would have embraced you as we do."

At that, the congregation inside and outside the building roared in a dozen different accents with love for Peter, for the great God he preached, and for our glorious faith.

Timothy and I carried a large basket of round loaves down the aisle and the church elders broke them up and gave them to Peter and John, who handed out the pieces. The recipients nibbled and passed the bread on so that all might have some from the hands of the disciples as they had received it that night from the hands of Jesus. Silas and Paul passed out small jugs of blessed wine filled from the skins outside. When we had made our way through the church, we went to the street, where many of the merely curious—unbaptized, I suspected—got a bit of bread and a dollop of wine. Then the love feast continued.

I drank moderately. I knew Paul was still testing me. I very much wanted to go on his next mission even though nothing on my journey northward had swayed me from my original preference for Peter. But the amicable way in which Gentiles were accepted in Antioch had fortified my resistance to circumcision for the sake of expediency. Besides, Paul's promise of far places was more inviting than trudging through dissentious Palestine—even with Peter. And I could still not see any way for me to go to Rome as a minster so long as Father was there.

I was moving among the feasters, happily breathing in the smells of cooking meat, fennel, anise, and cumin, when a young couple, the man in a *mestri* tunic, the woman unveiled and in a fashionably cut toga, stopped me. They asked me in good Greek about the trip north, and in a few minutes, there were other young people around me. One woman had the light looks I had seen on some northern Galatians, blond-brown hair, pale blue eyes, full even lips. She was not beautiful, but lush. As we chatted, her eyes told me as distinctly as if they were tongues that I might pay court on her if I sought it. But playing squire to a rich young Antioch Christian was not something I could risk.

As I walked to my lodgings, her image made me remember how good a woman's flesh felt to eager hands, how hungry their lips were in the toils of passion. I had suppressed lust for weeks, because when it came, it was alloyed with disruptive memories of Deborah. Tonight, lust had returned, not chained to Deborah, but as powerful and uncontaminated desire.

After Peter and John went back to Jerusalem, we settled in for the winter. Paul busied himself with every aspect of the Antioch church and wrote lengthily to the churches he had founded or strengthened on his missionary trips. Poor as the roads were—sea travel was impossible—he dispatched Timothy and Silas on trips of up to a week around Syria and Cilicia.

During these periods, I helped Paul with secretarial work, appeared for him at minor meetings, drafted routine letters. Paul's mind amazed me, grasping complexities before they were half spelled out, always aflow with ideas for money, for new missions into Arabia and Mesopotamia, for beneficial interchanges with city governments, churches, community leaders. Yet, occasionally, I felt that while Paul loved mankind, he was somewhat mechanical in his love of people. By that I mean if he saw a beggar or needy child, we had to restrain him from emptying his pockets. He was genuinely ready to die for humanity or even an individual if it served the purposes of God. I was just not sure that he was willing to *think* about individuals in order to understand what was in their hearts and heads.

All winter, even with his church tasks, he worked in a factory as a master tentmaker, true to his belief that ministers should pay their way, a practice I followed. I rented a small office near the tiered courthouse. Based on Paul's reputation, I soon had all the cases I could handle. I kept money for my needs and turned the rest over to Paul for the church and our trip, for as each day passed, I was more certain that he would take me.

I thought often of Deborah and, finally, although she might have

173

preferred I did not, I wrote her, telling of the trip to Antioch and the journey to come. At the end of my letter, after a number of false starts, I decided that truth was more important than walking on my toes around her feelings. I told her I still wanted to marry her and urged her to write.

On balance, it was a busy, productive winter. "On balance," because at times I went off balance. My cravings, following the fleeting encounter with the young woman at the love feast, had been symptomatic. Paul, as he had told me and for whatever reason, did not suffer from lust. How Timothy and Silas had banished it, or whether it had ever afflicted them, I did not ask. For my part, I burned, as Paul had put it, well into December. I prayed that my lust would be extinguished.

But it was not. Just as in Scythopolis and Lydda, I weighed the guilt I would feel in assuaging lust against the distress of my unslaked desire. Desire finally won. I found a brothel whose gold, marble, and flesh befitted the capital of the Roman middle east. It was well on the other side of the Corso from our church and the Christian quarter, therefore meeting a member of our church either as patron or practitioner was unlikely. My few visits left me physically more at ease, although I would have preferred to have taken up my ministry in Galatia and beyond with a less shadowed conscience.

XVIII

❖❖

In late winter, Titus, the follower of Paul who, I recalled, had refused circumcision, rode in agitated and weary on a large, ragged donkey. Titus was my age, a Greek Phrygian commoner with thick black brows and hair, and unkempt beard. Paul spoke with him privately, then summoned a meeting of the elders, Silas, Timothy, and me. I had never seen Paul so angry.

"Jerusalem"—he made it sound synonymous with "Antichrist"—"has dispatched a countermission to Galatia. So miserly, so selfish, that we had to beg for a decent gift for Damascus and Corinth, they are rich enough, *spiteful* enough, to try to undermine me"—he quickly corrected "me" to "us"—"in Derbe, Lystra, Iconium," ringing out the names as if they were his daughters who had been raped and murdered by savages.

The rest of us were almost as outraged as Paul. He had founded or rebuilt many of the Asia Minor churches in his first mission with Barnabas and a man named Mark seven years ago. On his second mission, which had ended at Jerusalem in the fall, he, Silas, Timothy, and, for part of it, a doctor, Luke, had shored up the same churches. Both trips had originated in Antioch with the assent of Jerusalem. So the countermission was, as Paul's tones suggested, a violation of Christly agreements.

Titus had been returning from a trip to northeastern Nabataea by way of Jerusalem and Peter had honorably told him the whole scheme. Titus had ridden night and day to Antioch, twice outrunning robbers, once swimming beside the ass through a stream swollen with floods that had torn down its bridge. He was clearly as tough as salted fish, and also resourceful.

He reported that Peter, supported by John and Philip, had vehemently opposed the countermission. But the majority had prevailed. One of their arguments had been Peter's own earlier one: that Jerusalem needed to branch out as Antioch had done. The leader of this raiding party was to be James, son of Alphaeus, who, Titus recalled, so mad he sputtered, had also instigated the move to circumcise him.

The countermission was going by land to Sidon, taking the first spring boat to Tarsus, then crossing the mountains into Galatia. This destroyed Paul's plans for a voyage around the perimeter of the Aegean, calling at port cities and making trips into the Galatian hinterland. For to reach the churches before the Jerusalem mission and brace them against what Paul saw as apostasy, we would have to abort the sea trip and make a hazardous crossing of the Taurus Mountains before the snows left the passes. Paul and the elders drafted an indignant letter to Jerusalem, then we began planning the overland trip.

The countermission brought other problems. Silas, usually so phlegmatic, wanted to meet with the Jerusalem mission and reason with them. Like Barnabas before him, he had been a legate from Jerusalem to Antioch, then worked briefly with Peter. The fervor Paul and the Antioch church generated had led him to switch his allegiances. Yet, I sensed in him a devotion to the ways of the Law, and to his vestigial bonds with Jerusalem. After discussion, his pacificatory idea was rejected by all.

We left in April, a light wind carrying in the warm sea air. We looked more like merchants than missioners: three of our donkeys were costly gray Muscats, the others powerful Lycaonians, all groomed by church members and garlanded by them as we left. I noticed Titus had joined our armed ranks. Strapped to his donkey at an easy reach was a thin, long Galatian sword.

The Roman basalt highroad took us through groves of myrtles, which gave way to oak forests as we reached the hills. On this route, so familiar to Paul, he pointed out Roman castles and gave us the histories of the small, busy ports along the coast. In Tarsus, Paul went alone to see his father, now senile and in the care of a cousin. Paul's only other close relatives, a sister and her son, both Pharisaic Jews, lived in Jerusalem and shunned him as an unbeliever, which I knew sorrowed him.

We learned from local merchants and port workers that the Jerusalem mission had not yet reached Tarsus. That night at supper, the five of us were discussing supplies and routes, when Silas again brought up the matter of reconciliation.

"Paul," he said, "they are brother Christians. We all know the nature of James, but surely some will be friendly. If they heed us and go back, good. If not, we are worse off only by a day or two. It may even be we can find some way to continue on together, each making allowances for the other."

Silas had shared all Paul's sufferings on the second missionary trip, even to being flogged and jailed with him in Philippi. I thought of him as submissive, but I also knew I did not fully read his thoughts. While my sentiments were with Paul, I felt Silas had a right to be heard out, his views reconsidered.

"Sylvanus, Sylvanus," said Paul with mild sarcasm, calling him by his Roman name, for Silas's family had also bought him Roman citizenship. "It is settled. We leave tomorrow." Silas looked sullen, but let his hands drop from the table into his lap as if to say, "What is the use?"

That noon, mounted travelers arrived from the east. They had turned back from the mountains. The snow was still deep and the gorges were passable only on foot. The news obliged us to sell our fine donkeys and much of our gear, and repack.

Tarsan Christians accompanied us as far as the last of the Cilician summer villas, taking turns carrying our packs. Next day, we labored upward, first through junipers and hardwoods, then Aleppo pines. As we climbed higher, the pines grew more gnarled from the unrelenting winter winds. Soon, small, low huts of woodsmen and goat herders were the only signs of habitation.

Paul would soon be fifty and looked older, Silas was forty-two, Timothy twenty-eight, and Titus and I both twenty-six. But the two older men set the pace and it was a brisk one. I carried my armor and it burdened me, but I would not leave it behind. Timothy, Titus, and I alternated shouldering the heavy three-man goat-hair tent we shared.

The Roman road was cobbled now only where the rainy season or thaws from snows would otherwise leave it a muddy swamp. Soon even these patches of stones ended and we were left with what was exaggeratedly called a military road. At a brief rest stop, Paul pointed to the snowy peaks ahead where we could see a ravine like a gray scar on a stern white face.

"The beginning of the Cilician Gates," he said with a smile at Silas.

"I thought when I first heard of them that they would be gates, with hinges on them," Silas said. I was glad to see things had become better between them.

As we entered the mountains, Paul recounted how the conquering armies of Xerxes, Darius, and Alexander had all traversed the Cilician Gates—albeit between late spring and early fall, when wheeled vehicles could pass.

Once into the valleys, we lost the sun early. The crashing streams beside us brought biting cold. At the end of the second day's climbing, Paul began to falter. He paused often, breathing hard, his face flushed. The next morning, he stopped to rest before we had traveled an hour. He sat panting while Silas gave him water from his goatskin and felt his head.

"How hot?" asked Paul leadenly.

"Hot enough." Silas sighed. "How bad is it?"

"Bad enough."

"There is a guardhouse soon."

"Two, three miles," said Paul, rising shakily to go on.

Timothy, just ahead of me, told me quietly that Paul had an attack of recurring fever once on the last trip. Paul thought it was something he had gotten as a child from the morasses of Pamphylia, perhaps malaria. Another half hour, and Paul had to stop again. He was wise enough to realize if we tried to go on, it would be dangerous for him. The day was overcast; the wind whistled down the gorge. Paul's face was as red as cooked beets from just his small efforts of the morning.

We started a fire despite the wind and heated a pot of bitter polygonum tea cooked in barley water. Silas gave Paul draught after draught. His eyes were bleary, but the potion gave him enough strength for us to half carry him to the guardhouse.

In the warm if drafty stone building, the four Romanized Gauls on duty made room for all of us. We were the first large group this year, for only couriers and a few hardy loners had preceded us. The countermission, we were sure, would now be close behind, but it was two more days before even Paul thought it was safe for him to go on.

Again on the way, as we climbed higher, the air grew thin and the defile narrowed in places to twenty feet. Wooden ramps built on ledges hewn into the rock wall had broken and fallen into the ravine during the winter. On hands and knees, we picked our way across the rocks where the ramps had been anchored. Far down in the crevasse, the stream roared so loudly we could not hear each other. Its spume rose like greasy smoke, making the trail slick. A misstep could send us tumbling into the torrent. On either side, limestone cliffs rose whitely for a thousand feet.

At last, the path widened and then opened into a small level area where flat stones blackened by smoke indicated that travelers had camped there. From the campsite, a rope and plank bridge crossed the ravine, guyed sturdily to iron spikes in stones. It was forty feet long and wide enough for carts, a small Roman engineering masterpiece.

Two hundred dizzying feet below, the stream crashed on rocks and plunged and foamed down waterfalls. I fixed my eyes on Silas's back, and crept along. At the other side, I relaxed, but caught a superior look from Titus, who had crossed the swaying bridge as if it were no more challenge than a doorsill.

A half mile onward, we came to another open place between towering cliffs. Paul was again flagging, and Silas called a halt. We built a fire and pitched our tents, then Titus went back down the trail to move his bowels. When he returned, he looked perturbed, but said nothing. Black Hades, not him, too, I cursed, believing he might be getting sick.

That night, as Timothy snored, Titus nudged me awake.

"Hunh? What?" I said with a start.

"Be quiet," he whispered. "Don't wake him. Come."

We squirmed out of the tent, I behind him. But our motion wakened Timothy. "What . . . ?" he muttered.

"Sleep," said Titus. "We have to piss. Keep the mat warm." Satisfied, Timothy grunted, pulled his cloak tightly around him and burrowed deeper under the camel's-hair blanket that served all three of us. From beside the tent, Titus took his sword and nodded for me to do the same.

"What is this?" I hissed as we left the campsite and headed back down the trail.

"Wait," he hushed me.

At the turning to the bridge, he motioned me to peer around. By the moonlight, I saw on the other side three large tents, a low fire in front of one. "Jerusalem?" I whispered.

"When I was easing myself, I thought I heard hammering. I looked. They were making camp. I saw James."

"You are sure?"

"I do not forget James," he said with quiet derision.

"We had best tell the others," I said.

"Tell *them?* Idiot! Not on your life. I am going to cut the bridge, keep them out of Galatia. For weeks. Make them go around by sea. And you are going to help me. If we tell Paul, do you imagine for an instant he will let me? Just think a minute."

My first thought was that Titus was out of his mind. It would divide Jerusalem and Antioch forever. On the other hand, if we told Paul, even he would feel there was no way to avoid a parley. If we agreed to go on together, dissension would burst out in every town. Or they would see that Paul was weakened by his illness, hypocritically wish us well, and hurry on.

Titus guessed my thoughts. "Don't think for one second that if that little rat-eye James gets a chance, he won't cut the next bridge as fast as he'd have cut my foreskin."

I smiled. Titus was not generally given to humor. But why should I endanger my position with Paul, so much less secure than Titus's? "Titus, just do the bridge yourself," I said.

"Coward talk! You saw those ropes. I could never cut them alone before they'd hear me and leave those tents like ants swarming out of a hill. It has to be done fast."

"Get Timothy."

Even in the dark, I could see his disgusted look. He did not need to answer. Timothy was too gentle for this work. I was not unflattered that he preferred me. "Eventually, Paul will find out. That will be the end of us," I said.

"No. I know Paul," said Titus again with scorn. "He will do *something*, but not permanently. Take the guy ropes on the left. Saw as far from the bridge as you can. If anybody comes out, stop sawing and hack."

I hesitated still, but he crouched and slunk toward the pair of guys on the right. Over the last two months, I had come to dislike Titus. And he reciprocated. But he also assessed me correctly. I would not let him down. I crept out to the ropes.

Our swords whined. Two-thirds through my first guy, the fibers began to untwine and the rope snapped, flinging the hank toward the bridge like a serpent striking. We listened, then began sawing again. In minutes, we had cut the four guys and started on the two ropes, thick as hawsers, that supported the treadway. Mine gave with a noisy clacking. The span was suspended only by Titus's, the boards pointing down like dried fish on a line. There was a cry from a tent. The first missioner plunged out of the tent, his cloak flapping around him as he grabbed up a scabbarded sword.

"Robbers!" he screamed as he saw us, thinking perhaps we had robbed his fellows and were preventing pursuit. Behind him came others, wielding swords and spears. One grabbed up a pitch torch and set it ablaze in the fire. Titus was still only halfway through. For me to try to synchronize sword strokes on the vee he had cut in the rope would only delay him. I backed up behind the rocks. In a moment, the whole party was there, a dozen of them, their shouts sounding above the torrent's roar. Their torch cast fitful light on Titus, who, all reason for silence gone, hacked away like a woodman gone mad.

"It is Paul's man," shrilled a voice I recognized as James's. "The Phrygian, Titus!"

A man in a caftan called in the resounding tones of an old prophet, "Brother, is this the way to treat fellow Nazarenes? Would you do this in defiance of all the master taught?"

"Heed him," shrieked James. "Let us pray together."

"Pray for yourself," Titus screamed as he chopped. "I *am* Titus, come to circumcise your bridge." The rope squealed and popped apart with a report like a catapult launch. The severed bridge lashed downward, its boards smacking against the opposite side of the ravine with a clattering that reverberated so loudly I feared it would wake Paul. Titus looked at his handiwork, sheathed his sword, and walked to where I hid.

"The curse of God on you, Titus." James's high voice rose above all the others. "The most awful curse of God on you!"

❀

We left early in the morning, Paul worrying more than ever about the Jerusalem countermission being close behind—even as it was making its arduous way back toward Tarsus. Titus and I kept our separate counsels. Two days after we cut the bridge, we reached the end of the Cilician Gates in weather so foggy we could not see fifty yards of the slope downward.

"The worst is over," said Paul.

In the morning, we emerged from the ravine. Sunshine flooded a wide green valley below us. There were tiny huts, and specks of white, at first almost indistinguishable from the patches of disappearing snow. Then I saw they moved. They were goats and sheep beginning their spring pasture. At this homey sight, my heart, so chilled by barren cold and misadventure, moved, too. The road broadened, parts of it cobbled as on the other side of the Cilician Gates. Like a snake, it twisted past hamlets of four or five dwellings. Shepherds and goatherds came eagerly to greet us. They remembered Paul from his journey three years ago and brought us cheese, pitchers of fresh goat and sheep milk, bread. Some walked a stadium or more with us as we passed on talk of the world on the other side of the mountain.

The entry of Paul into Derbe was like a little Antioch. There was a parade, the more joyous because hints of spring were in the air, the more colorful for its rural pagan overtones. There was the love feast, the Eucharist, and afterward a fest with local wines that would have tanned leather, assuming what we drank had not already been used for that purpose. Our hosts were peasants in goat- and sheepskin clothes, townsmen in the garb of the east, and a large number of converted Jews dressed as if for synagogue, and some few young people in Greco-Roman dress.

Most interesting to me were the Gauls, after whom Galatia was named. They were descendants of nomadic hordes which had streamed into Macedonia and Greece two hundred years ago and been invited into Asia Minor to help the warring Bithynians. They had stayed to plunder, and later were subdued by Rome. Many still lived outside towns in their own fortified villages. A few had been lured by the modest luxuries of Derbe, had let their druidic religion lapse, and had embraced Christianity.

By midnight, drunkenness, gluttony, and wenching were sifting the tares from the wheat. Some stuporous Christians of both sexes had been propped with rough amiability against the meeting house wall. Couples, arms around each other, laughing and unabashed, staggered from the yard into the fields.

Next morning, when we met with the elders, Paul was sour as an unripe persimmon. As a rebuke to his hosts, his beard was untrimmed and his streaky gray hair was uncombed. His eyes were slits over molten obsidian pupils. The elders were embarrassed by the derelictions of the night before, but were resentful and stubborn.

On Sunday, the Lord's Day, Paul spoke to a large crowd from Derbe and the countryside. In the long, storehouselike meeting place, he had to strain his voice to be heard.

"Oh, my beloved Galatians," he began, "it surprises me that I should be speaking to you with such a heavy heart." His voice dropped, and the audience leaned forward to hear him. "Oh, my foolish Galatians. Who has bewitched you? Who has clouded the picture I first gave you six years ago and then again only three years ago of our Lord, the crucified and risen Jesus? God is not mocked, oh, my Galatians. If you sow in the flesh, you will reap corruption. Drunkenness, lust, murder, licentiousness, impurity, and excess of all kinds, these, like envy, cruelty, rage, idolatry, will bind you in slavery and bar you from the freedom that awaits the good in the kingdom of God."

I squirmed, hearing him commingle gross sins like murder with the mild strayings of gluttons, drunks, and lovers. When Paul had exhausted this vein of sin, he moved from sins done to those so far undone, specifically heresies he expected among the fickle Galatians when the Jerusalem party arrived.

"Soon another great threat will try your faith," he warned. "Misguided men, believing they bear the message of Christ Jesus, will come from afar and tempt you. They will preach a Law I do not damn but caution you against, for it is dangerously outmoded. Before the spirit came, Jews like me were confined and preserved in this Law. It was our custodian. It told us that a man crucified upon a tree is the accursed of God. But I preach that this crucified man redeems us from fear and into freedom. For when we are baptized in Jesus, we are no longer Jew or Greek or Galatian, circumcised or uncircumcised, slave or master, man or woman, but one in Christ Jesus. We Jews were made as free from the Law as you, our Gentile brothers."

Inflammatory words! I was as thrilled by them as I had been dismayed by his earlier ones. If he had preached them in Jerusalem, he would have been stoned. Dry-voiced, simple even in his complexity, bearing so many scars of his belief, this small, determined, unbroken man, humble as a human can be, held out his hands to the audience: "The law of Jesus, oh, my beloved Galatians, is one of joy, peace, patience, kindness, gentleness, self-control. It is a law that has no tractates or codicils save only faith and love." There was no word, no applause. He held us in the silence of a place where God was.

❁

His theme announced, Paul instructed the elders and lay leaders and built up the cadre, passing over both those who were more extreme than he in opposition to Mosaic Law and those Jews who were still most attached to it. Titus worked with the ordinary Galatians, neighbors to his own country, I with other Gentiles, and Timothy with both Gentiles and Jews.

Silas went a separate way, arguing for Paul's beliefs among those who were likely to be most susceptible to the countermission when it finally came. Despite this loyalty, and perhaps because we no longer shared the rigors of the trail, strains seemed to recommence between him and Paul.

In the course of Paul's meetings, he learned of a small disorganized Christian community in Laranda, westward over almost nonexistent roads in the Taurus foothills. Ordinarily, he would have sent Silas with Timothy or Titus. But he passed over Silas and decided to send Titus and me. It was insulting to Silas, and far from artless on a second score. Paul knew by now that Titus and I did not like each other. I saw Titus as scornful, crude, jealous, and sycophantic. He could have come up with equally unpleasant adjectives about me. I suspected Paul saw our trip together as a test of our Christian capacities.

We set off on donkeys crawling with fleas, pathetic contrasts to the muscular mounts we had sold in Tarsus. Both of us carried swords and I wore my armor, somewhat to the disapproval of Paul, who liked the idea of pacifism even if he did not always practice it. The weather turned cold the morning we left, and by the end of the second day, a few snowflakes had begun to fall. That night, heavy snow blew in from the mountains and we awoke with four inches around our tent.

The snow fell all morning, and by afternoon the donkeys were exhausted. Just before dusk, we saw smoke and reached a cluster of rounded huts made of mud laid on crudely woven twigs. They stood among huge limestone blocks, remnants of some ancient city. Slovenly as the huts were, they would give us shelter.

"Hittites," warned Titus. "They hate everybody." I could scarcely believe it. The Hittite civilization supposedly had died out seven hundred years ago. Several women came from their huts in filthy half-cured goatskin garments. They called out "Water" in Greek and Aramaic so accented that at first I did not understand even that basic word. They were selling it in exiguous cups, about as mean a trade as anyone could practice. Their waterskins looked as scabrous as their own. "Better to drink scorpion piss," said Titus.

The men were camel sellers and camel-dung collectors. Their corrupted Hurrian dialect contained enough Aramaic for us to wangle lodging and a place for our donkeys in the communal manger. A dozen underfed camels and other pack animals including a scrofulous buffalo were resident there. When Titus's donkey balked at joining them, Titus took one of his long, delicate ears in his teeth and jerked the animal step by step into the shed.

Titus and I and five of the men ate around a fire whose smoke went up through a hole in the roof, thawing the snow that then dripped on the fire. The camel cheese smelled and tasted fetid, but no worse than the fermented camel milk that, save for Titus, who was abstemious, we drank from a common gourd. Its power loosened the men's tongues. They bragged of their descent from the Hittite kings. Yet, they spoke of themselves and their mates, some of whom I gathered were their sisters and aunts, with such depravity, that I could hardly believe I understood what they were saying. But the meanings of their leers and their hand and body gestures were unmistakable.

I tried to fit these dregs into my theology. Would Jesus have tried to convert them into Christians? I doubted they could be converted to humanity. In an aside in Greek to Titus, I asked him what he thought Jesus—and Paul—demanded of us in regard to people like these. "To pass them by," he said.

In the morning, we rode through what had once been a monumental gate with two massive pedestals. On one stood an eroded basalt lion, its wings and head long gone. A few paces on, almost covered by the snow, was a fallen bas-relief of bird demons with forlorn weatherworn faces and drooping wings. Their raised claws seemed to supplicate us—as if they were trying to dig out of the snow, but, too weak, were suffocating. Victims of every element, witnessed to only by degenerates, these gods had once been worshipped from the Bosphorus to Judaea. Would Jerusalem's Christianity come to that? Would ours?

XIX

In Laranda, we went first to our contact, a silversmith named Drobyta. He was a Lycaonian, like most of the eleven hundred inhabitants, some of whom had intermarried with Gauls.

The silversmith called together the Christians, and Titus gave them a firm talk somewhat like Paul's in Derbe, but without approaching Paul's emotional heights. Still, he got the points across. He conducted the Eucharist with dignity, as I assisted.

Drobyta told us that the town's Roman administrator, an alcoholic and the former lackey of some imperial counselor, had no real objections to their expanding the church. He was under the sway of his male lover, a paunchy Greek, who, in fact, was attracted to the aesthetics of a doomed but ever-returning God

The real problem, Drobyta said, was the hundred pure-bred Gauls who lived in a decrepit stockade just outside town. They had stepped into the vacuum caused by the weakness of the town's lone Roman and, although riven by dissensions, were the true governors. Their chieftain was one Thetorix, who called himself the "tetrarch." They practiced druidism, a creed of sun rituals, herb cures, belief in the immortal souls of people and horses, and the occasional sacrifice of enemies by disembowelment.

Next morning, we visited the Roman administrator, a wisp of a man, desiccated rather than fattened by his drinking. His Greek paramour sat beside him. Titus was political enough to let me deal with him. I told him we wanted to build our church more actively and he tried to look stern. "I will think on it," he said, "but, meanwhile, you

186

had best go see Thetorix. He is a Gaul to whom I have delegated some minor duties."

"Does Your Excellency have any recommendations on how to approach him?" I asked.

He looked to the Greek, who handed him a cup from which he drank deeply. "Carefully," said the Roman, "most carefully."

The Gallic stockade had military vestiges. Its fence, though full of gaps, was five cubits high and of hewn pine with platforms at the corners. By the gate, an ancient with a spear, fur jacket, leg wrappings, and a small round shield pointed us toward the settlement's single masonry building, which stood beneath a leaning watchtower. The stench of missing sanitation assailed us. Horses stood before sagging dwellings of wood and mud, fetlock-deep in their dung. Garbage, and human and animal waste decayed in ditches beside the street where vultures picked.

Thetorix sat behind a cross-legged table. He was a barrel-chested man of about forty who was missing several front teeth. Titus's biting of animals' ears was a regional practice, it seemed, with its attendant dental hazards, particularly for those who tamed horses. The tetrarch spoke ungrammatical Greek and had the hostile look of those new to authority. The silversmith had provided us with a gift, a silver medallion on a chain embossed with a crossed sword and spear. Titus presented it.

I remarked politely on a long Roman lance and a lark banner on the wall behind Thetorix. He said he had fought in Armenia as part of a Roman legion. I mentioned that my father had served in that area thirty-five years ago as a young man and had been wounded in a skirmish at Carana.

"Ah, a mountain soldier," he said, pleased. "I, too, but at Araxarta." He drew back the sleeve of his dirty tunic and showed us a great hollowed scar on his upper left arm. With consanguinity of sorts established, he called in an aide and gave him orders in an incomprehensible dialect.

"None for me," said Titus. "I have taken vows."

"You understand Tolistobogii?" asked the surprised Gaul.

"A little, a little," said Titus.

Thetorix was further pleased and I was impressed. Titus explained that a Gallic legion had been stationed in Phrygia and he had learned a few words. It was a hopeful beginning. The aide came back with the vile-smelling liquor and I took a swallow. It was a level up from the fermented camel milk, but still basically a disgusting milk brew. "Mare's milk!" said the tetrarch. "Not so tame as Roman wines, hunh, son of soldier?"

I sipped away bravely as Titus told him why we were here. The Gaul nodded intelligently. "You say you want to bring us a god. Unlike you and the Romans, I believe in men, not gods. Romans"—he looked at me—"make gods of fornicators because Romans are great fornicators. I once believed in druids," he went on, "wise men who could foretell the future. They told us the earth would be destroyed in their time by fire and water, but that meanwhile we should leave our homes and fight in Bithynia."

He curled his lips and took a gulp of the mare's milk, then signaled his hirsute aide to pour us some more. "So we crossed the Bosphorus and conquered for our allies and were then butchered by the Romans and are no longer a mighty people. And the world did not end from fire and water, nor from any other substances. My people still practice our druid religion, although Rome says Gauls may have no gods."

I recalled from my law studies that Tiberius had banned druidism because of the human sacrifices and the nailing of victims' heads, generally uncured, to porches. Thetorix, who like many other subject peoples was trapped in feelings of both love and hate for Rome, went on. "I am loyal to your emperor not because he is called a divinity, but because he is powerful, as we and our religion are not."

Titus replied, "Sir, your observations strengthen what we wish to propose. You say the Roman gods are fornicators and I agree. You say the priests of the Gauls failed to forecast the future of your nation, to your dismay. You say you tend to believe in men, not gods. We preach a man who was also a God. Our leader, Paul of Tarsus, has seen him and spoken with him, and sent us to speak to you of him. . . ."

Sly Phrygian serpent, I thought. That was what I hated about Titus: he was willing to stretch the canvas any way he could to cover the camel wherever it protruded.

Thetorix heard Titus out, then rose. "I will consider all you have said. For the time being, I do not wish you to preach this Jesus in Laranda. But we will speak again. Now, go to the Roman and register immediately on the tax rolls." He smiled, again showing the gaps in his teeth. "You *register* with the Roman. You *pay* the Gaul." He put on a gigantic broadsword, which he must have wielded as a Roman soldier and which he now wore as his badge of authority, and perhaps to discourage any rival in the clan from assassinating him.

Outside, a young woman of sixteen or seventeen with large breasts was astride a russet mare. She appeared more intelligent and less dirty than most of the Gauls. She stared at me and Titus with interest. Beside her, a groom held a black stallion.

"My daughter," said Thetorix proudly. "A good rider."

The stallion reminded me of my own in Borhaurus. I went to him, looked to Thetorix for permission, and patted his muzzle.

"You know horses?" he asked me.

"I had one like this," I said with a touch of nostalgia.

"Not like *him*. Do you ride?" he asked Titus.

"Not that one," said Titus, not unhumorously.

"Come tomorrow and ride him," the Gaul said to me.

On the way back to the silversmith, I asked Titus whether we should proselytize despite Thetorix's ban. Paul would not, he said, not while it was possible the tetrarch would relent and give us permission. The strategy was probably wise, but the question was not really whether Paul would, but whether Jesus would. Titus seldom distinguished between the two.

❁

I rode with Thetorix through primeval forests, handling the stallion charily. The trails were still slippery with spring rains. The tetrarch rode a roan gelding, almost as large and spirited as the stallion.

Talk is always effortless between dedicated horsemen, and although Thetorix was uneducated, he was intelligent, observant, and lonely He spoke of the frustrations of trying to keep order and quell dissension, of administering a town of Lycaonians in which he and his Gauls did not live.

"We Gauls drink; we farm poorly; we breed horses well; we mount the wives of our neighbors; we brawl; we live on the tribute of these peaceful drones. What else is there for us? But tell me of yourself. Why do you, son of a Roman officer, plod through barren foreign lands on behalf of a beggar god. You had everything. I—anyone— would trade a ballock for the kind of life you once had."

I told him of Andrew saving me from death, of my outrage over the blinding of the fuller, my conversion at the foot of the tilemaker's cross, our fight with the Roman deserter. I said I was now working on behalf of God and man, and often felt joyful. I said I thought it had something to offer him, too.

"Demas," he said. "Do not spoil our good ride and good talk by trying to twist me to your uses. Anyway," he repeated, "who could worship a dead Jew?"

"I am half-Jew, Tetrarch!" I said. I kicked the black stallion into a canter, spattered mud on him and shouted back, "And every drop of Father Abraham's blood as good as any Gaul's!"

Thetorix cursed in surprise at the challenge. He smacked the gelding and it, too, began to run. My initial lead kept me ahead at first. But the stallion ran heavily in the mud. When the road widened at a farm entrance, Thetorix galloped past me, all elbows and knees, giving me a shove as he went by that almost unhorsed me. Another stadium and he pulled up, the clear victor. Out of breath and genuinely happy for the first time since we had met, he said boisterously, "No Father Abraham, no Christus, taught you to ride like that!"

I was gasping too hard to retort. At the stable, his aide was grooming horses, but stopped long enough to pour us mare's milk. I felt we were now comradely enough for me to show a mild aversion. He said something in Tolistobogii and the aide brought me a silver cup of wine, Cappadocian, but an improvement.

"Rome did not give you a taste for wine?" I asked.

"Yes," he said quietly with a look at the men around the stable. "But to drink anything but this"—he dipped his chin at the mare's milk—"is to invite revolt. It is a penalty of tetrarchhood." As we wiped our horses, he said, "I am thinking of proclaiming a race next Sunday. Would you compete?"

"I would have to talk with my colleague."

His mood changed. He did not like to be crossed. "I decree it," he said. "Why would a Roman *ask* a Phrygian anything? Gauls and Romans *tell* Phrygians."

When I talked with Titus about it that night, he said, "It cannot hurt. Perhaps you can move him."

Next day, Thetorix sent word he had found me a chestnut stallion belonging to his uncle. I tried it out that afternoon. On the following day, I rode with the tetrarch and his aide while they laid out the course along roads and through woods. Thetorix said he was thinking of expanding the contest to other events. We drank again as we groomed our mounts, and by the third cup, he had become both expansive and confidential.

The competition had taken on political overtones, he said. Everyone could compete, but he believed it would winnow down to him and his nephew. There would be wrestling; the horse race; the hacking with swords of saplings and pigs. In case of a tie, the victor in the horse race would be declared overall champion. He seemed apprehensive over his nephew, so I asked him about it. Thetorix leaned toward me.

"I must swear you to secrecy, Demas, by the name of this god you take so seriously." With the tetrarch an oath proposed was an oath administered. "Mercka"—the nephew—"would like the tetrarchy, and I would give it to him if he were a better man. But he is wild, crazy.

He talks of killing this Roman drunkard, returning to the old ways, taking *all* the taxes, giving Rome none. Whoreson gods! There would be a legion here in a week and we would have to flee or climb trees." He spread his arms to simulate a crucifixion.

"He talks of marrying Gerta"—Thetorix's daughter—"marching on Derbe, restoring the priests, even the sacrifices." He shook his head and poured me more wine. "Who would not like to march on Derbe, but with what? We are finished as a nation. We have more freedom here than any Gauls in Galatia."

"So, the games . . . ?"

"Will show him up, disgrace him among the young who listen to him." The nephew, he said, might win the sword event, for he had an arm like a juniper tree, but he was a clumsy wrestler and rider. "Clumsy in the head, too."

"What you are saying is that you keep your power if you win. If Mercka wins, he gets your chair and your daughter and perhaps your head on his front porch. What do I get if *I* win?"

The thought had not occurred to him. "Money?" he suggested. "My daughter?" That idea intrigued him. I told him I had taken a vow to serve Jesus until I was well into my thirties. He nodded. Vows he understood as well as oaths.

"Not money either," I said, inspired by a proposal that would anger Titus, and would have been unacceptable to Paul. "You have heard from Titus and me what our religion is. You have seen that I am a reasonably happy man. I wake up every morning with hope. Can you say the same?"

"No," he said, grasping a hint of what I was going to propose. "But I refuse your invitation before you invite."

"Wait. I am not asking you to join. Just hear me. What has druidism got you? Priests making false auguries from the guts of sheep, deer, birds; herb cures that do not work; lies one on top of another to explain the failures. And filth. Your people live like vermin." Christianity, I said, besides all I had spoken of before, has rules of cleanliness—I did not mention that they were adapted from Mosaic Law. "If your people were Christians, they would take their excrement and trash outside the stockade instead of letting it rot in town. They would care about themselves because they would care about reaching the life hereafter. Unlike your old gods, Jesus is not hard to understand. He is as full of God as a honeycomb is of honey. He pours it out and it sweetens all our lives. If I won, I would not ask you to *decree* that people believe. If those you rule did not come to Jesus on their own, as soon as we left town, they would stop believing.

You would only give us permission to *talk* to them and give them *permission* to join."

Like every gambler, Thetorix was captivated by a new kind of wager. But it was not a wager unless I put something at risk. "And if you lose, you accept druidism?" He laughed.

I tried to shake the wine out of my brain. "No, but I would be willing to leave town in disgrace."

"Would you also give me that armor you came to town in? I have an armorer who could make it fit me."

I thought of Grandfather and how I loved the armor. Like a second skin. "Yes," I said grimly, "I would do it."

"And your sword? I would want that. You would have to leave town in nothing but your *saq.*" He was having a fine time.

"That, too. But Titus and the other Christians must not be hurt."

"Done," he said. We pledged the terms with a Roman clasping of forearms.

"Tetrarch," I said, "if you lose to Mercka, you lose all. If you lose to me, you and your people win a new world."

I tried to make Titus think that my purposes in competing were only for the sport of it, what Paul had called all those years ago a "perishable crown," and a desire to create a good image for Christianity in Laranda. But I was sure Titus suspected I had more at stake. Half of him, I believed, wanted me to do well. The other half wanted me to fall on my face.

In the three days remaining, I practiced downstrokes with my sword and galloped the chestnut along roads and forest trails. I wrestled any Gaul willing to risk a fall. Holds came back to me from the Xystus and Scythopolis that permitted me to lever the Gauls' strength against them. By the end of each wrestling match, I felt that if all that Christianity did was to bring Laranda's Gauls closer to bathtubs, mine would be a victory well won for God.

The contests were centered in the town square. The Roman administrator, as president of the games, sat in a stand of planks along with his Greek adviser, and the senile chief druid. With them were a few prominent merchants, Thetorix's wife, and, in a Roman robe of a few years back, his daughter, her pretty peasant face made up with powdered lead and rouge.

Thetorix's Gauls, all sober at least for the opening, acted as marshals, keeping the populace from crowding into the middle of the partially paved square. Even before the games began, the wine, barley-millet beer, and sweetmeat peddlers had made their first circuits. At the edges of the square, children smacked each other with wooden swords, while others wrestled as if the town's fate depended on them.

There were forty of us in the competition, some so old or so young or so fat that their entry could only be for the novelty and excitement. In the preliminary sword game, we hacked at saplings a palm thick. Mercka cleaved his with a stroke that would have beheaded an elephant. When the results were compared, two of the four finalists were Thetorix and Mercka.

Each of these four would now try to halve a pig with a single slash. For the Gauls, the contest was a surrogate for their human sacrifices. Two men held a rope tied to a ring in the pig's nose, two others a rope tied at the haunches. The four swine squealed and scratched at the cobbles as if they sensed their fates. The sword used was an immense, sharply honed broadsword. As winner of the first sword round, Mercka began. He looked confidently at the crowd and drew applause from a large number of young Gauls. I watched Thetorix as he shrewdly noted the most enthusiastic supporters of his rival.

Mercka braced his columnar legs and cocked the sword. His biceps and triceps were so pronounced they ought to have made snapping sounds. He nodded at the four townsmen holding the ropes and they tightened their grips, drawing even more vociferous shrieks from the pig. The sword flashed down, hewed through the pig's chine and hit the cobbles so hard with its remnant force that it clanged. The pig, its squeals instantaneously silenced, fell in halves, toppling all four men on their backs. The blood shot from the severed arteries as the two halves, their muscle contractions making them seem briefly alive, flopped in the blood at the end of the slack ropes. Mercka's claque cheered wildly.

It was hardly worthwhile for the rest to compete.

Wrestling was next. Only biting, hitting, and gouging were barred. Contestants fought to a surrender, disablement, or for thirty minutes when they themselves decided who had won. In a dispute, Thetorix and the Roman administrator would rule. By elimination, the wrestlers were reduced to Thetorix, Mercka, me, and to the town's delight and surprise, for everyone had thought it would be another Gaul or half-Gaul, a Lycaonian in his mid-twenties named Nistera, who had served in a Roman auxiliary. Thetorix held straws to the three of us and I drew the short one, making me his opponent.

The two of us fought hard but without real hurt. There were times when, with a sharp wrench of his arm, I might have used my purchase to snap his wrist. But I do not think I would have done it, even if I had known it was necessary to win. As our thirty minutes ran out, I had

193

immobilized him, my hand braced on the back of his neck, my weight across his back.

Nistera was as tall as Mercka, but a good fifty librae lighter. Still, for the first fifteen minutes, with grace and swiftness, he took down the Gaul time after time, making him look the fool as he fell like a tree to the mat. But Nistera could not hold him down. The Gaul simply broke grips with his mighty hands, or extended his loglike legs, or arched his back into a dromedary hump to lift his opponent and free himself.

After one such escape, Mercka dropped on Nistera, knocking the breath from him. With his knee in the Lycaonian's chest, the Gaul slammed his head to the carpet with its underlay of stone. Bloodthirsty Gauls urged Mercka on. Suddenly, I understood how real these games were for them. To establish national pride and his manliness, to puff his courage and thrill himself and the crowd, Mercka intended to murder Nistera.

He raised the Lycaonian's head to hammer it again, and at the same time, Thetorix and I rushed onto the mat. The tetrarch grabbed Mercka's shoulders, toppling him. I fell on his sweaty thighs lest he kick and injure one of us. Nistera's hands came feebly to his head. His knees went up and down as his feet made a drumbeat of agony on the carpeting

Mercka, for a moment, tried to fend off Thetorix and me and get back to his savage work. We subdued him sufficiently for Thetorix to help him to his feet and announce him the winner to the wild cheers of his supporters. Only then, did I understand why Thetorix had saved Nistera. Any kindly motive aside, the tetrarch had been politically astute: he had endeared himself to the Lycaonians, while alienating only Mercka's cruelest allies.

After a pause, it was my turn with Mercka and the crowd became quiet. He was forty librae heavier and almost a palm taller. Looking at his muscled arms, chest, and legs, and the hate in his eyes, I was afraid. If he got the right hold, he would kill me swiftly. And Thetorix would have no logical excuse to intervene. I glanced nervously at the spectators and saw our few Christians together, Titus among them. "Pray for me," I said under my breath, even as I prayed for myself.

The Gaul and I circled. In his fight with Nistera, he had led with his right leg. His stride was short and there was an instant when he was unsteady, vulnerable. I let him follow me to the edge of the mat to confirm what I had seen, then, as he lunged forward, I drove my shoulder into his stomach, threw him on the mat, and rolled him so I could get the grip that had tired and defeated Thetorix.

But he bulged his neck as I sought the hold and flopped over on me. It was all I could do to scramble away. He rose, and again I led him to the edge of the mat. This time, he was cautious. I invited a move at my left arm, and as his massive right arm came out, I grabbed it at the wrist, tucked it under my arm, and rolled to the mat.

The leverage crashed him down, for if he had tried to hold back, his forearm would have snapped. Before he could rise, I shoved him off the carpeting with my feet. If I could just keep executing these fast moves, I would win. But my tactics were not popular with the crowd. Aside from the fact that I was a foreigner and Mercka, for all his grossness, was local, this was an audience that wanted to see someone injured.

Mercka knew enough now to wait for me to come to him, where he could use his Titan strength. When I sought again to roll him, he pulled back his wrist and grasped me in a brutal bear hug. He jammed up his knee, trying to crush my testicles. I closed my thighs but the impact staggered me. Rules or no rules, he clubbed me to the carpet with his ham-hock fist, then dropped on me and hooked his arm around my throat from behind. I pressed my chin to my chest and gripped his arm to keep him from crumpling my larynx. The crowd shouted bloodthirsty Gallic war cries. It was my life that they were screaming for.

Jesus, I said under my breath, give me courage. But it was not my courage that was giving out. It was my neck muscles. My body was oily with sweat. I dug my first two fingers between Mercka's fingers, but none gave up their common grip. His arm, partially disembarrassed from my grasp, tightened on my larynx and windpipe. I began to gasp, to see blackness.

At that moment, my forefinger wedged between his little finger and the next one. With my last strength, I wrenched his little finger toward the back of his hand and it snapped like a string bean. He bellowed in agony and, greased as we were by our sweat, I slithered from his grasp. In an instant, I was behind him, my knee in his lower back, his disabled left hand in both mine. I twisted the wrist upward. If he used the bull muscles of his neck to try to break the hold, he would break his wrist with it. The crowd screamed at Mercka to get up.

I knew I could kill or cripple him if I rammed my knee into the back of his neck. But I had been spared. I could not kill or maim him needlessly. Through my hazy eyes, I saw the administrator studying the level of water in a clepsydra. At last, he signaled the end of the match. I released the groaning Mercka. He came to his knees, holding the useless finger in his right hand as if it were a dead baby. When he refused to concede me the victory, the administrator ruled in my favor.

It was midafternoon and we rested, the audience to swill beer and wine, munch cakes and bread and discuss the bouts, we to recover for the horse race. My defeat of Mercka meant that whoever won the race would be overall champion. The friends of Mercka were splinting his broken finger. The Lycaonian, although he appeared disoriented, fumbled with his bay's saddle. I rubbed my strained neck and my mat burns with oil and myrrh.

While I worked on my injuries, Titus, the silversmith, and the other Christians came to me. "We were praying for you," said Drobyta. I looked at Titus, who met my gaze without expression. But I knew he had too. "Thank you," I said, wanting to grip his hand, but not doing so.

Before we mounted, Thetorix said a few quiet words to me. "Be alert Demas. *Swing wide* if *anything* happens." I thought he meant that his nephew intended me harm. We formed a line in the center of the square, muscular stallions, wind-broken nags, even two powerful white Tyanar mules. Mercka was on a gigantic brown-and-white gelding, perhaps the biggest horse I had ever seen. We would return to the square when we had run the course.

Thetorix was first off, with Mercka behind him. I, with the rest of the pack, followed. We left town and swept onto the Derbe road. Ahead, I could see Mercka lashing his horse fiercely and the tetrarch beside him energetically trying to force him off the road. But slowly Mercka pulled into the lead. Thetorix hung on gamely, eating mud cakes from the hooves of the gelding.

Their drive left me thirty yards behind them, although I was well ahead of the pack. We held that order for a mile, then veered across fields toward the forest of pine, terebinth, and vallonia oak. Thetorix kicked and switched his horse to regain the lead. His brave stallion responded, stretching its neck to draw abreast of the gelding. Side by side, the two riders elbowed and kicked, Mercka even beating Thetorix's horse with his stick. When the battering ended, Thetorix was ahead.

The forest path was covered with pine needles and leaves and intersected by stunted laurels and treacherous roots. Tangled loops of wild grapes hung just above our heads. I kicked the chestnut and moved him closer to Mercka. The massive Gaul pounded up and down in his saddle like a mallet driving a stake. We entered the deepest part of the forest with Thetorix ahead of him by a mere length. Here the underbrush was sparse. Only rarely did the sun break through, then, obliterated by the treetops, it disappeared, leaving us in shadowed dimness.

On the trail, there were outcroppings of rocks and roots. We galloped under more vines, some as thick as my arm. Thetorix and I bent low to avoid the vines' twigs and leaves. Mercka, erect as a tent pole, lacked the skill to lean and blend with his mount, but held the reins in one hand, his other before his face to fend off the thrashing foliage.

Ahead was an ancient stand of oaks, menacing as the gates of a forbidding city. My chestnut slowed on its own. Thetorix, his face caked with mud but cracked along lines of ferocity like a mask in a Greek drama, looked back at his nephew. Then the tetrarch dropped his head to his horse's neck and unaccountably galloped through a narrow gap between two of the sentinel oaks instead of a wider place he should, by rights, have chosen.

The surprise shocked me back to his warning: *Swing wide if anything happens.* I swung my horse toward the larger opening. Mercka, still upright, followed Thetorix through the smaller gap. But only for an instant.

To my amazement, there was a crashing of wood above him and his huge body was abruptly lifted from his horse as if the unseen hands of Atlas himself had slipped under his buttocks and thrust him skyward. Mercka's fingers let go of his reins, his neck extended. His legs remained bent as if they still held between them the mighty horse which, neighing wildly, ran on, leaving him as helpless as a fish just jerked from a pond.

For a half instant, Mercka rode only on the air. Then, like a monument falling, he dropped to the forest floor. I glanced down and saw his protuberant eyes, his contorted face, his gaping mouth. Not even a mutter had escaped him. Above him was a large vine, all but torn from its tree, which Thetorix had passed under but which had garroted his rival.

Dumbstruck by Mercka's execution—for what else was it?—I let my reins go slack, but the chestnut continued gamely to gallop on his own. Thetorix's horse was twenty-five yards ahead as we left the woods. The watchtower of the stockade and the few three-story buildings of the town were in sight. I was fevered. How could I leave town with my God and myself naked and in disgrace, and I certain to be cast out by Paul?

I switched my stallion and he gallantly moved up on the muddy, braided tail ahead. In less than a minute, I was taking clods from the hooves of the black, and moments later, I swung out. Thetorix's eyes were crazed. He beat his frothing horse heavily with the switch, now broken to a mere butt.

"Pray to your god, Demas!" he shouted.

"Pray to him yourself!" I cried back.

I galloped past him, but his black horse hung to my right quarter, calling on its last reserves. The narrow road that led into the square was just ahead. I reached it first. My entrails seemed to fall out as the tetrarch, no matter how I flailed my steed, pulled up. With buildings on either side, I could have cut him off, perhaps unhorsed him against the walls. But I did not want to win the right to preach in Laranda by murder. Soon he was a nose ahead, then a neck. The crowd had heard our clattering and screamed with anticipation. I beat my horse into a final magnificent effort, but the tetrarch burst into the plaza and crossed the finish line a half length ahead. I reined up at the far edge and looked back. Thetorix had already wheeled his stallion and now crooked his arm upward in the Gallic salute. The crowd roared and whooped. His groom ran up to take his bridle. Thetorix leaned over, said a few words, and the aide hurriedly summoned several marshals. They would be going back to get his nephew, I was sure.

From the center of the square, Thetorix signaled me to join him. I was tired to the bone and heartsick. I had gambled with Jesus as my lots, and I had lost. I trotted my horse over to comply. The crowd shouted again as Thetorix gestured that I was to circle the crowd beside him and we set off, but I dropped back a half length, the position in which we had finished.

The other riders began to pound into the square. Almost all had appeared when the crowd went silent. The courageous Lycaonian favorite, Nistera, had arrived. He was slumped on his horse, barely holding on with his thighs. Thetorix and I rode to him and helped a group of townsmen to lower him from his steed.

Thetorix strode to the center of the square while I trudged toward the Christians. They would hear now how I had wagered our faith and lost. The voice of the tetrarch was hoarse but loud. He spoke a sentence in Tolistobogii, then repeated it in the Lycaonian dialect. I was sure he was telling about the bet. But Drobyta was smiling. Even Titus looked pleased. What was going on? Thetorix should be declaring himself victorious and me a plucky, but disgraced, exile. Drobyta saw I was perplexed and summarized what Thetorix was saying.

"He says you were on the verge of beating him and shouted for him to pray to your God if he wanted to win. He says that he would not pray, but did demand from your—our—God a sign that he existed. He says that forthwith his stallion drew fresh wind and was the victor. He said that Mercka had been injured or killed and remarked that his nephew had wanted them to return to the old gods of the Gauls. . . .

"But Thetorix said it was too late, that the gods of the Gauls had been lost in time and senility, and that the Roman, Persian, and other gods were unpredictable, perhaps weak, and certainly confusing. He said he is also not sure that your—our—God is the true God. But he said that because of the sign our God had given him, he wanted you to go among the Gauls and drink mare's milk with them"—I let out a shout of joy that even Thetorix must have heard—"and talk of your God to see whether any Gauls wanted to believe in him.

"As for the Lycaonians, he would not hinder you if you came among us likewise. He said he planned no decree on this whole subject, since he understood that if your God was not embraced voluntarily, he became poisonous."

I did not know where he got this last bit of theology, but it was, I suppose, at least metaphorically true. I would have run to the center of the square and hugged Thetorix if it would not have embarrassed him. Instead, I embraced my fellow Christians, even Titus, and rejoiced in my God of love, and strength, and humor and irony and sometimes violence.

The obsequies for Mercka were held the next day. Thetorix made a speech praising his bravery. But after his body was placed under a cairn by his bravest friends, it is noteworthy that most of them left town.

Titus and I worked long, dedicated hours in Laranda, I mainly with the Gauls and mixed Gauls, he with the Lycaonians. But only a handful came over to us. The tetrarch spoke with me on several evenings over wine, and I gloomily told him that despite his generosity, we were failing. One night, he told me that he had decided to be baptized.

"Why? You do not believe," I said with astonishment.

"Listen to me," he said. "I have thought many hours about this. Your God would be helpful both to Gauls and Lycaonians. However, I see it does not matter that I gave people a free choice. They will not come to your Jesus without nervousness unless I go first. So I must join your religion. Why not? I do not totally disbelieve. From my heart, I did ask your God for a sign, and I won."

"Do not lie, Tetrarch. You do not believe. We both know you won because your horse was stronger—and because you were the better rider." He did not argue, and I pondered what Jesus would do. What would Paul do? My suspicion was that Jesus would take Thetorix and Paul would not. "If we baptized you," I said, "you would have to pronounce the words of faith. Titus will catechize you as I have done, and if he thinks you do not believe, he will not accept you."

199

"Well, I will swear to it all—even that I am contrite over Mercka and that I believe your God came back from the dead. What does it matter if I lie to Titus? He is a Phrygian."

When Thetorix announced he was becoming a Christian, he was joined within days by dozens of Larandans, including his daughter, Gerta; Nistera, for whom she had begun to show fondness; and the senile druid priest. The old man appeared for baptism in his ceremonial robes and a coronet of laurel and gall oak leaves. I told myself that if we could let Thetorix join us, then this ancient man's credentials were no less valid.

In a short time, we had baptized fifty-four Gauls and Lycaonians in a cold pool at the bottom of a waterfall that crashed out of the Taurus Mountains. As many more were talking with us and would be ready for baptism, we hoped, in a week.

XX

❖❖

Back in Derbe, Paul was pleased with our numbers, but questioned us shrewdly on whether we had made certain all who were baptized had been thoroughly instructed and were sincere in their belief. Titus and I cloaked the new church members in as much regularity as we could.

The evening we returned, Paul dictated a long letter to the north-western Galatian churches, in part to Timothy, and when his hand cramped, to Titus. Generally, Silas helped take down these epistles. I wondered at his absence, but did not ask about it. Next morning, I rose early to breakfast at Timothy's. He was as much Paul's man as Titus, but he would not—could not—dissemble, much less lie. I had never seen him so distressed.

The differences between Silas and Paul had finally erupted. The issue again was whether to wait for and negotiate with the counter-mission. This time, when Paul demurred, Silas told him he was leaving to return to Peter. Titus and I volunteered nothing about our night at the bridge. I told myself that if Paul and Silas were this alienated, our confessions would not cement them together.

That night, the five of us were together at supper for the last time. With varying degrees of warmth—I, the warmest—all of us but Paul told Silas how sad we were that he was going. Paul picked spitefully at Silas in a way I had never heard him before with anyone. The poisons had obviously been festering for a long time. After the meal, Paul disgorged his bitternesses.

"I hope," he said to Silas, "if you encounter our brethren from

Jerusalem, you will not talk to them of our plans." I was confounded. He was saying he thought Silas might betray us. From the ugly writhings of his face, I could see he was trying to swallow his venom. But it would not go down.

"You know I do not betray people," Silas said, shaken.

"If I were more mean in spirit, Sylvanus, I would say your desertion of me when I need you is a betrayal."

Silas's face became red. Paul was attacking him where it was most unfair. Silas had nursed him when he was sick, and been through a dozen hells of persecution with him. Usually so mild, even deferential, Silas struck at the testicles.

"Like Barnabas betrayed you?" he asked scornfully.

Barnabas had been a schoolmate of Paul in Tarsus, vouched for him in Jerusalem fifteen years ago, been flogged with him, and pulled him from a ditch near death after Paul had been stoned. Paul had refused to take Barnabas's nephew, Mark, on the second mission; they had argued, and Paul pigheadedly had told Barnabas to go his own way. All of us knew these facts as we watched the blood drain from Paul's lips like wine from a crystal glass.

But even as he opened them for a crushing rebuttal, he dropped his head in his hands. When he raised his face, I was shocked. It was cleansed of hate as if Jesus had miraculously transformed him in full fury. Paul cleared the phlegm from his throat and said softly, "I did drive Barnabas away. I have driven you away, Silas. I am profoundly sorry and I beg you all to forgive me."

For Silas, forgiveness was always only a kind word away. He was about to make allowances, as was his habit, but he took a breath and let his candor speak: "Paul, you eat all your oldest disciples alive, any of us who want to be your friend."

Paul listened without interrupting, sunk in self-condemnation. Silas went on, but more gently: "You can work with young people, Paul, because they are not looking to you for friendship, but as a father. For those of us, like Barnabas and me—we who are more settled in our ways—you treat us in such a way that we can no longer serve you."

"Five years," Paul said, "you have been with me. And Barnabas thirteen, and the parting so bitter I never heard from him after he left for Cyprus. What kind of follower of the master am I if I cannot have a friend who is also my equal?"

It was becoming more painful for Silas to speak his unaccustomedly hard, true words than for Paul to hear them. Silas reached across the table and put his hand atop Paul's.

"The apostles were only with Jesus three years," said Silas. "It may be that he, that you, cannot treat other men as equals because we are not your equals. Perhaps you must build into your mission this necessity of expending friendships. Jesus had his problems, too. He angered people. He had his Judas."

"He angered Pharisees and Judas was a traitor. You and Barnabas never betrayed me. What I said was vile, vile." He turned to us younger men, his eyes anguished. "Go with Silas. Follow him where he takes you. He is purer than I am. He has spoken justly. I cannot help abusing those I love."

"I am going back alone, Paul," said Silas.

And indeed all three of us protested that we would not leave Paul. But in my heart I was torn, and I thought my own thoughts that night. Leaving Paul would not be just a matter of being able to pursue my suit again with Deborah. I liked, even loved, Silas. Working with him and Peter would be fruitful, exciting. I could make the symbolic gesture of circumcision more easily now. Since Jerusalem, I had made compromises with Christ—the whores in Antioch, the conversion of Gauls whose belief I doubted, the ruthless episode at the Cilician bridge.

I would be done with the anxiety of laboring for this complicated man, done with his discomforting hold on my life, done with working under the shadow of his disapproval. I would be more on my own, for Peter and Silas would give me great latitude. Even if I preached entirely as I believed, they would accept it. They knew that trying one's hardest was enough.

But the iron in me said I must not go. Where Peter and Silas would work, at least until Peter went to Rome—where I could not follow—was mainly Judaea, the little world. Paul's was the great world. My successes in Laranda were still fresh. I would not give up the soaring creative zeal I felt in bringing to Jesus Gentile and Jew alike without regard for an outmoded Law. Was this ambition, even hubris? Whatever it was, I would not abandon the search for souls under the Christian most able to do it.

❁

We worked through Lystra, Iconium, and then came to Antioch of Pisidia, named like the greater Antioch after Syrian kings who themselves had vaingloriously appropriated the name of Zeus's grandson, the son of Hercules. It lay at the foot of a mountain whose top was already dusted with snow. An aqueduct marched toward the city like a giant centipede with arched legs. On its gatehouse was a crude but forceful drawing of a god with horns growing from his shoulders, a lance in his hand, a Phrygian hat cocked on his head. It was the pagan god Men.

"Home again," said Titus.

The city smelled of tanneries, whose heated vats of skins had dyed the faces of the workers dark. Side by side with the common people's hovels were magnificent temples to Jupiter, Men, Cybele, with Greek architraves and fluted marble columns. The priests of Cybele, Titus told Timothy and me, were famed for their devotion: each cut off his penis when he put on the priestly robes and burned it as a sacrifice to the goddess.

We labored there as we had in Derbe. Titus replaced Silas as Paul's chief aide, and Timothy took up Silas's role among conservative Jewish Christians. I continued to seek members in surrounding villages among those who worshipped the Roman gods and the innumerable variations and native gods that the lavish imagination of Asia Minor had spewed up over the millennia.

There were always problems, and they were always different. But there was also always the joy of feeling I had clarified the yearnings of people so they could feel joy, too. Among those who came to us, there was initially suspicion, then curiosity, then hope, then acceptance. They were almost always sincere people, conscious of the importance of goodness, wanting to find it in themselves. By teaching them of Jesus, I knew I had helped them in that quest.

It was deep into January before we came to Colossae. We seemed pursued by sleet and snow. All of us had colds. One of the donkeys was dying. Paul's malaria had recurred. We were irritable. We had hoped to be in Ephesus by now, but we were so far behind that Paul decided we would winter in Colossae.

One night, we were joined for supper by a traveling Christian donkey buyer. He had seen the Jerusalem mission at Miletus and again at Laodicea. They were probably now in Pessinus or Ancyra, churches established a few years after the crucifixion of Jesus by the original disciples in their more venturesome days. As the merchant spoke, I cast a worried look at Titus, who gave me back a stony stare.

"Why did they decide not to land at Tarsus?" asked Paul. "We had thought they were only a few days behind us."

My palms broke out in sweat. I had lived so long with the guilt of our bridge-cutting that I had come to feel we would never have to pay the piper. The donkey man looked unhappy. Obviously, he had heard the whole story, and with the bias of the Jerusalem mission. Before he could begin, Titus confessed.

"I cut a bridge in the Cilician passes."

Everyone stared at him. Paul, for once, was voiceless.

"I cut the bridge to delay them. You were sick. They would have overtaken us."

"I helped him," I said.

Titus went on without a look at me. "I stopped them without hurting anyone. I would not have asked Demas to help if I could have cut the ropes fast enough myself."

Paul's face twisted with the fury that had been in him after the supper with Silas. "I have always thought of you as my true child in our common faith," he said harshly to Titus. "You betrayed me." It was the worst thing Paul could say about anyone.

Timothy clutched his hands, feeling a painful sympathy for everyone at the same time. The donkey buyer looked as if he wished he had never left his donkeys. Titus took Paul's words like a cur. It irritated me. If I had said to Titus what Paul had, Titus would have drawn his sword on me.

"It was a betrayal of everything Jesus taught us," Paul raged. "Once they had overtaken us, we should have broken bread with them as Silas urged, and talked together about what our common purposes were. Indeed, your madness cost me Silas." I had not been willing to accept this kind of abuse from Father and I was not willing to accept it from Paul. Besides, I felt part of his anger was neither moral nor religious but pettily based on our daring to step outside his control. "No one betrayed you," I said hotly. "Perhaps what we did was not Christian. But it saved us from incalculable trouble. I know you must punish us, but at least bring a little sanity to this."

Paul looked at me with genuine hatred. Suggesting he might be unbalanced was too much. "Those are words you will wish you had never spoken to me, Demas." But hearing his threat, he began wrestling with his fury. At last he was calmer. "Titus, I ache with this," he said. He put his head in his hand, thinking hard or praying or both. When he came up, he looked as if he might cry. "I will write a letter to Jerusalem. I will beg their forgiveness. I must banish you, Titus, and you, too, Demas."

I was shattered. Titus had said Paul would do something, but not anything serious, and I had come to believe it would be no more than putting us from him for a week or two.

Titus looked as if he had been given a death sentence. "I do not think I can bear that, Paul," he said humbly.

Paul could do without me. But could he do without Titus? Yet he had done without Barnabas, Silas. I could see his mind working in a convoluted, tortured way to square out justice, his notion of Jesus, and his own needs. I saw a way:

"Why not just write them that you banished us as soon as you heard the news. You need not say where to or how long. Then think it over and see if you cannot take us back."

"Roman lawyer," said Paul scornfully, nevertheless liking the idea. "Where would you go if I banish you?" he asked Titus.

"Do not ask," said Titus, wanting to leave Paul uncompromised, then unable to disobey him, he replied, "Ephesus, so when you come, I can try to convince you to take me back."

"I would have known anyway," said Paul. "But delay your arrival there until spring." He turned to me. I was still smarting, but he was in no mood to coddle me. "And you?"

"The same."

"Demas," he said, still unable to get what he regarded as my insults out of his craw. "I have never entirely trusted you."

If I lost my temper again, he would be done with me forever. I swallowed his insult—like a cur.

❀

Paul barred us from preaching, and Titus and I went separate ways, he south toward Lycia, I north. My long, cold circuit by way of Philadelphia and Smyrna was purifying in the way that I imagined Paul's sojourn in the deserts of Arabia had been twenty years before. As the donkey and I plodded through the wintry hills, I shivered and thought. I also gave legal advice, did arduous farm work in small villages, and talked, not just to those along the road, but to myself.

I began to find peace in this solitary life. At moments, looking at the frozen stars, I knew the warmth that filled me in the cold night was the almost overpowering presence of Jesus. It was a gathering joy and my first reaction when I felt it coming was to murmur, "Thank you, God, Jesus." In the midst of it, I prayed, feeling that if ever I was reaching them, it was then.

"I do not know with certainty who you really are, Jesus of Nazareth," I said one night looking at the starry heavens, "but I know you are in the people I am closest to, and at this moment, I know you are in me. I know you are part of the God of the synagogue who saved me from the well, and I know that at my best, what I am doing is in your and his name. I also know this is not enough. I know I must know you as Andrew did, as Dathan did, as Peter and Rechab do, as Paul sometimes knows you. I know that somehow I must find out better who you are!"

I could not invoke these moments of rapture. And they left me as suddenly as they came. But I knew that from them I was storing up energies for my work in the spring.

At other times, I thought of those same stars shining on Deborah far to the south. I wrote her from Philadelphia, knowing the letter would not reach her for months. I recounted my adventures, told her how I longed for her, asked her how she now felt about us and urged her to write me care of the church in Ephesus. I also wrote my family in Rome, Grandfather, Ezra, and Thomas. I did not write Rechab, for I was still ashamed.

In March, I rode slowly down the coast to Ephesus, where local Christians told me Paul had been further delayed to the east. I did not seek out Titus.

Paul and Timothy finally reached Ephesus in April and I went to the synagogue to hear Paul's first sermon. He had been conciliatory to the Jews on his last brief trip two years before. They were well educated and rich; indeed, Jews from throughout Asia had banked their money here for the rebuilding of the Temple in Jerusalem. And no less a lawyer than Cicero had come here ninety years ago to defend the Roman governor who had blocked the disbursement of these funds.

Curiosity about Paul had filled the synagogue with Ephesian Jews. They had even closed their eyes to a number of Gentile Christians who had come with their Jewish Christian brethren. Paul's face looked drawn by the long winter. Perhaps out of gratitude for the opportunity, perhaps out of prudence, since this was his opening sermon, he spoke moderately. He told of Jesus' life, identified him as prophet rather than Messiah, and ascribed his death to factionalism in Jerusalem.

Outside, a crowd gathered around him and Timothy. The inshore breeze, salted lightly by the sea, picked up the attars of the early flowers, a smell both beguiling and astringent. Paul was glad for the attentive audience and the day and, for all its wrinkles, his face was childlike with pleasure. He was going to succeed in Ephesus, it seemed to say, and people were going to love and revere him and, through him, Jesus.

The worshippers thinned, and he and Timothy saw me and made their way through to embrace me. Titus came forward, also smiling. I sensed he had already met with Paul, and I felt jealous. In this contest, Titus would always be first.

❀

Paul saw Ephesus as a glittering potential treasure for Christianity. It had been built into grandeur by Lysimachus, successor to Alexander. Its avenues and academies, its gymnasiums and parks, were legendary. The city was dedicated to Artemis, whose temple crowned high landscaped terraces. Her idol in it, however, was not a graceful huntress by Praxiteles or Phidias, but a smoke-blackened monster of vinewood, with numerous breasts, thick thighs on which were cut mystical signs, and in her hand was a cudgel, not a bow.

The debased and erosive influences of Asia Minor had thus transformed the virgin daughter of Zeus into the licentious Phoenician goddess Astarte, whose priestesses were lesbians, whose priests were eunuchs. Her hundred-columned temple was a sanctuary for criminals and an arcade for bankers, who, in my view, were indistinguishable from criminals anyway.

Astarte had infected the miasma of pagan sects with extraordinary sensualisms. The city was a witches' caldron of black magic, orgies with multiplicious perversions, thaumaturges of all kinds, fakirs, Orphic fanatics, beggars rotting on lewd and repugnant display from every imaginable venereal disease.

To further spice the brew, besides our and Jerusalem's adherents, there were a number of related cults. One was led by a handsome and cultured Jewish spellbinder named Apollos, once a disciple of Philo of Alexandria, who had tried without success to integrate Judaism with Platonism. Apollos was now trying to combine Christianity and Platonism. There were also followers of John the Baptist, who had baptized Jesus, saying in effect that Jesus was the Messiah. The Johnists in Ephesus, however, considered John the Messiah, and Jesus a usurper.

In this religious stew pot, everything was tolerated so long as it did not interfere with the main business of Ephesus, which was making money and pursuing pleasure.

It was amid the seething diversity of Ephesus that I fully recognized Paul's organizational genius. It was greater than Father's or any other Roman's I knew of, Augustus not excepted. Indeed, I suspected that Jesus already might be accounted no more than a local Judaean prophet whose words were on the way to oblivion if Paul had not

208

arisen to spread them. For Paul created churches in which Jesus' words would survive long after Paul himself was dead. It made me both proud and uneasy. I sometimes wondered whether by saving Paul on the road to Antioch, I had helped save the words of Jesus for the ages, or something different: Paul's notion of what he *thought* Jesus had said.

Soon the crowds at Paul's appearances in the synagogue were too large for the building. In addition, although the Jewish fathers had been hospitable, Paul's attractiveness to their members and his increasingly critical reference to the Law began to make him unwelcome.

At an evening service in early summer, Paul broke the cord. "I do not condemn the Law when it tells us older men to be temperate, sensible, serious, steadfast, sound both in faith and in love," he said. "Or when it tells younger men to exercise self-control and to forgo the devil cries of the flesh. Or when it advises older women to be reverent in behavior, to teach what is good, to avoid slander, nor be slaves in secret to drink. Or when it tells young women to be reasonable, chaste, domestic, kind and submissive to their husbands.

"No, my brothers in Abraham, the cicada does not preach against its old shell, nor the bird against its old nest. But even as I honor the Law of our fathers, I beg you to move on to the law of Jesus." From there on, he heated the irons. "It is true that our Lord told Jesus to speak first to the Jews. But our Messiah Jesus warned that if they persist in outmoded ways and scoff at him, then on the last day he will weed them out with the chaff, and consign them and their false sayings to the fire."

That week, the synagogue leadership let Paul know he would have to find a new rostrum. The local Christians hired for us a lecture room generally rented out to academics and other orators. By late summer, our church in Ephesus had grown from fifty to three hundred and fifty members.

At our first baptism in a pool of the Cayster, Paul defined the theme he had been developing for twenty years and would preach henceforth wherever he went:

"I, a tentmaker, see among you not master tanner and vat stirrer, stable owner and manure collector, farmer and handyman, master and slave, but all one person in Christ. As he is the body, so you are the members, each working for the good of the whole.

"I, a Jew of Tarsus, see the tunics of those who were Greek, the girdles of those once Phrygian, the leggings of those once Gauls, the short cloaks of those once Cappadocians, now all become one in Jesus. For our Lord is like a continent of many peoples. Yet a continent in which a single people is without sunlight remains a continent in the dark. For how can you sow and reap in sunlight when your neighbor is without light and can neither sow nor reap? Therefore, let us bind ourselves into a continent so shining that the sunlight of Jesus falls on our neighbor from the glow that is in us. . . ."

As the days passed, we went to the Pion and Coressus hills to talk to wealthy people from Ephesus in their summer villas. We sought new members in the markets, the hangouts of sailors, the countinghouses, even the Roman barracks.

Paul organized the members into parishes, each under a minister. Before setting up a parish, he visited the local Asiarch—the pagan leader in the precinct. He asked what site for a new meeting place would cause the least problems and whether the Asiarch would be willing to make common cause with Christians in asking the city for better sanitation, welfare for the poor, more market space, and better water supplies. In time, many of these rivals for souls came to respect him.

In his talks with the civil authorities, Paul asked their advice, assured them that while he might preach against the Law, he never preached against the law. He conferred with merchants', workers', and sailors' groups, everyone with power or influence in Ephesus. It was not that he could always agree with them, but rather that they should perceive him as reasonable, and that he would have his hand on the forehead of the city so as to know when it was calm and when it was feverish.

In the evening, when Paul was not at meetings, he wrote to the other churches he had founded or rebuilt. His letters were eloquent and fiery admonitions, always ending with news of his work and plans. He used as messengers young members who took on the assignment as a mission. A steady stream of them left from his quarters for Corinth, Beroea, Thessalonica, Antioch of Syria, Tarsus, the Galatian churches, even Palestine.

Paul's system insured his correspondence. Papyrus scrolls telling him of how his foreign churches were faring came from Aristarchus and Secundus in Thessalonica, Sopater in Beroea, Erestus and Sosthenes in Corinth, Luke, the doctor, in Philippi. These were able, well-educated people. They were merchants of Jesus. They laid out Paul's message as they would fresh pomegranates or fine textiles. They gave good value and they were paid in the currency of men's souls.

I had hoped also to hear from those to whom I had written. My letters were sent by ordinary means, with a note on them saying the addressee would reward the bearer. They were entrusted (along with an advance payment) to ship captains and caravan leaders, who often resold them. It could be several months between dispatch and reply—and many letters never reached their destinations.

In all of this, Paul, who was living with Aquila and Priscilla, a Christian couple who had come to Ephesus from Corinth, found time to earn enough money as a tentmaker to take care of his personal needs. He also made a point of visiting the sick, the aged, the mad, the beggars, those most ignored by Ephesus's other sects. And while I had always been skeptical of faith healing, I can attest to one remarkable occurrence that resulted from these visits.

One day, a cripple whose neighbors said he had not been able to walk for ten years asked Paul to pray for him. Perhaps he asked the same of every holy man who passed his way. Paul told the man to concentrate his heart, his mind, and his voice on asking Jesus to let him take just one step, and Paul prayed aloud with him. After a half hour, Paul helped him to his feet and supported him with an arm around his waist.

The man made a stumbling step before leaning against a wall. I could scarcely believe it, but I saw it. A small crowd had gathered and pushed closer, but Paul begged them to give him room and silence. He rubbed oil on the man's knobby, unused knees, and they prayed aloud again. This time, the cripple shuffled a few inches on his own before leaning against the wall.

"I am tired, Master Paul," he said, not quite believing what he had done, "but I will walk tomorrow." The crowd dispensed to spread the exciting word. On the next day, we went to the man's house. There were two hundred people behind us. The man's housekeeper came to the door, and, amazingly, we could see the man inside making his way around the wall. He took a step into the doorway, and awkwardly, without bending, snatched up Paul's hand and kissed it. The mob howled and fell on Paul, tearing at his clothes, trying to touch him and the cripple.

Subsequently, Paul returned at night alone for prayer and to anoint and massage the legs of the cripple. Soon the man was wobbling around his house on crutches and even out in town. Before long, Priscilla and Aquila were being importuned for bits of Paul's clothes or for tats of wool or cotton he had touched, even for snippets of his hair.

The rest of Paul's "miracles" seemed more the results of good advice. He told those afflicted with disabling sores to wash them with clean water and vinegar, men with eye troubles to rinse them with boric water, and cripples to exercise their limbs a little more each day and to get relatives to massage them with oil—all of this while praying. With the possessed, he held their hands, listened to them, spoke calmly with them, and did not so much exhort them as pray *with* them. Some of them stayed as deranged as they had been, but some were calmer.

Paul preached angrily against the "cures" of the medical frauds who proliferated in Ephesus: treatment of a woman's bloody discharges by making her sit at a road fork with a mirror in her hand and then, when she nodded, waking her violently with a shout; a remedy for paroxysms and ague that included seven hairs from seven dogs, ashes and wood shavings in a leather pouch hung around the victim's neck; having people with consumption eat a kernel of barley plucked from the dung of a white mule.

With Ephesus organized into parishes, with substantial men chosen as ministers and deputy ministers, Paul looked to the outregions. I once heard him tell a sea captain from Tarraconensis in Spain that perhaps he would set sail for there. To a Nubian freeman, he said he would like to go up the Nile. But for the time being, these were dreams.

More realistically, he sent us to Miletus, to Smyrna, to the manufacturing town of Magnesis, to Tralles, the fig and raisin center of western Asia Minor. He used his "veterans" as a wise general uses his elite troops. When we got back from one mission, he had another ready for us. It was on my return from Spigal, a fishing village south of Smyrna, that at last I found a letter. It had arrived overland from Grandfather, the first words from my life in Judaea for more than two years.

I skimmed the letter, looking for what was most important to me, found it, and groaned aloud: Deborah had left Modi'im; it appeared there might now be another man in her life. I read through it, this time engrossed. Grandfather's information had come in part from Ahiam, who had heard it from Rechab, and in part from Deborah's brother Bediah, with whom Grandfather and Ezra had supped when Bediah was in Borhaurus on business.

Deborah had not easily rejoined the church in Modi'im. I could imagine her feeling, perhaps unfairly, that Rechab regarded her censoriously. They had become more distant. Things had come to a head when Matthew had visited Modi'im and she had argued with him very much as we had argued with James in Borhaurus, but with more vehemence. On several issues Rechab had sided with Matthew.

To get her thoughts together, she had gone to visit an aunt in Raphia, a minor port south of Gaza. This aunt was the widow of a copper smelter and had kept up his small factory. Instead of returning to Modi'im, Deborah had decided to stay with her and had now been in Raphia almost a year. Bediah had advanced her money to buy into the business. She had told Bediah that she loved me, but that it seemed hopeless for many reasons. Moreover, she had written me twice and had gotten no reply. I crumpled the papyrus, cursing over my lost letters, then quickly smoothed it and read on. Deborah had come to believe I had at last become angry or had despaired over her refusal to marry me and had abandoned my love for her.

While remaining a devout Nazarene, she was disappointed in Rechab and in the Jerusalem church, and planned no leadership role in Raphia. Bediah had told her she should think of marriage before she became much older and her aunt had regularly made the same arguments. Somewhat to the surprise of Bediah, Deborah had begun taking some interest in the modest social life of the town. The man most interesting to her was a Christian Jew, older than she was, who supplied the factory with ore, crucibles, tools, leather pot handles, and fine stones. He was Raphia's leading importer of grain, oils, furniture, and other wares.

Grandfather would never have mentioned him unless he sensed it was a serious liaison. I cursed again. Why had she not written me a third, a fourth, a fifth time, given me a chance to talk with her before considering another man? She had loved me as much as she could any earthly man. I knew that. In our last torrid days, she had loosened her bonds to Christ. Now I sensed that working against me. Without her daily labors for the Nazarenes, I could imagine her rethinking her view that she owed Jesus not just her soul but her body.

I thought of trying to get to Raphia. It was winter, an overland trip all but impossible. By sea, some few coasters made short runs from one port to the next on good days, but that way was slow, unpredictable. Besides, coldly, ethically, to go would be dishonorable. I could not desert Jesus when my work for him had never been more important. I could not leave Paul when he had begun assigning me (without even fully trusting me) to important missions. If I fled to Deborah, I might possibly win her love, but I would forfeit my self-esteem.

Grandfather wrote that he had received letters from my mother and father saying they were contented. They were optimistic about the new emperor, Nero, who was a student of Seneca. Mother, too, wondered why I had not written. Perhaps no one but those in Borhaurus had gotten my letters. Father, I assumed, had not mentioned me or Grandfather would have said so.

I wrote a letter to "Deborah bas Sirach, owner, copper smeltery, Raphia," certain that would make the carrier click his teeth with expectation of a large fee. I repeated the urgings of my previous letters, begging her for a sign that when I could honorably wind up my work with Paul, she would marry me.

XXI

No answer had come to me by that summer, when Paul sent us beyond the mountains: Titus and Timothy to Macedonia and Greece, me over the passes of Mount Tmolus to Sardis. From there, I was to preach and organize all the way to Bithynia et Pontus on the Great Black Sea and then along its coast. The Ephesus church provided me with a Muscat donkey, young, stubborn, and strong. Paul held a small love feast and Eucharist for me. I was moved when from his gnarled hands I took the bread and the wine. On the morning of my departure, he and a dozen of our church leaders saw me off. I had come of age in Paul's eyes.

Once on my way, the adventure, the skies, the roll of my strong donkey, made me feel like a new person. Each town I visited had enchantments and peculiarities: the sour perseverance of the gnostic heretic in Sardis, a tailor, with his talk of spirit life between moon and earth; the fierce toughness of the old woman who led our little band in Thyatira; the jocose vulgarity of the Christian blacksmith of Pessimus. In each of these places and others, I bolstered the church, brought new Christians to our fold.

As I traveled from one town to the next, Deborah and Paul, my whole previous life, at times seemed like the existence of a stranger. Time and again, I felt the peace of Jesus, swelling me—I thought with laughter—like the inflated pigskins that buoyed the cargo rafts in the sluggish rivers I passed. I had felt lifted up in this fashion during my exile from Paul while I looked at the winter sky. Years before, I remembered, I had also had a sense of almost reaching heaven as I rode into fields of spring flowers on the black stallion Father bought me when I was fifteen.

And what joy, what love I had felt for Ezra, when I had once beaten him, the best of the carob pod *sicarii*. He had fashioned a prophet crown of paper and the Sadducee boys had crowned me as they and my Roman comrades cheered. And who could gainsay the love and joy that day when Father wept and embraced me in the herdsman's hut as I lay on the flea-ridden pallet.

Indeed, I had felt this kind of transfiguration when I was making love with Deborah. And, if I wanted to be entirely honest with myself, might I not have felt something similar in the pure ecstatic hotness, the bellowed coals, of Visilia Persullus? Except for the involvement of the flesh—oh yes, a great exception—my rapture with Deborah and her was not so different from these other moments of exultation when I had wanted to cry, "Thank you!"

In all these exalting instants, there were common denominators within Paul's expansive definition of love: a vanquishing of insecurity; a sense of freedom, courage, even derring-do; an openness and clear, perfect emotion; a desire to laugh gratefully; a love that, as Paul put it, "rejoices in right."

❀

The road to Ancyra, the provincial capital of Galatia, was scarred by earthquakes that had left craters, deep gulches, and steam holes giving off sulphurous fumes that took ghostly shapes as they climbed into the cold sky. Even the underbrush was dark, barren-looking. In Ancyra, we had heard, the Jerusalem delegation had made the most progress. The Paulists in Ancyra had been a minority, the majority of Christians being Jews who were still close to the synagogue. The Jerusalem mission had won over most of the Jewish Paulists. The remaining Paulist leader was a slightly demented orchardist who lived outside town but sold figs and dates in its agora.

The Gauls here were Tectosages, who hated Tolistobogii even more than they did non-Gauls. Up until fifty or sixty years ago, they had annually eviscerated a Tolistobogii captive and thrown him into the Sangarius River. The theory was that the corpse would carry a report of the Tectosages' heroism down the river, into the Black Sea, and across it to Gauls still living in their ancient homeland.

Some of these sanguinary Gauls had joined with local degenerates at a nearby village in an anachronistic cult of Anat, sister and consort of Baal. One of the cultists was brother to my most promising potential

Christian, a young woman named Coris, whose zeal, so like Deborah's, and dark beauty made me churn with despair and desire. Anat supposedly was a warrior-goddess who had slain her and Baal's son and enemy Mot, god of droughts and the underworld, cut him into pieces, made him into a cake, eaten him, and defecated him in a field to fertilize it. Surely, Coris begged, the powerful God I preached could make her brother see reason before the grotesque cult got him into trouble.

One dark night, she took me to where the devotees of the cult were holding their summer initiation, deep in the woods. I wore my cuirass and my sword. We watched from behind the caved-in wall of a broken, roofless temple to Sandan appropriated by the Anat worshippers. Although it was warm, I could feel Coris shivering beside me.

Forty people, mostly men, were in the temple. Its altar was a long table lit by a bonfire on a rude hearth. On the table was a wooden idol of Anat, two cubits tall, and skimpily leafed with gold. She had horns, wings, a bow, and quiver, attributes of Baal, but she also had breasts. From between her legs protruded a male head, Mot's, no doubt, in accord with the myth.

Also on the table were what at first looked like parts of a doll, but which I realized to my horror were the head and armless upper torso of a child. A man in a black robe, with emblems of plows, cattle, and corn sewn on it, stirred a pot suspended over a corner of the fire, chanting in a moaning voice. The audience stood as if drugged while the priest drew first an infant leg, then an arm, from the pot and put them on a silver plate on the table. I gagged, and quietly spat out my bile.

From the rear came a younger man in a decorated robe, an initiate, perhaps, who sliced the meat from the bones and helped the priest to mince it and mix it with meal. They made thin patties, put them in a covered baking dish and thrust it into the fire. The men and women began chants, grotesquely like the psalms the elders had sung in the synagogue and that we Christians sang at our own worship.

The older priest poked the dish from the fiery coals, and with a spatula put the cakes on the silver plate. They were going to eat them in replication of their goddess's obscene myth, but it was also a ghoulish similitude of our Communion. I watched as the priest first offered a cake to the idol, then took a bite and, as the younger man knelt, fed pieces of it to him. About half the cultists solemnly came forward and each in turn was given a piece, this time by the younger man.

One of the recipients was the brother of Coris. She took my arm tightly, letting it go only when her brother was back in the shadows. The older priest and his initiate threw the baby's bones, head, and chest in the fire, stoked it, and turned back to the congregation. To my astonishment, from the empty place that had once been the front wall of the temple came a woman wailing at the top of her voice with a crying infant in her arms.

At the table, the young priest's knife caught the light of the fire. The older priest came back to the table with the pot. They were going to make more cakes for those who had not been served, only this time I would be a witness to the sacrifice of the baby. My God did not want me to stand by for that.

I lightly pushed Coris toward the path back to Ancyra and ran into the firelight, sword drawn. I shoved the old priest into the young one, and hewed at the idol. It was of ancient insect-tunneled wood, and in seconds I reduced it to kindling and crinkled gold leaf. The young priest, sacrificial knife in hand, started toward me, but I roared at him, brandishing my sword.

He fell back and I clanged my sword on the pot, knocking it to the ground, then chopped a sizable gash into the ceremonial silver plate. The other men in the audience, stunned at first, rushed forward. I kicked the table over into them. Gasping for breath, I shouted, "Your filthy god is dead! Any sword can hack her to pieces!" Then I fled back through the fallen wall.

Next morning, I went to the Roman administrator and identified myself. I told him that I would report to Rome that he tolerated human sacrifice if he did not permanently end the Anat worship. He was weak, but not incompetent. He pretended he had known nothing about it, and promised to suppress it if it returned. I had done what I could.

As it turned out, Coris's brother did not waver from his devotion to Anat. And so long as even one of the cultists still believed in the goddess I had annihilated, my ministry was in danger of a premature end. It was time for me to leave Ancyra. We held a small secret baptism. During the love feast, I drank too much of the orchard keeper's execrable date wine. At the Eucharist, thanks be to God, I kept my hands if not my mind off Coris. Christianity already had enough problems in Ancyra.

❁

At the end of my journey through vineyards of giant mauve grapes and treeless mountains, deserts where the terrible khamsin wind filled the air with sand, and silent forests, I came to Heraclea, by the vast

218

inland Black Sea. It was a pleasant town with tamarisks and heavy flower scents. Its grainfields outside ran down to the water and were ripening for harvest. On my first night, I looked out to sea toward the mysterious lands on its distant northern shores. Andrew had told me that Simon the Zealot had gone insane on a mission to Asia Minor years ago and was last seen setting sail in a small fishing boat toward those same shores. Who, I wondered, would eventually carry the knowledge of Jesus to their peoples?

There was a Hellenized Jewish community in Heraclea and they let me speak in the synagogue. I found new members among both Jews and Gentiles. I sent a report to Paul with a ship leaving for the Mediterranean through the Propontis, and a copy via a camel caravan bound for Pergamum.

I traveled to Amastris, Sinope, all the towns along the coast. Without Paul listening over my shoulder, I spoke much as I had in Borhaurus. Unlike the people in and near Ephesus, those of northern Asia Minor were unsophisticated. They did not worry a great deal about resurrections, or holy spirits. They wanted assurances that Jesus was the son of God, without needing to know much about what that meant. And they wanted to be told that if they lived by the rules of Jesus as best they could, they would be more contented on earth and would go to heaven.

I had no problem except for the question of heaven. I was often asked whether the body went there, and I said I did not think so. I said most Christians believed their souls were immortal and would find in heaven the kind of joy and peace they felt on earth when they were most in touch with Jesus. When pressed on my own belief, I said I *hoped* there was a heaven, but would not know exactly what Jesus meant by the "life eternal" until I died on earth. I devoutly hoped word of my dubiety never trickled back to Paul.

One evening, from a second-floor window, I looked out at the sun dying upon the Black Sea, the light only a faint line on the horizon. I felt the isolation I had sometimes sensed in Paul. How very long he had been on his painful road. Where would it end for him? For me? I did not know. I only knew it would be where Jesus needed me. And then I felt sublime. Where he needed me was where I wanted to be.

A day's travel from Trapezus, my bowels became fluid and I grew feverish. By the time I reached the city, I could only seek out an inn and try to recover. Trapezus was at the farthest reach of Rome's territories, the capital of Polemonis, which strictly speaking was not part of the empire, but a vassal state under its own king. Paul had instructed me not to try to set up a church in Trapezus, but to go south expeditiously. The complex social structure of this ancient place, its self-indulgence and self-satisfaction, the fickle tyranny of its king, made it unripe for anything but a broad campaign like Paul's in Ephesus. It had not suffered enough to be ready for an easy conquest by Jesus.

As I began to get well, I found myself falling under the spell of this city of fables, capital of the Amazons, victimized by Hercules and Theseus. I walked in the bazaar, holding in my appetite lest I relapse. The grilled meats in the cookshops were redolent of spices I had never smelled. I scrutinized erotic ebonite carvings from India, indecipherable phrases on enameled vases from Cathay. I saw Scythian gold in such profusion on a black carpet that the tiny merchant, his Far Asian face as yellow as his wares, had hired a ferocious pantalooned guard with a scimitar to stand over it.

The villas and palaces had serpentine columns, gaudily inlaid walls, carved teakwood doors. In the morning, from my window, I could see camel caravans leaving for mountains whose foothills were forests of rhododendron. And at sunset, others, elephants swaying slowly among them, wound toward the city from far lands I would never know. Lulled by such sights, by the autumn zephyrs from the sea, I wanted a hiatus from this hard road Christ had set me on. I yearned for the luxuries I had enjoyed as a tribune's son, for fine wines, not rural dregs.

The women were so beautiful and I had been away from their bodies so long now, the smell of them, their creaminess, their thin fingers and long hair, their smooth legs and bellies. There were blondes with skins so pale I could imagine they never went out until after dusk; ebony Africans blown here by the trade winds, their lips luscious as fat black grapes; petite Orientals with dark almond eyes who smelled of jasmine. Others could flagellate themselves over lust or mutilate themselves. I had rationalized it in Antioch and that argument was still valid four years later here in Trapezus. I located the city's finest bordello. I wanted an interlude in the land of Lotophagi.

Outside, I debated with myself for an hour as I watched richly dressed men go in and out. Finally, cursing under my breath, I returned to my lodgings. I lay awake, sweating in the sultry dark like a man at the baths. I was sure Paul was wrong about fornication and adultery being *monstrous* sins. But, alas, he was probably near the truth about the body being the temple of God. When it was dedicated to love as mine had been with Deborah, then there was a seriousness and even a holiness along with the laughter and joy. When no love was there, then it was only physical excitement and relief, not *evil*, but a degrading of the body's higher purposes. Still, if lust itself was a sin, then I was a sinner.

220

Next day, I left Trapezus. For days, I traversed the cruel passes of the Pontic Mountains, which snows never left. The winds were mordant, and the thin air left me gasping. Then, when I thought I could stand no more, I descended into a desolate plain, an unpeopled place where the trees had been cut and even the stumps hacked up for firewood long ago. It was a land of broken temples, fallen and looted shrines, hovels long given over to underbrush. Donkeys, once domestic, now wild, ill fed and burred, brayed all night.

In the distance, I often heard wild dogs, and one morning five, their red eyes demented with hunger, attacked me. Gripping the bridle in one hand, my sword in the other, I wheeled and turned while my donkey flailed at the bedraggled mongrels with his hind feet. He stunned one, more wolf than dog, and I stabbed it. The animal slammed into the ground and gyrated as if to fling the wound from its breast, flecking the ground with blood. Smelling it, the snarling pack tore their fellow to pieces. I ran beside my donkey for five stadia before I felt safe.

On the northern borders of Armenia Minor, surrounded by straggly beanfields and raw iron pits, was Bayba, the last town Paul had assigned me. A new wooden arena rose on its outskirts. The city made Laranda's Gallic stockade look prosperous. Dogs and vultures picked over street garbage; families stared out at me from inside roofless mud-brick houses; beggars more scabrous than those in Ephesus swarmed me. The base of the temple to Astarte, the town's only marble building, was urine-stained, its tile roof fallen in, the head and arms knocked off its gilded statue of the goddess and no sign of priests or priestesses.

I passed a small synagogue whose marble door pedestal with Hebrew inscriptions gave it a flourishing air by comparison. This was a dying town. There were squatters at the address of the Christian Jew whose name Paul had given me. They said he had been gone six months, but when I asked where, they looked sheepish and would not answer.

In the local tavern, I drank a cup of wine flavored with an herb unknown to me. Arak, said the tavern keep. I asked him whether there was a Roman presence in the town. It would at least be a place to get information. I recognized his sly look and put a silver drachma on the table.

"The Emperor Deity Cremens," he said, touching his heart with his right forefinger."

"The Emperor Deity Cremens is the leader of Bayba?" I asked.

"You would do well," said the hosteler, "to touch your heart as I do when you say his name." I did not do so but resolved to talk around the name in the future.

"But how can he be an emperor? There is a king of Polemonis in whose territory your city lies."

"Quite true, but the king confines himself to Trapezus. Here we are ruled by our emperor." He explained that the emperor was of a prominent Lesser Armenian family. His father had been mayor of Bayba and had sent him to Rome during the reign of Caligula. He had excelled in martial arts, come to Caligula's attention, and been taken into the Praetorian Guard despite his Anatolian blood. He had come home with a Roman name and his father had unexpectedly—the tavern operator considered how to say it—"been called by the gods." The son had appointed himself mayor, formed his own Praetorian Guard, which acclaimed him emperor, and the priests of Astarte had swiftly declared him a deity. He had then disbanded them and closed the temple.

I told the tavern keeper I was a minister of God, and when he looked unbelievingly at my armor, I said I was of the army of Jesus. I explained briefly my beliefs and asked if he had heard of any other Christians in Bayba. Talking conspiratorially lest the three other patrons overhear, he said that such a man had come to town about nine months ago but had only stayed three months. I pressed him. He leered at my purse. I withdrew another drachma and he went on in an even lower voice. "The Emperor Deity Cremens' "—he made the absurd gesture with his forefinger again—"lectors . . ." I corrected him: "Lictors." But he said, "we call them 'lectors' here . . . came and made him part of the games."

"The games?"

"At the arena. This Christian would not fight a gladiator as he was supposed to do. He said it was his religion to turn the other cheek. So he was allowed to"—and here the tavern keeper erupted into laughter so fierce that he spat some of his wine on the table—"turn the cheeks of his buttocks to a wild bull that gored him in the rectum as he knelt."

"It killed him?"

"It is most probable. The lectors dragged him through the streets and left him outside the walls." He nodded that our interview was over and overcharged me for the arak wine.

The emperor Cremens ruled from a moldy brick complex. Beside it, he had built a sandstone shrine with his name in bas-relief on the marble architrave. In spite of letting the temple to Astarte run down, he apparently did not yet feel secure enough to install his godhead and cult in her stead.

I sent in my name and the fact that I was a Roman citizen. I did not mention I was a Christian, an implicit denial that I compared in my mind with the denial of Peter and found equally expedient. The emperor kept me waiting for an hour, then I was ushered into a room whose walls were of thin-cut, poorly polished local marble. Guards in full dress regalia, a clownish rural parody of the armor and casques of Roman legionnaires, stood behind the emperor, who sat on a purple-draped throne. He was clad in a toga with a braided gold belt and was, I judged, in his mid-thirties. He must have weighed five hundred and fifty librae. He wore a coronet of silver laurel. Beneath it, his eyes were like green grapes all but lost in suet.

"Welcome," he said in thick Latin, aberrational in itself, for Romans generally spoke Greek together outside Italy.

"Kneel," said one of the guards to me.

I inclined my head. I was a minister of Jesus and a Roman, and I was not going to kneel to this obese Anatolian unless someone physically forced me to. The emperor looked irritated but did not order the guards to act.

"I recognize your name, of course. What Roman does not know of the Faevolians." From the way he mispronounced it, I was certain he had never heard it. Perhaps he thought he should have. "What brings such fame to our poor city?"

I told him in some detail about Christianity, adding, to allay what I could of his apprehensions, "Jesus has said that what is Caesar's belongs to Caesar and what is God's is God's. My religion is no threat to you, Your Excellency." I told him I would like to tell the residents of Bayba about Jesus.

The obese man shifted. Insofar as I could see any expression under the flabbiness, he was intensely considering my request. At last he spoke: "How would you like to arm wrestle?"

As insane as his hero, Caligula, I thought. His challenge was not, as with Thetorix, a wager that might allow me to preach, but simply an invitation that I dared not refuse. I accepted and two men in togas whom I assumed were "lectors" brought in a table but no chair for me. The table was built so he needed only lean to rest his elbow on it. But if I kneeled, my arm would be too high, and if I stood, too low.

"Your Excellency has a very favorable table," I said as I kneeled, instantly wishing I had kept silent. He pulled up the sleeve of his toga. The fat hung from it in wattles. At the wrist, Roman style, was a silver bracelet embossed with scenes of battle. Even with this unequal angle, I could have beaten a weakling. But somewhere beneath the lard there had once been the muscles of a soldier. He slowly brought my arm to the table.

"Again," he said. This time he wrenched my arm so suddenly that I sprawled and rolled down the two carpeted steps that led to his throne. As I rose, he said peevishly, "You hurt me by what you said about the table. It was almost as if you were saying I was not fair." He waited for me to apologize and when I did not he went on. "We had a Christian here, but we already have a god. I am the Emperor *Deity* Cremens." He touched his pudgy forefinger to his heart as the tavern keeper had done.

"But can Your Excellency not imagine a spiritual God under whom Your Excellency would be the temporal emperor as well as a dependent deity?" I asked cautiously.

The green eyes closed, giving the face a malevolent cast like that of a gigantesque clay god I had glimpsed inside an Asiatic death cult's shrine in Trapezus. I had a feeling that somewhere back in that head of grease was a light that sometimes showed with dangerous hotness. He opened his eyes.

"To me, as a deity, everything is imaginable."

"You can imagine being a Christian, then?"

But he was tired of sparring. "If I let you preach your religion, you would speak against me. I know you Romans."

"I would preach only the peace and joy of Jesus. It is a message Your excellency could hear without being offended."

His head began to nod. I saw now he was sick physically as he was mentally. Perhaps a narcoleptic, or a heart simply unable to pulse blood to so much bulk. I do not know by what strange route, what forest trails and mountain passes, his mind went, but when his eyes opened, he said drowsily, "The Emperor Deity Caligula was my friend."

I waited for him to say more. When he did not, I asked him quietly, "So may I preach?"

"Preach," he said, more an echo than a mandate.

I took him at his word. In a simple tunic next day, on a corner of the town square like any itinerant orator, I called on citizens as they went by to listen to me. Soon I had four in front of me. I talked of Jesus' life and sayings, emphasizing the peace that he brought, the simplicity of living by his ethics, and the hope of Christian faith. It was a sermon likely to appeal to this decaying and malignantly beleaguered town.

One of the guards who had been in Cremens's throne room saw me and drew close. The plumage on his helm and his red-and-white cape looked withered in the sunlight. An old woman saw him and inquired of me, "Sir, if we heed your message, what will our emperor, the deity Cremens, say?" She made the sign of obeisance.

"It was he who told me to preach," I replied. "Were not those his words?" I asked the guard. He looked uncomfortable.

"Is it true, Ivakah?" asked the old woman. Spoken to directly by someone who knew him, the soldier nodded assent.

"Thank you for your honesty," I said to him and turned to my listeners. "If the emperor has approved"—I had purposely omitted the salute and felt nervous—"what have you to fear? If what I say touches your hearts, come and bring your friends tomorrow. . . ."

The slow-witted soldier made up his mind to act on my omission. He drew his sword, elbowed my four listeners out of the way, and put the point at my chest.

"The Emperor Cremens told me I might preach," I said.

"Curse you, foreigner, you just did it again," said the soldier. "I should kill you on the spot." He debated with himself as my stomach fell, then, to my relief, marched me across the square to the rear of the palace and down a flight of stairs. It was the jail whose jailer, a sere man with cruel eyes, wore a band of purple on his soiled toga and a haughty look. The soldier explained my crime.

"I was told I could preach," I tried again.

"You are not charged with preaching," said the jailer. "You are charged with failing to salute the emperor."

"I am a Roman citizen," I said, invoking a right accorded throughout the Roman empire. It required whoever held me to take me before a Roman magistrate, tribune, or other officer.

"We are not Roman," the jailer sneered. "We are of the Kingdom of Polemonis, liege only to the Emperor Deity Cremens"—full salute—"and the king in Trapezus."

Technically, he was right. Roman law did not apply to vassal states. I protested that if anything happened to me, Rome would be unhappy, a statement I had no reason to believe was true. Two malodorous guards led me down a tunnel. As their smoky torches passed the peepholes of cells, weak voices, some of them women's, called out for pity in Greek, in Aramaic, in languages I did not know.

For a day and a night, I was locked in a similar chamber, then was led to the end of the tunnel, where there were four large sunlit cells. Three were occupied, and I was put in the fourth. There was no impediment to my talking with my three muscular jailmates, and I soon learned they were Cremens's gladiators. I, like them, they said to my horror, would be defending my life at the weekly games in two days.

Two of the prisoners were brute hulks, sailors from ships calling at Trapezus who had drunkenly robbed and murdered four people. Cremens had purchased them from Trapezus. The third, named Belzek, had come from Bayba, and like Cremens had gone to Rome, but as a gladiator. He was an expert in *retiarius*, the net and trident. In his early forties, he had been awarded the *rudis*, the wooden sword signifying honorable retirement.

He had come home as a hero and for a few years had led caravans to India. But he had lost everything in a Bactrian dust storm, turned to brigandage, and two months ago had been captured with six of his men. The men had already been killed by him and each other at the games. The town would like to see him pardoned. But any popular figure was a threat to Cremens.

I came to like Belzek, at least as much as I could someone who was likely to kill me in two days. For one thing, he comically pointed his forefinger not to his chest but at his anus every time he mentioned the name of Cremens.

"They will keep putting me out in the games until I make a mistake or somebody gets lucky, maybe you"—he smiled—"and then . . ." He turned his thumb down, the imperial gesture signifying death for the loser.

Belzek's view of death was fatalistic. He had killed so many in the games, seen so many of his friends killed, even killed them himself, that the wonder to him was that at forty-seven he was still alive. I wished I could have taken as sanguine a view. I spent a good deal of time praying and, whether because of the real threat of death or not, somewhat to my surprise I came to feel hopeful about and even comfortable with the idea of some kind of afterlife.

Belzek had a curious mind and listened with interest when I spoke about Christianity. He, in turn, told me of his family in Bayba and expatiated on local politics. His brother-in-law, a man named Prebea, was a sergeant in the emperor's guard who sympathized with Belzek but had to be more imperious toward him than Cremens himself to protect his own life. The guards were divided on Cremens, Belzek said. Some wanted to kill him and put themselves under the less-chaotic rule of Trapezus. Others liked the power and benefits they had under Cremens.

XXII

❖❖❖

The day of the games was unseasonably cool for early autumn. We four who were to be gladiators plus seven ordinary prisoners, one of them a woman, were taken to a pen under the arena. These seven wretches, all starved, whereas we had been well fed, even wined, had been dressed in motley tatters to make them attractive prey for the animals. Two of them, from their babbling, were insane. I felt a duty to speak to the quieter ones of Jesus, but they were so abject, so fearful, that I could draw no replies, only moans.

The Bayba games were primitive. In Rome, three hundred gladiators might compete in a single day, many at the same time, using seven kinds of weapons. Another hundred prisoners might be dispatched by a veritable zoo of animals. Here, Belzek would have his net and trident, but no armor, and I my cuirass, helm, sword, and a small Thracian shield. The sailors were designated *hoplomachi*, with full suits of rusty armor, swords, and shields. I could see their eyes sparkle with fear behind their visors. Belzek and I, the celebrities, would not fight each other in the first round. The sailors both hoped they would draw me.

Above us, the boards of the arena creaked as the populace streamed in. Down the corridor, a bull began to snort and a skinny old madman in our enclosure began to wail hysterically. Cremens's exchequer apparently was not deep enough for such exotic performers as lions or panthers.

The seven miserables were taken out of our pen and we four remaining were allowed to stand in our entranceway to watch the animal event. The seats were filled with three thousand or so people. The old man who had screamed at the bull's snorts and the woman were led by a guard onto the sand-covered arena. With heads bowed, they were paraded past the audience. The crowd whistled and hooted at them.

At the end of the circuit, the old man collapsed. The guard kicked him, then flopped him over. Another guard brought out a bucket of water and doused him. When that failed to revive him, a guard with a knotted whip and then one with a hot iron came out and applied their resuscitative methods.

The fallen man was unmoved by their diligence. He had, I was sure, died of fear. As the guards dragged him out by his feet, I found myself praying, not for myself but for these pitiful people who were to be killed by the animals. I begged God and Jesus to let them die as painlessly as the old man.

A guard led the frail woman into the arena. The light wind fluttered her tatters as she stood waiting in the empty ring, bewildered. No woman's crime could justify this enormity. Under the grandstand, the bull had been tormented into ferocity with knife jabs and now he trotted angrily from an entranceway. Gore from his wounds ran down his back and muzzle.

The woman saw the bull and took a step backward. He had not seen her. The crowd taunted him and he smacked his horns against the wooden barrier. A guard blew a sheep horn on the other side of the ring and the bull turned. Alerted by the woman's trembling rags, he faced her and his tail went up, his head rose. The crowd went silent save for the shouts of a drunk. The bull ran toward the pathetically small figure, the bright scraps of her garments like flames in the breeze, then picked up speed and lowered his horns.

The woman put one hand to her breast, the other to her genitals. As the bull reached her, she turned slightly and the bull's right horn caught her in the side. He reared his head, snatching her up from the sand as if she were a dry leaf. He jerked her to and fro in the air. She was like a rag doll, thrown about by the great back and shoulder muscles of the bull as he tried to dislodge her. At last, he dropped his horns to try to rub her off in the sand, and she flopped from the horn.

"Thank you, God," I said, seeing she was unconscious.

The bull tossed her once, then again, and finding no movement, left her and looked up again at the taunting crowd. A steer tender led his animal into the ring, and the bull followed it out docilely. In a minute, the steer man returned and yoked a halter under the woman's arms. As the steer dragged her body away at a trot, it left a streak of blood in the sand.

The next victim was given a sword to fight a fresh bull. He took a feeble swipe at it as it came toward him, horns lowered. He was gored several times before his screaming died. The next man cringed by the barrier, but the bull found him and impaled him against it.

I began to pray aloud, feeling that if God spared them even a moment of agony as a result of my pleadings, then it was useful for me to witness this horror. Belzek and the two sailors looked at me curiously. As one after another of the prisoners were killed, I found my prayers for them mixed with prayers that God would give me strength against my opponents and would kill Cremens with the most prolonged and excruciating torture.

At last, the animal games were done. The crowd, in good humor, cheered the steer as it dragged a log back and forth to smooth the sand. Then, the four of us marched to Cremens's box and, as tradition decreed, guards handed up our weapons for his inspection. When my turn came, the obese man smiled pleasantly at me and made a clumsy swipe with my sword.

The combat began with a *praelusio*, a sham fight among us with wooden swords. It excited the crowd and allowed us to study the strengths and weaknesses of our opponents. For instance, my first foe showed a tendency to lay on heavily for a few moments, then back away and drop his sword to catch his breath. By lot, he and I went first. We walked across the sand to the center. Five yards apart, we looked at the emperor's box. Cremens was too porcine to stand unless he had to—Belzek had told me he had a hole in the seat of his throne through which he defecated. He raised his arm and let it fall heavily into his lap.

With a deep breath, I brought up my shield. My opponent, sword unwieldy in his nautical hands, came toward me with a yell and began slashing. I dodged and parried, taking no solid blows on sword or shield. Impacts could weaken me and, besides, I did not want him to shatter my sword through a fluke.

As in the *praelusio*, he stopped when he was out of breath, dropped his sword and backed up. With one good feint and slash, I could have hamstrung him as easily as I might have sliced cheese. But it did not seem to me Christ's work to execute murderers. If I could let him fight aggressively and then disarm him, he could beg the crowd to appeal to the emperor for mercy.

Twice his wild blows clanged off my helm, leaving my ears ringing loudly. The crowd cheered his manic energy. Whenever I retreated, they hissed and whistled. He was the favorite, the simple sailor against the Roman sissy.

I could not let him swing away forever. Avoiding his blows was taxing. I would need all my stamina for Belzek. After his next sally, I struck his rusty sword just above the hilt, intending to knock it from his hands. Instead, it shattered. He was left with only two inches of blade. I paused, hoping he would signal to the crowd with a raised forefinger that he wanted mercy. But fearing I would move in to kill him, as he would have done to me, he panicked and lumbered toward the box of the emperor. The crowd jeered.

Cremens struggled to get out of his seat. He screamed imprecations at the sailor. One prisoner had already affronted him by dying before he could be gored. My opponent made a stumbling turn when he heard Cremens's curses, and clumped along the arena fence. He tripped in the sand, laboriously raised himself in the heavy armor and leaned panting against the fence.

From one of the entrances, the two torturers with iron and whip came. The mariner saw them and began running, but again fell. The whip man beat his legs while the man with the hot iron thrust it behind his knees where the flesh was exposed. A few in the crowd whistled derisively at the torturers while the hapless sailor twisted and screamed in the sand.

Two officers had gotten Cremens to his feet. He shouted and shook his fat arms at a squad of soldiers beneath him. The soldiers ran out and I saw the flash of their knives and swords, the rise and fall of arms and elbows as they stabbed the helpless man through his visor and every other chink in his armor.

There was a hum of disapproval in the crowd, but no overt hissing or catcalling. For while Cremens might seem ludicrous to an outsider, in Bayba his grossness was synonymous with monstrosity. His ferocity and capriciousness made him an object of terror. Yet, I thought, when tyrants rule by terror and by spectacles, the terror must be total and the spectacles must never miscarry. That the restive thousands in this audience dared even a low drone of reproach against Cremens's orders meant that his tyranny was insecure. But that was the future. I had to worry about living through the next hour.

Belzek's entrance with the other mariner-murderer brought the games back to order. I watched every move Belzek made against his opponent, hoping to discern some weakness in him. He, I was sure, would already have noted the slightly rolling way I moved because of my mutilated toes. The sailor took a few tentative swings. The ex-gladiator studied his opponent with a practiced eye, then thrust his trident into the man's calf. The mariner fell. With a swirl of the webbing, Belzek enmeshed him and circled, tightening the net until the armored man was caught like a great carapaced beetle in a spider's web.

"*Habet*," went up the traditional cry—he's had it. Within the net, the sailor frenziedly jabbed up his forefinger, begging for clemency. But all over the audience were fists with thumbs down. Belzek looked at Cremens for a decision. The emperor, hoisted by his aides, came to his feet. It was a chance to reassert his dignity. When the eyes of the crowd were on him, he showed his fat fist, thumb down. Belzek thrust, once, twice.

❀

The retired gladiator and I faced each other in the center of the ring, waiting for Cremens's signal. Even from here, I could see the emperor's pallid skin was subtinted gray. His exertions had affected the system of tubes and viscera that was made for a man of two hundred and fifty librae—a hundred and seventy pounds—and was now working to keep functioning one who weighed well over twice that. His chin slumped into the rolls of fat on his neck. He turned to a lector and said something and the man quickly handed him a silver cup. It must have been strong medicine. His head snapped up, he stood, though again with assistance, and raised his arm for us to fight.

I looked at Belzek. Would Jesus have simply accepted death from his trident? Perhaps. But I had decided that God was not ready for my ministry to end. That meant I could not afford the Christian game I had tried to play with the sailor. Belzek was too much my superior for that. I could only try to kill him.

Belzek began cautiously attacking as the crowd cheered. I watched his steps, knowing my life depended on my finding an Achilles' heel. I had seen none in the *praelusio* or his bout with the sailor. He charged, net protectively before him, then spun it out. I dodged it and struck at him, but he parried far up on his trident and furled the net, ready for another throw. Again, he stalked me. For a half hour that was the pattern, he the careful aggressor, I pushing him back with short quick slashes.

Gradually, I began to think that when I moved sharply right, he shifted with me a little farther than he needed to. Or was I mistaken? Again and again, I moved hard to the right. Each time he shifted slightly too far.

Was he making this seemingly abnormal move because his vision

231

was imperfect in his left eye? Or was he just awesomely canny, letting me construct an offense on that possibility so that when I depended on it he could kill me like a dove tricked into a snare? But did I have any choice except to go against his left side anyway? There, I had his trident to contend with, brother to a spear, a weapon I knew. In his right hand was the net, more foreign to me and treacherous.

I focused on his eyes and moved rapidly to his left. Alert and agile as he was, he seemed to keep me constantly in sight only with his right eye. I thought about a double feint—left-right—that would show me definitively how far he would commit himself. My mind on theory, I relaxed my practice. The net unfurled like a striking snake and I stumbled backward. The skein scraped my helmet and face, and caught my shield. I jerked the shield, but it was snagged. I dared not hold on to it further lest he pull me into his toils. He plucked the shield from me with his net like a hungry man snatching a citron from a tree. I felt a stab of fear. Without my shield, I was naked. He steadily moved on me, keeping himself between me and my lost shield, his eyes glowing with anticipation.

I retreated. The crowd jeered, and when I was near the barrier, threw food on me. His stalking tired me. I had to counter him or die. I moved suddenly to his left, risking a full trident stroke. He thrust, but not precisely enough. His tine only scratched my leg. I slammed his bowllike helm with my blade, shaking him, and skittered past him toward the shield at the middle of the arena. Belzek ran, too, but the weight of his trident, net, and heavy helm taxed him. I reached the shield first. I was out of breath, but he was panting.

I was sure now of the infirmity of his left eye. I worked him relentlessly, circling right, drawing his thrusts, chopping or parrying, and often hacking the trident when he paused. I would have hewn its oaken shaft were it not so well made. Our ages at last had begun to speak. Soon he was waving the weapon outward in long sweeps, a sign that his arm had become weary from the impact of my blows on the shaft.

He hurled the net more and more. I could feel fatigue in my calves, forearms, shoulders. Sweat gushed from my body. But I was not as tired as he—when I breathed my second wind, he breathed his third; at my third, he would be on his fourth. We had fought for an hour and a half when my sword stroke slid off his trident and nicked his thigh. In a few minutes, I cut his shoulder. His breath was coming faster. He fought on, knowing all the steps to take, hoping his body would take them. The crowd had lapsed into intense silence, as if they were players for high stakes in a game of dice. They shouted only when there was a flurry of blows.

232

I thought I was in control, but I underestimated his strength and his daring: I moved in to slash, but he made a prodigious net throw, letting it sail entirely from his hand. I tripped as I tried to avoid it and it dropped on me. He grabbed the net and pulled me toward him as if he were a fisherman and I a great, struggling fish. I dug in my heels, and he stabbed at me with his trident.

I flung myself to the side. The prongs hit the sand beside me. I gripped the haft. He gave a massive jerk, and I let the trident go. Belzek tumbled backward, knocking the wind from him, and I wriggled from the net and struck the trident from his hand with my sword. Though still dazed, he rolled over and reached for the net. I snatched it away. I had not been able to kill him, but I had disarmed him. He could only scoop up the little shield. Now it was I who stalked him, sword in my right hand, trident in my left, ever interposing myself between him and his fallen net.

The autumn shadows glided slowly from the grandstands across the arena. Both of us were streaked with blood, which had mixed with sand as it coagulated. Belzek's left eye had begun to drift, but his right had not lost its cool concentration. I knew where I had seen that look before. Years ago, Father and I had closed on a wild boar with one eye. The dogs were nipping in at it, and it was doomed. But its little red eye showed no passion at all.

I jabbed at Belzek with the trident, slashed with the sword. His shield parried this way and that. We were at the imperial box. Cremens leaned forward, avid in spite of his bulk, studying the contest from the perspective of a long-ago time when he was in Rome and an athlete. Again at the center, I feinted with the sword at Belzek's left shoulder and he brought the shield across to block me, exposing his chest.

With all my muscle behind it, I thrust the trident. He moved the shield to counter, but the trident caught the shield's rim and drove it into his solar plexus. The power of my oblique blow snapped the trident head from its staff. Belzek's arms dropped and I thrust violently again. The blunted weapon rammed his chest hard enough to kill. He staggered, his trained reflexes keeping him on his feet even as his eyes rolled back. Blood flowed from the wound and down his bare abdomen.

His mouth opened, but I heard no gasps. He went down, first on one knee. Then his body seemed to lose all life. He fell onto his face, the spirit, the great vitality gone. I had, I was sure, killed him. I felt a shock of grief and remorse. I need not have struck the last blow that had taken his life.

The crowd was shouting, furious that I had slain their favorite. A few white handkerchiefs blossomed, petitions to Cremens to order Belzek spared. But most in the crowd did not wave. They could see it was too late for human mercy. Above me, I heard Cremens braying, "Stab him! Cut his throat!" His face of lard squirmed with hatred. Could he not see the man was dead? I would not dishonor his body. "He's dead!" I called up, loathing this monstrous sow—and myself.

The emperor shouted to an elderly man below him who teetered out as fast as he could. I helped the nervous old man, presumably the court doctor, roll the body over and he held a mirror to the mouth, looked at the eyes, and hurriedly felt the throat, heart, and wrist. "Dead," he said to me almost as a question. I nodded. The man hurried at a broken gait back to the imperial box and called up his finding to Cremens. It spread around the arena, stirring cries of dismay and anger.

But even as the doctor had left the body, I thought I had seen its hand twitch. Such things happened when corpses stiffened, but it was too soon for that. The blood and sand were already caking on his chest. The wound was not deep. Was it not possible that the impact had simply emptied him of air? I fell on my knees, and pressed hard on his chest, to make of it a bellows as I had seen soldiers do when I was in the field with Father and a comrade had the wind knocked out of him. I put my ear to his mouth, pressed again and felt a faint rush of air. "Breathe, curse you!" I said. "Breathe! God, let him breathe," I prayed. I put my lips on his open mouth and as hard as I could blew my own air into his lungs, continuing to pump his chest. In his throat, I thought I heard a gurgle. Was it life? Or just dead air? I blew again, and in seconds I heard a croaking sound in his larynx. Oh, Jesus, I said to myself, is he alive? I took my mouth away. His chest was rising on its own. Yes, he was alive. I was sure of it. "Thank you, Jesus," I said, beginning to sob. "Thank you, God. Thank you!"

So far no one in the arena realized what had happened. They had seen the physician examine Belzek, leave him for dead, and report to Cremens. They had watched me, probably assuming I was mourning a brave rival. Belzek's breath rasped. His eyelids compressed with anguish, then his eyes opened. For a few moments, they were lost. Then they steadied.

"Zeus's stones, you hit hard," he grunted.

I cradled his shoulders and tried to lift him, but could only get him sitting. Cries of disbelief began to come from the crowd. He crooked his knee and rolled and with my help came to his feet. There was a moment of awed silence. Even the emperor was stunned, his fat lips wordlessly open.

Then from across the arena, came the hysterical shrill of a woman. "The kiss of life! The kiss of life!" Others picked up her scream. In this superstitious land, miracles were often promised, but no one trustworthy had ever seen one. Now, three thousand people were sure a miracle had taken place before their eyes. Their cries of "Kiss of life!" rang tumultuously.

People began to leap from their seats and run across the sand. I had seen enough miracle worship when Paul was almost mobbed at the cripple's house to know that this crowd—if they grabbed at us for souvenirs—could do to us by veneration what Belzek and I had not done to each other in combat.

At the sight of Belzek rising, the emperor, sword drawn, surrounded by a dozen guards, began making his way down a flight of steps leading to the sand. His face was blotched. I was sure he planned to have the guards subdue us, while he administered *coups de grâce*. I half dragged Belzek toward the crowd, but as I looked back, I saw to my astonishment Cremens's mouth twist in a gigantic grin, then he collapsed sideways. Jerked by a mighty spasm, his thick arms flung upward. The sword arced from his hand, glittered in the sun, and dropped harmlessly on the sand. The guardsmen tried to support him, but he rolled from their arms and like a great globule of tallow oozed down the steps. With some reservoir of strength, he squirmed a few lengths on the sand, then lay still, surrounded by his shocked guards.

Before I could get Belzek to the mob, four of Cremens's guards led by a captain rushed us. Belzek's wound had reopened. I pushed him behind me and turned weaponless to face the soldiers. The captain's eyes, however, were not afire with battle, but with panic. He lowered his sword and shouted, "The kiss of life!"

They shoved me to where Cremens lay in the sand. The face of the emperor was so contorted that it looked like a twisted bread loaf. One eye squinted like a currant partially rolling from the bread. The other was buried forever within the yeasty face. The captain grabbed me by the back of my neck. "Give him the kiss of life!" he shouted in my ear.

Cremens's warped mouth was as fat and purple as a scavenger fish's. The guardsman let go of my neck, put his sword point where his hand had been, and cried, his voice cracking, "*Give him the kiss of life!*" Another push and the sword would stab between my skull and the top of my neck. If I wanted to live, I had to comply. I bent over the quivering and moaning lips, curved by his seizure into the revolting simulacrum of a seductive grin.

Suddenly, from the imperial box, six or eight guards began to shout down at us. Those around Cremens looked up. The mob saw something strange was happening and slowed their onrush. "Do *not* give him the kiss of life!" ordered a sergeant from the box. The guardsmen around Cremens drew their swords and the captain turned his blade from me toward the seats.

"Prebea! Do not be a fool!" he called up.

Belzek also shouted, "Prebea!" I recalled that was his brother-in-law's name! He was this rebel sergeant!

Behind Prebea, the guards seethed and gibbered. "Put down your swords," Prebea cried to the group in the sand. The captain looked indecisive for a moment, then rushed toward the steps, followed by his guardsmen, leaving Cremens in the sand.

The crowd was silent, spectators now of a combat that affected them far more than the contests of gladiators. The emperor's loyalists began fighting their way up the steps. But Prebea, above them, had the advantage. Evading the captain's jabs, he sliced into his neck, all but taking off his purple-plumed head. In a few minutes of strenuous battle, the rebels slew the guards on the sand while in the grandstand others chased and murdered the unarmed lectors.

Prebea ran to the fallen emperor. Cremens's one eye seemed to wink knowingly. His mouth opened. It was a brilliant pink inside and gave out small piglike grunts, as he tried to speak. But it was too late for words. Prebea, holding his sword like a dagger, plunged it into Cremens's chest and blood gushed up the blade. He pulled it out and held it high to the crowd.

"The tyrant is dead!" he shouted. He waved his men into the seats and they obeyed on the run. The rabble, a giant tidal wave, roared, mad with their freedom from Cremens's terror, and rushed forward. Belzek, enough recovered to limp rapidly, hurried with me behind Prebea's men into the stands. But it was not us that the mob sought.

The first of them, burly and agitated, scooped up the sword of a fallen guard. With a two-handed chop, he severed the great round head of the emperor and held it up by its hair. The second man snatched his silver coronet from the sand, the third tore at his belt. Others shredded the tentlike toga, fighting for a relic of the late emperor deity.

When the decapitated body was naked, the mob cut at it with knives or ripped off gobbets with their fingers. I looked with disgust and shock as they ran off in triumph with a hand, a fat gory foot. Like a school of voracious fish in a feeding frenzy, they swarmed the mountainous cadaver. From their midst, there came loud snaps and quarrelsome shouts. Men—and a few women—ran off with bones, bits of entrails, organs, babbling maniacally at their good fortune. When the bones were gone, the remaining seekers of trophies clutched up sand that Cremens's blood had soaked, running from the scramble with hands raised like bloody gloves. At last, the shouting ended. The crowd moved away from its grisly work. Where the body had been, there was only a shallow pit dug clean of sand to the dirt below.

I felt like vomiting. However much Cremens had deserved to die, I was appalled. I had never even imagined such savagery. The relics, I was sure, preserved in amphorae of oil, would be sold and resold. Counterfeits would be on the market within days. At last, the crowd calmed and gathered under the box where Prebea stood. Prebea summoned Belzek to him and the two, both sanguinary with combat, embraced. The crowd resumed their chant, "The kiss of life," acknowledging not just the miracle of Belzek's return to life, but the end of Cremens's tyranny.

Prebea held aloft the bloody sword that had slain Cremens. The crowd cheered. When they were quiet, he cried to them, "We will have no more emperors in Bayba!" and handed the sword to Belzek. The crowd screamed ecstatically. After they quieted again, Belzek said in a loud voice, "I do not choose to rule. I have no experience. I choose instead to be ruled in Bayba by Prebea, and in my heart and deeds by the God Christ Jesus who, through this young man, gave me the kiss of life."

The dramatic words of Belzek about Jesus did not establish a theocracy nor did the promise of Prebea about no more emperors create a republic. Prebea consolidated his power by massacring the former adherents and toadies of Cremens who had been too stupid to flee, a substantial number of their families, and a twelve-year-old whom Cremens had designated son and heir, along with the lad's mother. On the spiritual side, Prebea let me preach unhindered to a people badly in need of religion.

I sent a letter via caravan to Paul, and began organizing. Belzek was my first and best new Christian. For his baptism, I used a few drops from Andrew's flask. We began building a cadre. I instructed the Baybans on Jesus and his teachings. We labored fifteen, twenty, hours a day. The results, even giving due weight to the impetus from Belzek's return to life, were awesome. For the immersion, we led two thousand new Christians to a stream that ran cold and clear from the Pontic Mountains. I prayed God would forgive me for making part of the ritual a murmured, "The kiss of life," as I kissed each of them on the cheek. The ceremony and accompanying festivals took the best part of three days.

It was still two more weeks before I entrusted this huge new church to Belzek. But he, I knew, would be the best of regents for Jesus. Thetorix had become a Christian for practical reasons. Belzek had become a Christian because he was certain that Jesus, through me, had given him his life.

XXIII

❖❖

In Troas, I found a small coastal ship with a single trapezoidal sail that edged down the littoral on good days, and scudded into the nearest cove at the threat of bad weather. One morning, a snowstorm blew in and trapped us at sea. The waves were choppy and high. The next day was brilliant and icy. A week later, we hove into sight of Ephesus, the temple of Artemis as white as the snowy terraces on which it stood.

I went first to the house of Aquila and Priscilla and found Paul alone at his tent loom. His eyes teared and he hugged me with relief. "I had heard nothing since Sinope," he said. He looked thin and told me he had been eating the coarsest bread for breakfast and shrinking his lunches in order to combat the hubris he might otherwise have felt over his successes in Ephesus. He gave me a letter that my mother, wisely judging the surest route, had sent care of Paul instead of to my lodgings.

I was eager to read it, but put it aside as I told Paul of my journeys. He was pleased, and said that Titus and Timothy also would soon be back from their ministries. He also mentioned that James's Jerusalem countermission had circled from Ancyra through Cappadocia but was generally winning few followers.

"How fortunate they got such a late start in Galatia," I said, not daring to go further about the benefits of our bridge cutting. Paul frowned, then broke into a rare wide grin.

"Ah, you and Titus. Well, Menander"—one of the few Greek writers he liked—"says even dark acorns like you two may produce good oaks." His suggestion of forgiveness and the warmth of his humor

239

and shared erudition disarmed me: I could not, as I had wanted to, confront him with our growing doctrinal conflicts.

I read Mother's letter on the way to the shop off the agora above which I had lived and where I again would seek lodging. It was loving and gossipy, but gave no hint of Father's feeling toward me.

At the shop, there were two dirty, water-stained letters, one from Deborah, one from Ezra. I broke the crumbly wax seal on Deborah's. Could it be possible that I had not seen or heard from her in more than four years? Her letter had been sent almost a year ago, three months before I left for the Black Sea.

She wrote that until recently, she had received only one of my letters—from Antioch of Syria—where she had written twice, telling me of her uncertainties about our love. But she had heard nothing more. Then, my letter from Ephesus had come—almost two years afterward—and too late.

She was torn by hearing that I still loved her and wanted to marry her, for, certain I was out of her life, she had married the merchant of whom Grandfather had written. He was a forty-five-year-old bachelor, born a Jew but now a Christian with Roman citizenship. He had wooed her for two years, and gradually, reasonably, persuaded her to marry him. She helped him keep his books, he helped her and her aunt with the smeltery and copper-crafting business. They were hoping to have a baby.

I read on: "When I wrote and you did not answer, I sensed you had found in your mission what I initially found in mine. Your silence and your failure to come to me led me to believe that you were using my refusal to marry you as a knife to cut me from your heart. But even if you had loved me enough to leave Paul and come to me on the possibility we might marry, I would have been wise if I could have refused you. Although we were once everything in each other's lives, we shamed ourselves with a shame that I, at least, would never have been able to forgive myself for. It would have poisoned us as married people.

"And now the woman that I have become is not one who would want to marry a Christian missionary, always at the farthest reach of life. Nor am I a woman whom a Christian missionary would want to marry, although I am still a prayerful Christian. Through my prayers and with good fortune, I have found a way of living with some of the contentment that I want. My life is without blazing hearth fires, but also without terrible burns. And yet, oh Demas, even as I write these words, I burn."

She said nothing about loving her husband. Nor was there a vestige of her consuming love affair with Christ, the jealous love that had forced on us lunatic restrictions that in the end shipwrecked us. After we were caught, I thought angrily, did the Christ inside her reject her because she had strayed with me, a mere man? Or was that too Sophoclean? Better for me to believe she had simply been worn down and chosen Christian resignation over Christian passion.

And I? I was left with a raw cavity in my body and in my soul, a longing for a woman who I must bring myself to believe did not exist anymore. I thought of her long, smooth body in the arms of an older man. I thought of her gone from the home I had imagined, the kitchen, the infants' small room, from walks and rides. I was barred forever from her kisses, the smell of wine and food and spices on her breath, her laughter, her bravery, her competence in all things.

I did not even have the cold solace of absolute certainty. Deborah had changed from devout Jewish schoolgirl, to Grecophile adolescent, to zealous Christian, and now to thriving factory owner, rich merchant's wife, and mother-to-be. Might she not change again, for she had said she still burned for me?

Why had she not waited? But for people like us, there never was any waiting. We wanted things when we wanted them. She had wanted an end to distress and had married a man she did not love to find it. I had wanted the fulfillment of my work for Jesus with Paul, and had traveled the highways of Asia Minor in its pursuit, and lost her in the process.

I opened the letter from Ezra. He wrote that Grandfather had died in his sleep. I gasped, already all but broken by Deborah's news, and now triply burdened with grief over the death of Grandfather and with the heavy guilt of not having been in Borhaurus to ease his passing.

Next day, I went suppliantly to the synagogue, where the rabbi let me pray with him for Grandfather and agreed to conduct a small Kaddish. When I was young, Grandfather's heart had always been open for me. He had never let me down. Gently and wisely, he had shown me his God who had become my own God in union with Jesus. With Grandfather gone, I had no one to confide in, to counsel with in his special way.

Because I loved him so completely, and he me, his death left me sorrowing, but not inconsolable. In contrast, the loss of Deborah was an unhealing wound. I wanted the comfort of prayer. Yet I could not pray. I wanted the rapture of God's joy and calm, but I could not summon it. I seemed no longer of interest to Jesus and God, for I could not reach them and ask for relief from the torment of my grief, my anger and my guilt.

However overwhelming my personal pain, our cause prospered. Paul was well into a campaign against Ephesus's legions of sorcerers, necromancers, magicians, thaumaturgists, false prophets, and fakirs, preaching that "their words and writings will burn in the fires of the righteous like the filthy rags of lepers on the day Christ comes to judge."

Paul had only symbolic fires in mind, but his influence had grown so great that two dozen magicians decided to publicly burn their incantatory sheets, magic texts, papyrus slips for spell-casting, and other charms. They appeared one night at the agora, dressed in their outlandish skins and cloaks, and smelling vilely of the various ointments they used against evil spirits.

One wore a necklace of gallow's nails, another carried a crystal jar of locust eggs. A snake charmer in a saffron loincloth with a great snake around his shoulders wept as he beheaded the creature with a scimitar and laid it on the pyre. The leaping flames made the colonnades of the agora look like trembling ancient spirits—phantoms too feeble to protect themselves.

While Titus and Timothy were away, I worked as Paul's secretary, taking dictation. He sent the same basic messages to all the churches, modifying for local problems. To Corinth, for instance, he commented on a member caught in adultery with his stepmother. Paul, himself scourged so many times, told the church "to deliver this man to Satan for the destruction of the flesh, that his spirit may be saved on the day Jesus comes to judge."

I winced, thinking this sounded like an invitation for some fanatic Christian to have the man whipped or even killed. Paul felt my hesitation and looked up.

"Do you know how they will read that?" I asked.

He did not even accord me an answer, but gestured dismissively at my objection like a man brushing crumbs from the table with the back of his hand, and went on dictating.

His letters were not always so harsh. At times, as we sat in the cold by the flickering oil light, Paul would clear his throat and spin out words so moving I could hardly write them.

"Putting away falsehood," he once dictated, "let everyone speak the truth with his neighbor. If you are angry, do not let the sun go down upon it. Let all bitterness and wrath and clamor and slander also be put away from you, and all malice. Hate what is evil, hold fast to what is good, outdo one another in showing honor, be patient in tribulation. Whatever is true, whatever is just, whatever is pure, whatever is gracious, if there is anything worthy of praise, think about these things. Never flag in your zeal for them. Be aglow with the spirit. . . ."

He stopped, drained, waiting for the well to refill. I wanted to praise him, but did not I knew only that when he was speaking this way, he was being touched by something beyond himself. I knew the words came from his unique liaison with God.

It was now a few months before my thirtieth birthday, almost five years since I had left Borhaurus and Deborah and joined Paul. April, its freshness borne in from sea and mountain, had come to Ephesus. Paul was talking of moving on before winter, and I, too, was eager for Greece and the west.

He had managed everything with administrative excellence in Ephesus. The church was strong, respected, well-to-do, and was still growing. Soon it would rival Antioch in size. But Paul was uneasy. He felt increasingly that he had not addressed certain of the city's social horrors.

Among other things, there were kidnappings of children who were auctioned out of town to rich perverts for sexual use. In some cases, parents sold their own children for such purposes. The city also abounded in child prostitution, torture rings, gambling, child drunkenness, and the peddling of rotten, harmful goods to the poor. Slaves also concerned Paul.

We once passed the city slave pens with its retarded Phrygians and Cappadocians consigned to traders by relatives; its uprooted ebony Nubians; brown-haired Britons; gnomish Orientals. All were displayed as though they were fowl or animals. Wives in one pen called out to their husbands in another, children screamed for their parents. At this sight, Paul's lips tightened bitterly.

There was much else that he found shameful in the behavior of the Ephesians. Even more than Christianity, Judaism had taught him to abhor idols and pagan talismans. In May, the devotees of Artemis would convene in Ephesus from the whole empire for the Artemision, a festival held every four years. The celebration produced a Danaän shower of gold for the city's merchants. Tiny goddesses, coin-sized temples, huntress bows, moons, obscene fertility objects were sold at exorbitant profits.

Throughout April, Paul preached against the idolatry. Late that month, a delegation of silver-, gold-, and leadsmiths and other merchants came to beg him to suspend his attacks, at least during the Artemision. Their leader, one Demetrius, a leadsmith, said they had been building stocks of goods for a year and would lose hundreds of thousands of drachmas if Paul turned the celebrators away from their wares.

He showed Paul a miniature replica of the pocked black stone now in the temple to Artemis that supposedly fell from the sky several hundred years ago as a gift and sign from the goddess. A few cavities were drilled in the basalt pebbles to imitate the pocks. I was sure it would be sold for a hundred times what the labor cost. Demetrius, an excitable man, said his workers who made such trinkets were the very people Paul most sympathized with and that Paul was now driving them to beggary. Overcome by his vision of ruin, he threatened Paul.

More moderately, a goldsmith with at least an elementary idea of our religion suggested that later in the year, perhaps, the manufacturers could devote some of their production to Christian items. "We could make crosses of gold and silver, or of lead for the less well-to-do, or perhaps an elegant enamel plaque showing your deity vanquishing some demon of your choosing." Paul treated them as Jesus did the moneychangers, all but shoving them out of his room.

As it transpired, Paul's exhortations cut deeply into sales of the trinkets. By the second week of the Artemision, it was clear the merchants would suffer a disaster. One afternoon, Demetrius, supported by the other sellers, delivered an incitant harangue against Paul from the steps of Artemis's temple. With fire and eloquence, he convinced the huge crowd of visitors that Paul had defiled Artemis. "If he succeeds," he screamed, "our great goddess, worshipped throughout the world, will be cast on a dung heap! Forgotten!" The mob poured down the terraces, intent on murdering Paul.

I had been listening and ran ahead, stumbling and cursing, trying to get to Paul before they did. By the private baths of Artemis's ethnarch, the Megabyzos, the eunuch priests ran out, their suety bodies draped in towels, and watched with wide eyes. But they made no move to join the avengers of their patroness.

Paul was meeting in his lodgings with Titus and Timothy—who were now back in Ephesus—and, over his obstinate objections, we convinced him he must hide. We rushed him first to the house of an assistant minister, who hid us while he went out to find Paul a safer refuge. It was dusk when he returned with word that one of the Asiarchs with whom Paul had cooperated on a cloaca project would hide Paul in his cellar—ideal, for who would search for him at the home of a pagan dignitary?

After dark, Titus and I escorted Paul up the hill toward the house of the Asiarch. But a hundred yards away from it, a dozen men emerged from orchards on both sides of the street. We shielded Paul, but clubs came out of the night like unseen stones. When I regained consciousness, I found Titus slapping my cheeks.

"They took him," he said frantically.

I was sure Paul had been killed, but when we reached the house of the Christian minister, we learned Paul was in jail. The mob had not dared kill him, but had filed charges against him of provoking a riot. It was not until morning that we were able to see him. He was on a cot. The white-haired Asiarch had been with him for an hour. Paul's face was puffed almost unrecognizably, his right hand broken when he had shielded his face. The mob had not done it. A cellmate, now removed, had.

"He beat me until I could not bear it. Even the jailer, who had been procured, could not abide it," Paul whispered.

From Paul and the Asiarch, who had made inquiries, we learned that one of the Asiarch's servants (now fled) had betrayed Paul. A venal Roman magistrate, bribed we suspected by the merchants, had put Paul in a cell with a brute facing trial for mayhem. The felon had been made to understand that if he hurt Paul badly enough, his own sentence would be lighter. Titus and I looked at each other furiously.

"Do not harm him," Paul said and coughed, holding his chest, on which the man had stomped. "It is fortunate I believe in a God who raises the dead," he added with a wan smile.

"This is not the way of Ephesus, good Paul," said the Asiarch, dismayed that his servant and city had brought Paul to this estate, "not the way at all. I will not eat or wash until I have won your freedom."

Paul sat up and took the Asiarch's two hands and held them silently and again I saw the miracle of faith that Paul carried within him. The elderly pagan knelt by the bed, his rich gown rubbing on the dirty floor. Tears streamed down Paul's face, not of pain, but of gratitude. When his tears stopped, he prayed, "God, I thank you for this beating. Already, it has begun to bring Christ Jesus to one of the most honorable men of Asia Minor. What is my poor pain to such a happening as that?" The immaculate Asiarch and the dirty Christian, two elderly, brave, godly men, embraced, neither saying anything, in a tableau that would have stirred a stone to empathy.

The Asiarch convinced higher Roman officials in Ephesus that they could not keep a Roman citizen in a jail where he had been illegally beaten. Paul was freed, but the criminal charges still stood against him. This time, we hid him in the basement of a Christian barber to recuperate, pending his trial.

Later that day, I drew Titus aside to talk about how we could revenge Paul. Titus believed in an eye-for-an-eye as much as I did.

But we concluded that if we or any hireling of ours killed Demetrius, it would not take a dead man's finger magically pointing to reveal who was behind it. We nursed Paul for a week, and by that time he was restless and wanted to speak out before the Artemision ended.

"This Demetrius and his people will kill you." Titus reasoned with him. "It will be four years before they get an opportunity to make back their losses."

"Yes, and I will tell them that four years hence I will speak again against their idolatry."

"Paul," I said, "if you try to speak, you will not be alive in four years, not even tomorrow."

"This is not the time or place," Titus said. Mild Timothy joined in, along with two visiting Macedonian ministers, Aristarchus and Gaius who had been seized by the mob and had narrowly escaped being murdered. We argued that Paul should be leaving Ephesus anyway; that its church was strong enough to function without him, and, at this moment, might be more secure if he left, rather than inflaming the city against all Christians. The last argument was the most persuasive. Paul agreed to flee.

Our problem then became how to smuggle him out of the city. Lictors, legionnaires, city constables, bounty searchers, and the merchants themselves would all be watching to make sure he did not leave before his trial. We devised a plan, jointly forced it on Paul, and called in the barber. He cut the locks from a devout old woman, shaved Paul's face, and attached the woman's lank gray hair to Paul's with horse glue and pine resin. Giggling like girls, the old woman and an aged friend dressed Paul in ragged woman's robes and wrapped a dirty piece of cloth around his head as a turban.

"Walk around, sir. Let us see you," said the newly bald crone. Paul limped decisively around the room. "No, sir, like this," said the woman. She mocked her own slow gait, bending even further than was natural. Paul imitated her.

"Better, much better," she said.

"Now *think* like a woman," said the other aged woman. She lowered her voice and said as if she were a peremptory man, "You here, old mother, get your broom and sweep up those crumbs. Do you think I feed all the cockroaches in Ephesus from my table?" She handed Paul a broom while everyone laughed, including Paul, who, however, declined to sweep.

The husband of the shorn woman arrived and looked with amazement at his wife. After his role was explained to him, he said, "Well, then, good Paul, or rather Rachel, when we go out, walk a few steps

246

behind me, and if I speak to you, only nod, do not speak—for both our sakes and for our Jesus', too."

A caravan of women slaves was leaving that day for Persia. Its leader, a man with the blinkless, amoral eyes of a pit viper, was the brother-in-law of a Christian. The young and middle-aged were in one group, the older in another, all loosely tied together, less from fear that they would flee than for order. My gaze was drawn to a slave of astonishing beauty, her face perfectly contoured, Oriental at the eyes, perhaps from some ancient Kirghiz fused with her Phrygian blood. A guard said something to her, but she did not answer. I saw why. Her vague gaze and the loose quiver of her lips told me she was moronic. What Persian monster would she serve as paramour? What indignities would be visited on her childlike womanhood?

Paul was among the old women, shoulders hunched. He would not have brought many drachmas at auction. He and his fellow slaves trudged slowly through the avenues of the city, across the river and through the gates.

With Paul safely out of the city, Titus, Timothy, Gaius, Aristarchus, and I left separately. We stayed well behind the caravan for two hours, then drew up and reclaimed Paul and his donkey. Paul threw the rags and the wig far off the road and picked at the glue and resin stuck to his hair. "I would not be a woman," he said, "or a slave, either, for anything in the world."

"Seven years ago," Paul told us as we approached the stubble of masts in the harbor of Alexandria Troas, "I was here and thought of taking a ship for Rome, but God bade me do otherwise." I wished, oh, how I wished, that God would communicate his commands to me as directly as he did to Paul.

We were four weeks in Alexandria Troas, our last mission in Asia, then sailed to Philippi in Macedonia, a Roman military colony with full Roman rights. We called first on Luke, the doctor who had accompanied Paul on his last trip. He was tall, austere, and I doubted we would stir much warmth between us. But he loved Paul, and was as loyal to him as Titus and Timothy.

For the first time since I had been with Paul, we were lodged in a luxurious villa, one belonging to a widow named Lydia, a dealer in purple dyes and inks. She was the only woman I had ever seen Paul talk with as if she were his equal. She argued with him even when he was right. He had a bantam rooster look about him when he was with her. I almost imagined something might once have happened between them, although she was as lean as a battle-ax, with a face to match, and long hennaed hair. When Paul had converted her seven years before, she had immediately ordered her entire household to become Christians.

In his first sermon, Paul spoke to a group of Thracians whose ancestors had been brought to Philippi by King Philip of Macedonia to mine the gold in the hills nearby. They were morose and debased, and their women were overworked, resentful, and had the tongues of asps. Paul admonished the men to live more cheerful and moral lives, and then addressed the women.

"Be subject, you wives, to your husbands as to the Lord," Paul preached. "For the husband is the head of the wife, as Christ is head of the church. As the church is subject to Christ, so let wives be subject in everything to their husbands."

Afterward, Lydia poured a boiling deluge on Paul such as I sometimes wished I had the courage to. "Paul, you are totally out of touch with the world?" she said, so loudly any passerby could hear. "These poor male beasts do not need a stupid speech about their superiority to their wives. They need one about not beating them, or selling their little girls into slavery, or putting female babies out in the woods to die!"

"Lydia," he retorted, "do not tell me you spend your every waking hour studying the workings of the average Thracian household. If the men are cruel, frustrated, it is an outgrowth of drink, lewdness, even of their wives' belligerency. . . ."

"Wives' belligerency? How would *you* know about belligerent wives?" Paul looked hurt and Lydia, having intimidated the unintimidable, softened. "Paul, please, please, before you start solving the social problems of Philippi, briefly talk to me. Is that so great a thing to ask?"

"No, Lydia," Paul said straightforwardly in one of those recoveries of humility that so ennobled him. "I was a fool. Things begin to go well and I think I know everything. I embrace Satan and hubris. I am sorry."

"You are *God's* fool, Paul," she said, so mollified that she took his hand.

Philippi, except for the Thracian minority, was faring well and we did not linger. We rode out in the shadow of the Pangaeus Mountains, from which all but the uppermost caps of snow had melted. Streams crashed down, gurgling raucously in the culverts beneath the Roman road. Soon we crossed fields of hot, fragrant asphodel and flax. We entered forests of oak and plane and passed mountain lakes, and then hillside villas.

We came on Thessalonica around a bend in the coast road. It was the most beautiful city I had ever seen. Founded lost ages ago as Therma, it rose from its scimitar-shaped harbor in terraces like the bows of warriors. On its environs, a marble arena stood among fruit orchards. White city walls encircled its temples, the columned façade of its theater, its bathhouses fed by hot mountain water, the porticoes of pools shaded by cypresses.

On his last trip, Paul had realized that a church in Thessalonica could spread Christianity from its busy harbor to the world. Unlike Trapezus, the city was dedicated to accomplishment, northern in its energy, agnostic rather than atheistic like Athens, where Paul had one of his few failures. Thessalonica was admiring of genius, and thus receptive to Paul, although it found some of his tenets too confining for its exuberance.

We called first on Jason, an aging textile and tent maker who seven years ago had let Paul work in his large factory. Paul saw his old bench and the crone bending over the loom. She moved for him and he wove two rows, careful not to distort her pattern, while Jason and his workers stood by smiling.

I was enamored with the city's beauty, wealth, variety, its *rhythms*. Aristarchus, its minister, and his deputy Secundus attended us, taking us to small food shops, out-of-the-way markets, vistas of the sea we would never have found on our own.

I could have stayed in Thessalonica for months, perhaps years, but with fall coming on, Paul sent us out again. He gave himself the longest mission, first to Dyrrhachium on the Adriatic Sea, north to Illyricum, and then south to Nicopolis. He assigned me the region around Mount Olympus, and Thessaly. Aristarchus and Secundus were given eastern Macedonia. We were to rendezvous in Corinth by winter.

XXIV

✦✦

The Greeks, pacified for centuries by the Macedonians and Romans, were easy to preach to, but difficult to convert to Christianity. Their foreign rulers had forced on them many gods, and they had adapted to them all. They no longer believed in any. The only sincere piety in this part of Greece was among the Jews. There were seldom enough men to form a synagogue, so they formed a *proseuche*, a fenced grove where they met and discussed Judaism. The rabbis welcomed me on the basis of my maternal Jewishness and invited me to speak to their flock.

In a village south of Mount Helicon, I stayed a week with a rabbi and his wife. I made no attacks on the Law, but the eleven Jews and I argued vigorously and companionably over whether the Messiah I preached was the one promised by the prophets or merely a prophet himself. At week's end, three decided they were Christians, though they did not want to be baptized. I did not stand on ritual.

Our two religions were so similar compared to agnosticism and paganism that I was sure my three "converts" would maintain a felicitous fellowship with their Jewish brothers. Would that by some miracle I could have carried their touchstone of love to the cities and erased the bitterness between our two creeds. Why did we hate and clash, worshipping as we did the same God, different only in our views of his manifestation? Would it always be Jews against Christians, Christians against Jews? But if Paul with all his experience and wisdom could not find firm common ground for Jew and Christian, how could I?

250

On my way again, I was an hour from the village when I saw a work chariot pulled off the road. Four men sat beside it drinking, although it was still morning. They had not even bothered to unhitch their horses. Three or four more sets of legs protruded from under the chariot. In front of me a stretch of the uneven road had been partially washed away. This was a repair crew, made up of broken-down Roman military horses, and perhaps broken-down auxiliaries. My first thought was that Father would have had them flogged.

As I approached, I saw one of the drinking men say something to the two others and they got up and blocked my path. I felt for my sword, for all of them were armed with work knives.

"Persian?" the first man asked, trying to hide his respect for the workmanship of my armor with a disdainful tone. He had on a Roman cuirass, but was a country Greek. He muttered some word at me in what I assume he took to be Persian. I patted my donkey into motion. But one of the others took its bridle.

"Roman," I said, wondering whether to draw.

"Roman? With that nose?" said another of the men. I angered, but still hoped I could extricate myself without trouble. "We could sell that," he said of my armor.

"Give it to us as tribute," said the first man. The road menders gathered around me too closely for me to draw my sword. The man holding my bridle tightened his grip on it. If I gave these scurvy pirates my armor, they would kill me so I would not report it to the next Roman authority. Indeed, the man with the bridle reached into his girdle, where I saw a knife hilt.

I kicked him in the testicles with my right foot as I gouged my left into the donkey's haunches. The big Muscat broke from the group but almost plunged into the eroded cavity in the road. I looked back and saw all but the man I had kicked running for the work chariot.

The road ahead ran through a field before disappearing into a forest. In minutes, I saw the chariot behind me. Three men were in it, the Greek in the cuirass lashing the horses with the reins as if he knew what he was doing. Using my dagger, I cut my panniers loose. I looked back again, seeing my fine goat-hair cloak, my cook pot, my weighted gourd in the road behind. The chariot was gaining. I beat my donkey and he did his best, but the elderly steeds of the road crew were responding to the whipping. I heard the creak of the chariot, a light wooden box with latticed sides on two big wheels.

Suddenly, what looked like a spear clanged on a stone in the road just ahead of me, throwing sparks. As I swept over it, I saw it was a stone pry. When I glanced back, I saw the wild, unshaven faces of the trio. One man held a second pry, the other a mattock. Both leaned from the chariot, eager to strike at me. My heart beat against my ribs like a bat in a bushel. I drew my sword, giving up a hand on the bridle.

The chariot was soon only ten yards behind me, rocking crazily, almost tipping. The driver screamed, trying simultaneously to get the men on opposite sides of the box, to control his steeds, and yet to keep a hand free to lash them. The mouths of the nags were drawn back by the cruel bits in frothy parodies of smiles.

In moments, they would be beside me. I frantically surveyed the men and the chariot. Its left wheel was wobbling. Now they were abreast of me. I ducked as the man with the mattock swung and it whistled over my head. The next swipe would crush my skull.

Desperate, I turned the donkey toward the careening chariot. I thrust my sword into the wheel's unsteady spokes. The blade spun from my hand and jammed against the axle supports. The wheel hurled off with a shriek. The bare end of the axle raked into the road, pitching the box leftward as I kicked my donkey out of the way.

The horses fell in a tangle of reins. The chariot's momentum flipped it on its side, and the two men with weapons, screaming a terrified duet, soared out as if they had been catapulted. I ducked to avoid one of them, but he flew into me, taking both me and the donkey down with him.

When I came to, my head throbbed. I lay beside the road, my hands and legs tied with pieces of the reins. Dust from the crash and from the horses' thrashing hooves hung in the late afternoon air. The man in the cuirass and the man who had swung the mattock, both scuffed and dirty, stood looking down at me, the latter groaning from an injured arm. A few feet away lay their comrade, blood still running from his mouth, his head askew on his neck, dead. The two men over me saw I was conscious and began spitting in my face. I tried to think of a way to escape, but the heavy knots were secure. I closed my eyes while they spat and sought agitatedly for an argument for my release.

"My father is an official in Rome," I said to the driver. "He will pay you. Or if you send to my coreligionists in Corinth"—a day and a half's ride—"they will ransom me."

"And have the Romans hang us from a tree for our efforts?" he said. "Which is what we have decided to do with you, Man-who-calls-himself-Roman," added the injured man.

Up until now I had forced my mind to be calm knowing only that I was in danger. But the stark statement that I was to die on a cross panicked me and made me shut my eyes again, but this time so they

252

would not see my panic. When I opened them, I said, my voice unnaturally high, "No, brothers, there is money—"

The driver kicked me in the side. "There is money in your armor and your dagger and your donkey," he said. I saw he already had my purse in his hand. "Safe money."

"Take it. Spare me," I said.

"To sing to the Romans? No, Sir Killer-of-our-comrade, we will make a bird of you that will sing from a branch, but only for tonight, and in the morning you will be singing no more."

The second ruffian laughed. The words penetrated like a blade: they planned to let me hang all night and then kill me in the morning. What argument could I make? I shuddered. In a few minutes, the others in the repair crew arrived with the food, wine, and road gear that had been left behind and collected the tools scattered by the crash. One of the horses was sound and they freed it from the tangled traces. The other animal lay in the road, neighing in pain from one or more broken legs. The driver cut its throat.

Sobered by their work, they pulled the wreckage from the road. When they were done, the driver, who was their leader, and a second man hewed a thick seven-foot limb from a tree and put it beside me. One of the others looked at the limb squeamishly, but made no protest. I reasoned with him. "I have told your chief that I am offering money for my ransom. When I am missing, my friends will come seeking me. You will be caught. My father is a Roman official in Rome!"

"Silence, you," said the leader, coming to me and forcing a handful of dirt into my mouth. "Taste this. When we give it to you by the shovelful in the morning, you will taste nothing."

I knew all too well, beginning with that day I had seen my *sicarii* abductor on the cross, what a crucifixion was about. The fortunate ones, like the informer, were killed with a spear. Or the arteries in their hands or wrists accidentally were pierced by nails and they bled rapidly to death, or their legs were smashed with an iron rod—the *crurifragium*—and they died of shock or heart failure, or their throats were slit like Dathan's. The luckless ones were bound to the cross by ropes.

They dragged me well off the road and buried their dead comrade nearby. They spent the rest of the day eating, drinking, and sleeping. At dusk, when all travelers on the road would have passed, they built a fire. Their leader staggered up and sarcastically offered me wine, but I shook my head.

"Here, let me give you some that is better aged," he said. He raised his tunic, dropped his *saq*, and urinated in my face. The others laughed and did the same, and, my stomach already churning with alarm, I vomited, turning my head from side to side as the hot, stinking water spattered me.

While one held a stone pry to my face, they untied me and stripped my armor, joking, admiring it, estimating what it would bring. They took my shoes. One of them, seeing my mutilated toes, chortled, "Maybe we should be hanging him. Look how he is fixed to dance on air!" They tied my wrists to the limb—the *patibulum*—and kicked me until I got up. The limb weighed heavily and I hunched my shoulders to carry it.

They threw a length of rope over the limb of an oak near their fire. Then, four of them on the rope, they hoisted me and the crosspiece. I grunted in pain as my body sagged, supported only by the biting rope at my wrists.

The smallest of them stood on two of the other's shoulders and lashed the *patibulum* about five long cubits up the trunk while a third tied my feet to the tree. Then they knotted the hoisting rope to a second tree so I would not fall during the night. Customarily, a ledge called a *sedile* was put midway on the upright to support the body, but I was accorded no such luxury. The pain in my arm sockets was agony such as I had never imagined. I tried to raise myself to relieve it if for only a moment, but I could not. I tolerated it for a while, then started to beg them to kill me and be done with it. Even they had put the injured horse out of its misery.

Between grunts of anguish, I called down more appeals, but they amused themselves by throwing clods at me. I shut my eyes. An hour passed, then two. I prayed silently. Prayer was the only control over anything I had left.

Was it so odd that I reverted to the prayers I had said more than twenty years ago when I had been in the well? But this time there would never be a third day. My prayers and my pain became everything. More time passed. I heard the voices of the men only vaguely, even when they cast gibes up to where I hung. My bladder released, but I could not help that and made no effort to.

In my prayers, I told Jesus and God, who seemed sometimes like two beings and sometimes like one, that I was contrite for the foolish and cruel and thoughtless things I had done. I spoke of how I might have been more considerate of Father. I talked of my love affair with Deborah and of how sorry I was to have brought such distress to Rechab.

The pain became a constant, as much part of me as my talk to my Gods. God and Jesus, out of that pain, seemed to be talking back, forgiving me. My arms were numb now, and my gasping had dried my mouth. Vividly, I saw the purple tongue of the *sicarius*, heard his garbled prayers and appalling curses. My own tongue swelled. I knew that in time it could get so large it would choke off my breath.

I thought of Dathan, and how he had died for the precise reason that he had emulated Jesus, unlike me, who was dying because of a chance encounter with drunks. I thought of Jesus on the cross. Even as Father had implied, we were all suicides-in-waiting. For those who suffered the enormity of crucifixion, all other differences were insignificant. Was that also true of men who were not Christians? Did Christ become one with the two thieves on either side of him? My *sicarii* abductor? Was he a brother to Jesus, Dathan, and me?

I thought of Deborah being crucified and groaned. Then, briefly, I thought of her naked, of our lovemaking, feeling its sensuousness, but without lust, as something rich and soft. I had no apologies to God and Jesus for it.

Sometime in the night my senses failed and I drifted away from myself and awoke with my screams. Another time, blackness came, and I thought, yes, yes, I am to be allowed to die, but then lights broke in sharply. I saw God and Jesus as lights, and myself as a smaller light joining the greater one. Did this mean that for all my failings, I would be one with them?

I saw Andrew's face, and it become a part of Jesus' greater light, and Dathan's, and Grandfather's, although he was a Jew and a usurer, and then the dead robber's in the woods, and then the Roman deserter's with his eyes rolled up, all turning into the light that was now both Jesus and God.

I opened my eyes to darkness and pain, and realized, quite lucidly, that what I had seen as light was the feeling of water striking my face, thrown by the few drunks below me who were still awake. They did not even want me to have the peace of unconsciousness. Through the tops of the trees, the autumn sky was so thick with stars there seemed no place entirely black.

I faded again and became nothing, then wakened, in pain. Below me, the fire had burned down and I could see only the shapes of the road crew, at peace save for their snores. They had crucified me, but oddly I felt nothing for or against them. It was too late for either. My tongue felt even more swollen.

I began to have dreamlike thoughts. I was suspended not from a tree but in a great glass bubble named Pain and was talking from inside it to God on the outside, a person now, powerful but impossible to see in detail. He was saying, well, soon we will have you out of there, and with us.

At another time, I saw all of us, all the crucified men, leaving their crosses and walking in a long line toward Jesus. My eyes were closed. I could feel my breath rasping past my tongue. Yet I could also hear the sounds of the night, cricket and bird call and the wind in the trees, and the rubbing of one tree against another. I croaked and croaked for water, fearing my tongue would choke me, but no one heard.

I lost all sense of myself again, I do not know for how long, and then suddenly, as if struggling from a nightmare, I heard the sound of screams. Were they my own? But they continued and I became certain I was conscious. They came from the drunks below me. I heard the thud of blows, and the harsh angry cries of newcomers. I could see struggling and the dull flash of swords in starlight and, dimly, clubs that rose and fell. Vaguely, I saw some of the road menders blunder up and heard them crash into the forest. I understood these newcomers were my rescuers, and I tried to struggle back into their world. I was afraid they would not see me so I shouted.

The clamor below me stilled. I heard Hebrew words and saw a torch lit from the coals. I coughed from its tarry smell. Men were looking at the hoisting rope. In a few moments, I felt hands on the rope that tied the crosspiece to the tree and on the rope around my feet. Then carefully, but causing me extreme agony, for it was change, I was being lowered into the arms of the rabbi with whom, only the morning before, I had been comparing Gods.

One of his flock, as it turned out, had been returning late from the next village and had heard my screams. He had crept up and seen my Muscat donkey tied to a tree and understood what had happened. The Jews of Mount Helicon had survived in Greece by taking care of their own, and I had become enough of their own for them to organize a rescue.

I spent four days recuperating, and even then, I was so weak I could only ride at half pace to Corinth. The first winter winds had started to blow when I arrived. Paul and the others were already there. They embraced me and Paul held a special love feast and Communion to thank God for my safety.

Paul had delivered to Corinth's Christian elders the money that the Apostolic Council had given us for the Corinthian mission to Spain, and we were much loved in the city. We worked in Corinth as we had in Ephesus, Paul keeping in touch with his religious empire via his courier system. One of his letters was an appeal to all the Paulist churches for donations to the poor of Palestine. The offerings totaled six thousand drachmas, three times the amount grudged us by the Apostolic Council.

Paul received a letter from Peter, who had arrived in Rome, inviting him somewhat tepidly to come. Paul pondered whether to accept, but decided against it at this time. I felt relieved. Nothing had happened to make me think that my presence in Rome would not still endanger my family. For his part, Paul did not want to interfere with Peter, for the church in Rome was divided between followers of Antioch and Jerusalem and Peter was trying to bring them together. Paul also wanted to make peace with Jerusalem before he went on a lengthy mission.

He wrote Peter a long, loving letter saying he was going on to Jerusalem. He also said he was sending an epistle to the Antioch Christians in Rome, a copy of which he was enclosing for Peter as a matter of protocol. Paul spent a long time thinking out this epistle. It could not offend Peter, nor the Christian Gentiles of Rome, nor the Christian Jews, nor the emperor or other Roman authorities.

We all sat with him when he dictated it to a Christian slave named Tertius, whose penmanship and speed with a split reed were famous in Corinth. Without *explicitly* alluding to Rome's wayward Christians, Paul routinely denounced covetousness, malice, envy, murder, strife, deceit, malignity, gossip, slander, blasphemy, insolence, disobedience to parents, haughtiness, boastfulness, foolishness, faithlessness, ruthlessness, heartlessness—in that order.

I marveled once again at how he could put such different sizes and kinds of grain in the same loaf. I also thought that if Paul was correct, and even one of these sins could bar a person from the kingdom of God, then I was doomed to Sheol or worse for at least six of them. But neither I nor anyone else spoke up to Paul about his indiscriminate casting of stones.

As he dictated, his voice at various times droned, rose angrily, or chided. Gradually, this epistle that had commenced as an ugly hatchling became a swan. An hour passed, and I began to get the eerie feeling that I was witnessing the creation of a masterpiece, one as awesome and long-lasting as the shrine to Artemis in Ephesus or the Temple in Jerusalem.

". . . Rejoice with those who rejoice," Paul was saying, "weep with those who weep; live in harmony with one another. Do not be haughty but associate with the lowly; never be conceited. . . Do not avenge yourselves, but, leave it to the wrath of God, for he told us, 'Vengeance is mine.' If your enemy is hungry, feed him. If he is thirsty, give him drink. Do not be overcome by evil, but overcome evil with good. . . ."

He went on and on, a sublime amalgamation of all he believed about God, Jesus, and love. I was sure each of us in that room heard it as a letter to himself, so personal was its power. It made me ponder why I had not succored my enemies, even when I might have, why I had killed when I might have given water, why I had challenged when, without harm to myself, I might have turned away. Why I had been proud instead of humble.

Wearily, Paul began to finish. He had been dictating this stupendous act of memory, intelligence, and faith for three hours. He had soared into a mysticism that I often did not understand, but that this time was inspiring, transcendent. "None of us lives to himself," he whispered hoarsely, "if we live, we live in the Lord, and if we die, we die in the Lord; so then, whether we live or whether we die, we are the Lord's. For to this end Christ died and lived again that he might be Lord both of the dead and of the living."

It was what I had felt imperfectly at the foot of Dathan's cross. It was what I had felt in the well as a child, and again when I was upon *my* cross and submitted myself simultaneously to death and to God. For those who could understand it, Paul had made death unterrible and life, therefore, open to joy. How many others would find in it the same answer: in Rome, the world, and for all time to come?

When Paul was done, we sat speechless. He smiled, humble, exhausted, and fulfilled. Luke smiled back and, with the detachment that masked his fierce love for Paul, he said, "It is by this, Paul, that you will be remembered."

In mid-March, a ship was sailing for Palestine from Corinth's port of Cenchrae that would bring us to Jerusalem for Easter. Once more, Paul was haunted by the violence that had often overtaken him, but never deterred him. On the day before we were to embark, our Corinthian brethren picked up word of a plot. A cabal of Pharisee extremists, feeling that Paul had blasphemed God, had arranged for assassins to kill him.

We decided that Paul, Timothy, Aristarchus, Secundus, and several others would leave secretly that night for the port of Argos by donkeys, one of them my beloved Muscat. Titus, Luke, I, and the rest would leave by ship from Cenchrae as planned to put off the plotters. We would all rendezvous in Troas. We boarded, wondering what disappointed eyes on the dock belonged to the would-be assassins.

We found Paul as planned in Troas, and sailed toward home. During the long voyage south, the soft days and nights aboard ship gave me time to ache anew over Deborah. At Lesbos, looking out over the fields of fast-fading hyacinths and narcissus, I thought of Sappho, of how sweet life was, and of death and the gods. "Death is an evil thing," she had written, "the gods know this on high, for if it were a good, the gods themselves would die." And yet, I mused, entrapped as I was halfway between Greece and Nazareth, the God Jesus had chosen it.

We stopped at Miletus and met with ministers from neighboring towns of Asia Minor, whom Paul had invited. Some had known him from his first mission a decade ago, and, like him, they were growing old in the service of Jesus. After a love feast and Communion, Paul spoke tenderly: "I leave you for Jerusalem. From there, my path may lead to Rome and even the western reaches of the world. I know that after my departure fierce wolves will come among you, not sparing your flocks. And even Christians will arise speaking perverse things to draw your members away from you. But this will always be, this is our struggle."

We knelt and held hands for a last prayer. I felt our unseen God among us. He was in the tender winds of April playing in our hair, the smell of asphodel from the hills and of salt from the sea, the murmur of our voices, and in our acute awareness of all of us living and dying.

The night we made port in Caesarea, a Christian prophet named Agabus came to our lodgings. He was four long cubits tall, and he took Paul's belt, squatted, and bound his own hands and feet with it. In this awkward posture, he prophesied in a booming voice, "Thus says the holy spirit, so shall the Jews in Jerusalem bind the man who owns this belt and deliver him into the hands of the Gentiles."

It was a weird moment even for those of us who did not believe in prophecies. Agabus gave him back the belt, and Paul, fingering it, said irritably, "Imprisonment? What does it matter? And if it comes to dying in Jerusalem, then I will die there. It would mean God did not want me in Rome anyway."

Whatever our apprehensions, it was still with eagerness that we approached Jerusalem after our six-year absence. As we rode, we passed hundreds of pilgrims observing Hasartha, driving lambs and heifers for sacrifice in commemoration of God's gift of the Ten Commandments. We saw Persian Jews in chethomenes brocaded with silver and gold, Babylonian Jews in black robes that touched the dirt,

Phoenicians in dusty, striped pantaloons. As they walked, they sang songs I recognized from the synagogue: "I was glad when they said to me, 'Let us go to the house of the Lord . . . to Jerusalem where the tribes go. . . .' "

When at last we entered the city, I felt that surge of awe and kinship that its Temple and towers always excited. Jerusalem, Jerusalem, I said under my breath, mother of my blood, feed me in the ways of the Lord. The streets were swarming with pilgrims. I had once heard that Herod Antipas had demanded a kidney from every lamb sacrificed in Jerusalem during one of the major feast weeks, and wound up with six hundred thousand kidneys.

Paul lodged with an old friend, Mnason, a Cypriot, while the rest of us stayed with members of Jerusalem's small Christian Gentile church. Thomas would have been glad to take me in, I was certain, but I did not want to break our ranks. Nevertheless, I went by to see him. He was sleeker, handsome as a gray ram and, if anything, more cynical. His major news was that everyone was either writing the story of Jesus, or helping someone to write one.

"A frenzy of histories," he said as we sipped the fruity Samos wine, my gift to him from my journey. "They no longer want to preach, so they write."

"Everyone?"

"Matthew, Peter in Rome, even John. They all want to record it while they are here to do it. I ought to be writing, too, but I am too lazy. The rest of us are giving the ones doing the writing our best recollections."

"Have you seen any of them?"

"Well, no one has written much yet. Matthew showed me his first two pages. Surprisingly fair. John is going to let me look at his when he has a first draft completed."

"When Paul hears about it, he will start one, too. But what about Peter's? He can scarcely write," I said.

"Silas was helping, but he went to Palmyra when Peter went to Rome. Peter is using a secretary named Mark, another one who fell out with your leader." Thomas thought a moment. "I am surprised you have lasted so long. You do not fit the mold."

"When I agree with Paul, it is with all my heart."

"And when you do not?"

"Then I feel distressed. And a little guilty," I said.

At the Apostolic Council meeting, Titus and I, lest we stir up animosity by reminding them of the episode at the bridge, watched unseen through the crack of a door. We saw Paul give them the six thousand drachmas for poor Christians and heard him recite the donors, from metropolises like Thessalonica and Ephesus to small churches like Laranda and Amastris, from Dalmatia all around the Mediterranean to Tyre.

Everyone praised him, awed by the breadth of his ministry. But there was still old venom in the fangs of the council. When the plaudits ended, his enemies recommenced the debate over how much of the Law Gentile Christians should have to follow. Paul tried to placate the council, but Matthew, James, son of Alphaeus, and their younger allies among the Palestine ministers were unrelenting.

Thomas rolled his eyes, John and even Bartholomew looked depressed. Without the imposing presence of Peter, there was no one to roar "Enough!" and stay the acrimony. Some of the young ministers, who one day would be the council, nipped at Paul like feists at an old wolf. Finally, Paul lost his temper.

"You talk to me about the Law, but like you, my brothers, am I not a Jew? Are you descendants of Abraham? So am I. Are you servants of Christ? I am a better one than most of you, with greater labors, more imprisonments, with countless beatings, and often I have been near death. Five times I have received at the hands of the Jews the forty lashes less one. Three times I have been beaten with rods. Once I was stoned. Three times I have been shipwrecked. A night and a day I have been adrift at sea."

There were catcalls, but Paul's high, outraged voice rose above them: "On frequent journeys I have been in danger from rivers, danger from robbers, danger from pagans, danger in the city, danger in the wilderness, danger from false brethren. I have lived in toil and hardship through many a sleepless night, in hunger and thirst, in cold and exposure. And apart from other things, there has been the daily pressure upon me of my anxiety for all the churches.

"Who is weak and I am not weak with him? Who is made to fall and I am not indignant? I am afflicted in every way, but not crushed; perplexed, but not forsaken; struck down, but not destroyed; always carrying in my body the death of Jesus so that the life of Jesus may be manifested in my body. And, yet, there are those among you who hate me."

The finale silenced everyone for a few moments, but then they set to shouting and, at last, James, brother of Jesus, called for calm. "Paul," he said, clearing his rooster throat, "we want peace, not war, healing, not new hurt. We are moved by your words but many of us still want assurances that you are a child of the Law as you have just said. We in turn prayerfully accept your—and thus our—Gentile brothers.

"Four of our young members, still practicing Judaism, desire to become Nazarites"—a kind of lay brotherhood of devout young Jews—"and they lack the means to pay for the sacrifices themselves. Go with them to the Temple, Paul, pay their expenses so they can make their sacrifices, so their heads can be shaved. Purify yourself with them, so all may see you are, though a Nazarene, yet still a Jew who lives by the Law."

They were asking Paul to do what he had preached for years that people need not do if they not want to: strictly observe the Judaic Law. Not only that, but they were asking him to pay for up to a dozen sheep, a dozen baskets of bread, the same number of jugs of wine, not to mention a week's living expenses for these unknown people.

Ineffective, mean-spirited, false Christians, both the men who had walked with Jesus and forgotten who he was and these second-generation ministers who had not known him in person and would never know him in their hearts. They would hate us no matter how we abased ourselves. A pig eat their pricks! as Belzek would have said. Why did not the few decent ones stand up and spit out these gobs of phlegm? There they sat: weak Thomas, doddering old Philip, John half-lost in his mystic clouds.

Paul was more embattled than I had ever seen him. If he defied James, the council would spurn him. If he capitulated, he would lose some of our respect, and his self-respect as well. Ten years ago, he had faced them down over the circumcision of Titus. Why not again? He bowed his head in thought or prayer, glib words silenced by this dilemma. At last, he looked up and nodded that he would accede. I saw the fierce, wicked joy on the aging faces of his enemies and hated them enough at that moment to kill.

We gathered at the house of Mnason, none gloomier than Paul. "I did not want to leave behind a nest of vipers," he said without his usual assurance. "My concession will pacify them at least so they will not openly denounce me. I do not want them writing Peter and the Roman church that I am an outlaw. Our Gentile friends will understand it is a gesture I must make for the sake of some sort of unity."

"There is no unity in it," I said, since nobody else would. "They will always hate you because you are alive and they are defunct. Even if they could forgive you all the rest."

Our own meeting now began to break into argument. Paul brought it to a close. "Have we been poxed with their sickness? What I have done is done. I prayed for the guidance of God. I did not hear him and made my own decision. Unlike him, I am not infallible. The future will tell us if I did right."

While Paul was spending his seven days at the Temple with the Nazarites, most of our group visited Christian shrines. Golgotha, where Jesus was crucified, the Mount of Olives, nearby towns like Bethlehem, where he was born, and Bethany, where he supposedly brought a dead man back to life—these were becoming for Nazarenes and Christians what the Temple was for devout Jews. I had other things on my mind. I was struggling over whether to see Deborah. The problem hectored me unceasingly, even as I discharged my first duty: a visit to Ezra and Ahiam.

XXV

As I approached Borhaurus, memory, like hot sands, blew in my eyes, and although it was cool for May, my hands sweated on the bridle. I went first to Ezra. He had married and taken over Grandfather's business, but did not yet have any of his luxurious habits except for the serving of exquisite date juice and cakes. Since writing me about the death of Grandfather, he had sent me two more letters, but I had not gotten them.

"Just as well," said Ezra. "They were about the small patrimony he left you. You might already have given it away to the infidels." Now we sparred with words, as we had with carob pods fifteen years ago in the Xystus. But I was not ready for the blow he landed on me: "He left you forty thousand denarii," said Ezra, watching my mouth open.

It was beyond anything I had imagined. I had always known Ezra would be his heir and had assumed all the money would stay in the business. "He gave me too much," I said.

"He took care of everyone, Demas. Even I never thought there was so much. He said for me to give it to you all at once if you want it, but to try to talk you into taking it bit by bit so we do not have to dislocate investments any more than necessary. If you do give it to your sect, he said he will come back as a dybbuk and revoke the bequest."

I smiled, thinking of how Grandfather would have phrased it, and then suddenly was discomposed by sadness. Ezra waited for me to find myself again before he told me what news he had of my family. Mother had written that Father might be sent to Massilia, Gaul's great Mediterranean port, as deputy administrator. It was an eminent post in which he could finish his career. It would also make it possible for me to go to Rome with Paul. And Massilia was close enough to Rome for me to visit.

After our supper with his wife, a graceful girl of nineteen, Ezra nodded to her and she left the table. "There is something else," he said, leaning toward me. "I get a sense from your mother that your father is dubious about Nero. It is no more than my feeling, but I pass it on to you in case you or your Paul are thinking of going to Rome."

He poured me more wine and we reminisced. At last, inevitably, I asked him about Deborah.

"I suppose it would do me no good to suggest you forget her?" he said with a wise smile. When I shook my head, he went on. "I know only one thing of my own knowledge. This man she married has sold tainted wheat to the poor."

My heart seemed to stop for a moment. She could never love a man like that. That being true, it would mean she was open to love me again. "You are dear to me, Ezra," I said.

I spent a day visiting Ahiam, who mentioned that Rechab had asked after me. I called on other church people and friends from my youth. I should have stayed longer. I should have gone to Modi'im to see Rechab. Thinking of what Deborah had written, I feared he hated himself for discovering us, and somehow I wanted to let him know of my regard for him. I should have begun thinking about how my money could help Jesus. I should have gone back to Jerusalem in the event Paul needed me.

But I could think of nothing except what Ezra had told me about Deborah's husband. And so I set off for Raphia. To avoid Jerusalem, I took the shorter, rougher route through Gath, where Goliath had lived. In Raphia, I knew the honorable thing for me to do was to go to Deborah's and her husband's home, present myself to them, learn how her life was going and depart.

Instead, I hid around a corner that she would pass on the way to her smeltery. I saw the workers go in and then her and her aunt. Her face was half hidden by a hood. She looked heavier. On a small wax tablet, I scratched a note saying, "Meet me two blocks up the street. Demas," and paid a street boy to take it to her. Three minutes after the youngster entered, she came out, the rectangle of wax crushed in her hand. I saw that what I thought was heaviness was pregnancy.

She swept back her hood when she saw me, and I knew that law of Rome or law of God, I would never stop wanting her. Her face was no less beautiful than it had been six years ago. If anything, the new flesh had made it more wanton. Her lips worked as she strove against tears, the dark blue eyes glistening like wet lapis lazuli. She came to me but we did not touch.

"I knew you would come," she said. "We heard from Jerusalem that Paul had returned. I thought of asking Ezra to tell you to stay away."

"It would not have mattered," I said.

"No, I am glad." Her mouth began to falter. "Demas, I did everything wrong."

"Wrong?"

"There is no time to tell you now. I must go back. My aunt will wonder."

"Your aunt . . . ?" I felt batted like a child's ball.

". . . is kind but gabbles. Be in the market at noon. Near the cloth merchants. Talk to me as if distantly. Hoshea—my husband—knows everyone in town."

While I waited for noon, I walked to the port and watched the last boats come in from night fishing. She had done everything wrong, she said. On the way to Raphia, I had let myself consider her possibilities for a divorce. There were not many. Both Mosaic and Roman law made it almost unachievable for a woman except when the husband physically tortured her or their child, or had intercourse with animals or had a trade so repugnant that no wife should have to tolerate it. I recalled the hapless collector of dog feces in Borhaurus.

What if Deborah simply left with me? Both laws provided the death penalty for the lovers if the husband prosecuted. There were exceptions, but there were none for a man who took another man's child, born or unborn. Deborah's husband was rich enough to hire constables to chase us down. And if we risked it anyway? I imagined her giving birth in a wattle hut in Eastern Parthia or a freezing wilderness hamlet among the Goths in Far Dacia—places outside the Roman empire and thus beyond the reach of Hoshea. The vision jarred me back to the hemorrhaging woman in Borhaurus all those years ago. Was that the sort of primitive birth I wanted Deborah to venture?

Back in Raphia, the bustling market was full of fruits, vegetables, meats, wares of all kinds, in stalls, under canopies. Deborah was nervously fingering a loop of purpled wool. I strolled to where she stood. She bowed her head slightly, formally, but said urgently, "Can you come back in two days? He is going to Ascalon on business. At noon . . . ?" I nodded.

I felt desire so strong it made me dizzy. She flicked her sleeve as if brushing off an insect. It bought her a moment more. "Six stadia outside town on the coast road south is a fallen terebinth and a trail. Down it is a grove and a broken shrine . . . to Dagon." She smiled, more rueful than ironic. Dagon was a Philistine god dedicated to orgies.

For me to stay in Raphia would be conspicuous. In Anthedon, a fishing port to the north, I took a small house on the beach. I was feverish with the thought of seeing Deborah, even though it would mean I would have to catch up with Paul on the road to Antioch. He was certain to leave Jerusalem immediately after the purification. I felt disloyal both to him and Jesus, but neither feeling changed my resolve.

When I returned to Raphia, I easily found the fallen terebinth. The trail led through overgrown flax fields to a copse of kermes oaks, so old the Philistines might have planted them. The shrine was now only a half-dozen hewn blocks, thrones for brightly colored lizards who darted their tongues at me before skittering into abdication.

Before long, I saw the brown hood of Deborah's cloak spindling its way through the fields. I ran toward her. She hurried to meet me, her body awkward in her tailored robes. We met and our lips went for each other's as if they were famished and had lives of their own.

I smelled the nard on her, a rich wife's perfume, and on her breath the jasmine she must have chewed on the way out. She broke, gasping. My hunger for her was greater than any lust. I wanted the world to turn backward to a time and place where everything between us would be possible again.

Although we were on a path that others could take, our mouths were heedlessly gluing and ungluing, our hands finding accustomed places to touch and to hold, untying strings, working through loose garments to caress warm, necessitous flesh. Breaking from each other's lips only long enough to glance back for intruders, we half ran down the path past the shrine and into the farther part of the copse. There we stared at each other, saying nothing. Still without a word, she let herself down on the ground hand in mine, and drew me down beside her.

This was no lovemaking as we had known it in Borhaurus, a leisurely acceleration of touch, of tease until we ignited. We rushed to culminate as if our heads were to roll only seconds from now, killing us in the midst of coition. Legs spread so far apart there could be no chance of my not finding my way into her, no matter how precipitate I might be, she thrust her thickened belly upward. As I lowered onto her, she took me in her hand swiftly and not overly gently and guided me in, grunting sharply, not in orgasm, but with relief that finally it was done. Feeling the inside slickness of her, I spent and spent, our cries blending like the final extended syllable of a hymn.

❀

Gradually, we drifted back to the world. I saw the brown earth beside her linen cloak, the dead oak leaves. She would be seeing the sky through

267

the far tops of the trees. Cautiously, I rose from her. "Do you suppose we should have debated all this before we did anything again?" I said, glad we had not.

"No."

"I was heavy?"

"No," she said again.

We walked back to the stones and sat. There was no longer pomegranate freshness in her cheeks, or guilelessness and flinchless courage in her eyes. Her face had more depth now. It was as if it had grown bigger to house the more complex thoughts that lay behind it.

"I had forgotten what they did to your nose," she said. "I always remembered you as so beautiful."

"If I was, I am not anymore," I said.

"No. It is inconsequential. I no longer am as I was."

"You are beautiful, but different." I looked in her eyes and the recklessness I had felt for her all those years ago in Borhaurus engulfed me. "Deborah, come away!" I said.

She turned her face. "Don't say it, Demas. Do not even think it. Oh, God, I wish the seed from you that is in me could go to the baby and make it yours!"

"No, wait. . . ." Familiarly, I tried to cut off her words before she could say no, and thus set an unshakable course. "Is there a chance that if you told him you could not love him, he would give you up after the baby is born? Divorce you?"

"No, no, he would never give up the baby, and I . . ."

". . . could not either?" Were we implacably blocked? I turned my frustration on her. "Deborah, how could you marry . . . ?"

"No, Demas," she interrupted.

But all the bitterness of the years rose in me, all the ridiculous reasons she had found for not marrying me. "If you had only been as unsteadfast with Jesus when we were in Borhaurus as you became toward me!"

"Demas," she broke in again. "Do not do that to me."

I was almost in tears. "I don't even know why you married! Only what other people heard from still other people."

"I want to tell you. You don't let me begin before you reproach me. I want to . . . but first . . ." She reached up and touched my mashed nose, then brushed the damp hair from my forehead. "You must never be out of my life again."

"Nor you out of mine."

She touched my lips to put a brief seal of silence on me. "Just let me talk." She paused, and when I did not again try to speak, went on:

"The year with Rechab after you left was unbearable. What had been everything to me began to destroy me. Rechab and I were countermanding each other, disagreeing on everything, both of us trying to be so polite, knowing that was not even our real fight.

"What he felt in his heart was that he had led me to Jesus and I had betrayed them both. But *that* was never mentioned. After all we had been to each other, our feelings shriveled and became diseased. He was making me feel so guilty, Demas, and he was hating himself for doing it. His wife even talked to him, but he could not stop.

"I had always been able to believe that God, Jesus, could function in a world where good men like Rechab could lose an eye and a leg, and your beautiful face could be smashed, and even where Dathan could be crucified, as Christ himself was. I could imagine it because we were the people of God and were trying to get others to be like us and so there was certain to be a struggle with evil. But here was evil among us, Rechab and I hating each other, and nothing to be done. And in my hate and despair I was losing God, losing Christ, as I lost you."

"You do that," I said. "Instead of trying to work it out, you run away from it. And look what happens."

"Demas," she said, a trace of the past asperity when she was crossed coming back into her voice, "do not lecture me. The point is I did leave and I came here. And Hoshea was a kind man. He *is* a kind man. He worked so hard to make the smeltery efficient, profitable. And, after a long time, he began to tell me how he loved me, and after what I had been through, it was flattering. . . .

"So here was someone I could talk with, could tell everything to, an older person. And I did tell him, even about us, even that I was still in love with you, and that I could never love him as I had loved you. And he accepted. Can you see how that would be? Still, if your letters had come, I would have waited. But they did not, and as I said in my letter, I thought I was out of your heart."

"Never."

"Well, I understand that now," she said, touching my face. "Anyway, at last he asked me to choose . . . and I chose." She looked off into the flax fields, and fumbled for my hand. "There was no problem for a while. We had such plans. He talked of becoming mayor of Raphia. He made me feel like a queen. In you, I had a strange one, someone who treated me like an equal. . . ." She smiled. "Sometimes almost as if I were a man."

"Rechab did, too, all of us did. How could we not?"

"Yes, all of you. For Hoshea, though, I was to reign in the home and he elsewhere. We had our first big argument about the smeltery. He wanted a larger hand in managing it, and perhaps he would have been better at it, but my aunt and I liked running it our way. We won, but he sulked like a child. He does that every time I stand up to him. And while he is a skilled merchant, he is just not a very strong man."

I had to say it: "Skilled, perhaps, but Ezra has heard he sells tainted wheat to the poor."

"Not fair," she replied heatedly, then sighed. "But not entirely wrong. He buys what he can get and if some of the wheat is a little blighted, he sells it cheap."

"At no profit?"

"No, at a profit."

"You talked to him about it?"

"Yes, and got the expected argument. If he did not do it, someone else would and at a greater cost to the poor."

"So things became worse."

"But no worse than in most marriages."

"And now?"

"And now I have a husband who is good to me, and a baby five months on the way, and I am overseeing a factory. And the man I love has come to Raphia, and I am an adulteress and do not know what to do." She said the last part without shame, simply as fact.

"What we did has only to do with ourselves," I said. "It is Paul and the Ten Commandments that are wrong, not us."

It broke her somberness and she smiled. "Demas, Demas. And Jesus is wrong, too?"

"I do not believe he said everything Paul says he said."

She turned my head to her and kissed me, and I tried to make it a soft, gentle kiss, but I felt the passion in her. In a few moments, we were walking rapidly back to where we had made love before. It was more leisurely this time. An hour must have passed. The afternoon was at the full. She took my finger and touched it to her swollen breasts and her pudenda. "I have thought how you can spend the night."

The servants, she said, were Hoshea's. But her room was on the second floor and one window opened on a field. Four hours after sunset, I could climb to it by way of the sill of the first-floor window because it was the dining room's and no one would be there. I could leave the same way before dawn.

"Like a thief," I said.

"Like a thief," she repeated without laughter.

I scraped my knee getting into her room. She poured some fine Pulcinum wine she had opened on a handkerchief, knelt clumsily to clean the wound, and then pulled my head down to kiss me. Without words, I slipped her gown from her, and she my clothes from me, and we climbed into her deep bed. In Borhaurus, the fact that we risked dying on our ordinary rounds at the quick hands of some hater of Nazarenes had stoked our fervor. In the place of that ardor born of danger and hopelessness was this ardor born of uncertainty.

Yet, how swiftly all the learnings of our past came back. And now it was the freer for there was no fear of assassination—or pregnancy. I put my hand on her stomach and felt the occasional kicks of the child. Oddly at peace despite our confusions, we whispered in each other's ears.

"This is your own room? You do not share rooms?"

"No, not from the beginning."

"Is it good with him in bed?"

"Well, not perfect."

"You are hedging. How often?"

"Demas, in the name of the gods."

"Tell me, Deborah. No secrets."

"When he wants to. Maybe once every two weeks."

"That's lunacy. I would be at you every night."

"I know."

"You would like to with him more?"

"Demas, enough."

"Tell me, Deborah."

"I suppose so. It dwindled. When he found out he did not have the kind of wife he wanted, he faltered."

"Sometimes they look for someone else. Maybe he will find someone and set you free."

"No," she said.

"What is he doing in Ascalon? Maybe he has a submissive little widow up there that makes him feel like a man."

"Oh, God, things are bad enough. My brother drank too much when he was here, he wondered if Hoshea . . ."

I could see what she was trying to say. "Likes men?"

"I do not think so, really. There is always that talk about a man who is a bachelor that long."

"Any indication?"

271

She giggled. "I do not sense it. When he likes to make love, he likes to make love."

During the three days her husband was gone, I reveled in her. Her dark nipples atop breasts grown full, the softer sag of her buttocks, and even the quickened mound of her belly gave to her flesh luxuries that had not been there when her body was younger. My long need seemed to have made my passion endlessly resuscitative, and even between our couplings, we languidly touched and explored. In the midst of love or during our respites, our talk was as effortless as it had been by the fires in Borhaurus. We never spoke fraudulently.

Sitting together at the old shrine one day, as I told her of Paul in Ephesus, she asked me, not without spite, why I held him in so much greater esteem than I held myself. I ignored the animus and tried to give her an honest answer.

"Paul, with the exception perhaps of Peter, is the true weight of the church," I said. "The rest of us are breezes, not storms, mists, not rainfalls, candles, not suns. His letters . . . his sermons . . . if you could just hear him at his greatest . . . he goes down and down inside himself. There is no bottom. I cannot write or speak with depth. On the road, and in Borhaurus, I was effective mainly because I was a good organizer. You provided the intensity, the depth."

"Demas, you are far too hard on yourself," she said. "You have a busy mind, not a shallow one. Your thoughts are here, there, always in motion." She meant to support me, but in a sense, it was another way of saying what I had said myself. She saw my disappointment and took my hand. "There was no one with more depth, with more intensity than you when you brought Andrew to us, or on that night when we cut off Rechab's leg, or when you made love."

"I cannot go to bed with all my female parishioners," I said. "Why, I cannot even get crucified for the right reasons. With me, it is for kicking a drunk in his testicles. The only time I ever had depth was when I was nine years old—and was twenty cubits deep in a well."

"There it is," she chafed, "exactly what I mean. You blow a clown's horn every time you are in danger of finding a road down into your soul."

"Because, Deborah, when I try to find seriousness, there is a wall. I cannot break it down, or burrow under it or climb over. And people feel it. In me, they hear a man with the answers, but they do not hear a voice from God."

The only thing we *were* reticent about was the future. But, finally, on the last night, as we lay naked, exhausted for the time being, faces up and holding hands as innocently as four-year-olds, she indirectly brought up what was ahead.

"As wrenching as it was, things were simpler last time. If we had married, we could have stayed in Borhaurus. We might be there yet. Only my devotion to Jesus kept us apart."

"Only . . ." I began. But I did not want to reproach her. I was too Roman not to believe that she, both of us, had taken the paths we were fated to take, even to this moment. But she was right about the past simplicity and the present complications: Hoshea, the baby, Paul . . .

She sensed my thoughts and came up on her elbow so she could look into my face by the faint moonlight. "You are thinking that we are too entangled now with other things. I wonder, really, if you are brave enough to run away with me?"

"No," I said, "I would do it." The sense of certain death I had felt when I was on the cross had made me more willing to risk all for present joy. My body was in her arms, when, by rights, it should be food for Grecian worms. Like the near-naked prophet I had seen on the square that day in Ptolemais, I understood the wisdom of saying yes.

"But . . . ?" she persisted.

"But I would know it was wrong. I am committed to Jesus now. Perhaps, well, obviously"—I smiled, thinking of how it had been— "not as much as you were then. And to Paul."

Deborah was silent, her eyes too dark for me to see. At last, she said, "We are both married to men about whom we have doubts, but we must run out the string with them a while yet."

We had lingered too long. I promised to find a way to return in a few weeks. The gray predawn light scarcely hid my descent. When I was back at the inn, I felt her absence as if a vital part of me had been removed.

XXVI

When I got back to Jerusalem, the world was upside down. Paul was gone from Mnason's, who himself had fled to Joppa. I hurried to Thomas, who let me in nervously. "Your people have gone to Caesarea," he said. "I haven't seen this kind of madness since Stephen and James were killed." He poured us wine. "The Sanhedrin are thinking of condemning all Christians, the *sicarii* are looking for Paulists, and who knows whether they know which of us are which. The council is in turmoil."

He drank some more wine, bolted the door, and in a more or less orderly way told me what had happened. On the last day of the Nazarites' purification, while Paul was in the inner court arranging their final sacrifices, a Pharisee who had heard Paul criticizing the Law in Ephesus saw him and began shouting. Another man claimed Paul had brought a Gentile into the inner court, an offense punishable by death. In fact, the Gentile, Trophimus, had only been shown the outer court by Paul. An angry crowd dragged the protesting Paul to the outer court to stone him—almost exactly where Stephen had been stoned to death twenty-five years before.

A phalanx of legionnaires rescued Paul and let him try to explain to the Jews that he had committed no offense. But Paul went on to say he believed Jews and Gentiles were equal before God, and he referred to Jesus as "the Messiah." The screams erupted again. The wilder rabble tore off their clothes and threw them about. Others ripped at the cobblestones, but unsuccessfully: Herod had fitted them too well for that. Then everyone threw dust into the air. There was so much that it all but blotted out the sun.

Next day, Paul was taken before the Sanhedrin, the ruling Jewish body of Palestine made up of the high priest, Ananias, and his seventy-two councillors. The two shouted at each other, and Ananias slapped Paul in the mouth, an action signifying that the high priest no longer considered Paul a Jew. Paul, in turn, called Ananias a "white-washed wall," a way of saying both that he was a hypocrite and a wall dogs pissed against.

The Romans jailed Paul until they could decide what to do with him. That night, Paul's nephew, a devout Jew whose blood, however, was thicker than his dogma, told Paul he had learned from a scribe friend that forty Zealot assassins had secretly sworn to the Sanhedrin that they would not eat until they had slain Paul. The Romans did not want a Roman citizen to be murdered while in their custody. They sent Paul, protected by a troop of Roman cavalry and spearmen, to Caesarea to let Felix, the procurator, hold a trial of the case.

I left that night for Caesarea, brigands or not. Better that than compromising fearful Thomas or being impaled by *sicarii* knives. The misadventures of Paul, and my fears of robbers, occupied me for much of the moonless journey. But long before I reached the coast, my thoughts turned back to Deborah.

❁

Paul was in the guardhouse next to the palace of Felix, who had before him the report of the legionnaire captain, Lysias. It said that while Paul was charged by the Sanhedrin under *Mosaic* Law with various blasphemies and desecrations, Lysias found nothing felonious under *Roman* law. Ananias and several Sanhedrin members were coming to Caesarea in four days to try to convince Felix that Paul had also violated Roman law by agitating and by belonging to an illicit sect, and to propose that they be allowed to administer punishment, that is execute him.

I set about to counter that proposition. My labors made my absence from Deborah a little more bearable. Felix remembered Father—and me without rancor from the case of my smashed nose seven years before—and I was able to convince him to refuse the Sanhedrin's demand for a writ of summary judgment against Paul. But I failed to get the case dismissed without trial.

On the date fixed, the Sanhedrin delegation and their Roman lawyer, Tertullus, arrived. He put on his case first, praising Felix in his opening statement for his peaceful reign and his reforms, which sent twitches of cynical amusement across the face of the procurator. Felix knew all too well that his realm was torn by factionalism and bloodshed and that he was better known for cruel ukases than reforms.

Paul testified that far from agitating, he himself had been the victim of agitation. He also cited part of his letter to the Romans written in Corinth in which he had said, "He who resists the authorities resists what God has appointed." As to being a leader of an illicit sect, I pointed out that Paul had been beaten while taking part in purification rites that he had paid for himself for four Nazarites—all good Jews. I emphasized that many Christian churches still met in the synagogues, and with the approval of the Sanhedrin.

Felix asked Tertullus, "Do the Jews welcome an illicit sect within their holy walls and then come and tell me the sect is illegal?" Tertullus said the Jews were trying to end the practice, but conceded not much progress had been made.

I challenged Ananias to produce a single witness who had seen Paul bring a Gentile into the inner court. I had asked the aging Trophimus to be present (along with four other Christians who looked vaguely like him). Tertullus's witness peered nervously around, passed over the four decoys *and* Trophimus and selected a baker who had not visited Jerusalem in four years.

Felix should have dismissed the sorry case at that point, but instead he postponed a final ruling. He dared not provoke Jewish leaders that far. Ananias and the other Sanhedrin members left angrily enough as it was. They had hired a Roman lawyer who had made a clown of himself.

There was a saying that when you could not afford to bribe Felix with denarii, you could bribe him with obols. He was not just venal, but cruel and libertine. He had hired renegade *sicarii* to assassinate a high priest who had insulted his brother, Pallas, an adviser to Nero. When I went to Felix to argue again for dismissal of the case, he reminded me that the costs of escorting Paul to Caesarea had been high. He said that remitting these costs—to Felix—might incline him toward leniency. I took the offer to Paul, who shook it off as if it were a fly on his nose.

My inability to win the case for Paul and my absence from Deborah kept me dejected. It seemed sometimes that no sooner had we touched the soil of Palestine than all had soured. For life on the road had produced fine results. And how easy it had been. I got up and had only one thing to do: preach to the people in the next town about our brave, good religion. But it had been a long time since I had experienced the rapture that had possessed me on the road to the Black Sea: the rapture of God.

My longing for Deborah was combined with guilt, and my guilt gave me new reasons to resent Paul: his categories of sin that made adultery as evil as murder, his teachings on women and slaves, his peremptoriness, his hypocrisy—his failure (oh, yes, it was justified) to fully trust me. These feelings about Paul sometimes approached revulsion and they spread in me like a gangrenous infection toward Jesus and God. I was coming to feel that if a person like Paul was God's man, how could I be?

Six weeks after the hearing, Paul called us to him. What with his confinement and the way his plans had been aborted, he should have been as jumpy as a frog in a fire. Instead, he was affable, calm, even making little jokes. There were fifteen of us there, including the local church leaders. Felix, always unpredictable, had provided us with a wineskin of good Capernaum, which we drank with bread, lamb, marinated beans, and fruit. For the Eucharist, Paul had Timothy buy our own flask—the wine of Felix was potable, but not as the blood of Jesus.

"My legal counsel," he said with a warm smile at me, "believes we have exhausted our possibilities in Caesarea. As a Roman citizen from an imperial province, I can take the case out of Felix's hands and go to Rome for a hearing. But with me would go Felix's recommendation, and if I anger him that way, what with his brother's power, it would be off the boat and onto the cross for me. The alternative is to wait here until our good host"—Paul grimaced sarcastically—"frees me or is replaced. This is not the first time that God has asked me to stop and meditate on how to get a lucid channel to his mind and wishes, uncluttered by the everyday duties of the road."

Felix had assured him that he could keep up uninhibited correspondence with the churches and invite delegates. Besides, after I passed on word of the onset of literary ambitions among the original disciples, Paul had decided to do his own history. He and Luke had already put down some preliminary notes, and he wanted Luke to stay and help him with the writing. Timothy and Titus, he said, were to work in southern Asia Minor, Illyricum, and elsewhere until he was free.

He wanted me to stay within a day or two of Caesarea for any legal needs. When I was not working on the case, he wanted me to go from community to community in Palestine, trying to bring together the scattered Paulists, particularly Gentiles, and fashion them into a web of small cells and churches. Paul had said nothing in advance to me of this.

In my view, setting up Paulist parishes in towns and villages where Jerusalem had churches was an invitation to violence and failure. In

Ancyra, I had seen the proof of this. The devout Jews became upset because they sensed we were against the Law, the established Nazarenes because they accurately saw it as a raid on their members. Even Paul had not done well at it.

To make matters worse, however much I might agree with Paul's central message, my subsidiary doubts would leave me deviating, and doing so beneath his nose. Finally, there was my dejection that diminished my energies and my ambitions. Perhaps an important but brief assignment in Asia Minor would have lifted my mood—without keeping me too long from Deborah. But Paul's assignment only fed my depression.

By next morning, I was indignant and told him so. "I have come when you have bidden me, Paul, gone where you told me to. I have even saved you from harm. I deserve better from you than an impossible assignment without your even consulting me."

Paul knew he had acted arbitrarily and for his own convenience. Perhaps unfairly, I suspected Titus and Luke of encouraging him to do it. It was in such situations as this that Paul became most defensive when he was called to account. "Demas," he said, "I do what I think the master would want."

This piousness aggravated me all the more. I said what was on my tongue. "I do not mind taking risks when I must. And I can stand failure. But only when my work is not stupid on the face of it."

His brow contorted as it had that night in Derbe with Silas. "You have been sulking, Demas, hiding something ugly in your heart ever since you came to Caesarea. . . ." He was becoming even angrier, but then, with that amazing facility I had first seen that same night, his hostility waned. The fury disappeared from his ebony eyes. He sighed and spread his hands apart as if in surrender. "You are right, Demas, I have wronged you. I should have consulted, not ordered. I am sorry. Let us discuss it now as if I were inviting, not commanding."

Thus disarmed, I recovered my own equilibrium. I suggested that I *assess* whether we could bring over communities allied with Jerusalem. Only if it proved feasible would Paul decide what to do, depending then on whether he went to Rome, on who stayed behind, and on whether he thought his own little band or missionaries from Antioch would be better for the job. Paul listened, thought and agreed.

While I was composing a legal summary of precisely where Paul's case stood at this time, a letter came from Deborah.

"Demas, my poor darling," she wrote. "What kind of woman have you come home to? My pregnancy"—she would be in her seventh month—"is not going well. There has been bleeding and I am in bed.

Hoshea does not leave Raphia and at night a servant sleeps in the room next to mine so he can hear me if I call. I can think of no way to see you. Are my ills the wages of our love? Even if this were so, and although my poor body is of no use to you, I kiss you a thousand times in my mind. . . ."

The letter alarmed me and dragged my spirits down still further. I wrote her care of her aunt, telling her of my new assignment and assuring her of my love and concern.

Before I left on my mission, I went by Paul's cell. Historical and religious scrolls loaned him by friends and by Felix were stacked around the walls. I saw Talmudic writings, the Septuagintal text of the Hebrew Scriptures, Greek and Roman histories. He noticed my glance and asked amiably, "Do they meet with your approval?"

"Herodotus? Thucydides?"

He smiled. "Luke and I will need models. I am a better tentmaker"—he looked at the goatskin and thick thread Felix had sent him—"and he a better doctor than we are historians."

I asked if I could read what he had written so far and he handed me a scroll. It was a detailed outline in Luke's pedestrian Greek of tales Paul and the others told about Jesus, Paul's mainly derived from his talks with Peter.

"You are coming along handsomely," I said, wishing it did not sound patronizing. Paul did not miss my tone, but thanked me. Neither of us wanted to open new fields for argument.

❁

I rode down the coast, dutifully reporting back to Paul on Apollonia, Joppa, Jamnia, Azotus, Ascalon, and Gaza. These churches were subservient to Jerusalem and none were healthy. But winning them away from the Apostolic Council, I wrote, would invite fights that few local Paulists were eager to take on.

In Gaza, particularly, for it was close to Raphia, I thought of Deborah, and brooded over how I could visit her. My imaginings of her, belly and all, aroused me. But at best it would be months before I saw her again. Like Samson centuries ago here in Gaza, I was blinded by a woman and chained by my own indecision and disheartenment. But I had no will to pull down temples on the heads of the evil, much less on my own. Where was the fire that had consumed me at the foot of Dathan's cross?

For four months, I traveled the length and breadth of Judaea, its arid lands and its lush, its hill country and the declivities where salt was mixed with sand, There, my donkey's feet sunk in above the hooves, festering at night so that I had to wash and then rub them with oil. I wrote reports to Paul about every city, town, and village. If ever he decided to challenge Jerusalem in its own domain, he would be well equipped with names and information. I thought of visiting Modi'im, but I had reinstituted the sin Rechab had surprised us in, only now it was not merely fornication, but adultery. I could not go.

When I passed near Borhaurus, I went to see Ezra and my friends, hoping to find letters with Ezra. On one visit, Mother had written, saying they were content in Massilia, whose streets they found "safer than those in Rome." It confirmed what Ezra had inferred earlier about Nero. Mother said she had been in bed for a week with an "indisposition," which left me uneasy, for she never complained about her health. There was again no mention of how Father felt about our estrangement. Also with Ezra was a note from Paul praising my reports, saying his own case was *status quo ante*, and that his book was going well.

On another visit, Ezra handed me a letter from Deborah. Her child had been born, a boy who was puny and colicky. The birth had been arduous. For days, I was glum, hardly admitting to myself that it was because in the deepest, ugliest caverns of my heart, I had wanted the baby to die so that she could more easily leave Hoshea. I wrote her my congratulations, saying I was looking forward to seeing the baby. It was a lie in case my letter was seen somehow by Hoshea. But it would let her know I would come to Raphia when she wanted me. Meanwhile, I dispatched a report to Paul on the Galilee churches and headed north.

At last, I came again to Jerusalem, but did not make my presence known even to Thomas. My isolation from Paul, from preaching, from Deborah, made me feel fit only for the solitude of my own company. I went to the Mount of Olives, where Jesus had gone to pray as his agony drew nigh. There in a copse called Gethsemane, I looked at the stars and tried hard to reach God. I remained too much my father's son and Aesubius's student not to recognize that prayer might be sterile. Yet, even at its most bare and lusterless, I thought as I sought contact, it was an honest dialogue with the best part of myself.

I was unable to call down the joy and peace of Jesus that I longed for, and through which I thought I might find answers. But in those few hours at Gethsemane, I saw as clearly as I ever had that the years behind me had been largely reflexive rather than reflective. I had never planned anything much beyond matters at hand. On this hill, if not from God, then from the interstices between the stars, I began to see the pattern that my life at least *should* have. I *should* return to Paul, and urge him to let me take up my preaching with him. I could do it with honesty if he let me ignore or shade those elements in his preachings that were not the same as mine.

But if Paul demanded fealty to the letter of his dogma, then I should leave him and preach on my own. Nothing else I might do, not the law, nor the military, nor administration, could fulfill me. From watching Paul, from applying his system in Bayba and other towns, I knew I not only could bring people to Jesus, but could organize, so that my seeds would not grow mere weeds as Jesus' had in Shechem.

But did I really believe I could find wholeness without Deborah? I knew I did not want to begin a ministry without her at my side. That being true, the first thing I must determine did not involve Paul or even Jesus, but how to find a world for Deborah and me. I turned it over and over, and when I left Gethsemane, unlike Jesus in this garden, I had resolved nothing, nothing except that I must go again to Raphia.

XXVII

❖❖

So cautious was I when I went again to see Deborah that I lodged in Hyksa, a village northeast of Raphia. For a day, I lurked near her house and the smeltery without seeing her. At nightfall, I crept beneath her window, hoping she would open it to breathe the cool air and I could whisper up to her. But she did not.

Next day, she came from the house late in the afternoon, the baby in the arms of a nurse. She was thin, with dark moons beneath her eyes. I shadowed the little party like a cutpurse until they reached the market, where I mixed with the shoppers and caught her glance. Her mouth opened, then shut tightly.

She said something to the nurse and took the baby as the woman moved off toward a sweet shop. With a quick motion, Deborah let fall one of the boy's tiny booties and I picked it up. "Noon tomorrow, the shrine," she murmured with a polite smile as if she were thanking me. She walked away without another look and I returned to Hyksa, where I drank too much at supper yet still did not sleep until near dawn.

I waited by the fallen blocks as before. The weather was overcast and the unharrowed fields were stubbled with dead underbrush killed by winter's cold. I saw her coming, and ran to meet her. We kissed frantically, but there was no passion in her, rather an unphysical kind of hunger as if she needed to put herself in the safekeeping of friendly arms while she repaired some debilitation of spirit. As she held me, I felt against my chest her breasts heavy with milk.

"I am so unhappy, Demas," she whispered, "so unhappy it makes me afraid you will not want me anymore."

I tried to reassure her, but she overrode me and poured out her sorrows. The birth had been agonizing. She had been in hard labor for fifteen hours and the midwife had to cut her to free the baby. Her husband had tried to be sympathetic, but as a bachelor who married late, he found her female injuries repellent, her slow recovery incomprehensible.

"Micah"—Hoshea had named him—"has cried for two months, Demas, and I am not sleeping. I only eat to keep up my milk." She gave me a quick, sad smile. "You have become a tan prince—nose and all—and I an old woman."

"You look fine," I said. "All women with their first babies, particularly when they are older . . ." Her face fell and I realized my gaffe. "The Paulist school of tact," she twitted me. It lightened things, but only for a moment.

"There is more, worse," she said. "Hoshea is seeing someone in Ascalon. I have suspected it for weeks."

I seized on it. "Are you sure?"

"Yes. The last time he came home, his lips were puffed. When I confronted him, his face looked like a small wet rat's." She looked disgusted and heartsick at the same time.

I recalled the hint her brother had dropped. "Could it be a man? A boy?"

"I don't know. I don't know how much I want to know."

I argued with her over her squeamishness. Whether it was a man or a woman, this discovery could give her a reason to press him for a divorce. But only with reluctance did she agree that I could seek proof when he next went to Ascalon, which he planned to do in several days.

I rode the thirty miles up the coast the day before he did after extracting from Deborah a description of him and his traveling garments, and the address of his shipping agent. As stealthily as possible, I loitered around the port until Hoshea arrived at his agent's. He had the handsome bearing of a minor and partially corrupted Roman legate, his hair graying but mostly dark, an intelligent visage, a tendency toward portliness.

It was too much to hope that his friend would be in his shipping agent's office and, indeed, when Hoshea came out, he was alone. I followed him at a distance through the bustling streets to the city's academy. There, he waited outside while I dallied around a corner a half block away, fretting with my sandal as if I were trying to fix the strap.

In a short time, a youth with light hair appeared. He was skinny, somewhat pimply, if the distance did not mislead me, and obviously pleased by the visit of the older man. Hoshea had no feminine characteristics, but the boy, in conversation, gestured and swayed androgynously. In parting, Hoshea softly touched his friend's bare upper arm for a few moments, and drew an impassioned look and nod in return. Now I was sure.

I followed Hoshea back to his agent's. When he came out, I trailed him again. But I lost him in the noon-hour crowds, nor did I find him at the academy or at the port the next day. Where or whether he had set up a rendezvous with his young man, I did not know. But I had seen that caress.

On the day of my return, when Deborah came to the marketplace with the baby and nurse, she merely dropped her head in a concealed nod and I knew where to meet her. Again I ran to her as she approached the marble blocks. "It's true!" I said. "A boy. Not a day over seventeen." Her worried face fell. It irritated me. I had caught Hoshea and she was not pleased.

"You wanted to be rid of him. If you do not, say so."

"It is easy for you, Demas. You see a dragon, you kill a dragon. But I am not that certain about my feelings for him." She must have seen my hurt and surprise, for she added with an irked smile, "Oh, I am sure enough about my feelings for *you*. It is so complex. There is still the baby, for one thing. . . ." She was looking for reasons not to act.

Unassertively as I could, I suggested that a man who would sell tainted wheat, marry a woman without telling her he was a jack and jenny at the same time, and pervert himself with boys was a man who could be forced into compromising with us. She could bring up the youth with him and ask him reasonably for a divorce, with the baby to live with her. If he did not agree, she could threaten to ask the Roman authorities, since he was a Roman, for a divorce based on his homosexuality. To avoid the ridicule and scorn of the community, he might divorce her.

"He won't do it," she said. "He will not give up Micah."

We parted, our only accord that we would meet tomorrow. That, too, had its complexities. She could only leave the baby for two hours because of the nursing. She had to contrive a story for the servants about needing time for "reflection."

When we next met, we argued again about whether she would confront Hoshea with her new knowledge. How could she not? I demanded. Had he not grossly offended her? And while all three of our sins might offend God, his offended nature as well.

Perhaps it was just as well that I had to return to Caesarea to get my next assignment. I stayed there three days, talking briefly with Felix, who was immovable. Nevertheless, Paul still wanted me near enough to reach him quickly if he needed legal advice. This time, before he gave me a new task, he discussed it with me. It was to extend the inquiries I had made in Palestine to the neighboring regions of Peraea, Idumaea, and Nabataea.

During a trip to Jarda in southern Idumaea, I made a detour to see Deborah. We met at the shrine of Dagon and, lips pinched, she told me she had made up her mind to talk with Hoshea.

"Demas, of course I hate him for what he is doing. I feel betrayed, jealous. But there is good in him that I can see and that I can understand why you do not. He is suffering, too, just as we are." He had been raised a Pharisee, and his perverted acts, she was certain, had appalled this vestigial part of him even as they inflamed him.

She was speaking from a Christian feeling of which I was not capable. I kissed her, grateful our argument was over. I did not feel the dependency that had been on her lips before, but rather hunger. I held back my lust, thinking of what she had said about being ripped in birthing. "You cannot," I said.

"You are gentle," she replied.

It had been a long time. She felt me against her and moved her abdomen to put my body where it would be most comfortable for her. I began to gasp, and she groaned quietly.

"We must only do what will not hurt you," I whispered. I wanted her so much I thought I would faint. I helped her to the ground, and she guided me into her slowly, pausing when it hurt, then slipping me in a little farther. I spent, still careful not to force myself into her. She began to cry, not, I thought, from pain, and certainly not from orgasm, perhaps from the simple relief that we were together again.

Now that she had made up her mind about approaching Hoshea, I did not urge her to. In part it was my fear he would be adamant, in part, because no matter how he reacted, our blackmail would acknowledge what my soul already knew: the extent of my falling away from Jesus.

For the next week, my life centered on the few hours she could see me. When I was not with her, I rode into the badlands nearby. There, fifteen centuries before, the Hyksos, a small people extant only in the name of my little village, had perished defending their homeland against an Egyptian army that legends said "reached to the horizon." Nearby were the ruins of Gerar where Abraham had lived in an uneasy triangle of love with Sarah and Hagar.

The heat of Deborah's and my passion seemed to heal rather than exacerbate her rent flesh. After a journey of three weeks into the desert towns in Nabataea, I begged her to let me into her room at night, for now the door between her and the servant's room was closed. Why, I asked, could she not get a wet nurse for Micah, why could she not leave Micah and come away with me on the pretense that she needed a vacation?

To oblige me, she extended our time, a half hour here, an hour there. The frequency of our meetings created hazards. A young couple apparently also using the shrine of Dagon for seclusion once saw her coming back along the path—alone, for I always prudently picked my own way back through the fields.

But nothing chilled us. We were like copulating dogs I remembered as a child who had not stopped even when raucous boys kicked and threw cold water on them. Deborah once asked me wonderingly whether if we ever came to hate each other, we would still need to make love. I said that probably we would.

Paul, I told her ruefully, was prone to say that he suffered from a thorn in his flesh, meaning, depending on the context, his malaria, his nearsightedness, his hubris, even his hypocrisy. But the thorn he had never suffered from was lust. For him, there was no virtue in physical love, only dirtiness. For us, the very hotness of our love guaranteed its purity.

❀

On my next visit to her, even before I kissed her, she announced, "Hoshea suspects."

"How? Are you sure?" I demanded.

But perhaps the real question was why we should be surprised. The maids had told him she went out alone more often. She was eating better, looking better. "Besides, I have been happier," she said. "I suppose that because what he is doing makes him feel better, he assumes the same for me."

"What did you tell him?"

"I told him it was because spring was coming."

I was not altogether unhappy about his suspicions. I hated our paralysis and our deviousness. "I am tired of making love in ditches and fields," I said one day. Besides, in the long run, what were the alternatives to confronting him? To continue as we were? For me to leave her? To flee together? None were acceptable. After much discussion, we decided the two of us would talk with him. We reviewed what we would say as if we were practicing parts in a Greek drama—or comedy.

She told him that afternoon that I had come to Raphia to see him, and why. The three of us met in front of the fire. I was so suspicious of him that I asked him to switch goblets after he poured the wine. He resented the request, but, his lips compressed, he complied.

"Even outside Rome, I see we must do as the Romans do," he observed. When we were seated, he began. "Deborah has told me of your invitation to me to participate in my own blackmailing."

"We are looking for a way to oblige everyone as far as possible," I replied mildly.

"I gather my wife has been most obliging to you."

I felt somewhat as I had on entering the arena with Belzek. Then, I had sought flaws in his gladiator skills. Now, I sought them in Hoshea's resolve. For one thing, I saw he relished his bons mots at the expense of honest anger.

"There would be advantages to you in letting her go," I said. "You would be free to pursue your own course, and if you found you wanted a woman, next time you could do so without making false representations and maybe it would work out."

"Oh, but I do not want another woman. I prefer Deborah, for much the same reasons you do, although that may not be obvious to her. And there is Micah, of course."

"Why not give him to her and start again? There is another advantage to you: you would be rid of me. I do not intend to stop loving her and I think she feels the same way."

Hearing it put so baldly angered him. "Implicit in everything you say is the reek of the extortioner. Why not just admit that is what you are?"

"We can call each other names," I said. "But why do that? Why should we become enraged? It could only lead to monstrousness. You are a wise man. I have seen life, too. I am aware that if we leave here with nothing solved, hating each other, you could poison me or have me killed in some other way. And someone, if not Deborah, then one of my friends or relatives would do the same to you. Or I could contrive *your* death. But you, in advance, would have made sure the finger would point at me. I would die—or become a fugitive for life. All this is what I mean by monstrous. Why should we be driven to such things?"

"You put it very forcefully."

I shrugged. I did not think of what the Christian thing to do was. Jesus would never have gotten himself into a pig wallow like this, nor approve of anyone who did. I was in battle and I was in sin, and I could not turn back from either.

"Everything important is known among us," I said. "There is nothing we can do to wholly satisfy all of us. In fact"—and I let myself smile as I looked into his eyes—"you are wiser than I. I sought to point out advantages to you when I was sure it was wasted breath. You did not even bother."

"I am not complimented," he said with some fervor. "You are asking me to give up my wife and child. I will not succumb to a criminal, a blackmailer."

"Do you really want to infuriate me?" I said. "I did not call you a liar for not telling Deborah you were . . ." I started to call him a pederast. ". . . as you are. If you will not divorce her, perhaps she will decide to divorce you."

"Not possible," he said scornfully. Then he realized what I really meant: that she would publicly make charges against him. He paled, and his hand went to his forehead. He looked at the floor, too shaken to answer for a minute. But when he looked up it was with a determination that surprised me. "If you do that, I will fight it. I will disgrace us all."

Feeling coated with slime for doing what I had done, I nevertheless argued the case, but he was immovable. Did he want to ruin his chances for the mayoralty, to ruin himself in the church, to blacken himself in the town? Now it was I who was shaken. He was playing Leonidas. What did it leave us?

I said as reasonably as I could: "There are arrangements, we all know that, where the parties accept inevitabilities. There are women who accept the affairs of their husbands and even—"

"Hoshea," Deborah interrupted, taking up the dirty burden. "If I can reconcile myself to your . . . friend, then . . ."

Now his temper flared. "You are that insane for him? That much the animal? You would sanction my proclivities in order to retain this person, sleep with me whom you despise in order to . . ." He stopped, realizing he had backed himself into a corner.

"None of this would be easy for any of us," she said.

"For him," he said bitterly, "it is nothing. He is the ram who tups the ewe of the neighbor. For me, for you—"

"No," I broke in. "Nothing? I would be prevented from having the thing I want most in the world: a life with her."

"If you love each other so, why have you not simply left?" He knew the answer, but I treated his question as if it were ingenuous.

"You know she will not leave without her son. And if we took him, you could have her, and probably me, put to death for abduction." I

288

was getting more and more upset. "Look at it cleanly, we are all three trapped."

"Trapped by you!"

"I am trapped by love!" I burst out miserably.

Deborah stayed us both. "We are all three trapped by love," she said quietly.

Her words struck him at the best and most vulnerable part of him: his intellect. He understood the truth of it. He was trapped by his love for the baby, his paramour, and Deborah; she by her love for the baby and me; I by my love for her. I saw in his face the similarity of our thoughts. "I am trapped by more loves than either of you," he said nakedly.

Tears came to his eyes, and at that moment I recognized how lacerating this was for him. He was struggling to preserve all his loves. He must have known that Deborah, his own wife, and I wished he would die and solve our quandary. In the quiet, perhaps he saw in our faces how well we understood what he had said. He went on: "There is no way that any of us can make it any easier for ourselves or anyone else."

Deborah was able to say to him what I would not. "I will make it as easy for you as I can."

He got up and opened another flask of wine. This time I did not bother with the rigmarole of tastings. We had all three been shattered by the realization that none of us could possibly win. When he sat down, he was ready to eat the rotten fruit of compromise. We managed it mostly with euphemisms. Deborah did not say she would continue to have sex with him when he wanted. But she nodded when he said to her, "I assume we would continue, insofar as we do now, to share each other's bed."

I did not demand that he not subvert me with Paul, but I said, "I assume we will be discreet everywhere and with everyone." He did not tell me I could visit his wife in his house, but he assented when Deborah said she wanted to get a new nurse and maid of her own choosing. In return, I did assure him that I would see her only in ways that would not embarrass him. Anesthetized by wine to the immoralities of what we were doing, we covered the contingencies and I rose to leave. They had the dignity not to go to the door with me. But I knew from her half nod that I would see her at the shrine tomorrow.

When she arrived, we were almost childish in our somber, shameful lust. We made love as if it were a marriage ritual, my cloak on the moist ground, our bodies crushing the tiny spring flowers that rose among the shocks and weeds. Afterward, calmed, we stared at the pale sky. Hoshea, she said, had left for Ascalon with eyes red from weeping, perhaps to tell his adolescent lover what he had given up for him. We spoke with relief of not having to meet in the fields anymore. But we said nothing about the kind of bargain that had brought it about.

That night, I scaled the wall to her room, and spent the dark hours making love to her, the baby fitful in its crib beside the bed. Back at my lodgings in Hyksa, replete, I tried to fall asleep. But exhaustion, without forcing me to slumber, broke down my defenses against my conscience. I finally looked at the concordat we had reached with the eyes of a moralist.

Our passion, our need to slake it, my inability to leave her, or her inability to make me go, had pushed Jesus and God from our minds. I, who planned to be one of his ministers again, had conspired with her to sell her into whoredom. She had agreed to give her body to a husband she despised and her payment was the freedom to have me. I, as pimp, had accepted the proceeds from this barter: the pleasure of taking her sweet flesh, albeit it hot from the love gasps of her husband. We, who had made so much of our Christian morals in earlier days—indeed, had often talked of little else—had now joined a tormented man of little goodness in an agreement that was cheap, soiled, and entirely wrong. But these considerations did not prevent us from slathering her bed for the two nights he was gone.

The day after he returned, Deborah and I met outside town. She was well enough to ride her mare. I kept pace on my donkey, but planned to buy a horse so as to come back to her from my journeys more quickly. The tamarisks' flowers were pink and sensual, and the violet laurels were in bloom. We rode by marshes filled with plumed reeds and calamus, their fronds like the flags of children.

I had never seen an April so beautiful. On a desolate part of the beach, we tethered our steeds, then sat on a driftwood log. The beauty of her youth had bloomed, again, and more lusciously; her buttocks were more rounded, her breasts heavier, her face fuller. Diana had metamorphosed into Venus.

I asked her how her husband had seemed when he came back from Ascalon, and she said, somewhat reluctantly, that no sooner was he home than he wanted her. True to the concord, she had lain with him. It had been discomforting enough for me to think about this part of the agreement in theory. As implemented, it made me sick with myself, shamed for her, and jealously curious.

"What was it like?"

She shrugged and tossed a small shell toward the sea. "Do you want to know? I had thought I would not talk about it."

"I think I want to know."

"It gave me no pleasure. I looked on it as a matter of duty. I tried to be agreeable, friendly."

"Is that all?"

"Why know the details?"

"Because I want them."

She looked at me to see whether I was perturbed, and saw I was but would be more so if she did not go on. "He was anxious, afraid I would try to deny him his . . . rights."

"You mean he could do nothing."

"Oh, Demas, stop it!"

"I want to know. I want to know this one time so in the future I can fortify myself against thinking about it."

"I had to help him."

"As in fellatio with a boy? I want to know."

She looked dismayed, and said nothing, thus conceding it.

"How long did it take?"

"Not long. When it was over, he cried. He was grateful. He said he hated himself. Enough! Why must you take away what small dignity he has? Why do this to me?"

"Next time say no to him!"

"You know I cannot. It would violate . . . the agreement. Besides, he is my husband."

"What kind of husband? Where do you think he puts that thing before he puts it in you? It's nauseating."

She retorted angrily: "Listen, Demas, if you do not like it, then do not put yours where his has been." It was as if the April day had turned suddenly cold.

The months passed. Our passion burned ever hotter. Years ago, I had been willing to give up everything for her. Now I did. I no longer dared pray, nor did she, nor did she go to her church. As Jesus had driven Deborah from me so many years ago, so Deborah now drove away Jesus. Even when I was gone from her only a few days, I yearned for her lips, to touch her, to talk with her, to possess her body and her words. I preserved in the museum of my mind the Jesus I had discovered. But it was Deborah whom I worshipped.

I went less and less frequently into the sparse lands Paul had assigned me. I found a small house in Gaza and set up a practice. I wrote Paul that I was trying to work out what sort of Christian I was and where my work should be, and said I would be sending him fewer reports. I asked him to suspend judgment of me in the name of the faith he had seen in me. I told him if he needed my legal knowledge, I would come to him instantly.

We were careful about how we made love at the time of month when she was most likely to become pregnant. We did not want any more complications. Improbable as it may seem, Hoshea and I came to a *modus vivendi*. We were both locked into misery. He, like Deborah, stopped working for the church. He gave up his idea of becoming mayor. Deborah spent time with the baby and the factory and avoided Hoshea when she could.

Familiarity made our vice routine. I occasionally saw Hoshea in the streets of Raphia and we bowed. One day, he came to see me in Gaza. "I have a problem. It affects us all," he said, not without a semblance of courage. His lover's uncle was blackmailing Hoshea—for money. "Give me the name of the man and he will trouble you no more," I said.

I found the uncle alone in his rug-weaving shop in Ascalon. He was younger than I had thought he would be, a muscular man with the small angry eyes of a lynx. I told him I was on the way to Caesarea to have him prosecuted by Roman authorities for blackmailing a Roman citizen, a capital crime. Although I was no less guilty than he, I said without a pang, "My intention is to have you crucified."

He postured about Hoshea not daring to press the case for fear of the notoriety, and I reminded him that his nephew would also be smeared. "I will get a lawyer. You cannot—"

"I suggest that, like me, he be a Roman one," I said. "If he charges you half of what my fee is, he will have your shop before I can get possession of it for damages to my client." At last his belligerence wobbled.

"Your client is a vile man," he snarled.

"He is not a vile man charged with a capital crime under Roman law. You soon will be." That broke his will. I forced from him half of the money Hoshea had given him, and assured him that I would seek his death and property as readily as I now spat on his floor in leaving.

That fall, a reply came to my letter from Paul. He said he understood my decision, would never forget my services, and would welcome me back. But there was an intimation in his tone that while I might not be an out-and-out deserter, he nevertheless looked on me as deplorably weak in the faith. So be it. I sighed sadly.

Soon it was spring again. I would shortly be a third of a century old. I no longer wrote to Paul, nor went on my journeys for him. I lived in Gaza, but made my visits to Deborah more often, frequently under the pretense sanctioned by Hoshea that I was his lawyer. I felt wasted, a betrayer of both Jesus and the God of the synagogue. I brought my feelings up with Deborah one day when we had escaped to our old meeting place at the shrine. Around it now were patches of gladiolus and anemones in shades of brilliant red and crimson.

"I cannot do this much longer," I said. "I love you. I love to be with you, to touch you. But sometimes I feel like the chaff that the elders in the synagogue used to compare with fallen Jews—so light it swirls up every time a breeze blows into the threshing room. I have to be more than just your lover." She kicked at the dirt with her sandal, but did not respond. And we did nothing.

Often we talked on a "what if" basis, a way of airing our frustrated dreams. "What if" we *could* go on the road as missionaries? We examined every aspect of it, even though we had never been further from the eyes of Jesus and God. More often, we sought ways out of our quandary, some new argument. Finally, that spring, she agreed without enthusiasm to propose that Hoshea divorce her, keep Micah all year, and let her spend half her time here with him and the baby, the rest with me.

But before she could broach it, a letter from Paul reached me in Gaza. Felix, in putting down a riot by Zealots, had massacred a dozen innocent Jews by mistake. Jews throughout Judaea had responded with acts of terrorism. Rome had replaced Felix with Festus, a veteran administrator, giving him orders to restore calm as soon as possible.

Festus had gone immediately to Jerusalem to talk with the new high priest, Ismael ben Phabi, who had demanded in exchange for cooperation that Paul be returned to Jerusalem for trial by the Sanhedrin. Festus said he could not simply give over a Roman citizen, but agreed to retry Paul immediately. Paul had been given no time to summon me. The trial had been held on virtually the same charges as before. "I told them all," wrote Paul, "that if I, a Roman citizen, have committed wrong under Roman law, then I deserve to die under Roman law. But I should not be invited to die by the daggers of my enemies in a dark alley."

Festus knew that under Roman law Paul was innocent. But he did not dare acquit him. Instead, he recessed the trial for a few minutes, took Paul aside, and warned him that if pressures by the Sanhedrin continued, he might have to remand him to them. At best, they could keep Paul in jail forever with legalities. Festus suggested an appeal by Paul to Rome, the option Paul had always had, but had not taken because Felix would have spitefully sent along a negative report to Nero. But Festus, by making the suggestion, removed that impediment.

When the trial reconvened, Paul formally announced his appeal to Nero. Festus, with relief, ritually replied, "You have appealed to Caesar. To Caesar you shall go."

"I have prayed lengthily before writing you, Demas," Paul ended his letter. "We both know that Christ said faith is like a mustard seed. He might have added that some mustard seeds grow more slowly than others, and that the great trees they produce have different shapes. But in all of them the birds, as he said, sing with strong, beautiful voices. It is this voice in you that I need. Come to me in Caesarea. Festus knows your father. He is fair. Convince him to send the best possible recommendation to Nero, then come with me to Rome to present my case. I beg you in the name of the God we both serve."

I gasped. To Rome? And begging me? As Deborah and I had bound ourselves more closely together, I had all but given up the idea of rejoining Paul. But he needed me. I might be the sole means of saving him, and not just as his lawyer. In spite of his sermons about turning the other cheek, he would need his best sword to ensure he was not tossed overboard by some procured *sicarii* on the way to Rome.

On my knees beside my pallet that night, I sweated to reestablish contact with God. Finally, in the watch before dawn, I seemed in my weariness to sense him, if vaguely. "I cannot give her up. Make Hoshea let her go," I whispered. An answering voice seemed to say. "He will not. *You* must." Yet I was not sure the voice was not my penitent own.

Most of the next day, I wrestled with Paul's demand. By afternoon, I knew I must heed Paul. He alone was genius enough and strong enough to make certain that the infant church continued. If I deserted him, I put for all time the creed of Jesus in jeopardy. Intestines writhing, I galloped my gelding through a rainstorm to Raphia and sent the astonished servant in to call Deborah from the supper table.

She read Paul's letter and did not need to ask my decision. My desperate eyes told her.

With no regard for the protocol we three had set up, Deborah led me into the dining room. "I am sorry," I said to Hoshea, "I have something to discuss." I was sure I looked like a warrior from Hades in my dirt-encrusted armor, with my muddy face and my eyes red from wind and rain.

"Can it not wait until tomorrow?" he asked, less angry than taken aback, trying to maintain the forms.

"It concerns all of us," I said. "Could I wash and perhaps the three of us . . . ?"

He sensed I was on the defensive. We could meet, he said, after they had finished eating and Micah was in bed and he took care of some urgent commercial matters.

When we all sat down, I told Hoshea of Paul's need for me in Rome and of my and Deborah's proposal that she be with me half the time, and him and the baby half.

"I see no decision for me to make," replied Hoshea. "If you stay, this barely tolerable situation continues. If you go, I will, of course, be pleased." He twisted his mouth in a cruel smile. "I can always find myself another lawyer."

Deborah answered him quietly. "Why not simplify it for all of us in a way that makes it fully tolerable?"

"I would gain nothing from it. I will not do it."

"Let her go," I urged him. "She and you could put out that she is with relatives in Italy. After I finish in Rome, we could go far away, where no one would know her, where no one could send back word that would embarrass you."

"I am a shipper, Demas. Word would travel. With her in Raphia, even disliking me, I am not scandalized. I have been fair. Unpleasant as it is for me, it can continue if you do not go to Rome. It is you, not I, who are to blame for this crisis."

"I could simply leave with Demas," said Deborah.

"You would not leave Micah permanently, particularly with him ailing and so needy of you," he said scornfully. "Do not take me for a fool, Deborah. I am not sure you could leave him for six months if he were well."

"Why have a wife who cannot love you?" she said.

"You are still a wife," he said. "Why should I give you up for half the year?"

"I am a wife who is only a disguise for your love affair in Ascalon," she said. "I could assert my right to Micah, to a divorce. I could expose you in court as a parent unworthy of our child."

"The scandal would force you to give up your catamite," I added.

He flushed at the word, but kept his temper. "Come, Demas. How could Deborah declare me unworthy? What kind of fit parent is she, dividing her favors between her husband and her paramour?"

Deborah flared out at him: "There will be no more of what you call my favors for you, Hoshea. With you, never again!"

That, to my hateful pleasure, cut into him. "It would violate the agreement we three made," he said. "I would be justified in refusing to let your arrangement continue."

"Why should she honor this diseased and godless pact?" I cried. "My parting will end all that. Would that it ended your miserable life!"

Yet, I smelled defeat. Paul had done for Deborah and me what we had lacked the will to do for ourselves. Deborah and I looked at each other. She was so beautiful. In the light of the embers, I saw she was weeping. She rose and glared with hatred at Hoshea, then took my hand and led me in the direction of her room. It was a petty Parthian arrow, but the only one we had.

All night, we made love feverishly, unhappily. We knew we were separating for the same reason that we had before: because we did not love enough. She did not love enough to give up her son; I did not love enough to give up my loyalty to Paul and to God.

I slept heavily in the hour or two before dawn and awoke in the gray of morning. I turned to take Deborah in my arms one last time, but she pushed me off. I realized she had been awake thinking some time. I looked into her dark eyes, and to my surprise and dismay, I saw fear there, even panic.

"Demas," she said, "I cannot pretend to be brave any longer. I have thought about what my life will be when you are gone. Reconsider. Stay. Surely, what we have is better than losing each other again."

I tried to put my thoughts together. I loved her, would die for her, and never more so than now when I saw her need for me. But if I deserted Paul and he was killed aboard ship or executed in Rome, my guilt would make a locust shell of me. What would there be left for Deborah to love?

"Deborah, if he died, the only hope of Jesus on earth would be drained away forever. I could not face myself!"

But she was ready for my no, regardless of how I said it. "You speak of Paul's death, yet if our love dies, I die. You will be in Rome, I here, a corpse who walks, yet feels nothing. Is Paul more to you than I am?"

I argued that she could come with me if she would leave Micah. In that case, if Paul dismissed me, it would be his, not my, decision. I would be shriven of guilt. She shook her head, refusing any discussion of giving up her son.

"Something could happen to Hoshea," I tried. "Or he could change. Our love lives as long as there is hope at all."

"Paul has confused you, Demas," she said, unreached by anything I said. "You are not that vital to him. I have thought of every word in his letter. He uses you as a convenience, when it suits his purposes. For me, you are my life. Think of me with Hoshea for all the years to come. Dear God, why can't you see?"

She who wept so seldom began to sob. I tried again to embrace her, this time only for solace, and she thrust me away, now roughly. "If you go, I swear it is done forever between us. Be reasonable. You return to him as a clerk, not a missionary. If you stay with me, no matter how hellish our circumstances, it is as a man, as I, with you, am a woman."

"I go as a man, to protect Paul," I said as gently as I could.

"No, not as a man. And as a protector who in his heart hates the man he protects. You see yourself as an idealist for going with Paul. But that is untrue. The idealist was the man I fell in love with all those years ago. Even before you were a Christian, I loved you because you were struggling, Demas. You said that with me you were the chaff on the threshing-room floor. But with him, you are much worse. You give up your will to Paul. You serve him as an errand boy, a carrier-out of legal commands."

Her anger was breaking out as hysteria. Was she severing herself from our love with hate and resentment to shield herself from future thoughts of me—as she had thought I had shielded myself on the road with Paul from the loss of her? "If you marry Paul this way, Demas," she went on, her voice higher and louder, "you become like me, an appendage, grown onto a man you will not be able to bear, as I can bear neither Hoshea nor myself. If you become the slave of Paul, I will come to hate you even as I hate myself for staying with Hoshea."

"Deborah," I cried. "Stop. You are destroying us both!"

I grabbed her to hug away our catastrophic words, but she broke free, hitting out at me. She struck my nose and the blood spilled out on her hands, my chest, the bedclothes. Horror vanquished hysteria. She jumped from bed, picked up her shift and tried to stanch the flow of blood. When she had, she threw down her shift, and, naked and angry, a Fury, glared at me, more full of hate than she had been at Hoshea the night before.

"Go," she said. "Go forever!"

Numbed, I made my way north, passing through Jerusalem, too deep in woe even to bid farewell to Thomas and John. But I could not leave for Rome without saying good-bye to Ezra, to Ahiam, to my other friends in Borhaurus. Besides, I needed an advance from Ezra against my inheritance to use in Caesarea and Rome. My partings in Borhaurus were nostalgic, for I did not know when I would come that way again. But a more poignant visit was ahead: Modi'im, where I wanted to make my peace with Rechab.

I found him in his shop, as I had the first time, with the dank, honest smell of fuller's clay. He moved with such efficiency that I would not have suspected he was disabled unless I had seen the old scarred sockets where his eyes had been.

"Rechab," I said. He recognized my voice. His grizzled face tried to form itself into lines of control, but he failed and it broke apart, sobs without tears. Comrades again after far too many years, we hugged.

At supper and afterward, I recounted my adventures. But when his wife went to bed, I knew I could not escape telling Rechab of Deborah. "I loved her, Rechab. I will always love her." It did not answer the question I knew still lay between us. It was less that he was inquisitive, than that for there to be honesty in our reunion, I had to be open with him.

I sighed and said, "I do not know if God will pardon us, but married or no, we have been lovers. She does not love her husband and he has a youth on whom he dotes. It is a cistern full of snakes. . . . Her child is sick; she cannot leave him. And now she says she is done with me. I wish I had come to you with a neat package, one that you and God could countenance. But I cannot. I live with pain and confusion."

Rechab said nothing, trying to sort it out. At last, he said, "God has been good to me, Demas. I have been spared confusion and yet I see it everywhere. I can only tell you how grateful I am that you are here, and that in all my prayers I will ask the peace of God for you. And for her."

That was enough. We talked on, almost until dawn, and I slept a few hours. They fed me a peasant breakfast. Then all three of us prayed outside by Andrew's tomb. I parted feeling that a long-raw wound was healing over at last.

When I reached Caesarea, I went directly to Paul's cell. He looked fit. His hair and beard were trimmed, his tunic fresh. Festus kept him in light chains. Paul was all hope and business and hardly thanked me for my ride north before he plunged into his case. He had dispatched Titus and Timothy to the most important churches to inform them he was leaving for Rome and to bolster them.

I immersed myself in law scrolls, precedents, Jewish and Roman statutes. My memorandum to Festus must be so persuasive that he would not just write a neutral report to Rome, but a favorable one, and would give Paul maximum freedom on the voyage. If Paul arrived in Italy in heavy chains, in heavy chains he would remain. But if his armed guard was only a formality, he might maintain great freedom in Rome while he awaited Nero's action.

Yet, I worked as only half a man. I thought of a blind eunuch slave I had seen at the stall of a money lender in Trapezus. All day he sat, his face impassive, feeling coins between thumb and forefinger, tasting them, weighing them on scales. Perhaps such a person was more able than a whole one would be at his limited task. But what kind of life was that: talent without joy or meaning.

As I worked on the documents, King Herod Agrippa II, ruler of northern Palestine, arrived with his sister-lover Bernice to pay Festus a state visit. Agrippa, a Jew installed by Claudius, was a scholar of religions and was obsessive about Christianity, not without reason. His father had beheaded the apostle James; his great-uncle had done the same to John the Baptist; his great-grandfather had ordered all male babies in Bethlehem under two years old murdered when he heard that a child—Jesus, as it turned out—was born to be the Messiah.

Agrippa was interested in Paul's tangled case and wanted to hear him. Since the king had it within his power to request Nero to pardon Paul, Luke and I urged him to keep his remarks moderate. Paul was to speak at Festus's banquet for Agrippa.

Their dress epitomized their differences. The king was in a regal purple mantle, embroidered with his family crests in silver and gold thread. Bernice, breasts bare to the nipples, wore a girdle of woven gold, a pink tunic and necklaces of lapis lazuli. *Sikra* rouged her cheeks and antimony lustered her brows. Paul had on a simple tunic.

While we waited, the guests finished the last of their ortolans (small birds, eaten bones and all), piglets' vulvas, crayfish, braised lamb joints, and wines of every imaginable flavor. Paul was ordered in as they ate dessert. He came forward and, Greek style, raised his right arm, three fingers extended, to signal that he was about to begin. He spoke mildly of his own case, but went on dramatically to denounce the forefathers of Agrippa for their persecutions. Not surprisingly, the king did not intervene on Paul's behalf.

A week after the debacle with Agrippa, I presented my memorandum to Festus. I hardly dared breathe while I waited in an anteroom for him and his advisers to review it. At last, he summoned me in. "Paul will not go to Rome hobbled either by my words or by my chains," he said. When I told Paul, he embraced me with tears in his eyes. We were both certain I had saved his mission and perhaps his life.

Two days later, as I debated whether to make a final trip to Raphia, Festus informed Paul that a ship had put in from Alexandria and would sail forthwith for Rome with Paul and his party aboard. I wrote to Mother, joining Father's name to my salutations, and told them I was bound for Rome and would like to visit them in Massilia. To Deborah, I wrote a short note, repledging my love—and telling her I was on my way to Rome.

XXVIII

❖❖

Our ship sailed in a drizzle. Luke, Aristarchus, and I went as paying passengers. Paul's chief guard was a centurion named Julius of the Augustan Cohort, the far-flung imperial police. His other prisoners were two dozen Zealots and common criminals of varied race and specialities, all destined for the lions at the Circus Maximus. Rain followed us up the coast as the ship weltered along toward Sidon.

Rome seemed distant and Deborah, my wife in spirit, my love, drew farther and farther away to the south. I had often thought we would pay for the rapture of our lovemaking, would be punished for our immoral contract. Perhaps God would kill us, or strike us with a wasting disease, or let us be discovered and disgraced. Now I realized what God's punishment was: he had separated us, perhaps forever.

After six weeks, much buffeted by headwinds, we reached Fair Havens in Crete, still less than halfway to Rome. As we put on water and supplies, the sky grew dark and the mizzen sail began to flap ominously. Paul was on deck, and the captain asked him in jest, "How does your God feel about a run of fifty miles before the wind, if we hug the coastline?"

Paul, his gray hair and beard ruffled by the wind, looked up at the heavens. "Approximately as he did about Father Adam being tempted by the apple. You had best ride it out here."

The captain ignored the prophecy, and for an hour we scudded along smartly beneath Mount Ida, which looked down on us like a gigantic eyeless face. Then the sky erupted. Rain veiled the peak as the sailors muttered fearfully about the "euroclydon," rare and violent winds that blew up without warning from the northeast.

We could neither run with the euroclydon nor hold against it. The vessel, though of fifteen hundred tons, lurched and plunged. The passengers huddled below, the few small children screaming. The criminals and Zealots (leg-chained in a separate compartment) appealed to six or seven different gods. The entire belowdecks smelled of vomit and excrement.

During the night, we Christians prayed, did what we could for the children, and invited anyone who wanted to pray with us. In the third watch, we were suddenly soaked by an onslaught of water. The crew had opened the hatches above us and bellowed down for us to begin handing up our baggage and anything else that could be jettisoned.

I pushed my armor out of sight behind a stanchion, and slipped my dagger and the flash of Andrew's baptism water into my girdle. Aristarchus and I climbed the ladder to hand up the baggage and other belongings. On the crazily canting deck, the sailors were tied together at the waist to keep from being swept into the sea. They were flinging over sacks of grain, grappling poles, grinding stones, even the bricks of the ship's galley. At the mainmast, two men sawed, silhouetted now and then by lightning. Only the mizzen would be spared to give us locomotion if we survived the storm.

By now, Paul's pleas to "come before God believing in his only son" had convinced a dozen of those belowdecks, and three crew members, to declare themselves for Jesus. With all hope lost, they embraced the omnipotent God who had visited on them the storm. Why, when things are at their worst, do we turn to him who causes our woe? Aesubius would have called it the supreme triumph of emotion and will—that is, faith—over reason.

We baptized the new Christians with seawater, waiving any preparatory instruction. Our bread was soaked, but we gave to each a morsel and a sip of wine some passengers had saved. I pried open the door of the prisoners' rooms so we could carry our rites to them. Among them, only the Zealots angrily and utterly rejected our God. They reminded me of their dead brother of long-ago, my abductor who had died on the cross cursing.

All night, we bailed with chamberpots, halved amphorae, and basins, handing them up the ladder to the hatch. At dawn, the euroclydon still roared and Julius and the captain, both drenched, came below. They had remembered Paul's augur and pushed through the tangle of bodies to where he bailed and prayed. "What does your God say now?" shouted the captain. Paul debated whether to answer, then did: "Last night an angel came to me and said we need not be afraid, for God wants me to be saved so that I can appear before Caesar. All who are with me, he said, will also live."

The centurion and Egyptian captain looked at each other, said nothing, and climbed abovedecks again. Within hours, the winds began to abate, and by that night the storm was over. During the middle watch, in impenetrable darkness, the helmsman thought he heard breakers. He cast his plumb and found we were in twenty fathoms, then eighteen, then fifteen.

At first light, we saw the beach. Swells lifted us over the outer shoals, but for all the skill of the sailors at the steering sweeps, the waves drove us sideways and we were staved in on the next wall of submerged rocks. We swam and waded through the surf, the able helping the aged and the children. Not a soul was lost, just as Paul had prophesied.

We were on Malta, an island less than a day's journey from Sicily. But the straits were too choppy for passage. We were delayed until late winter at least, along with a grain ship that had made harbor and been able to stow its cargo ashore.

On an unusually mild day in late February, we sailed on the grain ship for Syracuse, then to Rhegium, my first port in Italy. The dark ultramarine sea was the color of Deborah's eyes as I had last seen them, angry at dawn. Yet I yearned for her to share my wonder as Buxentum, Salernum, Paestum, slipped by to starboard with their marble temples, porticoes, terraces, small theaters. Above their wooded hills where the summer villas of the wealthiest families in the empire nestled was Vesuvius, mythical home of Vulcan.

Crowds were at the wharf in Puteoli to cheer us and wave pennants bearing bread loaf designs, a ritual for the first grain ship of the year. On that first night in Italy, in this port fabled for its beautiful women, the bay breeze blowing through my window, I tossed in longing and wondered whether Deborah, with her body's accustomed needs and with Hoshea's persuasiveness, was as true to me as I was to her.

Next day, I roamed the docks. Great freighters cleared the port, low in the water with wine, fine furniture, marble and bronze statuary, silver- and goldwork. Tying up at the docks were blocky *oneraria* from Spain, sleek Phoenician-rigged traders with their two sails, *frumentaria* from North Africa laden with great blocks of Egyptian porphyry and bluish marble, an obelisk, the sarcophagi of mummies. The port was busy with the shouts of stevedores and sailors, the shrill of hawkers, the bump of the ships against the wharf, the smells of citrons, tamarinds, spices, human sweat, animal dung, Gilead balm, sandalwood. From triremes, fettered slaves trudged, surveyed by lines of dealers.

While Julius made arrangements to transport the prisoners to Rome, Paul took advantage of his freedom to visit the small Christian community in Puteoli, mostly Jews converted by Peter. From them, he learned that Peter was abed in Rome, ailing from dropsy. Priscilla and Aquila; Urbanus and Stachys, two elderly twins; Herodian, a distant cousin of Paul's; and others were also in Rome. Titus and Timothy were due soon.

We traveled by foot, and, through the Pontine Marshes, accompanied by nighttime concerts of frogs, by canal boat. A hundred stadia from Rome, we were greeted by Christians who had come out to meet us. Paul kissed the cheeks of Priscilla a dozen times. Strange man! How could he speak of women as if they were loathsome, and yet so love this brave, handsome matron? He did not stop smiling until the greeters reluctantly told us that Peter had rampant dropsy.

We passed into Latium and came to the Temple of Jupiter Latialis, where the military heroes of the empire paused to pay homage on their way to receiving triumphal honors in Rome. Paul, wizened and poor, without laurels, chariots, or booty, with nothing but his own God and a sense of irony, paused and prayed on the way toward what he believed would be his own triumph.

Seven days out of Puteoli, we saw Rome, embraced by the wooded Sabine and Alban hills. In the foreground were gray and brown shops and residences, then in the middle distance the glistening white shapes of temples, palaces, monuments. Great aqueducts seemed to stride from the city on arched legs.

"*Ecce Roma*," breathed Paul. "God be praised."

I was too bedazzled to speak. Never before, not at Antioch or Ephesus or Thessalonica, had I ever felt so much the provincial bumpkin. I had come at last to the megalopolis of the empire: the very center of the world!

The noises confounded my ears, the smells my nostrils. The streets were strewn with every imaginable kind of trash; the two- and three-story tenements crowded in on each other, many so poorly built that they bent at the top like old women frozen in mid-bow. Heavy carts loosened cobbles as they rolled cumbersomely through the business districts. Worshippers of Cybele and the Egyptian gods banged cymbals, wooden castanets, and gongs; beggars of indescribable odor clutched at our tunics and cursed when we did not give them money. Then, from this squalor, an avenue gave on a sunlit vista of overpowering beauty: one colossal temple after another of shimmering marble—to Jupiter, to his consorts, to the other Olympian immortals, to the emperors who had let themselves be acclaimed divine.

At Praetorium headquarters on the hill of Caelius, Burrus, head of Nero's imperial police, studied the encomiums from Festus and Julius and allowed Paul to continue in *custodia libera*. But he postponed setting a date for a trial.

We went directly from there to Peter's house in the suburb of Trastevere. A dozen Christians accompanied us. But only Paul and Luke, as physician, were admitted by Peter's wife, whose sour face and trembling lips made her look as if she were perpetually sampling vinegar. Paul's skin was gray and Luke was forlorn when they came out an hour later. I caught Luke's arm and he said in a quick, low voice, "Worse than dropsy. His kidneys are swollen."

The next day, I came back alone. I begged his wife to let me see him, and at last she relented. He was toothless, his cheeks caved in. Only his bushy beard seemed to have any vitality. The pockets of dropsy had been drained, perhaps that morning, for the loose skin lay on his throat and the inside of his elbows like yellow flags. His cataracted eyes examined my face. I saw that he recognized me as someone he knew, but it was only when I told him my name that he made the full connection.

"Demas, Demas," he said with wonderment, "won over for Jesus by Old Protokletos." He smiled, tried to laugh but succeeded only in a cough.

The tears came to my eyes. Of his generation, only he and Andrew had been good, deep earth. Only they had been pure water. None had Peter's humanity and only Paul his majesty. I might have been his disciple, and it seemed now to me I had chosen wrongly.

His wife entered with a cup of warm wine bolstered with an egg. From its smell, I could tell it also contained incense and sulphur. Peter shuddered at the taste. His wife raised a finger to me, indicating I must not stay long.

"I forgot about your nose," he said. "What a mess. For the cause." He rummaged in his mind for what he wanted to say. "Paul came by, you know. You are here with him?"

"Yes. I have been with him since we were all in Antioch. Almost nine years."

"So long?" he mused, seemed to fade and took a hearty gulp of the emulsion. "You stayed, did you? Barnabas, Mark, Silas . . . they left." He paused. "Mark and I are putting together a book. Tell Mark I said you could see it. We've tried hard to be fair. I would like to know what you think."

Fair? I thought. All of them would try to be fair. That would be the problem. They loved John so much that they would obfuscate in order

305

to avoid refuting his visions. No one would write that James and Matthew, sons of Alphaeus, were mean in spirit and therefore unworthy choices by Jesus. Or that Peter, if rumor were true, had whored, and that Andrew was a clown, if a dear one. And what was the truth about Jesus and Mary Magdalene, who had followed him right up to the cross? The facts would be swallowed up in fairness. None of the disciples, and certainly not Paul, wanted to remember or know the dark side of the truth, except perhaps Thomas, the least effective of them.

"I would love to see it," I said. "I have so many questions about what really happened. I have read some of what Paul and Luke are writing. And I have heard so many stories. I do not even know for certain about the resurrection. . . ."

Peter managed a grunt of humor. "*You* have a lot of questions? *I* have a lot of questions. Memory, Demas, oh, the beard of Abraham, memory . . . Mark and I are not even saying anybody saw Jesus after he was crucified."

He shut his eyes as if thinking about my question, but when he opened them, he stared dully at the single window. With a piercing sadness, I realized Peter had begun to listen mainly to the voices inside him, the voices of the dead.

"Paul writes that Mary Magdalene saw . . ." I said quietly.

That brought him back and he smiled, the diminished lips stretching across the toothless gums. He took another draught of the laced wine, and lowered his voice. Even at this remove in time, he did not want his wife to hear. "Ah Mary, Mary was someone very unusual. You have heard that sorry gossip: that she and the master . . . ?"

Peter was lapsing into an old man's lecheries. "I cannot imagine it is true," I said, "else he could not have preached as he did about the sins of the flesh."

"Maybe not, maybe not. They were so accursedly cautious. I never knew. She was someone," he repeated.

I had so little time. I wanted to draw him back to what he knew for certain. "Some say she told you and the others she never saw Jesus at the tomb, only a stranger. . . ."

"Well, that is also my recollection of what she said at the time, but the others say she said she saw Jesus. John is sure he came back in the flesh that night and is going to say so in his story. He told me that in a letter. . . ."

"But surely on that matter . . . ?"

"Demas," he sighed, beginning to fade again. "Who knows what they will say, or Paul and Luke, and Paul never even saw the master except for that unbelievable business on the road."

Peter's wife came in. Perhaps she listened at the door to make sure people left when his voice grew tired. But he wanted to make a few more points. "If I had to be put to a test by fire, I would say I don't think he was there that night in the flesh. But there *was* a presence. I can't describe it any better than that. I think even Thomas would say that much. . . . But the thought I want to leave you with is this: it doesn't matter. He is resurrected through us, and if it helps to simplify it for the people we preach to, then let them believe that he came back as meaty as a slab of oxen flank."

"But if it's not true . . . ?"

"Pigeon crap! Truth? It *is* true in the sense I said it was. He comes back to us, time and time again, and always will. We are not preaching to Greek scholars or Roman lawyers, Demas, we are preaching to people who are like we were. They can't read or write or speak even Aramaic or whatever else they speak very well. They must see things simply, and a god who does not come back from the dead and do miracles and so on is no god to them. Believe me," and his voice was now so low I had to lean to hear. His wife touched my shoulder and I rose, but he signaled with a flop of his hand on the bed that he still wanted to go on.

". . . Believe me, almost any message to them is worthwhile, any myth, so long as it gets them to love God and man. How can a myth be hurtful if it does that? So, Demas, go preach the Jesus you want to. That's what I did. That's what makes this"—he opened his hand, turned it toward himself—"going away so wonderful. I did what I was supposed to do.

"Soon I will be at peace, walking the road with Jesus and my brother again, laughing at nothing, sure that finally I am where I want to be. People of good will—you, Paul, John, so many, way beyond the numbers even Jesus thought of—will be preaching, each in his own way what they conceive Jesus wanted. He made it so simple, love of God, love of man, so what a person sews on to it is not very important when all is said and done."

He reached out his hand. It looked enormous on the thin arm. I took his hand and felt the love and began to weep, for he had wearily closed his eyes. His wife touched me again, and I carefully put the hand on the bed and left.

I went back the next day and the next, but he was feeling poorly. His wife was admitting only his closest associates, or visitors from the old, old days, or Paul. Luke saw him daily, and looked more pessimistic after each visit.

Two weeks after we got to Rome, word began to spread that Peter was dying. It was as if he had only waited for Paul to come so he could lay down his shepherd's crook. Sensing that this great, humble man was on the verge of death, Christians began a vigil outside his house.

Soon the crowd was so huge that it blocked the street and constables had to confine us to a vacant area across from the house. The pitch torches blew gently in the spring night air. All of us prayed aloud, a drone like millstones slowly grinding. On the fourth night of our vigil, Peter's wife came out and spread her hands helplessly. Her look of anguish said it all. There was a great wail, then another, and soon there echoed throughout the quarter the cries inherited from the Jews since Father Adam, the Jews from whom Peter, Paul, all of us, were descended.

As I went home, I recalled the story of Jesus prophesying that Peter would stretch out his arms and be girded and taken where he did not want to go. John had thought Jesus was saying Peter would be crucified. But given the figurative way Jesus spoke, he could have meant that Peter would stretch out his arms to embrace the whole city of Rome. And as to going where he did not want to go, perhaps Jesus had simply been wrong.

For all the love that people had for Peter, the church he left behind was chaotic. Some Jewish Christian parishes met in the city's twelve synagogues, rigorously excluding Gentiles. Other Christians gathered in taverns or shops, still others in homes or rented rooms. There was no liaison among the parishes, few written records, no community projects, no organized conduits to the city authorities or to the other sects.

Paul began reconfiguring the Roman church with the energy of a boy. It was what he had dreamed of doing for years. All the things he had learned in Ephesus and other cities, he applied to Rome. From the amorphous parishes, he structured clearly defined ministries, headed by the most competent Christians and all reporting to him. Within these new parishes, using me and his other veterans as his factotums, he set up alms and mission committees, catechumen groups, guilds for nursing the sick, for taking the Eucharist to the enfeebled, for finding homes for orphans, for conducting instruction classes for the young.

Paul established a central headquarters in rooms near his own. Here, he let the church pay his expenses instead of earning them by tentmaking. He was too busy weaving Christians together to weave goat hair. Titus and Timothy, who had reached Rome, and Luke served as his chief aides. I was once more supernumerary except on legal and other matters where I had special knowledge. I thought bitterly that Deborah had not been entirely wrong: I was often no more than an errand boy.

❀

Rome's Jewish leaders had been notified by the Sanhedrin in Jerusalem of its long-standing feud with Paul. But the Roman Jews needed him as a potential ally. Eleven years before, they had prevailed on Claudius to banish all Christians from Rome. Even though the order had been largely ignored, there had been several riots and the Jews had been blamed. Now rumors were abroad that Nero might move against both Jew and Christian. So, in spite of Jerusalem, the Roman synagogues wanted to explore whether the *modus vivendi* under Peter could continue.

The meeting started out well enough with Paul convincing the rabbis that Christianity for former Jews was not inconsistent with Mosaic Law. But then he began arguing that Gentile Christians could live generally within the Law. Even a sophist like Paul could not make that case. The rabbis were not fools. The more conservative rabbis among them said that the day the first Gentile joined Jewish Christians in the synagogues was the day the whole lot would be thrown out.

Paul lost his temper. "God was right in saying to your fathers through our prophet Isaiah, 'You shall hear but never understand and you shall see but never perceive.'" The rabbis tried to shout Paul down, but he shouted above them. "Let it be known here and now, that this salvation I preach will also be preached to the Gentiles. And *they* will listen. If circumcision was all it took for goodness and wisdom, I could cut the foreskin from a billy goat and call him a rabbi."

The Jewish leaders cursed Paul roundly, some spitting on the floor as they stalked out. They were not willing to buy tranquillity at the cost of swallowing insults. It would require a great deal of work to repair this day's damage.

❀

Luke was almost finished with his and Paul's tract on Jesus, and they were now writing a second work about the apostles' lives, Paul's in particular, after the crucifixion. Meanwhile, Paul had provided Mark with space at the headquarters to work on his and Peter's book. Packets of material came in frequently from Palestine to Mark, who had written to the disciples and to others requesting their best recollections. In turn, Mark was sending preliminary chapters to the Apostolic Council for those who might want to chronicle Jesus. So, by letting Mark work close by, Luke could keep an eye on what everyone else was writing.

Peter had said I could see Mark's draft, but Mark, who was engagingly droll, but weak, hesitated until one day when Luke was out. Mainly, it confirmed stories I had heard already. But it had the odd, fresh anecdote, such as one in which Jesus healed a deaf, babbling man by sticking his fingers in the man's ears and applying a coat of his own saliva to the man's tongue.

"Did Peter say he saw that one happen?" I asked Mark.

"*Seeing* something is not necessary for any of their histories," he replied, looking as if he wanted to say more. From his tone, I sensed he missed Peter.

"Cite me a 'for instance'?"

Mark looked cautiously out the door of his cubbyhole. "Well, there is this story Luke, or rather Paul, has about ten lepers between Galilee and Samaria . . ."

I nodded. Paul had used it in sermons to show the interest of Jesus in non-Jews. Jesus supposedly had healed ten lepers, but only one, a Samaritan, had come back to thank him.

Mark went on. "I asked Peter about it because if it were true, I wanted to put it in our history, and Peter said it never happened, that Jesus had sent all ten off to *pray* they would be healed, and that was the last they ever saw of them."

"So you left it out."

"No, let me finish. A few days ago, Luke asked me if I was using it. When I said no, he suggested I give it some more thought. He had heard Matthew and John were *not* putting it in, and Luke wanted it in Peter's book so as to corroborate his and Paul's because they *are* using it."

I thought about that a moment. "So will you do it?"

He looked morose. "I do not piss in a borrowed tent."

XXIX

Paul might no longer have trusted me to preach, but he was not one to underemploy his resources. The reporting I had done for him on the Palestinian and outlying churches had been thorough, and he had passed it on to Antioch. It contained names of leaders sympathetic to Paul, and of towns that most resented Jerusalem's emphasis on the Law. It listed the places where Nazarenes were most willing to accept Gentiles as their Christian brothers, and of where Nazarene leaders were corrupt or lazy, among many other facts.

The missioners of Antioch were already using it in and near Palestine to bring over Nazarenes and new pagan proselytes to Paulism, to the disquiet of the Apostolic Council. Paul, in order to consolidate the Italian churches, asked me to undertake similar surveys north of Rome in the towns where Peter had set up parishes. I accepted willingly.

I left behind my armor, but felt strange without it even though there had been no brigands reported for decades on the great Roman vias. Just north of Rome, the smells of the fruit orchards filled my lungs. I passed enormous columns, sculpted by Roman artisans, inching northward on rollers made of the trunks of trees and drawn by oxen. As the column moved from one roller, slaves carried the roller to the front and again put it beneath the great marble shafts.

I was on my own again, although still haunted by Deborah and our shameful alliance, an alliance I felt brought on my isolation from Jesus and God. But as each church, eager for news of Peter's death and Paul's ministry, greeted me with warm excitement, I began to feel loved and useful. Some invited me to preach, and at first I declined, for Paul's mandate to me was only to investigate. But when the requests continued, I gave brief homilies—humble ones, because I spoke from a burden of my own sin, a sin I would not repudiate.

In Vetulonium, a place of ancient Ertruscan ruins, and at Petrasancta, I extrapolated some of my own philosophy about Jesus into my short talk. The Christians seemed to like the questions I raised. Afterward, as I rode along, I formulated model sermons, preaching them for practice under my breath toward slaves in olive groves and at passing carters with bags of cinnabar, cobalt, and iron ore.

My final destination, Luna, two hundred miles north of Rome, was a sparkling seaport with marble temples, a theater, and a columned forum. The city had been founded only a hundred and eighty years ago with two thousand Roman citizens and was now owned by the emperor, but administered by a progressive and genial mayor. Its private houses were set among cypresses and artistically decorated with mosaics of demigods, animals, and birds. In the garden of one, I glimpsed a beautiful young matron in a diadem, leaning forward to console one of her children, her position outlining her thighs against the bleached linen of her robe—and I thought uncomfortably of Deborah.

The leading Christian was a glassblower, an artist whose aquamarine bowls, glasses, and jugs had made him a rich man even in this wealthy town. In his courtyard, under cloudless skies, I spoke to the fifty Christians. They were burghers and beggars, old and young, slaves and masters, mostly Jews, but at least ten Gentiles: the yeasty mix Paul loved. But when I spoke, it was not with the words of Paul.

"Nine years ago, at this time of year," I said, "through the kindness of God I traveled from Jerusalem with Peter, John, and my leader, Paul. To me, they represent the three great visions of our Christian church, disagreeing on some things, but agreeing on the most important of all.

"Peter, in my last talk with him before he died, defined this most important Christian belief when he said that Jesus' message of loving God and man is so simple that it hardly matters what we sew on to it. His breath was short, but even if it had been shorter, he could have said it all: 'Jesus is love.' It is love I would like to try to explore today.

"To begin with, I do not think love includes fear. John told me Jesus once said that perfect love casts out all fear. Fear, Jesus believed, has to do with punishment and menace. Love is the opposite of punishment and menace. Yet, we are often told to fear as well as to love God. I do not know how that is possible. How can we love what threatens us? If we fear God, how can we love him? We must choose. I chose, as Peter did, not to fear, but to love, God.

"No more can we love man or woman when we fear them, for if someone makes us afraid, we cannot truly love him. It also follows that if we carry within us like horrible weapons the things that make men fear us—viciousness, hatred, and the other great evils—then we cannot expect to be loved. Let us suppose, for example, that we are cruel to children, or to our wives, or other persons, or, indeed, even needlessly cruel to beasts. Does this not make us unlovable, not just to man, but to God? And if neither God nor man love us, do we not know in our hearts that we are unworthy and so we cannot love ourselves. The enormous sin of hating ourselves has made us fearsome. We are alone except for one companion: the huge, dumb brute of our sin."

I paused, suddenly struck. I felt the joy of Jesus beginning to suffuse me. He had come back after so very long. I felt dizzy, carried beyond myself. I fought to avoid spinning off into a vertigo I could not control. I reined in the nameless language in my heart without curbing my great joy. My words returned as if a wondrous gift had been restored to me.

"I myself have sinned," I said, "and I have let it make me hate myself. But I feel the grace of God stirring in me today for the first time in a long time—in spite of my knowledge that I will sin again. Our beloved Peter was a coward when he denied Jesus after the crucifixion, and I am sure that in his exuberant, impetuous life he sometimes erred in other ways.

"But do any of us doubt that if there is a heaven, Peter is walking there beside Jesus? Surely, if we aspire to the humanity of Peter, we are not lost. Far from it, we are on the way to being found. So let us cast out all hate, and pray as Peter did that we can overcome our sins, large and small, but that if we err, it be on the side of love. For if God and Jesus are love, then they are in us when we ourselves love, and we are therefore ourselves part of God and of Jesus. . . ."

I preached on, carrying the audience as I had never done before. I saw the frieze around the courtyard, terra-cotta faces of maenads, cupids, satyrs, gorgons. In my headiness, they seemed to blend with the rapt faces before me. I was going further than I had intended from Paul's ways, but I felt called by my exaltation to risk it. I was aware only that I was transported. And yet, when I ended and my audience gazed at me with amazed silence, I saw that I had transported others. It was then that I knew God had given me words beyond my own.

The glassblower kindly broke the spell. He had wine brought out in clear pitchers and served to us in stemmed goblets he had made. For the love feast, he also had cakes made of game birds, dates, whole nuts, and fruit. Beggar and banker alike, we ate as if we were royalty. During the feast, I was questioned.

"When Father Peter first came to us," said an aging slave with a strange accent, "we asked him about Christ Jesus coming back in the flesh and Father Peter said that our Lord had risen three days after he was crucified. But now we hear doubts. You have talked with the apostles, Sir Demas. Do they agree with Peter?"

I felt a start of annoyance at Peter. He had told them one of his useful myths, one that only weeks ago he had told me he himself did not believe. Now I must answer for it.

"Not long before Peter died," I said, "he told me that he felt Jesus came back more as a mystic presence than as flesh. There are different views. I do not think we will ever be sure, and I do not think it is important. He is here in our joy. He will be here when we celebrate his last supper. He is risen in us whenever we feel his peace which is his love."

"Is that really enough?" a scholarly youth asked. "If we are to believe, should we not be certain of such things?"

"We are unsure of many things," I said. "What are the stars? Pythagoras, Aristotle, Hipparchus, others, speculated that they are balls of fire, or holes in the dark screen over the world, or great jewels on the inner surface of a hollow globe. Do I need to know their composition or how they function to know they are stars and to be awed by them? Do I need to know whether Jesus came back as flesh or spirit? Or do I need only to know that he comes back each time we think of him?"

I journeyed back to Rome through the fields and farm towns at the foot of the Apennines. In Luna, I had spoken of love and sin and doubt and I had felt accepted. As I went south, I spoke on other subjects, often equally at odds with Paul. I described women as equals in a marriage, and, recalling how well Deborah and her aunt ran their business, said sometimes they made better employers than men. I said they had every right to be heard in the churches. In the face of Paul's horror of the flesh, I said I thought God made our bodies to be enjoyed no less than the most succulent fruits so long as we did not let that enjoyment cloy our lives or hurt the lives of others.

My words were more vague than Paul's on the coming of the judgment day—the end of the world. I told them I knew Jesus said he would be down to judge the living and the dead, but I had no idea when that might be. They knew as well as I that thirty years had passed and the warm sun was still passing across the good earth.

Many of those to whom I preached were slaves, some attending the services with their masters. Paul ordered these people to be "obedient to earthly masters, with fear and trembling, in singleness of hearts, as to Christ, rendering service with a good will as to the Lord. . . ." He accommodated slavery, I believe, because he knew harsh criticism of it would invite a Roman spear thrust in the direction of the church. Rome, since its founding, had been fearful of slave revolts, and, in fact, had almost fallen to one. Although he detested slavery, Paul would not speak against it.

I, however, was not so cautious. When I was asked, I said slavery was an unnatural state, one dictated, unfortunately, by the economics and politics of the world. If Vercingetorix had defeated Caesar, or Hannibal the Republic, I said, then it would be we who would be the slaves. As to why Jesus, at the end of his life, did not condemn it, I could only answer lamely that I did not know.

Each time I preached, I felt exhilarated. But I worried that this exhilaration would be short-lived. Rumors of my sermons had preceded my return, and in Veii, a town ninety stadia north of Rome, Titus emerged from the rear of the audience and I knew I was undone. He sat quietly through the love feast and the Eucharist and then mounted his donkey to ride beside my mare. "It's all over for you, Demas," he said as we departed.

I looked at Titus's leathery Phrygian face. "It was probably over when I preached my first sermon on this mission," I said. Yet there was something I had to know from Titus. Much could be said for his bravery, even his honesty. "Don't you feel anything?" I asked. "After all of our years of fighting for Paul, even for each other? And now you're no better than a spy."

His face tightened. "Demas, I did not like doing this. But Paul asked me to, and his way is my way."

"The sad thing is that most of the time, his way is my way, too," I said.

"So why do you fight him? I will be frank with you. I wish you were gone. I always have felt that way. I *knew* you were not like us. But Paul can use you. Why not change? He would forgive you."

"I cannot change," I said. "I have found I can preach Jesus *my* way and that people will listen."

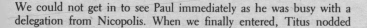

We could not get in to see Paul immediately as he was busy with a delegation from Nicopolis. When we finally entered, Titus nodded affirmatively to him. While Paul poured three cups of fig juice, I knew his gigantic brain, like a marvelous machine of pulleys, ropes, and levers, was adjusting from the Problem of Nicopolis to the Problem of Demas. I had been calm with Titus, for what was Titus to me? But with Paul, my leader for so long who was now about to decide the course of the rest of my life, I felt touches of panic. It had been one thing to take—at a distance—risks that might lead Paul to banish me. It was another actually to face Paul and that possibility.

"Demas," he said, when we were seated, "I heard that you were preaching an unknown doctrine in the north—doubly defying me, for I had instructed you not to preach at all. I sent Titus to find out about it. Clearly, you feel that you, and not I, know the true Jesus, that my belief is not the true belief."

"No, Paul," I said. "If I thought that, how could I have followed you all these years? If I disagree, it is only on interpretations, not because I doubt you know the true Jesus."

"Thank you," he said, "but if you say I interpret the words of the master differently from you, you are saying that, in your view, I do not *always* preach the authentic Jesus."

Put that way, he was right. I had equivocated. Did I not want to be able to say to myself as long as I lived that at this pivotal encounter I had been honest? Yet, to be honest might be to destroy myself with Paul. The moisture ran in my palms as I debated within myself. At last, I sighed. "Yes," I replied, "what you just said about my belief is correct."

"That in important matters concerning Jesus, I am wrong?" Paul wanted it said explicitly. He wanted everything.

"Yes, that is what I now believe."

"Demas," he said angrily, although he himself had forced me to be so blunt, "you *never* believed as I or anyone else did. Poor Philo thought he could marry Judaism to the Greek philosophies. Apollos thought he could do the same with Christianity. But no one besides you thinks he can make a marriage of all three. Jesus is not divisible. One cannot pick and choose from a God like one would from a bin of vegetables. My knowledge of Jesus comes from his revelation when he made me part of himself on the way to Damascus and from my many talks with the original disciples. It is presumptuous of you to challenge knowledge we have been gathering and interpreting for thirty years."

Now I saw that he had built a case for putting me away from him. The touches in me of panic were more insistent. Rationally, I had seen for at least two years the inevitabilities of a schism. But whatever my *knowledge* of Paul's unbending ways, I had always *felt* our parting would be on my terms, as it had been when I left him for Deborah in Raphia. I was unnerved. What, after all, was Christianity without Paul?

I tried to impose on myself an iron will such as I had so often seen Paul enforce on himself. I breathed deeply. "Paul, I seek only to tell the truths of our mission."

"I have heard what you call your truths, Demas," he said. "They are not my truths. They are not those of Jesus."

"Paul," I said, some desperation in my voice, "despite what you say, you know as I do that many matters are in dispute, even among the original disciples. Please listen to me."

"Well, let us deal with your—" he paused—"heretical ideas one by one. May we start with your view of the resurrection, since from what I hear, it is one of your favorite themes? I believe with John and the majority that Jesus returned in the flesh. I know that his voice *literally* spoke to me that day on the highroad."

I was relieved. At least, he would let me argue my case. Did I also feel that so long as we were talking there remained the shred of a chance that he would accommodate me?

"For my part," I said as mildly as I could, "I do not think a person needs to have your certainties to be a good Christian and a good minister."

"I assume you have the same uncertainties about the miracles?" There was no mildness in *his* voice.

I wanted to assert my own doctrines, not merely react to his inquisition. Yet faced with his implacable eyes and voice, I again rose to his question. "I have spoken with only a few people who claim they saw miracles. I am also sure some are hard to explain without a miraculous element. But, again, I do not think certainty about miracles is necessary. I do not *need* them."

He was getting angrier. "But you *do* need, from what I hear, to preach that such things as perversion, drunkenness, sloth, fornication, adultery, are not important, and that Jesus did not condemn them."

"To be fair to Demas, it is more complicated than that," Titus said. "He preached that Jesus said—"

"*I* will tell him what I preached." I cut off Titus, my reasonable tone beginning to evaporate under Paul's false charges, "I preached that Jesus cared far more about ridding the world of murder, rapine, rage, hypocrisy, greed, envy, hate—the great sins—than he did about those you mention, the sins of the flesh. Like you, Paul, I have seen drunks vomiting on the cobblestones, catamites parading around with flour on their faces, men and women with noses rotted off from their lechery. It is disgusting that such things happen and sad that children should have to see them. But I think Jesus believed there are more important fires to contain, such as the monstrosities committed by men like Cremens in Bayba—"

"Well,. I believe Jesus meant what he said"—Paul broke in ominously—"that all sins must be purged, and none are more insidious, more festering, than the sins of the appetite." Paul had become pig-eyed and suddenly I was wary. "You disagree also with my, that is Jesus', attitude toward women," he said.

"I think in many respects, given the opportunity, they can be our equals and perhaps our betters," I replied. I thought of Deborah in Borhaurus and Modi'im. But I did not want to give him reason to question me about that. "Lydia comes to mind," I said.

"Lydia is a magnificent woman," he said. "There are many others. Priscilla, Phoebe . . . I could go on and on. But you speak of them as equals. Did Jesus choose a woman as a disciple? Are you suggesting they preach? That is not their role. Nor was it under Jesus."

"It was not their role under Jesus because Jesus was preaching to Jews and the Jews would not have stood for it. You are preaching to Greeks and Romans, where women—"

"Demas," he said, "I do not need you to tell me who shall preach in God's ministry and who shall not." His tone was fierce, but in this question of women there was a defensive undertone.

My panic had disappeared. "You do not even like women, Paul. Only when they behave like men. As Priscilla did, who is stronger than her husband. In my view, women scare you. I have heard you say, 'It is well for a man not to touch a woman.' What kind of talk is that?"

"I have preached that touching a woman is only possible within marriage. I have often said I am glad I have never had that kind of desire for a woman. If that makes me a freak, so be it." He added wryly, "Nor have I ever had any desire for men. Nor had I ever thought it."

I knew from the intensity of his black eyes that I had pricked his pride. I had forced him to answer me with neither condescension nor didacticism. Now I knew he would attack me personally. It was his style. "You have made some harsh judgments of me about women, Demas," he said. "In the past, I have spared you, spared even questioning you about them. There were, however, reports that reached me after we left Antioch about your behavior there. I ignored them."

I looked at Titus. Had he, even then, followed me, found out I was going to the house of prostitution? He shrugged no. "I did what I did,"

I said. "If I have done wrong, it is I who must live with it." Did they know only of Antioch? Or did they also know of my greater sin in Raphia.

"No, Demas, you also asked *us* to live with it. Imagine the disgrace to us all if one morning a harlot was found beneath your bed. Are you so forgiving of fornication and adultery because they are sins to which you have often yielded?"

I hesitated. And in those seconds, Paul got his answer. But I did not want that silent yes to be all I had to say. "They are sins that Jesus found easy to forgive," I said. "Were even the apostles always so pure as you?"

"Demas, that is beneath you." Obviously, he had heard of Peter's straying with women, or perhaps knew of it firsthand from when they were friends in Jerusalem twenty-five years ago. "I gather from your answer you are also confirming the reports I have about you and our coreligionist in Raphia."

Stated this merciless way, his accusation took the fight from me. "Raphia is now a matter between me and God," I murmured.

"It is over, then?"

"It is over, by her doing, not mine," I said quietly, my mouth gone dry, my gallant posture blown to the winds.

"And you are contrite? It would help your case."

I had confessed. I would not tell him I was contrite, for I was not. "Paul, let it be," I said.

But it was not Paul's nature to let things be. "In that matter, you disgraced us," he observed. He waited for me to comment and when I did not, he continued. "In another matter, you endangered us. I am speaking of your sermons about slavery. You go too far. There are expedients we must follow to survive."

I was still shaken by his knowledge of Deborah and me. Intellectually, I now knew there was no possibility he would let me remain with him. Yet, I wanted to follow my rope to its end. "Paul, your life is a hymn to freedom. You were yourself briefly a slave. I have seen your hatred of slavery myself."

He knew he was on unsteady ground and chose another target. "You preach that Jesus may not come soon to judge the quick and the dead. What kind of madness is that?"

In this, he had reached the center of our differences: the opposing premises under which he and I accepted new members. It was an issue that had divided Deborah and me in Borhaurus, but we had resolved it by each preaching our separate beliefs. I thought her and Paul's emphasis on scaring people into the church by using their fear of imminent and eternal judgment was deluded at best, and at worst hypocritical. "Yes, I preach exactly that," I replied. "I simply do not know when Jesus will come."

"It is a tenet that his return is at hand," he said, as if to snap off the argument.

"A tenet only because it frightens the ignorant into joining us," I retorted. "Paul, are we to use any pretense we can to lead people to baptism? If they are afraid of the end of the world, are we to scare the hell—literally—out of them so they will come to us before it is too late? You even tell people not to get married a second time because it might confuse Jesus when he arrives to judge. As if he has a list in heaven that needs revising every hour while he is on the way down to earth. You know as well as I do that we do not know when he is coming."

"*He* preached his coming was near."

"Well, it happens that it was not near. But even if we did know when he was coming, there are so many other lies, so many half truths we tell to win people over. We tell the slaves Jesus wants them to be slaves because they will be free in the next world; we tell the guileless about resurrection, about miracles, about the holy spirit—whom I have never even understood. We tell traditional Jews we are at one with Mosaic Law and Christians that we do not believe in the Law. If people are poor, we say Jesus wants them that way so they can be rich in the world to come; and if they are rich, we tell them to pray hard and make donations and we will see if we cannot bring them, too, into heaven." I stopped. I had made my manifesto.

Paul was taken aback. He looked briefly at the window to regroup his arguments and my gaze followed. On the rough cobbled street, we watched two oxen switched along by a boy. When Paul turned back, it was to reply calmly, "Demas, this is leading us nowhere. I had my vision of Christ many years ago. I have followed it as I saw fit. I do not want a baring of scars." He smiled. "You saw me accept some of them and you have surely gotten your share in the years you have been with me. More often than not, Demas, you have been a child of God, and I know that your willingness to die for the master as you see him is exceeded by no one, by no one at all."

He was ending our interview. I had said more or less what I wanted to, and in the process had clarified how different our views were. I could put down my doctrinal sword. But that said, there was my heart. Paul had been my leader, my inspiration, at times a friend, at others a surrogate father. I again felt prickles of panic. "Paul," I said, "in spite of all I have said, I am grateful to you . . . I have loved you."

Why could he not accept me for what I was? And with that thought came a granule of hope, not from my brain but from my heart, that he would let me preach my way without estrangement from him. I voiced that infinitesimal hope. "Paul, take me as I am! I can help with the legal things, preach in outlying regions where others do not want to go. I have saved you with my sword, and with my words before Felix. I have been set on by dogs, robbers, imprisoned, crucified. Surely, my Christianity is better than none?" I stopped, riven by my emotion.

Paul, too, was upset. The compulsively loving Paul who had always hoped I would change vied with the intricately strung man of reason. The latter won. "You would be useful, Demas. You have done all the things you said, and more. But I cannot afford the luxury. The message you insist on preaching is a corrupted one. Already, I must send someone northward to correct what you preached on the resurrection, the miracles, the other things—"

"Corrupted only in your view, Paul. . . ." I began more as a plea than an argument, still caught up in my passion.

He waited, not unkindly, for me to calm. "Well," he sighed, "let me accept that. But I have had to make decisions. Even now I may have to excommunicate Hymanaeus and Philetus in Ephesus. They were loyal followers once. There must be purity of doctrine or we will be drowned in the false prophets, the wolves that Jesus warned against."

"I am not a wolf or a false prophet, Paul," I said, embarrassed at my outbursts, seeking again for my dignity.

"You are not a true one."

"Jesus will be the judge of that," I said resignedly.

The room was silent, uncomfortable. I was exhausted both in intellect and feelings. Dazedly, I tried to review the conversation as a lawyer, ticking off my arguments one by one. Had counsel for the defendant said what he needed to say? Yes. Did he have any further questions? No, alas.

"Paul," I asked, "can you at least give me your blessing?"

"Yes, Demas," he said, also relieved that finally it was done. "You have risked so much for Jesus and for me that I cannot send you away without sharing him with you." He fetched bread and a wine pitcher from his cupboard. It was like the little Roman pitcher Dathan had fashioned. I thought of it with its two companions stored in a box at Ezra's. My throat grew tight. Paul waited for me to recover, then gave me and Titus the Eucharist. Moved but dry-eyed, I silently prayed for the forgiveness of sins that I had committed and for the good deeds I had omitted.

321

"Pray for me, Titus," I said, remembering Laranda and his prayers then, and, oddly, it was at this moment that my tears came.

"I will pray for you," said Titus.

It was a measure of our Christianity that all of us, at least in this moment of farewell, meant every word we said.

XXX

When I was in the street, I told myself that I had morally and intellectually prevailed. I had broken with Paul without rancor and over high moral issues. I had been as bull-headed as he was. But even if these consoling thoughts were true, they did not give me solace for long. I was alone, far more than when I had broken with Father. Then I had left to join Deborah's and Rechab's energetic and close movement, and I was in love. In defying Paul, I had let a transcendent cause march away and leave me. I walked aimlessly. In the face of Paul's main message that men should love, not kill, in the grandeur of working for the salvation of humanity, just how powerful were my objections?

I passed the Circus Maximus and smelled the stink of the cages, row on row in the shadow of wise Minerva's temple. I heard the throaty growls of the lions, the snarls of panthers, the rumbling voices of the bears from within the barred cages. The adamantine Zealots aboard our ship and the prisoners we had hastily baptized had died here by now in Nero's games. I thought of Bayba. I saw vividly again the goring of the helpless woman, the torturer putting the red hot iron to the fallen sailor, the dismemberment of Cremens.

I had been a powerful aide to the one man in the world whose teachings and organization might have put an end to these grisly spectacles. Of all leaders, he knew best how to impress upon the hearts of men that savagery was a sin in the eyes of the God of decent mankind.

Certainly, I could *tell* myself I had kept my integrity intact. But was what I called integrity really any more than my stiff-necked pride? I badly needed someone to assure me I had done right. I needed Deborah. Or Ezra, or Grandfather, or Peter, Rechab, Thomas . . . or Father. But there was no one. And the man from whom I most needed support, Paul, had just dismissed me from his movement.

That night, I tried to recover my spirits. In Borhaurus, in Bayba, elsewhere in Asia Minor and Greece, I had proved I, too, was organized and persuasive. In Luna, I had moved people with the truth of Jesus as I saw it. I did not want to intrude on the ministry of Paul. But north of Luna was beyond his pastorate, as was northern Gaul, Spain, Numidia, Mauretania. I should choose a site and begin planning my campaign. But I did not.

In the next few days, I missed Paul almost unbearably. My intelligence, on which I had foolishly prided myself, had told me, and continued to tell me, that parting from Paul was for the best. But the rest of me was overwhelmed by the pain of my dismissal.

I roamed the city, watching firemen pumping water through their leather hoses to put out a fire at a draper's, workmen installing marble facing on Nero's new palace, boys racing in goat carts. I listened dully to a blind musician plucking modes on his kithara, sat overlong in the public lavatory, went to the baths, browsed in the library, or napped. At moments, I let myself, who had braved so much, be chilled by fear that Paul would denounce me as he planned to do to Hymanaeus and Philetus. Was not I, like them, an outcast, an enemy?

❁

One day, a letter arrived from Massilia, relayed by Luke to my quarters without comment. I recognized Father's handwriting on the envelope. It had been ten years. I tore the seal—and instead of hope I felt a vulture beak in my guts: Mother was sick and Father and my old tutor Aesubius were bringing her to Rome for treatment. Since Massilia had its own renowned medical center, I knew the trip could only have been prompted by desperation.

They would be staying with a friend, Farius Cralla, in his large house on the Street of the Pythian Victory. Each day I went there to inquire. I would wait a minute or two in the hall between the pool and the household altar, then sleek Farius, or his handsome wife, or his daughter Daphne, who was perhaps twenty, would come, tell me they had no news, and briefly chat.

My gloom was far more penetrating than when Deborah had sent me off with a curse, for there had soon been the excitement of the sea voyage and the renewal of my preachings. Even after Paul banished me, there had remained the sustaining thought of my family. Now, as if I were being tested by an inexorable and dreadful progression, my mother was coming to me, mortally ill.

A week after the letter, they arrived. I heard Father's feet beat rapidly down the stone stairs, and he rushed from the portico into the wide hall, arms outstretched. His distraught look gave way to surprise: he had forgotten my smashed nose. He was gray, his face worn more than the years warranted, his stern aspect deepened by agony. Only in his bearing was he the father of my youth: erect as he would be, I was sure, until the day he died. I flung myself into his arms, weeping.

"Demas," was all he said. "Father" all I could answer as we embraced. He led me up the stairs to where Mother lay in a bed with carved walnut legs, flanked by two three-legged tables on which were her medicines, her jewelry, a mirror and cosmetics. She had been a pretty, plump matron when I last saw her. Now unhealthy flesh rolled on her arms and beneath her chin. Her eyes shone with the old love, they alone giving life to the sad face behind its pathetic mask of pomade, kohl, and powder.

I held her, even now comforted by her familiar perfume. Aesubius toddled in, fragile as an antique amphora, and embraced me. Then, discreetly came Farius, his wife, and Daphne. Farius invited me to stay with them, and I gratefully accepted. That afternoon, a famous heart physician came to Mother. Downstairs in the hall, he whispered to Father and me that he would do his best, but he had little hope. "The beating of the heart is too faint, good Junius, too irregular," he said.

In the evening, Father, Aesubius, and I sat in Mother's room and I recounted my adventures. When I explained my break with Paul, Father looked smug, but kept his counsel. After a while, Mother fell gently to sleep and we three talked quietly by her bed until midnight. When at last I went to my room, I saw that as tokens of our reunion, they had brought from Massilia my worn primer of Herodotus, an ancient Jewish spearhead I had found in a field, the brass bit and spurs Father had given me for my first pony. Mother had kept them for me all these years.

In the next days, Father, Aesubius, and I, sometimes relieved by the wife of Farius or Daphne, took turns sitting with Mother. Indeed, the Crallas treated us as members of their family. Father went for a time each day to the Office of Imperial Provinces, and he and I met in the afternoons at the baths. We spoke companionably of Mother's latest prognosis, of Massilia, of the architecture of Rome, avoiding talk of

Christianity and politics. When we had been scraped by slaves and rubbed with oil, we walked and talked in the garden with its manicured trees.

Friendly as we were, nothing lifted Father's mood. In the old days, his Stoicism frequently was lightened by his dry humor. Now his face showed mere endurance. All his energies and thoughts were devoted to Mother, and to maintaining his dignity—and an appearance of courage that I had ceased believing in after Rechab's trial.

One evening, when Mother seemed stronger, we took her, wrapped in furs, to the Crallas' garden on a light wooden couch. There we grilled a small tunny on a brazier and afterward drank wine beneath more stars than I had ever seen. "I loved being on the road at night by the campfire," I said. "I missed you all then. Good memories seem so easy when the day is over and the fire is warm. But mainly I felt satisfied, tired but satisfied, because I was doing what I thought was right." I looked at Father.

"Our causes were so different, but I know what you mean." He sighed, with these words finally and quietly accepting me. Mother reached from her couch and took his hand. "When I was young," Father went on, "and in the field at Vendelicorum, I did not feel I was there for Tiberius, but Rome. And for myself. At the forest's edge, two thousand Germans opposed us. The sun shone hot on our armor. We knew how well we were trained, how sharp were our swords, how eager our horses.

"I felt just as you described it, Demas, better than almost any other moments of my life. I have not felt that way for a long time. If I were fighting for Nero today, I could only wish for death in battle. In my heart, I know that I have settled for a life without love for Rome, without love for anything." He looked at us. "No, not without love. I have settled for love of you, of your mother, of Aesubius. That is a great deal."

She had dozed off, warm within her furs, her hand still in his. Her face's sweetness, made young by the dark, reminded me of the lineaments of Deborah sleeping. Made stupid by this memory and Father's eloquence and rare emotion, I felt the tears come. He, too, might have cried. I could not tell, for he rose and poked the dying coals of the brazier.

Daphne's green-eyed prettiness was hard to ignore. When her parents were not nearby, she was flirtatious, and I was flattered by her attentions. Once when I came in while she sat with Mother, I saw her wiggle her toes and smelled the perfume of nard, surely from a little leather vaporizer in her sandal, a current fad. We took walks on occasion, and I liked her humor and her quick intelligence, which lightened these onerous times.

She also had a piquantly salacious mind and provocatively let me know she had just ended an affair with a wealthy married man. And once, she coyly cooed Sappho at me in her schoolgirl Greek: " 'The peer of Gods, you seem to me. When you smile on me blissfully . . .' " And then a parody I had not heard since my school days: " '. . . the sweat runs rivers down my ass which trembles like the springtime grass.' "

Sometimes at night I imagined Daphne's full body coiling and bucking against me like a great white snake. And by the time I had been in the Cralla household for two weeks, I was sure Daphne (how unsuitably named) was thinking of a dalliance or perhaps even marriage. But beneath her compliant flesh, I clearly saw the specter of bones, and not spirit. Perhaps once, her brightness, her dash, her money, would have led to a marriage. But she was sugar and froth from a world that for me no longer existed, nor had it for a long time.

I wrote Deborah, telling her that I was with my parents, that my mother was sick, and that I had been turned out by Paul. I closed without endearment. She had left me with none to give.

One day at the baths, Father led me to an unfrequented spot in the garden and, pale and nervous, handed me a scroll to read quickly and return. It was a copy of a general decree, written in the kind of administrative language that protects the writer if the initiator—Nero in this case—changes his mind. "A sect founded by one Jesus, called the Christus, deceased, of Palestine, has been active in Rome and the empire, preaching against The Divine Gods, and thus the Emperor. In Rome, a certain Paul, also know as Saul, of Tarsus, has activated a faction of this cult.

"The Emperor does not look on this sect with favor. He wishes no sanctions against those who openly renounce it or even, in his benevolence, those who take oath to let their practices lapse. But those who further it are regarded by the Emperor as in contravention of Statue IV, Section Twelve, Paragraph Two, of the Code. The rights of such violators and their protectors, including Roman citizens, may be temporarily suspended at the option of provincial and equivalent authorities if there is reason to think unrest may occur through their practices."

It was an invitation, even a suggestion, for official persecution of

Christians. But Father had more. In a low voice, he told me of a dispatch he had seen from Palestine.

"One of your leaders, James, has been killed by some Pharisees and scribes. They threw him from the Temple roof. He survived long enough to start praying, then some workers beat him to death with their tools."

At first, I thought it must be faulty information. James had been the conciliator who pacified the Jews by preaching adherence to Mosaic Law, and calmed the Romans by rendering whatever Caesar wanted rendered.

"Why kill *him*?" I said, sitting down. "He just wanted to get along."

"Our best intelligence is that the Sanhedrin put the perpetrators up to it, to cow the Christians and to show Rome their boldness and strength. As head of the Nazarenes, your James happened to be the victim best suited for that role."

Father dropped his voice even lower. "Furthermore, do not wager on the job expectancy of Burrus. Or his life expectancy. Or that of anyone else. Seneca is already retired outside of town. Tigellinus and Vespasian have captured the imperial ear. Father Tiber is soon going to have bad breath."

My stomach turned. He meant from the smell of corpses. Paul's could be among them. The oppression would also bring trouble for Mother and me and Christians all over the empire, and by extension for Father and other relatives of Christians.

"Father, what is going on? Nero seemed—"

"*Seemed* is right." Even in a whisper, his voice was acid. "He is blossoming into a lunatic. Like his mother"—Agrippina, a madwoman and poisoner—"like Caligula."

I did not see how Paul's case could succeed in the face of this. Just to stay alive, he would need the most cunning and thorough legal help. That night after supper, feeling the urgency of what Father had told me, I asked him whether I could inform Paul. He nodded solemnly, but his face had on it the drained look of a man who has learned of his secret sentence to death.

When I went in to Paul, he was cautious, but he had enough reverence for the parable of the prodigal son to try to seem welcoming. On my part, seeing him in danger made me want to save him. I told him of the document Father had showed me without mentioning its source. But Paul said in a whisper, "I know your father is in Rome"—he had heard it no doubt from some Christian in Nero's government—"God will not forget him for this." I would have liked to ask why he was not equally accepting of the man who had brought the news and was willing to risk his well-being to protect him from the threat. But I let it go.

"You must . . ." I began, then realized I was no longer his lawyer and could not utter legal "you musts" at him. "For whatever my opinion is worth to you, I feel you should get the case advanced immediately, before Burrus loses what little power he may still have. Let me get up a memorandum as I did for Festus and bargain with Burrus to settle for your banishment to Spain or North Africa or someplace."

Paul shook his head. "I have heard talk of Burrus leaving, and have thought about it. But we are in place, Demas. Peter gave the church of Rome love and I have given that love a form. God will let it stand. I cannot go."

He was being as stubborn as he had been at Ephesus. Nero, later or sooner, would kill him if he stayed. Paul, of course, also knew this was true. I thought of soldiers coming for him, of him being dragged out like an unresisting sack of flour and taken to woods outside the city and beheaded or tied like the *sicarius* or me on a cross to die.

"You have often said you were all things to all people, Paul. You are not the least changeable of men. Let me come back and try to get you out of Rome. I, too, serve Jesus. I would die for him. I would, if necessary, die for you." I tried to state it as mere fact, yet tears came over my yearning to help.

In his old, nearsighted eyes, I also saw tears. "Demas, we have never been closer. How well I know the dangers you would undertake for me. But I cannot afford to let you help me—" he tried to smile and failed—"much less die for me. Believing as I do that what you preach is heresy, I would be wrong before God." I was hurt and he knew it. "Do you understand why I cannot?"

"I understand," I said.

A few days later, I came back to the house with flowers I had bought for Mother at the Julian market. I found Aesubius and Father packing our belongings. Farius was protesting, but in his voice I heard a suggestion of relief. When Aesubius saw me, his tallowy face screwed up in anger and grief. "Oh, Master Demas, how could you have joined these Nazarenes? You see? Once again they have brought disaster on the house of Faevolian. Disaster!"

Father took the arm of Aesubius in one hand, mine in the other.

"Let be, Aesubius," he said, but his inward pain had twisted his face like a wrung garment. "I have learned that Nero is suspicious of me," he told me matter-of-factly. He did not need to explain that by treating us as part of his family, Farius would also be looked on with disfavor. We had to go.

We moved Mother on a litter to a third-floor apartment with four small rooms that Father rented near Vicus Tuscus. From our window, we could see the pines of the Palatines beyond the great vulgar palaces of Tiberius and Augustus. Mother could talk now only in a whisper and ate sparingly. Father, Aesubius, or I always sat with her. Three days after we moved, Father took me aside. "The noose tightens," he said. "My superiors have told me we are not to return to Massilia. I will be given an assignment here, but meanwhile I need not come to our offices."

"Father," I said, anguished. "It is as Aesubius said."

"You let be, too, Demas," said Father. True, he said, his change in status could be due to Mother and me being Christians. And if my visit to Paul had been reported by an informer, that, too, could have made his superiors mistrust him. "But in these days it needs no overt act. My presence in Rome is enough. Tigellinus has never loved me. He was in Judaea and may remember my hatred of Caligula. To talk of any emperor's death is to wish this one's."

He looked up with hopeless eyes, then, for only a minute, as of old, they became frosted and keen. "Yes, I would prefer to think that my past is the reason I am brought down: that I loved the idea of the Republic and hated tyranny. But under this Nero, it is no disgrace even to be destroyed for assisting the well-meaning worshippers of a crucified criminal."

Mother worsened. She slept most of the day and when I held her hand I felt the chill of her fingertips. Father generally was too depressed to talk to us. Even when Aesubius or I was watching, he sat in Mother's room, his head sometimes exhaustedly across her knees. When he did speak, it was to urge us to flee before some lackey of Nero found us and summoned us to exile or worse. His instincts were sure: through a messenger, we got a cryptic unsigned warning—from Farius, Father was certain—saying, "Soon the falcon stoops. Go!"

One night while Father dozed, Mother began to breathe rapidly through her mouth. I knew this was a sign of crisis, and felt her toes. They were cold. Anxiously, I took her fingers in mine. They were not just cool, but cold. Mother, I was sure, was dying. I grunted in misery and turned to rouse Father, but my touch had wakened her. I looked into her face. Her cheeks were purple in the soft oil light. Her lips quivered, then smiled. I leaned close to hear her.

"I am going," she whispered. I turned again toward Father, but she stayed me with her trembling fingers. "Before long, I will know whether what we say about God or what your Father says is true. Wake him, Demas. Give me Communion."

I began to sob. I woke Father, and when he saw my tears he knew Mother was dying. We called Aesubius. While he, Mother, and Father held hands, I blessed the bread and wine and prayed that God would take this good woman up to himself. Paul taught that no unbaptized person could be given Communion, but Father had become a good-enough Christian for me, and Aesubius, for all his atheism, had always been. I had more reason to doubt my own worthiness. I served the bread and the cup, and all took it.

Mother died during the night. Father softly said her name three times, the *conclamatio* of Roman custom, and then cleaned her poor wrecked body with oils and dressed her in a sadly fashionable toga of white and gold. On her bed, we put lilies and cypress. There would be no cortege or *laudatio*. Instead, Father dispatched messengers to his friends in Rome including five veterans of his time in Judaea who had retired here, inviting them to the funeral meal. He found enough spirit to send me out for the best wines, cheeses, meats, and pastries, although by convention we should not have held the repast for nine days.

Not even Farius Cralla came to the gathering, only the five soldiers and a few lower civil servants who had not yet learned of Father's fall. That evening, Father put his head across Mother's knees and sobbed brokenly. It was the first time I had seen him weep since the day I was saved from the well. All that night and the next day, he sat by Mother's body. Aesubius and I tried to get him to eat or take water, or at least to leave her side and let us sit with her. But he only shook his head.

At last, about the second hour after dusk, he asked me to get him some myrrh and poppy powder for pains in his head. I thought of arguing, but he seemed too lost within himself for me to cross him. Nevertheless, I ran all the way to the apothecary. I no longer trusted Father to be by himself. In his desolation, there lay danger. And poor flabby Aesubius would not have been able to restrain him from any madness he undertook. Waiting before the apothecary's door, I thought of abandoning my errand and returning. But at last, the medicaments in my hand, I ran back. I was still too slow.

In Mother's room, Father lay on the floor, his funeral robes bright red with lifeblood. I shook him violently. "No! No!" I shouted. I tore open his robe. Aesubius, as Father, I was sure, had ordered him, had pierced him through the heart. I looked for Aesubius. He lay by the chair in the corner. He had fallen on Father's sword, his body, like Father's, in disarray. Only Mother rested serenely.

I screamed now, "No! No!" The three I loved most in the world, for Deborah and Paul were gone to me, were all dead in this one small room.

I pulled the bloody blade from Aesubius's chest, found with my fingers the wild beat of my heart, and held the point there. What prevented me from driving it in? I do not know. A more spiritual Christian might propose that it was the voice of God, or Andrew, or Dathan reminding me I had not completed the tasks they had set for me. But I think it was the sight of so many dead whom I loved, and the simple corollary that someone must honor their bodies and go on with life.

I put down the sword and closed Father's eyes and then Aesubius's. I cleaned their bodies, and kissed their lips. Then I went to their rooms to find fresh robes. On Father's otherwise empty table, in his handwriting, was a poem in Greek whose author I did not know nor have ever discovered. Perhaps it was Father.

"Death is the butcher, and men his herd of swine.

"He picks at random from the squealing line,

"Then draws his knife."

Beneath it, he had scrawled. "It is better this way. Good-bye, Demas. I love you. Go onward."

❁

Nero had recently reinstituted the ancient practice of having the corpses of his enemies dragged by a hook through the streets and thrown into the Tiber. He had also revived an old law allowing the ruler to confiscate his foe's estates. There was nothing I could do to save my parents' house in Massilia, and the land I knew they owned there and near Rome. But the bodies of my loved ones would not be defiled. I had them cremated off the Via Appia, save for Father's little finger, which, as was customary for cremated Romans, I buried.

Above the site, I had a stone erected—far enough from the Via so his name would not be widely noticed. On the marble, rather than a line from the poem he left, I ordered inscribed one from Catullus, whose works he had given me so long ago: ". . . *Soles occidere et redire possunt* . . ."—suns that set rise again. I had his and the others' ashes put in a single simple urn.

My sorrow was now too deep for me to fathom or seek to overcome. I found a room near the decaying temple of Juno Lucina, well away from the Forum, where I would be anonymous. Alone there with the urn, I thought again of killing myself. These savage blows that God himself seemed to have contrived against me made life valueless. But the weight of grief was too heavy on me to act, even to rid myself of it. For two days, I lay in bed, taking a little water, waiting for a call strong enough for me to free myself as Aesubius had done. It did not come. My grief degenerated to despair.

Life and death seemed equally empty. I was nothing, a mere organism. Was it possible that only a few weeks ago, as I preached north of Rome, I had felt a return of the joy of Jesus? Now the last of my loved ones, Father, with whom I might have made some kind of life, was dead. I alone existed: a thirty-four-year-old man in a room with the ashes of his family and too immobilized to bury them or join them.

John had told us on the road that only once had he seen Jesus so melancholy that they could not reach him, and that was in the garden of Gethsemane. "My soul is sorrowful unto death," he had told them. And yet it was from that point that Jesus had come fully to understand his life.

That night, I thought again of the half-naked prophet in Ptolemais I had heard ten years ago on my journey to Antioch with Paul, Peter, and John. He had preached the God of Yes, and Paul had scoffed at his rags and his wild message. Lord in heaven, if such a one could preach a gospel of hope, why could not I?

I tried to pray for strength to cast off my apathy, as I had when Deborah had left Borhaurus, but hordes of insidious thoughts defeated me. Paul had gone into a time of paralysis for years in Tarsus after his conversion. What made me think I was a better man than he? Why should I try to recover? If God wanted me to know him again, why did he not give me a clear sign? These and other ruminations chewed up my infant resolve, and spat it out as thin whey.

I could sink no more profoundly into woe. Beyond this, there was only one step, death, and twice I had almost invoked it. If I did not want to die, but to live, I knew I must soon begin to fill my emptiness, my sorrowfulness unto death, with life, with some kind of truth.

For days now, the urn, resting on the floor, had been my only focus. I walked around it when I rose from the bed. No matter where I looked, my eyes came back to it. Honoring these ashes with burial, I knew, was the one thing, the only thing that I must bring myself to do, my sole imperative. I had thought that if my will ever returned, I would bury the ashes beneath the stone outside Rome where I had already interred Father's little finger. But, as time passed, I recognized that was a thought of convenience, for the earth in and around Rome was poisoned soil.

I came to feel I must take the urn to Borhaurus. That was where Father had lived his most productive years, and, unlike his native city, Borhaurus had valued him. It was Mother's birthplace and we had been a family there. Until I had laid to rest these three, this enormous part of my past, in the soil where they had once been happy, I could not seek a future. Gradually, the knowledge that I had this burial mission forced me to prepare for it. I went out to buy food with some regularity; I washed, shaved my face, now so bearded I hardly recognized it; I took my clothes to a fuller. At last, I packed what belongings I had, and, using a false name, took passage from Puteoli to Palestine.

In Borhaurus, Ezra took me in, provided me with a servant and all the luxuries of his life, and heard me out. It was not until I had been with him three days that he said with a smile, "I have concluded that you would prefer to live rather than die, so I want to tell you something I have withheld."

Watching me closely, he told me that from Bediah he had learned that the uncle of Hoshea's lover had tried to blackmail Hoshea again. When Hoshea refused, the uncle had revealed Hoshea as a pederast. Hoshea had prosecuted the uncle, who had been flogged. The youth had been forcibly severed from Hoshea, who had sworn to Deborah he would never again give in to his weakness. The scandal had not died down and they had sold their holdings in Raphia and left for Spain. Ezra shook his head and told me the worst: Deborah was pregnant again. For an instant, I imagined the baby was mine, but too much time had passed. Despite her vows, she had returned to Hoshea's bed.

In telling me the news of Deborah, Ezra had shredded whatever chimera I had that Deborah and I might ever reunite. If, during all this, Deborah could not force a divorce on Hoshea, then one was not possible. Of that I was certain.

"Now," I said, "there is truly nothing."

"Until there is something," Ezra amended.

Father's problems in Rome were not known of in Borhaurus. The people here remembered him as a fair man who had laid the groundwork for the calm in the town. Few cities in Judaea had been as free from violence in recent years. Ezra used his considerable influence so I could bury the ashes in the courthouse square beneath a modest marble stele with the three names on it, and with unostentatious Christian, Sadducee, and pagan rites.

I was moved by the love Ahiam and the other Nazarenes showed me, despite the fact that they knew Paul had dismissed me. His esteem was great even in towns paying allegiance to Jerusalem. But old ties were stronger. I did not tell them my alienation from Paul was part of an inundating deadness I felt toward Jesus. I worshipped with them at the site of the still-unbuilt meeting place. But my prayers fell from my lips and to the ground.

I stayed a few more days, but there were too many tragic memories in Borhaurus and nothing now to keep me. Besides, I had a longing to see Thomas, who had opened the door for me to Christianity. He had been a kind and worldly witness to my joys and pain within its walls. I dared hope he could counsel me on how to shape a new life from one that had no meaning. I drew out more of Grandfather's money, bought a fine donkey, more the mount of a traveling scholar than the stallion I would have preferred, and donning my armor against robbers, rode to Jerusalem.

XXXI

❖❖❖

When Thomas came to his door, my armor startled him but he covered it with a jest: "*Ave Caesar, morituri . . .!*" Thomas spoke no more Latin than the others, but sometimes pretended to erudition. Age had begun to accelerate in him as it sometimes seems to do in those we once expected to remain eternally young. His face had in it a permanent weariness.

"Caesar has some money," I said. "Can I buy us some respectable food and is it safe for you to lodge me for a night?"

I changed into a tunic and we went to a cookshop, bringing back a feast of lamb, wheat bread, goat cheese, lentils and lettuce fried with olive oil and cumin, a honeycomb sprinkled with locust powder. We ate on the roof in the cooling evening, the voices from passersby in the street below hushed, the first stars in the dark purple sky. Over the rich food and wine, I told him all that had passed since I had last seen him except as regarded Deborah. I let him know of the depths of my depression and of my alienation from the mission.

He nodded sympathetically. "Paul drives you all away," he said, "but he gives you courage and thus spoils you forever for us." The Apostolic Council, he said, was more timid than ever since the murder of James and his succession by Matthew. The supine attitude of Matthew had inflamed his more antagonistic brother, James, who had broken with the council and was fuming at home in Tarichaea.

"They all seem more interested in writing books about Jesus than about preaching him. But the truth is, none of us can remember accurately all he said, or all he did."

"I am more confused than ever," I said. I told Thomas how during my estrangement from Paul after he banished me for cutting the bridge, I had prayed to Jesus to let me know who he was. "I was sure then that I knew how I felt about him—how much his presence meant to me. I do not know that anymore, much less the facts about his life."

"And no one ever will with certainty," said Thomas.

That night, we returned again to the deepening mystery of Jesus, how little was known for sure of his childhood and youth, how everyone's memories had been clouded by time. The oil lamp limned the lines of Thomas's face still deeper.

As he became thrall to the wine, he said expansively, "You know, Demas, you could be of great use to Nazarenes and Christians alike. Who better than you to find him again? You know the country where we walked. You went all over it on this reporting mission for Paul. You know us who knew him best. You have time, for you said yourself the future means nothing to you. You have money. You are a lawyer. Suppose you went about it the way you prepare a case, questioning witnesses, asking them—us—to discriminate between what we *saw* and what we merely *heard* from others?

"You could weigh the credibility of those you speak with. From the many stories you could amalgamate not my Jesus, or the Jesus of Paul, or Peter, or the rest, but something closer to the true Jesus of history. You could *write it down* in good Greek. We would have a more accurate life of Jesus than all the scrolls being written, better than Peter's, Paul's, Matthew's, John's. . . ."

The idea was instantly appealing, but I felt my lethargy, my depression, drag me down. "You do it, Thomas. You are enough of a skeptic to change your views if the facts dictated it."

"Ah, Demas, Demas, no, no," Thomas said, pouring himself yet more wine.

"Suppose just for argument I did do it," I speculated. "Would you go with me? Between the two of us . . ."

Thomas considered that, and for a moment, I thought he might agree to my suggestion, but he finally replied, "I am too tired, too ailing, too everything. I do not have the will."

Dear God, did he think that I did? Still, as we discussed the idea, I thought of all the questions such a series of interviews, such a quest, could answer. Did Jesus come back from the dead? I might well be able to find that out, assuming it could be known. Did he ever prove he was the son of God? Did he really do any miracles? What *did* he think about the comparative weight of sins, about women, about slaves?

Even his most important speeches, his sharpest parables, his most pointed conversations were described in different ways. What—and the thought pained me like a knife prick in an old scar—would he truly think about Deborah and me? And even if I had some ideas about what Jesus was as God, what did I know of him as man? Did he like cumin or beach bathing or yellow gladiolus? When I found this Jesus, would I be able to preach him? And would God give me the desire, and strength and skill, to do so?

I went to bed slightly drunk, but less so than Thomas. The unusual amount of wine made me sleepless. In the darkness, the lines of the poem Father had left came back to me. His Stoicism had not even given him the strength to kill himself. He had thrown his death off on his slave, a braver man. For all my talk of what Jesus had done for me, though, was I any braver? Had my faith proved any more valuable to me than Father's? Thomas was right. We had all become ministers of a Jesus we did not even know. Perhaps Jesus *was* the man Paul adamantly preached he was. Or was he as Peter said? Andrew? John? Was he the strict, loveless Jesus of James, son of Alphaeus. Could one ever know the true Jesus?

Well, I thought, in one sense, yes. Dathan had known him during those moments before the mason killed him. I had, too, of that I was sure, when I was closest to death on my cross. Was it proximity to death that brought us to know Jesus and God? No, not necessarily. Dathan had also known him before that. None of us, however, had needed to know him in an intellectual way any more than Rechab had. Because, for all my supposed rationality, their way of knowing him by feeling him had ultimately been mine.

It had *felt* so simple, turning people toward Jesus. It seemed the best thing anyone could do for another person. But, in the end, this *feeling* that I was doing good had not been enough, and its limits had shipwrecked me and mine.

Jesus was a jumble for me now, perhaps even the architect of my misery. Yet, in my heart, and, now, in my mind, I knew if there was an answer, it was he, the more so after my talk with Thomas. I also knew that if I was to find him, it had to be in a new way, as much a discovery of the mind as of the heart.

In the morning, we took breakfast in the single large room that served for living, sleeping, and cooking. Thomas had two armchairs, one with a cloth bottom, the other of woven straw, and we sat in them and talked by a window in the neatly whitewashed wall. Thomas recommenced his urgings, this time without benefit of the vine. "What would it hurt just to talk with a few people around Jerusalem?" he said. "If you did no more than write down in an orderly way what John and I told you, Jesus would be better served in the future."

Again, I felt a quickening interest. And, in fact, what better venture did I have to occupy my time? Besides, suppose I discovered even a particle of my lost feeling for Jesus, with its concomitant joy and peace? I agreed at least to put down Thomas's memories. For his part, he agreed to borrow the latest draft of Matthew's recollections about Jesus from John who was now reading it. I was sure Matthew would not help me directly.

Over lunch, Thomas and I talked of the other original disciples. "Andrew you spoke to," he said, "at least the one night, and James, the brother of John, left nothing behind in writing when they beheaded him. You have already seen the early drafts of Peter and Paul. Bartholomew will talk, but is getting confused, and he was not with us on the road every day." He smiled. "He and Philip forget they were often home with the boats. Philip is dear, but half senile. James, son of Alphaeus, probably would not talk, least of all with you."

"Where are the rest?" I asked.

"Well, Judas of Kerioth is not where you would want to look for him. Jude Thaddeus simply disappeared a few days after his father, James, was beheaded. Simon, well, you know that tale: he said good-bye to Matthew one morning in Galatia and left for the Black Sea and Scythia." He paused, and his tone changed from the instructive to one of gratitude. "Demas, need I tell you how glad I am that you are serious about this kind of undertaking?"

"Somebody," I said, "should have written this history before now. Thirty years is too long to have let it lie fallow." Yet, if I merely defined Jesus more accurately than anyone was doing now—even if not perfectly—I would, as Thomas had said, be doing him and Christians everywhere, and myself, an enormous service. Perhaps Thomas was right. Perhaps at this moment and in this place, there was no one better suited to do this task than I was.

Next day, I found Thomas had visited John early and borrowed Matthew's scroll. I took extensive notes from it, and then, using letters and numbers, keyed them to what I recalled of Paul's and Luke's, and Peter's and Mark's, writings and tales of Jesus. Such a system would let me compare separate versions of the same incidents.

In the morning, Thomas called up his memories as we looked out on the Valley of the Cheesemakers, where once Jerusalem's famous cheese market had stood. I slowed him when he got ahead of my stylus, sometimes catching up when he got discursive.

"Everyone tells the story of the last supper much the same way," I prompted him at one point. "I heard Peter tell it years ago in Antioch and Matthew has—"

"Yes, well," Thomas quickly replied, "Jesus *was* inspired that night. He was unforgettable! 'This is my body, eat; this is my blood, drink.' Simple, yes? And perfect."

"But on other things, divorce, for instance, are there not chasms of differences between the stories? Matthew and Luke and Paul say Jesus was intransigently against divorce and yet Andrew . . ."

Thomas looked sly. "Well, Andrew would remember what Jesus said differently because of his brother."

"Peter?" What was Thomas trying to say?

"Peter wanted to divorce his wife. She made life miserable for him. She wanted him to leave us. She carped about Jesus—and everything else—even though Jesus performed a cure on her mother. Jesus still told Peter divorce would be totally wrong. Maybe Jesus was right. They stayed together."

"And adultery?" I tried to sound academic. "Andrew did not seem to think it mattered that much to Jesus. But Matthew and Paul seem to think he saw it as a deadly sin. And since Paul got most of his stories from Peter, then . . ."

Thomas leered. "If Jesus had seen adultery as deadly, he would have had mostly cadavers for disciples. Now don't put this in your book unless you wait until we are all gone, but I confess I was no saint. Peter certainly was not. Or Jude Thaddeus. People like Paul and Matthew and James, son of Alphaeus, can afford to make a fuss over it. What woman would want to go to bed with any of them? Talk to John. He has some very interesting ideas about physical love for an ascetic."

"Peter? You? Half the disciples . . . ?" So the rumors were true. They were no better than I was. "But Jesus?" I persisted. "How did he feel about this?"

". . . That it was untidy, broke up families, fouled a person's mind. Jesus was orderly and felt that any kind of illicit activities like this got in the way of orderliness."

"But as a major sin?"

"Not in a class with the worst. You do know," he added pedantically, "that most of those old stories in the Torah that wind up anathematizing adultery are really metaphors for the love affairs of Israel with false gods. In practice, the ancient Jews were far more lenient about adultery and fornication than we are today."

"So Paul and Matthew on this subject . . . ?"

"Are entirely full of camel dung. They classify these fleshly sins coequally with the sins of the spirit to give their kind of religion a focus, an exclusivity, a goal of complete virtue that other religions do not aspire to."

"But if future generations accept their views as the views of Jesus?"

"Then so be it." Thomas eyed the sun, saw it was noon, and poured wine. "You sound like a man in a state of adultery looking for a Jesus who condones it," he said. "You will not find him."

I tried to conceal how well he had hit the target.

"Ask John," he said, "to tell you the story of Mary Magdalene. You did not find it in Matthew's draft. Matthew would say he omitted it because John was the only one there, but, of course, there is a bushel of other secondhand incidents that Matthew *did* put in."

I pressed Thomas on the story, but he refused. "Well, where is she now?" I asked.

"No one knows. Peter, John, and I wanted her to preach, to be part of the council. Her mind was that exceptional, but the rest objected. She tried preaching on her own, but gave it up. I lost touch with her fifteen years ago."

"She would only be about forty-nine, fifty?"

"Correct. And a treasure coffer of information. She would know how Jesus truly *felt* about these issues. Ask as you go around, maybe someone will know where she is."

We talked of other matters in dispute, including Matthew's assertion that the mother of Jesus was a virgin. Paul agreed with him sometimes in sermons, although he did not argue the idea in private. "You never heard James, Jesus' own half brother, say that sort of thing," Thomas said, "and she certainly did not remain one. There were two younger brothers, Simon and Jude, and two sisters, Mariel, and one named Reba. . . ."

"And a second half brother?"

"Joseph, dead now, by the first wife who died, named after the father. You know, or do you, that Jesus' mother is still alive? Alive, but senile."

What would she have said about this talk of her being a virgin? I wondered. "Did Jesus ever claim that she was?"

"Never. People like Paul and Matthew need phantasms for manipulating the *am-ha-arez* and others at the lowest level. For them, Jesus could not be just the son of a carpenter. Our Messiah had to fulfill a prophecy: Isaiah, eight hundred years ago, said a virgin would conceive and the child would be called 'God Is with Us.' So Jesus must be born of a virgin. But you do not hear Matthew or Paul preaching it in towns with any worldliness, like Jerusalem or Athens or Thessalonica, do you?"

I sighed. "Is it any stranger than the resurrection?"

"Now wait. You are talking about something completely different. You can have Christianity without a virgin birth, even though it helps, but not Christianity without resurrection."

"You are saying the resurrection happened?"

"No, I am saying it *did not* happen. But it should have. Gods have to be gods. The Assyrians had gods who died and were resurrected, the Egyptians one that came back every spring after he had been cut to pieces. The Greeks needed one not born but springing from the head of her father. Gods have to be born amid portents, surrounded by prophecies, oracles, omens."

I stopped him. "Thomas, I have never told anyone that Jesus physically came back from the dead. And I have brought thousands of new members to us."

"Demas, don't play pure with me. I know that busker game. I would wager you do say he came back, meaning in the spirit of others, and that you do *not* crudely say he died like everybody else. Did you ever hear of a successful god who was not immortal? Osiris? Jupiter? Dagon in his heyday . . . ?" I flinched at the thought of Dagon.

"When gods *stop* being immortal, when they are proved temporal, powerless to live forever, they are no longer worshipped. When Moses ground up the golden calf the Jews had fashioned, they saw it did not have the power of immortality, saw it was just so much yellow powder. You Romans still win the wars, but your gods are dead. They died when we saw they had no power to stop the Persians and Gauls from throwing them down. They died when the Germans tossed the portable gods of Julius Caesar . . ."

"Varus," I said. Though well read, Thomas showed gaps in his knowledge.

". . . of Varus in their latrines and shit on them."

In the morning, I questioned Thomas further about the resurrection, beginning with the day Jesus was crucified, a Friday. "He was buried that night, just as everyone says?"

"By Joseph of Arimathea, a Nazarene, in his own garden."

"And no one went to the tomb the next day?"

"I think Mary Magdalene or his mother did. One of the women, anyway. It was a cave cut out in the rock. They found it had been closed with a big stone."

"The following day, Sunday, is when the controversy begins."

"Begins, my boy, and continues world without end." Thomas was fresh and in good spirits. "Just before dawn, Mary Magdalene, and, if I remember rightly, his mother and a third Galilean woman, Joanna, went back to the tomb. It was not far from Golgotha where they crucified him. They let themselves in through a gate—"

"Thomas, may I interrupt? Joanna is where?"

"I don't know and I don't know who would know. She was almost as old as Mary, his mother. She may be dead. So, they found the stone was rolled back and Jesus was gone. Mary Magdalene ran back and told John and Peter, who were hiding together in a broken-down wine storehouse. They went with her to the grave on the run and found the linen shrouds there, but no Jesus. John and Peter came and told the rest of us—we were in the cellar of a lampmaker. We were dumbfounded, scared.

"Who could have taken the body? we asked ourselves. A friend? An enemy—the high priest's men or the Romans to keep it from being venerated? Had they thrown it in the burial pit on Golgotha where they put the two thieves crucified with him? About that time, Mary Magdalene came up. She had stayed behind at the tomb. She was out of breath. Now, Demas, she *said* she had looked in the tomb again and there were two angels in there. . . ."

"You did not believe her."

"Of course not. But I knew she was not a liar. I thought perhaps she was hysterical over seeing Jesus killed in that horrible way. She was certainly wrought up."

"So she said . . . ?"

"That the angels asked her why she was crying and she said because Jesus had been taken away. She heard something and looked around and saw a third person and thought it was Joseph of Arimathea's gardener. And he asked her why she was crying. Now, remember, it was still almost dark and he said, 'Mary,' and when he said her name, she saw it was Jesus and she said, 'Teacher.' "

I started to interrupt and say that Peter, I was sure, had recalled Mary Magdalene's story otherwise. But Thomas was going on. "And the man in white told her Jesus was going up to heaven and for her to tell us. I do remember none of us believed that either, except possibly John and poor crazy Simon."

"So . . ."

"Well, that night I went to Bethphage to hide at my twin brother's. When I came back the next day, they were still in the cellar. And they said Jesus had come to them down there the night before. They said the lampmaker had just brought them an onion-and-mutton stew and wine and they were talking about what they should do next, and all of a sudden he was there, among them."

"In *body*?"

"*Not* in body. In *spirit* . . ."

That was just as Peter had remembered.

"And even if John said at the time, Jesus was there in body, then I have forgotten it, and it is not the kind of thing a person forgets."

"And did you say something about not believing he had come back unless you could put your fingers in his wounds?"

"Never. If I said anything, it was something like that I wished he *would* come back, but that I would not believe it unless I could touch his wounds. That's very different from what you hear today."

"Then how did the story about the bodily return get started?"

"Think about the atmosphere. The body was gone. Mary Magdalene had come back with this disturbing tale. Jerusalem was in even more commotion than usual, everyone looking for followers of Jesus to put on the cross. We had been praying in cellars for two days. I can well imagine John getting one of his visions, saying Jesus was among them. John *was* the closest, even closer than Peter. And the rest would say, yes, yes, Jesus is among us, thinking John meant in spirit.

"Then, as the days passed, John probably came to feel Jesus really had been there in body and, in fact, it *was* about then, if my recollection is correct, that John began to say that Jesus had been there *in corpore*. And who was going to correct him? He was the most distressed of any of us. Nobody wanted to argue with him about details."

"Details? Whether a man comes back from the dead?"

The aging face of Thomas creased into a broad smile. "It seemed like a detail then."

"A week later, you met again."

"Eight days, I think. At the same lampmaker's."

"The doors were locked?"

"Probably so."

"And Jesus appeared again."

"Never. Never, never, never. I was there that time."

"Then what . . . ?"

"We were still trying to work out how to carry on the ministry. We were frightened, confused, and not getting very far with new ideas. We thought Judas might be betraying us. He had not hanged himself at that stage. Peter was doing his best, but he was only a man, even if the best of them. John said something like, 'If we pray together, maybe he will come among us and tell us what to do.' So we prayed and John said he again felt the presence of Jesus. He said he heard Jesus say that he wanted us to go forth and forgive sins and baptize.

"Well, we all started talking at once. James, son of Alphaeus, got very excited. 'Where is he? Where is he?' he asked John. 'If you hear him, why can't I?' We went back and forth over it for the best part of an hour. And John said we should pray that he would come to each of us." Thomas went silent.

"And you did?"

"Yes, and nobody said he had come to them. But, then, we went back to what we should do, and—I swear this is true—we did work out our plans, that same night. And they were along the lines John had said, forgiving sins and baptizing. That week, Peter talked with James, Jesus' half brother, who was managing the family carpentry business and he agreed to help us. We needed him. He held us together—you know, cool, dedicated. I think James came to see Jesus that way, as a sort of wise accountant."

"Somewhat like he is himself."

"Yes."

"There were supposed to be other appearances."

"Demas, the two instances I told you about are the only ones with anything to them. Oh, I know when everyone gets their stories down on papyrus, it may *sound* like Matthew or John or whoever witnessed other returns by Jesus. For instance, one story has it that Jesus came to us while we were fishing in Galilee and told us where to catch fish and then ate with us. It comes from a night when we were catching next to nothing, and we sat down with a stranger and shared broiled fish with him. He told us where he had been finding them, and when we told him who we were, he said he was a Nazarene and we all prayed together."

"Did you catch fish?"

"We caught fish, a boatload of them. But that is not the same as seeing Jesus."

During the next two days, I talked with Thomas about the other supposed miracles of Jesus, which, as I knew, were as much a staple for Christian preachers as the resurrection.

"All right, let us examine the most famous first: Lazarus," said

Thomas. "We hear nowadays that he died of a fever and was resurrected by Jesus after he had been in a tomb for four days. But at the time, Mary and Martha, Lazarus's sisters, both said he was only in the tomb two days. I was there and helped pull him out and he became conscious very fast, I can tell you."

"So what do you think happened?"

"I think the cool in the tomb took away the fever."

"Any other theories?"

"Maybe just getting away from Martha. Visit her. She still lives in Bethany. Mary has died. Or better yet, talk to Lazarus himself, in Beth Jesemoth."

We went through other "miracles" Thomas had seen. As with Lazarus, as with Paul's cure of the cripple in Ephesus, all could be plausibly explained—if sometimes barely plausibly—as having been worked by nonmiraculous means.

"Do *you* believe they were miracles?" I asked at the end of our last day of interviews. "If you do, you believe he is God." Thomas was worn out by his words.

"I no longer know, Demas. My *mind* tells me he was only a man. But that is totally irrelevant to my conviction that he was and is God. You cannot imagine him, Demas. He had this wonderfully clear intellect. He had an instinct about what could be done. And once he felt he had the word of God in his ear, then he had the courage to do anything. At the end, we begged him to leave Jerusalem. He had infuriated every leading Pharisee and Sadducee in the city. But he felt God wanted him to die for mankind, as an example of what man could do. He felt God had picked the time and the place and he kept the appointment.

"Demas," he said, begging me to believe him, "I cannot tell you how . . . grand he was. I am not brave. If I were, why would I toady to this verminous council? But I would have died for Jesus if he had asked. The very night he was killed, all of us but John denied him. But *if he had asked* . . ."

"I believe you."

As I listened to this once idealistic man, now so humanly tainted, it struck me that it was not just James who remembered Jesus like himself, or rather as he wanted to be. Thomas did, too, and Andrew, and Paul. Did I also see Jesus in *my* image: a dilettante who knew a little about everything, a headstrong man, self-indulgent, yet wanting still to do right?

When I visited John, he told me many of the same stories Thomas had, and in the same way, but when I recapitulated Thomas's version of the return of Jesus, he grew defensive. "I love Thomas in a most special way," John said. "But he is a . . . disappointed man. I assure you, Demas, Jesus was as much in the room on those two occasions as you are now. We questioned him and prayed with him. Thomas is also forgetful about the fishing episode. When Peter saw Jesus on shore, he jumped from the boat and swam toward him. Could I make up details like that?"

John was so pure that to cross-examine him seemed crass. What he believed, he believed unshakably, although I was convinced that time had made true some things he only devoutly wished were true. But there were areas where his views were astringently practical, almost as practical as my own. One concerned the fleshly sins. I told him Thomas suggested we talk about Mary Magdalene. Unlike most mystics, John had a sense of humor. "Is he suggesting I had eyes on La Magdalena?"

"Certainly not, least of all you," I assured him.

"Well, I am not sure I like that any better!" he said, pretending to be insulted. "Mary was beautiful. She was young, eighteen, nineteen, still married to a rich drunkard who had beaten her. She had left him and was soliciting men in order to earn a denarius or two. Jesus and I were at the Temple one day and she was cringing on the street in the dirt. A crowd was going to stone her, as is condoned by the Law for adulteresses, especially if they are also prostitutes.

"Jesus said the first stone should be thrown by whoever among them was without sin. Not a one would throw, knowing the rest would call him a hypocrite. They just slunk off. Jesus told her not to sin anymore and to be on her way. But she wouldn't leave him. At first she followed him around like a puppy. However, there was mettle in her. She was intelligent. And brave. You know she was at the foot of the cross when Jesus was crucified. They loved each other."

"Of course," I said, "he loved everybody," but more from John's wise old eyes than from his words, I realized he did not just mean that generalized love. He meant something else.

"He was in love with her?" I asked incredulously.

"Not in the ordinary sense. It was not possible." He was pleased to have put me back on my heels, but I was sure he would go no further. Still, I could not leave him unquestioned.

"What are you saying? That he lusted for her?"

"I have said all I will, Demas. You are seeking the true Jesus. I have told you a great deal about him. You are right to let your love of him

347

carry you on this mission. And because I love the truth of Jesus, I love you for it. Now, let me make a few observations. I have never drunk save for a very little wine and I have preferred not to eat meat. I was, am, a celibate. I am a tidy old man. But as I grow older, I tend to think that such things as slovenliness, sloth, too much food and wine, are sins of sadness, evil only when they seriously affect others.

"As to the carnal sins, I have always felt—and only as an often perplexed bystander—that they are a little like gold. If adultery, for example, is hoarded, made the object of greed, used as a bribe or committed at the expense of others, then it is evil. Yet, generously given, I am not sure but that it, too, may be an expression of love."

I could hardly believe he had said it, this celibate so different from the celibate Paul. "That is radical talk for a member of the Apostolic Council and the closest disciple of a man who was so harsh on the sins of the flesh."

John rather liked the idea of being thought radical. "I think Jesus saw that radical element in me, Demas, and approved without entirely agreeing with my views. But, remember, his message was love, and I have thought a great deal about where that message leads. Jesus was only thirty years old when he was crucified. I wonder if some of his views were not still forming. I felt him moving toward my belief that if love, mental, spiritual, carnal, does not hurt others and is not on the face of it base, then religion perhaps does best to leave it alone."

"Base? Do you mean homosexuality. Bestiality?"

"Not homosexuality. I myself have a natural repugnance toward it, but I can imagine that two men could love one another. One thinks of David and Jonathan. No, I mean . . . what you suggested, bestiality or people injuring themselves or each other in perversions . . . gross perversions."

We talked on, John evading further talk of Jesus' personal life, but eager to answer other questions of historicity. I left him late, my fingers cramped with note-taking. Our conversations had been intense. What were the implications of his comment about the love of Jesus for Mary Magdalene? How does a God love a woman? And in that and other regards, did John, like the rest of us, also see Jesus in his own image?

I felt each time I left any of these aging disciples that I might never see them again. My generation would be the last to know them, the only living links with our dead master. Their deaths would remove the availability of truths about Jesus. What intimations, what spirit of Jesus, would they take with them?

Even with Bartholomew, I felt that way. He was as guileless and loyal as Andrew had been, but he lacked Andrew's zest and humor and he was not bright. His allegiance was most often to Matthew, but he had been close to Philip and walked daily with him. One day, Bartholomew invited me to come along.

Philip recognized my face. Kind and befuddled, he recalled with pleasure the day he had baptized me and my wife in Hebron. I did not correct him. He was a cheerful man, at peace with himself. In him, Christ's message of goodwill had taken firm root. As we walked, he told me a story that he must have recounted often. He had once told Jesus that he wanted to see God, and Jesus had said, "Why, when you can see me? As you see God in me, so live that men may see the son of God in you." In Philip, as in so many other Nazarenes and Christians, I saw Jesus. How I wished that my life were such that men and women could see Jesus in me.

The three of us walked to the garden of Herod's palace. An aqueduct trickled water into a pool before the bench where we sat. Behind us, the vines of summer softened the high walls into cascades of green leaves. When I questioned them, even Philip remembered details of the last supper. More than anything else, that shared meal was fastened in their minds.

I also went to see Matthew, who had little time for me. I was of Paul, and had been one of the ogres of the Cilician bridge. He pointed me to an uncomfortable chair, served me a cup of fig juice, but no cakes, and spent most of the time with a monologue on his troubles with Ananias, the high priest. I asked him explicit questions about Jesus, but did not tell him I had read his draft. He scowled and said, "I am composing a history of the master. But it will only be useful to those who can read Aramaic." Since we were speaking Aramaic, he had to assume I could read it. I knew he was snidely saying I was uncircumcised, and thus contemptible.

"I will look forward to it, but could we also . . . ?"

"Perhaps you can translate it for Paul," he sneered, an equally nasty way of saying Paul had forsaken his Jewishness. I started to snarl back. But that was what he wanted.

In the morning, I returned to Thomas and we chatted about what I had learned. When we parted, I embraced him, feeling how thin, how fragile, he had become. Only his mind was taut and young. His will, his heart, his body, were failing.

That afternoon I took the Dung gate to Bethany. My pursuit was beginning to lift me out of my soul's dark night. My investigations into Jesus' life were beginning to give me not just knowledge, but purpose. Each evening, I studiously transferred my notes from the wax tablets to papyrus.

XXXII

❖❖

Bethany was an attractive town on Kidron Brook. There the Nazarene minister obligingly directed me to the house of Lazarus's sister, Martha. She had a wrinkled-apple face like Paul's and had been married and widowed since she had known Jesus. What with the Miracle of Lazarus a centerpiece of the story of Jesus, Martha was a person every Christian and Nazarene tourist stopped by to see. Her eminence unfortunately had gone to her head. She had a rote recitation that she offered me, and in most particulars it was the same as the usual Lazarus story I had heard before. There was no doubt in her mind—indeed, she was immovable as granite that her brother had been dead four days before Jesus raised him.

"But, Thomas," I persisted, "whom you must know, told me you and your sister said at the time that it was two days."

"Who cares what *he* says?" she replied haughtily. "You know how the others feel about *him*. A grumbler, a naysayer. I talk to *that* kind all the time."

"But there were mourners still there when Jesus arrived. Would they have stayed four days?"

"Why would they not? Everyone loved my brother."

"Your sister, did she leave any written memoirs?"

"None, only her sweet presence." Martha composed her wrinkles in a pious expression. "That angel once anointed the feet of the master and dried them with her beautiful long black hair. Before she died, she let me cut it off and I have built a little shrine here with donations from followers of our Lord."

351

She had guessed from my handsome donkey and my clothes that I was not impoverished. I dug in my purse and found four denarii, more than I needed to give her. She took me to the "shrine" in the back of the house. The room Jesus had slept in was Spartanly clean. In one inlaid casket was her sister's hair, and in a second one, some of her brother's cerements. "When times were hard I had to sell some of his burial things to a rich Gentile. But the hair is all there. . . ."

She moved around the room with alacrity, showing me a cup Jesus had drunk from, a clay lamp with an intaglio lamb he had given them as a house gift, a flowered wooden comb he had used, a stone skin scrubber, a discarded sandal. I was moved by these simple objects that Jesus had touched. In them was sure proof of his humanity.

My generous donation heartened Martha so much that she gave me the names of people who had also been in Bethany when Jesus was here. They offered no definitive information. The other person I was eager to find in Bethany, a man named Simon the Leper, whom Jesus supposedly had cured, had gone to Jerusalem, Martha said, but she had no idea where I could find him there.

I crossed the Jordan next day just north of the Dead Sea, where the river was broad and fordable, and rode into Beth Jesemoth at sunset. Next morning, I met with Lazarus at his wool storehouse. He was a spry sixty-two-year-old, well groomed as an old pampered pony. He summoned a slave to bring cakes just as Grandfather used to do. I told him of my research. With polite, incisive queries, he quickly determined I was a follower of Paul.

"If you are questioning the authenticity of my miracle, you have come to the wrong man," Lazarus said. "I was dead thirty years ago and now, albeit a bit infirm, I am alive."

"In your circumstances, I would also not question miracles." I smiled. "Nor would I be as gracious as you are to one who does."

Lazarus chuckled. "Oh, I am willing enough to question miracles, but only those that happened to others."

"Yours is the miracle most often cited as true," I said. "An important element of it is how long you were . . . thought to have been dead."

"Well, I know the arguments. If it was four days, I was dead, if two, I was not dead. Let me assure you at the outset. One, I was dead. Two, it was two days. Martha, poor woman, and most of the Apostolic Council prefer it to be four for obvious reasons. 'Venerable lies make youthful truths': Zeno of Elea, I think." Lazarus was pleased to have an attentive captive audience who might recognize his classical allusions.

"You never chose to dispute publicly those who insist it was four days?" I asked.

"Why? At the time, it was important that Jesus be seen as a miracle worker. Our family was believable: good burghers, not like our other miracle of Bethany, Simon the Leper."

I broke in politely. "I tried to find this Simon to ask about his cure. Your sister said he had gone to Jerusalem. . . ."

"You will not find him. He is dead."

"Of?"

"Of leprosy," said Lazarus with an ironical smile. He went on: "I believe the question of miracles is best viewed in terms of politics and economics, of which I am an eager but inept small-town student. The Sanhedrin saw Jesus as a challenge to their system, a man who won Jews from Judaism by doing miracles on the Sabbath and insulting rabbis. If he became successful, it would mean dwindling rentals of stalls for sacrificial animals, unsold animals. It would mean that moneychangers—for remember, all fees have to be paid in Temple coins—would be unable to give the Sanhedrin their *baksheesh*.

"With loss of income would go the Sanhedrin's power, for what would happen if they held a Passover and no one came? So Caiaphas, the high priest at the time, found means to do away with Jesus. And since Jesus was, in the end, determined to die, they were partners." He grew more thoughtful, less glib. "One day, we Nazarenes—Christians—will wear the shoes of power. Like the Sanhedrin and Rome, we will martyr those who seek to dismantle *our* cadre structure."

I mentioned that Paul understood the uses of power as well as Rome or the Sanhedrin. Was he, I asked, the kind of leader Lazarus meant who would martyr fellow Christians? It set Lazarus off on further speculation.

"I have known two great rebels in my life, Jesus, and much less intimately, although he stayed with me ten, twelve years ago, Paul. What do you suppose would have happened if the two had met and worked together?" I started to say that Jesus would have been better served than he was, that his message would have spread faster. But was I so sure? Lazarus was not.

"Jesus was not a poor organizer, but he was essentially a prophet. He was certainly not one to organize an empire. At this time, when the church is turning toward Gentiles, Jesus would have been an anomaly. Then, too, remember this: he was every bit as self-assured as Paul. But he was less dogmatic. There would have been a power struggle. I am not sure Jesus would have won. When all is said and done, he was not the schemer Paul is. He was not simple, but he was simpler.

"Paul is woven more from the cloth of Caiaphas. Paul's miracle of epiphany, for example, I regard as no miracle at all. Recall that he had been guarding the coats of the Pharisees as they stoned Stephen to death. My theory is that Paul was ready for some enormous change in his life, and that he felt so guilty about Stephen that on that hot road to Damascus he fainted from *guilt*, fell off his donkey and had some sort of vision."

Lazarus had business to attend to, but he invited me to stay at his house that night. His wife, who was as opinionated as he was, prepared a feast such as I had not eaten for months. Afterward, the three of us sat before the fire and drank a honeyed local wine.

"What was Jesus like as a person?" I asked. "You are a rarity, you know, a Nazarene who saw him as host, not disciple."

"Yes," he acknowledged, flattered. "I venture to say our relationship was unique. But perhaps all acquaintances of great men say that. Jesus was the most articulate man I ever knew, though you could almost smell that horrendous Galilean garlic in his accent. He had only a few words of Greek. He had no Latin. But he was capable both of extraordinary directness and subtlety. His parables exemplify his honesty, his tact. He veiled them precisely so he could get his messages across without being seditious. Nevertheless, he took great chances, telling these stories of dissent and hope before his most dangerous enemies."

"They always sound didactic to me."

"Yes, because you hear them secondhand, devoid of his magnetism. But before an audience, his delivery elevated them to the level of writ. And before the fire, told amongst friends, they were entrancing. He drank a little wine, laughed, and told his tales with a sort of self-delighted expression as if he were waiting for the moment when one of us would get the point, the truth within the parable.

"Mary, my sister, may God bless her, loved to listen to him. She had fantasies about marrying him. After all, he was a skilled carpenter, at the top of the working classes, a handsome man, none of that northern Palestine coarseness in his face. He was spruce, beard always trimmed, robes clean. My guess is whatever woman was in a house where he stayed could hardly wait to wash them. He had that direct way of looking at you. And what really made him attractive to women was a reckless something they saw in his eyes. They knew he would do what he wanted to do, that the stubbornness in him was based in self-confidence."

I thought of how I had accused Paul of getting on with women only when he could use them in men's roles, of his being afraid of women and not liking them.

"You are saying Jesus *liked* women? As *people*?" Lazarus nodded in agreement, so I risked, "There was a woman, Mary Magdalene. . . ."

"She was a cryptic presence," Lazarus said. "She stayed with the other disciples when Jesus was in town. But I do not believe the stories about her. Certainly not as regards him. Women in that aspect were complications he could not afford."

It was not something even he wanted to talk about, and I veered to a subject about which he did. "You are a learned man, well read. How well read was he?"

"You are too kind. I am a dabbler. To answer with brutal frankness: Jesus would not know Aesop from Aeschylus, but he knew the Torah. Of that I can assure you; I studied under Gamaliel in Jerusalem, a few classes ahead of Paul, by the way. I loved to argue the Law with Jesus, and no one, *no one*, could talk him under. And no one was more graceful than he when he won a point. It was different, of course, when he was arguing with certain Pharisees. He was not the same man around bigots."

❁

On my way north toward Galilee, I passed through Jericho. Luke had a story in his scrolls about a dwarf named Zacchaeus, a rich tax collector, at whose house Jesus dined. Jesus ate and stayed where he pleased, a Pharisee's one day, a leper's the next, a shopkeeper's the next. His inconsistency was not without point: all were children of God. Zacchaeus, a provincial Judaean servant of Rome, I thought, might have an interesting perspective.

It turned out the dwarf had been dead ten years. His wife, a fat, vapid woman, recalled menus she had drawn up for Jesus' visits, but not his talk. Their son was the assistant tax collector of Jericho and I located him, a brash, busy man, at the central depot for balsam, Jericho's main crop.

He remembered Jesus: ". . . An outgoing fellow. He ruffled kids' hair . . . masculine, direct, no nonsense about him." How unlike the subtle dialectician Lazarus had described. I smiled.

"What's funny?" he asked.

"Everybody I talk with sees Jesus as himself. You see him as bustling, a man's man, forthright. . . ."

"Is that right?" he interrupted brassily. "Do you suppose my old man saw him as a dwarf?"

Neither he nor any other Jerichoans recalled anyone who had known Jesus well, but several mentioned an old balsam farmer outside town, a follower of John the Baptist. The farmer had lost a debate with Jesus and now headed a minuscule sect that venerated John *and* Jesus. Despite the eccentricities I had seen among the Johnists of Ephesus, I was unprepared for this one.

Emulating his leader, he wore a rough tunic of camel's hair. And he looked and smelled as though he had gone bathless and unbarbered since John—who had been beheaded thirty years before—had baptized him. His balsam trees were ragged and the yard in front of his mud-brick house was littered with broken toys and furniture and torn cloth. He hospitably invited me to lunch with his young wife and clutch of children and prayed weightily to John the Baptist, Jesus, and God over the meal of honey, water, locusts, and peasant bread.

The coming of Jesus, he explained, had been predicted by John. Judging from the debate my host had with Jesus, he had concluded that Jesus had always been God, never man. The crucifixion had been a charade by Jesus to cover his return to heaven. Like his father, the ancient Jehovah, Jesus was a vengeful god. Knowing the old man would talk theology all afternoon, I broke in to ask about Jesus' forty days in the wilderness, supposedly spent in these parts.

"Satan is said to have offered him the world from that mountain right over there." He pointed with a sinewy arm at a hill higher than those surrounding it. "John said he never believed a word of that Satan story. Why would Satan offer the world to God? It doesn't make the least bit of sense."

John the Baptist's mother, long dead, was a second cousin to the mother of Jesus, and I asked the farmer whether there were any other family members nearby. A look of extreme foxiness transfigured his face. He knew something important, or thought he did. The more I questioned him, the more secretive he got. I reached for my purse: considering his penury, it was surprising how long it had taken me to think of it. I had become too accustomed to the scruples of Paul and the original disciples.

"I would like to make a contribution to your work, if only you would trust me enough to confide in me," I said, giving him two denarii. He bit them both with good, white teeth.

"Did you know Jesus had a sister?" he asked.

"Two, one is Mariel, and another, Reba."

"Well, Reba is a member of our church."

I could not believe it. Surely, she was an impostor. "She lives here? When will she . . ."

"*She* comes when she feels like it."

"But when was she last here?"

He looked unhappy, as if he were not giving me good wares for my money. "Two years ago."

"Where does she live?" Oh, let her be alive, I thought.

"She says Adamah." It was a town two days to the north.

"What does she do?"

"She lives in a cave. I should not be telling you." I gave him still another coin. "I know nothing more . . . except that she drinks. I got her to pray with us to give it up, but after the Communion she got into the wine and I could not get her out."

"What does she say about Jesus?"

"I dare not repeat it. The God Jesus would doom me to his hellfires if such blasphemy as she speaks ever crossed my lips."

"It was that bad?"

He nodded. "Bad," he said. But no matter how I wheedled, even offering him ten denarii, he would not tell.

❁

Adamah was the Jordan's east bank at its most deteriorated. It had once been a great fortress, the staging area for the army of Joshua when he crossed over to Jericho. Now, as I rode past the crumbling city gate, I caught the stench of standing swill, heard the buzzing flies even on this cool day.

There was no synagogue, no tax office, no shops open at midday. From the shadow of the town fountain, whose bowl contained scummy water, a leper saw me. Without even murmuring "Unclean! Unclean!" as the law required, he chittered for money, Adamah's only sign of commerce. Flies crawled confidently on a toeless foot. I stood away from him but tossed him an obol. The three fingers remaining on his right hand captured it, furtive as a crippled insect.

"There is a woman named Reba who lives in a cave near here," I said. "She drinks a great deal. Where is she?"

His hand made a circular twitch for more alms. I dropped several quadrantes and he thrust his booty into his filthy *saq*, which only a desperado would stoop to ransack. "More," he said. My heart beat faster. I threw him two more obols.

"A mile along the wadi," he croaked, pointing, "in a cave in the hill

357

if she survived the bad wine she bought last week." He grinned, his toothless gums gray-white.

The trail by the wadi was without vegetation and was cut so badly by erosion I had to dismount and lead the donkey into and out of the ditches. The caves, a quarter of a mile away across the badlands, were dark holes in a brushless hill. At the first, I called "Reba!" An urchin came to the cave mouth and stared. I dug in my purse. The child's hand sprung out and, with one motion, he closed on the quadrans and pointed to the left.

In a moment, other cave dwellers came out and pleaded for money. This was the land of the outstretched hand. I waved them away and called "Reba!" at the cave the boy had indicated. At last, a crone appeared in the orifice, her stringy hair a garish crimson from oak insect dye. Like the balsam farmer outside Jericho, she wore a dirty camel's hair garment. Her face was coarse as wet sawdust, small broken veins showing through the smudges on her cheeks; her eyes were wary and hostile.

"Reba is not here," she rasped, her accent strongly Galilean, but with a trace of gentility that belied her looks.

I was sure it was Reba, the sister of Jesus. Careful, I thought, my heart again thudding, be careful. "I brought her some wine," I said. I took my wineskin from my saddlebag.

"Leave it there." She pointed to a spot between us.

"I do not want to play children's games with you," I said. "I know you are Reba. You wear the coat of a follower of John the Baptist. I want to talk with you. You want my wine. I will be brief."

"You are a soldier,"

"No, I wear armor against robbers."

"You want to talk about God," she said.

"Well, in a general way."

"How do I know you will not hurt me?"

"If I wanted to hurt you, I could take out my sword, walk up, and chop you to pieces. Why would I offer you wine, good wine, if I wanted to hurt you?"

Her face became crafty. It was the look of the devoted drunk who has woven all her skeins into a single design: how to get the next cup of wine. The neighbors still watched.

"Let me come at least to where we can drink and talk without the whole world listening."

"These people are not the world," she said, assenting.

We sat at the mouth of her cave, and she took a preliminary draught of the wine, found it was better than what she was used to, and said

358

mildly enough: "You are a follower of John the Baptist? My brethren told you where to find me?"

For the first time on my quest, I misrepresented myself, and badly. No, I said to both questions. I was a Roman scholar doing a history of John the Baptist and why his appeal to people was growing even though he had been dead thirty years. I had heard of her from a beggar in Adamah. I filled her cup, went to the donkey, got mine, and filled it, too. She seemed to begrudge even that diminishment of the supply.

"I will leave my wineskin when I go," I said. The idea relaxed her. I asked her how she perceived John and she spoke of him much as the cult leader had. When I cautiously inquired about the position of Jesus in her religion, her mental shuttle went off the loom.

"As John is the human side of God, trying to be good, so this other"—she meant Jesus—"is the evil side. He causes all the bad things." She made a rotating gesture with her hand as if to indicate not just her own plight, but everyone's.

"How does he do that? Is he a god?"

She made a long speech to the effect that he was, but had not always been. He had schemed his way into God's favor, she said, and now caused all the grief in the world, which John worked tirelessly, but somewhat ineffectually, to remedy.

"I can see you believe that heaven is like a human family. There is the father, and the good child, and the bad child, who is Satan. Now in your own family, who was Jesus?"

She paused. I poured her some more wine, guiltily hoping it would liberate enough of her hatred for her to start talking of Jesus as her brother. She drank deeply, and said, "The bad child, but seemingly good. Oh, you will never know how bad. He tricks everybody."

"But what exactly did he do?"

When her cup went down, I filled it again. It gave her a feeling of being waited on. She began to welcome this opportunity to talk to someone besides cave dwellers. She was showing me blocks of truth amid the rubble of her ramblings.

"He tried to tell us all what to do. I hated it."

"What did he tell you to do that made you hate him?"

She hesitated again, then went on firmly, "I don't care if he strikes me dead for saying it." The wine had made her bolder. "For instance, when I was ten . . ."

Her story, when I weeded the malignancy and irrationality from it, was of an unstable girl in a traditional Jewish household. Jesus was the favorite: prodigiously intelligent, vibrant, even as a child. She was three years younger than he was, and bright herself. He was reading all

359

the holy books, in love with the Torah, even the tractates. And Jesus had great plans for Reba. He had actually drawn up rules in writing for her and her sister Mariel based on his readings.

Mariel, the youngest child, had done what she was told. Reba had rebelled. When she refused to obey Jesus, her mother had punished her, kept her in, sometimes even spanked her, for the rules Jesus had written for Reba had come out of the holy books, so how could they be wrong?

"Do not go out at this time of day," she recounted, "wear these clothes on the Sabbath. I hated it, hated it. But when *he* disobeyed, they didn't even scold him." For instance, the family had gone to Jerusalem and Jesus had talked to the elders in the Temple. On the way back to Nazareth, Jesus had slipped away from the caravan and gone again to the Temple, and their father had to go all the way back to seek him. "And Father was *pleased to find Rodent there.*"

"You mean Jesus?"

"*Rodent!*" she repeated.

As the sun and the wine went down, and she saw she had an uncritical listener, she unraveled her whole tawdry and fascinating story—as she saw it—full of epithets against Jesus and most of the family. All save for her, her younger brother Jude, and occasionally James had been in awe of Jesus. She, far from living by his rules, had continued to defy him.

It was as if she had been the testing table for Jesus. How heavily he must have pressed on her when she balked at becoming his first disciple. Had he felt an angry sense of failure as she resented, then hated, him? Certainly, he had learned from it, for he had never been tyrannical later with his apostles.

"Did anyone ever tell him to leave you alone?" I asked.

"Father sometimes, but he was decrepit, a coward, oh, such a coward." She pursed her lips and made a farting sound.

When she was fifteen, a man of forty had wanted to marry her and her family had been more than willing. The man was feeble-minded, not brutal, but manipulative. She had one miscarriage after another. Unable to bear a live child, disgraced by what seemed this ultimate insult, she had started to drink. Jesus, now working in their father's carpenter shop, had begun to grow up. He sought her out and gently, I gathered, tried to reason with her. But the hatred in her was too deep.

Once, after Jesus had begun his ministry, their mother and the two full brothers had begged him to cure her besottedness as he had cured others. He prayed over her, but to no effect. He had not really wanted to help, she was certain. Yet, when he was crucified, she had wept.

In recent years, she had lived with a man in Adamah who had died, leaving her enough income for simple food and cheap wine. She had heard of the balsam farmer in Jericho and gone to him to be baptized, then had returned a second and last time two years ago, she was not even clear why.

She was drunk. I could no longer understand her, only hear the tone of the toxins she continued to spit out. She asked me slurringly for money and I gave her twenty denarii. Guilt money. I left the wineskin, hoping it would keep her in the cave until tomorrow, when I would come back.

I lodged in Adamah's vermin-infested inn, and next morning just after dawn went to her cave. She was gone, her neighbors did not know where. I asked around Adamah for her, stayed another night, and went back to the cave. She had not returned.

XXXIII

In Nazareth, the Apostolic Council had a strong ministry that cared for and venerated the mother of Jesus. Here, there was no disguising my investigations. I had met the minister, a former rabbinical student, during my journeys for Paul. At my request, he took me to the house of Mary. For years after the crucifixion, Mary had lived in Jerusalem with John. But as she aged, she had wanted to come home and the church had bought back for her the ample old family house. One room was a small chapel where visitors could pray (and make donations for its upkeep).

The room Jesus shared with James had been kept intact. Jesus' crib was in a corner. The shelves held a boy's spinning top, a snakeskin, an abacus, a wooden ball with paint chipped; a child's goat-hair greatcoat, a cap, robes, hung on racks. The coat with its wool tassels at the four corners—the zizith—and the Hebrew cap with its fringed point reminded me that Jesus had been raised a strictly devout Jew—a fact I had sometimes tended to forget during my years working with Gentiles.

By the wall was an ambitious chest he had made, an ornamental candlestick, two chairs, a small table, a whimsical clotheshorse for a child. They were all well fashioned, but not so that one recognized the touch of the Almighty in them.

In the garden outside, one arm of the cross, now oiled, with a nail still in it, lay in a simple marble sarcophagus. Beside the marble box was the prow of a boat from which Jesus had fished and where he had stood to preach to a large crowd ashore.

The memorabilia affected me much as the simple items at Martha's had. These were the material things of Jesus' life. He had made them or touched them, and in the case of the cross, he had bled and died upon it. And yet my feelings were less intense because here the objects had been formalized into a museum by the church of Nazareth. They were not just odds and ends from casual visits.

Jesus' mother was sleeping in the rear room she had shared with Joseph, the father, who had died when Jesus was sixteen. The minister opened the door reverentially. The woman in the clean, neat bed was ghostlike. Her head was like an egg with only wisps of finest white hair on it. Her lips, as pale as her face, trembled minutely as if she were carrying on a silent conversation with herself. Yet I knew it was only the involuntary twitching of tiny muscles. Her eyes, half shut, were faded, a pellucid blue, her nose refined like carved ivory that has been rubbed until it softly glows. Her small ears seemed too fragile to touch.

"She is eighty, we think, perhaps seventy-nine," the minister whispered. She was beautiful, not in a human way, but as a work of art. Her head was perfect, its translucent skin unblemished—age had turned it into velvet.

"I am awed," I said at last. And so I was. From the womb of this ethereal being a God had been born. She was already three-quarters joined with him in a heaven far beyond our imagination. What thoughts, if any, still lingered in that eggshell head, I could not dream, nor could she ever say.

"Did she speak of him . . . before she became like this?"

"Not much. I am told she did a little housework, talked with her younger sister, with friends. But, remember, this was a simple woman battered by the blows of one son crucified, a stepson, Joseph, killed at Sepphoris, a daughter who became a drunkard, two sons gone far away. . . . Only Mariel, the younger daughter, and James, her other stepson, came to see her regularly. He was killed . . . after she became like this."

I did not confide in him about Reba. I had violated her enough by priming her with drink. One son he had spoken of, Simon, who lived in Tyras on the Dniester, had written to her up until the last few years, he said. Jude, the other, was thought to live near Theodosia. The family, like many others, had flown asunder under the pressures of unsettling times.

Jesus' aunt Judith was a tiny widow, stringy and energetic, who lived in a small, ordered house. The lightly fermented date juice she served me was as good as any I had ever tasted except for Grandfather's.

"Why are you doing this?" she asked. "You are not even a Nazarene from the looks of you." She meant that I was not a Jew.

With Judith, there was nothing to be won by indirection. I told her I had been a disciple of Paul but was no more, and that in my travels I had heard many inconsistencies about Jesus and wanted to determine the facts. "I would like to find out what he really said, what he really did, who he really *was*."

"So would I," said the old woman emphatically, cocking her head like a parrot. "So would we all. Even his mother is not, well, was not sure." She stopped, then remarked, "She is sure of everything now because she is sure of nothing."

"Are you saying he said contradictory things?"

"No, I am not saying he did or didn't. What I am saying is that when he was here, we all heard what we wanted to hear, so now, thirty years later, his words are all twisted. *Somebody* ought to write down what is left of them or in thirty more years *nobody* will be able to tell Jesus from Jehosophat."

Well, I thought, there were enough people, including me, who were writing things down now. Whether it would make Jesus any less complicated remained to be seen. "There are *some* things everybody says he says," I said.

"Oh, yes, love God and your neighbor. That's *too* simple to forget."

I asked her what she remembered of Jesus as a child and she served up a bland gruel of virtues—he was kind to his parents, brothers, sisters, brave, truthful, and so on.

"Was there *nothing* wrong with him and the family?"

"Well, no family is perfect."

"What do you mean?"

"Young man—I didn't catch your name. . . ."

I told her.

"Demas, I am not one to wash the dirty linen of my sister in the streets of Nazareth."

"Well, this is hardly the street. I only meant that there are conflicts among children in every family." I could not have misread Reba entirely. Something had happened to make Reba what she became, and that something had to do with Jesus.

"There were problems," she said, "but they were mostly the other children's makings and, the truth is, Joseph and my sister's. But I am not going to talk about them to a stranger."

"Then why not consider me a family friend?" I cajoled. A witness like this would not come my way again.

"No, I am more likely to consider you a snoop."

"Could you tell me what he was like as a young man, say, in the shop of his father? And I am sorry if I seem a snoop."

She took it as an apology, or at least a promise not to root around in the family's closets. "Well, at eighteen, he was in charge of the shop. James had bought his own carpentry shop in Sunem, and was most often over there. There was more money in Sunem. Jesus had the two young boys and Mariel with him—"

"And a second sister . . . ?"

"Reba. Don't start me on her. She would not lift a saw *or* a broom. She would not lift a thing but her skirt." Judith dismissed her with a hand wave. "Since then, she has gone, disappeared. . . . Anyway, when James ran the shop here and wanted things done by the younger children, he calmly said it would be done, and if it was not, he kicked their little bottoms and that was that. Jesus liked things his way, too, but he set down written rules. He would tell little parables to make his point or try to reason. The two younger boys had seen Reba defy Jesus and get away with it, so they defied him, too. When Jesus was, oh, say twenty-two or twenty-three, they went to James's shop in Sunem."

"Even though James was just a half brother?"

"Well, you see, *James* didn't meddle with their *minds.*"

"And Jesus did, in the way you described?"

"Yes, Jesus was shaken to the bone by Reba going, why deny it, and when the boys told him they were going, it set him back on his heels. So that night he came to talk to me and my husband, God rest him. We had no children, so we loved all of them. And I was not a doorway rug like my sister. I think Jesus knew in his heart that he had driven all three children away. He wanted us to assure him he was wrong, to tell him that Reba had been incorrigible and the boys had been ungrateful, foolish.

"Azriel, my husband, started to give Jesus the sugar teat and say, 'Now, now,' but I butted in and told Jesus he simply had to learn— and this may sound funny now—that he was not God. I said people did not want a lecture every time they drilled a hole a needle's breadth out of true. They preferred a smack."

"How did he react to all this?"

"Well, his mind was still trying to find an argument that would convince his heart, you know, but there was no escaping it, and my husband, once I had spoken up, sided with me. So, finally, Jesus stopped arguing, and his face bunched up and he said, 'Thank you,' in a little croak and began to cry."

"Cry? You said he was twenty-two?"

"Perhaps twenty-three. My husband and I went to him and put our arms around him and pretty soon we were all three weeping, just sobbing, as if it was for all the things that had not worked out the way we wanted them to. . . . After that, Jesus got more humble, letting other people finish what they had to say before he commented, and thinking more before he spoke, things like that."

"And happier . . ."

To my surprise, I saw tears well up in her eyes, and she brushed at them with her sleeve. When she had her control back, she said, "No, not happier. Less. More considerate, more thoughtful, but more . . ." She looked for the word. ". . . more private. He was not as close to us anymore, or to anyone. And I would say *that* was when he began to become . . ."

"God."

"I don't like to put it that way. He read more, went away alone, prayed more. He began speaking with John the Baptist—you've heard of him, a distant cousin who some people thought was the Messiah. Then, when Jesus was twenty-six or twenty-seven, he went to the Jordan and this John baptized him. A month and a half later, he came back, very determined, and told us about the baptism and that he had talked with God in the wilderness. . . ."

And here she looked uncertain, like a person who has bitten a seed and does not know whether it has broken a tooth. "And that he had also talked with Satan, who had offered him the dominions of the world and that he had fasted and prayed and would soon be leaving to preach throughout Palestine."

"Did he say what he would be preaching?"

She got the same expression, but less pronounced. "That he was the son of God and that people should love God first, and their neighbors as themselves, and many of the other things that we Nazarenes, and you Christians, too, believe to this day."

"And what did his mother think?"

"She was tearful, worried about what would happen to him, with good reason. Azriel was the only one who wanted to follow Jesus, and I begged him not to, and Jesus said to my husband, 'Azriel, you have a greater love here than I with all my ministry can bring you.' It made me very proud . . . of both of them."

"You would have made a wonderful disciple yourself."

"Yes," she said without self-pity. "I would have. But by the time I let myself realize it, he was dead fifteen years."

"And the woman who did follow him?"

"Mary, from Magdala, over by Galilee? What about her?" She had the same note of spite in her voice as when she had spoken of Reba. "She was the kind of disciple he did *not* need."

"She was loyal."

"Oh, she was that. And she knew how to take care of herself, even if it was on her back."

"Not with Jesus."

"No, but not from any virtue on her part."

"So where is she now?"

"Living like a queen with some Roman shipper, the last I heard. Sidon, or Tyre, or Alexandria. I don't know."

"Do you know his name?"

She looked astonished. It had just dawned on her that I wanted to talk about Jesus with Mary of Magdala. "Ropsius, or some such," she said and then smiled. "Be careful of your vows."

Next morning I went to see Mariel. The carpenter she had married was no match for the carpenter who was her brother. A stocky, graying man, he sent Mariel into the bedroom while he questioned me about how a non-Jew could follow Jesus when Jesus had avoided Gentiles. His brother-in-law, he said, had been a strict adherent to the Law of Moses, as were he and Mariel, although they were both Nazarenes. "I met the master only once," he said, "I am from Baina." Finally, he summoned in Mariel. She had some of Reba's lineaments, but instead of dissipation, her wrinkles bespoke defeat. She recited the standard encomiums under the intimidating eyes of her husband.

With nothing to lose, I asked why she stayed behind and worked in the carpenter shop when Jude and Simon went to James. She looked at her husband and I saw the bile rise in his face. "You have been talking to our aunt. She does not know how to keep her mouth shut," he said. Mariel looked as if she feared her husband might do something violent. It occurred to me that he probably beat her. People like him were the reason Galileans were held in such contempt by the rest of Judaea.

In Nain, I found a maker of musical instruments who had gone to school in Nazareth with Jesus for three years. Jesus had led the class two years, he the other. "I won that year only because he was argumentative. Jesus felt that just because the Halakah"—the interpretations of the Law—"stated something, that did not mean it was true. Jesus was correct, but no rabbi wants to be brought up short by those who are supposed to be worshipfully sitting at his feet."

In Tarichaea lived James, son of Alphaeus, who could tell me much if he would. I found him sitting on the front stoop of a house that Matthew and he owned on fallow farmland, throwing corn to pip-afflicted chickens. When he saw me, he screwed up his face belligerently. I was deferential and asked whether he could spare me some water and would let me pause to chat a while. His bellicosity gradually turned to self-pity, the exiled rustic longing for recall to the big city.

"I never blamed that dirty business at the bridge on you, Demas. I knew it was Titus. . . ." He said the name as if he were spitting out bitter persimmon seeds. Finally, he brought out a clay pot of millet beer and asked me with fake heartiness how matters were in Jerusalem. I preferred him surly. That was his honest mode. I told him what Thomas had passed on to me.

"So now you are doing a little spying for Paul?" he said, unable not to be nasty even when he intended cordiality.

"He banished me," I said. When James perceived me as a fellow exile, his talk came easier. I pointed to Mount Hattin, actually only a hill. "There must be as many versions of what the master said there as there were listeners that day," I said.

James felt pedagogical stirrings. "I remember it as if it were yesterday," he said. "The master talked a good deal about the meek, the poor, the persecuted. I am all for that, of course, and everybody remembers it. But they forget the backbone of the sermon: there is a Law we must follow. He said he was not 'abolishing the Law of the prophets but fulfilling it.' "

I cautiously asked whether in that sermon Jesus gave equal weight to all sins. Yes, he said, from first to last. Here, James was more Paulist than Paul, for he was a disciple who wanted to see mankind suffer thoroughly for its sins.

"The exact words of the master were that 'not an iota, not a dot' in the Law can be ignored. I agree. He said that to lust after a woman was to commit adultery. I agree. He said if our hand or any other member offends the Law, we should cut it off. That may be going too far, but not by much. If every iota and dot of *that* was followed, we would be a nation of castrati which we act like we are anyway." He chuckled at his wit.

"John, and Peter, too," I ventured, "feel strongly that some of the sayings of the master were meant more as guidelines, things we ought to follow, but that not all of us could."

James turned red at the mere suggestion. He looked as though he was torn between ending our talk right then and letting me stay so he would have an ear into which he could pour his venom. Meanness won out over integrity.

"John and Peter, Peter and John! That's all you hear. I tell you, between being forgotten among the other Jameses and having to hear 'Peter and John' all these years, I have been worn down. I was there, too, not like some of them that took off a month at a time. I shared the hardships. I believed in the master as much as they did. And where does it get me? They call me James the Less behind my back."

"Everybody deserves credit. . . ." I said, hoping to mollify him so I could get him back on the subject. But he had an audience and his hate had flowed over its banks.

"John was a dreamer, nothing but a poet. He dreamed up half the stories we wound up preaching as true. And Peter was a whoremonger! *Twice* we had to pull him out of whorehouses. Drunk as a tavern sponge. The master was furious. He should have banished him. But then he would have had to kick out your friend Thomas, too, and that lunatic Simon and Jude Thaddeus. They were just a little more discreet and a little less drunk about it."

He spat disgustedly into the scrabble dirt by the stoop.

"Peter was the one that sided with the master over letting that little Magdala slut stay around when some of us tried to get him to send her packing. A disgrace! But the master had to keep her on as evidence he could forgive anybody. But don't think Peter didn't have it in his heart to tumble her. And the master said if you have it in your heart . . ."

I could see the pasty white froth in the corners of his mouth. He was working up to a rage.

"You say John made things up. You mean he had visions?"

"You can wager your skimpy beard he had visions."

"You mean the resurrection? It would mean a great deal for me to hear about it from you. You were there."

The strain of recollection calmed him. He, like the others, except for John, was genuinely unsure. "The first time, I *thought* he was there," he said, "but we were hungry, afraid. All those years when I was preaching, I said that he came back to us. But you have asked me direct questions and set me thinking. So I would say the second time, no, definitely not in body."

However, there were other miracles that he was certain had no natural explanation. He had seen Jesus turn wine to water at Cana, seen him cure a madman in minutes, steady the trembling of a palsied woman, even bring back from the dead the daughter of a Sadducee named Jairas. "Sometimes something *did* happen. Other times, nobody knows and nobody will ever know. At Gamala, a lot of people were fed. Now some say they just reached in their shirts and pulled out their food and shared it. Others say a fish bone turned into a fillet, a crumb into a loaf. All I am sure of is that there was a lot of bread and fish.

"I remember Andrew," he said, and even this spite-laden man smiled fondly, "what a clown he was, passing out one loaf, taking a bite from the next. But if you ask some people, they will swear it all happened at Bethsaida Julias. Even if you ask them there, because he *did* speak there a few times. Do you see what I mean? Do you see how confusing all the stories become? I could help clear things up, but Matthew and I are not getting on, as you know. He has not even asked me to help with his book. They call themselves Nazarenes; do you know you are the first person with even the rank of minister to visit me? But I tell you, the simple people of Tarichaea know. They come. I'm surprised we have not been interrupted already."

As if he had willed it, from the dusty road a man turned in. James looked hopeful. But the man had only come to say there would be no delivery of goat's milk today because the goat had eaten garlic grass.

James had seemed most convincing about the "miracle" at Cana, two miles north of Nazareth, where at a wedding, the wine ran out and Jesus was supposed to have turned water into more wine. John also vouched for the story. Thomas had been drinking hard and could remember only that people said Jesus had produced wine from water. I went to Cana, where the bridegroom, now in his fifties, his heavy wife nodding in agreement, attested to the story.

I questioned the husband about whether his father might not have had a second delivery of wine brought in when the first started to run out, or whether a friend might not have provided some without telling anyone, but he shook his head. He had dealt with skeptics for thirty years and was not riled by them. I talked to a half dozen of the guests and all remembered the evening approximately the same way. It was possible I was witnessing a kind of mutual self-delusion, but if that was true, it was surprising I had not found even a needle hole in the various stories. I was faced with the uncomfortable probability that a true miracle had taken place at Cana.

There was no dearth of other miracle stories among the hundreds of hills and by the misty lakes of Galilee. An old flax farmer told me Jesus had come to him at night, roused him and helped him harvest his flax. A crone said Jesus had told her where her dead mother had buried a crock full of drachmas, but that the devil in the form of her nephew had dug it up before she could get to it. A formerly barren couple said Jesus had struck a bargain with them. They would have twins, but the girl was to be sold as a slave in Joppa and the money given to the synagogue. They had kept the bargain. The son was alive and well in Japhia.

I was wading in a marsh of miracle stories: people cured of boils, of paralysis, of epilepsy (one epileptic was lowered through a hole in a roof because Jesus was surrounded by cure seekers), of devils, of "lion's mask" (leprosy that so disfigures a face it looks like a lion's), even of venereal diseases.

370

The strangest story was told to me by a man who lived in a field with pigs. Wild-eyed and filthy, he talked through the fence in sounds like oinks. He had been covered with pustules and Jesus had broken bread with him and said if he would live out his days with pigs his skin would heal. He was to eat their food and leave the field only to celebrate Passover. His skin cleared and this was the man's thirty-first year with the pigs. He had no intention of giving up their company. Indeed, he was celebrated. People came from miles around to push their ailing friends and relatives through the fence for healing.

An elderly rabbi who had been in Capernaum at the same time as Jesus had seen with gentle disbelief the cult of miracles developing in this city. I questioned him about the daughter of Jairas, whom James had mentioned was brought back from the dead by Jesus. "Jairas," said the rabbi, "was an able official but given over *entirely* to superstition. Once Jesus got all the faith healers and musicians and dying lilies and fumigants out of her room and a little fresh air back in, small wonder the poor thing revived. I could have done that one myself." He smiled.

"In another case," he continued, "done on the Sabbath in my own synagogue, Jesus took the withered hand of one of my parishioners in both of his and started kneading it, and soon the man was flexing his fingers as surely as I am flexing mine now. I cannot deny a miraculous element was present. A visiting Pharisee, long since in Abraham's bosom, asked Jesus loudly, 'Is it lawful to heal on the Sabbath?' And Jesus—now you understand we are talking about a young Nazarene basically without higher education—said, 'Which of you if his best sheep falls into a pit on the Sabbath will not lay hold of it and get it out?' Well, what could the Pharisee say?"

As to the cure of Peter's mother-in-law, the rabbi shook his head in dismissal. "She was a tiresome old woman who had a cold and Jesus probably told her to steam up cassia bark. We Galileans are full of magic and miracle stories. Let a fog blow in from the sea and half the people of Capernaum will swear the ghosts of the dead of Sepphoris returned in the night.

"In sum," he said, "Jesus was a remarkably gifted healer. He knew instinctively where to touch, what to say, what to recommend. It is *almost* as if he were in direct contact with God. But, my dear young man, had he been the Messiah, he would have healed us of our benevolent affliction—our Roman occupiers. Nor did he heal himself from a most unpleasant end, for which, I can tell you, I am heartily sorry."

XXXIV

✠✠

Trying to recapture all the words of Jesus, I realized, would have been as futile as trying to chart all the stars in the firmament. From my hundreds of interviews—if those with groups were counted—I began to create in my notes a pictograph of only the most prominent stars, that is, the most significant words of Jesus. When someone repeated for me the transcendent music of his sentences, I was aware I had heard and was recording thoughts as awesome and eternal as the most majestic stars.

In the Galilee village of Beth-yerah, for example, there was no mistaking the accuracy of the recollections of its elders. The remembered words of these fishers as they spoke to me in the shadow of the mimosas and oleanders were far beyond the vocabularies of men whose lives were boats and bait and hooks. Jesus had stood in a boat a few feet out in the sapphire waters where now among the reeds stood a crane, eyes searching for carp fingerlings.

"Do not," he told the fishermen, "lay up treasures on earth where moths and worms can eat them and where thieves break in and steal. But lay them up in heaven by your good works. There neither moths nor worms eat and thieves do not break in. For where your treasure is, there your heart will be. Look at the birds. They neither sow nor reap and yet your heavenly father feeds them. Are you not of more value than they? Or consider the lilies of the field. They neither toil nor spin. Yet Solomon in all his glory has no raiment to rival them."

At other times, angry words of Jesus had branded the brains of his adversaries forever. In the guise of a Roman historian, I went to an old

Pharisee at Genessaret who spoke to me in bitter tones. "I saw no harm in inviting him with some of my friends to continue the debate that followed his sermon," he said. "The first thing he did was to sit down without washing his hands." Jesus, of course, knew that the washing of one's hands before eating was an ironclad rule among devout Jews. One of the guests reproached him. The Pharisee, shaking anew with outrage, described what followed.

"He told us, 'You Pharisees cleanse your hands and the outside of your cups and dishes, but inside you are full of extortion and wickedness. Do you not know he who made the outside made the inside, too? You tithe mint and rue and every other herb, and neglect justice and the love of God. You covet the best seat in the synagogue and salutations in the marketplace. You are like hidden graves. Men walk over you and the earth gives way and all manner of innocents are swallowed up.'

"I asked him to leave. He stood at the door and shouted at us. 'You breed of vipers, how can you speak good when you are evil? On the day of judgment you will render account for every word you say. You are blind guides. And if a blind man leads a blind man, both will fall in the pit.' He meant us! Well, sir," and, although panting, the old Pharisee's lips slowly parted in an acid smile, "I wrote the Sanhedrin in Jerusalem saying this man had best be handled as the old-time Jews handled *their* blasphemers. And you can see that I still have not fallen in the pit, while he has been moldering in the grave these thirty years. I wish you Romans had crucified him twice."

More often, Jesus spoke in parables, which, as Lazarus had commented, were extremely subtle. If he had stated the message of the parables baldly, the Pharisees and scribes many times over would have had him scourged—or worse—as a blasphemer.

At several places, people remembered an allusive parable urging them to desert the old Mosaic covenants in favor of the new convenant of Jesus: "No one sews a piece of unshrunk cloth on an old garment; if he does, the patch tears away making a bigger tear than before. No one puts new wine into old wineskins; if he does, the wineskin bursts and both the wine and skins are lost. But new wine is put in fresh wineskins, and both are preserved. And what man, after drinking new wine, would want to taste the old again?" He had no need to explain.

Not even Paul came remotely close to Jesus in giving wings to parables. "The sower sowed the seed," began one he told in the grain districts. "Some of it fell by the path where birds ate it, some on rocky ground where it sprung up, but the soil was too shallow for it to take root and the sun scorched it, and some fell among brambles, which choked it. But some fell in good soil and yielded grain by the hundredfold.

"The sower sows the word. Those merely along the path ignore it and Satan snatches it away. Those on rocky ground greet it with joy, but when they are persecuted and give up, it does not take root and dies. Those in luxury welcome it, yet their need for money and worldly things stifles it. But those with good soil hear it and are rewarded a hundredfold."

Or again: "Those who are well have no need of a doctor, but only those who are sick. I desire mercy, not sacrifice, for I am here not to call the righteous, but the sinners. The righteous are already content in God. They need no repentance. Which of you, if you have a hundred sheep and lose one, will not leave the ninety-nine grazing and go after the one that is lost?"

Or: "What father among you if his son asks for a fish will give him a serpent, or if he asks for an egg will give him a scorpion? If you who are sinful know how to give good gifts to your children, how much more will the heavenly father give to those of his children who ask."

He used children as similes often, and always with precision. Asked once who would be first in heaven, he pointed to a child. "Whoever is as humble as this child is the greatest in heaven. Unless you become like her, you will never even get there. For whoever receives a child in my name receives me, but whoever corrupts a child would be better off with a millstone around his neck and thrown into the sea."

Yet sometimes I thought of Reba and felt that Jesus, like Paul, preferred children as symbols rather than as small beings to dandle on his knee or sport with in the street dirt or give a sweet to, as Peter might have done.

✿

I was engrossed in what I was doing, but I was lonely. At night, the low-hanging stars seemed to whisper their Grecian myths of heroism and magic. I thought of Deborah. By now her baby would be born. Only with her did I want to talk about the loves of Andromeda, the lusts of Orion. I thought I had bound her in the strong box of my memory, but starry nights liberated her and made me yearn. By day, I turned my thoughts to Jesus and my discoveries. I wondered whether I would ever preach again.

In this context, when anyone told me he had heard Jesus speak of family, I asked what he had said about women, divorce, and fleshly sins. The consensus was what most of the disciples remembered, and thus different from what I had hoped. Time and again, people recalled his saying, "What God has joined, let no man put asunder." Sometimes he added, "Whoever divorces his wife, except for unchastity, and marries again commits adultery."

John felt Jesus was gradually modifying this view, but in all my talks, I found only one morsel of supporting evidence. An otherwise virtuous divorced man had asked Jesus bluntly whether what Jesus preached meant he could not get into heaven if he remarried, as he wanted to do. Jesus questioned him earnestly, and apparently satisfied, smiled and said, "Not all men can receive this saying of mine, but all who can receive it should: all things are possible for God." The man had interpreted it as consent and had remarried.

I also found Jesus making allowances for harlots, tax collectors, cowards, and thieves. A quote from Isaiah that he used over and over again was that God "will not break a bruised reed or quench a smoldering wick." But he gave no hope to the wantonly violent, the arrogant, the true haters, child abusers, gross hypocrites, and those who victimized the poor.

I did not know what to think when I discovered that one group he excluded from any possibility of salvation was lawyers. An old attorney in Chorazim had jotted down this tirade: "Woe to all lawyers. You load men with burdens and then turn your backs on them. You build tombs for the prophets whom your fathers slew. You take away the key of knowledge so you can keep the law to yourselves. Those who try to learn it, you destroy."

"There are lawyers and lawyers," I commented. The old man looked at me cynically and replied, "That is what we always say."

Jesus had carried his ministry through Tyre and Sidon and the lands southeast of the mountains of Lebanon. Parts of this same journey I had ridden with Paul, Peter, and John almost seven years ago. Then it had been summer. Now the road was frozen and I shook as I rode, even though I wore a woolen shift beneath my armor. The qadim, a chilling east wind, blew every night, making the air as cold and clear as the icy streamlets I crossed.

The heatless sun spangled the sea and gave the mud-brick towers of Tyre the luster of thin, colorful silk. As I knew from my trip to Antioch six years ago, the churches from here north were Paulist. The most famous miracle of the area, and one Paul understandably often mentioned, involved Christ's rare healing of a Gentile, a Syrophoenician girl. The Christian minister of Tyre had done his own investigation of the case a few years ago.

A woman devotee of Astarte had broken through a crowd of the sick around Jesus, thrown herself down, and grabbed his calves. "Lord, son of David," she said, "be merciful to my daughter. She is possessed by a demon." The daughter, she said, screamed almost incessantly, ran out of the house, often naked, and lacked control of her bowels and bladder.

As kindly as he could, Jesus said, "I am sent by my father to preach only to the lost sheep of the House of Israel." He meant, most likely, the sick Nazarenes and potential Jewish followers around him. But still the woman persisted, jerking at his calves. Jesus lost his temper. "Woman, is it just for me to take the bread of the children and throw it to the dogs?"

Hysterical as she was, the woman was shocked by this harsh remark. "Yes, but even the dogs under the table eat the children's crumbs," she replied.

Jesus removed her hands from his legs. "Let us go," he said to the disciples. "For that saying, she gets her way."

The child was living in filth, tied to the bed, and was bruised from beatings by her mother. Jesus and the disciples cleaned out the room. Jesus himself took a statue of Astarte outside and smashed it on the cobbles. He talked with the girl for two hours, and she began to calm. Next day, he spoke with her again and, convinced the mother was more the problem than the child, he found a Nazarene matron willing to be her foster mother. The mother agreed to give up the child, but was allowed to visit daily. The child's symptoms slowly disappeared and years later she married. I would like to have spoken with her, but she and her husband had moved away and the mother was dead.

Before I left, I asked the minister whether he had ever heard of a Roman shipper named Ropsius. He knew those in Tyre and along the coast to Sidon, but none with a name like that.

On the way south, I branched off to see Rechab, then went to Borhaurus and visited a day with Ezra, Ahiam, and my other friends. From Ezra, I withdrew some more of Grandfather's money. To my delight, he also wrote me a note for a second cousin of ours in Jerusalem who worked for the Sanhedrin and would have access to records about the trial of Jesus.

As I approached Jerusalem, I discovered that the closer Jesus drew to the city of his crucifixion, the more often he spoke of himself as the son of God. In Beeroth, according to a Greek public scribe, he had said, "If you partake of the flesh and blood of the son of God, I will live in you, and you in my father in whom I live forever." At Gibeon, once the center of Philistinian Baal worship, the townspeople had been so enthusiastic about Jesus' claim to Godhood that they had proclaimed him king of Judaea. They forced him onto a makeshift throne so they could march with it to Jerusalem, five miles away, and two disciples were pummeled in extricating him.

When I arrived in Jerusalem, I found Thomas and John were gone to Ashdod on the coast to enjoy the first warm weather of March. I journeyed there and found them in a small villa Thomas had borrowed from a Nazarene market inspector. They were eager to hear of my investigation. It yielded good conversations, good memories for them, but not much new material for me except for one elucidating anecdote on Jesus and Gentiles.

"One time," John said, "I reminded him that God had urged Isaiah, Jesus' favorite prophet, to bring over not just the children of Israel but everyone, including Gentiles. Jesus was sensitive about our failure to work among Gentiles, and made a little joke of what I had suggested. 'Isaiah had eighty years to do it,' he said, 'and he never got one Assyrian to become a Jew. I have had two years and I already have among my followers one Syrophoenician, thirty-five Samaritans, four Romans and'—he smiled for Jesus meant Judas of Kerioth—'a Judaean.' "

Before I left, Thomas told me he had a clue to where Mary Magdalene was. An old Nazarene sea captain, retired in Ashdod, had thought he had seen her, although aged considerably, in Rhinocolura, a small deepwater port in Nabataea a hundred and fifty miles south on the road to Egypt. He had seen her while visiting a Roman shipper named Robezius. I gasped. It could only be the shipper "Ropsius" mentioned by Jesus' aunt.

I resolved to travel to Rhinocolura as soon as I saw my second cousin who worked for the Sanhedrin and for whom Ezra had written the note. The cousin was able to give me permission to see records developed by the Sanhedrin to convince the Romans to crucify Jesus in case their verbal appeal to the procurator, Pontius Pilate, had failed.

The file room was deep beneath the Temple's Court of the Gentiles. I reached it by a circular stone staircase that led to an ancient cedar door into a musty low-ceilinged room lit by oil lamps. The scrolls were sealed in pottery vessels. There thousands of words of hearsay, rumors, pertinent and extraneous facts, and opinions had been collected by the three scribes who had assembled the case against Jesus for alleged blasphemy and other crimes.

"Said accused overturned duly authorized tables of the Temple moneychangers, caused benches of purveyors of sacrificial pigeons to be feloniously broken, accused eminent Pharisees and scribes of being 'whitewashed tombs, outwardly beautiful, but full of putrefaction and dead men's bones,' worked miracles and did other illicit labors on the

Sabbath, slanderously and injuriously said tax collectors and harlots would enter heaven before the chief priests of the Temple," read one extensive bill of charges.

Among the many documents, I found an informal note from Annas, a high priest, to a Sanhedrin member describing his talk with King Herod Antipas. Herod had asked Annas who people thought Jesus was. "Some say he is Elijah come again," Annas quoted himself as telling Herod, "and some say he is John the Baptist brought back from the dead." "Not possible," Herod replied agitatedly, "I had the Baptist killed myself and saw his head on a salver." "My own opinion," Annas told the king, "is that he is a talented rabble-rouser who will cause trouble to Rome and Judaea alike until he climbs a tree"—is crucified.

For two days, I took notes from the miscellanea. One item copied was an opinion written by a Rabbi Jochanan ben Zakkai, who had spoken with Jesus early in his ministry; it said, "In the beginning, he was a prophet, and had he remained loyal to Jehovah he would rank now with Nahum, Haggai, and Habakkuk. But he became a deceiver and is now only another false Messiah."

The road to Rhinocolura took me through the mountain country of Eshtaol, Beth Jibrin, Lachish, lands where Samson and David and Goliath had lived, haunted now by ruined walls, fallen Philistine temples, long-razed villages. I came to the coast at Gaza, then, groaning over my memories, went on through Raphia and down the long sea road to Rhinocolura.

The beautiful little port brightened me. It had a jewel-box harbor, mud-brick buildings tinted pastels, canopies of many hues over the stalls, and crowds of well-dressed people in its seaside marketplace. A ships' chandler pointed to the villa of Robezius among olive trees on a prominence overlooking the port.

Nervous as a virgin, I gave my name to the servant and said I was a Roman scholar from Scythopolos who wished a word with the Lady Miriam—the formal name for Mary. I had expected a worn but still attractive woman with a bit of residual tart in her face, but the woman who came to the foyer was a tall matron of stately bearing. She had auburn hair streaked throughout with gray, a single dimple in her left cheek and steady brown eyes.

"So, Roman scholars now appear in Parthian armor?" Her Greek was lilting but still had the accents of Galilee. My heart jumped. It could only be Mary Magdalene. Her smile drew down one side of her perfect lips.

"Your robbers down here are as famous as your beauties," I said, trying to hide my excitement with a quip.

"Hear, hear," she said. "But, in fact, as you obviously know from my accent if you are a scholar, I am not Nabataean but Galilean." She led me into the house. "Well, then, Sir Demas, you have come a long way from Scythopolos. What do you seek?"

"I have been doing research on—" I began, but broke off the subterfuge. "I am a lawyer and a Christian of no small confusion, once a follower of Paul of Tarsus. Thomas, a disciple of Jesus, urged me to talk with those who knew Jesus and to make a true record of what I was told so that Christians could know him better. I find there are as many Jesuses as there are people who knew him. Of all those important in his life and still alive, you are the only one I could not find. His aunt . . ."

As I talked, the sophistication with which she greeted me fell from her like an actor's mask. Her expressions, clear as wall drawings, changed from astonishment to suspicion to nervous interest. In her eyes, I saw her deciding whether to turn me out with a pleasant word or talk with me. I spoke more rapidly.

"I mentioned Thomas and Paul. It was not they through whom I first encountered Jesus, but the disciple Andrew."

Again her face showed surprise. Then she smiled with almost girlish happiness at hearing Andrew's name. "Andrew. Protokletos," she said. She mused a moment, then went on. "Next to Jesus, he was the best loved. They, we, all made fun of him." She had regained her gently mocking tone. "But how could dear Andrew have converted you? He was the worst of missionaries." She squinted at me. "You are *that* Roman?"

I was flattered that through some Christian talebearer my presence at the death of Andrew had been relayed to her. I told the whole story. The tears welled in her eyes, but she did not weep. She merely nodded as I spoke. When I was done, she said quietly, "Andrew has bought you my confidence."

She led me onto a small patio that looked out on the coasters moored at the new quay. The air smelled of summer flowers and sea salt. She had a servant bring us wine diluted with cool water and flavored with jasmine.

"Where shall I begin?" she asked.

At the beginning, I might have said. But in the first flush of her frankness, before she became entangled in storytelling and perhaps

379

embellishments, I wanted the truth of the central mystery. Mary Magdalene would remember it uncorrupted by the politics and usages that had made Thomas, John, Peter, all of them, no longer reliable witnesses.

"Begin, I beg you, at the foot of the cross," I said.

She looked surprised, but acceded. "There were four women—we thought they would not harm women: Jesus' mother; John and James's mother, Salome; Joanna, who was from Jerusalem, and me; and John whom no one made afraid. We stayed there until the soldier pierced Jesus with the spear and then they shoved us away. On the Sabbath, we women went to the tomb. We had spices and oil to anoint his body, but the tomb was closed with a stone. We went back the next day to pray, except his mother."

"But why not . . ."

"She was too upset; grief was mounting in her. At the tomb, the stone was rolled away. I looked in and his body was not there. . . ." She closed her eyes briefly to summon back remembrance. "All three of us ran to where the disciples . . ."

". . . were hiding."

"Yes. Peter and John were the only ones there. We told them and they ran ahead. They thought the body of Jesus had been stolen by the Jews or the Romans so we could not venerate it. Peter and John went back to find the rest and the other two women went with them, but I stayed behind just . . . to be there. I looked in the tomb again and thought I saw two shadowy forms and I may have said something to them like, 'Where is the master?' but now I think I was just so afraid, so distracted by it all, that perhaps I only imagined I saw the forms.

"But I did sense someone behind me, and I looked around and saw a man all in white. I thought it might be a Roman, or an agent of the Pharisees, or perhaps a gardener. But then I thought, What would any of those be doing dressed all in white? I said, 'What did they do with my Lord?' And the man said that he had gone to heaven." She stopped.

"You are sure he, too, was not an illusion?"

Her tone had become hesitant. She went on, but in a duller voice. "No, he was real."

"And that was all he said? Did you recognize him?"

"That was all he said, and, no, I did not know him."

"You did not see him again? You did not see Jesus?"

"No, and I never said I saw Jesus. Only the two forms about whom I could well have been . . . hysterical, and the man in white." She looked up at me sternly and said, "Sir Demas, you are playing lawyer. I am not a witness in a trial."

"I am sorry," I said, feeling so bewildered and empty that I wanted to cry. I had come to the final authority on the resurrection. She had turned the mystery back to me. I would never know. I could not believe she had told me all she knew.

"But they, some of them, say Jesus *did* come back."

"I know. John." She shrugged. "Everyone was in turmoil. They wanted him back. But even John did not say he thought Jesus had come back in the body until a week or two later. Now it seems accepted by them all."

I could prod nothing more from her memory. Although I was almost sure now Jesus had never physically returned to the disciples, I would have to live with the enormous vacuum of uncertainty. "And in the first days afterward . . . ?"

"I wanted to stay with them, to preach," she said. "I understood his message. But I was only nineteen, and there was also what I had been before I joined them. To tell the truth, most of them did not want me. And Jesus' mother had never been happy with me. Andrew and John were the only ones who really thought I could be an apostle to women, although Thomas would have agreed, but the rest felt 'What does Andrew know?' and 'John is such a mystic,' so I was out in the cold."

"Peter?"

"Would have let me stay but for the wrong reasons."

"On *that*, you do not want me to play lawyer?"

She broke her earnestness with a smile. "The witness wants to respond. Nothing happened. Peter wanted to . . ." Just as James, son of Alphaeus, had said. "Who can blame him with that wife of his? Anyway, I left them and tried to preach on my own, but things got out of hand. The Jews were talking about stoning me; the Nazarenes were shocked at a woman preaching. So I talked individually to women, but they found out what I had been . . . I saw I could not talk of Jesus in Palestine."

She had gone to Antioch to preach, but had not been accepted there, either, and had given it up. A married man she had liked became her lover and she had lived with him for four years. After him, there had been others, all substantial, each leaving her funds as they departed for home and their wives. She had met Robezius ten years ago, and by then had enough money so she could stay with him from choice, not necessity. His wife lived comfortably in Rome, but they had tired of each other and Robezius planned to live out his days with Mary in Rhinocolura. He was now on business in Alexandria for a week.

The flowery wine had begun to sit heavily on my stomach. The sun was sinking, making a yellow highroad to us on the Mediterranean's blue-black surface. Mary invited me to stay for supper and the night. I looked up, thinking to my shame that, in spite of Deborah, in spite of everything, if this woman of majesty offered me the opportunity . . .

She saw it on my face and burst out laughing. "I am offering you *a* bed, Sir Demas, not *his* bed." I blushed, tried to say a word of gallantry, stammered, and shut my mouth.

At supper, we ate slices of grilled baby lamb, thin wheat bread, lettuce and cucumber with oil and vinegar, delicate honey cakes. And we drank a great deal more wine. I asked her how she had felt about Jesus. Had she revered him?

"Not revered, because he was not priestly; he was not distant . . . even though toward the end he talked a great deal about being the son of God. And why should he not? You could not see these cures, these phenomena, without being awed, without thinking that even if they could be explained, there were just so many of them, so we thought he *must* have supernatural power."

"But you saw him . . . ?"

"Not as a God, but as a man in whom a God dwelt. He was very much *with* us, stubborn, funny, sometimes bad-tempered, but always so—" she looked for the word—"compassionate, even though a leader, even though in command. I loved him as a man. . . ." She stopped, thought, and then took a long draught of wine that made her shudder. "Loved him as a woman loves a man. I was in love with him, you see, and he was sometimes in love with me."

The wine had taken control of us both. But I was shocked almost sober by what she had said. Yet was it not what I had wanted to hear, wanted to believe? So that I was justified and sanctioned in my love for Deborah. "All along, I had hoped he loved you," I stumbled, "even that you and he . . ." I could not finish the question, no matter how much I wanted its answer.

Mary studied me, then smiled a tipsy smile. "You poor bumpkin. You are like the rest of them, in a stew because a woman is gnawing at you and God won't let you have her." My eyes must have popped. But she sighed and went on. "Well, with us it did not happen. Not that there was anything wrong with him. In his mid-twenties, he had . . . there had been a woman in Nazareth, a widow, but after her, I don't think anyone. I imagine giving up women that way was anguish for him."

"Then why did he?"

"He *had* to. He could not be like the rest of us. He had to set the example. Peter, with that harpy he was married to, he couldn't stay away from women. These were men on the road, in danger of stoning, death, at every town. What do you expect?"

"Well, I am in no position to condemn them," I protested.

"Remember, we were working mostly in rural areas and small towns. The Jews we were bringing to us were strict about that sort of thing, or at least it was the Law and they felt their rabbis should be. If the Pharisees could reproach him about a red-haired former— That would have been the end of it. He would have been just one more fraud claiming to be the Messiah.

"Jesus took a dangerous gamble simply by letting me be with them. I was no pasture virgin, you know. I had already been threatened with strangling"—an alternate punishment, I knew, for adultery—"and I was not being stoned for stealing goat dung when he saved me. Besides, how could Jesus say anything to *anyone* if he and I . . . ? So I was as protective of him as he was of himself."

"If all this is so, then why did he preach so fervently against fornication, adultery, divorce?"

"He *didn't*. Perhaps on adultery more than the rest, because it can disrupt families. But people like Matthew, and Jesus' brother, James, who was not even with him, and that little insect, James, son of Alphaeus—they make it sound like anything to do with physical love was anathema to Jesus. . . ."

"And Paul," I said.

"Yes, Paul," she said scornfully, "very much so. He may be a great organizer. I am sure he is. But he is also a great prude and a great misinterpreter."

Mary had become intense and very sure of herself, the way some people are when they have drunk too much. "Demas"—she had dropped the twitting "Sir Demas"—"do not ever trust a man who does not like women, and I mean physically. I hear Paul is like that. Judas was, too. I am not comparing the two except in that one way. I am just saying that you cannot trust them."

The thought sobered me, at least briefly. "I can trust Paul to be Paul," I said gloomily.

"Well, if the history of Jesus is left to men like that, it will be wrong because they will cut him to their own measure."

I interrupted to say that was what I had found in all my talks with those who had known Jesus: *everyone* cut him to their own measure. I did not add that she was doing the same thing.

"They will reduce him to themselves," she went on. "The true Jesus will not even be known to the next generation. Already, he is all but unknown to this one."

"Perhaps my collection of stories . . ." I began, but a thought intervened. "Is it possible that your cantankerous, unpredictable Jesus, for all his genius, all his appeal, all his humanness, is not the kind of person a church *can* be built on?"

She gave me a lovely, off-center smile. "Perhaps if it cannot be built on a person like that it should not be built at all. Or perhaps you are right. It may be better for it to survive with Jesus distorted, even if it means hundreds, thousands, of years of false impressions, than for him not to come down to posterity at all. Maybe Paul's version is all people in the future will have. After all, what Paul and the others say about loving our neighbors is just what Jesus said. The rest"—and here I heard the ringing echo of Peter—"we can forget."

She tried to fix me with her unfocused eyes. "Demas, I fail as a Nazarene not because I live with the husband of another woman, but because I do not love my neighbors as I love myself. I do not do enough for the old, the insane, the poor of Rhinocolura. I do not influence Robezius to do more. *That* is my sin. Jesus saved me from stoning as an adulteress, and he would do that again. But I am not sure he would save me if I were stoned for turning my back on those who are suffering."

Mary clapped her hands for a servant, said words to him in the Nabataean dialect, and motioned me to follow him. He led me to a room looking out on the dark sea where small lights of ships at anchor twinkled like faint stars. The servant put my lamp in an alcove, and I sat on a cross-legged stool, wondering how I would make it to the low Roman bed where I could collapse.

❁

Mary and I greeted each other at breakfast with pulsing headaches and some humor. Over a strong herb tea, we talked on the second-floor patio again. I told her many of the stories I had collected and she confirmed some of them, amended others.

"And now that you have discovered Jesus," she said with a trace of gentle mockery, "where will you preach him?"

She had read in me what had been growing gradually, the feeling that I would begin a new ministry. With all that I knew, how could I not want to tell other people about it. Her question was pregnant. Where? In Italy, Nero's flames could burn any church I set up, and besides it would be an intrusion on Paul, as would any work I did in Asia Minor. North Africa, Ethiopia, Illyricum, Spain were all foreign to me and, prohibitively, Deborah was in Spain. Nor did I want to infringe on the Apostolic Council in Palestine. Greece, Macedonia? There was where my imaginings most often took me.

As if she were still reading my thoughts, Mary said, "Go to Greece or to Thessalonica. They will adapt to anything, even you. And the persecutions of Nero will be mild there."

It was time for me to leave her. She kissed me on my cheeks and I smelled the jasmine scent, richer by far on her soft skin than in the wine. In the noon sun, her face, though dauntless, was drawn by our drinking. She looked her age.

❁

Once outside Rhinocolura's small, breezy bay, the weather turned hot. My donkey's tongue lolled, but he paced gamely on. The country on either side of the road grew arid, although broom, mustard, wormwood, and some woebegone acanthus gave me some shade when I stopped to drink from my water bag and tear off chunks from the loaves I had bought in Rhinocolura.

During the evenings, before the chill forced me into my goatskin coat, I began to put my notes in chronicle form, combining what was repetitious, footnoting, occasionally adding my own speculations about a witness's veracity or want of it. I was certain I had collected more data on the life of Jesus than anyone ever had done before, and I had done it more methodically.

In my notes, I also jotted down some of the events of my own life, the well episode, for example, my visits to the synagogue, my practice of law, a discreet mention of Deborah. If there should be some future reader, he might like to know the professional and personal credentials of the gatherer of this mass of exegetic material on Jesus Christ.

❁

In Jerusalem, I spoke again with Thomas and John. Both encouraged me to take what I had learned to audiences, to use it to win people to Jesus. I journeyed to Borhairus to see Ezra and Ahiam, and spent two days in Modi'im with Rechab. By now, I was sure I wanted to try to preach again, at least for a while. With each, I discussed where I might take a new ministry.

At first, I decided on Thessaly, so much of it unvisited by any Christian mission. But, in the end, I fixed on Thessalonica. The church there had fallen lately into disorder. Paul had written harsh letters urging it to change. "It is not a place," he had once said, "where one can suit the fare to the eater." But perhaps my fare was what the eater there needed.

In Borhaurus, I dipped deeply into my inheritance, and got from Ezra the three pitchers Dathan had given me. I packed the gold and pitchers carefully along with my few other treasures. Then, I left my native city again for far places.

I was finding it easier to select a place to preach than to choose a message to preach there. As I made my way first to Caesarea, then by ship toward Thessalonica, I considered the Jesus I had discovered, a God different in so many ways from Paul's or even from the Jesus I had preached before.

I had found no proof that he returned in body. That lacking, I would not preach that an event so far outside nature was true. I also had difficulty with the concept that he was truly the son of God. The "holy ghost" notion, too, was beyond my reason. The miracles of Jesus were a more difficult question. Some, such as Jesus' turning water into wine at Cana, seemed genuinely supernatural. Perhaps there were facts unknown to me, yet ascertainable, that would make wine always wine, water always water, but I had not found them. So, while I would not preach the plethora of miracles that Paul and the disciples did, I planned to say that I had found the hand of God in several of them.

Even the discoveries that ran jaggedly across the grain of accepted Nazarene and Christian belief had made my faith in God and in Jesus more stable and vigorous. I was more certain than ever that the presence of Jesus pervaded the disciples after his death, sending them like great shooting stars into the world to preach his commandment and to forgive sins in his name. I was convinced by my findings that Jesus felt unshakably that there were gradations of sins, those of the flesh being far less destructive than those of violence, and of the spirit.

Jesus had forgiven drunks, gluttons, homosexuals, adulterers, and those who lusted. Indeed, for that last sin, if Mary Magdalene was right, he had forgiven himself, and I was sure he forgave Deborah and me. My quest had showed me a Jesus who preached forgiving, not condemning, mercy, not justice, love, not the withholding of love. This Jesus extolled freedom and said that in the name of love exceptions could be made to all his rules, save his Golden One. This was a God I could love, a God whose message I could preach as long as I had breath.

XXXV

❖❖❖

I had first come to Thessalonica with Paul five years before. We had arrived in sunlight through fields of flax and asphodel, and then I had thought it was the most beautiful city I had ever seen. How much had happened to me since then: my crucifixion, the two years of wooing Deborah again, then losing her, my joy and disasters with Paul, the death of my family in Rome, and my months of questing in search of Jesus.

This time, I arrived in Thessalonica by sea and stood on deck in a rainstorm, watching our dory crew draw us to the quay. I found a temporary room in a harbor lodging house for sailors, then went to Aristarchus, who was as doughty as I had remembered him from our desperate hours bailing for our lives in the ship off Malta. Secundus, his deputy minister, whom I had known in Corinth, but not well, was with him, grown fat.

They had heard during the winter of my break with Paul and were not happy to see me. Yet they listened with interest as I summarized my investigations of the acts, words, and feelings of Jesus. I told them I realized my conclusions ran counter to Paul's in important ways, but I added that I considered that God, not Paul, was God. They, too, I reminded them, had been censured recently by Paul for what he considered deficiencies in the way they were managing the church in Thessalonica.

For *minor* deficiencies, they hastily added. This Jesus *I* intended to preach, they said, would disrupt their church (which nominally had eight hundred members) at a time when pressures from outside were likely to grow. They tried to persuade me to find another city for my ministry. But when all their arguments failed, they—and I—began looking for honorable compromises.

Both Aristarchus and Secundus had advantages I lacked. They were experienced Christian leaders in their forties. They were Thessalonians. And although both were Jews and their church was half Gentile, they were trusted, even loved, by their members. But I also had strengths. I had been close to Paul for nine years, had done more organizational work in more different places than they had, and had a better feel for how Nero's changed tack would affect Roman policies.

After more polite argument, we agreed they would write Paul little more than that I had arrived and that I was determined to stay. For my part, I promised to spend most of my time organizing—where they conceded much work needed to be done—and to preach as moderately as I could. In fact, even they did not always preach pure Paulism. To insist in Thessalonica, as Paul did, that there were insurmountable impediments to salvation for sinners of the flesh would be to exclude most of their current worshippers.

Once we had struck the agreement, the whole idea of working for Jesus in Thessalonica began to invigorate me, much as it had in Borhaurus ten years ago. When I had been here before, I had been under Paul's thumb. Enthralled by his genius, I had also been inhibited by his doctrine. This time I was more free.

As I plunged into the life of the Christian community, I discovered that besides Paul's strictures against immoralities, a related part of his message was causing problems. When he first preached here, he had sought to give the Thessalonians an emetic of fear that would make them disgorge their twin vices of superstition and sensuality. He had therefore put frightening emphasis on Jesus' words about Parousia, preaching that the end of the world and thus the judgment day was imminent.

It was not the first time I had met a group absorbed in the terrifying concept of personal and universal death. In a Galilean village during my inquiries about Jesus less than a year ago, I had found a cult of apprehensive old people who were still sure the world was going to end any week and that Jesus would come to judge them. Their relic was a parchment copy of a sermon by Jesus, which their scribe had taken down and which the hamlet elder had taken from a bejeweled leather case. The words on the scroll he unrolled for me in his trembling hands were as follows:

"The day of judgment is at hand when all who are of this world and all who are in the tombs will come forth. Those who have done good will be resurrected to life. But for those who have done evil to themselves and others, it would be safer in Sodom and Gomorrah. The angels of God will throw them into the furnace of fire to weep and to gnash their teeth."

Paul had done Thessalonica no favor by adopting Jesus' threat. Bigots within the church were still using Paul's doomsday prophesies to cry hellfire at other Christians who were not rigorously pious. Aristarchus and Secundus had taken an expedient approach. A small tidal wave, a landslide on Mount Olympus, which towered with Jovian dignity above the city, an unusual increase in miscarriages—all were cited by them as *possible* portents. Many Christians—because the end of the world had *not* come—had made it a reason to become dubious about a variety of other aspects of Jesus' creed.

The confusion had led some Christians to quit the church entirely and join small sects of Johnists, humanists, and pragmatists.

First, to combat this fragmentation, we concentrated, as Paul would have done, on setting up a trustworthy cadre of believers from all levels of society. We named subministers in the port; in the rich suburbs whose villas climbed toward the Kalamarian heights; in the workers' areas; in the alluvial plains of the Vardar and Aliakmon rivers, inhabited by the poultry and grain farmers; and in the foothills of Mount Khortiatis, where herdsmen produced great quantities of hides, wool, and meat.

Aristarchus and Secundus, despite their years in the city, had made few constructive contacts with the government and the non-Christian community. This negligence had left the church more isolated than its precepts naturally dictated. I began opening conduits to the city fathers, starting with the six elected politarchs. They had evolved from the hoplites, who, centuries ago, were drawn from the peasantry, elected their own leaders, and ruled under a rudimentary democracy.

In my visit to them, I proposed that we Christians be allowed to take a more active role in the municipality, serving the city without favor or venality on sanitation, port, market, aqueductal, and other civic committees. Next, I conferred with lesser civil authorities at the harbor, constabulary, agora, waterworks, and other city agencies.

The politarchs were subject only to the veto of the Roman governor, whose small force of auxiliaries and lictors enforced his few orders. My Roman name got me in to see him. He was a man thin in body, intellect, and outlook. I was suitably humble and he suitably haughty consonant with the new rules from Rome about Christians. We talked at length, and I thought he deemed me reasonable. I left believing that he did not feel the new edicts required him to stir up the volatile city with a bloodbath of Christians—at least not yet.

✳

I spoke with the few open-minded leaders of the synagogues and sought areas where we could work together on behalf of the community, such as refuse disposal and health services.

I found the greatest resistance to Christianity among the pagans. With them, even limited cooperation was difficult. In their dozens of religious beliefs, they made up the majority of the polymerous population: Greeks, Romans, Galatians, Asians, Thracians, Egyptians, and numerous other races. They were fermenting with disagreements, and most of their sects were too extreme for us to work with them. Often they were also too unhitched by opium derivatives, myrrh and more obscure drugs, including aphrodisiacs made from blister beetles.

But we did reach civil accords with a very few, including a cult of devil worshippers. They agreed to share a new well with one of our parishes, although at first I was disconcerted by their leader, whose forearms were pierced with gallows nails and who wore an amber hippopotamus on a gold chain ringed through his lower lip.

Soon we were building new meeting places. Baptisms had increased, Communions were crowded, and, most important, our members were interested in what we had to say. The new activity even began to encourage numbers of Johnists, pragmatists, and humanists to drift back to us.

When I was questioned by members, I tried to give moderate answers. After an outdoor sermon beneath Mount Khortiatis, for instance, a burly hide-curer called at me angrily, "Paul, whom you say you followed, told us the end would come in his lifetime. He is old now, so unless he lied, Jesus is at hand. Yet you say even the young among us may live to be old. Where is the payment for our life of sinlessness?"

Several other of these rough hill people joined in, shouting other words they thought Paul had said about archangels and the trumpets of God being almost within earshot.

I had to raise my voice to be heard. "How often have you waked in the night and thought dawn's first light was nigh only to toss for hours before the cock crowed? If you who live by the setting and the rising of the sun can be mistaken about the coming of day, how much easier for men to be mistaken about so great and unknown an event as the date of the end of the world."

"But," one of herdsmen argued back, "Jesus was the son of God. He would know. And he would tell Paul."

"Jesus came to earth as man," I rebutted. "Surely, he sometimes made the mistakes men do, as when he spoke of the future, else how would he be human?"

In sermons, I felt looser now, more at ease. I was discovering when to pause for effect, when to use anecdotes about how Jesus, the country boy from Galilee, had tied the Pharisees in knots time and time again, when to speak at length, when briefly. From my quest, I was able to speak of Jesus almost as an acquaintance. I could cite episodes from his life to show his bravery, his quickness, his wisdom.

In spite of my promises to Aristarchus and Secundus—and ever more confident in my message—I gradually began to preach more fully the Jesus I had discovered. On the resurrection, for example, I told my audiences, that while most Christians believed that Jesus returned in the flesh, "I am sure that Jesus and God can love us whether or not we believe in the actual resurrection of Jesus' body."

And of miracles, I said, "Some of them defy all rational descriptions. I heard of them from the mouths of those who saw them, and even from some of the healed. And so I tend to believe. But let us imagine there was not a single miracle: we are then in the presence of something even more remarkable, a man so good, so magnificent, that through love he could transmit his own health to others." For Paul, heresy, for me, freedom.

One rainy day, I prevailed on Aristarchus to speak with me to an audience of Jews on a street in their quarter. I could almost imagine that the synagogue, only a hundred yards away through the slanting drops, was listening, its dark window slits the ears of some massive, timeless creature. When I had finished my talk of Jesus as Messiah, and of the joys of his new and simple convenant, five Jews stayed behind to speak with us. As Aristarchus and I made our way out of the quarter, he commented, "Three of them will join us, one of them a spy."

Our efforts to bring Jews to the church did not make me popular with the city's Jewish Council. They were so perturbed when a dozen young Jews joined us that a Pharisee council member took revenge by refusing sale of construction materials to our parishes. I stirred up similar hostility among the priests of Cybele and Astarte, the best organized and most violent of the pagans, when I condemned "gods of clay and spittle coated with gold." Yet the peaceful alternative to this tension would have been to remain silent about the message of Jesus, something I could not do.

The ultra-Paulists, those who were convinced Parousia was near, remained our thorniest problem, for they were in our midst. After my first two months of preaching, however, and to the dismay of Aristarchus and Secundus (but somewhat to my relief), two hundred of the most unbending of these from the alluvial plain and hill country broke with us.

They found a place to meet and preached that we were apostates who denied the resurrection, the miracles, the imminence of the world to come, who denigrated the holy ghost and approved adultery, drunkenness, gluttony, sloth. . . .

Aristarchus bravely went alone to one of their Communions in the hills to try to recapture them. They denied him the sacrament and drove him away, threatening to stone him if he came again. We decided to let them boil in their small pot of hates, but we tried all the same to undermine their rigid leaders.

I had thought by now we would have heard from Rome. I had written to Borhaurus and Modi'im and gotten letters from Ezra, Ahiam, and Rechab. I had also written Belzek, Drobyta, and the leaders of the other churches in Asia Minor and Greece that I had visited as a missionary for Paul, telling them I had now branched out on my own. All had written back, telling me their news, asking for information about my ministry. Some inquired whether this meant I was no longer preaching the dogma of Paul. I answered yes and no, and spelled out my differences, and why they had arisen.

XXXVI

In October, just before winter shut the sea lanes, the last of the big freighters from Italy dropped sail in the harbor. From the steps of the new meeting house we were building off the agora, Aristarchus, Secundus, and I watched it tying up at the quay. They, I suspected, were hoping that Titus or some other emissary from Paul would be aboard in response to their letter telling Paul I was in Thessalonica. Although they had been, by and large, patient with me, I knew that they still wished I had not come and would welcome my departure. Someone from Paul, they thought, might expedite it.

Their faces fell when, not Titus, but a grimy sailor with crafty Phoenician eyes sauntered up with a letter for them. He held it fast until he had extorted seven drachmas from us. They read, their lips moving as I stood by uncomfortably. When they had finished, Aristarchus handed it to me.

After the usual greetings to the two of them, Paul wrote that several of the church leaders were imprisoned and his own liberty had been curtailed. While he was still allowed to go out during the day, he was manacled and guarded, but the guard was changed daily lest he fall under Paul's spell. Timothy was on the road, but Titus, Luke, and Mark were free for the time being and in Rome. They were helping Paul prepare for his trial, which was to take place in three or four months. Burrus had retired, and the trial would be held before some new appointee of Nero.

Paul then turned to the letter Aristarchus and Secundus had written about me. "Demas," he said, "has deserted me for the things of this world, and so I have informed all who have asked. His faith is sincere, but it is as much the faith of the earth, the city, the roads, and the streets as it is of God. It is with pain that I say this, for, as you know, he has given the blood of his veins and the blood of his mind for me, preserving me with his own body from death.

"By doing so, he has given me a few more years to carry the words of Jesus to our brothers. I looked on him as a son, although always as a prodigal, for as he was prodigal with his sword in protecting me and with his wits before the legal powers, so he was prodigal in sowing an errant gospel. Yet, like the father who prayed for the return of the prodigal, so I pray for Demas. So far he has not chosen Jesus' path back to me.

"I urge you therefore to discourage him from preaching. For he is like the squatter-bird who comes to a nest built by wrens and lays her own coarser eggs there so that her offspring can be raised by wrens. Just as squatter-bird chicks take the food of wren chicks and starve them, so would the message of Demas starve new Christians. If he will not fly away when you urge him, you must drive him from your nest, without harming him, if possible, for even a squatter-bird is lovely in flight and not an adder that crawls on its belly in filth."

Paul closed his letter with a long sermon admonishing the Thessalonians about their morality and faith. I noticed with bitter satisfaction that there was no mention of the day of judgment.

When I had finished, Aristarchus said anxiously, "You see, he says you must go." Secundus, perspiring, looked at me irresolutely, seeking some way to support Aristarchus without offending me.

They were kind men who saw how unhappy I was. They also were brave men who would die for Jesus and probably for Paul so long as the issue was uncomplicated. But neither liked dilemmas and Paul had forced one on them.

"You must go, Demas," Aristarchus repeated. And this time, Secundus nodded in agreement.

"I would like a day to think about it," I said, and added with the beginnings of defiance, "and to pray for guidance."

Aristarchus noticed my combative tone, but Secundus did not and gripped my arm briefly in Christian sympathy.

Supperless, wineless, I knelt in front of my pallet, seeking some communication from Jesus or God. In Thessalonica, I had felt a return of the zeal that had inspired me in Borhaurus, Laranda, Bayba, Luna. . . . That being so, I asked God whether he really wanted me to stop my ministry again? Paul's simile of the two birds was powerful, but unfair. True, I *was* a squatter-bird, but the nest I had invaded was

394

in disrepair and I had made it stronger: the wren chicks had been hungry and I had fed them.

If I left Thessalonica, would the women, the young people, the alienated, the Jews and pagans I had brought to Christ, be fulfilled with the sermons and leadership of Aristarchus and Secundus? Would the slaves to whom I had spoken honestly be satisfied at being told again their condition was a natural state? Would those trying to be better people who drank too much, or lied or were lazy, or obese or, for that matter, who fornicated for the sheer joy of it be served better by being shamed or even, if Paul had his way, driven from the church?

I had told all these people they, too, were the children of God. I believed Jesus *wanted* them as much as he wanted those with strong wills and unquestioning hearts and minds, those who never became drunk and made fools of themselves, never became desperate and slept with their neighbors' wives, never simply became demoralized and gave up—with Jesus their last, only friend.

My mind began to get fuzzy and I felt I had lost contact with God, without any answer to the question of whether I should stay. I got up from my knees and crawled onto the bed and slept until just before dawn, when I arose, washed my face, brushed my teeth with my frayed beech stick, drank some cold water, and got down again on my knees beside my unmade pallet. By the time the sun had risen enough to light my room, I was finding answers. They did not flash like Paul's epiphany, but came so gradually that I only became aware of them when I realized I was no longer debating.

I went to Aristarchus's house early. We walked to Secundus's and then we three strolled to a hillock that looked out on the glitter of the Thermaic Gulf.

With such beauty in the world, I thought, why was there also such contention? Rome was persecuting us and would soon, I was sure, also suppress the rebellious Jews in Palestine. In our own church, the extremists in the hills and the plain hated us, plotted, no doubt, our downfall. Among the pagans, an Oriental Hades cult had been caught kidnapping infants whose fat was used in candles for their ghastly ceremonies of initiation. We had demanded that the governor disband them and they had taken vows to kill our leaders.

What kind of God did we believe in who made Thermaic Gulfs and at the same time allowed the death of innocent babies at the hands of Satanists? What kind of world was this with its fury, and love, and hate, and kindness and laughter, and deceit and cowardice and courage all jarred in together? The three of us sat in the autumn sun, they perhaps thinking not unsimilarly. Their silence forced me to begin:

"Paul is right in saying I am an interloper and that I preach some things differently from him. But you two know I am different from you and yet I love you. We have been through tribulations that have tested us. We have not found each other wanting. Why cannot we go on as we have been going on?" I asked. "You can preach as you do, I as I do.

"If people question why we are sometimes at odds, we can tell them to look to their own families: not every family member believes exactly the same thing, but they remain a loving family, closer than they are to anyone outside their home. We can cite the many things we agree on. We take Communion together; we are all baptized; we all live and die in Jesus."

They looked at each other and Aristarchus replied earnestly, "I will never be able to argue as well as you, Demas. I wish I did not even have to try. We already have Rome, the Jews, the extremists, the pagans against us. We do not need internal trouble. If you left, it would simplify things."

I felt guilty about my inability to control the situation, to make them want to accommodate themselves to me. I felt frustrated, but not angry. "I prayed all last night," I replied. "I do not think God wants me to go. I think he feels I have done good, not evil, here."

"Demas," said Secundus, "I sometimes think you and I pray to different Gods. Yours always seems to agree with you."

Aristarchus was annoyed. "You are dressing up politics as piety. Be practical. If you stay, what can we write Paul?"

"You could write him that I refused to go and that you felt it was better to keep the church together, so you were not trying to expel me."

"He would excommunicate us, too."

"No," I said, "he would write you another letter, an even stronger one, and ask you to read it to the congregations. Or if he could afford to, he would send Titus or Luke. And, believe me, if Titus comes, you will not have to worry anymore because Titus will just take over your followers in this church. Then Titus and I would begin a head-chopping contest that would make the murder of the innocents look like a circumcision."

Aristarchus pondered that a while, then said with bravado, "We could just declare you no longer part of the church."

"You could try," I conceded. But we both knew a large number of the most active members would follow me out the door. I watched him as he chewed on his problem, so much more difficult than mine, and he less able to handle it. Paul, who could help them, was far away. I was here.

"We could ask Paul for his advice," Secundus offered.

Aristarchus sighed and finally nodded without enthusiasm. "That will buy us a little time again," he said.

I thought of also writing Paul. But we were now foes. His next move would be to excommunicate me. I was not going to wait for destruction as did those poor wretches gored to death in Cremens's arena. When Paul responded again, it would be even more sternly and I wanted the Thessalonian Christians to be loyal to me, and to what I believed.

In the meantime, since Aristarchus and Secundus had joined Paul in bluntly saying I should go, I felt no more obligation to temporize. At the opening of our new meeting house, Aristarchus and I both preached. He gave a fine sermon on our growth and our hopes without mention of Paul's chastisement of me. When it came my turn to speak, I broke forever with Paul and Paulism.

"Often," I said, "you have heard me preach of cruelty and violence, vicious lust, continuous hatred, resentment, greed. My brothers and sisters, these are the mighty sins in helms of bronze that stalk us with fire and swords and slay newborn decencies and sturdy old goodnesses alike. If we cannot overcome these terrible sins, then we are destroyed and eternally damned.

"There are also lesser sins. I, you, all of us are guilty of them. They are the sins of our flesh and senses. Just as Paul has always said, Jesus wants us to purge ourselves of these sins, too. But what Paul does not tell us often enough is that Jesus, from his humanity, knows our human nature. And when Jesus sees us truly striving to rid our hearts of rage and destruction and ignobility, he forgives us our minor transgressions.

"In recent months, as I have told you before, I went through the lands where Jesus walked. I talked with those who, thirty years before, had known him. The Jesus I discovered was not the same as the harsh God that Paul preaches. One day, for instance, a woman broke in on Jesus while he ate at a Pharisee's home and anointed his head with oil and washed his feet with her tears. She told him she had prostituted herself on the Sabbath and had stolen food for her children. She begged for God's forgiveness.

"The host haughtily demanded why Jesus even let such a woman approach him. But Jesus ignored the Pharisee and instead asked the woman, 'Did you hate, or lie, or slander the good name of others, or mistreat your friends, or your husband'—and he smiled—'or your pet sparrow?' 'No, Your Honor,' she said. 'I have never done these things, although my husband is a drunkard, but rather I have tried to be happy, and, often foolishly, have tried to make others happy, even my sparrow.'

"Jesus turned to his host. 'When I came into this house, you called me rabbi, but did you give me water to wash my feet or oil for my hair? This woman, out of love and a desire for forgiveness, anointed me and washed my feet.' Jesus lifted up the woman, told her to sin no more and said, 'I tell you, sirs, her sins, which are many but not great, are all forgiven, for she has loved much. Indeed, a man who sins little but also loves little, may not be forgiven so easily.'

"This is the Jesus I preach! Do you understand what he was saying? He did not condone her behavior. But when love is present, he forgives frailty. Gluttony he also deplored and drunkenness, but he walked among men who ate too much and drank too much and he did not consign them to Satan as he did uncontrite murderers and hypocrites. He preached against laziness and prodigality, but he did not think these built walls around salvation so high that we poor humans could not climb over them.

"Suppose a man or woman are not married or are each married unhappily but cannot divorce and yet love each other and bring each other joy and peace amid their sorrow? Are we to believe that Jesus who loves us would curse them for all time? No, he would feel their love was more important than their sin so long as their love did not intrude on others. If this were not so, why in the calendar of his years, did he not tell us that this unfortunate but common situation was a sin that doomed us forever?

"I believe the same thing of the love of man for man or woman for woman. If such people do not seek to turn children to their aberrative ways, and if their love is honest, then are they beyond saving? If they are, then why did not Jesus tell us so? I do not speak of these fleshly and lesser spiritual sins in order to encourage people to practice them." So deep was I in seriousness, that the audience's laugh at these words surprised me. I stopped to smile with them, then went on.

"But if we are told, as Paul says, that these sins are as certain to bring us to Satan as the towering trespasses of which I have spoken, then—since all but a few saints are afflicted with *some* transgressions—we may despair of ever finding our way to God. We may abandon our quest."

When I was done, I glanced at Aristarchus. His face was red with rage, Secundus's gloomy and sagging. A public declaration of war could not have disconcerted them more. From here on, I knew, I must take care of my faction in the church. Let Aristarchus and Secundus, if they chose, take care of theirs.

❁

I spent more and more time among the members, curtailing my administrative work. I visited the homes of the poor, the ailing, the dying, the public sick house and the asylum where the city dumped its imbeciles, hopelessly retarded, and epileptics. If there was a hell such as Paul preached, these two rat pits must resemble it. Even so, Thessalonica was more humane than other cities that simply let the mad and the sick die on the streets or carted them outside town to starve.

One of Paul's earliest converts had been a wealthy Jew named Amos, married to a Macedonian woman. He had been the retailer for the tents and textiles of Paul's elderly friend, Jason, now dead. This couple had a twenty-one-year-old son, crippled and dumb from birth, who was now considered insane. They did not send him to the asylum, but took care of him at home. They had baptized him as David, but called him "Son," even when speaking to others, as if calling him by the name of the Jewish king was stating their disappointment each time they said it. When he was younger, they had hired teachers of the classics. He had listened year after year with dull or closed eyes, completely without response. One instructor after another gave up, and in six or seven years the parents did, too.

Because street children jeered at him, and he, in turn, glowered back with what they called an "evil eye," the parents took him out only once a day. One or both accompanied his four-wheeled cart, which was drawn by a servant.

One afternoon, I was visiting Amos in hopes he would add to his already generous contribution for the new church building. I heard servants shout in alarm and we ran to David's room, where his long, emaciated form alternately scissored and stiffened on the floor in what looked like an epileptic seizure. His mother and Amos stood as if stunned. Obviously, this attack was new in the poor lad's pathology. The one thing I knew about epilepsy was that something had to be put between the teeth of the victim to keep him from biting off his tongue.

I snatched a napkin from the tray of food a servant had been feeding him, balled it slightly, grabbed David's head and shoulders in one arm and thrust the cloth into his mouth. His eyes were rolling and his arms and legs were flailing, showing, I thought, a great deal of muscle action for a cripple. In less than a minute, he was calm, exhausted, his eyes shut, his skinny arms and legs outstretched like a man on a cross. His mother, father, and the two servants looked at him with eyes bugging.

Then, as we watched, his legs tortuously entwined at the ankles, locking together, his arms twisted and closed onto his chest, his hands bent outward like claws—until he was again a grotesque cripple. While the servants carefully lifted him back onto his bed, Amos told me this was the first time his son had ever had a seizure. It was also the first time his body had not been contorted since his youth, when day by day it began to assume the pathetic shape it had now.

I came back two days later, both about the contribution and to see how David was. The servant was readying the cart and I walked along with Amos. I could see why passersby were unnerved, for the young man cast angry looks toward everyone. He seemed to gaze with least hatred at the poor, especially lepers and other beggars. His most rancorous glares were for the wealthy and for adolescents. I sensed he was self-conscious about my studying him, because he gave me the ugliest looks in his repertory. Insane he may be, I thought, but not imbecilic. There was a spark inside that large but not ill-shaped head.

As we passed through a lower-class neighborhood inhabited by votaries of Heracles, Ares, and several other pagan gods, a group of youths came from a courtyard and began to jeer. One of them shouted the Anathema of Alecto, a vicious pagan street curse supposedly proof against malign spirits. In a moment, a thick-necked lout came out of the courtyard, blocked our way, and bawled in our faces, "Go another route! Why bring your evil garbage to our neighborhood, dirty Amos?"

The marriage of my friend to a Macedonian had made the whole family abominations to this class of pagan. Amos signaled the servant to turn around. In David's eyes, I saw a look more frightened than angry. I assessed the man blocking us, his clumsiness, the flatfooted way he counted on size to enforce authority. "Sir," I said, "we wish to take this young man the shortest route home."

The servant had already started to back up the cart so he could turn it around. A crowd gathered and some, mostly women, urged the bully to leave us alone. Amos put a hand on the cart, countermanding his order to retreat. The oaf saw we would not move, and lumbered past the front of the cart, I thought to let us go by. But instead he shoved it with his foot, tipping it over and rolling David onto the cobblestones, where he lay like a giant knotted rope hank.

I grabbed the man's arm and spun him. He brought up his pig-haunch fists, but with all my might, I struck him a blow in his belly, my first in anger in many years. He doubled up, swayed, and dropped to his knees, then pitched onto his face. A youth snarled and came toward me. I reached instinctively for Ezra's dagger, which I no longer carried, then cocked my fists. He fell back. We righted the wagon and lifted David back in while the hulk groaned and rolled in the street. As we passed through the quarter, the residents watched us go by in silence.

I thought about David that evening at my supper. Most of the miracles of Jesus and the others had two things in common with medical cures. They came at a time of crisis in the disease and the victim generally wanted very much to get well. The little Syrophoenecian girl with her thrashing, filthiness, and naked dashes into the street was a perfect illustration, most mad and also in her soul most mad for a cure. Perhaps David's epileptic attack, with its release of his skinny limbs from their curlicue, was a crisis. Maybe that scintilla of fear in his eyes today was a hint that he badly wanted to live.

Next day, busy as I was, I went by to walk with David and his father again, partly in case the bully's confederates came out in force—today I carried my knife inside my tunic—and partly to take another look at David. As we walked, I talked mainly to Amos, but said a few things to his son in a conversational, almost reflective way.

For one thing, I told him, if he kept up his angry looks, I would eventually meet someone who would wind up knocking the straw out of me. What David did when I was not around was his business, but when I was, I said, I wished he would carry flowers between his teeth and try to look pregnant. There was not a change in his expression. Looking him in his eyes, I drew Ezra's dirk. He started with surprise, or perhaps fear.

"If you do not like flowers"—I smiled—"you can carry this in your teeth and look *really* fierce."

He blinked, perhaps merely relieved that I was not menacing him. Or, I thought hopefully, could it have been a split second of dark amusement? Up to now I had been curious, empathetic toward his parents, but not much more. Now I viewed his condition as a challenge. Two days later, Amos let me take David out alone. We went to the hillock where Aristarchus and Secundus and I had talked. I sat in front of the cart and looked him in the eyes again. "Listen to me, David," I said. "I have a theory that something is going on in your head, something that has been deadened a long time."

I said I knew from his thrashing during his seizure that his muscles worked. They were not withered. Why not learn to make them work, I asked, at his own bidding, not just his seizure's? At times, I said, I saw him trying to break out of his cocoon. Yet at others he seemed to be trying to punish the world.

For answer, he only glowered.

It was becoming chilly. The wind had shifted from the sea to the north and the mountains. I threw a shawl over David's shoulders and pulled my light cloak around me. I started to speak of my own disappointments, then broke off and chuckled, but not happily. I would be confiding in a mute, one too tangled in the head even to indicate he was listening. Still, the only other confidant I had was God. Talking to God straightened out my thinking, but, like David, he did not give fathomable replies. I grunted with laughless humor again. On the other hand, God and David were trustworthy. Only cadavers were more discreet.

On our next outing, I did begin to delve into my problems. "I do not know whether those teachers that no one thinks you listened to started you on Hesiod like mine did, but you may recall he said a whole city reaps the fruit of an evil man. And Paul, whom I revered and whose life I even saved, is now saying I am that evil man. I know that is hard for you to believe. It's hard for *me* to believe."

David's mask did not relax, but I went on anyway. "I see myself as an intelligent, not too profound, decent, diligent, sometimes straying man who truly wants to be more godly and feels happy and worthy when he tells people about Jesus. I am not an *evil* man. I have never said this before out of respect for Paul and for how God probably regards him, but I am beginning to feel that Paul, despite all his talk about love, wants to squash me like a tomato bug. Every night I pray, I pray hard, for help."

I was surprised at how easily my fears and hurt feelings came out when I was talking with, or more accurately at, David. I looked at him. He had closed his eyes. "No," I said, "not you too? I knock down this Goliath who dumped you in the street. I bring you out here on a nice walk, I pour out my woes to you, and you fall asleep on me or worse, just shut me out, like Paul."

His eyes blinked open, the anger gone for an instant and replaced by something like confusion. Then the subdued glare I was accustomed to came back. Something was happening in David.

I began making it a daily habit to take him for an hour's walk at noon, when all business in Thessalonica stopped for lunch. Part of my reason was that I was sure he liked it. But it also gave me some minutes to steam away anxiousness, to clarify what I had done well and poorly during the last day, to plan against the difficulties. Every day, later in the afternoon, one or both of his parents took him out, giving him a double sojourn in the brisk winter air.

As time went by, and almost without my noticing it, David's choleric look changed to one of inward focus. Sometimes it seemed as if one part of him was talking to the other about who each of them was. Once I spoke to him about how Paul had come to represent my father, about my own father, even about Rechab and how I seemed to reject people who had filled paternal, judgmental roles in my life. Or else I forced them to reject me. I looked up and was sure he wanted to say something. He had that intent stare, only turned more outwardly than in the past.

"You know," I said, "sometimes I can tell you want to give me some good advice or express an opinion. Why not? You could tap once for yes"—I tapped once on his cart with my knuckles— "twice for no"—I tapped twice.

As good folk as his parents were, the problems that sent him into his long night were probably bound up with them. They wondered why I spent so much time with him. I said it helped me to organize my thoughts to talk to him, even though he might not understand. To the community, the walks also looked strange, but then all Christians seemed strange to most Thessalonians. Aristarchus and Secundus saw my attention as charitable, but perhaps partly for show and money: a church leader assisting the insane son of a rich parishioner. "When anybody asks, I say you are working a slow miracle," said Aristarchus dryly.

One day, David and I went to the port and paused to look at the small moored skiffs, and the coasters that made short winter voyages, although never out of sight of land. I thought of a glorious day with Paul sailing among the isles of Greece, then my mind drifted to Sappho, to Daphne, and finally to Deborah. I sighed and recommenced our walk. The sailors stared without malice at David. One, in a sloop filled with kegs, offered us wine. It rippled goldenly in the cup. David drank nothing alcoholic, but I drank heartily. It was rich as honey.

"Where from? Samos?"

"Aye, Samos, where else? Give some to the lad."

I offered the cup to him, and he hesitated before turning his head away. "David," I said. " 'With wine, let us drown care'—that's Vergil's advice if I am not mistaken."

He gave the cart two thumps on the side, the code that I had taught him for "no." His thin lips almost smiled. I was excited. What was he trying to tell me? "Not Vergil?" I asked. Two more thumps. Then I remembered. The quote was from Horace. He had caught me out in my pedantry. More to the point, his "no" opened up a mystifying chasm. How much else did he remember from those years when he was taught but no one thought he had learned?

A week later, I asked him if he wanted to see the people I gossiped to him about, and invited him to one of my sermons. After a few moments' consideration, he tapped "yes." We were having joint vespers for three congregations next day, and I arranged for Amos to bring him. Our new church building by the market was filled with members from our three parishes. Amos and his wife wheeled David into the rear. But a few noticed their entrance and soon everyone craned to try to see him.

My sermon was on the meaning of the story about Jesus and the woman at the well, and when I was done, an older man, one who I thought had deserted us for the ultra-Paulists, called out, "Jesus did many miracles and we all know about Paul's Miracle of Ephesus"—for Paul's healing of the cripple was renowned, no more so than in Thessalonica, which envied its great Mediterranean rival. "But where is the miracle of Thessalonica?"

I had been at Ephesus and knew Paul's "miracle" may have been no more than the consequences of kindness and wisdom, thus only indirectly a cure by the Almighty. There were shouts from the audience of support for the question. I gave my standard reply on the irrelevance of miracles, but got loud dissatisfied grumbles from several people, none of whom I knew. Nervously, I began to suspect that the ultra-Paulists had seeded the audience.

Aristarchus with the wine, and Secundus and I with the bread, started into the crowd. The first heckler shouted again. "If Demas is right and Paul is wrong, then do a miracle on Evil Eye!" We went on serving the Communion, but the cries multiplied from the interlopers. "Evil Eye! A miracle on Evil Eye!" Soon there were calls, many from several of our own more excitable parishioners: "A miracle, Demas! . . . On the son of Amos, a miracle! . . . A miracle on the crippled boy for Thessalonica! . . ."

I tried to see David. The church was beginning to churn into turmoil. There was no way Amos would be able to get him out. I agonized for him. His first excursion, one I had invited him to, and I could not protect him! I imagined his panic, and groaned. We tried to continue the Eucharist, but it was hopeless. The parishioners were pushing me toward David. By mistake, someone knocked the basket of bread out of my hands and with dismay I saw the symbolic flesh of Christ fall to the floor. Aristarchus, wine jug sloshing, was shoved along with me.

Soon we were just outside a ring of parishioners of all ages gathered around David. His eyes were shut, his body drawn in on itself, arms and legs as serpentine as a Persian column and hands turned out like flippers. I was thrust up beside him, a piece of bread still clutched in my hand. There, Amos was trying to press back the mob.

Amidst the hubbub, I said, "David, I am sorry, so sorry to have gotten you into this." He blinked to make sure it was I, then shut his eyes tightly. For weeks, the congregation had seen me taking him out for walks. Now they were like rapt front-row spectators at a freak show. My heart was beating wildly out of rhythm. "Help him, God, Jesus," I prayed to myself, "there just is not any time or room right now for a more elaborate conversation with you. Please, just help." At the same time, my mind began working frantically on how I could help myself.

"Aristarchus," I said to him, where he stood disconcerted outside the circle. "Bring me some wine." The mob parted to let him in and I held the cup while he shakily poured it half full.

"David," I whispered, "I need your help, too. Badly." He made no response, not even opening his eyes. I put a morsel of the bread to his mouth. "David," I said, loud enough for all to hear, "this is the flesh of Jesus Christ. Eat it." Abruptly, at these familiar words there was silence in the church, not a cough or a baby cry. Fathers held children on their shoulders. For a long time, David was paralyzed, his face expressionless.

Then he opened his mouth just enough to take the bread and chewed. Thank you, Jesus, I thought. Thank you, David. Thank you both, thank you, thank you. All around me, I heard the suspiration of breath and a few soft comments of relief.

"David," I said, "this is the blood of Jesus. Drink it and think of him." I held the chalice to his lips. I thought of him turning his head away from the wine of Samos at the port. "David," I said, "I need this so much," then a wild thought swept into me and I said, "David, Vergil wants you to drink it, Horace wants you to, Jesus and God want you to, and I, oh, how I want you to."

A twitch crossed the lean face. He opened his eyes. I saw their concentration, deeper than I had ever seen before, void of anger, fixed on the profound heart of that internal conversation that he carried on with himself. His lips began to quiver. I drew back the chalice. Some of those closest to him retreated apprehensively.

David's eyes shut again and his upper body jerked forward, then heaved back against his father so hard that had there not been people behind Amos, it might have knocked him over. I feared David might have a seizure such as the one that had introduced him to me. I still had a chunk of bread and made ready to push it into his mouth as I had the napkin to keep him from biting off his tongue. His body came forward again, but less spasmodically, and stopped in an erect position.

To my astonishment, his fingers unfroze from their clawlike position and writhed like so many small snakes. They calmed and the hands dropped, relaxed, no longer odd useless outcrops of skin and bone. The spectators gawked. His arms began to untwine. The right one swung spastically through the air, slapping the man nearest him on the nose, then lashed back, but did not retwist. The right hand rose, trembling so much it shook the whole body. The crowd gasped and murmured unbelievingly. Who had not seen this silent, deformed body wheeled through the streets, and now it was becoming almost human.

The right hand, on the thin stem of its forearm, reached toward me, the fingers and thumb forming a U. I edged the cup toward the hand. That was what David wanted, or at least what most of him wanted. The crowd held its breath. Outside in the street, I heard a dog bark, the rumble of a wagon as it passed. The thumb and fingers closed on the cup, then lost their hold and the arm swung wildly again until the left hand gripped the arm and returned it. Once more, the fingers touched the cup.

I was sure they had it. As I let it pass to him, I felt a quivering in his fingers. The left hand maintained its grip on the other arm, and the cup zigzagged toward David's closed mouth. Wine splashed over the brim and onto his white tunic. Suddenly, his mouth gaped, and the right hand made a swift, unsteady rush for it. Desperately, the left hand tried to guide the cup. It smacked against his upper lip, and spilled some into his mouth, although most drenched his tunic.

David's face was like a grotesque of Bacchus, the small spurt of blood from his injured upper lip mixing with the darker red of the wine as it ran into and around his mouth and down his chin. He gulped at the blood and wine and I grabbed the cup, drained it, and held it up in gratitude to God, Jesus, and my improbable savior, David. I embraced his shaking body, hearing small, strange sounds in his throat. Then a bleat, half gurgle, half scream, like the birth cry of a Titan, burst from him.

"Dee-math! Dee-math! Dee-math!"

The supposed mute had not just spoken, but roared.

"My God, a miracle," said Amos in quiet awe.

Those nearest us, as if coming out of a coma, began to repeat, "A miracle," and the cry spread from the rear of the church to the front. Above it, David yelped, "Dee-math!" until the mob picked that up and screams of "Demas!" and "Miracle" rang deafeningly from every quarter of the building.

David's shouts ended in breathlessness and I looked at the face, the eyes closed, but simply in exhaustion, the arms at his side, the long skinny legs flopping out of the cart like those of a child who has outgrown his toy wagon.

"Zeus's stones," I said softly. "God be praised."

XXXVII

❖❖

It would, of course, have been a better miracle if David, from that day forward, had begun loping around Thessalonica with a jug of wine in one hand and a loaf of bread in the other, giving Communion to the bedridden. As it was, when I went by next day, his arms and legs were twisted into the old position.

"David," I said. "You truly saved me. You made a miracle of your body and voice." I smiled, but he scowled. The devils in him who wanted him to spend his life as a cripple had reasserted their control. But, as the days passed, it became obvious that they were now too weak to maintain that hold. Muscle by muscle, David's limbs again began to relax.

Eventually, with my help, he began to voice words, as he had first done in screaming my name at the church. With mulish determination, he built up his vocabulary. The same powerful will that had kept him like a conch deep in its shell now propelled him toward the world. David took his first steps on crutches. He began to make visits with me to the sick house, and to the asylum where he spent hours talking to those children who were least disturbed. The servants who had once tended him were now his assistants, carting him on our rounds, helping him out of the wagon and following as he lurched through the asylum on his crutches from child to child.

To the people of the city, who had been accustomed to seeing him as a contorted creature in a cart, he had become "the Miracle of Thessalonica." Wherever he went now, the sick, hoping to find a cure from his cure, reached out to touch him. But at first he withdrew, even cringed.

"What would it hurt to let them touch you?" I asked. "Perhaps a touch, a blessing from you would reach something in them that would make their pain easier. Half the miracles you hear about are no more than that." Gradually, he relented.

The "miracle" increased our church membership. It also established me as the first among equals in the leadership. More and more, Amos, initially from gratitude and then from zeal, became my elder partner in the church, supporting his work with more largess. I felt secure enough to rent a medium-sized house where I could hold meetings and bring houseguests, using drafts on my dwindling inheritance to pay for it.

Our church sent out missionaries, four men and one woman, avoiding areas near Philippi and Beroea, where there were strong Paulist churches, for we did not want to invite antagonism. They worked in northern Macedonia among the Axius River settlements, and into the hinterland. In these sparsely populated regions, there were Christians who had been out of touch with any large churches for years. The missioners reported back that although the fields had been long untended, their seeds were taking root.

Their enthusiasm caught at my heart. If Aristarchus could ever turn from Paul sufficiently for me to feel secure in leaving Thessalonica, someday perhaps I, too, could go on a mission toward the Bosphorus. Along that vast littoral, small Christian cults proliferated, many faithful to the teachings of John the Baptist. They were not subject to Paul's epistles and visits. If I could convince them my view of Jesus was correct, it would mean thousands of members, all loyal to our church.

With the abundance of our success, I was ready to put into effect another of my dreams. "I want to hold a convocation," I said to David on one of those increasingly rare days when his expansion into life gave us time to talk at leisure. He was now able to walk with a cane. His speech, while comprehensible, was peculiarly economical.

"I want to invite Belzek here," I said, "and Drobyta from Laranda, and Ahiam and Rechab, if they will come, and the others I knew from Asia Minor, and perhaps a few from Thessaly. I would like to invite Thomas and John as honored guests, even if they do not come.

I can begin to do on a small scale what Paul has done to establish a dogma."

"And will you invite Aristarchus and Secundus?" David asked.

I discussed the convocation with them, and Aristarchus said it would put the church at Thessalonica even more at odds with Paul. Beneath this objection, I could feel his resentment of my gradual usurpation of his powers. Secundus looked woeful and wrung his hands. But they lacked the power to oppose me. And Paul remained mysteriously silent now when they most needed him.

I sent out invitations by land and sea, asking the ministers to come in September, which would give them time to return home by ship. In my heart, as I did, I knew that one Christian would be missing and that her absence would outweigh the presence of all the others. I had never heard from Deborah. And although I had asked Ezra to get her address from Bediah, Bediah had declined.

I heard from Belzek, Drobyta, from the leaders in Sardis and Pessinus. The ministers in Heraclea and Amastris also said they would come. Ahiam said he and Rechab were making every effort, although he cautiously said they could make no doctrinal commitment without speaking first with the Apostolic Council. And, to my delight, Thomas said he would come; John, however, was ailing and could not.

※

Late one day, from my window, I saw David approaching my door at a fast, strong limp, assisted only by a cane, for his left side would never be fully able. It was hard to remember him as that great spiderlike creature casting his bilious glance from the four-wheeled cart. Yet, even this new David was exhausted, favoring his right leg even more than usual.

"Your convocation will get you trouble," he said when I had poured us both wine.

"How do you know?"

"Say nothing about it—the father of one of our children." That would be, I knew, a Romanized Jew who was secretary for the governor's intelligence service and whose once-mute daughter David was teaching to say a few words.

"Trouble from whom?"

"Khortiatis, the alluvial plain." These were the Paulist extremists. "The Macedonian Ethnarchs"—a league of pagan high priests who worshipped Nero as a divinity. "The Zealots and *sicarii*. Word of your convocation has spread. They all see it as an avalanche intended to bury them. Cancel it," David warned.

But I could not, even if it were not too late.

***

Thomas was the first of our conferees to knock at my door. I cried out with joy. He was leaner than ever, his hair white. At supper on the terrace as the sun set, he said, "It was the wisest thing you ever did, Demas, breaking with them all. How I wish I had done it years ago. . . ."

He probed me about Paul, my travels, about Thessalonica. He told me, and I felt a whiff of pride over it, that the Antioch church was using the research I had done for Paul to win over Nazarenes in Palestine and beyond. The subject brought him gloomily to the Apostolic Council.

"It dies a little every day. Matthew spends all his time revising his scrolls. John has just about enough energy left for his. . . ." Indeed, John had sent with Thomas a copy of his work so far. "The rest of us . . ." His shoulders dropped. "All around us, talk of a Jewish rebellion. Rome makes concessions to the Zealots one day, and crucifies them the next. It will all tumble down like towers in an earthquake in a year or two."

Before the others arrived, I got Aristarchus and Secundus to come over and eat and drink with us.

"Why can't you accept Demas?" Thomas asked them bluntly.

"It would be easier if we could, good Thomas," said Aristarchus, "but who better than you, an original disciple, understands loyalty. . . ."

"There are not that many doctrinal differences between Paul and Demas," said Thomas. "I cannot agree with everything either of them says. We disciples did not—do not—agree with each other. That is the beauty of Christianity."

"We feel," said Aristarchus obdurately, "that without Paul's strictness, things do not hold together. We need to preach discipline"—he smiled—"even though we do not seem able to get anyone to practice it. The views of Demas—and I am not trying to start an argument—are too marshy to stand on."

Thomas was enjoying the dialectic. "Concede though, Aristarchus, none of us knows precisely how God wants us to find our way to heaven, whether Demas's or Paul's or yours or my views most please him or most offend him. Can you not be looser?"

Secundus, as he was wont sometimes to do, came out of his diffidence to sum things up. "Paul and we preach, 'Be good, there is a judgment day.' Demas, and I gather you, preach, 'Be good, there *may* be a judgment day'—a world of difference."

"Secundus," said Thomas, "Paul will not be with us much longer. Nero will be casting around for someone to blame for something; Paul will come to mind, and like that"—he snapped his fingers—"he will be on a cross or chopping block."

"Then," said Secundus, "all the more reason for us to be loyal to him." There was a sublimity in his quiet principle.

Two days later, Belzek arrived with his deputy, a bushy-bearded spice merchant. Belzek, his scarred face, broken chin and teeth, and strongman's build anomalous among the ministers, gave me a hug that crushed more wind out of me than I had ever breathed into him. Prebea, he said, had been a harsh but fair ruler. When criminals were caught, whether they were murderers or his own underlings dipping into the exchequer, they paid with torture or death or both. The favorite parable of Prebea was the one on rendering unto Caesar. "I do a great amount of rendering unto my brother-in-law," complained Belzek, "and he does very little rendering unto Jesus."

Drobyta, the silversmith of Laranda, came next. His spare, straight body had wasted in the ten years since I had seen him until his shoulders turned in like a man carrying a heavy sack of ore. He had a growth in his chest so large I could see its outline. We both knew this would be the last time we would see each other this side of the hereafter. I introduced him to Thomas, an honor he wanted. Thomas, never less cynical, prayed quietly with him in an empty room while the rest of us pretended nothing was happening.

Nistera, the young Lycaonian who had competed at the games, had come, too, with his wife, Gerta, the daughter of Thetorix. They smiled as they presented me with the ethnarch's gift: a garnet-incrusted jug of fermented mare's milk. Thetorix, they said, still embraced Christianity after his fashion. He continued to mix it with vestigial elements of druidism. When his black stallion died, Thetorix required Drobyta to give it a Christian burial. The Gauls, all now nominally Christians, had been pleased to hear from Thetorix that the horse was now in Jesus' stable—beside the simple donkey on which he had ridden into Jerusalem—in case Jesus wanted a more spirited ride in the holy meadows.

The former gnostic of Sardis and the blacksmith of Pessimus arrived, followed by the ministers of Heraclea and Amastris, both dressed in the Persian style. Four more delegates came from Asia Minor and two from Thessaly. The last to arrive were Rechab and Ahiam. They and Thomas stayed with me. Our own missioners had come back for the convocation. From town, there were Amos, David, and several of our church leaders. To my satisfaction, Aristarchus and Secundus attended, although they were there only to observe. They honestly advised me they planned to report back to Paul on the gathering.

We held our first meeting at two long tables on my terrace and I felt a surge of pride as I looked at these thirty brave and good people. Paul must have felt something similar in Antioch when he first realized that his lonely work had become a movement. Thomas opened the convocation with a prayer.

Then, I told them of my journey to find the truth of Jesus and of my conclusions. I said that if I could convince them that the Jesus I had discovered was the true Jesus, then there were imperative reasons for us to go forth zealously and preach this Jesus. At present, a confusion of Jesuses were being taught—by the leaders of the Apostolic Council, by the followers of John the Baptist, by Paul.

"Paul is my main concern," I told them, "for he is the most persuasive. He was my greatest teacher, but I am alienated from him, although his shadow, sometimes bright, sometimes dark, still is over all my thoughts. Paul tells us he speaks from a flash of revelation. I can offer nothing so romantic, only the hard work of a lawyer. How much easier it would have been for us and for the church at large if I had found it was all as Paul said it was. But I did not. Therefore, to have stayed with him would have been, I felt, a betrayal of Jesus. A choice was forced on me and I chose Jesus."

The group I had called together were rebels: pagans against paganism, Jews against the Mosaic Law, Roman citizens against emperor worship, Paulists against Paul. I had asked them to believe in a Christ who forced them, more than other Christians, to become even greater revolutionaries.

The scorn of Jesus for slavery, his support of the poor against the powerful and rich, ran counter to the whole Roman system. So if our convocation accepted the Jesus I espoused, that would enroll them not only against Paul and the leadership of the Apostolic Council, but against an increasingly dangerous Nero. With so much at stake, they drummed me with questions. I did my best to answer them until my voice was little more than a croak. We broke up well after midnight, still just getting started.

It was not until the fourth day that we arrived at a credo broad enough for all of us to accept, with Aristarchus and Secundus, of course, abstaining. Thomas had been magnificent, a word to moderate me here, a word to bring along Rechab there. Even so, Rechab had several of the Apostolic Council's tenets about the Law in his gorge

413

and he would not spit them out. We made several exceptions in our credo for him and Ahiam.

On the fifth day, we dealt with organization. We worked on maps, laying out on them the regions where each would work. We saw opportunities without openly challenging Paulists or the Apostolic Council, not just in places where we were already working, but in Cappadoccia and Galatia. There, many Christians had lost touch with Jerusalem, Antioch, Ephesus . . . and Rome.

Belzek had more than enough work in Bayba, but was willing to free the spice merchant, a water wheel of energy, for a mission across the Black Sea to Theodosia and neighboring cities. Nistera and the smith of Pessinus talked of sending a joint mission to Armenia and possibly on into Parthia.

At the church building that Sunday, the visitors each said a few words. The crowd overflowed into the streets. Thomas, dressed in a white linen tunic with an intricately worked leather girdle, the gift of Ahiam, said, "These delegates have been called by Jesus as he called us long ago beside Galilee. Henceforth, what you say of our Lord in your families will be the same words received by our brothers and sisters from Tanais on the great Black Sea to Carana in distant Armenia and back. In this way, we share the love of Jesus Christ with others in whatever language and beneath skins of whatever color."

I spoke last and most briefly. "We send out a new line of Alexanders from Macedonia," I said, "this time not armed with swords, which only temporarily conquer, but with the words of Jesus, which are eternal. Thus, in our dispatch of these brave men and women, we ourselves become the conquering word of God."

We held the love feast in a grove, the autumn colors already in the trees that sheltered us. The air was savory with the smells of grilling fish, of an ox haunch turning over the coals, of fennel, dill, and rosemary. Everyone drank heartily of the resinous red wines of Macedonia and the golden ones of the islands. Aristarchus and Secundus joined Thomas in serving the Communion cup. The daughter of Thetorix, and the woman missioner we had sent along the Axius, passed out the bread.

These were among the happiest hours of my life. The fields were heavy with the harvest, and we were deploying intrepid men and women to reap Christians in the world's far places. The drone of bees on the remains of our feast, all the smells and sounds of fall, and the beautiful, hopeful, varied voices of our community seemed an antiphonal hymn to the God who sent us his son. Aristarchus and I stood apart briefly.

"If only it were always so," I said.

"Yes"—he sighed from the heart—"if only."

As the delegates departed for their home churches or the life of the road, I yearned to be going with them. I missed that time in the morning when I had left my tent or hut or room to take up my pack and march with Paul. When I thought of the road, I also thought of how I had longed for Deborah in those days, and of how much I missed her now.

The convocation had a volcanic effect on the extremists of the mountain and the plain. From our parishioners who still had friends among them, we learned that a vagrant soothsayer and necromancer, one Simon of Aegae, had seized on our meeting to feed their strangeness and hatred. He had prophesied that our evil apostasy had so fired the wrath of God that God had fixed the second Sunday from now as the day when sulphurous fire would descend from heaven and destroy Thessalonica and the world.

The extremists sent secret emissaries to our most conservative members urging them to leave us while there was still time for salvation. Others among them prayed in a frenzy of hate for our eternal damnation because we had precipitated the end of a world they were not quite ready to leave.

On the first Sunday after Simon of Acgae's prophecy, we held a love feast and Communion on our newly cobbled grounds behind the church. Our ministers were circulating among the congregation with bread and wine, when from the street in front of the building we heard first one scream, then another.

At the same time, a mob, all dressed in Lord's Day finery but armed with rocks and clubs, rounded the corner of the church. I recognized two or three ultra-Paulists from Khortiatis. The two hundred people at our Communion scattered, women running toward the streets behind the church with robes flying like a clothesline suddenly caught by high winds. Aristarchus led a group of men and some women into the building to defend it.

Amos, I, and others grabbed knives we had used to cut our meats and cheeses, pokers, grates, even long stirring spoons. The insurgents rained rocks on us. Our youngsters snatched them up and handed them to older youths or men to hurl back. We outnumbered our assailants, and I took a step forward to lead a counterattack. But a stone hit my chest and I fell. Amos pushed in front, a huge pot lid in his hand as a shield. "Hold the rocks," he shouted.

The attackers came at us with clubs. "Now throw," Amos bawled. Our stones slammed into the first rank, knocking down several of them. Amos's militia charged, picking up the fallen clubs and striking, sinewy Amos pounding heads as if they were fence posts. Overwhelmed, the invaders retreated. I staggered up and went with the others to aid our friends in the church.

The Khortiatis mob filled the rear, hurling stones at our defenders, who were behind a barricade of benches we kept in the church for the old and disabled. Several of our women, bending low, dragged our wounded men to the rear door. Aristarchus and his group had picked up hurled stones and empty wine jars and awaited the assault. Leading the hill people was a cadaverous man of forty with a forked beard and braided hair. He wore a royal blue robe and held a dagger he had drawn from a gold sheath on his brocaded girdle.

It was Simon of Aegae, I was sure. In a shrill voice, he urged on the attackers. A man beside him, a defector from our church, saw me and screamed, "There he is, Demas, the Anti-Christ!" Soon the rest had picked it up.

"Go, Demas!" Aristarchus said, trying to shove me back.

"Kill the Anti-Christ!" the soothsayer screamed. "Do the work of our Lord Jesus while we can!" He was nothing if not fearless. They were six arm's lengths from us. To my left, side by side, were a bent seventy-year-old and a boy of twelve, both with looks of eagerness. No one was turning the other cheek.

Simon, in his eyes, a glitter of power, even cruel majesty, pointed his dagger at me where I crouched behind our barricade. "We seek only to destroy the Anti-Christ," he called. "You other sinners we will only scourge and forgive. Push him out where we can give him the justice of God."

Our flock paid no attention to him. At Aristarchus's whispered order, we braced to heave the barricades over on them. The slowly advancing wizard opened his lips to cry again, but Aristarchus shouted, "Push!" and we shoved with all our pent-up might. The benches catapulted onto the floor and trundled into the marauders. Those in front tumbled down.

We rushed them and crashed our stones and pottery jars on their heads. The men behind them, off balance, could swing their clubs only awkwardly. The necromancer fell, but was hoisted erect by his followers. How I wished for my knife. I would show that a magician whose magic cannot protect him is no magician. My heavy stone cocked, I went after him. He cut at me.

I heard the ghastly "conk" of a cudgel on the head of Aristarchus beside me. Someone had clubbed him from behind. He spun, his arms instinctively coming to his head lest another blow fall. The hill man who had struck him was drawing back for a second swing when I banged my stone on his nose, collapsing him. I scooped up his club and fended off the blows of a second man.

Seeing me beleaguered, the soothsayer took a girlish swipe at me with his fancy dagger. I pushed off my immediate adversary and lashed the cudgel at Simon, striking him a glancing blow on his upper arm. I grasped his gown and it tore, baring the pale flesh of his skinny chest. He knew no more about self-defense than a pet finch. When he raised the knife to stab, he left his face fully exposed. I rammed the club into his mouth, smashing his front teeth. The blood poured from his lips, and he cawed like a dying crow. His dagger arm came down feebly and I grabbed his wrist, twisting violently. The elbow made a loud pop and he dropped the blade. His caws became shrieks and then I was shoved and wrestled away from him by his retreating allies.

In a few minutes, the last of the invaders were running down the street, chased by our stalwarts. Behind them they left three unconscious men and one dead. A number of our own, among them Aristarchus, had been stunned and we had our share of aching pates. I found the necromancer's dagger. Its blade was chased with moons and snakes, its gold pommel was a salamander's head with amethyst eyes. I gave it to Aristarchus as a keepsake.

The second Sunday in November, Simon's Doomsday, came and went with Thessalonica and the world still blundering on. The disappointed extremists, as we had expected, drove Simon of Aegae from their midst and hated us all the more because his prophecy had been wrong.

XXXVIII

A few days later, a messenger brought a letter in Deborah's handwriting from Cissusaea, just two hours' sail down the Thermaic Gulf from Thessalonica. I could not believe it at first. Surely, it had been simply missent from Spain to the little harbor town from which someone was forwarding it to me. But the wrapper was clean, virtually unhandled. I took it from the hand of the skiff man, forgetting his fee, and read it for a moment while he stood by, then, embarrassed, overpaid him.

"I arrived in Cissusaea an hour ago from Italy," it said. "I am lodged with my daughter at number seven in the Street of Carders. My son is with God. Not knowing how things might be with you if I came to Thessalonica, I thought it safest for you to come here. Hoshea agreed to let me go, through an agreement less strange than our last one. I love you. Hurry."

I stood in shock. Deborah just across the bay? Micah dead? Deborah free of Hoshea, free to love me, to marry, to live with me? That was what I had yearned for since that day fifteen years ago when I had seen her rubbing scent on the dead face of Andrew. What pernicious impediments there had been in the path of our love since then. Now they were gone.

Then why didn't I shout for joy instead of trembling with concern? I stood wringing my hands. I knew the answer. I had convinced myself that her return to Hoshea's arms was overwhelming evidence of her capriciousness and treachery. Her distress on the morning we had parted was proof of her hysteria, her instability, her cruelty. I had told myself that our love was only a series of betrayals, sins, and selfishness.

By forcing my mind and heart to accept these and other negative thoughts, I had made of our love a thing of stumps, as thoroughly cauterized as Rechab's leg. I had protected myself from hope and hurt by making her undeserving of me, and by convicting our love of being a thing of shame.

I saw as clearly as if they were before me the lines of Catullus: "*Orci, quae omnia bella deuoratis . . .*" I had invited in the master of hell, who devours all things beautiful, and he had eaten the sweet, pure, unfulfilled love Deborah and I had at first, as well as the more difficult love we had found in each other's beds.

Yet for all his and my efforts, I thought, Deborah's letter still in my hand, the ravening teeth of Orcus had broken on the innermost core of my love. Orcus had withdrawn, defeated, and I, no longer protected by the safety of distance from my lover, nor hidden behind my shield of resentment, could think freely again of Deborah's lips, her body, her quick, prickly mind, her emotions that swung from passivity to compulsive energy in a single day, her dedication, her will to achieve what she would. This Deborah was just across the bay, here, entire, like me, with all her sins and virtues upon her.

The imposing house where Deborah had taken a room was of limestone with marble steps. She was obviously not without funds. She let me in, the baby in her arms, reserve in her voice and a desperate hope in her eyes. Once we were inside, she put the baby on the bed and fell into my arms. She held me silently and powerfully, her face against my shoulder.

"So awful," she said, "so awful."

At an uncommon loss for apt words, I said, "Thank God, you're here. I never dreamed . . ." I stopped, constrained.

Deborah broke away and fixed me with her eyes, which seemed darker, more cautious than they had ever been. "You are sorry I came. I can see it."

"No, I am glad. But I am desolated about the boy. I have you only because he died. And I sorrow that this has been a period in hell for you."

"My coming makes things difficult for you."

Of course it did. Why lie? "Yes." I could feel us coming unstuck, separating. I could not let that happen. It was not possible that it would happen. "It doesn't matter," I added hurriedly. "And how could it be helped if it did? You are part of my life, the way my blood is part of my life. . . ." I paused, aware that years ago, she had said the opposite of what I was about to say: " . . . The way that Jesus is part of my life."

She gazed at me, understanding the criticism, even my old resentment at what she had done then. I saw the gray hairs at her temple, which she had unsuccessfully tried to darken away with kohl, and the wrinkles at her eye corners that did not tend upward as they do in people who are growing older happily.

"I only know," she said, "that I am here because it would be impossible for me not to come to you when I found I could."

Her way of speaking was so familiar. My love for her made my voice weak. "You are here because I brought dead Andrew to Modi'im and because you were there and I saw you."

She turned her face up to me and we kissed, not hungrily, but firmly, a pledge. "So much, so much has happened, and none of it good," she said. With the baby cradled in her arms and I across from her in a chair, she filled in the great gaps.

The changes in Hoshea began when their daughter was born. Deborah had underestimated how much Hoshea wanted a second boy, a healthy one. He tried to love the girl, but could not conceal his disappointment. He reinvested his love and hopes in the ailing Micah. The boy grew weaker, and Deborah forced herself to admit he might die, but Hoshea refused even to imagine it.

When it happened, Hoshea's grief put him beyond the reach of Deborah. He was quiet, polite, but distant. He made gestures toward consoling her, but they were only that, while she felt that her sympathy for him was genuine. In the last months, he made no pretense of wanting her. One night, he expressed what she, too, had come to feel and what also afflicted me.

"We killed him with our sins," Hoshea told her.

That night, they made love for the last time. In the darkness, he requited, she unable to be, she said, "What happens to us, to me and the baby? There is no longer any love here."

"I do not know," he said. "I cannot think."

But perhaps he did know. A month later, he said he had been called away to Carteia, a day's journey, to handle a shipment of ceramics. He was absent for a week. "You have gone back," she said when he came home. She forced him to say enough for her to infer that it was not even a respectable homosexual or bisexual, but an expensive male whore. So that was the end.

With Hoshea enfeebled by self-disgust and the unhealing wound of

Micah's death, Deborah was able to wrest from him an agreement to divorce her. They said to their few friends in Malaca, where they lived, that she was going home to nurse her aging and ill mother and wanted him to be free to remarry. He paid her the *kethubah* of the divorcing man and she left, first to seek me in Rome. But Christians there told her that Paul had put me from him and that I had come to Thessalonica.

"Demas," she said, "even as I sailed, I worried lest I bring to you not only my love, but my ill luck, my misfortunes."

I rose and she moved the baby carefully to the rug, cushioning it with a pillow. She opened her arms and I entered them. At first our kisses were consolatory, but they soon quickened into passion. Frantic as the sailors on the ship throwing over everything movable, we jettisoned our clothes onto the floor. Her heavy breasts leaked milk on me as, from groin to lips, we clasped ourselves together.

Late that afternoon, we walked to a shady spot by a wall whose crevices cascaded rue and arbutus. We sat on my light cloak, the child, Zephra, babbling good-humoredly while Deborah—then I— dandled her gently. I told Deborah about Thessalonica and we discussed the problems of me marrying a divorced woman.

Jesus had said such remarriages were adultery, but when it came to cases, he had seemed to give permission to the divorced man I had spoken with. Mosaic Law said unequivocally that a divorced woman could remarry. But I could only use that latter argument carefully, for I had rejected so many other aspects of Mosaic Law. Those in the congregation who already found me factitious would have grounds to defame me as a hypocrite and even parishioners partial to me might turn on me.

A breath of chill blew in from the bay, and I knew it was time for her and the baby to return to their room. "Can you stay?" she asked. Nestling to her on this first night of our new life was a compelling attraction. But it was also a faulted one. If, after I announced my plans to marry Deborah, it became known that I had spent the night with her in Cissusaea, I would be doubly damned. My remaining conservative parishioners, no matter what their own wanderings, would flay me. If I could say I met my love by day, but left her before night, it would help our case.

"Saint Demas the Politician," she said, following my thought. "When will you be back?"

"In a day or two. With a plan. And a chaperone."

I made my arguments to Amos and David. Neither was happy about the situation; both promised to do whatever they could to help me. I spoke at length to Aristarchus and Secundus. I could see they felt it would weaken my standing with the church. But they were sick to death of controversy. They promised they would not publicly denounce me.

Before I returned to Cissusaea, I also spoke to a dozen of our elders, both men and women. Since none had known of Deborah, they were confused. But they were also, I felt, somewhat in spite of themselves, curious to see this woman who, with her child, had come so far to marry their minister.

Amos and David—his first boat trip—went with me to Cissusaea. Deborah was warm, gracious, dignified, everything she could be at her best. We talked strategies for an hour, then left for the harbor. The boatman had spread the word that the Miracle of Thessalonica was in Cissusaea. By the time we were prepared to board, we had a crowd of fifty or sixty around us, several of them cripples brought to the dock by relatives.

David had progressed a long way since rejecting the touch of those who sought cures from him. He put his hands on the heads of the cripples and said, "I have no special powers, but my feelings are with you. May God help you as I was helped." For David, that was a long blessing.

The next Sunday, I told the congregation I wanted to marry. I said I had met Deborah at the burial of Andrew and that we had worked together as ministers in Borhaurus. I told how we had separated, feeling we could not serve both God and marriage. I said she had married and her husband had twice left her for liaisons considered unnatural by both Christian and Mosaic Law and that now he had also left the church and divorced her. I made the case for her remarriage, using the precedents from Jesus and—circumspectly—Moses. I did not say that we had been adulterers.

"I want to continue as one of your shepherds," I said. "I beg you, if you feel critical of my wishes, yield to them only for the time being and then monitor Deborah's behavior. Let her speak with you. See whether she helps the poor, whether she ministers to your loved ones when they are ill, whether she comes to you in the cold, dark watches of the night when you are in dread, whether she is by you when your loved ones are dying. If you find her wanting in these things, drive her and me from your midst, for she will not have deserved your trust and I will have misled you. But if you find her as I do, then take her to your bosoms and let us go on in the love of Jesus."

I asked the congregation to talk among themselves for an hour and then vote either to let us try to prove ourselves, or to reject us. If they rejected us, I would leave Thessalonica forever. If they did not, I would marry Deborah in two weeks. The meeting place was a Babel for that hour, but when I returned and asked for the vote, a heavy majority raised their hands in favor of us. Only my most dedicated partisans did so with much enthusiasm. Aristarchus and Secundus kept their hands in their laps, and a fair number who had looked toward them for guidance did likewise. Aristarchus, I knew, would send a report to Paul. There was nothing I could do about that.

When in two weeks there had been no groundswell against me, Amos married us. He had recently been made a deputy minister by the congregation, coequal with Secundus. David crushed the ritual pomegranate in his strengthening fingers; his mother, tears in her eyes, broke the traditional vial of scent. It was attar of hyacinth, named for a mortal whom the God Apollo loved and mistakenly slew.

Deborah and I settled into my house. Our life together began with more apprehension than ardor due to the contrived way I had made it possible, and our feeling that the whole Christian community was watching us. Still, at day's end, when Zephra was fed, we could go to our bed as man and wife at last. Most of the romance and much of the relief got swallowed up for me in the first week by my efforts to adjust to life with another person. I had been a bachelor thirty-six years, used to the space I lived in, great or small, being my own.

Now, instead of merely *my* footsteps, *my* whistling, *my* belches and mutterings, *my* door closings, there were baby noises, clothes rustlings, furniture shifting—foreign presences. The old woman who cleaned for me was soon getting new orders from Deborah, all without consultations with me. Even when Deborah's warm body was beside me, the spell was broken by the baby in the crib beside us who whined, then yelped for milk.

One morning, Deborah, her face, like mine, puffy from lack of sleep, looked at me shrewdly. "How do you feel about married life?"

"Bewildered," I said.

"Second thoughts?" She felt secure enough to ask.

"No," I said, knowing that mine were the classic complaints of the fallen bachelor. I was sure that our love would prevail, aware in my heart that I liked being married more than being single. And soon, we were finding again the pleasures of Raphia, in some ways more ecstatically because we were unhampered by the danger of exposure, by the uncertainty of not knowing how long we could stay in each other's arms, by the unhealthiness of our contract with Hoshea.

The ordinaries of my life kept me from her more than I liked. The church had advanced money for the missioners from our building fund. To finish the church building and to construct a small meeting place on the western outskirts, I had to knock again on the doors of our wealthier members. More than ever, I had to keep up my personal visits to our flock lest it appear I was more interested in power, in foreign missions, in marriage, than in those who relied on me, and on whom, in turn, I relied.

Deborah was weaning the baby early, and integrated herself quickly into the parish work. She went with David to the asylum and began accompanying me on calls to the sick and the dying. A blessedly limited outbreak of plague in a poor quarter along the old Mygdonian road frightened us for ourselves and even more for Zephra. But the risks had to be taken: Deborah and I visited and comforted the dehydrated victims, dripping water into mouths blackening with the fatal disease.

On some few evenings when there was no chill in the air, we went to the beach and waded, listening to the plaint of the waves, and watched the day die. Often we talked of the old days, but more often of what lay ahead. I began to think that by spring, if Paul did not intrude and nothing unforeseen happened, we three would be able to take the road to Bithynia for a month or two, leaving Amos as suffragan in Thessalonica.

Violence was in the wind and the madness of Nero began to blow over the Adriatic and the Greek peninsula. The governor called in Aristarchus and me one day. He was not so haughty now. We had become a stronger and therefore a more dangerous group. He knew of the battle at the church and how hard we would fight. Yet he had gotten orders from Rome that affected us and that he dared not disregard.

First, he was instructed to send his few auxiliary legionnaires to Palestine. This would leave only constables and lictors to keep the public order. Even these poorly trained functionaries were to be used mainly to protect Roman property, and, as the new decree put it, "in no case to suppress rioting among the sects, particularly if it is directed against the cult of Jesus, called the Christus." Nero was taking the lidded pot off the hob and putting it on the fire, where it would boil toward a scalding overflow.

This new hazard made us work all the harder to strengthen our church. Yet, in spite of the labors of recruitment, I did not neglect the writing I had begun in Palestine and had continued in Thessalonica. My latest idea was to write two separate works.

The first would summarize my discoveries about Jesus and my observations about Paul and the other disciples. I would include in this scroll the happenings of my own life. My reasoning was that if—unlike Paul, Luke, Matthew, John, and Peter, through Mark—I stated unabashedly what my life had been, then my readers would be better able to decide whether the Demas who presented this Jesus and these apostles was a fair or biased historian. All would know my *bona fides*. How much more Plato, with whom I did not compare myself, would have meant to us if we knew him as a person, knew the context in which his great brain worked. Did he stray with women? What wines did he prefer? What adventures did he have as a young man?

The second scroll would be a detailed compendium of all the stories I had heard about Jesus, with the sources listed, and with my assessment of how authentic I thought each one was.

I would send these two scrolls to the churches I had helped establish or revitalized. In addition, I would send them occasional epistles in the manner of Paul's exhortations, encouragements and polemical arguments. These epistles would contain news of other churches and of Christianity at large. In effect, I would be challenging Paul at his own game.

In beginning my first scroll, I used Herodotus and Livy as my models, for, like them, I was curious, skeptical, and credulous by turns, cynical and naïve. If only, I thought, I could write half as well as either. I found a talented student at the academy to help me. He transcribed my manuscript on scrolls of parchment. We proceeded at a rapid pace. Deborah, fascinated, made it a joint project, balking only at some of the details about us. I left them in, agreeing with her to take them out if, at the end, she still strongly objected.

My greater problem was that my writing seemed so shallow compared to the work of Paul and Luke, Mark and Peter, John, even Matthew. When I complained of it to Deborah, she replied much as she had that day at the shrine of Dagon.

"Demas, you are sniveling. Why speak of depth? A man like you can work as hard for Jesus, love him as purely, please him as completely, as Paul or anyone else. You can live as gloriously for Jesus, or die as gloriously. You almost did. The writing you leave behind can be just as important if the people who read it feel that it touches their own lives. A man who is not created on this grand scale you talk about, not a genius like Paul, or with native depth like, say, Dathan or Rechab, can be every bit as much a beacon for Jesus. Or just for goodness. And for all the ages to come."

I was moved, yet unable to respond except in a bantering tone. "Thank you, Deborah, but name me one shallow person in history who fits that description."

"Adam." She smiled.

"Adam didn't *do* anything," I said. "He was *done to.*"

"All right, Noah, Jacob, Ruth, and Esther. They never became Jeremiahs or Ezekials, but we remember them."

"Job?" I joined in the game. "He began as weightless as I am. But adversity *made* him heavy. It just makes me grumble."

"Aristophanes?" she said.

"Thank you. Aesop?"

"Augustus?"

"Aphrodite?"

"See? All shallow, useful, and immortal. And not even finished with the *a*'s." She had made her point.

XXXIX

One night by the fire, we read the section about our life in Borhaurus, arguing about the accuracy of our memories. She, exhausted from a day with a woman in her first labor, kissed me and left me to correct the places where she had convinced me I was wrong. As I worked, the old servant came in.

"There is a man named Titus below who says he knows you. He wears a sword."

I was as astonished as if I had been splashed with icy water. "Let him come up," I stammered.

"His sword?"

"As he is."

I tried to put together my thoughts as Titus's forceful steps thumped on the stairs. By the time he entered, along with consternation, I felt a kind of relief: the *praelusio* was over.

"Hello, Demas," Titus said, not offering his hand, though I had stretched out mine. His hot determined eyes took in the room, so comfortable by our standards of the road. "Are you surprised to see me?"

"It had to be someone," I said, motioning him to a chair.

"A nice place," he said with his familiar scorn. He looked at the scrolls I had been working on at the table. "The Gospel according to Demas?" he asked.

"No," I lied. I folded the notes and rolled up the scrolls and pushed them to the far end of the table.

"Make it good," he said as he watched me. "Paul and Luke have

427

decided to cut you out of theirs." Was he saying they had excised me from their record of Paul's life and work? For an instant, I did not believe Paul would be so petty.

"Everything?"

"Just that you were someone who deserted him." I could see how pleased Titus was at my hurt and tried not to give him the satisfaction of seeing it. "But I'm not here for that," Titus went on, "Paul is in serious trouble. Little by little they are taking away his freedom. Such friends as we have near Nero tell us he thinks of destroying our leadership in Rome." Titus said it without fear, concealing any other emotion.

"I begged him to leave," I said, still hurt that Paul would omit me from his story. "I thought I could have convinced them to exile him to Spain or someplace."

"It's useless for anyone to try. Even if Nero would let him go, Paul would not do it. You can imagine. He says if they decide to . . . do away with him"—Titus was not quite able to say "kill him"—"then that is what God wants."

I thought of the physicality of death, the tired gnomic body limp on the cross, or the severed head a pace from the bloody shoulders, Paul dead, the spirit flown. "I am not ready for Paul to die," I said softly.

"Suppose it would save him, would you quit preaching?"

In my heart, something said, yes, if it would save Paul. But Titus and I, not Paul, were asking that question. Thanks be to God, therefore, I did not have to answer it. "You are not saying that my quitting would persuade him to save himself? I do not think you are."

"No, of course not, I am only curious about how much this journey of yours into hubris means to you."

"Well, you will have to stay curious," I said.

"He could die, if he must, so much happier," Titus went on moderately. "Paul loves the Thessalonians. He thinks of you undoing all his work here and trying to do the same in Greece and Asia Minor. He sent me to ask you to quit preaching. That is why I am here. I told him, Luke told him, that you do not have the brains or the following, so he should stop worrying."

Wait and see, I said to myself. But I, too, remained mild. "Except for Thessalonica," I said, "we are not fishing in waters where he has churches."

"Demas, I know you. That will not last. Nothing is ever enough for you. When Paul is gone and the rest of them with him, you will become greedy, even if you cannot digest what you chew."

"The rest of *them*. You mean you—"

"He wants me and Mark to leave Rome."

"And he wants *you* to get me to leave Thessalonica so you can step in and take *my* place?" My choler bubbled up: "Who, by all the shades of Hades, do you think you are, Titus? You spy on me in Italy; Paul forces me out of Rome; he cuts nine years of my life out of his history; and then you come down here and snap your fingers and think I will strip naked and sit on a column in the desert so *you* can have Thessalonica?" I got myself under control. We both sat silently, I still breathing hard. "I am sorry," I said at last. "No matter what he has done, I would do anything to help free him. But I will not leave."

"Not even to take this thorn out of his flesh?"

"Once, yes, not now. I have work that I must do. I am not willing to quit preaching for Paul, not willing to obey him anymore. I never looked on it as the same as obeying God and Jesus anyway. . . ." Malice made me add, "The way you do."

The blood rushed into his face. I was accusing him of heresy and impiety, even apostasy, by worshipping Paul in the same way he worshipped Jesus. "That's exactly the kind of camel turd thing a half-breed traitor *would* say," he snapped.

"Yes, to a Phrygian sandal licker," I shot back. I thought he would swing on me. Then, clenching his teeth and forcing control on himself, he said, "Enough."

We both sat tensely, waiting for the boiling to subside. I spoke first: "Titus, I am sorry, sorrier than you can believe, about Paul. I am sorry about Luke, and Timothy, particularly about Timothy. And all the rest. And it may soon be my turn. And yours, wherever you are. Because once the Furies are on the wing . . . well, you know that. But if anything is going to happen to me, it is going to be here. Rome is where Paul makes his stand. This is where I make mine."

Titus hated failure as much as I did, as much as Paul did. "Then I will work with Aristarchus and Secundus and anyone else here to thwart you," he said. "Because, when Paul is gone, I plan to preach his doctrine in Corinth, and Philippi and Ephesus and here, too. And I cannot have you preaching perversion and drunkenness . . ." He paused, calculating how much it would cost him if he gratified his desire to truly injure me. "And practicing adultery in my own backyard."

My instinct was to strike him, but somehow I held myself in and instead burst up like a water spout at sea. "You would not know what adultery is, Titus, or anything else to do with flesh. The devil never bothers to tempt people like you. You are neither good nor bad because you are nothing, a mindless yes for Paul. His man-with-a-knife. Paul's worst part . . ." Titus spluttered with rage. My voice rose enough to dominate him.

"When he says chop, you chop. When he says put your tail between your legs, you oblige. Timothy may be his puppy, but you are his mad dog, a Phrygian street mongrel. I tell you this: before I would turn a single Christian over to you, I would personally consign him to Satan incarnate."

Titus was rabid. "Satan? Satan? You *ought* to know about Satan! You turn this place into a turd-heap of corruption and sin and—" he was so full of fury, his words slurred—"bring your whore in and your bastard and then preach Jesus."

I was up and crossing the room as he finished, and hit him in the mouth with my fist as he rose to fend me off. He rocked back in the chair, but as fast as a cat rolled off its side and put the table between us while he recovered from my blow. Still enraged, I launched myself across the table, but with both hands he tipped it, me, wine and cups, my papers, all onto the floor. He rounded the litter swinging, and smacked me obliquely on the head. It opened him up for me to elbow him in the chest, knocking some of the wind from him, and he fell. I dropped on him, grasped his head in my hands, and slammed it against the bottom of the overturned table.

The impact jarred my thumb down his cheek and he clamped it in his bloody mouth. I tore skin and flesh, screaming as I tried frantically to extract it before he gnawed it off. Then with all my strength I drew back my other fist and clubbed him so hard on his cheekbone that his jaw popped open, releasing me.

All my hate for him and my frustration over the years with Paul poured elementally into my hands. I clutched his throat, ignoring the agony in my thumb, and began to strangle him. He grabbed at my wrists, found them iron with my mania, and reached up to try to claw out my eyes. I jerked my head to escape his fingers, and he bucked me off and rose to draw his sword.

I grabbed up a chair and swung, knocking him down and sending his blade clattering across the room. Suddenly, from behind me by the door, I heard a scream: Deborah's. She stood in her nightgown, open-mouthed, eyes wide at the sprawling stranger whom she must have taken for an assassin, and at the blood all over our faces. My sword was in the corner. She ripped it from its scabbard and cocked it over Titus for her downswing. Titus looked up in terror at the blade.

"No! No! No!" I shouted. "It's Titus!"

He tried to rise, but I jumped on him. Deborah dropped the sword, and like a panther threw herself on us. Between the two of us, we finally subdued him. His eyes were as small and mad as a wild pig's, running with tears of hate, rage, and frustration. Deborah, braids undone and in her face as pugnacious as any warrior, gripped his hair in one hand, his throat in the other. We held him on the floor until he stopped struggling and then let him rise. His face was a smeared, bloody mask, his chest heaving. He eyed us both with loathing.

"Get out," I said. "Never come back."

Aristarchus and Secundus now had forced on them an ally who, though he did not have the vision and intelligence of Paul, nevertheless had his unshatterable will. On the first Sunday that Titus was in town, he took the church platform and in Paul's name denounced me on every issue from divine birth to Pentecost. His bruised face—word of our fight had circulated through Aristarchus and Secundus—and his strident voice had an effectiveness I knew well from our days on the road. He began by reading a letter from Paul to the Thessalonian church.

" 'I know you are concerned for me as a prisoner for the Lord,' " Paul wrote, " 'and I am grateful, but I fear that you have been timid in your testimony for Christ Jesus. For there is one among you who you are aware has turned from me. To the names of Alexander, Hymenaeus, and Philetus of Ephesus, who preached heresies against the word of Christ Jesus, and whom I have severed from the church, I must now add Demas.' "

I felt a paralyzing anxiety and chill as I heard my name among these others. I was excommunicated.

" 'Demas has preached,' " Titus read on, " 'that sins of the flesh are of no importance. Yet a man is not two entities, one of flesh and one of the spirit. The spirit cannot be separated from the flesh like an olive from its pit or a citron from its skin. Demas has cast doubt on the resurrection and on the miracles witnessed by the apostles and saints who walked with Christ Jesus. He questions the holy ghost, the sanctity of marriage, the roles of men and women in our church, the day of judgment for both the quick and the dead promised by our savior.

" 'We all know that in a great house there are vessels of all materials, all consecrated and useful to the master of the house. Yet some of the finest may crack and be dirtied with stains so foul they cannot be washed out. These vessels are not useful and the master casts them

431

away. God grants that those who are cast out and then by the miracle of his cleansing love become perfect and wholesome again can rejoin his house.

" 'Even men snared by the devil himself may escape and again do the will of God, for whom all things are possible. But until such things happen, those who canker us with foulness must be cut from our bodies, which are the fleshly temples of God, lest they infect our members and bring us to eternal sickness. I urge you, therefore, in the presence of God and of Christ Jesus to convict, rebuke, and repudiate Demas lest he turn you away from the Lord with false teachings. . . .' "

The denunciation was complete. Genius Paul! He had read the situation with eerie accuracy. He had couched the letter so Titus, Aristarchus, and Secundus would have the best weapons possible to convince Thessalonian Christians of all persuasions that they should drive me away.

After a taut pause to let the message of Paul sink into the audience, Titus began his own execration: "Demas tells you of a new Jesus he discovered, claiming he spoke with men who knew our Lord. Paul and we who follow him have spoken for years with the men who walked with Christ Jesus. *They* saw him on the cross and tell us that he returned and ate and spoke with them. *They* attest to the many and marvelous miracles he performed. *They* preach him as the son of God. *They* pass on to us his words.

"Demas has preached that adultery is among the least of sins, but the Law of Moses punishes it with death; the Lord Jesus calls it the curse of the generations and equates it with murder. Paul tells us that it is as evil as idolatry. . . ."

And so on and on. Aristarchus had briefed him well on what I was preaching. Wisely, Titus did not directly besmirch Deborah. She was already revered for her visits to the plague victims, for her willingness to be wherever anyone in need called her to be. At the end, he announced that on the next Sunday, the church must choose between me and Paul, between Satan and Jesus. Aristarchus and Secundus, looking as if they had come fresh from their own whipping, supported him.

I was numbed. Yet, the congregation looked at me to answer. At least, thanks be to God, I had anticipated that. Two days before, I had spoken with David, who now made his laborious way forward from the rear. Row on row of eyes followed his determined limp. He paused at the platform, put his cane forward, and lurched onto it. Who could see that performance without recalling the crumpled monster in the cart?

He spoke, his locution still marred, his words spare, sharp and hard:

"We have gotten letters from Paul. We have gotten words from Titus. From Demas, we have gotten love. When we are assaulted, he risks his life and sheds his blood for us. When we are in anguish, he and Deborah come to us no matter how starless or moonless the night."

He paused as if it were difficult to go on. I was not sure whether it was the actor in him or the saint, or simply that he needed a deep breath. "When we are silent, he teaches us words. When crippled he tells our limbs to move. Because of Demas, our children who were like me have hope. Our old people go to the Lord in peace because their hands are in the hands of Demas and Deborah and, yes, of our brothers Aristarchus and Secundus. Now a great man sends someone to denounce Demas. The great man is in Rome, ready to die for the Lord. We pray each night for him. But Demas is here, needing us to reach our hands to him as he has so often done for us. I reach out my hand to Demas, our minister and my beloved friend."

With the jerky motion to which all of us had become accustomed, he extended his hand toward where I stood with Deborah in the first row. I came onto the podium and, bandaged thumb and all, took his hand in mine. Together we stepped down, I to my place, he at a shuffle down the aisle to his.

❁

During the week, Titus sought out those in the church who opposed me or whose support was wobbly. Amos, David, other loyalist leaders, and I spent the week bolstering our friends. We were helped because Paul had become identified to some extent with the extremists who had rampaged that Sunday into our church. Titus, although he had visited Thessalonica in the past, was seen now as an alien and disruptive presence.

On the next Sunday, the meeting house was crowded, and late-arriving Christians from all over our area were in the streets outside. My heart was clogged and leaden.

"We are at a dividing place," I told the members. "Even though we still flow to the same sea, we have become two rivers. If the majority flows with me, let us stay and work from this church. But let us diligently help our brothers build their own church, for that is the way of Christ. If the majority flows away from my teachings, then I pray that you who do remain with me will help me to build our own church. No matter what decision you take, let our daily prayers be that we may find some way to rejoin and again be a single river in Jesus."

As Aristarchus and I drew straws to set the order in which the vote would be cast, my gullet felt as if it would spasm. If the count were close, it would be worse than if we lost. Then the contention would never end. Aristarchus drew the long straw, and elected that those favoring my dismissal would be first to raise their hands. He stated the question bluntly. The hands shot up, for haters are ever more ready for action than the moderate. But there were nowhere near enough for him to win.

As the majority raised their hands for me to stay, I felt a relief so strong that I closed my eyes lest I grow dizzy. I opened them and looked at Deborah. Her expression was also relieved, but somber.

There were shouts of anger among the losers, but none of joy among the winners. Titus accepted the verdict with a veiled look of detestation at me. Before trouble could occur, he, Aristarchus, and Secundus left the front of the church and filed to the door. My followers made a way for them, and the defeated flock, some of them jostling their erstwhile fellow worshippers, fell in behind them and left the meeting house.

In the ensuing weeks, we stuck to our bargain. I delivered the building funds to Aristarchus, glad Titus was not with him. In Aristarchus's looks, I saw his misery. One day I went by, as many of our parishioners had, to help with the actual labor. Secundus was there, but not Aristarchus or Titus. Gently, Secundus told me that they did not want my help on the structure. I could almost hear Titus spitting out how my sinful hands would defile this new house of God.

Secundus said quietly to me, "Titus is healing the breach with the—" he looked for a way to say it that would not be disloyal to Titus—"hill and plain people."

For a moment, I was furious. Titus was inviting men of violence and hatred into a church based on love. "He is sowing noxious seeds, Secundus, and we will have to pluck poisonous berries, all of us, once he is gone."

"I don't think he is going," Secundus said dismally.

❁

During this time, if Amos and David were my strong right and left arms, Deborah was the rest of me, and whatever soul I had outside of the part that belonged to God and Jesus. I often came to bed late and snuggled into her warmth. As if in a dream of love, she turned her body and lips to me, waking even as we proffered our first soft kisses.

434

In the darkness, the turbulent spheres of anxiety, of danger and grief, of cunning and intransigence, ceased colliding. The world became calm. The quiet of our room and the night outside let my senses focus entirely on her sighs and whispers, on her silken flesh whose rippling surfaces lay over the caverns of her soul.

I could not believe our passion did not come from God. I thought of the first book of Moses, where he urged men and women to be as fruitful as the stars of heaven. Surely, there was a reason for that wise man—who said he was quoting God himself—to use the image of lush fruits and shimmering constellations when he talked of men and women populating the world. Else, when he spoke of making love, why did he not use the analogy of chickens or rabbits or goats?

If I was right, and acts of loving passion were manifestations of God at his most splendid and powerful, then it made no sense that Jesus had forgone this kind of love. Would Mary Magdalene have told me if they had made love? No. Did that mean she had lied to me—that they did? No, again.

Zephra was a year and a half old. Deborah and I wanted a child of our own. The perilous eddies in Thessalonica gave that desire immediacies we would not have had in a more tranquil time and place. We did not even say it, but, put brutally, we wanted a baby before something happened to us. Nowadays, there was an accumulation of possibilities that, in the language of gamesters, cast the lots against permanence. Nero, the ultra-Paulists, the *sicarii* and their secret Jewish supporters, the dangerous pagan fanatics, all were free-flying arrows.

At times, such thoughts on our mind, we imagined taking the remainder of Grandfather's legacy and what was left of her *kethubah* and going to some far safe place. Father had once told me there were blue lakes in Italy north of Mediolanium with villages beside them and mountains looking down. Villas there, he said, could be bought cheaply and came with tenancies that were ample to support a small family.

"You could finish writing your story there," said Deborah.

"Who would want it? It would be a story without a moral or an ending."

"We could raise our children, make love, farm and fish, grow old gracefully and at eighty die in each other's arms," she said. "That would be a moral and an ending enough."

At other times, we dreamed of a day when our internal problems were resolved, Titus gone, the extremists scattered by their eschatological insanity, Nero dead, and an emperor no worse than Claudius in his place. Thessalonica would be the Christian center that Rome was unlikely to be. My writings and my sermons, winglessly constructed as they were compared with Paul's, would be accepted over his as the true legacy of Jesus.

❁

One day, David limped up at a near run. His eyes were wild and he was out of breath. His friend in the office of the governor had told him that the official weekly summary of events in Rome contained an item saying Paul was dead. There was no mention of the others. Shaken, all but shattered, I went to Titus to share the news with someone with whom I had shared Paul. I found him at the new church laboring beside several of those who had broken with us. When he saw me his brows lowered. He would never forgive me, for anything.

"Paul is dead," I said.

His face went blank; his lips moved without a sound. Finally, he whispered, "How do you know?"

"It doesn't matter. I am sure."

"The others?"

"I do not know."

Again he was expressionless, almost moronic. His hands still held the sledgehammer with which he had been sinking posts. His fingers tightened, and his face with them, and I stepped back in alarm. "Ahhhhh!" he screamed, raising the hammer, and bringing it down so hard that the head buried in the earth. He left it there and fell to the ground, his hands clutching his face, his body curled into itself like a mummy's in a funeral urn. The others looked at me in alarm and I distractedly gave them the same message. I stumbled to Aristarchus's, informed him, and we went together to Secundus.

Next day, more news arrived. After two and a half years of legal preparations by Paul and his lawyers, the trial, before Tigellinus, had lasted thirty minutes. Soldiers had taken Paul in chains out the Trigemina gate, probably to avoid any Christians in the Aventine quarter. He had been beheaded near the Salvian marshes, his head and body left in the muck. There was no word about how the others were killed, but they were listed: Luke, Timothy, Priscilla and Aquila, Urbanus and Stachys, Herodian. Mark was not named and I assumed, as Titus said would happen, that Paul had sent him away while it was still possible.

"Timothy, Timothy," I muttered. He had been so innocent. All the things his intelligence and industry had let him do for Paul in Corinth and elsewhere he had done without an iota of guile or meanness. To kill him was to spear a pet lamb. I went again to Titus. He was not at the building site, and I went to his lodgings. By now, I was sobbing, for Timothy, for Paul, for all of them, remembering Priscilla and Aquila in Ephesus and again on the road from Puteoli with the others, all so full of laughter, so good, and now wasted, gone. When Titus saw me weeping, he knew the rest.

"All?"

I stuttered the names.

"Only Mark alive," he said. No tears came from him, although his agony must have been even greater than mine, for he had known them longer. But his grief was less complicated. For he was guilty only of being alive when they were dead. He had been faithful to the dead while I had deserted them.

I stood by the doorjamb, coughing with great sobs. At last I had been able to feel my enormous grief, my guilt, my despair. I longed for a word from Titus to acknowledge that what I felt was something that he, and only he, in Thessalonica, could understand. But there was nothing. He comforted and was comforted by those who had followed me to his house.

When I pulled myself together, weak from my sobbing, and turned to go, he broke briefly from his friends and came to me.

"I am sorry, Demas," he said tightly. "I cannot help you."

All these executions made life smell of death. A huge piece of Jesus Christ had died. None in our city had known Jesus. Only a tiny number of us had known any of the disciples. But many of us had known Paul. He had brought Christ to the city. In traditional Jewish mourning, we did no work for three days. Nor did we exchange greetings in the street, another Jewish custom. Some of our Jewish Christians, reverting to even older rituals, wore dirty clothes and went unshaven.

"Leave the dead to bury their dead," Jesus had said.

Paul had gone further. In Thessalonica, he had said, "Do not grieve as others do who have no hope."

But we grieved, we grieved. Sadly, it was a mark of our alienation that none of the three factions mourned him jointly. I fell uncontrollably into the kind of depressed lassitude I had felt in Rome when Paul had thrust me out and my loved ones had died. Deborah, who had never understood the grandeur of Paul, tried to bring me out of my anguish and was irritated with me when she could not. For a week, I trudged through my duties perfunctorily, and then slowly and dolefully began to recover. It was David who jolted me back into reality.

"It's time," he told me one day. "Any more is luxury."

When I came back, unlike the aftermath of my family's death in Rome, it was as if, unknown to me, I had been storing energy. I rose early and worked late. Titus was also back at his labors. He was doing more than merely driving our two factions to the Antipodes. We learned he had talked with pagan priests of Ares and Zeus, and even fringe fanatics dedicated to Attis, Astarte, Cybele, and Isis.

As a Phrygian, he was, in fact, the best man to convert them to Christianity. But that was not what he was about. Instead, he was goading them into violence by describing our strategies to win over their youth, and thus sap their ability to survive. Paul, even at his most manipulative, would have barred such inflammatory tactics.

Titus also kept up his liaison with the Paulist rabble from hill and plain, reminding them that I had refused to heed the last message of Paul and abdicate. They would see this as a mortal sin against the dying wishes of their principal saint, an act that only compounded their hate for me over the fiasco of Simon of Aegae. On hearing of Titus's treachery, I was first shocked, then incensed. Surely, he knew that in encouraging these unstable people, he was inviting them to kill me.

We also had problems unattributable to Titus. Paul's exodus from Thessalonica twelve years ago with the Pharisees angrily at his heels had made it hard initially to find followers among well-to-do Jews. My break with Paulism and his death had helped us to attract young disaffected Jews from such families. This gave the more prejudiced and hostile among their elders even more reasons to hate us.

One night, two adolescents from our congregation were set on by Zealots. And each day, more *sicarii* arrived, driven here by the ever-more-draconian stringencies of the Romans in Palestine. I did not wear armor, but regularly carried my dagger. When Deborah made her rounds of those in need in the evening, an armed church member went with her. Once again, it was as it had been in Borhaurus, or worse.

In late March, news came that Mark was in Crete. He had carried from Rome the final manuscripts of his and Peter's book, and Paul's and Luke's life of Jesus and acts of the apostles. Paul had told Mark to disseminate all three books, but Mark was not really capable of that task. Of the surviving Paulists, only Titus had enough contacts, enough knowledge of where copies should go, and, most importantly, enough steadfastness, dynamism, and ingenuity. These scrolls were Paul's and Peter's legacy to the church and to posterity. Titus decided they were more important to Christianity than the church in Thessalonica.

He left without bidding me good-bye. However, I learned from Secundus that he had a chastening session with him and Aristarchus in which he said at all costs I must be unseated. He also told them that from Crete he would go to Corinth, Ephesus, and Antioch. That meant, happily for me, that it would be a long time before he turned again to Thessalonica.

On the Sunday after he left, I went in my simplest clothes with Amos, David, and Deborah to the unfinished church of our rivals. We drew hostile looks, but we took Communion from the hands of Aristarchus and Secundus.

Next week, with the traditional colleagueship that even warring rabbis accord each other, I was permitted to speak briefly to their congregation. When I saw the size of the audience, I was sad, although also relieved. There were only a few at this unusual event, meaning their membership had waned. I said only that our next Lord's Day would be devoted to prayers that we could reunite. I begged Aristarchus and Secundus to come and said I would relinquish the platform to any of their members who wished to speak to our congregation.

Aristarchus did not accept the invitation, but Secundus did, and spoke vaguely about the Christ in all men. Two others roundly denounced me. And another three said we should pray for Paul and talk about unity. Soon there were daily reachings-out between our two churches, and, finally, a decision that we should worship together once a month while our elders worked to restore the *status quo ante*. We also agreed that their new building could be converted into a school for David's disabled children.

The movement toward ecumenism offered both an opportunity and a reason for Deborah and me to take the road and preach as missioners as we had always dreamed of doing. By going, even temporarily, I would be plucking out the rebels', pagans', and Jews' main burrs, giving them a chance to heal now that Titus was no longer here to infect and reinfect them with fevers. Amos and David had proved they could work with Aristarchus and Secundus. Our cadre was so devotedly behind Amos and me that there was no danger that Paulism would resurge. And Zephra was old enough to travel.

Deborah and I were deep in our planning when the time came for her monthly bleeding, generally so regular—and it did not come. Two weeks later, she was sure she was pregnant. I was exultant. We would, of course, postpone our trip. But Deborah's mind was made up. When again, she argued, would the time be so ripe? Besides, we had let it be known that I would take the road for a few months as part of the healing process of our church.

"I can travel for six months," she said. "After all, we are going by ships and mules, not racing chariots. A month or two before I am due we can get lodgings. I do not need to have it in a manger," she added irreverently.

In the weeks before we were to go, I did everything I could to leave things in order. We realigned our alms committee, our religious education leaders, our youth and elderly groups to make sure the returning rebels were fairly represented. My two erstwhile colleagues could not have been more cooperative.

We met with the governor, urging him to try to recall a legionnaire unit, or at worst to assign some of the lictors to police duties in case there was any kind of sectarian turbulence. He nodded, said he understood our concerns, but promised nothing. We tried unsuccessfully through the few Jews with whom we had continued dialogues to get the Pharisees and scribes who most hated us to meet with us. The fanatics among the pagan cultists and the ultra-Paulists also spurned our overtures.

❀

On the day before our departure, the church planned a Sunday baptism at the river and an afternoon love feast. But three days before the festivities, our informants began to bring in disturbing reports. The first, as irony had it, came from the pagan merchant who supplied the herbs we planned for our spitted ox. The most volatile of the extremist pagan priests, he whispered, were talking of assassinating me before I left to "spread my poison" in Bithynia, a stronghold for their rites.

A young Jew, a new Christian, told us his father, a drover, and several others like him were planning a *proper* good-bye for me with the help of the *sicarii*. Next day, we heard that the Paulist fundamentalists were going to attack me before I could become the Anti-Christ and Anti-Paul of the Propontis.

We tried to see the governor again, but to our heightened concern, he refused. We had to settle for expressing our worries to his chief lictor, who told us his own spies had picked up similar, if less pronounced, signals. When we asked what he planned to do, he looked defeated and gave us evasive answers.

That night, David got more word from his friend in the governor's office. "The Romans are going to *let* it happen," David said. "They *want* it to."

"Let *what* happen?" I asked.

"Let *whatever* happen. Every lout in town with nothing to do will be out to watch—or to help."

I sent for Amos, Aristarchus, and Secundus. We four and Deborah met in the room where Titus and I had fought. We considered calling off the ceremonies, and sneaking Deborah, Zephra, and me out of the city at night as we had done long ago with Paul in Corinth. But Corinth had not been Paul's headquarters. If we did not openly meet bias and hatred against us in Thessalonica, what kind of religion were we?

Nevertheless, next morning we polled our parishioners. The elders and other cadre scurried around the city, to homes, to the market-place, to the shops and factories, to fields, to tavern and dock. The consensus was that we must go ahead with our plans. We got word through intermediaries to the groups who threatened us that if we were attacked, we would fight. Even the most demented would know from the battle at the church that a fight would mean casualties among them. But did they care?

That evening, our leaders gathered at our house again. As they walked through the streets, they had seen almost no one. The town was closed down, uneasily awaiting the confrontations of the morrow. We had done everything we could to prevent them—and everything we could to meet them. We worked until midnight, picking positions and squad chiefs for our armed men. We would parcel off some of our "soldiers" to guard the church and the feast preparations while we were at the river.

Then we sat together over Deborah's stew of lentils, chicory, and lamb and talked of how to avert future troubles. All we could do, I thought, was to seed our enemies even more numerously with spies, as Father and Grandfather had done.

"I was naïve not to have done it before," I said. "We would be better prepared."

"To be naïve these days," Amos said, "is to be dead."

"Yes, to be dead," said Aristarchus seriously. "But how Christian are we in our efforts to push that away? We revert so easily into men as savage as the men we fight. Why, we were battling Simon and his followers—our fellow Christians—like so many Joshuas, and yet we worship this man of peace. When I was still groggy from that club, I thought of Jesus taking the blows of the scourgers. But what I really wanted was for one of you to take revenge on the man who hit me from behind. Demas did and so answered my prayer.

"The truth is perhaps we should have given them our meeting place, humbly, and then patiently started work on another, praying for time to finish it, for time to keep going. We pray for victory, and for help, and in gratitude. . . . Why not pray for a few more years to put one foot in front of the other? Isn't that what our life really should be?"

Aristarchus's rare eloquence left us silent. I thought about what he had said, about what tomorrow held. I saw Deborah thinking, too, her face, softened by the oil light, the same face I had fallen in love with over Andrew's quiet body. Yes, I would pray for just those few years.

"I am so happy," she said in the silence. I could not guess what path had led from Aristarchus's reflections to her saying that. But I felt the same calm joy, the same presence of good, and I saw in the faces of the others that they did, too. How easy it was for us, all bound together, at least for now, in love and trust, to sense another guest at the table, the Jesus who had brought us together.

Impulsively, Deborah took my hand, and then Aristarchus's, and held them. "I would like to say a small prayer," she said. She looked around and, feeling our assent, began, "Jesus, thank you for letting us be alive. Help the children who come after us to find love such as we have right now without the complexities that have afflicted us."

Secundus added quietly, "Help us find a way to carry on our ministry, to make peace with our brothers in Christ whether they are here or in Rome or Palestine, to spread your words as best we understand them. Let us work as long as we can for you and have an easy death when it comes, one that will serve your purposes in some way."

After they had gone, even curled up against Deborah's warm body, I could not sleep. It was the same for her. "Demas," she said, "suppose something does happen?" I was nervous myself, not in the best state for calming Deborah's fears.

"Well, something *is* going to happen," I said, trying to sound reasonable. "There is going to be a move against us and we are going to repel it and carry out our ceremonies."

"I mean suppose . . . ?" She let it hang in the air, and I knew she meant suppose one or both of us were injured. Or killed. I did not want to talk about that. She was silent awhile and I tried again to sleep, but she sighed and said, "When we come back from Bithynia, it will be the same thing all over."

Well, what was I supposed to do? My father had weathered Caligula. We could weather Nero. "Deborah, we will do what we have always done. We will think and pray and try to figure out what God wants us to do and then go ahead and do it."

She thought about that awhile, then came up on her elbow.

"Demas, please don't make any speeches to an angry mob. That's the kind of stupid thing Paul would try. Just stay back. And let someone else do the fighting for a change."

I did not plan to carry anything I could fight with except Ezra's knife beneath my tunic. I could not wear armor and a sword while I conducted the baptism and officiated at a Communion celebrating the man of peace. I did not want to behave as though the church were in a state of war. I thought of Aristarchus and his talk of how hard men fought to push their death away. I had lived through numerous tests before: the well, the two sets of robbers, the arena at Bayba, the storm at sea, and, most important, my crucifixion. With God's help, I had staved off death many times, and I wanted to keep staving it off.

I thought with a smile of Deborah. If I were to die now, would she try to take over the leadership? But, no, that was unfair. She would defer to Amos. What would happen to our baby if I died? There was still a bit of Andrew's water left. I would hope when Zephra was ten or eleven, Deborah would use some to baptize her, and the rest when our own child was that age.

I thought with yearning of my father and how I wished I could have baptized him as a Christian. How terrible for him to have died with only that cold fatalistic poem in his mind. But there had been all these reasons that he had not believed, and all these reasons that Mother and I had.

I thought of Paul and of his long great letter to the Romans. He had said that to die in Christ was to live in him forever, for in his resurrection, we were also resurrected. Then I had believed it only in the sense that the death of Jesus, and of Dathan, Paul, and the others, would always live in our acts and our memories to inspire us. But now I did not know. Perhaps Jesus did exist after the crucifixion in a way less evanescent and mystical than I had once thought. Certainly, I felt a closeness to him I had not felt when I was younger.

I chuckled quietly. Was I saying that my mind, my cold, clean, Roman mind, was less trustworthy than my heart? No, not yet. But it was something to think about, to argue with Deborah about on the road to Bithynia.

She turned and again we tried to sleep, and after a long time she did. But I could not. I eased myself out of the bed and she sleepily

443

mumbled, "Where are you going?" and I told her I wanted to jot down a few notes and for her not to wake.

I brought my manuscript up to date with the events of the evening. I glanced through it at random. It was such a poor thing compared to what Luke and Paul had done, and what Mark had written about Peter's story. Soon Titus would have copies of these scrolls flying out to all the corners of the Christian world. And Matthew's and John's would also be on their way. It was time for me to finish mine and send it out, too.

Then I would begin my great compendium of Jesus' words and acts, and my epistles, dispatching them by couriers and via our missioners to all the Christian world. It was my hope that my words would modify Paul's, bringing them more into line with what Jesus really said and felt. I thought of those missioners we had sent already, there in far lands under the stars, enjoying the freedom of the road. I had spent many years doing as they were doing. I had walked a long way with Paul, and before that with Deborah and Rechab.

I had walked with Dathan, too, carrying him with me in my mind, my heart, my bones. I thought of his three pitchers in our bedroom. I began to nod. The places and the words all blended in the beginnings of a dream. I put my head on the desk and dozed. After a few minutes, I shook myself awake, wrote these last few sentences, and went back to the warm security of my bed.

Endnote by
Professor Jones-Haarwijk

With those words, ". . . security of my bed," the Thessalonian Apograph ends. From the scroll, we were unable to determine whether there was more, and the ancient copier simply broke off his work there, or whether the Apograph in its present form was all Demas (or False Demas) wrote. Further research may or may not yield answers to these important questions.

Meanwhile, I proffer the following datum for speculative purposes, although it is lacking in contemporaneity. It is from the Tiflis Microapostolic Fragment, an uncanonical papyrus scroll discovered in 1902 in the Autocephalous Georgian Orthodox monastery in Tiflis, now of the Union of Soviet Socialist Republics, by Professor Vladimir Koltrasov (1850–1913).

Scholars have long been acquainted with the Fragment. It purports to list the fates of a number of minor disciples of the apostles, many mentioned in earlier apocryphal material, along with some who also appear in the canonical books.

The Fragment's ink was carbon-dated in 1977 by the Soviet Academy of Learned and Historical Research as blended not earlier than A.D. 300. N.B. This is some two hundred forty years after the hypothetical date for the final pages of the Thessalonian Apograph, and one hundred and fifty years *before* the ink in the Apograph was carbondated. The relevant section reads in whole:

". . . and Demas of Jerusalem [sic], in the ninth year of the reign of the emperor Nero Claudius Caesar, was stoned in Thessalonica for the second time and died with the name of the Lord Jesus upon his lips."